T5-BCL-992

The Letters of Fanny Hensel to Felix Mendelssohn

Illustration 1—Pencil drawing of Fanny Hensel by Wilhelm Hensel, n. d. [Staatliche Museen Preussischer Kulturbesitz, Nationalgalerie, Berlin (West)]. Frontispiece.

The Letters of Fanny Hensel to Felix Mendelssohn

Collected, Edited and Translated
with Introductory Essays and Notes
by Marcia J. Citron

PENDRAGON PRESS

Musicological Series by Pendragon Press

Aesthetics in Music
Annotated Reference Tools in Music
Festschrift Series
French Opera in the 17th and 18th Centuries
Giovanni Battista Pergolesi: The Complete Works/Opere Complete
The Historical Harpsichord
The Juilliard Performance Guides
Monographs in Musicology
Musical Life in 19th-Century France
RILM Retrospectives
The Sociology of Music
Thematic Catalogues

Library of Congress Cataloguing in Publication Data

Hensel, Fanny Mendelssohn, 1805-1847.
Letters of Fanny Hensel to Felix Mendelssohn

Prefatory matter in English; letters in German with English translation.
Bibliography: p.
Includes indexes.
1. Hensel, Fanny Mendelssohn, 1805-1847.
2. Composers--Germany--Correspondence.
3. Mendelssohn-Bartholdy, Felix, 1809-1847.
I. Mendelssohn-Bartholdy, Felix, 1809-1847.
II. Citron, Marcia J. III. Title.
ML410.H482A4 1987 786.1'092'4[B] 84-26364
ISBN 0-918728-52-5

Table of Contents

*To my mother,
Leah Semiatin C.,
who has always been
interested.*

Acknowledgments

Several people lent their generous support to this project. Miss Margaret Crum, retired Assistant Librarian in the Department of Western Manuscripts at the Bodleian Library, Oxford, kindly permitted me to consult the page proofs of her invaluable *Catalogue* to the Green Books collection during the initial stages of research, and expressed enthusiasm at the prospect of the publication of Fanny Hensel's letters to Felix Mendelssohn. Later she agreed to check a few manuscript problems *in situ*. To Dr. Rudolf Elvers, director of the Mendelssohn Archive at the Staatsbibliothek Preussischer Kulturbesitz in West Berlin, go my thanks for permission to view the many autograph documents by both Fanny Hensel and Felix Mendelssohn residing in the Archive. The insights conveyed by Dr. Cécile Lowenthal-Hensel, historian and great-granddaughter of Fanny Hensel, during my last visit to Berlin provided much food for thought.

Of the several readers, Professor R. Larry Todd of Duke University deserves special mention. Not only did he go through the entire book and offer general comments, but imparted his vast knowledge of Mendelssohniana in numerous and detailed identifications and bibliographical references. His care and thoroughness are greatly appreciated. Others who read the manuscript and offered helpful suggestions are Professors Philip Gossett of The University of Chicago, Jurgen Thym of The Eastman School of Music, and my colleagues, Jeffrey Kurtzman and Anne Schnoebelen of Rice University. In addition, thanks are in order to several scholars who generously shared their expertise: Dr. Cecilia H. Porter of Chevy Chase, Maryland, for her knowledgeable perspective on music in Düsseldorf; Professor Douglass Seaton of

Florida State University for his detailed information on Mendelssohn's canons; the late Professor Boris Schwarz of New York for his identification of several Paganini compositions; and Dr. Victoria Sirota of Brookline, Massachusetts, for her biographical clues to members of Fanny Hensel's circle.

Deep appreciation is extended to Professors Michael Winkler, Margaret Eifler, and Klaus Weissenberger of the Department of German, Rice University, for their care in reading through the transcriptions and translations, and their many helpful suggestions. Ms. Kay Mittnik, also of the Department of German, spent a great deal of time proofreading the retyped German texts. Anna Marie Flusche, O.P., lent her editorial expertise in the final stages of manuscript preparation.

I am most grateful to the Bodleian Library for its cooperation in making Fanny Hensel's autograph letters available for on-site investigation, and silver-print photographs for subsequent examination. It also graciously granted permission for the inclusion of several facsimile reproductions, as did the Staatsbibliothek Preussischer Kulturbesitz and the Nationalgalerie, both in West Berlin. Generous financial assistance was provided by Rice University, the Shepherd School of Music, and the Deutsche Akademische Austauschdienst (DAAD). The enthusiasm of Mr. Robert Kessler of Pendragon Press for the project has continued to be a source of great satisfaction. And finally, I wish to express special thanks to my husband, Professor Mark Kulstad of the Philosophy Department, Rice University, for his wise counsel and continued interest in Fanny Hensel.

27 July 1984
Houston, Texas

Bibliography Sigla

ADB	*Allgemeine Deutsche Biographie*, 56 Vols. Leipzig: Duncker & Humblot, 1875-1912.
Alexander, *Letters*	Boyd Alexander. "Some Unpublished Letters of Abraham Mendelssohn and Fanny Hensel," *Mendelssohn Studien*, 3 (1979), 9-50.
AMZ	*Allgemeine musikalische Zeitung*. Leipzig, 1799-1848.
BAMZ	*Berliner allgemeine musikalische Zeitung*. Berlin, 1824-1830.
Bartlitz, *Works*	Eveline Bartlitz. List of Works to "Felix Mendelssohn," *The New Grove Dictionary*, 12. London: Macmillan, 1980, 152-56.
Bill, *Darmstadt*	Oskar Bill. "Unbekannte Mendelssohn-Handschriften in der Hessischen Landes- und Hochschulbibliothek Darmstadt," *Die Musikforschung*, 26 (1973), 345-49.
Boetticher, *Briefe*	Wolfgang Boetticher, ed. *Briefe und Gedichte aus dem Album Robert und Clara Schumanns*. Leipzig: VEB Deutscher Verlag für Musik, 1979.
Chorley, *Autobiography*	Henry Chorley. *Autobiography, Memoirs and Letters*, ed. H. G. Hewlett. London: Bentley, 1873.

Chorley, *S & M*	Henry Chorley. "Mendelssohn's Sister and Mother," in W. A. Lampadius, *Life of Felix Mendelssohn Bartholdy*, ed. & trans. William Gage. New York: O. Ditson, 1865. Rep. Boston: Longwood, 1978, 210-12.
Citron, *Hensel*	Marcia J. Citron. "Fanny Mendelssohn Hensel: Musician in Her Brother's Shadow," in *The Female Autograph*, ed. Donna Stanton, Vols. 12-13 of *New York Literary Forum* (1984), 171-79.
Citron, *Influence*	Marcia J. Citron. "Felix Mendelssohn's Influence on Fanny Mendelssohn Hensel as a Professional Composer," *Current Musicology*, 37-38 (1984), 9-17.
Citron, *Letters*	Marcia J. Citron. "The Letters of Fanny Hensel to Felix Mendelssohn in Oxford's Green Books," *Mendelssohn and Schumann Essays*, ed. Jon Finson and R. Larry Todd. Durham: Duke University Press, 1984, 99-108.
Citron, *Lieder*	Marcia J. Citron. "The Lieder of Fanny Mendelssohn Hensel," *The Musical Quarterly*, 69 No. 4 (Fall 1983), 570-93.
Crum, *Catalogue*	Margaret Crum. *Catalogue of the Mendelssohn Papers in the Bodleian Library*, 1: *Correspondence of Felix Mendelssohn Bartholdy and Others*. Tutzing: Hans Schneider, 1980; 2: *Music and Papers*. Idem, 1983.
Cullen, *Baubiographie*	Michael Cullen. "Leipziger Strasse Drei--Eine Baubiographie," *Mendelssohn Studien*, 5 (1982), 9-78.
DB	Depositum Berlin. A cataloguing designation for some items in the Mendelssohn Archive of the Staatsbibliothek Preussischer Kulturbesitz in Berlin (West).

Devrient, *Erinnerungen*	Eduard Devrient. *Meine Erinnerungen an Felix Mendelssohn-Bartholdy.* Leipzig: J. J. Weber, 1869.
Eckermann, *Gespräche*	J. P. Eckermann. *Gespräche mit Goethe*, ed. H. H. Houben. Wiesbaden: F. A. Brockhaus, 1959.
Elvers, *Acht Briefe*	Rudolf Elvers. ''Acht Briefe von Lea Mendelssohn an den Verlag Schlesinger in Berlin,'' *Das Problem Mendelssohn*, ed. C. Dahlhaus. Regensburg: Gustav Bosse, 1974, 47-53.
Elvers, *Nachlass*	Rudolf Elvers. ''F. M. B.'s Nachlass,'' *Das Problem Mendelssohn*, ed. C. Dahlhaus. Regensburg: Gustav Bosse, 1974, 35-46.
Elvers, *Quellen*	Rudolf Elvers. ''Weitere Quellen zu den Werken von Fanny Hensel,'' *Mendelssohn Studien*, 2 (1975), 215-20.
Elvers, *Staatsbibliothek*	Rudolf Elvers. ''Neuerwerbungen für das Mendelssohn-Archiv der Staatsbibliothek 1965-69,'' *Jahrbuch Preussischer Kulturbesitz*, 7 (1970), 308-20.
Elvers, *Verzeichnis*	Rudolf Elvers. ''Verzeichnis der Musik-Autographen von Fanny Hensel in dem Mendelssohn-Arkiv zu Berlin,'' *Mendelssohn Studien*, 1 (1972), 169-74.
Fétis, *Biographie*	François Joseph Fétis. *Biographie Universelle des Musiciens et Bibliographie Générale de la Musique*, 2nd ed., 8 Vols. Paris: Firmin Didot Frères, Fils et Cie., 1873-75. Rep. Brussels: Culture et Civilisation, 1972.
Forchert, *Marx*	Arno Forchert. ''Adolf Bernhard Marx und seine Berliner Allgemeine musikalische Zeitung,'' *Studien zur Musikgeschichte Berlins im frühen 19. Jahrhundert*, ed. C. Dahlhaus. Regensburg: Gustav Bosse, 1980, 381-404.
GB	Green Books collection of letters

	addressed to Felix, in the Bodleian Library, Oxford: MSS Margaret Deneke Mendelssohn (MDM) b. 4 (Vol. I), and d. 28 through d. 53 (Vols. II-XXVII).
Gilbert, *Bankiers*	Felix Gilbert, ed. *Bankiers, Künstler und Gelehrte*. Tübingen: J. C. B. Mohr (Paul Siebeck), 1975.
Goethe, *Dichtung*	Johann Wolfgang von Goethe. *Dichtung und Wahrheit*, in *Goethes Werke*, 10. Hamburg: Christian Wegner Verlag, 1959.
Goethe, *Reise*	Johann Wolfgang von Goethe. *Italienische Reise*, ed. George von Gravenitz. Leipzig: Insel-Verlag, 1912.
Grimm, *Wörterbuch*	Jacob & Wilhelm Grimm. *Deutsches Wörterbuch*, 16 Vols. Leipzig: S. Hirzel, 1854-1954.
Grossmann-Vendrey, *Vergangenheit*	Susanna Grossmann-Vendrey. *Felix Mendelssohn Bartholdy und die Musik der Vergangenheit*. Regensburg: Gustav Bosse, 1969.
Grove, *Mendelssohn*	Sir George Grove. "Mendelssohn," *Grove's Dictionary of Music and Musicians*, 2nd ed., Vol. 3. London: Macmillan, 1907. Rep. Philadelphia: Theodore Presser, 1916, 110-77.
F. Hensel, *Tagebuch*	Fanny Hensel. Unpublished Tagebücher, 1829-1834 (in MA), and 1839-1844 (copy; formerly on loan to the MA by Eva Roemer).
S. Hensel, *Familie*	Sebastian Hensel. *Die Familie Mendelssohn (1729-1847)*, 3rd ed., 2 Vols. Berlin: B. Behr, 1882.
S. Hensel, *Family*	Sebastian Hensel. *The Mendelssohn Family (1729-1847)*, 2nd ed., 2 Vols., trans. Carl Klingemann. New York: Harper & Brothers, 1882. Rep. New York: Greenwood Press, 1968.

S. Hensel, *Lebensbild*	Sebastian Hensel. *Ein Lebensbild aus Deutschlands Lehrjahren*. Berlin: B. Behr, 1903.
Hiller, *Mendelssohn*	Ferdinand Hiller. *Mendelssohn Letters and Recollections*, trans. M. E. von Glehn. London: Macmillan, 1874. Rep. New York: Vienna House, 1972.
Hirschberg, *Marx*	L. Hirschberg. "Der Tondichter A. B. Marx," *Sammelband der Internationalen Musik-Gesellschaft*, 10 (1908-09), 1-72.
HSZ	*Spenersche Zeitung* (= *Haude- und Spenersche Zeitung*).
Hyatt King, *Collectors*	Alexander Hyatt King. *Some British Collectors of Music c. 1600-1960.* Cambridge: Cambridge University Press, 1963.
Klingemann, *Briefwechsel*	Karl Klingemann. *Felix Mendelssohn-Bartholdy's Briefwechsel mit Legationsrat Karl Klingemann in London*. Essen: G. D. Baedeker, 1909.
Köhler, *FMB*	Karl-Heinz Köhler. *Felix Mendelssohn Bartholdy*, 2nd ed. Leipzig: Reclam, 1972.
Köhler, *Mendelssohn*	Karl-Heinz Köhler. "Mendelssohn," *The New Grove Dictionary*, 12. London: Macmillan, 1980, 134-56.
Köstlin, *Lang*	H. A. Köstlin. "Josephine Lang: Lebensabriss. Verzeichnis der Kompositionen," *Sammlung musikalischer Vorträge*, ed. P. Waldersee, Series 3 (1881), 51-103.
Krautwurst, *Hensel*	Franz Krautwurst. "Fanny Caecilia Hensel," *Die Musik in Geschichte und Gegenwart*, 16. Kassel: Bärenreiter, 1979, cols. 658-62.
Kupferberg, *Mendelssohns*	Herbert Kupferberg. *The Mendelssohns: Three Generations of Genius*. New York: Charles Scribner's Sons, 1972.

Kurzhals-Reuter, *Oratorien*	Arntrud Kurzhals-Reuter. *Die Oratorien Felix Mendelssohn Bartholdys*. Tutzing: Hans Schneider, 1978.
LC	Library of Congress, Washington, D. C.
Ledebur, *Lexicon*	Carl Ledebur. *Tonkünstler-Lexicon Berlin's von den ältesten Zeiten bis auf die Gegenwart*. Berlin: Ludwig Rauh, 1861. Rep. Tutzing: Hans Schneider, 1965.
Lowenthal-Hensel, *F u. F*	Cécile Lowenthal-Hensel. "F in Dur und F in Moll, Fanny und Felix Mendelssohn in Berlin," *Berlin in Dur und Moll.* Berlin: Axel Springer, 1970.
Lowenthal-Hensel, *W. Hensel*	Cécile Lowenthal-Hensel. *Preussische Bildnisse des 19. Jahrhunderts. Zeichnungen von Wilhelm Hensel*. Berlin: Nationalgalerie, 1981.
MA	Mendelssohn Archive of the Staatsbibliothek Preussischer Kulturbesitz, Berlin (West).
Mahlung, *Musikbetrieb*	Christoph Helmut Mahling. "Zum 'Musikbetrieb' Berlins und seinen Institutionen in der ersten Hälfte des 19. Jahrhunderts," *Studien zur Musikgeschichte Berlins im frühen 19. Jahrhundert*, ed. C. Dahlhaus. Regensburg: Gustav Bosse, 1980, 27-263.
Marx, *Erinnerungen*	Adolf Bernhard Marx. *Erinnerungen*, 2 Vols. Berlin: O. Janke, 1865.
MDM	Margaret Deneke collection of Mendelssohn documents at the Bodleian Library, Oxford.
Mendelssohn, *Briefe*	Felix Mendelssohn Bartholdy. *Briefe aus den Jahren 1830 bis 1847*, 3rd ed., part 2, ed. Paul Mendelssohn Bartholdy and Carl Mendelssohn Bartholdy. Leipzig: Hermann Mendelssohn, 1875.
Mendelssohn, *Briefe-L*	Felix Mendelssohn Bartholdy. *Briefe aus Leipziger Archiven*, ed. Hans-

	Joachim Rothe and Reinhard Szeskus. Leipzig: VEB Deutscher Verlag für Musik, 1972.
Mendelssohn, *Briefe-RE*	Felix Mendelssohn Bartholdy. *Briefe,* ed. Rudolf Elvers. Frankfurt: Fischer Taschenbuch Verlag, 1984.
Mendelssohn, *Goethe*	Karl Mendelssohn-Bartholdy. *Goethe and Mendelssohn*, 2nd ed., trans. M. E. von Glehn. London: Macmillan, 1874.
Mendelssohn, *Reisebriefe*	Felix Mendelssohn Bartholdy. *Briefe aus den Jahren 1830 bis 1847*, 3rd ed., part 1, ed. Paul Mendelssohn Bartholdy and Carl Mendelssohn Bartholdy. Leipzig: Hermann Mendelssohn, 1875.
Mendelssohn, *Verleger*	Felix Mendelssohn Bartholdy. *Briefe an deutsche Verleger*, ed. Rudolf Elvers. Berlin: Walter de Gruyter and Co., 1968.
A. Mendelssohn, *Erinnerungen*	Albrecht Mendelssohn-Bartholdy. "Erinnerungen an Felix Mendelssohn," Festbeilage to the *Neue Freie Presse*, No. 27166 (19 April 1925), 29-30.
MGG	*Die Musik in Geschichte und Gegenwart*, ed. F. Blume, 16 Vols. Kassel: Bärenreiter, 1949-79.
Mintz, *Melusine*	Donald Mintz. "Melusine: A Mendelssohn Draft," *The Musical Quarterly*, 43 (1957), 480-99.
Moscheles, *Leben*	Ignaz Moscheles. *Aus Moscheles' Leben*, 2 Vols., ed. Charlotte Moscheles. Leipzig: Duncker & Humblot, 1872-73.
Moscheles, *Letters*	Felix Mendelssohn Bartholdy. *Letters of Felix Mendelssohn to Ignaz and Charlotte Moscheles,* ed. and trans. Felix Moscheles. Boston: Ticknor and Co., 1888; Rep. New York: Benjamin Blom, 1971.
NBA	J. S. Bach. *Neue Ausgabe Sämtlicher*

	Werke. Kassel and Basel: Bärenreiter, 1954 --.
NDB	*Neue Deutsche Biographie*. Berlin: Duncker & Humblot, 1953 --.
NGD	*The New Grove Dictionary of Music and Musicians*, 20 Vols., ed. Stanley Sadie. London: Macmillan, 1980.
NYPL	New York Public Library collection of c. 700 autograph letters from Felix to his family, 182[0] to 1847.
NZM	*Neue Zeitschrift für Musik*. Leipzig: 1834 --.
Oxford, *FMB*	Margaret Crum, ed. *Felix Mendelssohn-Bartholdy*. Oxford: Oxford University Press, 1972 (Bodleian Picture Books, Special Series No. 3).
Planché, *Recollections*	James Robinson Planché. *Recollections and Reflections,* rev. ed. London: S. Low, Marston and Co., 1901.
Pritchard, *Cantatas*	B. W. Pritchard. "Mendelssohn's Chorale Cantatas: An Appraisal," *The Musical Quarterly*, 62 (1976), 1-24.
Quin, *Hensel*	Carol L. Quin. "Fanny Mendelssohn Hensel: Her Contributions to Nineteenth-Century Musical Life," unpublished Ph.D. dissertation, University of Kentucky, 1981.
Reich, *Rudorff*	Nancy B. Reich. "The Rudorff Collection," *Music Library Association Notes*, 31 (1974-75), 247-61.
Schnapp, *Brief*	Friedrich Schnapp. "Felix Mendelssohn Bartholdy's Brief an seine Schwester Fanny Hensel vom 26./27. Juni 1830," *Schweizerische Musikzeitung*, 99 (1959), 85-91.
Seaton, *Sketches*	Douglass Seaton, "A Study of a Collection of Mendelssohn's Sketches and Other Autograph Material Deutsche Staatsbibliothek Berlin *Mus. MS.*

Autogr. Mendelssohn 19,'' unpublished Ph.D. dissertation, Columbia University, 1977.

Sirota, *Hensel* — Victoria Ressmeyer Sirota, ''The Life and Works of Fanny Mendelssohn Hensel,'' unpublished Mus.A.D. dissertation, Boston University, 1981.

Staatsbibliothek, *Dokumente* — Rudolf Elvers, ed. *Fanny Hensel, geb. Mendelssohn Bartholdy: Dokumente ihres Lebens: Ausstellung zum 125. Todestag im Mendelssohn-Archiv*. Berlin: Staatsbibliothek Preussischer Kulturbesitz, 1972.

Sutermeister, *Reise* — Peter Sutermeister, ed. *Felix Mendelssohn Bartholdy. Eine Reise durch Deutschland, Italien und die Schweiz*, 2nd ed. Tübingen: Heliopolis-Verlag Ewald Katzmann, 1979.

Thieme-Becker, *Künstler* — Thieme-Becker. *Künstler Lexikon*, 37 Vols. Leipzig: E. A. Seemann, 1907-50.

Todd, *Education* — R. Larry Todd. *Mendelssohn's Musical Education: A Study and Edition of His Exercises in Composition: Oxford Bodleian MS. Margaret Deneke Mendelssohn c. 43*. Cambridge; New York: Cambridge University Press, 1983.

Todd, *Ossianic* — R. Larry Todd, ''Mendelssohn's Osslanic Manner, with a New Source—*On Lena's Gloomy Heath*,'' *Mendelssohn and Schumann Studies*, ed. Jon Finson and R. Larry Todd. Durham: Duke University Press, 1984, 137-60.

Todd, *Review* — R. Larry Todd. Review of Two Mendelssohn Recordings, *The Musical Quarterly*, 67 (1981), 445-51.

Todd, *Symphony* — R. Larry Todd. ''An Unfinished Symphony by Mendelssohn,'' *Music and Letters*, 61 (1980), 293-309.

Walker, *Oxford*	E. Walker. "Concerning an Oxford Collection of Mendelssohniana," *Music and Letters*, 19 (1938), 426-28.
Weber, *Weber*	Max von Weber. *Carl Maria von Weber*, 2 Vols. Leipzig: Ernst Keil, 1864.
Weissweiler, *Komponistinnen*	Eva Weissweiler. "Fanny Hensel," *Komponistinnen aus 500 Jahren*. Frankfurt: Fischer Taschenbuch Verlag, 1981, 183-204.
E. Werner, *Letters*	Eric Werner. "The Family Letters of Felix Mendelssohn Bartholdy," *New York Public Library Bulletin*, 65 (1961), 5-20.
E. Werner, *Mendelssohn*	Eric Werner. *Mendelssohn*, trans. Dika Newlin. London: Collier-Macmillan Ltd., 1963.
E. Werner, *Sources*	Eric Werner. "Mendelssohn Sources," *Music Library Association Notes*, 12 (1954-55), 201-04.
J. Werner, *F. and F.*	Jack Werner. "Felix and Fanny Mendelssohn," *Music and Letters*, 28 (1947), 303-37.
Wolff, *FMB*	Ernst Wolff. *Felix Mendelssohn Bartholdy*. Berlin: Verlagsgesellschaft für Literatur und Kunst, 1906.
Worbs, *FMB*	Hans Christoph Worbs. *Felix Mendelssohn Bartholdy in Selbstzeugnissen und Bilddokumenten*. Reinbek bei Hamburg: Rowohlt, 1974. (The list of works was compiled with the assistance of Rudolf Elvers.)

List of Illustrations

Introduction

Abraham Mendelssohn once said, "Formerly I was known as the son of my father; now I am known as the father of my son."[1] His daughter Fanny Hensel might have said that she is known as the sister of her brother. Both, of course, are referring to Felix Mendelssohn. But despite the disparity in the siblings' fame, Fanny Hensel and Felix Mendelssohn developed an extremely special, close relationship based on common musical talents and interests that exerted a profound influence on their musical and personal lives. Fanny's letters to Felix from the Green Books at Oxford, spanning a period of twenty-six years and almost entirely unpublished,[2] reveal the depth and breadth of their relationship, and chronicle its decided impact upon Felix's compositions and Fanny's activities as a musician. In addition, the letters hold out a mirror to Berlin cultural life between 1821 and 1847, and make a significant contribution to the social and intellectual history of the nineteenth century.

Fanny Mendelssohn Hensel (1805-1847) was the eldest of four children born to the prosperous banker Abraham Mendelssohn and his culturally sophisticated wife, Lea Salomon. Fanny was four years older than the next child, Felix, and exhibited a protective, almost motherly attitude towards him in their early years. Both were musically precocious, and their shared training and activities set the stage for their close relationship. At birth, Fanny was described by her mother as having "Bach fingers." This observation proved prophetic. At the

[1]S. Hensel *Familie I*, 72.
[2]See "The Edition."

age of thirteen, for instance, she surprised and pleased her demanding father by playing twenty-four Preludes of *The Well-Tempered Clavier* from memory when he returned from an extended business trip. Fanny, like Felix, studied piano with Ludwig Berger, theory and composition with Zelter,[3] and became a member of the Berlin Singakademie.[4] They both received instruction from the renowned piano pedagogue Marie Bigot when Abraham took the family to Paris in 1816. Fanny, like Felix, began composing at an early age; her earliest extant piece dates from 1819, a lied in honor of her father's birthday on 11 December.[5] Autographs in the Mendelssohn Archive, the largest public repository of her music, reveal an outpouring of pieces in the early 1820s. This creative stream diminished markedly beginning in the 1830s, and probably was due in no small part to her new responsibilities as wife (1829) and mother (1830). Yet her musical grasp and influence were expanding as she became increasingly involved in organizing and conducting the lively and sparkling "Sonntagsmusiken," or Sunday musicales, especially after Felix embarked on his lengthy *Bildungsreise* in 1830. These entertainments had become major events after the family acquired the estate at Leipziger Strasse 3, near the Tiergarten, in 1825. The main house contained a large hall with columns and vaulted ceiling that was eminently suited to such gatherings. Lea and Abraham had long served as salon hosts to the intellectual and artistic luminaries of Berlin, but now music took on a more central role in their gatherings. True to her training in the Berlin tradition and intrinsic musical conservatism, Fanny emphasized the music of the masters, especially Bach, Handel, and Mozart. Beethoven was also a favorite. Of course, Felix's music formed a staple of the repertoire, and Fanny's was introduced to the public through this conduit.

Fanny wrote well over four hundred pieces—an estimate, since very few of her compositions were published, and a sizeable proportion of her manuscripts are in private possession and thus unavailable. Her compositions lie in the various genres current at the time, but there is an overwhelming preponderance of lieder and piano works.[6] The first pieces to be published appeared under Felix's authorship: three

[3]For a study of Felix's exercises with Zelter see Todd, *Education.*

[4]See Appendix B for a biographical outline of Fanny and Felix.

[5]Catalogued as DB Manuscript 3.

[6]Fanny herself claimed that lieder suit her best (letter 67).

lieder each in his Opp. 8 and 9 collections (published 1827 and 1830, respectively.)[7] Early in 1837 she contributed a lied, *Die Schiffende,* to an anthology issued by Schlesinger. It was not until late 1846 that her first collection of pieces was published, and six additional *opera* appeared shortly thereafter: Opp. 1 and 7 are lieder, Opp. 2, 4, 5, and 6 are piano pieces, and Op. 3 consists of choral pieces. A few years later four posthumous works were issued, which include two collections of lieder (Opp. 9 and 10), one collection of piano works (Op. 8), and a Trio (Op. 11).[8] Reviews of her works were mixed. A lied by Fanny was deemed the best of the second half of Felix's Op. 8.[9] The review of Op. 1 praised "the entire musical execution"—including the harmonies and the elegance of the accompaniment figuration—but discerned a lack of inner feeling.[10] Some notices made mention of her sex, such as the review of Op. 2, which asserted that the pieces do not betray a female authorship.[11] Some reviews alluded to her connection with Felix,[12] and some compared her style to that of other male contemporaries, such as Robert Schumann.[13]

Even though the great majority of Fanny's works were not published and thus not widely circulated, compositions were introduced to many a famous contemporary through private performances arranged by Fanny or Felix, and thereby garnered respect and praise. Goethe expressed his admiration for Fanny's lieder when Felix performed a few in Weimar in 1821.[14] John Thomson, the Scottish musician and critic for the *Harmonicon,* wrote a flattering appraisal of Fanny's music after his visit to Leipziger Strasse 3 in the summer of 1829.[15] An-

[7]In Op. 8 are *Das Heimweh* (No. 2), *Italien* (No. 3), and the duet *Suleika und Hatem* (No. 12). In Op. 9 are *Sehnsucht* (No. 7), *Verlust* (No. 10), and *Die Nonne* (No. 12).

[8]All issued by Breitkopf & Härtel c. 1850.

[9]*AMZ,* vol. 29, col. 815.

[10]*NZM,* 1 Feb. 1847, 38.

[11]*NZM,* 11 Jan. 1847, 14.

[12]For example in the review of Op. 6 in the *NZM,* 29 July 1847, 50.

[13]In the review of Op. 7 in the *NZM,* 19 Feb. 1848, 88.

[14]Goethe even sent Fanny a poem, *An die Entfernte,* to set to music, but she never did. See Mendelssohn, *Goethe,* 24 and 9.

[15]"She is no superficial musician; she has studied the science deeply, and writes with the freedom of a master. Her songs are distinguished by tenderness, warmth, and originality: some which I heard were exquisite. Miss M. writes, too, for a full orchestra by way of practice" (March 1830, 99).

other critic from the British Isles, the Englishman Henry Chorley, became a devotee of Fanny's pieces.[16] Ignaz Moscheles, Felix's close friend and colleague, also held her music in high esteem.[17]

It is understandable that lieder and piano pieces constituted the bulk of Fanny's works, since her instrument was the piano, and women were traditionally associated with genres suited for domestic performance. Fanny played only for private gatherings, with the exception of a public appearance in February 1838 at a charity benefit (letter 104). At her musicales she performed as soloist, chamber music partner, and accompanist, and frequently collaborated with the many famous musicians who passed through Berlin. She apparently conducted mostly from the keyboard. One contemporary stated that although Felix was the better technically, Fanny's expressiveness was superior.[18]

Yet despite her musical achievements, the high quality of her compositions, and her significance as leader of a flourishing salon in the 1830s and 1840s, Fanny has generally been relegated to the role of sister-of-a-famous-composer rather than treated as a musician of historical significance in her own right. Notable exceptions are two recent unpublished doctoral dissertations,[19] the biased and often factually incorrect section in Weissweiler's study of female composers,[20] and several studies by the present author.[21] Sorely needed are reliable editions of the voluminous documentary material—Fanny was a prolific correspondent and a conscientious diarist.[22] A significant yet indeterminable proportion is in the hands of family members, and undoubtedly a great

[16]Felix communicated Chorley's delight with Fanny's music and playing in a letter to her of 24 October 1840 (DB 9). See also Chorley, *S & M*, 210-11.

[17]Two of Fanny's unpublished lieder elicited Moscheles' praise and orders for copies, as described in the above-cited letter from Felix to Fanny. See also Moscheles, *Leben I*, 93, 309.

[18]Marx, *Erinnerungen II*, 117-18.

[19]Sirota, *Hensel* and Quin, *Hensel*.

[20]Weissweiler, *Komponistinnen*, 183-204.

[21]See Citron, *Hensel*; Citron, *Influence*; Citron, *Letters*; and Citron, *Lieder*.

[22]S. Hensel, *Familie* presents the greatest number of excerpts from Fanny's documents but is cavalier in its policy of changing wording and even names, and occasionally inserting material from one document into another. An exhibition of representative holdings in the Mendelssohn Archive is described in Staatsbibliothek, *Dokumente*. Fanny kept a diary from at least as early as 1829; the autograph diary from that year through 1834 is in the MA.

deal has been lost. But no reasonable assessment can be made until more documentation is available and reliable editions of her music are issued.[23]

The one hundred and fifty letters here are a start in this direction. But they illuminate as much about the recipient as the writer. Fanny, dubbed "the cantor with the thick eyebrows" by her brother, functioned as Felix's chief music critic, and her letters discuss his new pieces, pieces undergoing revision, and performances. Many of the critiques are relatively brief, passing references (e.g. 55). Typical of lengthier assessments are the discussions of the second movement of the *Italian* Symphony (60) and the sacred choral works of the 1830s (67). The most exhaustive critiques involve two major pieces: the *Melusine* Overture (52) and the oratorio *St. Paul* (80). Her remarks about the latter constitute our only clue to the specific nature of many of the pieces in the original version.[24] Occasionally Fanny takes Felix to task for general compositional practices: revising pieces capriciously (60) and writing solo numbers that are not serious enough in his sacred works (67). She is often requested to offer advice on other aspects of his pieces (e.g. 38). In a few cases Fanny's letters furnish additional information on the chronological history of a piece (e.g. 20). As expected, some letters touch on Felix's music much more than others, such as letter 52, which comments on five pieces: the *Melusine* Overture, *Reformation* Symphony, *Walpurgisnacht*, *Volkslieder*, and *Calm Sea*.

Fanny naturally does not neglect her own music. Several letters mention her song cycle of 1829, particularly in connection with her husband's allegorical drawing that adorns the first page of the manuscript (20; Illustration 3). Occasionally the references are very brief, as in the description of her F-major Sonata in 1821 (2). Concern over the publication of her music and her strengths and weaknesses as a composer occupies space in many letters.[25] In a similar vein, Fanny chronicles her successes and problems with piano performance. Her public presentation of Felix's g-minor Concerto in February 1838 (104) and

[23]Fanny Kistner-Hensel, pianist and family descendant, is presently editing many of Fanny's unpublished piano pieces in preparation for publication.

[24]The music to the first version is lost; see Kurzhals-Reuter, *Oratorien*, 96.

[25]See "The Relationship between Fanny and Felix" for an analysis of Fanny's attitudes towards her compositions and their publication.

her oft-requested performances in Italy in 1840 (117) rank as memorable high points.

Typically, reports of her piano playing occur in connection with her Sunday musicales or other performances at Leipziger Strasse 3. The accounts abound with the names of the musically famous in Berlin: Pauline Decker, Auguste Fassmann, Carl Bader, Auguste Thürrschmidt, and Louis Bötticher, to name a few. Before 1830 the names of Eduard Rietz, Julius Rietz, and Ferdinand David grace her descriptions. Foreign artists also perform at the musicales, for example the English sopranos Clara Novello and Mary Shaw, and the young French violinist Henri Vieuxtemps.

These performers, as well as others, do not escape Fanny's scrutiny. Although many are praised, many more are targeted for criticism, such as Thalberg, described as a boring big shot (107); Novello, a vain person who tells lies (112); Rungenhagen, a blockhead (100); and Taubert, a musical imitator (132). Spontini and Zelter are characterized as incompetent and bumbling (23, 12). Those fortunate enough to receive a balanced assessment are Chopin, Franz Hauser, Pasta, Fassmann, Bötticher, Liszt, Paganini, and Marx.

Fanny's view of Berlin musical life extends well beyond personalities, however. The Singakademie is frequently criticized for its poor performances and lack of musical momentum (e.g. 19), concerts presented by Karl Möser are boring and repetitive (87), and the opera has an incompetent management (84).[26] Berlin audiences are portrayed as fickle (94). Furthermore, Fanny is not fond of the city's music critics, implying that they are overly critical (52), and in the case of Ludwig Rellstab, professionally dishonest (14). Yet Fanny herself is highly critical, and in this respect stands squarely within the Berlin tradition, as she readily admits to Felix (134). Her conservative views about music also mark her as a Berliner: she finds some passages too modern in Part I of *St. Paul* (80), discloses steadfast loyalty to first versions of pieces and an aversion to their revision (52, 60, 126), and expresses displeasure with many aspects of contemporary music (68, 94, 107, 112).

Fanny's marriage to the court painter Wilhelm Hensel provides the opportunity for her to observe the leading figures and trends in the Berlin art world. She frequently describes the machinations and intrigues associated with the exhibitions of the Academy of the Arts

[26]Felix also holds a negative opinion of Berlin's musical leaders and institutions.

(86), as well as the rivalry between the Düsseldorf and Berlin schools (85). Foreign art movements also come under her purview. She assesses the quality and influence of contemporary French painters (85), and in several letters from Italy comments on the local art scene (e.g. 116). Sprinkled throughout the correspondence are references to Wilhelm's portraits of society's brightest and wittiest (e.g. 13) and family members (e.g. 22).

Everyday plans and events naturally occupy a significant proportion of the narration, but there emerge some enlightening observations on life and mores in Berlin in the first half of the nineteenth century. Several major technological advances take place during this period: the advent of the railroad, invention of the telegraph, and introduction of gas lighting. Leisure-hour pursuits involve family members in cultural endeavors, such as reading aloud from the latest literary rage, or presenting dramatic representations (*tableaux vivants*) based on a popular painting: activities far removed from today's immersion in electronic media. In addition, childbirth practices differ markedly from today. Women are confined to bed for several weeks both before and after the birth, may use their eyes only sparingly during this period, and are severely restricted in their allotment of food after birth. Perhaps most surprising is the practice of hiring a wet-nurse to feed the baby, and the widespread belief that siblings might grow to resemble each other if nursed by the same wet-nurse (150).

The letters cover the years of the so-called "Vormärz" period—a time of relative political stability for Germany. Sebastian Hensel's retrospective comments about Fanny's limited interest in current events are borne out in the Green Books: she concentrates on her world within the estate at Leipziger Strasse 3, occasionally focuses on events taking place in other countries and parts of Germany, and only rarely turns to politics in Berlin.[27] Her foreign allusions often touch on England, in letters to Felix in London. When she writes about German politics she displays liberal sympathies, as in her joy over the protest of the Baden parliament against the Crown (97), or her tacit approval of the Frankfurt student actions in 1837 (92).[28] Expressions of nationalistic feeling

[27]S. Hensel, *Lebensbild*, 2-3.

[28]Fanny is supposed to have adorned Sebastian's baby pillow in 1830 with a ribbon containing the colors of the French flag as a sign of support for the revolutions (S. Hensel, *Lebensbild*, 14). Wilhelm, on the other hand, was a royalist and actively sided with the monarchy in the uprisings of 1848.

face only infrequently and are mild in tone. Religion plays a negligible role: it is clearly a secular age.

Stylistically Fanny describes her world in a direct, straightforward manner. She, like Felix, avoids abstract modes of expression, although she can, on occasion, wax philosophic about a musical, or even personal, issue (64, 94). People who do express themselves in a vague, high-flown manner become targets for criticism (11). Literature and literary allusions figure prominently (e.g. 83, 1)—not surprising considering the strong humanistic tradition in the family, the comprehensive education afforded the children, the literary-minded age, and the numerous poets and writers of her social circles.

Another characteristic feature is the deployment of puns, although most get lost in translation. For example, in a letter from June 1829, Fanny inquires about Felix's song *Ist es wahr* (Op. 9 No. 1) by beginning the sentence with those very words, which mean "Is it true" (20). Fanny also peppers her writing with numerous foreign words and expressions. French is the most liberally applied spice—not surprising since French culture still held sway over Germany in that period and signified a special cachet in sophistication and elegance. Many French words had been Germanified and taken into the language as part of the regular vocabulary, such as "parliren" from "parler," and some had even been adopted unchanged and, if nouns, provided with an initial capital letter, such as "Saison" and "Plaisir." Another manifestation of the French connection was the use of French words in their original guise, and Fanny's generous sprinkling of French—with words like "maussade" and "renommège," and expressions like "moutarde après diner" and "rat de ville"—is typical for a person of her education and class. But other languages crop up as well: English, Latin, and Italian,[29] the last mostly in her letters from Italy. The occasional presence of English can be attributed to Fanny's heightened interest in the language after the inception of Felix's close ties with England in 1829. Furthermore Felix would frequently insert English words and expressions in his letters, and no doubt introduced English words in conversation. Fanny did not study English until the mid 1830s and lagged behind her sister Rebecka in this department.[30] Her usage be-

[29]Felix also used foreign words generously.

[30]Rebecka displayed a great talent for languages, and occasionally corresponded with Felix in Greek.

surface only infrequently and are mild in tone. Religion plays a negligible role: it is clearly a secular age.
trays an extremely limited knowledge of the language and is generally restricted to a word or very short phrase, such as "rather," or "never mind," or "at an end." Sometimes her construction is grammatically incorrect and clearly marks the author as a foreigner, as in "MAN MIDWIFE."[31] Latin words occur relatively infrequently.

On the personal side the letters convey the very strong bonds of familial loyalty and duty taken for granted by the Mendelssohns. In this respect the family was definitely not an isolated case, as such devotion has been a staple within Jewish tradition over the centuries. And even though the Mendelssohns were converted to Christianity, they retained many social values from their Jewish heritage.

Fanny died in May 1847, at the age of forty-one, from a sudden stroke. According to the information available she had not been suffering from any serious illness and had not had a previous stroke.[32] Certain remarks from the last year strike an ironic note in light of her unexpected death. For instance, in letters from June and December 1846 she declares how happy she is with her life (143) and proclaims a zest for living (148). But we also sense an autumnal flavor permeating letters from this period, almost as a premonition of the end: letters 145 and 146 from the fall months are laden with imagery of the harvest, of the bountiful crop of grapes grown at Leipziger Strasse 3 that year. She was to pass through one more winter and expire in the midst of the season of awakening.

[31]English words found in the original letters are realized in upper case, to distinguish them from the English translations.
[32]See Sirota, *Hensel*, 119 n. 3, for a modern medical opinion suggesting that Fanny had high blood pressure.

The Relationship between Fanny and Felix

The letters in this edition span twenty-six years, 1821 to 1847. At the beginning of this period Fanny is almost sixteen and Felix is a boy of twelve, who is, however, being accorded the very special honor of visiting the great and revered Goethe. At the end Fanny is forty-one and mother to a son as old as she was in 1821, and Felix is a celebrated composer and father to five children. Fanny's letters chronicle the diverse phases of their adult years, but, just as important, disclose the myriad and often subtle changes in their relationship—a relationship of far-reaching personal and musical consequences.

In the first few letters, from October and November 1821, Fanny views herself as mentor, protector, and even parent to her next sibling. In the first letter she dubs herself his "House-Minerva" and expects him to do justice to the training she has given him in her role as tutor. Letters from Felix arrive in the next few days, and on 3 November she both praises him and doles out criticism: "Meanwhile I can't refrain from praising you for your two lovely letters. They were equally well conceived and expressed (the latter is usually not your forte), and in every way therefore welcome and pleasant. . . . But since Goethe says that praise and blame go hand in hand, I can't help finding fault with two things in your letters, although they are very minor. First of all, my dear son, had you checked your agenda . . . you would have found that there was never a *32 Oct.*; you placed this date before the end of your letter. Secondly, within the address of your letters, you must write the place *on the right*, and not on the left as you've done so far. These are in themselves very minor observations; I trust you will not receive them unkindly, for you really know that they're well meant." Note Fanny's use of the term "dear son;" it reveals her role in relation to her younger brother. This maternal attitude invests her with greater control over Felix and the right to partake more fully of his exciting musical experiences.[1]

Felix's trip to Paris in 1825 prompts the next group of letters. He is no longer a boy but a young man of sixteen with four additional years of musical experience and gained confidence. Fanny and Felix have continued to share an especially close relationship, but the passage of four years has narrowed the age difference, which is evident in the more adult tone of address adopted by Fanny. Nevertheless we see some strong vestiges of a parental attitude, as in her criticism of Felix's behavior in her letter of 25 April (7).

Eighteen twenty-nine is a momentous year: Felix embarks on his first extended trip as a professional, and Fanny is engaged to be married. Fanny comments on the great changes about to take place in their family life.[2] There is a voluminous outpouring of correspondence by all members of the family during Felix's eight-month trip to England.[3] Fanny no longer functions as surrogate parent, although on occasion she lapses into the role (e.g. 14). Instead she idealizes Felix through exaggerated expressions of affection and allegorical imagery: all typical Romantic conceits. Characters from literature and other fanciful figures act as symbols. Fanny seems to be viewing herself as some Romantic heroine yearning for the unattainable—in this case some vague, spiritual union with her brother, whom she verily adores. Although we might be tempted to regard such a wish as some abnormal tendency between sister and brother, it can best be understood as the utterance of a young woman in the full bloom of romantic love and engaged to be married, so impressionable and seeped in the idealism and excessive emotionalism of the age that she transfers them to her long-standing confidante, her brother Felix.[4] Perhaps women were

[1]A statement of 1822 conveys Fanny's involvement: "Thus far I've possessed his full confidence. I've seen his talent develop step by step and have even contributed to his musical education to a certain degree. He has no musical advisor besides me. In addition, he never commits an idea to paper without my having examined it first. Thus, for example, I knew his operas by heart before even one note was written down" (Sutermeister, *Reise*, 299).

[2]Entry of 4 January 1829 in F. Hensel, *Tagebuch*; see note 18 to letter 12.

[3]See Crum, *Catalogue I*, 4-7.

[4]Eric Werner views the situation differently: Fanny's emotional exaggerations border on abnormal physical tendencies towards Felix, and she is extremely jealous and possessive of his love (*Mendelssohn*, 76).

more susceptible to such influences; assuming the identity of fictional characters provided a means of escape from domestic confines and entrance into a world without limits.

"I have a deep silence within me when I hear noises, am in the middle of conversation, and am busy doing everyday activities, and I never stop thinking about you" (13). "None of us is as good and clever as you. . . . You are our alpha and omega, and everything in between. You are our soul and our heart, and our head as well" (17). "You are a kind of angel— for God's sake, don't change" (19). These idealizations of Felix are often couched in animal symbols: the lamb representing his gentle side, the rooster his strong, masterful side (e.g. 31). Yet another part of the idealization is given expression in real or imagined pictorial representations in which Felix is the focal point around which the story turns, just as Fanny implies that her world revolves around him. The most literal realization of this scenario is Wilhelm Hensel's drawing entitled *The Wheel,* executed with Felix *in absentia* in July 1829. Described in great detail in letter 27 and featured as Illustration 5, this drawing depicts the close-knit circle of friends, called the wheel, to which Fanny and Felix belong. Felix at the hub is the focal point and group leader, and the other members form the spokes. Their clothes, poses, props, and the ornamented alphabet characters over their heads symbolically elaborate the story. Several refer to Felix's activities, including his future return from London and his relationships with the wheel members. Fanny's fiancé Wilhelm, formerly an outsider, is catapulted into the wheel and thus accepted by the closed group.[5] In letter 24 Fanny inserts a fanciful tale into a factual account of the family's anticipation as it awaits a letter from Felix some Wednesday. Here she paints the image of the family sitting in the kitchen, like servants, doing servants' work, shelling peas. She exaggerates their great anticipation in the midst of their humble activities: Felix's letter looms as the only worthwhile thing in their lives. And then she describes the moment when it arrives, with the resultant spilling of peas and clattering of plates to the floor. Interestingly, in another letter Fanny relates the moment when his letters arrive, and here she compares the attendant excitement and confusion to an opera finale—another fanciful construct (29).

But even more striking than the allegorical idealizations are the

[5]See also letter 23. Other allegories appear in letters 20 and 22.

numerous exaggerated declarations of love for Felix. These utterances begin in the fall of 1828 and culminate on the morning of Fanny's wedding, 3 October 1829. In October 1828 she writes that she intended to write him last evening, but was "afraid of my sentimental feelings" (11). Her emotions come to the surface often in the 1829 letters and are fierce in their intensity. It seems inconceivable that Fanny actually expects Felix to accept such statements at face value, but she might intuitively assume that he is aware of the Romantic tendencies of his sister and adjusts accordingly.

"By the way, believe it or not, when we're together [she and Hensel], you, and then you again, are always the topic of our conversations" (19). "Your *Hora* is really beautiful. How do I arrive at that conclusion? I've been alone for two hours, at the piano. . . . I get up from the piano, stand in front of your picture, and kiss it, and immerse myself so completely in your presence that I—must write you now. But I'm extremely happy and love you very much. Very much" (22). A theme that pervades many of these intense declarations is Fanny's assurance that her marriage to Hensel will not change her love and devotion to Felix, although sometimes it sounds more as if she is attempting to convince herself. Perhaps Fanny is afraid that the happiness of her previous world—times spent with Felix at Leipziger Strasse 3—will disappear with her marriage (24).

The letter written the morning of her wedding is a personal catharsis (32) and a turning point; afterwards her relationship to Felix takes on a different tone. It is also one of the three emotional climaxes within the collection:[6] "I am very composed, dear Felix, and your picture is next to me, but as I write your name again and almost see you in person before my very eyes, I cry, as you do deep inside, but I cry. Actually, I've always known that I could never experience anything that would remove you from my memory for even one-tenth of a moment. Nevertheless, I'm glad to have experienced it, and will be able to repeat the same thing to you tomorrow and in every moment of my life. . . . You will find everything here the same . . ." (32). Fanny is crying as much for her youth and the happy times of the past that can never occur in quite the same way again as she is for her fear that Felix might not love her as much now that she is married, or any confused

[6]The other two are her letters of 2 June 1837 (94) and 9 July 1846 (144).

sense of losing Felix because he is being replaced by Hensel in her affections.[7]

But there is also a playful side to the idealization of Felix in the late 1820s, and a third person enters the picture: their younger sister Rebecka, or "Beckchen," as she was nicknamed. In the typical scenario, described in several letters, Fanny and Rebecka display fits of jealousy, or rather mock fits, over their favorite, their lamb-rooster, their Felix: another manifestation of role playing. Letter 11, from October 1828, presents perhaps the most extreme case of this exaggerated behavior. Here Fanny and Rebecka literally grab the quill away from each other, insert lines within the other's paragraph, and compete fiercely to have the last word. Felix himself plays no small part in promoting this mock jealousy; for instance, he calls both sisters his fish-otters and his "Geren." The latter term, now obsolete, and translated in the letters as "dear girls" or "girls," meant "honeycombs,"[8] and Felix might have been attracted to the image of swarming associated with it. His practice of applying symbolic names, although much more limited than Fanny's, also places him squarely within the Romantic tradition.

Fanny's passage into adulthood occurs during Felix's trip to England and the months in 1830 before the birth of Sebastian. After June 1830 the allegorical trappings and intense declarations of love disappear.[9] Fanny plants both feet in the real world as she manages a household and raises a child. Nevertheless, the years of idealization will have a residual effect on her future life. She has come to expect perfect

[7]One wonders whether Felix had comparable fears of losing Fanny and her love when she got married. Sirota, *Hensel*, 42, asserts that Felix was jealous of Fanny's relationship with Wilhelm, and offers Felix's criticism of Hensel's portrait of Fanny as proof (see note 9 to letter 21). I find the evidence unconvincing and the conclusion unfounded, especially in light of Felix's remark in another letter that he considers it unfair to Hensel to postpone the wedding (see note 1 to letter 22). Wilhelm apparently had some difficulty in accepting Fanny's strong emotional attachment to Felix, or at least her utterances about it, as revealed in Fanny's letters to her fiancé written in the summer of 1829 (especially of 23 August, DB 106).

[8]Grimm, *Wörterbuch IV* 1b, col. 3592.

[9]Eric Werner makes a similar observation, stating that as Fanny grew into the role of wife and mother, "these tensions and pseudo-Byronic effusions vanished entirely" (*Mendelssohn*, 77).

behavior from Felix, especially in his conduct towards her, and her high standards demand a great deal from him. Throughout the course of the next seventeen years several occasions will arise when Fanny is hurt or disappointed by Felix because his actions do not live up to her lofty expectations.

With the letters of 1833 we enter the next phase of her correspondence.[10] Fanny and Felix are more mature; Felix is beginning to make a major name for himself in the world of music and is happily ensconced in a position, at Düsseldorf; and Fanny has been assuming a more active role in organizing and directing the Sunday musicales. From late 1833 to late 1834 her letters are animated by several discussions of musical or topical interest.[11] These interchanges are some of the most stimulating in the entire collection and reveal a relationship between equals.

The first issue to emerge is the Goethe-Zelter correspondence, issued in six parts between the end of 1833 and the end of 1834. Hardly any non-personal issue provokes as much anger. Fanny's letter of 1 December 1833 introduces the topic (49). We hear of it next in a letter from the end of February (52). After a disparaging reference in a letter of November (62), Fanny bares her anger again and takes another forceful poke at the work. Another ongoing discussion concerns Felix's *Melusine* Overture. Although Fanny has long given Felix detailed critiques of his pieces, this is the first extant example (52). It also proves influential, as Felix later declares that he has adopted many of her suggestions.[12] Incidentally, this is the letter in which Fanny piques Felix's anger by requesting additional information on the Melusine tale and thereby sets off a minor tiff that is continued in her next letter.

A discussion of another sort—an aesthetic argument—is pursued in letters from the last two months of 1834. Once again the impetus comes from a letter of Fanny. On 4 November Fanny comments that one finds Lafont, a violinist, outmoded merely by looking at him, and goes on to state that Paganini has effected a drastic change in violin playing (61). Her next letter makes it clear that she thinks Felix has no

[10]Letters from late 1830 through 1832 were removed from the Green Books. See "The Edition."

[11]An observation also made in Grossmann-Vendrey, *Vergangenheit*, 57.

[12]See note 10 to letter 52.

grounds for bawling her out for saying that it is man who brings about change: a classic case of the man-shapes-history vs. history-shapes-man argument. A few months later Fanny takes cognizance of the more mature tone of their recent letters and concludes, "It's fine with me if it stays this way" (67).

It does stay that way. During the next three years the oratorio *St. Paul* occupies considerable space in their correspondence. In 1834 and 1835 the references are brief and focus mainly on her curiosity about the evolving work (57, 60, 68). In January 1836 Fanny is already organizing private performances of certain sections of the work (77, 78). At the end of the month Felix solicits her advice as a colleague as to "fifths, rhythm, and voice-leading; as to conception, counterpoint, *et caetera Animalia*."[13] On 4 February Fanny begins her letter by adopting Felix's wording and then proceeds to render a detailed, moderate, and well-reasoned critique of the second half of Part I that includes praise as well as criticism.[14] Fanny's enthusiasm for the work is even greater after she attends the premiere on 22 May in Düsseldorf—she wants to know everything about its future course (82). During the summer she is kept abreast of the revisions and offers her opinions about the latest changes (84). Her letters from the last third of 1836 point towards a private performance for the family on Christmas day (85, 89, 90). The true culmination, however, is the Berlin premiere of the final version at one of her Sunday musicales, on 22 January 1837, which is a great success (91). One year later the Singakademie presents the work to the Berlin public, and Fanny is called in as advisor during the final preparations. Her vivacious narration of these rehearsals cannot fail to have amused Felix (100). In her next letter she renders a fairly positive evaluation of the performance (101; Illustration 8), but Felix is skeptical and attributes her favorable reaction to family bias.[15] In general, Fanny's long-term involvement with the oratorio again shows her to be a valued and supportive musical confidante.

In the autumn of 1836 there begins a period of approximately one year in which their relationship undergoes a severe strain. In October Fanny complains that Felix has not written in a long time and adds that

[13]See note 1 to letter 80.
[14]The significance of Fanny's comments to our knowledge about the music of the first version, now lost, is underscored in Kurzhals-Reuter, *Oratorien*, 96.
[15]See note 2 to letter 101.

a relationship cannot be sustained when communication is one-sided (85). Felix is courting Cecile during these months, and his response tells of augmented responsibilities as a correspondent.[16] Over the next several months Fanny repeatedly expresses her desire to meet Felix's intended before the wedding. The meeting never takes place, however,[17] and may be one of the reasons why Fanny and the rest of the immediate family do not attend the ceremony in Frankfurt on 28 March.[18] Anger and hurt fester for a few months and finally receive expression in an emotional letter to Felix dated 2 June 1837 (94). The collapse of plans for Felix and Cecile to visit Berlin in the summer adds fuel to the fire. Another possible factor contributing to the strain is Felix's lack of encouragement for the publication of Fanny's music.[19] After the passage of several months, however, the wounds begin to heal, Fanny becomes accustomed to Felix having a wife, and their correspondence resumes a congenial, if not as intimate, tone.

Fanny's trips to Italy of 1840 and 1845 dominate her letters over the next few years and vividly convey her keen excitement at being far from home and in that land of special enchantment for Romantic poets and painters. Fanny pays attention to Cecile in her letters after 1837, but primarily with respect to family matters. Sometimes we sense a note of hypocrisy towards Felix's wife. Between 1840 and 1845 there are several gaps in the correspondence, largely attributable to Felix's appointment to King Wilhelm Friedrich IV in Berlin. But Felix's attention to his growing family plays a role, for it precludes the kind of relationship shared with Fanny before his marriage. They are still close but each is becoming more involved in his own sphere of activities and may have less of a need, and possibly inclination, to bring the other into his world. The death of their mother at the end of 1842 also changes the relationship: childhood bonds are broken, and the concept of Leipziger Strasse 3 and what it represents is now gone forever.[20]

The summer of 1846 produces two successive letters startling in their cathartic intensity (144, 145). Fanny announces that she is about to have her Opus 1 published, and in the process discloses her fears of

[16]See note 2 to letter 85.

[17]See note 5 to letter 94.

[18]The only relative on Felix's side present is his Aunt Dorothea Schlegel, who lives in Frankfurt.

[19]See the discussion below.

[20]See letter 126.

her brothers and deceased father, and her lifelong attempt to please all loved ones. Only partially concealed resentment towards Felix's negative opinion of her publishing plans surfaces in her statement that "I trust *you* will in no way be bothered by it, since, as you can see, I've proceeded completely on my own in order to spare you any possible unpleasant moment, and I hope you won't think badly of me" (144). In her next letter she expresses outrage at the idea of starting to publish at such an advanced age, and admits that she has had a guilty conscience towards him, given his negative attitude. These statements reveal long-standing strain in their relationship. Moreover she declares that "an entire oratorio of yours [*Elijah*] is being introduced to the world again, and I don't know a note of it. When will we hear it?" (144). If one compares this situation to her intimate involvement with *St. Paul,* one realizes how considerably their relationship has changed over the course of ten years, and how markedly Felix's dependence on her musical advice has diminished.

Although the letters chronicle numerous changes in their relationship from 1821 to 1847, several themes permeate the collection as a whole. One involves Fanny's attitudes towards her musical activities: her lack of self confidence and need for Felix's approval.[21] Fanny is particularly unsure of her creative ability (23, 42, 67, 116), and also sets little store by her talent as a pianist.[22] For example, she writes that the prospect of Felix asking her to play in Düsseldorf when she visits later in the spring of 1835 fills her with anxiety, since the Düsseldorfers will probably have heard Felix play any pieces she might perform. In addition Fanny declares that "I'm so unreasonably afraid of you anyway (and of no other person, except slightly of father) that I actually never play particularly well in front of you, and I wouldn't even attempt to accompany in front of you, although I know I'm very good at it" (70). Here her lack of confidence derives from a comparison with her brother; in Fanny's mind she clearly comes out the lesser of the two.[23] Thus it is with particular satisfaction that Fanny reports how well she performed at her first public appearance, in February 1838

[21]See also Citron, *Influence*.

[22]See Hiller's glowing report of Fanny's rendition of a Hummel piece at a gathering in 1822, and Fanny's negative view of that same performance, as quoted in Sirota, *Hensel*, 15-16.

[23]Her statement about her fear of him and of their father is echoed eleven years later in her emotional letter of July 1846 (144); see the discussion above.

(104). There is only one letter in which Fanny describes her conducting with a baton, and she makes it clear that lack of confidence prevented her from doing a truly fine job (57).

Why, despite her considerable talents, does Fanny doubt her ability? One reason is that she never received an evaluation by any first-rate musician.[24] Perhaps even more important is that in spite of her excellent and comprehensive musical education she knew she was not being groomed to be a professional musician because she is a woman, and women have other responsibilities. This message was inculcated by her father. As early as 16 July 1820 Abraham writes to the fourteen-year-old Fanny: "Music will perhaps become his [Felix's] profession, while for *you* it can and must only be an ornament, never the root of your being and doing . . . and your very joy at the praise he earns proves that you might, in his place, have merited equal approval. Remain true to these sentiments and to this line of conduct; they are feminine, and only what is truly feminine is an ornament to your sex."[25] And eight years later: "You must prepare more earnestly and eagerly for your real calling, the *only* calling of a young woman—I mean the state of a housewife."[26]

Yet Fanny does continue seriously with her musical activities, although she also fulfills her responsibilities as wife and mother. Since she does not receive validation and approval for her music from the established musical world, she turns to Felix for such support. Although she is clearly dependent on him as early as 1821, as in her claim that "you're my right hand and my eyesight, and without you, therefore, I can't proceed with my music" (1), her need for his approval seems greatest once he has established himself as a professional musician—i.e. after 1830. In this way Felix serves to put a professional stamp of approval on her music and link it to the established musical world.

Fanny seeks Felix's approval of several facets of her life: "I don't know exactly what Goethe means by the demonic influence, which he mentioned very often near the end, but this much is clear: if it does exist, you exert it over me. I believe that if you seriously suggested that I become a good mathematician I wouldn't have any partic-

[24]Abraham took Felix to Cherubini in Paris in 1825 for an assessment of his musical talent.

[25]S. Hensel, *Family I*, 82.

[26]S. Hensel, *Family I*, 84.

ular difficulty in doing so, and I could just as easily cease being a musician tomorrow if you thought I wasn't good at that any longer. Therefore treat me with great care'' (84).[27] In another letter Fanny complains about a lack of musical stimulation in Berlin and then declares how glad she is that Felix likes her recent piano pieces (87). The importance of Felix's approval also extends to the publication of her music.[28] It is telling of Abraham's influence on his children that Fanny does not publish any pieces under her own name until after her father's death, and Felix inherits his father's view that women should not become professional musicians. Fanny first broaches the subject in October 1836 (86). From a remark she makes in a letter from the following month it is clear that Felix is opposed to the idea (88). Fanny proceeds with her plan to have a lied, *Die Schiffende,* published in a Schlesinger album in early 1837; afterwards Felix sends his congratulations on its success and his gratitude for its publication.[29] The issue apparently remains alive through the summer of 1837. Even though no mention of publishing appears in their correspondence, the subject is brought up by their mother. In a letter to Felix of 7 June Lea asks Felix to encourage and assist Fanny in having her music published.[30] Felix responds that he cannot in good conscience encourage her, a woman, in this endeavor, although he is willing to offer assistance if she decides to go ahead with it.[31] Whether or not justified, Felix here evinces a protectionist attitude towards his sister, a view consistent with other family decisions and society's attitudes towards women. He has determined the extent of her capabilities and the nature of her role and is echoing his father's statement uttered some seventeen years earlier. Perhaps Felix feels he has to stand in for his father and perpetuate his views. One might be tempted to infer that Felix senses real competition from

[27]The demonic imagery is a typical Romantic conceit; see also note 13 to letter 84.
[28]See Citron, *Influence*.
[29]See note 4 to letter 92.
[30]''Permit me a question and a request. Shouldn't she publish a selection of lieder and piano pieces? For about a year she's been composing many excellent works, especially for the piano. . . . That *you* haven't requested and encouraged her to do it—this alone holds her back. Wouldn't it therefore be appropriate for you to encourage her and help her find a publisher?'' (unpublished letter, GB VI 44).
[31]Letter of 24 June 1837 (NYPL), incorrectly dated 2 June in Mendelssohn, *Briefe I*, 88-89. One interesting line was omitted from the published version: Felix asks Lea not to show his letter to Fanny and Wilhelm. Thus it is likely that Fanny never read these lines.

his sister if she publishes and thereby gains a professional foothold, but there is no evidence to support such a claim. Furthermore, Felix seems very glad after the fact and is always supportive of her compositions and salon activities. Another possibility is that Felix wants to spare his sister the difficult experience of being subjected to the malicious pen of the critics.[32] It is interesting that Lea Mendelssohn, someone of the older generation, believes Fanny should publish her music, yet not surprising considering her sophistication and training as a musician—perhaps some of her own aspirations would be realized in her daughter. Fanny's letters from the summer of 1846, when she writes Felix that her Op. 1 is about to appear, reveal that Felix's views on the matter have not changed.[33] One is forced to conclude, therefore, that Fanny would probably have published more music had she been encouraged by Felix.

Another theme centers on Fanny's immersion in Felix's musical world, suggesting that she is living through him, perhaps vicariously. For instance, during his early trips to Weimar and Paris, Fanny insists on knowing all the details and claims she will be angry if he does not tell her everything. One might detect a note of envy in many of Fanny's lines from this period, such as, "You are really lucky to study from him [Hummel] again" (2). Fanny might wonder why she, given essentially the same musical education as Felix, is not being afforded these special opportunities. As the two siblings enter their maturity, they both establish a way of life in which music plays a major role. Fanny, like many well-educated women of the early nineteenth century,[34] cultivates a salon. Based in the home, it is an avenue open to sophisticated, witty women who are largely excluded from the economic, social, and political institutions of unlimited horizons.[35] As Fanny's salon is a microcosm of Felix's musical world, she is supremely interested in communicating its activities to a kindred soul as well as finding out everything about his sphere of activities. In this

[32]A view proposed by Dr. Cécile Lowenthal-Hensel, great granddaughter of Fanny, in a conversation of 1983.

[33]Letters 144, 145; see the discussion above.

[34]Such as Rahel Varnhagen, Sara Levy, and Fanny Arnstein. The last two are both great aunts on her mother's side.

[35]The difference between the scope and frequency of Felix's travels and Fanny's travels is immense. See Appendix B.

way she keeps in contact with the professional world of music and also enters that world herself through Felix. Thus she feels very badly when she is excluded—for example, when she expresses regrets about not being asked to work on the piano arrangement of *St. Paul* (84). To Fanny's delight Felix occasionally pulls Fanny into his world by having her act on his behalf. She functions as Felix's stand-in in the capacity of expert musical advisor at Singakademie rehearsals of the *St. Matthew* Passion (12) and *St. Paul* (100). Fanny twice carries on negotiations with singers at Felix's behest: for the Lower Rhenish Music Festival (111) and Felix's concerts in Leipzig (106). She is also requested to visit Rungenhagen at the Singakademie to find out if the institution possesses certain pieces that Felix wishes to use at his series of historic concerts in Leipzig (119).

The affection between Fanny and Felix shines forth in their correspondence. Fanny—the sister whom Felix dubs Fance, Fenchel, fish-otter, and "the cantor with the thick eyebrows"[36]—is very fond of her brother. Certain letters disclose her special sisterly concern in a touching manner, such as that from July 1829 in which she attempts to allay Felix's fears about a forthcoming letter from their father that will castigate Felix for omitting the surname Bartholdy in England (25). Sprinkled through her letters are pet names for Felix: lamb, clown, Felixelchen, and "my son."

Fanny's last letter to Felix honors his birthday in February 1847; three months later she succumbs to a swift fatal stroke.[37] Felix's closest lifelong advisor is now gone. Devastated by the loss of his beloved Fenchel,[38] he goes through a difficult period and his health begins to deteriorate. At the end of October Felix suffers the first of a series of strokes that culminate in his death on 4 November. Although it is nonsensical to assert that Fanny's death was a direct cause, it nevertheless

[36]Perhaps a reference to J. S. Bach.

[37]The autograph of her last composition, the lied *Bergeslust,* appears as Illustration 13.

[38]An unpublished letter to Rebecka of 19 May 1847 (NYPL), five days after Fanny's death, exposes the depth of his shock, disorientation, and remorse: "God help us all—I don't know what else to say and think . . . God help us, God help us! . . . Alas, if only we hadn't been apart! That causes me such bitter regrets! And the only thing that helps a little is to cry a lot—if only one could do that all the time. . . . Alas, dear sister, I can't write or think about anything except Fanny. It will never be otherwise as long as we're here on earth."

played a major role in his general decline and should be considered a contributing factor. Perhaps Fanny meant more to him than he realized and was as important to his well being as he was to hers. In any case, such an unusual sister-brother relationship may be unique in the history of music.

The Edition

The Green Books collection of letters addressed to Felix contains over 5,000 items. It constitutes a major part of the Margaret Deneke collection of Mendelssohniana at the Bodleian Library in Oxford, and its contents have been catalogued by Margaret Crum, retired Assistant Librarian in the Bodleian's Department of Western Manuscripts.[1] Letters meant a great deal to Felix, and, like other members of the family, he was deeply committed to their preservation. They were bound in green leather on a fairly regular basis. Although Felix attempted to reflect their chronology, many were displaced; some were inadvertently divided and therefore given a seemingly incomplete status.[2] The collection dates from 1821 through 1847, with some noticeable large gaps: the years between 1822 and 1828, and the last half of 1830 through all of 1832.[3] Regarding the earlier gap it is conceivable that Lea Mendelssohn took parental charge of many of Felix's youthful letters.[4] The latter is not so easy to explain, however; no one has suggested a reason to account for these missing letters. They apparently disappeared after 1844, when they were listed in an inventory of the collection. In addition, other letters have been removed over the course of the years. Felix himself is known to have distributed several letters as presents (*Albumblätter*), and his grandson Albrecht may have sold some complete letters or excerpts.[5]

[1]Crum, *Catalogue I.*
[2]For example, letter 58. See Appendix A.
[3]Elvers, *Nachlass*, 43.
[4]Elvers, *Verleger*, xxv.
[5]Elvers, *Verleger*, xxiv.

The Green Books remained with the Mendelssohn family until the death of Paul Victor Mendelssohn Benecke, grandson of the composer, in 1944. The collection had been passed down to Carl, Felix's eldest son, upon the death of Cecile in 1853, and then to his son, Albrecht, upon his death in 1897. Albrecht, like many Mendelssohns, married a first cousin, Dora Wach, the daughter of Felix's youngest child, Lili. Dora and Lili prepared an index to the Green Books, building on Carl's numeration of the letters.[6] The next owner was Benecke, the son of Marie, Felix's second child. Benecke lived in Oxford and was a Senior Fellow at Magdalen College from 1891. Upon his death in 1944 he entrusted the Green Books to his good friend, Margaret Deneke, herself a musician and avid collector. She, in turn, donated them to the Bodleian in 1959 on indefinite loan. In 1969 Deneke died, and the collection was bequeathed to her sister, Helena. Four years later, upon Helena's demise, the collection became the property of the Bodleian.

The Green Books consist of twenty-seven volumes; the first twenty-six contain the letters in chronological order.[7] Family letters predominate in the earlier volumes, and it is possible that other letters from those years were not always retained. Beginning in the mid 1830s, however, Felix seems to have preserved all letters.[8] From 1835 to 1847 we see an enormous increase in the range of correspondents and the sheer quantity of correspondence. Because of the bulk, each of these thirteen years is divided into two bound volumes.

Letters authored by Fanny appear in the first twenty-five volumes—from October 1821 to February 1847. She is represented by two hundred and seventy-nine letters, one of the largest groups by any correspondent.[9] One hundred and fifty letters are included in the present edition—almost 54%. Although it would seem advantageous to publish all of Hensel's letters, there are two main drawbacks: they are of uneven

[6]Carl's numbers are still in use today. They form the basis of the entries in Crum, *Catalogue I*, and appear in the "Listing of the Letters" (Appendix A).

[7]Volume 27 contains miscellaneous papers, including suggested texts to be set to music (Crum, *Catalogue I*, 266).

[8]Elvers, *Verleger*, xxv.

[9]This number counts a letter with separated fragments as one item, even though each segment has its own catalogue number. There are also two non-letter items from Fanny to Felix: a list of Felix's music, books, *et al.* (GB IV 204), and a copy of a poem (GB IV 210).

value and interest, and the edition, which contains both English and German versions, would be too long.

Certain criteria were applied in the selection process. Letters that contain information on any aspect of music—be it composers, pieces, performers, performances, or performance practices—are included, as are those that touch on aesthetic issues. Also chosen are letters that show the siblings' relationship as musical colleagues, point up significant personal issues between them, or chronicle their changing relationship. In addition, an attempt is made to provide chronological balance within the twenty-six-year time span. Conversely, letters are omitted if they contain only routine family news, such as reports of minor illnesses or Sebastian's progress in school. Letters that concentrate exclusively on the art scene are generally excluded. Letters from Italy of insignificant musical interest, albeit conceivably of general interest as travelogues, are passed over.[10] Many letters constitute nothing more than a brief note of thanks or an accompanying note in a package; these are omitted as well.

The question might well be posed, why include the German versions? The answer is clear: with very few exceptions[11] Fanny's letters in the Green Books have never been published. Without the availability of the original documents the letters in English translation lose their credibility as faithful renditions of Fanny's thought.

The letters in the Green Books constitute nearly all of Fanny's known letters to Felix that are extant and accessible to the public.[12] Three letters not part of the Oxford collection were published by Sebastian Hensel, and the location of the originals is unknown.[13] Several letters are probably in the hands of private owners, perhaps family descendants.

[10]Fanny wrote similar descriptions of the sights and sounds of Italy in her diary and in letters to other family members. Substantial excerpts from both appear in S. Hensel, *Familie II*, 69-176.

[11]See the discussion below.

[12]Within the NYPL collection are four letters from Fanny to some undetermined member of the family, from July and August of 1841 (Nos. 505, 507, 509, and 516); it could be Felix.

[13]Letter of 15 April 1829, in *Familie I*, 200-01; of sometime in the spring of 1838, in *Familie II*, 43-44; and of 7 December 1840, in *Familie II,* 179-80. Sebastian Hensel was not permitted to view the Green Books, and thus no references from the collection appear in his book (*Familie I,* vii).

The return correspondence assumes two forms: a section specifically designated for Fanny within general letters sent to the entire family,[14] and private letters addressed to her alone.[15] It would be impossible to publish Felix's return correspondence here given the general and wide-ranging character of a high proportion of his return correspondence, not to mention its sheer size. Another reason is that Felix's letters will be published elsewhere, by Rudolf Elvers, who has undertaken the mammoth task of compiling a *Gesamtausgabe* of the thousands of letters that Felix wrote.[16] Fanny's letters, however, do not take on proper meaning without specific reference to Felix's letters; thus the letters in this edition allude frequently and generously to Felix's missives.

The chart opposite tabulates the chronological distribution of Fanny's letters in the Green Books and also presents the statistics on the ratio of letters included and omitted.

The condition of Fanny's manuscript letters is reasonably good. One encounters only a few tears, usually caused by the removal of a wax seal, and an occasional smudge. The ink has generally remained dark enough for legibility, although in a few cases faded to the point where reading becomes difficult. The two most serious problems are bleedthrough, and obliteration of words or characters because of the binding.[17] A significant proportion of the letters contain the outer address and postmark, not surprising considering the custom of folding and sealing the sheets of the letter without the addition of a separate envelope. The size of the paper shows wide variation—from the note-card size utilized in brief letters (e.g. 120), to the 5 1/8'' x 8'' typical of most letters after 1829 (e.g. 101 and 144 [Illustrations 8 and 11]), to the

[14]The NYPL collection. Felix made it clear that letters addressed to a parent are intended for everyone, and he does not have the time to write individual letters to each member of the family. See his letter of 14 July 1824 (NYPL).

[15]Mostly in the Mendelssohn Archive, which has at least fifty-six such letters. Numerous excerpts appear in S. Hensel, *Familie*, and Mendelssohn, *Briefe*, although with extensive editorial ''corrections.'' In the NYPL collection are seven addressed to Fanny alone, of which two are brief fragments, and four addressed to both Fanny and Rebecka.

[16]Elvers, *Verleger* is volume I of this series. The more than seven hundred letters of the NYPL collection are to be issued next.

[17]This problem is often exacerbated when Fanny writes sideways in the margins after she has run out of space, as shown in Illustration 2.

Chronological Distribution of Fanny's Letters

Year	*Included*	*Omitted*	*Totals*
1821	4	0	4
1825	4	0	4
1827	2	3	5
1828	1	2	3
1829	24	22	46
1830	7	12	19
1833	7	3	10
1834	15	11	26
1835	12	14	26
1836	14	9	23
1837	9	11	20
1838	7	4	11
1839	8	6	14
1840	6	5	11
1841	4	6	10
1842	1	3	4
1843	6	5	11
1844	3	4	7
1845	4	7	11
1846	10	2	12
1847	2	0	2
TOTALS:	150	129	279

large, 9 1/4" x 12" size prevalent in the lengthy family letters of 1829 (e.g. 12 [Illustration 2]).

Fanny's letters are presented complete: there are no excised passages. Many letters, however, contain sections written by other members of the family—a practice especially prevalent before 1830. Because the purpose of this edition is to present the letters of Fanny Hensel and not the writing of others, these sections are not included but indicated by the name of the writer(s) enclosed in brackets. In addition several letters after 1833 contain a section in which Fanny writes for Sebastian; these, too, have been omitted and marked with brackets.

This book constitutes the first volume devoted exclusively to the letters of Fanny Hensel. To date only two of Fanny's letters from the Green Books have been published in their entirety,[18] and the overwhelming majority—over 95% of the total of two hundred and seventy-nine, or 92% of the one hundred and fifty in this edition—has not been published at all. Ten letters, all included here, have had sections excerpted for publication. The majority of such excerpts (in seven letters) has amounted to only two or three sentences,[19] two are quite extensive,[20] and one lies somewhere in between.[21]

The English translations constitute the focus of the book; the German originals are present primarily for referential and documentary purposes. Substantive annotations are appended to the English translations; only textual problems receive explanation in the German versions. Biographical information identifying individuals is reserved for the Glossary and Index of Names at the back, an arrangement that helps avoid clutter and needless repetition. There are also indices to Hensel's compositions and Mendelssohn's compositions. Appendix A lists each of the one hundred and fifty letters and gives its catalogue number within the Green Books, its date and place of origin, its destination, and its

[18]Letters 84 and 144 (30 July 1836 and 9 July 1846), in Citron, *Hensel*, 176-79.

[19]From letter 1 (Mendelssohn, *Goethe*, 6), letter 22 (E. Werner, *Mendelssohn*, 77), letter 24 (E. Werner, *Mendelssohn*, 77), letter 32 (E. Werner, *Mendelssohn*, 77), letter 46 (2 passages; Grossmann-Vendrey, *Vergangenheit*, 58, 64), letter 86 (Grossmann-Vendrey, *Vergangenheit*, 141), and letter 91 (Kurzhals-Reuter, *Oratorien*, 149).

[20]From letter 7 (A. Mendelssohn, *Erinnerungen)*, and from letter 12 (Grossmann-Vendrey, *Vergangenheit*, 30-31).

[21]From letter 90 (Kurzhals-Reuter, *Oratorien*, 110); see note "a" to the German version of that letter.

page number. Appendix B offers a biographical summary of Fanny and Felix by year.

The Transcriptions

Fanny's letters appear in a typical nineteenth-century German script.[22] Like the hand of Felix,[23] Fanny's is exceptionally clear, although not as elegant, and relatively few crossouts appear. Her earlier script is less fluid, and for this reason the writing in the letters from 1821 is slightly more difficult to decipher.[24]

The general policy has been to retain as much as possible from the original: all spellings, even in cases where it has changed over the last one-hundred-plus years;[25] all abbreviations, all underlining, all punctuation, all dating, and all musical notation. The reader will often note inconsistencies in Fanny's practices. Her spelling of proper names is often variable: Heyne or Heine, Ritz or Rietz, Frank or Franck, to list a few.[26] She seems to spell many words incorrectly, such as "Schooßhund" for "Schoßhund," or "Corespondenz" for "Correspondenz." She does not make a uniform practice of capitalizing the first letter of "Ihr" and "Euch." She is inconsistent in her use of a hard "c" versus a "k," as in "Singacademie." Some of the variability in spelling, particularly the interchangeability of "c" and "k," is symptomatic of the fact that German spelling was not standardized during this period, and foreign languages, especially French, had a strong foothold in many areas of the language.[27] One difficulty in transcription arises from Fanny's habit of lifting the quill in the middle of a word and

[22]See Illustrations 2, 8, and 11.

[23]See an example of Felix's handwriting in Illustration 9, an autograph letter to Fanny of 13 November 1843.

[24]For example, the final "f" in a word such as "auf," and the similarity between the uppercase "R" and "F."

[25]For example, verbs now ending in "ieren" were spelled with "iren," as in "interessiren"; an "h" was commonplace after a "t" in words such as "thun" and "Thaler"; and "ei" combinations were often, although not always, rendered by "ey," as in "seyn."

[26]Felix is much more consistent in his spelling of proper names.

[27]See also the "Introduction." Early editions of Mendelssohn letters, such as Mendelssohn, *Briefe* and S. Hensel, *Familie*, made a standard policy of Germanizing foreign elements in the language.

thereby leaving a space, which usually is no smaller than her normal spacing between words. In most instances one encounters little difficulty in demarcating words, as context makes the reading perfectly clear. But there are several occasions when that small space causes problems, such as in the middle of an infinitive with a separable prefix, such as ''stattfinden,'' which could be written as ''statt finden'' or as one word.[28] Because the language was not standardized and Fanny tended to be inconsistent, it is virtually impossible in some cases to know precisely which version is meant. In general, when the spacing seems equivalent to nearby spaces separating words, then the prefix is separated from the stem.

An exception to the policy of keeping Fanny's text verbatim involves the transcription of the ''m̄'' abbreviation as ''mm.'' In addition, no designation has been made to reflect when Fanny utilizes Latin script instead of German script. Whereas Felix is consistent in his use of Latin script,[29] Fanny is not. She will regularly combine Latin and German characters within the same word, thereby making distinctions in transcription very sticky, and, unlike Felix, she does not write all proper names in Latin script. Incidentally, it is often her Latin script that creates the greatest difficulties for transcription.

Despite the general clarity of her hand, a few passages occur where her writing is illegible. These are rendered by brackets, as are passages where a tear, smudge, or pasteover obliterates text, or the binding conceals parts of words or entire words. Fanny makes careless mistakes on several occasions, such as writing ''Sie hast'' instead of ''Sie hat'' (110). In such cases Fanny's version appears as is, and a footnote using a lower-case alphabet character is inserted as explanation.

The Translations

The chief principle guiding the translations has been the attempt to strike a reasonable balance between a faithful representation of Fanny's style, and readable, clear English. In many cases her phraseology, constructions, and syntax can be retained, whereas in others they must be

[28]To confuse matters further, one finds a third version for this word: ''Statt finden.''
[29]See Mendelssohn, *Briefe-L*, 17.

modified, sometimes substantially, to read well in English. The other goal has been to reflect the informal tone of her letters—she is, after all, corresponding with a very close relative. One device that evokes the informality is the deployment of contractions, such as "I'm" and "we've." Colloquial expressions are rendered in colloquial language in English, but care is taken to avoid modernisms.

The greatest challenge facing the translator is the sentence construction. Fanny regularly fashions sentences consisting of a string of independent clauses that are separated by commas and lack conjunctions. Here is a typical case: "Mittwoch Mittag aßen Caroline u. Auguste hier, tête à tête mit Mutter u. mir, nach Tisch kamen Märckers zum Kaffee, die gingen dann wieder fort, u. nun hätte ich Dich hergewünscht, um zu sehn, wie im Zwielicht Onkel zwischen Caroline u. Auguste auf dem Sopha saß, u. gräulich Cour schnitt, als ich mich über heiße Ohren u. kalte Hände beklagte, nahm er die Mädchen erst bei den Händen, u. dann bei den Ohren, um zu versuchen, obs ihnen auch so wäre, nachher zeichnete an Beiden" (13). It would make very poor English syntax to retain the multiple independent clauses demarcated with commas. The policy adopted in such cases separates the independent clauses by means of a semicolon, period, or dash, depending upon context and flow, generally without the addition of an intervening conjunction. Conjunctions exert great influence on how a sentence will be understood, and the translator runs the risk of altering the meaning of the original. With regard to sentence length, care has been taken to reflect the length of the original as much as possible, but, as we have just demonstrated, that is often impracticable.

Typically, certain problems arise from grammatical differences between the two languages. In German a person of the female sex is often designated by the feminine definite article before her proper name, e.g. "die Decker." No comparable construction exists in English. To make a decision to use Miss, Fräulein, or Mlle.—or Mrs., Frau, or Mme.—is to intervene with a definition of the woman's marital status as well as her social standing. In almost all passages where this construction is found, the woman's identity is obvious enough so that her last name can stand alone. In the few instances where her identity can be confused with a male with the same surname, an appropriate title of address is inserted in brackets.

Another inherent difficulty is encountered in the concept "you." English constitutes the culprit: "you" denotes both singular and plural, and often leads to confused meanings. Although a distinction in translation could be made by using a term such as "all of you" or "both of you" when a German plural is used, this option was rejected as general policy because of its clumsiness. Instead, for the sake of flow, the imprecise "you" is employed to render "Du," "Ihr," and "Sie," with the exception of the few instances in which context demands absolute clarity in number. Then a qualifier such as those just mentioned is used.

Fanny usually omits quotation marks when quoting other people directly.[30] In most cases context determines the placement of the quotation marks, but occasionally variant placement is possible. For this reason the reader is advised to refer to the relevant passages in the originals. In addition, Fanny usually leaves out quotation marks when citing the title or a line of a poem, or the title of a vocal piece, but context generally clarifies the intended meaning.

People's names also give rise to occasional ambiguity. Fanny frequently writes about minor figures such as neighbors, servants, tradespeople, and acquaintances, and because the first letter of both common and proper nouns is capitalized in German, confusion can result if the noun could be the name of an insignificant figure for whom biographical information is lacking. Once again context plays a decisive role, and explanations appear where dual readings are possible.

The edition eliminates variable spellings of names and adopts the most commonly accepted form: for example "Heine" for "Heyne" and "Heine."[31] The diminutive suffix "chen," utilized frequently, is dropped, and its endearment quality is reflected in a qualifier, such as "little" or "dear." The chief exception is "Beckchen," which is used as often as "Rebecka" to designate Fanny's younger sister; it serves as a second name and thus is retained in the translation. Names of cities appear in the form best known to English speakers, with modern spellings. Titles of journals, books, plays, and compositions generally appear likewise. On occasion, however, there is good reason to retain Fanny's less-familiar title—for example Mozart's *Don Juan* instead of the more familiar *Don Giovanni,* as it shows that the Italian version was

[30]In contrast to indirect quotation, where the so-called German "Subjunctive I" clarifies the reading.

[31]The reader may wonder about the absence of an accent mark in Cecile's name, which is contrary to Felix's practice. Fanny, however, consistently writes her name without the accent and therefore that is the policy adopted here.

not prevalent in Germany. German titles that are retained, such as *Spenersche Zeitung*, are not declined grammatically. Foreign titles of address, such as Kapellmeister and Herr, are preserved. With the exception of signatures at the end of letters, standard titles of address such as Mlle. and Mme., and Op. for Opus, abbreviations in the German are filled out to complete words. German names, titles, and quotations use "ss" instead of "ß."

As in the German letters, the integrity of Fanny's paragraphs is preserved but her nonsystematic practices of indentation are regularized into a consistent pattern, for greater clarity. Numerical quantities are in figures or words as in the orginals. English words in Fanny's letters appear in uppercase in the translations; underlined words are realized in italics, as are foreign words. Two exceptions are "adieu" and "addio," used so frequently that they are clearly part of Fanny's everyday vocabulary. Titles of vocal pieces, any portion of an instrumental title that is descriptive, for example the *Melusine* Overture, and titles of plays, art works, and books—all are italicized. No parentheses are introduced in the translation, although the placement of the parenthesized phrase is often shifted within the sentence to effect a smoother reading. As in the German versions, brackets reflect manuscript problems or illegible handwriting; they also enclose presumed readings in the face of such difficulties.

Whereas in the German versions the intent is to reflect exactly what is present in the manuscript, even if that means the absence of a date at the beginning of a letter, the English translations aim at giving the reader the fullest information possible with regard to dating. If no date appears at the top, the abbreviation "n. d." is inserted, followed by a presumed date in brackets based on evidence at hand. This evidence can be internal, culled from the contents of the letter or from dates that appear within the body,[32] or external, such as a postmark [PM]. When the internal evidence is obvious, then no additional explanation of the presumed date is offered. But when it is not, an explanatory annotation is appended. Months are always spelled in full, and years always have all four digits.

[32]A substantial number of the letters were written over the course of several days.

The Annotations

The substantive annotations refer to the translations. As mentioned earlier, a few textual problems occur in the German versions, and these are denoted by lower-case alphabet characters. Basic biographical information pertaining to people mentioned in the letters is found within the individual entries in the Glossary and Index of Names.

The annotations quote extensively from Felix's largely unpublished return correspondence and other unpublished documents. Unpublished material is rendered in both the original German and English translation; published material appears in English translation only, as the original version is available. A special policy covers excerpts from the NYPL collection: they are presented in English translation only, as Rudolf Elvers' edition of the originals is forthcoming. Translations of material in unreliable published editions[33] are based on the manuscript version, but the citation gives both the manuscript and published references whenever possible. Furthermore, there are several instances in which a quoted passage derives from a letter included in a published source, but the particular passage has been omitted from that source. When this occurs the publication is not cited.

As a general rule all translations are by the present author unless otherwise indicated. And finally, to distinguish between published and unpublished diaries of Fanny, the German "Tagebuch" is used in reference to her unpublished diaries, and the English "diary" for her published diaries.

The Glossary and Index of Names

All the names that appear in the letters, the annotations, and the introduction, with the exception of modern scholars and Fanny Hensel and Felix Mendelssohn, are listed in the Glossary and Index of Names. Many names are those of minor figures, such as neighbors, acquaintances, and tradesmen, and these present formidable problems in obtaining biographical information. Fanny often refers to such people by their first names, and unless some other biographical source happens to mention the complete name, the surname remains a mystery. Another

[33]Particularly S. Hensel, *Familie*, and Mendelssohn, *Briefe*.

problem with relatively unknown figures is the difficulty in finding their birth and death dates, and every reasonable effort has been made to acquire the basic biographical information for these people. When a surname cannot be located brackets stand in its place, and the item is alphabetized under the first name. There are also many people for whom Fanny uses a last name only. In the case of major figures this practice naturally presents few problems for identification, but difficulties arise when they are historical unknowns. In these cases the last name is listed, followed by Fanny's title of address in brackets, such as "Weber, [Herr]." The few cases where Fanny omits a title almost all involve men, and here an indication as to sex, such as "Herr," has been inserted, also in brackets. There also occur some lone surnames for which found biographical information is possible, or even probable, but not certain, especially if the surname is relatively common. In such instances some of the basic information—the first name, the dates, or the brief description—is enclosed by brackets.

The descriptions appended after the name and dates vary in length. In general, very well-known figures—such as Beethoven, Mozart, or Schiller—receive brief description, as do highly obscure figures because of the problems entailed in obtaining information. An attempt has been made to link the figures with Fanny and Felix, yet not unduly duplicate information contained in the letters or their annotations.

With respect to alphabetizing, umlauts are treated as if an "e" occurs after the umlauted vowel. Royalty are listed under their country or province: for example, "PRUSSIA; Friedrich Wilhelm IV, King of." Women are generally listed under their most common surname in the letters: for example, the name Pauline Schätzel occurs in the early letters but then appears with much greater frequency as Pauline Decker, her married name, and thus is listed under "DECKER, Pauline." In such a case cross-indexing refers the reader to the main entry. Maiden names are included wherever possible in entries listed under the married name.

The Letters

1–150

The Letters

1

28 October [1821]

[Paul, Rebecka, Boucher]

Do you perhaps still know the words to this lied of Mozart's son?[1] Then it will be easy to explain why I started my letter with it. You're really missed, dear son! Music in particular doesn't come easily without you. Now I'm thankful many times over to our friend Begas for painting the dear face so naturally on the canvas, as though it were actually standing here before us.[2] It seems as if I'm not to be ahead of you in Academy attendance, because since yesterday I've been so sick that I can't even think of singing, and I cough like an old woman in a hospital. Mother is also not feeling well today. She has a mild cold but nothing serious.

How is your present Minerva—your Professor Mentor—satisfied with you? I hope (to put it like a tutor) that you acquit yourself *reasonably* and do honor to the training given by your *House-minerva*. When you go to Goethe's, I advise you to keep your eyes open and prick up your ears, and if you can't relate every detail to me afterwards, I will consider us ex-friends. Please don't forget to sketch his house, for I would like that. If it's a good likeness and well done, you'll have to copy it into my musical album. Herr Berger was here last night, but I didn't see him because I had to go to bed at 7.—Father told you about Lipinski's concert and the fate of the *Stralower Fischzug*.[3] I don't know whether he wrote you that he was out today for fifteen minutes.—Regarding *Freischütz* there's still no mention; perhaps it will appear tomorrow in the newspaper.

There are two very long reviews of the *Fischzug* in the newspaper today. Father presumes that one is by Caspar. I think it's also very probable that he will never learn to hold back the ink! They placed an obituary for poor Lipinski in the newspaper, which won't help him at all. There's now hardly any critique that doesn't contain at least a subtle jab at Boucher. In the end I shall be proven right, and all his friends will be fed up with him.—You haven't written us what kind of an instrument Goethe has. Pay close attention to his room, for you have to give me a detailed description of it.—The dear, wonderful Rösel has returned and announced himself through a charming and very funny note that starts with the words, "Petz is here again!"[4] Strangely enough, Koreff pulled the same joke when he arrived a few days ago.—In the evening when the staircase door is opened for tea time, we often call out together, "That sounds as if Felix is coming." But stay away for a while; it's better that we get along without you a little longer and you gather the most wonderful memories for your future life. Another letter will arrive on Tuesday, and until then the time will seem enormously long, as though a month had passed.—Rietz sends his best, and asks me to tell you that he's glad you heard the Symphony and retained the theme so well.[5] I probably won't go to the Academy while you're away, for despite my protests the doctor is making me stay at home. My friends upstairs will think I've traveled with you *incognito*, and Fanny was even here recently to convince herself in person that I'm still around.[6]

Adieu, my little Hamlet! Think of me when I turn 16. One more thing—you must secretly take a swig of wine for my health, I impress it upon you. I take full responsibility for any red rash that might result. Adieu. Don't forget that you're my right hand and my eyesight, and without you, therefore, I can't proceed with my music.

Your truest, coughingest Fanny. Marianne has instructed me to send you her warmest greetings.[7]

[1]By Franz Xaver Wolfgang Mozart. According to *NGD XII*, 754, he composed c. 35 songs. A lied published in Hamburg (1820), whose opening line is "Weit in nebelgraue Ferne," by Schiller, might be Fanny's example, as the words fit the situation.
[2]Oil sketch in the Bodleian Library; see Oxford, *FMB*, 11 and 23.
[3]*Volksstück mit Gesang,* performed on 28 October. See the *AMZ,* 21 Nov. 1821, col. 795, which states that only Berliners can understand its local color and humor.
[4]Petz = the bear, as in the fable.
[5]Eduard Rietz. Probably Mozart's *Jupiter* Symphony, as Felix recently wrote a four-part canon on the C-D-F-E theme of the last movement for Zelter, which was also intended for Rietz. See E. Werner, *Mendelssohn*, 17.
[6]Perhaps Fanny Caspar.
[7]Probably Marianne Mendelssohn, but possibly Saaling.

2

n. d. [29 October 1821]

[incomplete at beginning]

I can tell you nothing about Rietz because I haven't seen him since you left.[1] The young Ernest Fürster sends his greetings. I saw him yesterday at the Frazkels, where I sat next to Elise. Tomorrow is Paul's birthday. You'll probably think about it, and now I can tell you that you've given him one-third of a very nice party, together with Beckchen and me, which comes to 8 gulden per person. He's invited a whole pack of young people; the fair sex, however, is excluded. In 10 years we'll want to inquire again.—The first movement of my F-major Sonata is copied.[2] The corrections are a pain in the neck and proceed slowly. I hope, however, that they will all be made by the time you come home.—How do you like Boucher's letter? Yesterday Caspar read us Boucher's autobiography, which is quite curious. I assure you that he places himself above Bonaparte, and within the company of the greatest men of all time: Shakespeare, Corneille, and Molière. But in between he relates how his enemies have dubbed him the Don Galimathias *du violon*. I find this epithet extremely fitting. Meanwhile, he exhibits an undeniably cheerful countenance. He played at poor Lipinski's concert yesterday and was the only cellist at the rehearsal. I haven't seen the Lithander girls yet[3] because our very unmusical coughs have thus far prevented us from inviting the whole flock of foreign virtuosos to our house. I can also calmly await such an event; it is only Lipinski whom I would like to hear again.

Adieu, *mon fils*! I must stop because my eyes hurt and my head is throbbing. Maybe I'll add a few more lines tomorrow.

The 30th. Paul had an amusing day. He received many lovely gifts.—We see in today's newspaper that the Gugels are in Hanover and played a concert there. It would be very nice if they came through Berlin. Now I'll say good-bye for the second time and ask you, my mature boy, to send my best to all the children, to the dear Herr Professor, and to his daughter.[4] Please remember me to the friendly, loyal Hummel if he still remembers me. You're really lucky to be able to study from him again.

Your truest Fanny

[Lea]

[1]Presumably Eduard Rietz. In letter 1, Fanny implied that she had seen Rietz.
[2]According to Elvers, *Quellen*, 216, this piece might be contained in a Sammelband in private possession that includes miscellaneous lieder, other vocal works, eleven piano pieces, etc., dating from 1820-21.
[3]Performed a piano four-hand Polonaise in a concert on 18 October (*AMZ*, 21 Nov. 1821, col. 796).
[4]Herr Professor is Zelter, and his daughter is Doris.

3

3 November 1821

[Dr. Caspar, Marianne Mendelssohn]

It had been my intention, my dear son, to write a long and detailed letter today, but as Father said yesterday, "Man proposes and the cough disposes." This unwelcome guest has tormented me for so many days that I'm completely exhausted and am not permitted to do much. Just consider that I haven't even played the piano in three days. Meanwhile, I can't refrain from praising you for your two lovely letters. They were equally well conceived and expressed (the latter is usually not your forte), and in every way therefore welcome and pleasant.[1] How good it is that you've gone directly to Weimar rather than wait for the celebration in Wittenberg. You are deserving of this time and will know how to use it wisely. I'm very glad that you've made such progress on your opera.[2] But write me whether the numbers I don't know were successful. Also don't forget to tell me what you've performed each time and what was the most successful, for you know that such things cannot be told too elaborately when directed at a *sister*. When you come home you must tell me verbally about Hummel's instruction.—The story about Herr Professor's dream is very touching—see how much this splendid man cares about you.[3] But your letter shows that you are also good and attentive towards him. But since Goethe says that praise and blame go hand in hand, I can't help finding fault with two things in your letters, although they're very minor. First of all, my dear son, had you checked your agenda—you set it up before your departure—you would have found that there was never a *32 Oct.*; you placed this date before the end of your letter.[4] Secondly, within the address of your letters, you must write the place *on the right* and not on the left as you've done so far. These are in themselves very minor observations; I trust you will not receive them unkindly, for you really know that they're well meant.

When I had just closed my letter recently, *Der Freischütz* arrived. I didn't scream for joy—I couldn't—but crowed. If you had been there we would have had a very pleasant hour. I only enjoyed half of the fun because I was all alone and helpless to sing even one note. I consider Seidler's aria rather unique; it's very beautiful. Yesterday *Freischütz* was performed again and is said to have been splendid. A brand-new report (from Heinrich) claims that Spontini has been robbed of his power again, and everything is back on the old track. One attributes this good deed to the Crown Prince.[5] What do you say now, [ ]?

Poor Lipinski was here recently to say good-bye. He left without a second concert but had the dignity to express his satisfaction with the Berliners.[6] Today is Hartknoch's concert, which I fear won't go well. You'll have a report on Tuesday.—I'm very curious about the text from Vienna that Mother has told you about. A sentimental, naive opera wouldn't be so bad if it were otherwise nicely constructed, for it usually contains very pretty cavatinas, choruses with the required bellowing of cattle, and similar rarities. But all joking aside, I like that type very much if it's done well. Swiss braids, milk pails, Alpine cowbells, glaciers in the twilight, and homesickness are all musical and beloved things that will certainly exist in abundance in your new text. And how nicely Mme. Robert will sing the part of the languishing shepherdess. I tell you that I look forward to it completely. Count on Caspar, strained through the report, to put out his best effort and deliver a new, really beautiful text.[7] Then you can be carefree for a long time. Adieu, dear boy. Rejoice that you are in Weimar and can breathe in the poetic air that wafts around you. You must take note of his native city for your finale.[8] You're very fortunate to spend some time in Goethe's house and see him in familiar surroundings with his friends. Send my greetings to him and the good Doris, and the *gutissimo* Hummel, and remain fond of your Fanny.

[1]Of 30 October (Mendelssohn, *Briefe-RE*, 19-21) and probably 1 November 1821 (NYPL).
[2]Presumably *Die beiden Pädagogen.*
[3]Zelter tapped Felix when he was in bed, and Felix asked Zelter if he could fetch him some water, whereupon Zelter replied: "*Oh no, I dreamed you had been stolen from me, and then I wanted to see whether you were still there*!!!?______" (30 October; 20).
[4]Letter of 30 October; the last section is dated "32 Oct." (in the MS, NYPL).
[5]Probably Heinrich Beer. Regarding Spontini, the *AMZ,* 21 Nov. 1821, col. 797, reports: "In a cabinet order the King has handed over everything in connection with music in the theater—the orchestra, the hiring and firing of Kapellmeisters, the performance of opera and operetta, ballet, etc.—to the exclusive control of the Generaldirector of Music, Herr Spontini, so that the Generalintendant, Count von Brühl, tends only to the tragedies, comedies, and dramas. So now each person, at present sharing the authority with the other, will reap sole honor and blame for the performances."
[6]Felix says it's a shame that he won't see Lipinski again (6 October 1820, *sic* for 6 November 1821; Mendelssohn, *Briefe-RE*, 22).
[7]Caspar wrote the libretto, based on Scribe, for *Die beiden Pädagogen.*
[8]Frankfurt.

4

Berlin, 6 November 1821

[Abraham, Lea, Beckchen]

What one doesn't experience in one's life! Would I ever have thought that my Felix would become a *talented* traveling correspondent! But it's true, and we have your numerous lengthy and elaborate letters as proof. The arrival of these letters constitutes the only major event in our house at present, in which life is very quiet and routine. Nothing significant is happening. My Felix isn't here, I haven't seen Marianne once in 10 days,[1] and if it continues, life will be very boring. Tell the Herr Professor that I find him very disloyal. He writes only to his fair-haired boy and doesn't send even one greeting to his earnest, best, [female student]. But send him my warmest regards anyway, for I won't repay him in kind. This week I still have to miss the Academy, but in a week no doctor will be able to keep me at home.—You must have experienced a fascinating type of impatience and expectation during Goethe's absence. Please tell us what sort of an impression his initial appearance made on you.[2] He is said to have a very imposing presence. You're very fortunate to live so close to him. You know that I was involved in reading his life aloud to Mother[3] when I came down with this hateful cough. Now Rebecka reads a few pages to us every night, but this snail's pace is making me very impatient. All our friends send their best, especially Frau Bing.

If the young Frau von Goethe still remembers me,[4] please send her my best. Remember me also to the Herr Professor, Doris,[5] and Hummel. Remain fond of me. Your Fanny.

[1]Marianne Mendelssohn.

[2]"On Sunday the sun of Weimar, Goethe, arrived." Felix also narrated how Frau von Goethe asked Goethe if he wanted to hear some of Fanny's lieder, and he agreed to listen the next day (6 [November 1821], Mendelssohn, *Briefe-RE*, 21-22). In a letter of 14 November 1821 (NYPL), Felix wrote that a Mde. Eberwein sang Fanny's lied, *Ach wer bringt,* which prompted Goethe to reply, "*Listen, the lied is quite beautiful*" (Mendelssohn, *Goethe*, 24). The lied is *Erster Verlust,*

based on Goethe's poem. There are two extant settings by Fanny; this early one is probably the version in autograph in Düsseldorf at the Goethe Museum.
[3]*Dichtung und Wahrheit*, published between 1811 and 1833.
[4]Goethe's daughter-in-law.
[5]Doris Zelter.

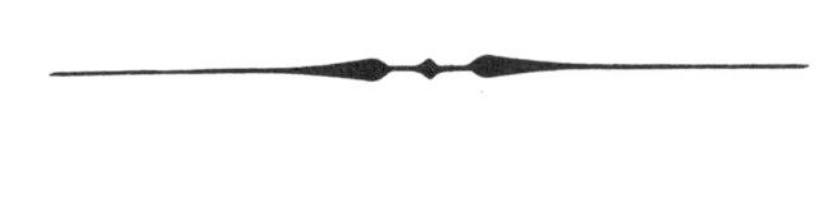

5

n. d. [8 April 1825][1]

After expressing a bitter complaint over the lack of letters this week, dear Felix, I must send you the newest Berlin *bon mot* in haste, which calls *Alcidor all-too-droll*.[2] Your sharp articulation during the telling of this joke will probably be of help. You would have been glad to hear your Alto Scena sung by the lovely Mme. Müller.[3] She has an abundance of feeling, and is a *dear person* to speak with our Rösel, who moved in again. You both are certainly everywhere at the same time, and Father is overdoing it. That's not right, for he should come back to us strengthened and not tired, whereas you can withstand a great deal. Your change in the Sonata is accepted—my general staff and the additional medical advisor have decided so[4]—and I also like it better when it's performed than when it's viewed on paper. I send my respects to all of you.

FMB

[1]A date suggested in Crum, *Catalogue I*, 3.
[2]Opera by Spontini (Berlin, 23 May 1825). See the review in the *AMZ*, 15 June 1821, cols. 404-06.
[3]Possibly *Che vuoi mio cor?* for mezzosoprano and strings. Autograph in the Deutsche Staatsbibliothek (Bartlitz, *Works*, 155).
[4]Of the extant Sonatas in public purview, one possibility is a Piano Sonata in c minor from July 1824. The autograph is in MA Ms. 34.

6

Monday, 11 April [1825]

You will wonder why I, out of my blissful rest, repeat the word unrest as an echo from your fast-moving world.[1] And yet it's so, with interruptions and disturbances—a hundred interruptions—and I'm not able to put down three words in succession. Therefore I'm starting early in the day for once and will immediately ask whatever strikes me first. Do Onslow (not Onzlow) and Schuhu know Beethoven's cycle of 33 Variations on a Waltz?[2] Otherwise you would gain honor from it, since you meet with these gentlemen alone in their studios, as a scholar and theoretician as well, to introduce them to our bucolic countryman.[3] You haven't mentioned Drouet yet; isn't he there? It almost seems as if you've hardly seen anything because you've already heard about everything. You haven't uttered one syllable about the Tuilleries, the museum, the city, and your walks.[4] I hope to find them, however, in your diary. And in fact, so far you've only heard nothing but salon music—*tout comme chez nous*—and the talents are just as trite as here. You've remained silent on Italian opera and the Concert Spirituel, except for a few words on the orchestra, which surprised Rietz a great deal.[5] He merely said that these instruments had always been Rode's delight. Won't he take the fiddle in his hand?—Father's letter from the 2nd and 3rd just arrived, dear Felix; we're very concerned that Father seems so ill and disgruntled. Is he as ill as his letters imply? Aunt Jette thinks he's happier and healthier than he's been in the last few years.[6]—Boucher moves me, in spite of his extremely mad madness. With his sense of superiority, how does he stand the general disdain in Paris?[7] You've also seen the *vieille* Muse once again.[8] Father talks about the Bigots' house, but omits mention of the nobility, who interest me very much. I would like dear Father to remember me warmly and with all modesty to Mme. Deloi—formerly Emilie Riedel—once again, and to Mlle. Milan. I send them my best wishes. It's a shame that you haven't met the charming Müller. She's spent almost every morning with us this week. We let her rest and that was fine with her, for she would collapse everywhere else. We made music together and my accompaniments seemed to please her. She had your Alto Scena and *povero cor* copied, although the latter is too high for her.[9] She also sang my *Spinnerlied*, which didn't lie in her range, with difficulty, but it sounded nice after I had changed a few passages for her.[10] I had offered to transpose it for her, but she declined. Yesterday morning she came here with her husband to hear one of your Quartets. Franck,[11] however, stayed away and we persuaded Julius Rietz to play the part from manuscript, although Eduard didn't want to do it. He far exceeded our expectations: he exhibited a good tone, a strong bow stroke, no rhythmic mistakes, and only a few wrong notes. Therefore he could have given lessons to your *Professor* at Trémont's.—After dinner Rietz and I performed your f-minor Sonata for her again, and he played the Adagio exceptionally well.[12] Then the dear people left and we played a great deal more music together. Will you show your opera to anyone?[13]

Today is our Backfisch's birthday.[14] We'll have a lovely young gathering and the improvisor will be here. Since I've heard how he wants to slaughter the *Eroica*, I'm very angry at him. One year ago we had a large ball—do you still remember how Lindenau took the violin in his hand and we all jumped? There's a letter for you from Lindenau that we will keep here because it's very thick. You'll be very pleased with the quick dispatch of your second Double Concerto. I hope you'll find the opportunity to play it with one of the 10,000 virtuosi, and that you'll come across someone who can master the last movement better than yours truly.[15] I'd be so happy if you would have the chance to hear your Symphony.[16]—The Baron Trémont reminded us all of Baron Bagge when we read the letter.[17] Everyone here sends his best many times over, and I send my compliments as well. One more thing—I've received a letter from Friederike Robert, who sends her best, and asks me to tell you that she has a lied ready for you. Robert was offended that you, dear Father, sent no greetings in [Mme.] Varnhagen's letter, but Mme. Varnhagen said, "It's nonsense! it's madness!—because Herr Mendelssohn is so good as to take the letter with him, he is obliged to add something to it," etc. Paul was very cute during young Rietz's debut. His eyes sparkled with delight and he stood behind him and continually nodded to the others to make them attentive.

After every piece he ran around praising him to everybody and was thoroughly delighted.

April 12th. The little gathering, despite our intentions, [has grown] into a small ball . . .

[letter is incomplete]

[1]Response to Felix's letter of 27 March 1825 (NYPL).
[2]On 1 April 1825 (NYPL), Felix wrote he met Onzlow at Baron Trémont's. Reicha is the "Schuhu," a word not easily translatable, which connotes someone very finicky and critical. The Beethoven is the *Diabelli* Variations, Op. 120.
[3]Beethoven as composer of the *Pastoral* Symphony.
[4]The letter of 20 April 1825 (NYPL) is Felix's response, in which, among other things, he takes Fanny to task for her incorrect spelling of Tuileries.
[5]Felix says he has written a great deal about these two areas (20 April). In his letter of 27 March, Felix wrote that the orchestra of the Italian opera "is very good, but not excellent. The strings are extraordinary, but the winds, especially the brass, are worse than average, and play out of tune and sound fuzzy." His letter of 6 April 1825 (Mendelssohn, *Briefe-RE,* 43-44) included basically the same observation.
[6]Aunt Jette = Henriette Mendelssohn.
[7]Felix saw Boucher and Onslow at Hummel's on Monday.
[8]Mme. Kiené.
[9]See letter 5. Uncertain whether *Povero cor* is extant.
[10]The actual title is *Die Spinnerin* (Tieck); autograph dated September 1823, MA Ms 34.
[11]Hermann Franck.
[12]Op. 4, composed 1823.
[13]*Die Hochzeit des Camacho* (Klingemann, after Cervantes), published as Op. 10; composed 1824/25.
[14]A nickname for Rebecka.
[15]Concerto for Two Pianos and Orchestra in A-flat (1824). In his letter of 20 April, Felix stated he will perform it soon with Hummel or Herz, but not publicly.
[16]In c minor, Op. 11 (1824).
[17]Trémont's singular manner of playing the viola was described in Felix's letter of 1 April.

7[1]

25 April 1825

Alas! You both travel to Paris and hear no decent music, or very little, and we stay calmly at home and are forced to stretch our ears. In one week we've had *Jessonda, Alceste, Samson,* and the *Pastoral* Symphony, and the last two will be on Sapupi's concert on Good Friday the day after tomorrow.[2] What do you think? This much seems clear: your talent for fickleness develops brilliantly in Paris. My son, your letters consist of nothing but criticism. Marx will be happy with you. I hope that time will cast a rosier tint on many things that now darken from the dust of prejudice, for if everything were really as bad as you now see it, the trip would be a great loss.[3] You characterize Kalkbrenner very well, and thereby conjure up a lively image of the amiable piano wizard, whom I wanted to hear thunder across the keys one more time. Rode's expression, "with the *exécution foudroyante*," is extremely apt. Has Kalkbrenner still not said anything *recently*? Tell him hello in any case; I'm very happy that he still remembers me.[4] You poor Tantalus! To see Rode every day but not partake of any harmony from those spheres! But I must confess that I find it really comforting to know that he's in Paris, where a reunion is rather possible, instead of a corner in Bordeaux.—Oh, what beautiful paintings you've seen! Why no word about them? Nothing on public gardens, the city, the buildings. I almost think that the tiresome salon music has killed off every ounce of enjoyment for you. Now, you will like our powerful music, when we saw away at your Symphony for the first time in our large, vaulted garden hall.[5] Oh, how I look forward to it! Your story about the six who always applaud the seventh is very good, and how Rossini and Meyerbeer, Hummel, Moscheles and Kalkbrenner found themselves together and exchanged pleasantries, yet who probably wish that one of the others would go to the devil.[6] We have the most beautiful summer sky now, and green trees as well. On Sunday afternoon we were in our garden with the young guard, in which a recruit was found, young Herr Schubring from Dessau, who brought us warm letters from the Wilhelm Müllers.

We all crouched along the ground and looked for violets, including Klingemann, who made fun of us. We claimed that he *dug up* violets. In addition, he had put on his glasses and then lowered himself on a chopped-off tree trunk to arrange the flowers, earth, and grass gathered in his handkerchief. Can you actually picture this grandiose figure? Our garden is already splendid; how wonderful it will be in May, when the lilacs will be blooming. But you're like a Vandal, for you're not even aware of green trees. *À propos*, have I, or have I not mentioned that Klingemann has already taken 3 violin lessons with Rietz? One has to admire his zeal. We've convinced him to become the main pillar of the symphony society,[7] and he believes it, and now mistreats poor Klotz who is under the aegis of the steadfast Rietz. Rietz has also received 3 female students: our little, talented neighbor Eda Benda, whom he inherited from poor Lauska, and the two little Blancs.[8] Mozart's Requiem was performed for Lauska yesterday. I couldn't attend because of my tormenting cough. Zelter's was performed at the Academy.[9] Next Friday we'll probably sing the one by Hasse at Zelter's.[10] It's too bad that Sebastian Bach didn't write one. Is Reissiger in Paris? If so, then why haven't you ever run into him? Or Drouet?

Don't you think it an incredibly good idea to perform the *Pastoral* Symphony before *Samson*? Samson was JUST such a man of nature, with knapsack, quail, and nightingale. And so, reversed as they may be, I look forward to both. And now adieu. The first viola corrections have just arrived. After we receive an answer from Weimar, the entire matter will be settled in 2 weeks.[11]

Dear Father, I greet you a thousand times over, and also Aunt Jette, and Rode, whose letters have given us great pleasure. Farewell. If only we could meet up with you in Potsdam.

Fanny

[Lea]

[1]A substantial portion of this letter is published in A. Mendelssohn, *Erinnerungen*, 29.

[2]A term apparently referring to Spontini, presumably disparaging and coined by Fanny. The *AMZ,* 11 May 1825, cols. 314-15, mentions that the concert on the 27th was directed by Spontini, and was a benefit for him. *Jessonda* is an opera by Spohr; *Samson* is an oratorio by Handel.

[3]Felix's strong response merits lengthy quotation (9 May 1825, NYPL; S. Hensel, *Familie I*, 147-48): "I was rather angry over your previous letter and decided to send a scolding your way, which was also not to be conveyed yet. But time, the beneficent god, will probably soften it and pour balsam in the wounds that my flaming anger directs at you. You write me of preconceptions and prejudice, of grumbling and 'Schuhuismus,' of the land where milk and honey flow, as you call this Paris? Just consider a moment, I beseech you! Are you in Paris or am I? That I must know better than you! Is it my style to judge music with preconceptions? But if it were, then is Rode prejudiced when he tells me, 'C'est ici une dégrengolade musicale!' Is Neukomm prejudiced when he says to me, 'Ce n'est pas le pays des orchestres.' Is Herz prejudiced when he says, 'Here the public is only able to understand and relish variations.' And are 10,000 others prejudiced when they complain about Paris! You—you are so prejudiced that you believe less in my highly impartial reports than in a charming image which you have concocted of Paris as some Eldorado. Pick up the *Constitutionnel*: is anything other than Rossini being given in the Italian opera? Pick up the music catalog: is anything other than Romanzes and Potpourris being published? Come over here and hear *Alceste*, hear *Robin des bois*, hear the *soirées* (which you furthermore confuse with *salons*, for *soirées* are concerts for money, and *salons* social gatherings), hear the music in the Royal Chapel, and then judge, then scold me, but not now, when it is you who are prejudiced by preconceptions and completely blinded."

[4]Fanny wrote about him (presumably in her diary) in 1823 and praised him as a performer and person (in S. Hensel, *Familie I*, 136-37).

[5]This vaulted garden hall is undoubtedly the large concert-giving room at Leipziger Strasse 3. Either the family has already moved there, or will do so soon. Standard Mendelssohn sources are vague on the time of the year, or else attribute the move to late summer.

[6]In his letter of 18 April 1825 (NYPL); their insincere remarks were uttered as they sat in an adjacent loge at a Concert des enfants d'Apollon. Pixis is also in this group.

[7]According to Mahlung, *Musikbetrieb*, 51, Rietz established the Philharmonic society—an amateur instrumental group—in 1826. Fanny's statement may imply that she and Rietz are planning to set up such a society. See also note 3 to letter 50.

[8]Lauska died on 18 April (*AMZ*, 11 May 1825, col. 315).

[9]Either the Requiem of 1803 for Fasch (lost), which Ledebur, *Lexicon*, 670, claims was later revised; or *Ein kurzes* Requiem (1823).

[10]Hasse composed several Requiems.

[11]Possibly for Felix's Piano Quartet, Op. 3, published by Laue. See Mendelssohn, *Verleger*, xix.

8

29 April [1825]

Oh yes, my son—the *Pastoral* Symphony (*Hirtensymphonie* in German) is very beautiful, and if you don't believe it, I advise you to be quiet, listen, and then judge. I can tell you *nothing* more except that Mother was delighted with it and asked me when it was over, what comes now?[1] Clarity and truth, richness and unity from start to finish. The scene at the brook is truly the epitome of grace, the entire movement shaded with cheerful, bright hues; only the heavy storm provides the necessary shadow in the landscape. It's too bad that my favorite passage, the scene at the brook, was completely spoiled by the unreasonable tempo, which was too fast, even much faster than in Möser's concert.[2] The orchestra had a better sense than Möser for the right tempo and therefore didn't comply, with the result that certain passages were glaringly slower than others. The piece possesses infinite charm, and displays the grace of the instruments more effectively than any other piece I know. Mother has probably already told you about Sapupi's sublime serenity.[3] Except for a few nasty placards, *Samson* went rather well. Milder was unsurpassable.[4]

You are making us languish in vain today—release us tomorrow. I hope you'll be back with us in a little over 2 weeks, and perhaps these are our last letters. You're receiving Rietz's letter so late, dear Felix, because he brought it over an hour after ours had been mailed. Dear Father, I wish you luck with the leasing of the middle floor—may your success be heralded with a flourish of trumpets and drums. Speaking of trumpets and drums, how is it possible for you, extraordinary *Wunderkind* and much-loved baby, to live 6 weeks without writing a single note? I can't understand it.

[Rebecka, Caspar, Klingemann, Rebecka]

The 30th

Since Klingemann and Beckchen took a breather, I want to take up the quill again to thank you for your sensible letter from the

20th. I'm just glad that you've finally performed with a decent accompaniment, for up to now I've pictured you starving in the land where milk and honey flow. Before I forget again, I want to ask you a question that's been on my mind for a long time but which I've forgotten to ask every time I've had the quill in my hand, namely: why, amid all the matinées, dinners, suppers, and whatever else is dished up for *art*, have you never played your Sextet?[5] Is there only one person in that Parisian society who can read alto clef? Dear Felix, I really wish that you and Father had your dear mother, wife, daughters, and your own beloved sister there. My mouth waters when I read about your *rational* pleasures. But don't get the idea that everything is quiet here. Yesterday evening we suffered through a pleasure as good as yours—we were at a soirée.[6] It was as hot there as only Paris could be. We were there with Ivan Müller and the improvisor Wolff.[7] I got into a long discussion with the former as he explained his improvements on the clarinet and alto clarinet. He claims that his inventions, which consist of additional keys and a somewhat modified construction of the instrument, make all tonalities possible and connect the sounds. He thus notates every tonality in its natural position and in respectable tenor clef. Imagine my joy at the mere prospect of seeing most scores notated in this way. If some Müller appeared out of the blue and improved horns in such a way that they would all be notated in bass clef, I would read scores for you like water. If you have the opportunity, inquire into Müller's clarinet. He claims that his improvements have been generally adopted in Paris. They have already begun to make some of his instruments here under his supervision. You must admit that it would be very advantageous to have all tonalities available on one clarinet.[8] I thoroughly dislike his playing. His tone is actually very nice, but his interpretation so tasteless that one becomes quite disgruntled. In the middle of his ridiculous little trills, runs, and cadenzas, he will hold one note so long and with such varying strength that one runs out of breath trying to jump back quickly into the flow of the piece. I can't adjust as fast, and therefore I feel nothing but a splitting headache when he plays this penetrating instrument in the room. Wolff improvised very well in spite of tropical heat, Josty's ice cream,[9] cake, and a throng of humanity hanging on to his neck, and I was very happy that he selected a theme that I had written down for him. Dorn did an adequate job with the accompaniment. He had a few excellent musical ideas from the poem, which really surprised me.

The next piece, a lied from the Tyrol, was accompanied on the guitar. I find this combination much better because the guitar's thin tone doesn't cover up the voice.—I've just come out of Father's room where I heard Rietz giving little Benda a lesson. She plays Cramer Etudes and must dutifully repeat them.—Rode's wish, which is to live together with us, I'm echoing a thousand times. If he did come here, it would make a lovely home for him and his wife and children. Then we could rejoice:

> "When the vaults resound
> One feels mightily the elemental power of the *violin*."

And our whole house would resound. But unfortunately that won't happen. What do you think about the great violinist Klingemann becoming our tenant? Rietz has warned us against it: "It is very dangerous to arouse the lion, etc.; Klingemann is the worst of the worst in his madness, namely in his violin madness, and as a reversed Amphion would scare off animals, humans, and gods."[10] He said good-bye yesterday in the midst of his numerous pranks, and traveled to a wedding today.—You can imagine how happy we were just to hear that Zelter received a personal letter from Goethe, and how anxious we were after hearing rumors of his illness and even his death. May God keep these two alive a long time. Amen.—And so farewell. I praise you, I love you, I praise your letters, and hope that we will have our dear trinity again soon. If only I could give out clever answers in a quantity commensurate with the number of times people ask the same question about you. Adies.

[11]

[Rebecka, Lea]

[1]27 April 1825 (*AMZ,* 11 May 1825, col. 314).

[2]Möser conducted the *Pastoral* Symphony on the 14th of April, and Spontini the same piece on the 27th (*AMZ,* 11 May 1825, col. 314).

[3]See note 2 to letter 7.

[4]Sang in *Samson* (*AMZ,* 11 May 1825, col. 315).
[5]Piano Sextet in D major, Op. 110 (composed 1824).
[6]Letter of 6 April 1825 (NYPL) discussed soirées.
[7]The *AMZ,* 11 May 1825, col. 314, also admired his tone, in a concert of 21 April.
[8]Felix agrees with Fanny that playing in all keys would be an advantage, but he does not entirely agree. He asserts that the person who could invent a different clarinet for every key would be a genius. The boast about Müller's clarinet invention being generally accepted in Paris is "Nego Factum!" (9 May 1825, NYPL).
[9]Josty's was a famous Berlin café (S. Hensel, *Lebensbild*, 7).
[10]Amphion was a son of Zeus, who with his twin brother Zethus built a wall around Thebes by charming the stones into place by playing on his magic lyre.
[11]The identity of the melody is uncertain.

9

Berlin, 16 February [1827]

Motto: Alas! how cold!

I wouldn't have thought that I'd receive news about you while you're still here. A coincidence—although there's really no such thing in real life—or actually a predestined fate led me to a performance of *Cortez* last night to meet Herr Simon's sister, a Leipzig woman who has heard your Symphony.[1] She assured me that it went very well, was received with excellent applause, and that the concert was one of the most well-attended in Leipzig. In addition, Weber's *Jubel* Overture[2] and one of his cantatas were given—you were thus in good company. Because I'm freezing cold yet thinking loving thoughts in a warm room, I can well imagine how you may be thinking loving thoughts of me while freezing on the Landstrasse. There are still a few hours left before I can accompany you into Stettin.[3] Moreover, I'm repeating once and for all that *Cortez* is the most boring fare I've ever tasted. And such a performance! It was horrible, except for my homily, which is beautiful, by God! Your proof correction is ready, and besides a touching note to Adolph Martin with regard to the title.[4] If I had seen one of your friends I would have him greet you. The best lied in the collection is obviously *Lass dich nur nichts nicht dauern*.[5] I assure you that if the third verse hadn't struck me in the first strophe, I would have inserted mistakes so that there would be some substance there. I wanted to let you know about this and more in the dumb contraption, so now leave me in peace. Say hello to Loewe, who is really a lamb, but you needn't tell him that.[6] Rejoice in your youth, guard against courtship, don't freeze your nose, and have a full concert and great success in Stettin. Don't drink too much beer and still less wine. Think of me as you travel.

Your  [7]

Mother just wanted to hear your *Pilgerspruch*, I'm embarrassed to admit.

[Rebecka]

What great luck that I received this note today.

[1]Premiere performance of the c-minor Symphony, at the Leipzig Gewandhaus, on 1 February. See the *AMZ,* 28 Feb. 1827, cols. 156-57. *Cortez* is an opera by Spontini: second version, Paris, 1817; third version, Berlin, 1832.
[2]Op. 245.
[3]Felix traveled to Stettin for a performance of his *Midsummer Night's Dream* Overture. His letter from Stettin of 17 February (NYPL) announces his arrival.
[4]Schlesinger, who issued Felix's lieder collection Op. 8, in which three were composed by Fanny: *Das Heimweh* (No. 2), *Italien* (No. 3), and the duet *Suleika und Hatem* (No. 12).
[5]Felix's lied, *Pilgerspruch,* Op. 8 No. 5.
[6]The composer Karl Loewe. Fanny is making a pun on his name, which means "lion."
[7]Possibly a reference to the opening of Beethoven's String Quartet, Op. 131.

10

n. d. [after 16 February 1827]

The cold weather is getting worse, and with pleasure I note that you're in Stettin, and with displeasure far from Berlin. We had a jolly time yesterday, and in the evening Therese Devrient and Rebecka sang a great number of lieder. If I were able to hear the duet *Suleika* sung only once by Loewe and Therese I'd never forget it.[1] Her rendition is unsurpassable. Franck, who really lost the 12th part,[2] sends his best. Everyone else likewise. Guillon, who played yesterday at Schlesinger's, is still not finding favor, to my great astonishment. Kohlreif accompanied him. Einbrodt, David, your Steinbeck, Sisen, etc. were here. Your Schnitter also appeared.[3] Little Rösel just dropped in, so you therefore know with certainty that it's 12:05 on Monday. This evening I'll brave the cold at the Academy because I'm hopeful about your *Te Deum*.[4] But it will certainly be very empty and go badly.

Your 

[S. Rösel, Rebecka]

[1]Karl Loewe. Fanny's duet published as No. 12 in Felix's lieder collection, Op. 8. The autograph is dated 28 April 1825, MA Ms 35; fair copy in MS MDM b. 2. See also letter 90.
[2]Hermann Franck. A literal translation of "welcher die 12te Partie wirklich verloren," which likely is an obsolete idiom having a very different meaning.
[3]Probably a nickname, but the person's identity is unknown.
[4]Composed 1826. Published in the Leipziger Ausgabe of Mendelssohn's Works: Series VI, Volume 1, ed. Werner Burkhardt (1976).
[5]See note 7 in the previous letter.

11

n. d. [PM 25 October (1828)]

We're happy, dear lamb, that you're so well and cheerful, but in truth I'd like to go with you sometime to a small city and listen to you play as much as I wanted.[1] For good reasons nothing like that can happen here, and it sometimes makes me very distressed and anxious towards you, like last evening, when I certainly would have written to you if I hadn't been afraid of my sentimental feelings. What you say about the chorale fantasy, which I should know by heart, is very nice, but I'd like to have heard it played because I haven't heard you improvise on the organ in 7 years—thus not at all.[2]

Ulrike wasn't here yesterday;[3] she's supposed to come today, and Marianne Mendelssohn in the evening. The day before yesterday Marianne Saaling ate here and stayed until 9. Then came Rietz, David, and Heydemann from the symphony society, where David is said to have played a Concerto by Spohr very beautifully.[4] Gans arrived later. His stories of students and imitations of Wittengenstein practically made us sick from laughing. The Mass in G major was performed at Zelter's yesterday[5] and there was a great fuss because the contrabass was misplaced and Zelter searched for it high and low. After dinner we went to Aunt Meyer's for a while. In the evening the Roberts, Varnhagens, and Hensel came over and we had a wonderful time. I'm now so tolerant that [Mme.] Varnhagen's most horrible *dictus* (or "tas," or whatever) didn't bother me. I sat next to Beckchen and we exchanged bad, private jokes and talked about Cluricaun.[6] Among the others, the exhibition was the only topic of conversation. Someone would speak, the Roberts would illuminate the matter philosophically, the Varnhagens technically. Hensel sat there with his sheep's face that you know and we stared at our feet under our respective chairs. It wasn't so bad. Sometimes there is even conversation here about the art of music in which *we* open up our mouths and listen with our noses. I've just begun a fugue on a theme. It's serious and there are to be contrasting sections. What a person won't take on. Ask old Steinbeck to compose a canon for my album on the words "Ach, was soll der Mensch verlangen?"—You can also leave out the words. I think the old man will do it. But why haven't you written anything about the bride?[7]

There will be *tableaux vivants* at the theater tonight, among them *Rinaldo* and *Armide* based on Sohn.[8]

[sentences divided between Rebecka and Fanny]

[Rebecka]

Farewell, oh brother! Don't consider this the end (no, not the end), but the end of your [ ].

I wish the best for the newlyweds. Beckchen is standing next to me and just had the dumb idea of trying to take the quill away from me—her fingers are itching for it. That one of us has to have the last word is an impossibility.

[Rebecka]

Our letters in proximity actually sound like Schlegel's conversation with another person,[9] for no one answers the other.

[Rebecka and Fanny mixed]

If I were Steinbeck and also had 2 pianos, I would really play something.

But I wish that you could have heard Carl twittering during the bewitching hour of midnight last night; Herr Felix would have requested the Trio in D major.[10]

[Rebecka, then Rebecka and Fanny mixed]

Adieu, dear heart! Cluricaun, you will have to pay for postage again, for, alas, no person is going to post a letter any longer, excepting exceptions, i.e., *Stadtpost scriptum*.

[Rebecka and Fanny mixed]

[1]Felix wrote that he's played on the organ several times (undated, from Brandenburg; NYPL No. 51).
[2]In the same letter Felix wrote: " . . . then I improvised on the chorale *Christe du Lamm*, which I first played with the flutes, then gradually fuller (because I did the registration myself in the absence of the organist), and finally I attempted to close with the soft chorale. (By the way, if you should have the desire to hear this fantasy, dear Mother, then I refer you to Fanny; she surely knows it by heart already, as she is familiar with my style.)"
[3]Ulrike Peters.
[4]Concerto unknown.
[5]Identity unknown.
[6]In the last paragraph of this letter, the German grammar "Cluricaun mußt" implies that Cluricaun is a name for Felix (substituting for the "Du" pronoun). The name is close to an alias of a Romantic author, H. Clauren (for Karl Heun), with whose works Felix was well acquainted. See a later reference in a letter from Felix to the family of 6 November 1829, in S. Hensel, *Familie I*, 267.
[7]Felix was attending Steinbeck's wedding. Steinbeck was a regular member of the Mendelssohns' social/musical circles in at least the first part of 1829, for his name appears consistently in Fanny's Tagebuch entries from January through April 1829, and then in August 1829.
[8]*Tableaux vivants,* popular at the time, were live theatrical representations of paintings or poems, done with elaborate costumes and scenery.
[9]Possibly in reference to Friedrich Schlegel's "Gespräch über die Poesie," in dialogue form, in *Athenaeum*, III (1800), 58-128, 169-87.
[10]The identity of Carl is uncertain; perhaps he is a servant. The trio is Beethoven's Trio in D major, Op. 70 No. 1 (*Ghost*).

12[1]

Berlin, 18 April 1829

I would have liked to start this letter, the first one that greets you in London, with the three-voiced trumpet fanfare.[2] But at the present moment you haven't arrived there yet,[3] the weather is bad here, and I don't want to tempt God. But if I knew that you had, I'd draw on all the registers of my heart, blow all the trumpets within my lungs, and send forth a music that you would have to hear on the British Isles. JUST on the day of your departure the Emancipation Act was passed, so this is the most interesting time for a journey to England.[4] Now I want to tell you about the topic that will for the

Illustration 2—Autograph letter from Fanny Hensel to Felix Mendelssohn, 18 April 1829 (first page) [Bodleian Library, Oxford: MS Margaret Deneke Mendelssohn b. 4, letter 39].

moment move you even more than emancipation, departmental law, and a Spanish earthquake—I mean our Passion from yesterday.[5] Here's the direct verdict: the performance far surpassed my expectations and lagged far behind yours. I didn't want to write you about the rehearsals on Monday and Tuesday and thus spared you the torment that filled my soul. Zelter himself played, and you can well imagine what he created with his two fingers and his *complete lack of knowledge* of the score. Discord and fear spread throughout the chorus, and your name was intoned many times. Thursday's rehearsal wasn't sufficient to allay that anxiety. Zelter didn't conduct the accompanied recitatives, but only the choruses, when he didn't forget. Stümer worked miracles and constantly kept his place alongside Zelter's almost continually incorrect accompaniment. To cite a few particulars: Devrient was so confused that, among others, he inserted only half the Lord's Supper and immediately started "trinket Alle daraus" in F major.[6] Milder upset the duet as usual and Schätzel slaved away in her aria. The brief choruses "der rufet dem Elias" and "halt lass sehen" got worse and worse.[7] Zelter reacted badly to that, was very angry, and always became confused at the reversal of the Golgotha pieces. Long pauses resulted. Then Stümer, with more discretion and composure than I would have thought him capable of, quietly reprimanded him. Devrient sat there like a perfect *Ecce homo*. At 4:45 the rehearsal was over and we came home beside ourselves with fatigue, exhaustion, and fear. Before that I had had a little advisory session with Devrient, Rietz, and David and we had agreed that Rietz would conduct throughout,[8] and David should pause as if his life depended upon it because the second chorus had to fend for itself at subsequent entrances. After these pointers it went extremely well. As to your suggestion to use 4 clarinets,[9] Rietz had tried it out in the rehearsal and I had heard the chorus, but we didn't find it effective; it sounded too pointed, and detracted from the character of the organ. Thus it remained as in the original in the performance. Eda Benda, whom I saw, said that the chorale sounded wonderful. The first chorus went generally well. Rietz beat time and the instruments entered almost precisely at the word "Jesu," which was amazing. Milder sang the aria very beautifully, actually swallowed the entire length of an eighth-note, but the flutes waited for her. The Lord's Supper very lovely. "O Schmerz" too fast, and the pianissimo in the chorus lost.[10] Devrient sang ''Siehe er ist da, der mich verräth'' as instructed.[11] The duet, contrary to expectations, excellent, the chorus weak. You can understand how Zelter finally atoned for his pleasures and conducted during the fermatas, but even they weren't quite precise. The final chorale without piano, the flutes excellent. The alto aria good amid the choral entrances, the tenors were the weakest throughout. The short choruses good. ''Wahrlich du bist auch Einer'' lacked the flutes at the start.[12] Schätzel made the same mistakes in ''Erbarme dich'' that she did in the rehearsal, but they were so subtle that probably only a few people noticed them.[13] ''Was gehet uns daran'' was the only chorus that was very shaky at the start,[14] ''Der du durch Tempelgottes'' much too fast; Rietz stopped, but it was already too late.[15] Now came the great scandal, which was inevitable: ''Ach Golgotha'' started on the 8th eighth-note instead of the 4th.[16] As per the expected outcome, Milder remained a half bar behind *during the entire recitative*, although Zelter played the correct part with all his might on the piano. Rietz went over to the basset horns and brought the parts together, but only in the last measures, and such misery has seldom been heard. With wondrous symmetry she spoiled the first piece the first time, the second piece the second time, and the third yesterday.[17] When it was over, many people surrounded me and cried out for you—Bader and Stümer in the forefront. Stümer became very gentle and said, ''It must have been an odd feeling for you today.'' In kind, I gave him the greatest compliments, for he was really admirable, especially since he held his own while Zelter often accompanied him with the wrong chords. Rietz also worked miracles, for Zelter conducted only when it occurred to him, and when he couldn't grasp the baton quickly enough, he used his hand. And when he also forgot to do that, the choruses would enter by themselves. Considered as a whole, it was a very good performance for the public, but everyone in the orchestra knew what was weak. During the entire evening I could only think about the steamship.[18] By the way, it was very full, the King was present from start to finish [ ]. I must also note that Devrient had received the score after the rehearsal and cleanly stuck the omitted pieces together with his spit. He is taking it away again and of course your score hasn't been tarnished at all. Rietz played splendidly. And now I think I'm finished. A few theater anecdotes that I've already collected for you will be sent next time via embassy mail, where I can write at even greater length.[19] You poor young man, how seasick you must be now! But what splendid hunger you'll have after your arrival. We live *stillissimo*. This evening Milder's portrait will be finished and I've quickly phrased your aria for her.[20]

[Lea, F. Rosen]

One more thing: I'm having your Octet copied. If you also want the Double Concerto in A-flat major copied, I need immediate instructions to that effect.[21] While I wait, let me convey many best wishes from Mosevius, who was just here. He came from Breslau with 3 other Breslauers to hear the Passion, and listened well. He brought me a pretty little letter from Franck.[22] Adieu, dear brother. Next time some more. I think we've filled up this sheet as if it were intended for the English mail system.

[1]See Illustration 2 showing the first page of the autograph.
[2]Perhaps Fanny is referring to the Trumpet Overture, Op. 101 (1825), which begins with a fanfare-like motive.
[3]Felix left Berlin on 10 April with Abraham and Rebecka, who journeyed with him to Hamburg, where he stayed a few days.
[4]The Catholic Emancipation Bill was passed in England on 10 April 1829, the day he left Berlin.
[5]Fanny's Tagebuch entry of 20 April 1829: "In France a departmental and communal law revoked. . . ." ("In Frankr. Departemental- u. Communalgesetz zurückgenommen. . . .") And there was an earthquake in Spain "which swallowed up two cities with all their inhabitants." (". . . welches zwei Städte mit all ihren Einwohnern verschlungen hat.") The Passion is the *St. Matthew* of J.S. Bach. Felix had played a major role in bringing about its revival, on 11 March 1829.
[6]Part of *NBA* No. 11. "Trinket Alle daraus" is in C major, whereas a previous parallel section, "Nehmet, esset," was in F major.
[7]"Der rufet dem Elias" is *NBA* No. 61b; "Halt lass sehen" is *NBA* No. 61d.
[8]E. Rietz's Symphony Society provided the instrumental accompaniment, just as it did at the work's revival under Felix, on 11 March.
[9]In letter from Hamburg of 14 April 1829 (Mendelssohn, *Briefe-RE,* 60).
[10]*NBA* No. 19.
[11]Part of *NBA* No. 26. Felix's instructions were for Devrient to sing c double-sharp instead of c-sharp on "mich" (14 April).
[12]*NBA* No. 38b.
[13]*NBA* No. 39.
[14]*NBA* No. 41b.
[15]*NBA* No. 58b.
[16]*NBA* No. 59.

[17]"Stück" often used by Fanny to denote "phrase," so she may have meant "phrase" here instead of "piece."
[18]Fanny considered Felix's trip a major event in her life, as she recorded in her Tagebuch on 4 January 1829: "This year will form an important chapter in our family history. Felix, our soul, is going away; the start of the second half of my life lies before me." ("Dies Jahr wird einen wichtigen Abschnitt in unsrem Familienleben bilden. Felix, unsre Seele, geht fort, mir steht der Anfang meiner 2ten Lebenshälfte bevor.") In a later entry (20 April 1829): "I'm so sad that I won't be able to write, and yet must write. . . . It's really difficult. Very difficult." ("Mir ist das Herz so voll, daß ich nicht werde schreiben können, u. doch schreiben muß. . . . Es ist doch schwer. Sehr schwer.")
[19]The Hanoverian embassy in Berlin was located on an upper floor of the Mendelssohns' house, and thus the family could send mail to Felix which would be forwarded by Klingemann, an official at the Hanoverian legation in London. See Cullen, *Baubiographie*, 51.
[20]Fanny told Felix how absurd she thought Milder's request, in a letter to Rebecka in Hamburg of 15 April 1829 (S. Hensel, *Familie I*, 201).
[21]Felix requested Fanny to have parts from the Octet and the Double Concerto copied for Klingemann (14 April).
[22]Hermann Franck.

13

Berlin, 24 April 1829

Today we expect our dear ones back, my Felix, and I really look forward to fooling around with Beckchen, with variations on the theme "Schatz verloren," etc. Actually, I'm only now feeling normal since you were in Hamburg. My jealousy over your being alone with Beckchen gave me little peace. How the child has it over me now! So one week alone. She's already written many details of your last days, but I want them detailed again, and greatly fear that I won't be free from envy over this week, but at least you can remove it with a calm letter, which I eagerly await. In Hamburg all of you warned somewhat confusedly, "Keep the important things in mind, don't be seriously distracted, the crazy girl is quite boisterous, they may have already made a courtship for her." One saw that in every line of your letters, which foamed over with high spirits.[1]

We have had our ups and downs. On the first holiday evening during your sea journey, a few close friends were here, namely Marx, who faithfully comes and is receiving Mother's special treatment, and the Heydemanns. Droysen isn't back from his trip yet. On the second holiday we received news from Hamburg of your boarding and were at the Fränkels—*horribile dictu*—in the evening. But Rosa was there and so everything was all right.[2] Tuesday we moved into the garden, where thus far we've been freezing for the fatherland. If April cuts such sour faces for you as it has for us, it will not be a proper manner to receive a foreigner. Caroline and Auguste ate lunch with Mother and me on Wednesday, *tête à tête*.[3] Afterwards the Märckers came over briefly for coffee and then they left again. Then I would have wished you here to see how uncle sat between Caroline and Auguste on the sofa in the twilight and flirted horribly with them.[4] When I complained about hot ears and cold hands, he took the girls first by the hands and then by the ears to find out if they were similarly afflicted. Later he sketched both of them. In the evening I emancipated myself in the manner of the Catholics.[5] I had arranged some music for Mosevius, but unfortunately Rietz was slightly ill and had to cancel. David kindly offered to play your Quartet,[6] as I wished, and brought Landsberg and Kudelsky along. It far exceeded my expectations and David in particular played very well (but without comparison to Rietz). Marx was also very taken with him. I'd previously played the Beethoven Trio in D major and was supremely satisfied with the instrument; it sounded splendidly full and strong. The uncommonly tender piano that one can bring forth put me in a very good mood, and I played well. Then Devrient sang a few more beloved lieder, among which the *Glutverlangen*, in particular, thrilled Ulrike.[7] Besides the above-mentioned the Heydemanns were still here. I asked Albert to take Paul's place at the second table, since he had had so much to do during the day that he didn't come over. He discharged his duty very well and would've done it even better if Caroline hadn't sat next to him *dos à dos*, his heart divided between hosting and courting duties, and his collar would have been turned around often.

Marx heard Paganini and is thoroughly thrilled by him.[8] He didn't find Hensel's drawing adequate and had a lengthy conversation with him about it.[9] He gives concert after concert, and is currently performing at the opera, with high-priced tickets and a sold-out house. In addition, young Praun is here now, who makes great claims, plays the same things as Paganini, and is said to have stated that he wants to follow him everywhere. He performed yesterday. I still don't know with what degree of success, since we attended a ball at the Bendemanns yesterday in which a large number of people from the other world were present—more than I've seen in respectable society. Rosa's former clothes were present in abundance, as were faded flowers with faded faces. August Oetzel was the only good dancer. The prettiest girls were Anna, Luise Oetzel, and Victoire. Hensel had invited first Pauline and then Victoire for the second waltz, but Victoire forgot and danced with the painter Remy instead, and felt very bad about it.[10] Martin is still not feeling quite right—Alexander as well—and I believe the Polish loan has traveled to their limbs.[11]—Paul has too much to do between now and his confirmation. He worked until 2 and 3 the last two nights after a full day at the *comptoir* until 9. His proprietor had chased off the supplier of the storeroom and Paul has moved into his position, and since he understands none of it and must ask questions at every turn, it takes a lot of time and therefore he must be there by 7 in the morning. I hope it won't remain so difficult.

The newest theater gossip is that Spontini, after announcing *Alcidor* ten times and then having to cancel, finally decided to write a formal letter of apology to Bader, which he sent to the directors.[12] Redern read the letter to the committee and Bader later asked whether he would settle down over the matter. He was not especially inclined to do so until Redern approached him: "We've had enough of this; what else does he want?" Even now it says in the newspaper that *Alcidor* has been canceled for the twentieth time and *Oberon* has been substituted,[13] allegedly because of Mme. Schulz's illness.

Saturday. Yesterday our family was reunited. Father is uncommonly cheerful and boisterous—with Beckchen that goes without saying. We've already shared much gossip. Oh Felix, your absence will now be felt more keenly, for thus far it was as though you would return with the others. The curtains on your windows are still there, and during the day I diligently looked over to see if you were still there. But in the evening it's dark. In general, people probably hear a kind of inner music during the deepest silences. For me, however, the situation is now reversed. I have a deep silence within me when I hear noises, am in the middle of conversation, and am busy doing everyday activities, and I never stop thinking about you. Take very good care of yourself, and let yourself become quiet and reflective at times in the midst of London's great noise. What pleases me about that journey is that one arrives in London before one arrives in England—one steps down directly into the largest capital city of the world without first entering an antechamber. Farewell. You will receive reports from us weekly through the mail, and gossipy letters later through Reden.[14]

[1]The courtship may refer to Salomon Heine's daughter; Felix, Abraham, and Rebecka stayed with the Salomon Heines in Hamburg before Felix embarked for London.
[2]Probably Rosa Fränkel.
[3]Probably Caroline Heine and Auguste Wilmsen.
[4]Presumably Joseph Mendelssohn.
[5]A reference to the Catholic Emancipation Act passed in England earlier in the month. See letter 12.
[6]Presumably the String Quartet in a minor, Op. 13.
[7]Part of the opening line of Felix's lied *Geständniß,* Op. 9 No. 2 (published 1830). Ulrike Peters.
[8]Marx's review of Paganini in the *BAMZ,* 6 (18 April 1829), 125-26. Before giving his lengthy and witty comments, Marx states: "It is difficult to solve the riddle of this phenomenon, perhaps even more difficult to state the solution in a permissible manner. Because here we are squarely faced with the impossibility of separating the person in all his manifestations from the innermost essence." He closes with "a great genius imprisoned in virtuosity." Fanny first heard Paganini in early March. She wrote in her Tagebuch on 9 March 1829: "Wednesday Paganini's first concert. I'll take the time to write more about this truly miraculous, unbelievable talent, about this person who has the look of an insane murderer and the movements of a monkey. A supernatural, wild genius. He is extremely exciting and piquant." ("Mittwoch Paganinis erstes Concert. Ich werde mir Zeit nehmen, mehr über dieses höchst wunderbare, unbegreifliche Talent, über diesen Menschen, der das Ansehn eines wahnsinnigen Mörders, u. die Bewegungen eines Affen hat. Ein übernatürliches, wildes Genie. Er ist höchst aufregend u. pikant.")
[9]Fanny's Tagebuch entry of 19 March 1829 states that Paganini ate at their house and then Hensel sketched him after dinner. Today the drawing is in Volume VIII of the Berlin Nationalgalerie's collection of over 1,000 drawings by Wilhelm Hensel.
[10]Anna Fränkel; Victoire may be Victoire Bendemann; Pauline = Pauline Bendemann.
[11]Alexander Mendelssohn, a banker; Martin is presumably his partner, perhaps a relative.
[12]Opera by Spontini; see letter 5.
[13]Opera by Weber.
[14]As head of the Hanoverian embassy located in their home.

14

1 May 1829

O Felix, even if I could bleat profoundly in writing I still wouldn't be able to express my joy. Yesterday your 2 dear letters arrived, and today the one arrived that you sent directly to Berlin in the mail, which took the longest.[1] You can't imagine how good it made me feel, especially after my horrible mood the entire morning (I'll tell you why later), and now I'm so soft as butter that I could be spread on any piece of bread. You poor thing—you must have gone through a lot. On Easter Monday I followed you continually in music and thought, and blew the three trumpets much too soon. In church I heard nothing during the entire sermon except the streaming of the Thames, and couldn't wait for it to end.

You've already heard many times that Paul was confirmed on the 29th, and there's nothing special to report. Wilmsen spoke well but the service was horribly long, exacerbated by the numbing coldness in the church. I'm very happy to be able to tell you that we're all extremely pleased with Paul. The strenuous work and the forced distance from us does him a great deal of good, and when he comes home at night he's actually very tired, but his sweetness and kindness make us truly happy. The sudden removal of a commissioned agent has given him the chance to advance quickly, and his proprietor is very pleased with him. Because our last dear sibling was sent out into the world in that recent church service, I'm again very much aware of the great changes that have taken place in the last few years—changes that have pushed us together and yet apart!

Today is the first of May and our room has become bearably warm after two attempts at heating. Storms have been the predominant weather recently, and thus the trees haven't become thicker in the past 2 weeks.

O Felix, great censor! Will you consider me lost beyond reasonable bounds, and entirely out of character when I voluntarily confess that I will have tea with the Redens this evening? And that this is the reason for my bad mood on the first page? Tell me instead, which will help much more, that I (in this case) am as clever as you and should look at the lighter side rather than be upset about it the entire day. But how I'll feel when I go there and how awful it seems that—

Here I was interrupted yesterday by Hensel, who came over. It was never more difficult for me to suppress my laughter than over there last night. After preparations lasting many hours, Frau von Stosch improvises in B-flat major, a sweet hint of *Per valli per boschi* wafts through the room, and now the lyre is really plucked, in an unbelievable way, etc.[2] But during the entire evening I thought of your letter, and I assure you that I had the courage to go anywhere, and if someone would have given me a slap on the cheek I would have held out the other. You write in such detail that I can't admire you enough, and if you continue at even half this pace you won't need a diary and we will still have the pleasure of experiencing everything. Mother, who's still in bed (it's still early, but we must mail the letter immediately), wants me to thank you for your punctuality and thoroughness, and tell you that she had an excellent conversation yesterday with a moldy English couple, on account of relatives in England. She also wants you to know how wonderfully Fräulein Reden and Herr von Röder performed the duet from *Matrimonio* yesterday.[3] Father, who stood behind my chair, sang along because he was nervous, Fräulein Elise was very hoarse (when hoarseness is hoarse, what is it?), and Mother and I dared look at each other only once—more would have been dangerous.

Marx has written a very nice essay on Paganini.[4] That Paganini's concert for the Danzigers was overflowing,[5] and that he performed new 4-part Variations on *God Save*, I'm reporting to you herewith from hearsay, like Rellstab, for it was Paul's confirmation day and we were quietly at home. This evening we'll hear him at Heinrich Beer's.[6]

Please write out for us at greater length, and more often, the invitations you receive. This evening you'll be in *Messiah* and it's really nice for once to be able to picture where you're likely to be.

At Marx's instigation I've set Klopstock's "Willkommen o silberne Mond" for instruments, namely contrabass, 2 cellos, and viola.[7] What! Contrabasses only go to a? You must extend their range down to an f.[8] What's happening otherwise with *Calm Sea*?[9] Farewell, my dearest. Hensel sends his best, and he'll finish your picture today. He could have shown us something much more unpleasant than this picture.[10]

Say hello to Klingemann, Rosen, Moscheles, and her, and be careful—not to the extent that you don't go among the coaches, but rather that you don't travel too often in a cabriolet, for he might become jealous again. She seems to respect you. But what does that mean? I'm not very happy about your behavior.[11]

The elder fish-otter

[1]Two of them are 21 April (Mendelssohn, *Briefe-RE*, 61 and 64) and 25 April 1829 (NYPL).

[2]Conceivably a line of text from a composition.

[3] Presumably *Il Matrimonio segreto,* by Cimarosa (1792).

[4]In the *BAMZ,* 6 (18 April 1829), 125-26. See letter 13.

[5]There was severe flooding in Danzig.

[6]In Fanny's Tagebuch (5 May 1829) she reports on Paganini at Heinrich Beer's: "Saturday at Heinrich Beer's with Paganini, who gave a splendid rendition of a Sonata, his *Glöckchen*: Rondo, and *Nel cor più non mi sento.*" ("Sonnabend bei Heinr. Beer mit Paganini, der eine Sonate, sein Glöckchen, Rondo u. nel cor piu non mi sento, göttlich spielte.")

[7]The poem "Die frühen Gräber," which Fanny set for voice and piano on 9 October 1828 (copy in MA Ms 31), and which was later published in the posthumous Op. 9 collection of her lieder (1850). The location of this new instrumental setting is unknown.

[8]"The devil take the contrabasses and Dragonetti *á la tête;* its lowest tone is—a!!" (25 April).

[9]"What am I to do with *Calm Sea*? Am I to reform the English? I'd love to. Will they stand for it? That is the question. It disturbs me" (25 April).

[10]Felix thanked Hensel for his portrait; Klingemann and Rosen are delighted with it (25 April).

[11]Felix wrote that he had given himself that same advice (25 April). It probably relates to his stay in Hamburg. See letter 13.

15

n. d. [c. 6 May 1829][1]

Oh oh, dear lamb, summer is here. From now on write about all the streets, places, and squares on which the people live to whom you have letters of introduction, because we possess a map of London, which Hensel gave us, and know everything. But we'd really like to know the name of the cross street near your residence on Great Portland Place, for the map doesn't show numbers.

This letter will reach you via Herr Werner, a nephew of Werner and Nephews. Please do everything to make his stay in your city pleasant and profitable. I'll consider every kindness shown to him my own, and am ready to reciprocate in kind.

If only the postman came now and delivered your letter, we could still answer it today and that would be nice. But I fear he won't have anything. Every letter that you'll receive today will reverberate with Paganini. What should I add? Namely this—that Beckchen flirted horribly with him at Betty's.[2] After she had gone up to him several times and addressed him, and he had munched on some oranges, we went to the table. A place was vacant next to us, and when the great Heinrich triumphantly led in his minister Paganini, the imp leaped up, ran up to him, and asked him to sit next to us. He nodded, followed, and when she had just sat down again, he turned around and went to another table where the other young ladies sat—Hofrath Herz's wife, Mme. Beer, Mme. Henning, etc. Anger and jealousy overpowered the imp and pealing laughter made her feel worse. Indeed, she swore in her anger not to lead him to the table today again (he's eating with us). Hegel was also there and paid many compliments to Anna and the others, and to Beckchen as well. Oh dear Felix, since you've been away no one has made up any idiotic sayings; we're still staying with the old ones, and in this respect, when you return, you'll find us similar to the Austrians: stagnant and dull.

Your letter to Paul just arrived, dearest Felix, and Father thinks we'll still receive another one today, from Friday. Certainly we are writing you every week through the mail; Father has already obtained very large sheets of paper. The embassy letters you'll receive are a bonus. That conduit is very nice when you'll want to send something to someone. We really wanted to send you some cake with Herr Werner, but at the moment when it was time to ask, I was overcome by shyness and so it didn't happen.

I had planned to have some numbers from the second Passion sung on Monday and had invited all the necessary forces, but since a horrible rain fell the entire day, nobody came but the Rietzes and Marx, whom wind and weather had not deterred. After his journey he walked around here without a coat, in his shoes. And we really sang from the Passion. A few times I had to laugh out loud particularly at Rietz, who bellowed out the alto part next to me. I thoroughly agree with Marx regarding the *St. John* Passion: when I know it better I'll be very enthusiastic about it.

Yesterday Paganini was the embodiment of the devil. He played a so-called *Canto appassionato* in e-flat minor, with the orchestra in broken tremolos. Suddenly he takes the whole thing into E-flat major, in order to fall back immediately into minor. It was very beautiful and seemed as though he was plumbing the depths of his soul and yet simultaneously ripping the heart out of the poor violin.[3] The *Hexen* Variations, in which he imitates the chatter of hoarse old women, are disgusting.[4] He finished in a very ordinary way, which was a shame.

Beni and Rosa say hello—they have taken a trip.[5] If one looks at the behavior of both of them, one would be forced to believe that she belongs to the family originally and he only got there because she was always the friendly one, and he probably held her back from everything. He certainly possesses that particular family flaw to the utmost. He's not even acceptable to us. There are always a few unfortunate elements in families, and I even have my own little ones. But that's an entirely different matter (and a redundant one).

Farewell. The fellow is standing there waiting for the letter, so we can't wait for a possible one from you. Take very good care, my lamb.

[1]Crum, *Catalogue I*, 5, claims this letter is part of GB I 46, dated 6 May 1829.
[2]Betty Beer.
[3]The *Canto appassionato* in e-flat minor is probably the *Sonata appassionata* of c. 1829.
[4]*Le Streghe* ("Witches Dance," 1813), based on a popular ballet tune. I am

grateful for the assistance of the late Boris Schwarz for the identification.
[5]Benjamin and Rosamunde Mendelssohn.

16

7 May 1829

My beloved Felix, although this letter will arrive with those from next Wednesday, I'm sending it out tomorrow to comfort myself. I can't tell you how the business with the parts torments me and how I've been reproaching myself over the distress I've caused you through my carelessness. You certainly told me where you put the parts, and certainly instructed me to take them, but dumb me can't find them. It's as if they've disappeared from the face of the earth. I've looked through everything and even took Rietz along because I didn't trust myself. But nothing has turned up.[1] And now on Monday you'll be annoyed at your dumb sister who distresses you over there in London and who transmits clever advice from here—advice that you certainly must have given yourself a long time ago. I wish everything would go smoothly, but only God knows where the copyists live and where you can get a hold of them. In the end I'll be responsible and inconsolable if the *Midsummer Night's Dream* isn't performed. Dearest Felix, Wednesday is more than one week away, and until your reply arrives I'll worry constantly. I assure you that it wasn't necessary for you to send an admonition to Hensel for him to encourage me to search. When he read your words, he got up from the table and wouldn't be calmed when I repeatedly stated that the parts could not be found. Moreover, I want to tell you that your 3 letters—from the 28th, the 30th, and the first—all arrived on the same day, Wednesday the 6th, so I don't understand why you haven't received any letters from us—we've written every post day.[2] Oh! dear Felix—we can't refrain from writing, and you will also surely receive a batch of letters from us all at once. That will probably last for a while and become tedious, whereas if we spent five minutes together we could catch up on news in no time. Yet I still have hardly told you how sorry I am that I haven't found your parts.[3] Woe is me!

I'd rather reserve the little writing space that remains for tomorrow, because today I can't think of anything except parts and more parts, and I've gotten into such a bad mood over the parts[4] that I'd better stop.

Saturday. Yesterday when I went to Zelter's and greeted your window in the courtyard, I saw something white in front of it that seemed as though you had just discarded a piece of paper or lost your handkerchief. When I came closer the dove flew away. It was a brief, lovely illusion.—One morning recently, Hensel sent me a drawing after we had had a little argument. I'd send it to you if it weren't so horrible. It's entitled *Misunderstanding*, and it is you, in a state of *understanding* with a *Miss* whom you are taking home. This morning he invited the entire family over for breakfast to see your finished picture, which will be brought to our house later. You will reside over the fireplace, behind me when I play the piano, but otherwise command a fine view of the entire room. Zelter, who is here often, sends his best, as do all your friends who faithfully ask about you. Farewell.

[Rebecka, Lea]

[1]In his letter of 30 April 1829 (NYPL), Felix wrote that he had asked Fanny from Hamburg to send all the string parts to the *Midsummer Night's Dream, Calm Sea,* Symphony in c minor, Trumpet Overture, and the Octet. But he has only received the Octet parts and those of the Trumpet Overture. He wants the other parts sent immediately, as he needs them for concerts taking place very soon. He says that Rietz [Eduard] might have the parts if they are not at home, and enlists Hensel's assistance in finding them, for, as Madame Moscheles said, Fanny is a bride and therefore may be unusually distracted.

[2]The letter of the 1st is published in Mendelssohn, *Briefe-RE*, 64-68.

[3]Felix wrote that he is sorry about the entire matter concerning the parts and of having given Fanny and his mother in particular such a burden. It turns out that he had more of the desired parts than he had thought, and he was very disturbed by Fanny's letter (30 April).

[4]The translation "bad mood over the parts" is a literal rendition of the German pun, "und bin über all die Stimmen in solche Stimme auch gekommen."

17

20 May 1829

Your fish-otters have just returned from a stroll through the garden—called a WALK—which they took out of their boundless joy over your very gay letter,[1] since they couldn't have done otherwise. The chestnuts sparkle, the lilacs are fragrant, the lilies-of-the-valley stand tall and fresh as first youth out of the ground. We chose this pleasant summer weather to initiate these little diary reports to you, which we intend to continue to send, one after the other, either weekly, via the embassy, or through personal envoy.[2]—This morning the chimney sweep woke me up at 6, an hour at which I usually don't get up. The result of my surviving was a good lied, which will make you rejoice, and by use of this expression you can't have any doubt that it's by Droysen.—[3]

[Rebecka]

Saturday, 23 [May][4]

The child is so funny that it's difficult for the old cantor with the thick eyebrows to keep up.[5] Let's see whether the following story is to your liking. When I arrived at Zelter's yesterday before 12, as befitting my vice-directorship, Goroncy was gurgling away in the lower hall. I entered and she sang a Swiss lied for Grell, who then excused himself. I stayed downstairs a moment, and then when I climbed the stairs, I heard the same lied upstairs in a moving rendition. I enter the room, Grell is seated at the piano, and is delighting himself with reminiscences. Incidentally, we celebrated our Friday with a Bach Concerto in E major, *Herr gehe nicht ins Gericht*,[6] and the first chorus from the *St. John* Passion. Hellwig, who didn't know about it, constantly danced around the piano before we started and was surprised at my impertinence as I remained standing next to it. When it was over he asked whether Rungenhagen was supposed to play at the keyboard, then I said I was in charge, and the matter was dismissed.

The day before yesterday Rietz came over with his violin; but Cotta came also, as well as our old uncle,[7] and so nothing happened except the completion of Cotta's portrait sketch.

Yesterday evening the eldest Lewenhagen, who will be away for 3 months, paid a visit, as did Herr von Boguslawsky and Märcker.

[Rebecka]

Wednesday, the 27th. There's nothing much to report these days, so I should keep quiet, but instead here I go. Yesterday I learned of Hensel's charming idea to have the chair from your picture made up for me—not as he wished me to find out, but rather because Mme. Robert, who has moved in here, naturally entertained nothing less than the idea of selecting this chair for herself, thereby interfering with us. I went to her today to ask her to select another, but for Hensel, of course, the pleasure has been spoiled. Overall we're busy with trifles, as usual. I'm hardly bothered by such things, for I previously took care of many details for you and am doing the same for Hensel, whom details affect almost as adversely as you. Mother has never learned to say yes to something, and that still produces extremely unpleasant moments. Just recently we had a terrible scene regarding my marriage.[8] Of course, when one views the entire situation, things are well and good and couldn't be better, and the minor flaws disappear. But none of us is as good and clever as you, and therefore no one gets anything from Mother. You are our alpha and omega and everything in between. You are our soul and our heart, and our head as well—the rest can go hang itself. We're fine when you're away, but less useful. You are a type of special rooster, and we possess those qualities to a significantly lesser degree. We now play the piece often: we take the little Titania in our hands and say "blessed mealtime," but with an "oh" before it.[9] To me there are actually two categories of people: you and everyone else. Beckchen will read that, but it only embarrasses me a little; she knows that she is here, and Hensel and a few other persons as well, and she can write it too. So now I've spun a yarn and perhaps spoiled an hour of your time, but now I'm satisfied. Only one more thing—what's to happen with the d-minor Symphony?[10] Are you thinking about it? I play your *Scottish* Sonata often.[11]

[Rebecka]

[1]Letter of 15 May 1829 (NYPL).
[2]These are generally written on much smaller sheets of paper than those used for composite family letters during this period (see Illustration 2). Also, Fanny and Rebecka are the main contributors, although Hensel joins in occasionally. Felix responds enthusiastically in his letter of 29 May 1829 (NYPL). On 11 June 1829 (NYPL) he writes: "I also received your dear diary, Fanny and Beckchen, on that Tuesday, and thank you most warmly for it. I'll send a detailed response soon, in the form of a similar rhapsody." His letter to the sisters of 25 June 1829 (NYPL) is such a diary letter.
[3]This lied is not part of the MA collection of Fanny's manuscripts; it could be in the autograph Sammelband containing thirty-eight lieder from 1826-32, in private possession (Elvers, *Quellen*, 216).
[4]Fanny mistakenly wrote "23 April" instead of "23 May."
[5]A term of endearment Felix applied to Fanny, especially in her role as an accomplished musician.
[6]Bach Cantata, BWV 105.
[7]Joseph Mendelssohn.
[8]This was not the first such scene, as Fanny's Tagebuch entry of 9 March 1829 shows: "Sunday afternoon there was a very unpleasant scene with Mother concerning our marriage, as a result of which I couldn't calm Hensel down again." ("Sonntag Nachmittag gab es eine sehr unangenehme Scene mit Mutter wegen unsrer Verheirathung, über die ich Hensel gar nicht wieder beruhigen konnte.")
[9]Possibly a pun with the double meanings of playing the piece and playing the game. Titania is a character in *A Midsummer Night's Dream,* and "gesegnete Ma[hl]-zeit" seems to be a private joke among the siblings. For example, Felix writes on 19 June 1829 (NYPL) regarding the possibility of writing a separate letter to his sisters: ". . . and what am I to write in it? 2 pages of nothing but 'blessed mealtime?' " (Mendelssohn, *Briefe-RE*, 71-72).
[10]Eventually completed in 1830 and entitled the *Reformation* Symphony.
[11]The Sonate *écossaise* in f-sharp minor, Op. 28. Worbs, *FMB*, 134, lists the date as "before 1830." Bartlitz, *Works*, 153, lists the date as 29 Jan. 1833, which appears on the autograph in West Berlin—presumably the completion date.

18

Berlin, 27 May 1829

Since Beckchen and I started the diary, we will have little more to do with letters. You'll receive the first *livraison* through Herr Deetz, who will depart on the second steamer. We've been rejoicing all week over the balls you've attended; you have, however, forgotten over ten new ones. The description of the Sir Alexanders will probably arrive today.[1] I picture a very lovely scene to myself—out of the raging chaos, in which there's nothing to grasp except one's thoughts, you come home in the evening and gradually come in contact with your heart's innermost feelings again. Then each of us appears in turn and embraces you, and then at the end, shortly before you fall asleep, the full image of home flashes vibrantly, until everything dissolves into a serene mist and blur. Who accomplishes the monumental task of waking you each morning? Milder is giving her concert for the Danzigers today, in which she will sing your *Maris stella*.[2] We were very surprised not to have been invited to the concert until we found out that Bach had taken care of the invitations,[3] which explains a great deal. Grell frequently complains about him, and was not even able to rehearse his piece, since he locked the organ right in front of his nose. Some musician! Devrient was here briefly yesterday and said that he wants to write you a very long letter, but his wife has been ill and he must spend every morning in the city. *Agnes!*[4] Milder chirps like a sparrow, we get along horribly, and she appeared at breakfast this morning and called for Hensel. What do you think of that?

[Rebecka]

I gave the child the quill because the hair dresser came, but now I'm taking it back merely to announce that Rietz doesn't flutter around anyone any longer except Eda Benda, and on her account has completely cut off his social engagements with us.

[Lea, Abraham]

[1]No mention appears in Felix's letters between 19 May and 29 May 1829 (NYPL).
[2]See the *AMZ,* 8 July 1829, col. 456. *Ave maris stella* was composed in 1828.
[3]August Wilhelm Bach.
[4]Opera *Agnes von Hohenstaufen* by Spontini (Berlin, 12 June 1829). See the *AMZ* review, 5 Aug. 1829, cols. 509-10.

19

3 June 1829

On Saturday your letters arrived at the embassy, my son, and you're doing the right thing in making use of this channel.[1] But please be so kind as to send such a dispatch with your next letter through the mail, for then we won't be waiting for it and instead will have the patience of a saint. We also sent you a letter last Saturday and tomorrow you'll receive letters from Zelter, Milder, and Devrient. Zelter also came for dinner Saturday and shared your entire letter with us. Devrient came afterwards and read us snippets from his. Rietz came over the other day and mentioned only a few things. Marx still hasn't been here, for he's very busy. In spite of the weak footing of the theater, his Festspiel for the wedding will be given, and on Sunday alone he held three different rehearsals of it.[2] The empress, who will arrive on Friday, is the only thing anyone cares about now (especially your father, the city councillor), and enormous preparations are being made for her visit.[3] Not only will the entire magistracy greet her, but he's also had to arrange for 76 white maidens. We both refused on account of the uncertain weather (it's already pelted down for four days without a stop). Father had to provide poetry, and he went to Rellstab, Förster, and Fouqué. Then he procured Anne Fränkel for the host of maidens and is bringing her here today to show her the sample dress and suggest that she be one of the leaders. He's opposed to Fräulein Büschleg because she's short and unattractive. In short, you're finding out wondrous things.—Today we're hoping for a long letter from you, since the last two were very brief. Oh dearest Felix, persevere in your good practice; you have no idea how necessary it is to us. For you are really a Phoenix. Whoever asks us how often we hear from you and is told, once a week, is astounded, and can't get over it. You are a kind of angel—for God's sake, don't change. And please send a short personal letter to your fish-otters some time and pine for them. Also send us the lied in which you sang your dear heart out last week, and the A-major lied—Caroline's lied—which I had to play last evening for the Wilmsens.[4] It was touchingly naive how the Wilmsens, who had come over the day before, arrived at 7:30, and how Baur, who hasn't been here since you left, came at 8. And how we all laughed—Auguste also—and how the three trotted off gaily around 11, as if it were fated for them to do so. Try to transfer this scenario to other people and it just won't work. This indescribable childlike quality resides only in the Wilmsen family. The Heines are in Charlottenburg and have all contracted a fever again. Two of Marianne's children have it also. Aunt Meyer, who sends her best, hasn't gone to Charlottenburg yet. I visited her recently and showed her some parts of your letters, which gave her immense joy. Gustav Magnus was also here recently and sends his best. We invited him to come again, provided that he could tolerate boastful people,[5] but we're on the best of terms with him.—Hensel has now found a place for his studio in the Luisenstift and I'm very happy that it's fairly close. He awaits only the confirmation of the King. I become involved in his affairs and push him a little, and think that I'll gradually cure him of this shortcoming, especially since he's given up and yet taken on so much because of his love for me. By the way, believe it or not, when we're together, you, and then you again, are always the topic of our conversations. You mentioned Lord Sandon in your last letter.[6] Have you still not seen Aunt Mine Bute yet?[7] Aunt Mine is called Aunt Marianne here now, who is one of Eda's aunts. I tell you, the business with Eda isn't entirely unclouded. He's in love as never before and always calls her "the little one."[8] We, on the other hand, tease him and ridicule him.—The Academy is stagnating and so boring that it's practically unbearable. Milder received the confirmation of her pension without the increase she requested and is furious. The theater is absorbed exclusively with *Agnes.* In Königstadt Mlle. Vio is successful; I haven't heard her yet.[9] That's just about everything. *À propos*, in a passage in your letter to Devrient where you say it's too bad that his impressions of the Passion are blurred or spoiled, we've concluded that he must have written you an extremely negative letter.[10] Don't place much stock in what he says right now. Since the rehearsals of *Agnes,* every *Ecce homo* is a tight-rope walker around him and he's not capable of making reasonable judgments. On the contrary, ask Rietz, who says that when Schubring goes home at night he sings from the Passion; ask Baur, who doesn't go to church on Sunday but plays from the Passion; and ask us—we also play and sing from the Passion.—Your splendid letter with news about the c-minor Symphony just arrived.[11] You poor knave, what slipshod work they've done for you. I'm very glad that you're now beyond all that, and I never doubted your success.[12] The news of it hasn't surprised me, but has nevertheless put me in a pleasant and light-hearted mood. You will create a *furorissimo* with the *Midsummer Night's Dream.* The story about Malibran isn't so bad.[13] Now I also have to tell you since [ ] recently lost a bet that concerned Malibran because he [ ] the Overture from *Figaro,* which you performed at a party. I was just quarreling with Rebecka and saying that I'd like to write another time when your letter has arrived, and the others could begin. And she was saying that they always say everything there is to say, so that she wouldn't have anything left to write afterwards.

[Rebecka]

Everyone here says hello and rejoices over your success; they're proud of you. Just tell me this: is Moscheles completely clear of these intrigues against you? From your letter, his involvement seems at least possible.[14] Take very good care.

[Rebecka, Abraham, Lea]

[1]Presumably referring to Felix's letters of 19 May and 22 May 1829 (NYPL).
[2]*Undinen's Gruß:* Festspiel (Fouqué), performed 11 June 1829 at the Königstadt Theater. The *AMZ,* 5 Aug. 1829, col. 809, responded negatively to the piece. The event was the wedding of Prince Wilhelm of Prussia and Princess Augusta of Saxe-Weimar.
[3]Empress = Czarin of Russia, the former Princess Charlotte of Prussia.
[4]Caroline is presumably Caroline Heine. The lied could be *Geständniß,* Op. 9 No. 2. There are also two other A-major lieder in Op. 9: *Frage* (No. 1), and *Im Herbst* (No. 5).

Illustration 3—Autograph fair copy of Fanny Hensel's song cycle, *Lieder von Fanny für Felix, 1829,* with Wilhelm Hensel's drawings (first page) [Bodleian Library, Oxford; MS Margaret Deneke Mendelssohn c. 22, fol. 22].

[5]Presumed translation of "mit kleinen Spiegeln."
[6]On 19 May, Felix reported that Lord Sandon visited him that day and led him through Parliament.
[7]"Aunt Bute is still in the country" (19 June 1829, in Mendelssohn, *Briefe-RE,* 73).
[8]Eduard Rietz.
[9]See the *AMZ,* 5 Aug. 1829, col. 511.
[10] Devrient had written Felix on Good Friday "about the dull performance" of the Passion (Devrient, *Erinnerungen,* 79n).
[11] The pride refers to Felix and the highly successful performance of his c-minor Symphony: "the success last evening was greater than I ever would have dreamed" (26 May 1829, NYPL).
[12] She writes the same to Klingemann on 4 June 1829 (S. Hensel, *Familie I*, 210).
[13]The rumor says that he is courting her passionately, but he wrote that he has not even been introduced to her (26 May). In a later letter (11 June 1829, NYPL), he writes that the rumor was started by one Herr Keferstein, who inferred that Felix was in love with Malibran because Felix had declared that she does excellent ornaments. According to Robert Schumann, Felix considered writing a Requiem for Malibran after her death in late 1836 (*Erinnerungen*, 32).
[14]Letter of 26 May. For a summary of the intrigues and their resolution, see E. Werner, *Mendelssohn*, 146-49.

20

[Rebecka]

4 June [1829]

I was out when your second letter arrived yesterday, and when I came home it was too late to answer it.[1] And now it's already the 6th of June and no longer the 4th, and it's raining continuously, and we sit—*horribile dictu*!— in the warm, heated room. I've just finished notating my 6th lied for you and want to copy it immediately on the yellow blotting paper, with terrible oaths directed at Herr Schwarz, who deceived me so fearfully with said blotting paper.

The 7th of June, Pentecost Sunday—a grey, rainy, cold Pentecost, in which there's not much to do—for us, lonely and routine. Two cornflower wreaths are hanging on the mirror, and we're still divided on whether we shouldn't put them on, because you're not here, or whether we should, for we would if you were here. We will probably choose the former—it's not weather for flowers, after all. I've just finished writing out my lieder and ask you not to treat them as if they came from far away, for that gives them only relative value, but rather as if they were lieder with both good points and bad points.[2] Please give them a critical evaluation. One is among them that I consider one of my best lieder, and we shall see if you feel the same way. You will sing them very beautifully. And you can also see that Hensel, although the laziest correspondent, is nevertheless involved with you.[3] I'm still not certain whether you'll like the drawing of Mother.[4] It wasn't quite right at first, but now that we've gazed at it, or that, through much effort and other things, the good has replaced the bad, we find it very good.

We really want to write the dumbest farces for you, but alas!—we haven't been coming up with them.[5] Sometimes I amuse the little imp by telling her what various people think of her.[6] Marx, Rauch, Heine, and Milder have made the following observations, respectively: she embodies the ideal of womanhood, she sports a happy face, she sports a tragic face, she resembles Old Testament figures.

[Rebecka]

Yes, you are the most clever one. I recently sat down at the piano and played through the scherzo of the Octet and tried to imagine where the airy D trumpets might appear.[7] Tell us some more about the dear scherzo and how you've spruced it up. In any case, I can have the honor of assuring you that you're the most decent of all mortals—not that *I* ever doubted it. But just don't think that other people doubt it. I was rather annoyed to learn from your letters that you've received all kinds of comments from home, but they write them so that you won't be spoiled. Everyone here is extremely pleased with you, and Father wonders constantly why you still haven't accepted any money. Do you remember how I once raged because Zelter thought your *Calm Sea* should begin with a few contrasts? And you calmed me down with "Now, now—don't enrage yourself so, my dear girl."

[Rebecka]

The 10th: at a time in London when you prepare your Symphony for the second time. How I envy someone like John-Bull, or rather Ox, who is bored by your scherzo.[8] Truly, your presence is needed, for Rietz doesn't take after anyone in the family at all. Indeed, I predict that during your absence I won't hear your Quartet, for which my mouth waters.[9] For I've already asked him three times in vain, and I don't ask more than three times.—Now I must elaborate a bit more than Beckchen did on the reverse side about Betty's purse. She made it for one of the many women's clubs which sold things for the Danzigers.[10] We immediately resolved to acquire it for you, in fine competition with both Fritz junior and senior.[11] I was actually there with Betty during the first hour of the sale and captured the purse. Both Fritzes were left empty-handed.

Now I ought to clarify the margins.[12] Oh good, the lieder have already been packed up and I must, like a minstrel, sing them from memory hereafter. First of all, Hensel asks forgiveness for his letter; he wrote it yesterday evening at the round table while we and Marx made a great deal of noise nearby. Secondly, he's sending you his loveliest drawing—the one of Beckchen—and has only kept a sketch, from which he wants to reconstruct it.[13] You'll receive a copy of mine with the next letter. Isn't it enormous proof of my selflessness and lack of envy that I only had Beckchen's drawing sent, especially since I could have easily intrigued to have hers left behind through my connections with the artist? Reward me for it. Give me the order of the red eagle, third class, with or without the oak leaves, and make me a privy councillor. But the margin: HEAR, HEAR! In the front we are sitting like children and playing. Hensel claims to have absolutely captured my grimaces when I hit single bass notes in between. It probably won't elude you that the good Pegasus has a treble clef in his tail. We move along further and enter the first lied.[14] You are roused. Here I don't know whether the artist has succeeded in properly expressing the Herculean work and especially the requisite exertion on the face of the rousing one. The rooster sits sadly on the column, against which a walking stick is leaning. From the roof of the main house (in which the title resides) two well-known animals, the good storks, look down into the bedroom. Then, the summer comes and someone writes to you from the garden (poetry) *Tulpen und blaue Wieden*, and the *Vöglein in der Linden* are in attendance.[15] The girl sits on a trellis, whose fruit will be known to you.[16] Is it true that you once composed a lied and then composed a Quartet from this lied?[17] And that others extract a great deal of substance from this Quartet and make ceaseless allusions to it? Look at her foot. It doesn't sit on a storm but on a sixteenth-note. Have you ever seen a more gracious footstool? Now the world is thick with cypress trees, sea, and ship; six lieder flutter over there—*Hochland.*[18] The Scot in that company looks around in amazement as you climb up with your other music, but now all of you will really get along with each other.

The lowest drawing is rather self evident. But please don't laugh over my naiveté in the three-part lied. I know very well where it originated and you do too, but that is precisely the joke. Is it my fault that you already had the idea last year?[19] Even though it's so clear, hardly anyone will understand why we're sailing from the grey past into the golden future in the drawing.[20]

Farewell. I once again conclude a diary entry consisting of trifles. May our dispatch give you as much pleasure as we had making it together. Amen.

[Wilhelm]

[1]Probably 29 May 1829 (NYPL).

[2]*Lieder von Fanny für Felix, 1829;* text by Droysen; fair copy MS MDM c. 22, working autograph MA Ms 31, 22-28.

[3]His drawings appear around the edges of song No. 1; see Illustration 3.

[4]According to Lowenthal-Hensel, *W. Hensel*, 71, Wilhelm did two drawings of Lea. This one presumably in Vol. IX, No. 3 of Hensel's vast collection of drawings at the Berlin Nationalgalerie. Felix acknowledges its receipt in a letter to Paul of 3 July 1829 (NYPL).

[5]Felix said he welcomes them and eagerly looks forward to them (29 May).

[6]Rebecka.

[7]Mentioned in Felix's letter of 29 May. Felix orchestrated the scherzo from the Octet to replace the original minuet in his c-minor Symphony.

[8]In Felix's letter with the en-route Hamburg postmark of 9 June (NYPL), he declares "I am a John Bull" after describing how he has given up a concert and a visit with a young lady in order to attend the horse races. John Bull is a nickname for the average Englishman. In Fanny's satirical usage it carries the connotation of a cultural Philistine. See also note 3 to letter 21.

[9]Presumably the in-progress String Quartet in E-flat (Op. 12), completed 14 September 1829 (Bartlitz, *Works*, 153).

[10]There had been several floods in Danzig. Betty is probably Betty Beer, but could be Betty Pistor.
[11]Identity of both Fritzes uncertain.
[12]Of the first page of Fanny's song cycle; see Illustration 3.
[13]According to Lowenthal-Hensel, *W. Hensel,* 76, it could be one of the following in the W. Hensel collection at the Nationalgalerie: Vol. VIII, No. 17; Vol. IX, No. 9; or Vol. IX, No. 31.
[14]Its text begins, "Stören möcht ich Deinen Schlaf nicht."
[15]Both of these lines appear in the second song of the cycle.
[16]The lush grape trellis in their garden.
[17]Pun on "Ist es wahr," the first line of Felix's lied, Op. 9 No. 1, from which the a-minor String Quartet, Op. 13 (1827), is derived. The opening motive of the lied is notated to the right of the girl in Hensel's drawing (see Illustration 3).
[18]No. 5 in the cycle.
[19]The three-part lied is No. 6, *Wiedersehn*, which has the same melodic line, although with varied rhythm, as the second theme of the main Andante section in Felix's Sonate *écossaise* (m. 43). This offers a solid piece of evidence of 1828 being one year during which Felix's piece was composed. In Felix to Paul of 3 July, Felix writes that there is no similarity between the two pieces. See also letter 26.
[20]In his letter to Paul of 3 July, Felix praises Hensel's arabesques and finds them so unforgettable that he knows them by heart.

21

Thursday, the 11th [June 1829]

[Rebecka]

Hooray! the first summery day is here today, the 13th of June, when one can finally sit outside and write to you. As Beckchen wrote on the preceding page, the blockhead is still in Potsdam, but he was here and said the stupidest things and got me angry, especially since I still can't come to an agreement with him about anything.[1] For he was a poet once and one can't find anything about him that rings true, for not even his vanity is genuine, and yet he

Illustration 4—Pencil drawing of Fanny Mendelssohn by Wilhelm Hensel, 1829 [Staatliche Museen Preussischer Kulturbesitz, Nationalgalerie, Berlin (West)].

believes himself the most straightforward person. Solve this riddle for me, my dear gospel, as Hensel alluded to you today in relation to me. I mainly know that he loves me because he respects my love for you and gladly even gives it precedence to a certain extent.[2] I assure you that I feel very good; I fared well with you and then with him and finally with both of you, and there is something to establish with both of you. You both grab hold of art firmly and use it to express your individual creative instincts. Don't change. Felix, I think your detour into D major isn't at all bad and I can imagine all sorts of things in it, but it would be very difficult for me to reconstruct it—perhaps I can.[3] Do you know what we girls are now reading? *La nouvelle Héloise* (the little one without my consent). I'm actually reading the entire book for the sake of one passage that you once liked: "vivre et mourir sans elle! vivre sans elle!" The Italian verses that occur in almost every letter don't please me at all. Actually one shouldn't read any novels if one is experiencing such things, but since we, blessed with reason, in reality live the life of a housewife, we would then have to leave these morsels unread, and that would be a real shame.

[Rebecka]

Tuesday, the 16th of June Your dear letter arrived the day before yesterday. Hensel brought it to dinner Sunday along with the pretty garden chair. I've found a little place for it in the garden, since the arbor is lost to us. Hensel can't stop getting angry over it, so please don't mention it—it belongs to the category of things that don't touch malicious people. But what helps us is that your picture is good, and we—Beckchen and I, your dear girls—sit in front of it for hours and wait for it to move us. It does indeed move us, but not literally, and thereby does its duty. Yesterday morning I visited Zelter. He sends his best and comes here very often to find out how you are. The Medem family was here last evening. Auguste still loves her old friends Felix and Klingemann and is informing them that her wedding is on the 6th of July (Hensel's birthday, I may add) and she will leave for Mecklenburg a few days afterwards.[4] Drink a toast on Monday, the 6th, to all born and married people. I want to convey herewith Auguste's greetings to Klingemann on my own behalf. Marx was also here yesterday and enjoyed talking philosophy with Auguste, and we invited Droysen and Albert for dear Jette and Constanze.[5] Since the day before yesterday, we've been in the habit of saying a *fine soul*, and so sometimes when we imitate you we claim that you have a fine soul. It's such a small pick-me-up. Adieu.

[Rebecka]

The other morning. The thunder came upon us fearfully: a crashing storm full of flashing lightning, smashing hail, and pouring rain—the worst in recent memory here. Few windows in the good city of Berlin were able to withstand the hefty impact of the hail. On a brief inspection with Hensel in the garden after the stormy night, we found all the paths strewn with acacia blossoms, and large twigs and branches on top of everything. Our 200 greenhouse windows had become at least 2,000. What will happen next? We are not FASHIONABLE and do not travel to Epsom Steglitz, although Father just rode there. Now something ridiculous—in the excitement of the first of the three readings of your letter yesterday, we thought that the concert of the *Midsummer Night's Dream* and various items in E-flat major took place yesterday, and as a result immediately began to get excited. (Our excitement often consists of us girls throwing our arms around each other, and hugging each other, and then running up to your picture and making faces.) But suddenly it occurred to me that the concert probably wasn't yesterday, and then I received your letter and realized I was right.[6] Next Wednesday I will have to play Beethoven's E-flat Concerto at the Heines in Charlottenburg, if I play at all. Yesterday I was involved with the *Midsummer Night's Dream* when Zelter arrived, and your letter shortly thereafter. You can't be surprised that your letters arrive late sometimes, for the same is occasionally true of ours even though we send out our little letter regularly every Wednesday afternoon. Our entire family lives together once again in the Kameke house in Charlottenburg. Aunt Jette, the last to move there, was the recipient of a party instigated by Aunt Meyer. To wit, Herr Tilenius and Herr Wigand were dressed as white maidens and recited a poem, line for line, about Aunt Meyer's factory, while the others had stationed themselves as triumphal arches. Aunt Jette is said to have laughed herself to tears.

[Rebecka]

Saturday, the 20th of June. Miltiz just left here. He told us that two of the thieves, as well as one of the stolen items, were found, and that the servant is innocent.[7] Although you will smile and shake your head in disbelief, let me confirm that this very unfavorable story has placed him in a very favorable light, and he's become *l'enfant chéri de toute la maison*. We wanted to go to the opera this evening to see Schechner as the Vestal, but unfortunately we didn't get tickets.[8] Hensel will probably complete my picture this evening. Despite my protests he's placed a wreath on my head again, which will lead people to believe that I was born with such a contraption.[9] Do you know who's the most respected man of our entire circle? Who always elicits the most tender consideration? M[ ]. You would enjoy seeing it, and likewise enjoy seeing how nicely and amicably he and Hensel get along. Tomorrow is the flower exhibition and he has received our only dispensable ticket. Tuesday is the flower academy, last year was your *Te Deum*. I must start to close now, for with the end of this page the diary comes to a close and I must run upstairs right away to substitute for Herr Klingemann. Give him our best and tell him we would love to have him here. Write sometime about your Covent Garden AFFAIR. Do you know anything yet about the text?[10?] Farewell, oh dearest, oh lamb. Are you corresponding with Wilhelm Horn? I'd consider it infinite *haut goût* if you slipped away for your trip to the northern coast of France and traveled to Paris for 24 hours *incognito*. I know I couldn't resist.

[1]Referring to Droysen.

[2]That Fanny's intense feelings for Felix constitute an issue is shown in a letter from Fanny to Wilhelm of 23 August 1829 (DB 106): "I love both of you so very differently, and yet so similarly; I feel it's impossible to spend a happy life without either of you . . . , and may you also feel this blessed trinity as strongly. . . ." ("Ich liebe Euch beide so ganz verschieden, und so ganz gleich, ich fühle die Unmöglichkeit, mein Leben ohne Einen von Beiden glücklich zuzubringen . . . und mögest Du es auch fühlen, diese selige Dreieinigkeit so stark. . . .")

[3]Felix notated a piano lied for Fanny in his letter of c. 6 June 1829 (NYPL): "Just think, dear Fanny—a lied in A major, very tender, which closes with the opening material, and when one is sick of hearing it, it's still sweet (see Shakespeare, who also was a John Bull) and makes the following detour to D major at the close: . . . [then 8 bars of music]. If I were you, Fanny, and in the mood, I'd make a decent

lied at this closing, which excites me (Felix), for which I (Fanny) would receive a text from Droysen." Later he discussed how it could be orchestrated, and joked about how he prohibits her from using more than 300 horns on low C.

4Presumably Auguste Medem.

5Albert Heydemann, and possibly Jette and Constanze Medem.

6Performed on 24 June. Beethoven's *Emperor* Concerto, with Felix as soloist, was also presented at this concert.

7In a Tagebuch entry dated Tuesday, 23 June 1829, Fanny writes: "Thursday the unfortunate story that Miltiz was called away from his performance here because someone had broken into his house." ("Donnerstag die fatale Geschichte, daß Miltiz vom Spiel hier weggerufen wurde, weil man bei ihm eingebrochen hatte.")

8In Spontini's opera *La Vestale* (1805).

9In the same Tagebuch entry as note 7, Fanny writes: "Friday and Saturday Hensel drew me for Felix." ("Freitag v. Sonnabend zeichnete hensel für Felix.") Felix gives his reaction to it in a letter to Fanny of 10 September 1829 (DB 3, 2): "Fanny's large portrait is also beautiful but I don't like it. I see how splendidly it's drawn, how closely it resembles her. But in the pose, clothing, gaze, in the totally sibylline, prophet-like quality of the adoring exaltation, my cantor is not present. In her case the exaltation doesn't point upwards, but inwards, and doesn't manifest itself in the outstretched arms or the wild wreath of flowers, because anyone can see that at first glance! But he must not, and instead only gradually become aware of it. Don't take it badly, Hofmaler, but I've known my sister longer than you, carried her in my arms as a child (exaggeration), and am now a regular, ungrateful bear at times." ("Auch Fannys größes Portrait ist schön, aber es gefällt mir nicht. Ich sehe, wie herrlich es gezeichnet, wie sprechend ähnlich es ist; aber in der Stellung, Kleidung, im Blick, in der ganzen sybilligen Prophetenhaftigkeit der schwärmenden Begeisterung ist mein Cantor nicht getroffen! Da leigt die Begeisterung nicht so oben auf, mehr immer drin, u. zeigt sich nicht in gen Himmel sehn, oder im Ausstrecken des Arms, oder im wilden Blumenkranz, denn alles das sieht einer auf den ersten Blick! Das muß er aber nicht, sodern erst nach u. nach draus klug werden. Nimm mir das nicht übel, Hofmaler, aber ich kenne meine Schwester doch länger als Du, habe sie als Kind in meinen Armen getragen (Übertreibung) u. bin nun mal ein ungeleckter, undankbarer Brummbär.") It apparently bears some similarity to Fanny's likeness in Illustration 4, also executed in 1829. A less idealized representation is shown in Illustration 1, an undated, although probably later, portrait by Hensel.

June 1829 (Mendelssohn, *Breiefe-RE*, 74). He then writes in his letter to Paul of 3 July: "The Covent Garden matter proceeds calmly, and two submitted texts are next to me. But I've considered everything carefully and don't want to return here next year. I don't think it right that some such proposal divert me from my travel plans. I think it better to go to Italy and write the offered opera there, and then in 1831, when I go to Paris, also visit London again. . . ."

22

Berlin, 29 June 1829

First of all, my dear Felix, thanks very much for the petition for our wedding.[1] It made us so happy that it's as if it were already beginning to take effect. Furthermore, your return home was never the topic of discussion in this regard; it is and remains set for September or October. Paul told Hensel yesterday that he instigated your request, but since your last letter can't possibly contain a response to his request, it's a coincidence that pleases me, coming from both brothers. I'm so anxious to see what your private diary for us will contain that I can hardly wait.[2] Once again I need your assurance that you're happy. Sometimes it's as necessary to me as air is to life, and then it will tide me over for a while. We had a lovely time yesterday and this morning. Hensel spent the entire day Sunday painting your picture, and this morning between 6 and 8 worked on the background, mostly outside. Nearby we had a nice picnic at the outdoor gymnasium and it was pretty. Today he placed your picture in complete sunlight, where it looked splendid and incredibly vivid. Recently he gave me a poem that he thought could be sung in the garden, although it's actually too lengthy for that purpose. I convinced him that it can't be set to music and am now composing it for his birthday. I hope it will be finished by then. It will consist of 8-part chorus, with the women's chorus and men's chorus first antiphonal and then together.[3]

One Evening.

Your *Hora* is really beautiful.[4] How do I arrive at that conclusion? I've been alone for two hours, at the piano, which sounds especially nice today, playing the *Hora.* I get up from the piano, stand in front of your picture, and kiss it, and immerse myself so completely in your presence that I—must write you now. But I'm extremely happy and love you very much. Very much.

The 2nd of July. We just received your dear letter from the 25th, one day late. We're thrilled about the success of the *Midsum-*

mer Night's Dream, but disturbed over the preceding frustrations.[5] We're also distressed that the things sent via the embassy take so long, for you've received only one of the 4 or more diary installments we've sent you, and we really have been writing to you once a week via the embassy, just as we do through the regular mail. Now we're sending you the little engraving that you've requested—a slightly larger one will have to remain behind. We've set aside one for you that shows an area with a wheel and lambs, but unfortunately the actual lambs' house is not visible. In the front, on the bridge, a rendezvous or an encounter is taking place, which refers to you—that should please you. Now, buy a batch of cherries from the woman street peddler with her cart; provide for one of the itinerant men with a long nose, for another with glasses and a Pomeranian accent; and call the third one, who is leading a woman, Louis, and the woman herself, Minna.[6] And I'd wager that you're in the back of that scene in a carriage, going home to Leipziger Strasse No. 3, asking for a stamp.

That scenario, as well as many others, will probably be acted out again. Among other things, I plan to have many scenarios acted out in the winter garden house, and to have some GENTLEMAN drink coffee here every morning, for otherwise I might not have the opportunity to see him before he goes out.[7] It will be a nice time, please God—so lovely that I don't want to see anything beyond it. Farewell. Mother sends a thousand greetings. I mistrust everything we send out because I don't know how long it will take and whether it will reach you in London.

[Rebecka]

You can also say hello to little Einbrodt for me—I allow it. How the whole group has been scattered to the four winds!

[1]In his letter of 19 June 1829, Felix wrote that the wedding should take place soon, for many reasons, including the fact that Hensel must be getting impatient (Mendelssohn, *Briefe-RE*, 72).
[2]An allusion to the diary type of letter he is writing to his sisters, begun with his missive of 25 June 1829 (NYPL). This practice is a response to their diary letters to him.
[3]*Nachtreigen,* dated 29 June 1829; autograph MA Ms 70.
[4]*Hora est* (composed 1828).

[5]This performance took place on Wednesday evening, 24 June (to sisters, 25 June). It was a great success, but the accompaniment to the Beethoven Concerto (No. 5), which he performed, was scandalous. His rendition from memory occasioned some surprise.
[6]The wheel = their circle of friends; the lamb = their pet name for Felix; the man with the long nose = Albert Heydemann; the man with the glasses and Pomeranian accent = Droysen; Louis = Louis Heydemann; and Minna = Minna Heydemann.
[7]Felix.

23

1 July 1829

Today your letter was expected with greater impatience because it contains the story of the *Midsummer Night's Dream* and probably a response to the lieder and drawings.[1] I'm pulling myself together with difficulty to write you now, since I have to go out later and the letter will make the rounds then. Last Wednesday we were really cheerful. The wheel gathering consisted of Minna and Albert Heydemann—Louis [came] only after Hegel[ ] [ ]—Auguste Wilmsen, Droysen, and us.[2] Mälchen Märcker had also come. The wheel occupied one side of the table and a great deal of nonsense flowed back and forth. After dinner we sat down on the elevated place on the street, which you know, and then the lovely letter that you still don't have was concocted,[3] and we laughed so much, namely over Hensel, who was in such high spirits, that Droysen and Heydemann in particular really lost their breath and ran into danger of suffocating to death. We went into the garden behind the house later, around 8, the presumed starting time of your concert.[4] We became solemn, the girls pulled out each and every cornflower from their wreath and pelted you with it, everyone received you with applause and *bravo*. Beckchen and I intoned both flute parts—unfortunately the clarinets were missing—and during all these events Albert and Louis sat on a tree, like cats. The day was extremely pleasant, the little gathering was lively and in good spirits, and every joke went over well. When we picked up Mother and Father at Marianne's in the evening,[5] the entire wheel came along, Louis Heydemann carrying coats and umbrella (it was a dry heat, with no hint of rain). And when we wanted to separate, the wheel, struck with enthusiasm, selected Hensel to be one of its members, right on the street, by means of a ceremonious round wreath of roses and the holding up of the opened umbrella. On Monday we were once again in Charlottenburg at Fanny Magnus's, where we also had a very good time. Martin and Gustav asked me to convey their best regards to you in this letter.

[Rebecka]

The most awful jokes are circulating about *Agnes von Hohenstaufen.* The best among them tells of the theater porter mistakenly bringing Blume the part from *Alcidor* to the last rehearsal and the error not being especially noticed; instead, the part is sung through to the end. Rellstab wrote a malicious review, and what will become particularly painful for Spontini is that he notes how the third performance was already empty, and how, in spite of unfavorable conditions such as heat and the like, the 20th performance of *Stumme* was overflowing. *Laissons là ce monde*.[6]

On the day when you receive this letter, we will be celebrating Hensel's and Droysen's birthday.[7] The day before yesterday I took on yet another musical work for Hensel—an 8-voice composition based on one of his poems. It won't be much but it will be something, and now it lacks only the last movement, which I'm thinking of making into a fugue. You know how concerned I always am that my imagination will run away from me, so therefore I'm happy if I succeed in writing down some notes, without having much of an idea at the start as to how it will turn out afterwards. Later, of course, I fret if it's bad. Adieu, my dearest Felix. I'm leaving you so that I can say good-bye to the Fränkels, who will depart for Switzerland and Italy tomorrow. Recently, Anna paid you several compliments in front of your picture; I assure you, your upbringing was good.

[Lea, Abraham]

[1]The letter describing the concert is 25 June 1829 (NYPL), and that giving Felix's reactions to the lieder and drawings is addressed to Paul, 3 July 1829 (NYPL).
[2]The term for Fanny and Felix's close circle of friends, centered around Felix. See letter 27.
[3]Letter 27, actually sent in mid August.
[4]Of the *Midsummer Night's Dream.*
[5]Marianne Mendelssohn.
[6]*Alcidor* and *Agnes von Hohenstaufen* are both by Spontini; the second version of *Agnes* was premiered on 12 June 1829. Rellstab had written malicious reviews of the first version in 1827 (*Vossische Zeitung*, No. 128 and No. 129; *BAMZ,* No. 23, No. 24, No. 26, and No. 29). *Die Stumme von Portici* is by Auber (1828). Fanny had attended the premiere of *Agnes*/2 and written to Felix on 17 June 1829 (GB I 61): "Friday *Agnes*, which, so to speak, was a fiasco—i.e., as only an opera by Spontini can be a fiasco—incurred general displeasure, with the exception, however, of the scene in the church. . . . The Czar of Russia declined the dedication because of Spontini's earlier offense against him; Raupach's disgrace may also be responsible." ("Freitag Agnes, welches so zu sagen, fiasco gemacht hat, d. h. wie eine Oper von Spontini fiasco machen kann, allgemeine Mißfallen erregt, wobei jedoch die Scene in der Kirche ausgenommen wird. . . . Der Kaiser von Rußland hat die Dedication abgelehnt, außer Spontinis früherem Vergehn gegen ihm, auch wol Raupachs Ungnade Schuld seyn mag.")
[7]6 July.

24

n. d. [PM 8 July (1829)]

[Hensel, Droysen, Rebecka]

For God's sake, what rubbish the girl writes! Really, when she lets her mouth run on sometimes she should be placed in a stockade, for otherwise she would be Beatrice.[1] Shakespeare is the only mortal who knew of such tomfoolery. But now I'm asking everyone individually not to read what follows, as it contains great secrets. Since you're traveling and unfortunately the embassy takes so long, the statements in the diary are now at an end. And now on to the silver anniversary. We also have great plans, but they are rather nebulous and you must help them to crystallize.[2] This much is certain, please God: the anniversary-eve party will be celebrated in the garden house—our place—on the 25th of December with a small, young, gay group and as many farces that can be found in the realm of humor. That day will pass, and on the anniversary day itself, the various well-wishing authorities will be received. At noon the royal family will eat with us here, because one shouldn't let oneself become too tired in light of the great musical festivities that will take place that evening at your house. The *Highland* Symphony is included, the scherzo with the airy d trumpets, and the *Midsummer Night's Dream* and *Calm Sea* will remain unforgettable. Regarding the eldest otter, she would rather show off her little talent at the anniversary-eve party, a small gathering, because in the first place she is dull, secondly idiotic, and thirdly she can do absolutely nothing. But she would like to set some of her husband's poetry to music. The young court poet Droysen has also offered his services, and the more the merrier. You, oh brother, must once again work on a [childlike] symphony that makes Mother die laughing before it's finished, and it must constitute the beginning of everything. In the following week a ball might take place at the silver anniversary couple's house. The London child will probably utter no wish in vain. That should be a wonderful time, Felix—a wonderful time! I assure you that I can hardly conceive of it and life beyond it: every moment a holiday, not one dull moment. And I can also assure you that you will play undisturbed at my house—no mouse may touch you. All the touching will be from within. Hensel is a good man, Felix, and I am content in the widest sense of the word, happier than I ever imagined possible. For I dreamed and feared that such a relationship would tear me away from you, or rather alienate us, but it is, *if possible*, just the opposite. I've gained more awareness than before, and therefore am closer to you. I reflect more often and therefore I reflect on you more often. And the more I have now and will have in the future, the greater I will have you and need you. It's not possible for you to ever take any of your love away from me, because you must know, as I do, that I can't do without even the smallest part of it. I'll repeat the same to you on my wedding day, because thus far, I've never known any emotion or situation in which I wouldn't have thought and said the same thing.[3] Everyone thinks your picture looks very warm and lovely. Considerable progress was made on it yesterday, which was Hensel's birthday.

Today he's coming back to touch up a few details on one hand, and I'm to pose for it. The matter regarding the atelier is now as good as settled. We really couldn't have wished for anything better, as the Luisenstift is very close and the paths through the gardens quite pleasant (in case permission has been granted for the breaking through of the doors). I've kept two places, one for myself and an extra one. Because the girls are so wild about the little father, you must impose order on the situation from London. It's really crazy. If Caroline and Beckchen can't sit next to him, they don't want to eat. They're making him vain and as a result he'll have to be trained again.

Wednesday. The only thing I have to report is a miserable performance of *Iphigenie*. Mlle. Schechner suddenly became indisposed before the start and was thrown on the good graces of the public, which she actually needed in great measure.[4] Furthermore, when one hears a performance in which every nuance deviates from one's conception, it's truly an awful experience. Adieu, my Felix. I'd like to continue writing but I've just thought of something you've always said, but which is untrue, namely, that one cannot write from home. I believe, however, that men must write on trips and women from home. Women will describe every well-known fleck on the carpet, which gives pleasure to those who are away. This evening the Devrients are coming over. He liked your letter very much and will probably bring it along. I finally just thought of something that Zelter requested a while ago, which I've always forgotten, namely, if you come across German motets by Handel in London, please send him the titles and other pertinent information.[5] Farewell. Your

Fanny.

[Lea, Rebecka]

Zelter has just sent a letter to you that I will mail with the next embassy dispatch. But I don't think that it will catch you. Oh dear Felix, I'd like to tell you so much more, and whenever I ought to stop I think that everything that's been said is so inadequate. But everything boils down to a single phrase: we love you. You are so smart and good that you haven't needed our advice yet. But we mean well, and you take it in the right spirit. Adieu. The weather is awful, but the sun has just peeked out a little and I want to frolic in the garden for a while. In Klingemann's splendid letter, the difficulties of the vacation frightened us. I hope they have been straightened out by now and you will both have a wonderful time. If only your coastal journey could have come through.

[Lea]

Now thank God, my secret writing on the other side was one of the three things that it could be, namely unnecessary, after the nice things that Mother just wrote you. Also, I assure you that I should've waited for your letter before writing to you, because the depression is now over.[6] You can't imagine anything more absurd than the situation on Wednesdays before your letter arrives, and then when it's there. Today, for example, we sat sentimentally in the kitchen, shelling peas, because—the postman comes through the court. And then he came, that good man—from here until the *dal segno* it's lies—and we sprang up, sending the poor peas rolling swiftly all over the kitchen, the bowls containing them not far behind. The plates also had trouble rescuing themselves from our haste. We fell upon the man and tore the letter from him—*Mother opened it, and while she read the 2nd side, I read the first side briefly. Then I couldn't continue because I howled and embarrassed myself in front of Father. So I didn't read of your joy in black and white because Father, who of course was less impatient than we, nevertheless tore the letter from my hand, and by means of his right as the stronger, took it with him in the carriage and will bring it back around noon. Mother told me, however, about a bet that's floating on some measure 21. She'd forgotten the lied, but I've checked in the meantime and found that it must be in the third where the voice has b, a, g on the word "leiden," and both hands in the accompaniment have f, "fa." How could it be anything else? Have I erred on the passage?[7] In haste I'll also report that your picture received two kisses on your birthday from the two dear girls who signed their names at the beginning of this letter.[8] Mother asks you not to respond to what she wrote at the end of her letter.[9] And now, for the six-thousandth time, farewell.

[Rebecka, Lea]

[1]Character in Shakespeare's *Much Ado About Nothing.*
[2]In a section directed to the sisters in his letter of 19 June 1829, Felix had written that he has ideas for the festivities, which he will convey in his diary letter for them (Mendelssohn, *Briefe-RE*, 72). In the diary letter of 25 June 1829 (NYPL; S. Hensel, *Familie I*, 214), Felix continued: "But above all: what is your opinion of the program for the silver anniversary in December? Send me your ideas right away; but if the thing won't be at least as dazzling as your royal parade, I'll remove myself from everything and not join in the festivities. A great deal of music with new Scottish compositions, for which you, o eldest otter, must also write something (HEAR HEAR! CHEERS, HURRAY—ORDER, ORDER!), I humbly suggest; Braham can also sing an aria and Neate play a concerto, etc. In addition, nothing can transpire without comedy, masquerade, dinner, and a ball (the left side, HEAR); even though I praise quiet weddings, silver anniversaries must be loud." He then asks for reasonable suggestions from them. In a later communication, this time from Scotland (11 August 1829; DB 3, 1), Felix writes: "I also want to bring many things to the silver anniversary. . . . But I'd love to write occasional pieces as well, and the children's symphony alone won't do, although I've already gathered splendid materials for it and know the BAGPIPE, *Rule Brittania,* and nationalistic melodies in it by heart. They must be occasional pieces, and in fact for voice. And with that, go to my favorite poet—my poet of the morning and the heart, Johann Gustav Droysen—and bid him 'Good day' from me, and might he recall what he promised me before my departure, and I need it now. Namely, he is to send me the text—fantastic, sweet, and just as he pleases, long or short, serious or gay (or both), old or new. In short, he should compose some music in words for me, to which I then make the text in notes. This is what Johann Gustav is to do for me." ("Ich will auch mancherley zur silbernen mitbringen; Instrumentalmusik, Spuk, Seltsames, . . . ; aber ich möchte gern auch Gelegenheitsstücke dazu schreiben, u. die Kindersymphonie allein thuts nicht, obwohl ich schon prächtige Materialien dafür gesammelt habe, und die darin vorkommende bagpipe, rule Brittania u. Nationalmelodien sammt andren schon auswendig weiß. Gelegenheitsstücke müssen's aber sein, u. zwar für Gesang, u. somit geht zu meinem Lieb-, Morgen- u. Herzdichter, Johann Gustav Droysen, u. sagt ihm guten Tag von mir, u. nun möge er sich erinnern, was er mir vor dem Abschiede versprach, und ich brauchte ihn nun. Er soll mir nämlich den Text schicken, phantastisch, süß, u. ganz wie er mag, lang oder kurz, ernst oder froh (oder beides) alt oder neu gemessen, kurz er soll mir eine Musik in Worten componiren, zu der ich den Text denn in Noten mache. Das thut mir Joh. Gust. schon.") Felix also wants a short, quiet lied for the celebration, for two voices without accompaniment. And for the large one, he wants as few words as possible.
[3]See letter 32.
[4]She was generally excellent in this opera, as the *AMZ,* 26 Aug. 1829, col. 560, reports: "Meanwhile, Iphigenia in Tauris was perfectly realized in Gluck's magnificent tone poem. This performance showed the true, high calling of the excellent singer for the declamatory, serious opera."
[5]In his letter of 17 July 1829 (NYPL), Felix states he will write to Zelter via Mühlenfels, who is returning to Berlin, to receive instructions on his copying of

Handel pieces from the sixty thick volumes of Handel manuscripts in the King's private library. This detailed list from Felix to Zelter, dated 20 July 1829, in private possession, is published in Grossmann-Vendrey, *Vergangenheit*, 38-39.
[6]Lea's section mentioned that Felix's letter to Paul, of 3 July 1829 (NYPL), has just arrived.
[7]It is No. 3 of Fanny's song cycle, mm. 21 and 22, which have an f-sharp. Felix wrote in his letter to Paul of 3 July: "Dear Fanny, a bet was just made whether there's supposed to be an f or an f-sharp in the bass in the 21st bar of your 3rd lied, *Grave.* Your manuscript says f-sharp; your verdict decides a dinner."
[8]Unclear what is meant by Felix's birthday, as it occurs on 3 February.
[9]Lea wrote about several issues in her last section, but since her last statements were general rather than specific, the particular issue to which Felix is not to respond is unclear.

25

n. d. [PM 8 July 1829]

I just finished my contribution to the large family letter to you, dear Felix, and must now add this small private dispatch, whose contents are as follows. It's suddenly come to Father's attention that your name was mentioned merely as Felix Mendelssohn in several English newspapers.[1] He thinks he detects an ulterior motive in this fact and wants to write you today about it, as Mother, who tried to dissuade him from doing so, told us yesterday.[2] I don't know now whether or not he will still carry it out,[3] but last night Hensel and I decided to write you this letter in any case. If it's unnecessary, then it won't hurt you—possibly it could be of value; and if it's unpleasant, then you'll forgive me.—I know and approve of your intention to lay aside someday this name that we all dislike, but you can't do it yet because you're a minor, and it's not necessary to make you aware of the unpleasant consequences it could have for you. Suffice it to say that you distress Father by your actions. If questioned, you could easily make it seem like a mistake, and carry out your plan later at a more appropriate time.—The real purpose of this letter is to dispel much of the apprehension, attendant with time and distance, that Father's writing may generate. As you yourself so recently wrote, alphabet characters are very cold and lifeless, and thus it's easy for the intended message to be misunderstood.[4] Father, in particular, always writes more harshly than he thinks, and thus we wanted you to receive a few friendlier words in this matter. It's possible that you'll be deeply annoyed when you read here for the third time what Father for one, and perhaps Mother as well, has written. But, as I said before, you'll forgive us for a poorly executed good intention. We understand each other, I think, and thus things will be the same between us. It gives me little joy to think that you, who sends only good things our way, are subjected to unpleasant news from us so often, and that, in this regard, you are leading your daily life so far away from home. I earnestly wish it were otherwise. But it is this way now, and, please God, may it lead to many good things.—How will things proceed during your upcoming trip? Will we receive letters as regularly? I remember with horror that first Wednesday when one didn't come, for if noon rolls around and none has arrived yet, we start getting quite unruly. Now you will worry. Adieu, my Felix. I'm sending this letter to Hensel, who wants to add a few lines and then mail it himself. You know how it always used to upset you when our parents concealed their satisfaction from you. Father makes us upset in the same way when he appears so indifferent and stoic, but then we'll catch him reading your letters three or four times and telling people how happy he is about everything you do. Only we're not supposed to know it. But we do know it. And so be well and happy. As I've been writing, two eyelashes have dropped on the paper, and if they arrive in London, you'll know who the letter is from.[5]

[Wilhelm]

[1]Bartholdy had been added to the family's name, upon the suggestion of Lea's younger brother Jacob, when members of Abraham's family converted to Christianity.

[2]Lea wrote Felix in the general family letter (see letter 24) that Abraham would write Felix about the matter, and she advised Felix to answer gently and comply with his wishes.

[3]Abraham did write to Felix (GB I 71). Almost the entire letter is published in E. Werner, *Mendelssohn,* 36-38.

[4]"Alphabet characters, which one writes, are very cold, dear girls; speaking is better" (19 June 1829, in Mendelssohn, *Briefe-RE*, 72).
[5]Felix's response to Fanny and Hensel is from Glasgow, 11 August 1829 (DB 3, 1): "How grateful I am for the dear private letter that you wrote me, and almost as grateful because it wasn't necessary." Felix writes that he received their letter in the midst of his hasty departure from London and read it in the wagon, "and it touched me doubly how you had spoken in such a precautionary and conciliatory manner, especially since it didn't require conciliation. For it would never in my life occur to me to want to oppose Father's will, and over such a trifle! No, believe me, it doesn't enter my mind, and I think there should be few misunderstandings across the Channel that won't be easy to clear up, and in the same manner as this.—" ("Wie danke ich Euch für den lieben Privatbrief, den Ihr mir schreibt, u. fast noch mehr danke ich ihn Euch, da er nicht nöthig war . . . u. doppelt rührte es mich, wie Ihr so vorsorgend und so ausgleichend gesprochen hattet, da es doch der Ausgleichung nicht bedurfte; denn es soll mir wahrlich in meinem Leben nicht einfallen, etwas gegen Vaters Willen durchsetzen zu wollen, u. nun gar solch eine Kleinigkeit! Nein glaubt mir, es kommt mir nicht in den Sinn, und ich denke es soll wenig Misverständnisse über den Canal geben, die nicht leicht aufzuklären wären, u. auf ebenso ge[re]dene Wege, wie dies.—")

26

Monday, 13 July [1829],
during your concert[1]

This time I'm starting to write very early because I have a great deal to tell you, my dearest Felix. First of all, I'd like to thank you for the great pleasure I derived from your letter, and that is actually the main point. I read your letter over and over again, as you did my lieder, and know it by heart just as well.[2] And when I'm at the end I always think of an additional coda for it that goes like this: "How am I, poor sheep that I am, so fortunate to have been able to give you such joy," and then I sing to myself the end of the 2nd lied, which to be sure has always pleased me the most, and find it quite good. I'm glad to know, however, with whom you made a bet about the wrong notes, since no one but Sir George has seen it, and you wouldn't bet a dinner with him.[3] You can hardly believe what a marvelous effect your letter has made on Paul.[4] I find him fundamentally changed since that day, and I must confess once again with immense joy that you are the constant embodiment of the invigorating, reforming, cleansing principle that teaches through love. As long as we're reflecting on Paul, what I've always valued about him is that he possesses no trace of envy towards you—only love—although he is well aware that you are both talented in different ways. He is diligent and upstanding now, and when things sometimes become a bit difficult for him, it is good for me to remember that Herr Vonhalle is not an agreeable man, and that apprentice years in general aren't rosy, unless they are like those of Wilhelm Meister,[5] but I'd rather see him learn a bit more. I despise the fellow, not like all rogues, because Shakespeare had better rogues. I was very sorry that I wasn't able to let you know Wilhelm Horn's address a week ago.[6] The letter came too late. You need only use Baron Delmar's address, where Horn, to my greatest surprise, is now replacing Becker, for the latter has returned to Germany. At the same time here, Horn inquired about your address—your letters, therefore, must not have reached him. What arrangements are you making for your Scotch journey; will we continue to write to Doxat?[7] It's nice how we are both living now as we wish: you're looking at the world with a fresh countenance, moving among three kingdoms because one may be too confining, and I'm looking ahead so quietly and serenely towards my new life, which is establishing itself very calmly and slowly at present. I've been thinking about looking at the world as well, because Hensel is determined to take me to Italy if you're there. Although this plan always seems impossible to me, I nevertheless find it very attractive. You pull us along—we, Mother and Father, and the child, who isn't permitted to stay here alone. I'm less fearful for Paul; he will find his way in the world alone, and perhaps farther than we. Then all kinds of nice things could develop, but we'll discover how many of them might actually happen. *Tuesday* Betty Pistor just left. We performed the lieder for her, after we'd recited a long prologue of yours. We recalled old times and many walks, and particularly one, when Gans and a certain Pole had left us, and we wandered around the streets and would speak of the present as well as the future. Then came the lieder, and then a long epilogue recited in front of your picture. You must imagine how it looks: the picture sits on an easel in front of the secretary, against the window, in the hall. And if you recall, there's a row of chairs at the window, on which we sat, next to which the picture was nicely placed. One cannot stand up without seeing it, and that is quite agreeable. If one could only become unaccustomed to sitting around expectantly the entire Wednesday morning and cutting the longest and most tasteless faces until the dear man—the postman—comes, and brings the dearer man—the letter. This "dear man" had an experience which was deleted by the speech censor himself because of abuse, but since revived with even greater liveliness.—A thousand greetings to you and Klingemann from Auguste von Le Fort, who departed yesterday and paid us a long farewell visit. She is extremely happy and indisputably a lovely person. Please tell Klingemann that we recall very clearly that last year all of Europe conspired not to send him a billfold for his trip, but since we've presumed a similar plot this year in Scotland, we've circumvented it and provided one. Unfortunately, it won't reach him in time and he will probably find it upon his return from Scotland. As you will Marx's music, dearest Felix. So far I haven't been able to force it away from him, but now I hope to receive it soon (namely, the revised Overture to *Ondine*), and then I'll send everything with the next embassy dispatch.[8] Until now [. . .]

[Rebecka, Lea, Abraham, Rebecka, Lea]

It's Wednesday morning, and that is significant because we've just received your letter in which, unfortunately, you've again complained about not receiving ours;[9] we do, however, send them punctually in the mail. I'm not happy that our correspondence will become more irregular from here on. But it is indescribable how much we look forward to Mühlenfels,[10] and I truly fear that we will fling our arms around his neck. Yes, my child, we will spoil him, we will have his favorite dishes made, we will respect him and be respected by him. In short, he shall have a good time. Your cadenza concoction is splendid. As soon as I've finished writing, I'll go and reflect where it belongs. I've already concluded that Moscheles is playing my part.[11] Fanny Magnus and Victoire asked about you yesterday with great interest—we were in Charlottenburg for Aunt Meyer's birthday.—How do you like a Jew from Mainz who was put away for deceit, named "Jewish Man Beer Doctor?" I've written it in block letters, for otherwise no Christian soul will believe it. Adieu, my life. To a certain extent I'm taking my leave of England; this letter will no longer reach you there. May things go well for you evermore. In England you are in fact an angel, but don't be a pea in Scotland nor an errant in Ireland, but only good.[12] Farewell.

[Rebecka]

[1]The charity concert for the Silesians, in which Felix is a participant (to Paul, 3 July 1829, NYPL).
[2]Felix to Paul of 3 July: "It [the package] laid the foundation for a day that I would call the happiest of my life had I been with all of you. . . . I think it's the loveliest music that a person on earth can create. Nothing has ever enlivened and gripped me, at any rate, so totally. . . . Yesterday I played for myself the close of the 2nd with the *Vöglein in der Linden* very quietly, and then did crazy things in my room, and hit the table, and may also have cried a lot. . . . That is the heart, the very heart of music. And if I start to play the ending, I have to sing them all, for none is weak. I can never stop. At the end I sing the first once again, in which the words are spoken; and then when the *Heimkehr* swings up to B major and I sing my soul out, when it gets hold of the *Hochland* so strangely; and the trio at the end!! . . . And then the *Grave,* which is very bitter! I've never heard such music. I'll never create anything like it in my life. That doesn't work when it's been uniquely expressed. Truly, there are few people who are worthy of knowing the lieder; Fanny ought to sing them only to a few. By the way, I wasn't able to listen to them critically; nothing came of it because they stand way too high above it. But yet only a few should get to know them, and only those who understand them." Felix did share them with others. He played *Hochland* for Sir George Smart, who thought it "beautifully and artfully harmonized, and melodious as well. OTHERWISE I would have thrown him down the steps." Klingemann's enthusiastic reaction to Fanny of 5 July 1829 appears in Klingemann, *Briefe*, 55-57.
[3]Sir George Smart. See letter 24.
[4]It's an unusually warm letter of encouragement and affection (3 July).
[5]*Wilhelm Meisters Lehrjahre*, by Goethe (1796).
[6]In his letter of 3 July, Felix requested that Louis Heydemann be informed that he's written to Horn twice, without an answer. Felix wants his address.
[7]Felix advised them to address letters to Doxat (10 July, in Mendelssohn, *Briefe-RE*, 77).
[8]Felix found it strange that he had not received any music or response from Marx (3 July). The Festspiel *Undinen's Gruß* was premiered on 11 June.
[9]For example in letters of 11 June and 25 June 1829 (NYPL).
[10]In his letter of 10 July, Felix wrote how wonderful Mühlenfels has been to him, and how he made Felix feel at home while he was alone in a foreign country. Felix asked that the family treat him well. Mühlenfels will have many merry stories to tell them in Berlin (76-77).
[11] In his letter of 10 July, Felix described the first rehearsal of the Double Concerto

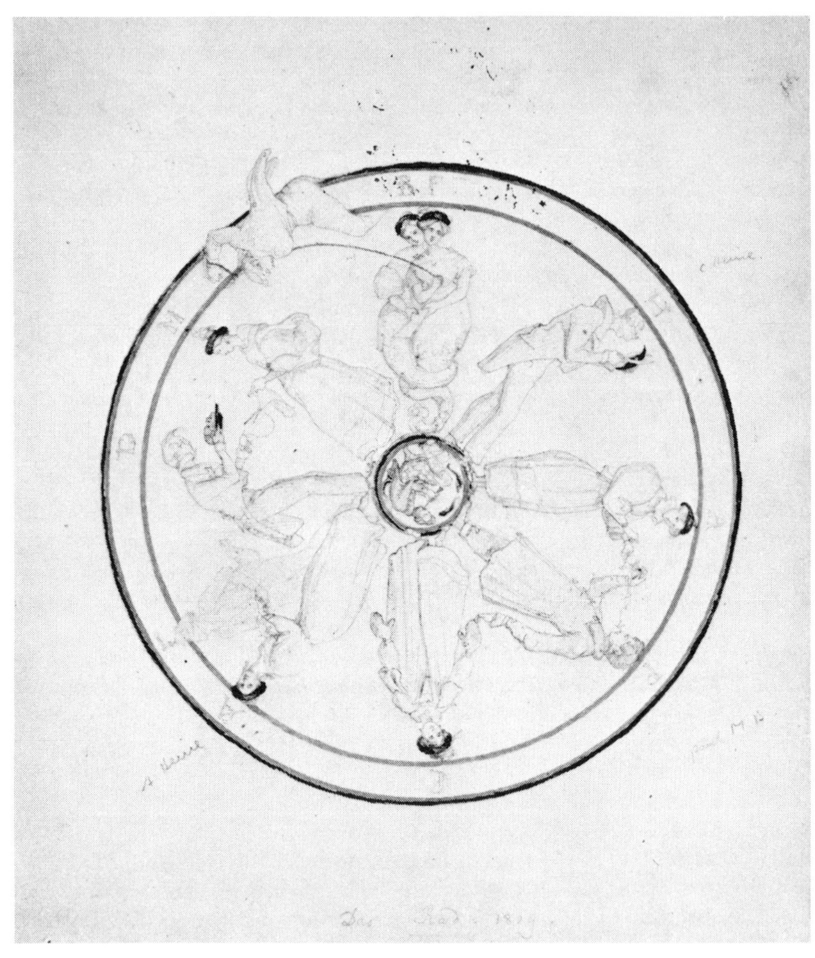

Illustration 5—Pencil drawing, *Das Rad,* by Wilhelm Hensel, 1829 [Staatliche Museen Preussischer Kulturbesitz, Nationalgalerie, Berlin (West)].

for the benefit concert for the Silesians: "Moscheles plays the last movement really brilliantly; the runs seem to shake loose from his sleeves. When he was through they all thought it was such a shame that we hadn't done a cadenza, and then I immediately dug out a passage from the last tutti of the first movement where the orchestra has a fermata, and Moscheles was forced to volunteer, *nolens volens,* to compose a big cadenza. Then we considered, among a thousand jokes, whether the last brief solo (*vide* Fanny) could remain, since people would have to applaud! 'We need a tutti section between the cadenza and the final solo,' I said. 'How long should they clap?' asked Moscheles?—'10 minutes, I DARE SAY,' I said. Moscheles bargained me down to 5. I promised to deliver a tutti, and thus we measured it, patched it, turned it over and lined it with wadding, inserted marmeluke sleeves, and formally tailored a brilliant concerto. Today is another rehearsal. It's a musical picnic, for Moscheles is bringing the cadenza, and I the tutti" (75).

[12] This last phrase is a literal translation of an untranslatable German pun.

27

Berlin, 15 August 1829

The wheel.

What is the wheel?[1] It is self-explanatory, also self-evident, and is a moral person. The accompanying scenario was written for you at a gay get-together in Charlottenburg, on Midsummer's Day,[2] and its dispatch was delayed because the following scenario, a pictorial representation, had been sketched on that day in free outline, with large strokes, and later worked on towards its completion.

Does it require an explanation? Don't you know the youth in the middle, the hub of the wheel, in English jacket and Scottish accessories?[3] Doesn't he look like a regiment oboist here? But the entire fine company revolves around him and dances to his piping. Fish cut him off from the continent, and a curious dolphin munches on the freshly-written music in his pocket. The person who treads on his head is unmistakably a member of the authorities in a blue coat;[4] she put it on that day even though it was very hot, and the enormous gloves protected her hands against mosquitoes. The C over her head containing the moon with the man in it will disclose what you don't know yet. The dainty figure next to her dances a galop with your shadow since you're not on hand.[5] The A represents a little fruit tree on which a little man climbs up a ladder. The F is a signpost with the inscription "Berlin."[6] The friendly man, who holds his neighbor's ball of yarn in one hand and presents a silver bowl (Klara Ponsin) with the other, carries your favorite dish—a "Mohrenkopf"—over to you.[7] Unity of time and place is, as you see, faithfully observed, because according to this plot the scene would have to be this Sunday evening in the Leipziger Strasse, but someone in the D retells a wheel story in which it is known that actually no Jew, but rather an Oberlehrer, fell into the water.[8] He stands with outstretched arms and is seen yelling, while a mermaid grabs for his feet. The ball of yarn leads us straight away to the knitted socks and their mistress. I think you won't mistake nose's sister.[9] Her M strides up and down like a respectable minuet. In a bold leap he surges into the wheel and at the same time treated himself unjustifiably as an impediment, for he is truly no impediment to this wheel, he does not need my applause nor be introduced, because what does that have to do with me?[10] In fact, I have the leash in my hands to which he is attached, but what does that mean? (I was also adored one time.) I won't waste any additional words over the two dumb, entwined fish-otters,[11] for it can't escape you that the B consists of two strangely grouped little goats, and the F looks through a telescope towards London. When it was drawn, it was true, and when you open it, it will be true again. The next nice man, when he was portrayed, had just cut silhouettes out of limewood paper, and looked quite eagerly at his work with his nose.[12] The paper face has become a silver moon, and otherwise it's been copied *tale quale*. His H displays two modern ballet dancers. I'm silent about the other; everyone, however, knows about it. Moreover, the letters above are not without meaning, because on that day the nice man wore black socks and shoes with long laces leading to white unspeakables, which looked especially good. The short person with the large mameluke who is approaching now buttons up her sleeve—you will probably still know why (but I don't know why two persons reach up their hands to a friendly *A* over her head) she holds a flower that grows towards the nose on Herr brother, who puts a dewdrop in the calyx.[13] I always claimed it was a silver coin.

The little boy above blows into his alphorn and calls out, "Hule, hule, little goose—come home."[14]

Of other things and more personal news nothing in this letter, which comes into your hands too late.[15]

[1]Drawing representing their closed social group; see Illustration 5. See also Lowenthal-Hensel, *W. Hensel*, 15-16, 68.
[2]See letter 23.
[3]Felix.
[4]Caroline Heine.
[5]Auguste Wilmsen.
[6]The F is over Felix's shadow's head.
[7]Droysen is holding the yarn of Minna Heydemann; Mohrenkopf = a small chocolate-covered cream cake. The identity of Klara Ponsin is unknown.
[8]The D is over Droysen's head, and the story relates to Droysen falling in the water during a gathering of the wheel at the Heines', as related by Fanny to Felix in a letter of 22 July 1829 (GB I 74).
[9]"Nase" = Fanny's nickname for Albert Heydemann; see, for example, letter 29. His sister is Minna Heydemann.
[10] Wilhelm Hensel.
[11]Rebecka and Fanny, intertwined because they are so close. Fish-otter was one of Felix's affectionate names for both Fanny and Rebecka.
[12]Albert Heydemann.
[13]Albertine Heine and Paul Mendelssohn Bartholdy facing each other. Mameluke was a very puffy sleeve fashionable then.
[14]Probably telling Felix to come home.
[15]Felix's reaction to the drawing as conveyed in a letter to Wilhelm Hensel of 10 September 1829 (DB 3, 2): "My goodness! What pleasure. And let me take the opportunity, o Hensel, to tell you that you're a great man. Your wheel drawing is truly heavenly and makes me feel warm and happy when I look at it. For that is what it does. It is so ingenious, and beautiful, and yet bears such a striking resemblance, and yet funny, and so forth. Droysen's portrait is the closest resemblance I've ever seen in my life; he obviously just said 'Perhaps.' And how you swing yourself in, and Caroline with the enormous gloves! But what is the meaning of the moon with the man in it?" (Mendelssohn, *Briefe-RE*, 92-93).

28

Berlin, 21 August 1829

I just wanted to sit down to write you a letter of another sort but can't start the day without the answer. Felix, brother, angel, what am I to tell you? Nothing has been considered or discussed, but Beckchen read me your letter and I'm happy to be able to tell you that Hensel and I made up our mind a long time ago, as you already know.[1] But I still don't know how—but it should happen, it must happen. Hensel has left the decision up to me. What's been holding me back is partly the worry over too long a stay, and partly Beckchen, whom I haven't been able to decide to leave at home. For I am her *vieux* Felix—it makes me happy to hear that. Regarding this concern I refer myself to you, and in regard to the other, I just don't know. Everything seems so bright and clear today, as though there were not a care in the world. Regarding your love for Beckchen as you wrote in her letter, I take my half of it, just as I have always given half to her, for we are the dear girls and you are the CLOWN. If you ever stopped sitting between us on the sofa—between us, do you hear? But that will not stop, I think, and so let's explore another subject.[2] Hensel and I have sketched out the following: when we're traveling together to Naples and Mother and Father are fearful about the sea journey, the four of us will board the ship again and travel to Sicily. And when we've seen the sights there we'll board the ship again and travel to Malta. And when it's hot there and very blue and oranges hang over our heads and we see the white coast of Africa in the middle of the day, you'll tell us about Staffa and the Hebrides.[3]—I think we've arranged our lives well, and if the dear God approves and lets everything work out, we can expect to see a few nice years. And now, after all that, the quiet reunion in Berlin, where we, I mean you and Hensel, will reach out far beyond the Leipziger Strasse; it will be tolerable.

[Rebecka]

The 25th of August. You yourself are familiar from past experience with certain chains of events—i.e. days and weeks when so many events coincide that one would like to think of only one thing at a time. The days in which your letter arrived were like that for me, as everything got muddled together. One aspect is now resolved and the other proceeds slowly. The determination of our wedding day is still the same, the last notice having been on the 20th, since Father is still in Hamburg, the entire apartment still has to be furnished, and, in addition to pots and pans, your favorite dish has to be prepared. Thus the exact date can't be settled upon yet.[4] But consider what I've asked you, dear Felix. I have a good idea of my organ recessional: G major, beginning in the pedals. Overall I'm happily convinced that my impending wedding hasn't hurt my compositional activities. If I've made even one good piece during my engagement, then I'm over the hurdle and can expect further progress. Don't you agree? I haven't composed anything better than the lieder I wrote for you, and the piece by and for Hensel isn't bad either.[5] But I'd rather not tell you anything about my plans for bigger and better things for fear of remaining stuck at square one. But what the heck, I want to tell you—listen closely. Johann Gustav Droysen told me once a while ago that he didn't think it a bad idea if lieder were constructed with a certain inner connection with each other, a thread, so to speak. He asked whether I would permit him to seek such a thread as the basis for lieder. I agreed. Then he returned after a while and asked me if the saga of the Lorelei would be all right. I assented, and then he brought me his plan. But it was too undramatic for a play and too dramatic for a saga: in short, neither fish nor fowl. At the same time, since I saw that it was becoming serious and lengthy, I expressed a strong desire to have my fiancé participate in the work. And so Hensel promised, at my request, to write a second part if Droysen could make his first more dramatic. In short, the affair grew and extended itself until I now have a large piece in three parts in front of me—actually a sketch of it—which we're constantly repairing and tailoring and hope to deliver to Droysen soon.[6]—We've passed on your instructions to him.[7] On Sunday we left the party, which was in the hall, and went towards the blue room with him, and imagined things quite vividly. He will write.—And now let me take a moment to rejoice over the present and the future. Hensel is dearer to me every day and, thank heavens, I believe he will be even happier. And when he returns from the Netherlands, our family will lead a very nice life.[8] You will bring lots of new things with you, discover lots of new things, and I promise that the time won't be long now. Listen: your *Hebrides* is all right and both violins don't stay on f-sharp too long.[9] I would be oddly cheered by it, as you are. We remain as always.

[Hensel]

[1]Felix's letter to Rebecka dated 10 August 1829, from Glasgow (DB 3, 30), and sent as a page insert in a letter to Fanny and Hensel of 11 August 1829 (DB 3, 1). The decision concerns the Hensels traveling to Italy shortly after their wedding. Felix discussed the trip in his letter to the Hensels. He would love to have them join him in Italy, and hopes that such a temporary stay there would fit in with their plans; Wilhelm should convey his opinion on the matter.

[2]A special intimacy is communicated in his letter to Rebecka (10 August). In the course of relaying his main plans for the near future, Felix makes it clear how fond he is of Rebecka and how much she means to him. In addition, only she is to know about his plans, but if she wants to tell Fanny and Hensel it's all right.

[3]Felix's response is his letter of 10 September 1829: "Fanny's ideas regarding Naples and Malta are lovely. I'll probably tell of the Hebrides, where the people are hard and raw. But are you really going to travel to Italy? And for a short time?" (Mendelssohn, *Briefe-RE*, 93).

[4]Their bans were read on 6 September and the wedding date of 3 October determined. In his 11 August letter Felix wrote: "Fanny writes a great deal about the wedding, but not *when* it is to take place. How can I settle on the chorale and the prelude, or even compose, if I don't know the time? Write me in detail about everything; I'm determined to take an interest in both of you." ("Fanny schreibt mir viel über die Hochzeit, aber nicht, *wann* sie sein soll; wie kann ich den Choral u. Prelud. bestimmen, oder gar componiren, wenn ich nicht die Zeit weiß? Schreibt mir alles genau, ich glaube fest, ich nehme einigen Antheil an Euch.")

[5]*Lieder von Fanny für Felix, 1829,* and *Nachtreigen.*

[6]Uncertain whether Fanny ever composed such a piece.

[7]See letter 24.

[8]Abraham, or possibly denoting Felix.

[9]Fanny is referring to the first four measures of the *Hebrides* Overture, in which the first and second violins are holding an f-sharp an octave apart. Felix's letter of 7 August 1829 contains the famous sketch of the opening of the work (Mendelssohn, *Briefe-RE*, 84-85). See also Todd, *Ossianic*.

29

n. d. [31 August (1829)]

[Rebecka]

The 31st of August You have a friend named Eda who plays the violin reasonably well. Yesterday was the last quartet gathering before David's departure. They played incredibly: the C major of Beethoven, the a minor of Felix, and the *Wanderer* Fugue.[1] Oh Jesus, oh Jesus, oh Jesus, how they did play! David is leaving on Thursday. He was emotional yesterday. Eduard is currently undergoing a phase of extraordinary playing, similar to his level of playing on the evening before you left. Friday we also had a quartet here (including David), which played a Haydn, the Rietz a minor, and the Beethoven f minor,[2] but it wasn't as beautiful as yesterday. I've just heard a great piece of news, but it will cause the wheel to dissolve into tears. You won't find Albert Heydemann here any longer, for he's going to Stettin on the first of October to serve his year as Oberlehrer at the Gymnasium there. How can a "Nase" be anywhere other than a Gym*nas*ium? He's very happy about it and looks forward to viewing Berlin at a distance for once; we're not as happy about it. But Louis also thinks he wants it very much, and so we should be happy for him. We're experiencing another period in which many things are ending and none are beginning. We must try to hold the remainder together. All things considered, when you return you'll find more things reduced than changed. David and Heydemann are going away, Gans comes less often, numerous unimportant people have also moved away, and no one new has arrived. On the other hand, many strangers have recently brought their momentary lives just like migrating birds, and you'll find their tracks in Hensel's sketching books.

I don't know if I've already written you that Hensel has started to paint Fräulein von Heister in court array and great splendor. Now he's dressed a marionette in her clothes and is painting her from it, but is annoyed that it sits so terribly still. He even thinks a sitting of

Gans would have been preferable. It's really horrible that Beckchen makes fun of me right down to my toothache. Do you find it funny that I've been suffering on both sides the last 2 weeks, had a tooth pulled out for nothing, and walk around with my head bound up? If you were here, I bet you would take my head between your two hands, shake it gently, and feel sorry for me. I told Rietz yesterday that I hoped you heard it in Holywell—I was referring to the high c in the E-major Quartet[3]—and later he played similar notes in your Quartet and the close of the *Wanderer* Fugue. Mr. Thomson said that you played the Quartet at Mr. Hogarth's. He wanted one of your manuscripts so I gave him the lied *Lass dich nur nichts nicht dauern.* It was the only dispensable one.[4]

[Rebecka, F. David]

The 2nd of September. The above-signator David now has an obvious depression regarding his departure and he's leaving reluctantly. I've had to promise him on every instrument and blessed thing to send him your Quartet in B. P. major, as Klingemann says.[5]—Marx shared the first sections of his Russian Festspiel with me and I gave him my opinion of it. He concurred with my criticism—namely, that many phrases don't end properly, and, thrown into the conversation, are too short—but put the blame on Droysen.[6] Furthermore, you're familiar with his music and thus know how much beauty it contains. September has begun without nice weather and I fear we must give up all hopes for this year. I assume that this letter will reach you back in London, and I'm glad to know you'll be on the Continent soon, since the storms are arriving early this fall, or rather, haven't abated at all. The rest will pass quickly, and before we turn around, December will be knocking at the door and with it a traveler who doesn't need to knock. Then we will sing, "O lovely wintertime." Father has been writing us very gay letters with all kinds of news, but without any word about his return or subsequent travel.[7] Do you know anything more about this? You seem to know things even before they are decided. Now not even anyone denies that Pauline Bendemann married Hübner. You've said for a long time that John Thomson and I have pelted music at each other. He left many published things and a handwritten rondo here, and in exchange I gave him a MANU-

SCRIPT OF MINE. If you ever have the chance to see it, you'll die laughing.

[J. Thomson]

The above-signator just came in when I was writing two hours ago and since he is rained in here and I don't foresee the end of his farewell visit, I'm grabbing the opportunity to continue this letter in his presence. Wednesday is always a very busy day, and when your letters actually arrive, the scene resembles a finale, for everybody pushes against everybody else and makes a fearful noise. Since Father has been away, we two have been sleeping with Mother in her room and always do very silly things. This morning Mother and Beckchen laughed very hard because I said as we were still in bed, "Today both Malon and a letter will arrive." Malon is here, and the donkey stands in the courtyard with a serenity worthy of emulation while it rains cats and dogs, but the letter isn't here yet. This isn't coming out very well because an English conversation is taking place nearby. Take good care. From now on I'm not to be held accountable. Hensel sends his greetings seven-hundred thousand times and asked me to send them along today in writing. Adieu, my soul, say hello to Klingemann many times for me. He already knows that he should be sending a nice response soon to our last letter. I don't know why I've written just about nothing over such a long stretch and can't find an ending. It's as though I were standing near you in the upstairs room, holding the door handle, disturbing you while you have too much to do, and then not leaving. By now you've probably received that certain funny drawing that I'm not naming in case you haven't.[8] I hope you'll enjoy it and I'm certain you'll recognize all the people in it. Adieu then for the thousandth time.

[Rebecka, Lea]

[1]Beethoven's Op. 59 No. 3, Felix's Op. 13. The *Wanderer* Fugue may be a string quartet Fugue from 1827 (in E-flat), or one of the 12 Fugues for String Quartet (1821).

[2]Uncertain identity of the Haydn; presumably by Eduard Rietz, and possibly an unpublished composition; Beethoven's Op. 95.

[3]Possibly another Quartet by Eduard Rietz.

[4]This lied is *Pilgerspruch* (Op. 8 No. 5); see letter 9. Fanny elaborated on Thomson in her Tagebuch entry of 31 August: "I must mention a young Scot, who arrived a week ago, by the name of John Thomson, who brought a letter from Felix, is musical, told us a lot about him, and whom I like best among all the Englishmen I know. Friday we took him to Zelter. In the evening there was a quartet here. . . . Hensel sketched him at home." ("Eines jungen Schotten muß ich erwähnen, der Donnerstag vor 8 T. eintraf, John Thomson heißt, Brief v. Felix brachte, musikal. ist, viel von ihm zu erzählen wußte, u. mir am besten v. den mir bekannten Britanniern gefällt. Freit. brachten wir ihn zu Zelter. Abends war bei uns 4tett. . . . Zu Haus zeichnete er Hensel.") In a letter to Hensel of 11 September 1829 (DB 3, 31), Felix responded to the family's delight in Thomson: "I found it very amusing that you all find J. Thomson so nice, and that Mother writes that she knows no Englishman as pleasant, lively, etc., because I never dreamed he would strike you that way. Furthermore, I am, by God, familiar with Englishmen who are much more pleasant, more lively, etc; but he probably conducted himself particularly well when he was with you." ("Daß Ihr J. Thomson so liebenswürdig findet, u. daß Mutter schreibt, sie kenne keine so angenehmen, lebhaften etc. Engländer, hat mich sehr amüsirt, weil ich mir es nicht im Traum hätte einfallen lassen; auch kenne ich, bei Gott, viel angenehmere, lebhaftere, etc. Engländer; er muß aber wohl bei Euch sich ganz besonders zusammengenommen.") John Thomson is undoubtedly the "J. T." who wrote about the Mendelssohns in *The Harmonicon*, 8 (1830), 7, 97-101. Fanny's musical talents are praised on p. 99.
[5]This is the Eb-major String Quartet, Op. 12, which was originally dedicated to Betty Pistor, although she thought this dedication was meant as a joke. See Felix's letter to David of 30 April 1830 (Wolff, *FMB*, 55), and 13 April 1830 (Mendelssohn, *Briefe-L*, 129); see Reich, *Rudorff*, 251-53, for a summary. A probable reference to the Betty Pistor connection appears in a letter from Fanny to Felix of 17 June 1829 (GB I 61): "What's the status of your Quartet to B. P.? Do you still feel the urge to have two new movements? She was here Sunday and I played that most assuredly absurd Scherzo for her. She laughed." ("Wie steht es denn mit Deinem Quartett an B. P.? Hält die alte Neigung noch für zwei neue Stücke? Sonntag war sie hier, u. da spielte ich ihr das gewiß absurde Scherzo vor; sie lachte.") In a letter of 22 September 1829 (NYPL) Felix announces that the Quartet "to B. P." is finished; see letter 31 for Fanny's reactions to the piece. The reference to Klingemann probably concerns a pun he made on the tonality of B-flat major in the second movement, from his letter to Fanny of 7 July 1829: "A new Quartet in B- P- major is found in the Adagio" (Klingemann, *Briefwechsel*, 57).
[6]Since Russian royalty attended the performance of Marx's Festspiel *Undinen's Gruß* on 11 June, it could be the piece in question. But Fouqué, not Droysen, is the librettist, so the determination is clouded.
[7]From Rotterdam.
[8]*The Wheel;* see letter 27.

30

Leipziger Strasse No. 3
21 September [1829]

[Rebecka]

Tuesday, the 22nd of September If your eldest girl is sitting with a bound head once again, it's because a third tooth had to be extracted. But don't think that this missing tooth, or this swollen cheek, has put me in an antisocial mood or been able to spoil our conferences about the anniversary-eve celebration. I have total mastery of myself and have accepted the situation (*patetico*). Having been removed from my post and subordinated to my younger sister, I've retired with dignity into the serenity of my private life and operate there unseen.[1] Felix, neither self-interest, greed, ambition, nor many other things influenced my decision to spend the anniversary-eve celebration in a certain family, but rather all the reasons that my superior cited on the previous page. Meanwhile, since we're convinced that you have such a good suggestion in your pocket, we're preparing to agree to your plans. Hensel wants to celebrate 3 weddings: the first, the silver, and the golden.[2] But haven't you reckoned on too much for the anniversary-eve celebration with three pieces?[3] And what do you intend to do with the one you've ordered from Droysen?[4] It doesn't appear in your plan. We don't know what we will do with all our treasures, because I find your plan for the first opera so charming that I would reluctantly cut numbers from them if I miraculously became Zerbino right now.[5] It's such a characteristic idea of yours that no one else in the world could have conceived it. But anyway, don't think that I will desist from an instrumental evening. What madness! We must, however, hear your new things! But we can do that later. Ponder everything, take the solemnity of the evening into account, calculate the rehearsal time, consider our needs, and send us your ULTIMATUM. Then we'll write further.[6] I'm not very happy that you won't be meeting Father.[7] Now you'll understand the many innuendoes in our last letters, for we were under the clear impression that you would return with him. Thus your letter to Father (he sent it to us) was almost painful—not only for you and Father but also for me. In this connection I want to impart a confidential piece of information that I actually can't swear is true, but which I firmly believe, namely, Father undertook the trip only in hopes of seeing you, as he couldn't bear the separation any longer. But the good thing is that now the trip is accomplishing part of its aim, which you should have effected: he is returning encouraged and in the best of spirits. Today we received a very funny letter from him, from Amsterdam. And now some more on our travel plans. The only factor that could deter us, the Hensels, would be finances. Since it's part of the very essence of your plan that our parents not know about it, we naturally are not mentioning our intentions, which thereby would seem even more unfounded. But now I'm worried—a feeling I can't shake—whether our parents will rightfully disapprove when we immediately go off and enjoy a costly pleasure that would, in the best case, consume an entire year's income, instead of economizing at the start of our marriage, living quietly, and fulfilling our obligations here. If we wanted to do it another way—as you know, Hensel was thinking of looking for a position there[8]—then a very long stay would result, which brings other serious considerations into the picture. In short, dear CLOWN, give me some sensible advice. You can imagine how miserable we'd be if we saw all of you embark thus and we had to protect the house. A circumstance that otherwise would be unpleasant but which could be advantageous to our present plans is that Hensel has been refused the use of the atelier in the Luisenstift because the palace is being furnished for Prince Albrecht. Begas and Ternite also have to move out. Hensel will apply for the 400 talers as compensation for a royal atelier. And now, dear Felix, you know all our domestic concerns. After a few months I'll be able to judge how much I will need and therefore what I can spare. If we decided (Hensel is certainly the more enthusiastic) to behave like vagabonds, spending everything and starting over later on, I fear our parents wouldn't be very pleased with such a plan, and without their consent (and this certainly has yours) we wouldn't do anything. But in case the trip actually came to fruition, Hensel would have to fulfill a historic commission from the King and another, which he is in the process of finalizing, for the Grand Duke of Weimar.[9] He would actually do these paintings in Italy from sketches he would take along. But you see how slowly such things progress here: he received the answer regarding the atelier only after several months, and a royal *Resçoipt* takes 4 days from Potsdam, almost as long as a letter from London. We therefore hope that you accelerate your return and then postpone your departure, so that we can be together, first just us, then with our parents, and lastly with the regime. Tell us your opinion, give us your advice, and send us another divisible private letter soon. It's always splendid when the letters are thus torn apart, but you must address yours to Hofmaler Hensel, Leipziger Strasse No. 3, because he's moving in on the 3rd of October. See, my young man, I've told you everything. I guess I get carried away when I see a sheet of white paper in front of me and feel good enough to converse with you for 24 hours, and when I need only to get up from my writing desk to look at your image. Another reason is that you love your dear girls so much. It certainly would be nice if one of your dear girls could go with you and the other stayed here.

[Hensel]

[1]In his letter of 10 September 1829 to Hensel, Felix wrote regarding a committee to oversee the festivities and stated that Rebecka is now the president, since Fanny is no longer impartial enough to hold that position. Hensel, Fanny, and Felix are members, Droysen an honorary member, and Klingemann a foreign member (Mendelssohn, *Briefe-RE*, 91-92).

[2]Hensel, the author of the text of Fanny's Festspiel, created three characters, each representing one of these three important anniversaries (Lea to Klingemann, 30 December 1829; Klingemann, *Briefwechsel*, 70).

[3]In his letter of 10 September, Felix suggested *Soldatenliebschaft,* his old work; a new Liederspiel by Fanny; and then "an idyll" by him, which turned into *Die Heimkehr aus der Fremde* with its comical characters (92).

[4]In his letter of 10 September, Felix requested that Droysen hand over the poem that Felix had asked him to write for the occasion (92).

[5]Presumably Prince Zerbino, the title character in Tieck's comic play of 1798, whose central theme is a journey in search of good taste. The eclectic style of the work is captured in Friedrich Schlegel's sonnet, "Zerbino," in *Athenaeum,* III (1800), 237.

[6]Felix wrote the Singspiel *Die Heimkehr aus der Fremde,* on a text by Klingemann. It was performed on 26 December 1829. After Felix returned to Berlin in early December, he encouraged Fanny to write an orchestral work, and she composed a Festspiel in eight days, based on a text by Hensel. The writing of the work is

narrated in a letter from Fanny to Klingemann of 30 December 1829 (Klingemann, *Briefwechsel*, 72).
[7]In Felix's letter from Llangollen (Wales), dated 25 August 1829 (Mendelssohn, *Briefe-RE*, 89).
[8]Wilhelm considered the establishment of a Prussian Academy in Rome, similar to the French Academy (S. Hensel, *Familie I*, 274).
[9]Karl Friedrich had recently become the Grand Duke of Weimar (1828). The exhibition catalog of 1830 of the Berlin Academy lists six oil paintings by Hensel, some of which are portraits. Two non-portraits are *Vittoria of Albano at the Fountains* and *Genzanerin [?] with the Tambourine,* one of which may have been commissioned by the Grand Duke of Weimar.

31

Berlin, 28 September 1829

My dearest Felix, I want to attempt to write you, although I can hardly concentrate. Despite all the efforts to take care of things in advance, things pile up towards the end, and I can't clearly distinguish what is wearing me down the most: the fatigue of last week, the upcoming events, or the severe toothache that I've had for a while but now, thank God, have lost. Father arrived Saturday evening in good health and was tremendously pleased with his trip. He already knew of your accident because of his conversation with Einbrodt in Rotterdam.[1] But our good Father said nothing to us about it since we hadn't received your letter yet. It arrived Sunday morning, and although we're not particularly fearful, we nevertheless await your letter on Wednesday with some impatience.[2] Because it will be your last letter before my wedding, I'm especially hopeful for good news.[3] For the good lap dog with the bandaged paw belongs yet in another way to the animal kingdom: he is first a lamb, second a rooster, etc. It seems that one doesn't come from London unharmed. Father himself asked Einbrodt first, on his honor, whether he should travel there, and then also sent Moritz Levy and Carl to him, and they had to repeat the same question on his word of honor. But his answer was the same; it's not necessary, and no trace of danger is present, thank God, and Klingemann emphatically echoes that assessment. It's very nice how he and the members of the embassy sit with you, and his loyalty is felt beyond the Channel. May God grant me good news by Wednesday, for how could I be in church next Saturday if it's otherwise? But Felix, I don't want to get myself excited, and prefer to give you a factual account, just as you like it. First, let me set the stage: Beckchen just started to read *Werther* and immediately stopped when Hensel arrived. She's embroidering now, Hensel is sketching, and Mother is reading the paper. Two lamps are on the table. It's 7 o'clock but I'm continuing to write because I didn't get to it during the day, and by chance we have a minute alone. Our furnishings are ready and very lovely: extremely tasteful, suitable, and nice. Father was completely satisfied with everything. My dowry is ready and I think my outfit will please you. This winter I'll look like a member of the authorities in a *blue* coat, just as certain other people wear them. On Wednesday there will be a small display of my dowry and the girls will stream in to see it. Thursday said dowry will be placed in my new closets, Friday Hensel will move his things in, and Saturday there will be a big commotion. On that day I estimate I'll have a quarter of an hour to myself in which I hope to write you a few lines. The crown ceremony begins around 1, Betty Pistor comes earlier, then, o *plaisir*! I had chosen Mine Stetzer as a bridesmaid, but she's getting married on the same day and thus can't come. Betty chirps like a sparrow as she complains about the dear family, and we've decided that when Beckchen gets married, Aunt Alberti will get married for the second time on the same day so that she won't have to attend. Another bridesmaid has made me very happy by stepping in; it is Hensel's sister Minna, whom we expect any day. I can't conceal from you that my crown adorns a new bride, dear Felix.[4] Two years ago I would've hesitated to share this news with you, especially with your little foot wound, out of fear of increasing your fever. But ever since the time when the entire Lake Sacrow, together with its house, garden, vineyards, heliotrope fragrance, vanilla tea, and people, was transformed into a quartet, you can probably hear with coolness that I—don't venture that—o Rietz!— Victoire—and—Rudolph (not Gustav) Decker—not

Magnus—Oh no, now it's out, and it's very likely that you're falling into a dead faint.[5]

[Lea]

The 29th of September It's 2 in the afternoon and I'm dead tired after an entire morning consisting of dress fittings. Felix, I'm not as frivolous as I sound, and I assure you that my thoughts extend beyond my *toilette*. If the sick lap dog were here now and the gig had been a hackney, two dear girls would have found time to sit at your bedside and tend to you until your friends came and drove them away. But unfortunately we can't do that. My organ piece is finished, and after I finished writing you yesterday I copied it for Grell. If I only had yours![6] Now I'll pick up the thread from yesterday. At 1 the crown ceremony will take place, and at 3:30 the marriage ceremony, for which the family will gather in the church. Later *we* will spend a few minutes at Aunt Meyer's, as she can't go to the church but still wants to wish us well. Then we go home, where we will spend the rest of the day quietly. I'm disturbed because I think I didn't announce the hour to you. But what I can't possibly describe are Mother's activeness, cheerfulness, absolute delight in everything, and her enormous kindness towards me. There is no end to her shopping, making arrangements, and furnishing, and I've never encountered such a completely prepared household. Father has made all the principal arrangements and we're very pleased with them, as you can imagine. In short, there's nothing else to say, for you know our parents, and that tells it all. I'll probably send you a lied that I'm thinking of composing before my wedding. It will be the last piece before my marriage, and I think the first afterwards will be a sonata.[7] Mühlenfels was just here, saying good-bye. He might come to dinner again, since he missed Father and Rebecka, but I don't think so. Rosen asked me to write you whether you could meet him somewhere between Brussels and Ostend between the 20th and 23rd. Adieu for today.

[Rebecka]

Just a few more words in a lucid moment—your letter just arrived and is nice, but the absence of an organ piece is not nice.

For who is supposed to accompany me out of the church? The old Bach or I myself? Where shall I find the time to write one? I would be very happy if you had at least chosen one for me. But it's nice that you want to come home in 2 months.[8] The story of the marmolade is also nice and I like everything except the gig, which is a devilish contraption. The *Hebrides* is very lovely and will give me a great deal of special pleasure. I look forward to the Quartet very much.[9] My thanks to Klingemann, whom I'll write at the first available opportunity after I'm married. Felix, my wedding dress is really lovely and we will all look like GENTLEMAN, but since I believe that for you the wedding will sit *here* (I'm holding my hand at my throat), and Father needs some room to write, I'll take my leave. Farewell, dear Felix. I'm glad that we can look forward to yet another letter from you. *The Afternoon*. We now have your other two letters, dear Felix, and if I let myself go I could be very distressed by the last one that I am to receive before my wedding, for it sounds as if you're disgruntled and ailing.[10] But I don't *want* to do that. Instead I am convincing myself as emphatically as possible that 2 weeks have already passed in which, with God's help, you will have recovered from the accident and blood-letting, and that I may hope that you will spend a free, happy, and healthy 3rd of October with Klingemann. I hope it with all my heart and have the courage to be optimistic. A thousand heartfelt greetings from Hensel, who has been painting strenuously the entire day so that he can complete the picture of Countess Arnim in the next few days. Also a thousand greetings from Mother. There isn't enough time for all of us to write to you, therefore I got up from the table. Mother asks you to take every possible precaution, listen to Dr. Kind, and do anything else that can help you. May heaven grant me a healthy, happy letter as the first thing in my wedded state. And with that, farewell. Everything will remain the same, including me.

[Rebecka, Abraham]

[1]Felix injured his knee in a fall from a carriage on 17 September, and first announced the accident in a letter of 18 September 1829 to his father in Amsterdam (Mendelssohn, *Briefe-RE*, 94).
[2]Felix wrote on 22 September 1829 (NYPL) that he is all right and well tended.
[3]Last letter before Fanny's wedding: 25 September 1829 (Mendelssohn, *Briefe-RE*, 95-97).

[4]Poetic way of stating that she is a virgin.
[5]Lake Sacrow is a lake west of Berlin, just north of Potsdam. The Magnus family had an estate at Sacrow. This imagery is undoubtedly a private joke involving their circle of friends.
[6]Felix never sent her the promised organ piece, although he seems to have been working on it. On 10 September 1829 (NYPL), he wrote that the organ piece for the wedding should be finished very soon. It was later incorporated into the Six Sonatas, Op. 65.
[7]The lied and the Sonata are unavailable or lost. They could be in a Sammelband in private possession (see Elvers, *Quellen*, 216-17).
[8]As he wrote on 22 September.
[9]"The Quartet is finished, and I think the ending isn't so bad!" (22 September). A few days later Felix wrote that he still has to add some finishing touches to the piece (25 September; 97).
[10] Felix wrote that he is very weak (25 September; 96).

32

n. d. [3 October 1829]

My dearest Felix! Today is the third of October and my wedding day. My first joy on this day is in finding a quiet fifteen minutes, which I've wanted for a long time, so that I can write you on this very day and tell you once more everything that you've already known for a long time. I am very composed, dear Felix, and your picture is next to me, but as I write your name again and almost see you in person before my very eyes, I cry, as you do deep inside, but I cry. Actually, I've always known that I could never experience anything that would remove you from my memory for even one-tenth of a moment. Nevertheless, I'm glad to have experienced it, and will be able to repeat the same thing to you tomorrow and in every moment of my life. And I don't believe I am doing Hensel an injustice through it. Your love has provided me with a great inner worth, and I will never stop holding myself in high esteem as long as you love me. There are only six more weeks and I think you will be pleased with the way you'll find things here, especially the very lovely layout, and only when you see it will I know whether it's suitable. Just as my room came alive yesterday when pictures were brought in (the sketch of your picture hangs over my desk), the pictures themselves will come alive when you come in and romp on the blue sofa in the arms of your dear girls and feel on top of the world.

You must visualize the scene: me at my desk, where everything looks colorful, and where ink and *eau de Cologne* exist in blissful harmony, and Beckchen at the window, preparing floral bouquets for the maidens in the crown ceremony. For you know that I am distributing flowers, that three of the bouquets contain myrtle, and that the holders of myrtle are the next brides. The weather is beautiful and all the little details have gone well so far. Yesterday I had a very nice day. I met Grell at the Parochial Church in the morning and heard him play my piece—I had been to the organ last when you had played—and enjoyed myself.[1] The piece sounded good and I had the greatest desire to play the organ but couldn't because of a lack of time. The rest of the day was occupied with miscellaneous errands and details. I had to tend to Hensel's sister's *toilette*, make visits, receive presents, move Hensel's things in, etc. At eight the family gathered for tea and a quiet pre-nuptial celebration. Louis Heydemann also attended and didn't spoil anything. Father had suggested the *Pastorelle* for the recessional, but I couldn't find it and Grell didn't know it.[2] Then, around 9 o'clock, Hensel suggested that I compose a piece, and I had the audacity to start to compose in the presence of all the guests. I finished at 12:30 and don't think it's bad.[3] I sent it to Grell this morning and hope that he'll agree to play it. The pre-nuptial celebration was very nice. It's in G major; I already knew the [key] because I had already devised one before you promised to send me one. But the style is conservative. It's starting to get very lively around here now. Soon it will be 11. At 1 my crown ceremony begins, after 3 the wedding ceremony. I think about you constantly, as calmly as before. Hensel, who was just here, sends you his best regards, and I'm at peace with everything because I know he loves you.

The usual Wednesday report coming via Hamburg speaks of all the love and warmth that we feel;[4] I think I won't forfeit my rights of collaboration with this sheet of paper. Adieu. I'm sending my most heartfelt greetings today to our Klingemann, who has earned new laurels through his caring for the sick. I don't doubt that you are lively and happy and cheerful today. Could I believe otherwise? Now farewell, and stay the same. You will find everything here the same, even the new things. For the last time

Fanny Mendelssohn Bartholdy

Beckchen greets you a thousand times. She has a cold and is suffering a great deal. My wreath just arived and is splendid; it's very thick, fresh, and green, and has many, many flowers. It was a present from Beckchen.

[1]An organ piece in F major, whose autograph is dated 28 September 1829 (LC). It is recorded on Northeastern 213 (1984).
[2]Presumably by Fanny. The only available *Pastorella* by Fanny dates from 1846 (Sirota, *Hensel*, 311).
[3]Possibly the Präludium in G major, in private possession (Elvers, *Quellen*, 216).
[4]The family's letters to England were routed via Hamburg.

33

Berlin, 8 October [1829]

[Rebecka]

Dear lamb, I'm writing as a guest at Mother's house,[1] my husband is sitting at the table and sketching, it's evening, and I'm happy and cheerful and feel very, very close to you. Oh, how I look forward to having you here—if only it were soon, very soon, my beloved Felix! Oh, if only I didn't have to visualize you as bed-ridden and ailing! We are living very pleasantly. Our mid-day meal after 5 would, or rather will, please you, and everyone likes our home. Louis Heydemann says hello. He visited us today and pulled his sister's handbag, full of potatoes to try out, from his pocket, because he had recommended his own potatoes so highly. He will be in Brandenburg for two weeks, at Steinbeck's, and when he returns he'll take his exams.—I had to stop yesterday because it was too noisy at the table, and I'm continuing in my own house. It's strange, but it seems that we've moved farther apart because you aren't familiar with my surroundings, and because I don't know with certainty if I should picture you caught up in London's whirlwind. And yet the time is drawing ever nearer, and it will be nice. Oh, my dearest Felix! I'm extremely happy that Rebecka and Minna are eating here today, for the first time.[2] Mother doesn't want to eat here yet and has flatly refused to do so, but will have tea here sometime—I'm hoping this week—and I look forward to that. This semester Gans is lecturing on Thursdays at 4. Father wants to attend his lectures and then eat with us. Perhaps you'll be able to attend his lectures too.

Nothing much else is happening. We're receiving a wealth of visitors, Hensel is painting, and I'm starting to work on something again, which I hadn't been able to do thus far. Yesterday I completed a funny piece of work. Tomorrow is Betty Beer's birthday and Hensel has made a drawing for her on a little box. He wanted me to make a musical mounting around it. I found the idea too pretty for the purpose, but he thought we didn't have to preserve pretty ideas for ourselves, so I wrote a piece that fills four lines around the picture. Perhaps I'll start on my Sonata again today.

I have an inexpressible longing for the *Calm Sea* and would love to play it again! Rietz hasn't visited me yet and I await him with great impatience,[3] for if he didn't come it would be a shame, and then I'd have to chuck music-making—not music itself—to some extent. I am blameless; I haven't missed an opportunity to be friendly to him, and Julius has also had a very friendly visit with me. He's becoming good; he's happy, mischievous, capable, and plays very well. Last Sunday we had a brilliant gathering, with the Mendelssohns, Betty Beer, Mme. Ridderstolpe— formerly a very beautiful woman—Englishmen, and many strangers. Felix, I must tell you that since my marriage, I've been receiving many compliments. I have a bonnet that brings me luck and I want to keep it until you return. It has a green ribbon and no wilted face. Yesterday Mme. Heine visited me with Caroline, an extraordinary kindness from the woman. And now farewell, my dearest. Remember me fondly. That's all for today.

[Lea, Abraham, S. Rösel]

[1]Fanny and Wilhelm set up house in the garden house, which was parallel to the main house across a court and gardens. See Cullen, *Baubiographie*, Illustration 4.
[2]Minna Hensel.
[3]Eduard Rietz.

34

n. d. [PM 3 November (1829)]

[Rebecka]

Dear young man, it is with particular pleasure that I take up this letter, in the strong hope that it's one of the last. Yesterday at the Academy I held a part of *Inclina* in my hand, but singing became difficult because I visualized your return. But all at once I made a decision, put the part aside, sat down, and proceeded to daydream undisturbed. Nobody has told you yet that there's a concert today for the benefit of the Silesians, in which your *Hora* will appear, and that, thanks to Grell's care, it will go well, and in a series of rehearsals has become a LION of the Academy (oh no, it's called a DEAR [ ]).[1] Grell sends his regards, as do Zelter, dear little Rungenhagen, and the entire Academy; people are incredibly curious about your little leg. Beckchen didn't tell you how we will suddenly break out in a dance, accompanied by obbligato pinching, and want to have the CLOWN there when it happens. I should tell you Hensel's Gans joke? When he wanted to put his name on the picture, he suddenly said that he wanted to write it in the hat, for that would be similar to how Gans had taken his—namely the Drücker—the day before, and only sent it back this morning. Hensel is painting a little picture for me, but I'm not permitted to see it until it's finished. Yesterday marked one month that we've been married; I have every reason to hope that we'll be this happy after one year. It's certainly nice how you've also seen Mühlenfels, who saw us. I'd really like to have been there to hear how he'd tell you, or not tell you, but rather bring out everything bit by bit. If you talk to him about us, I'm calm.[2] Send him and Rosen and Klingemann my warmest greetings. Rosen saw our house on the day of his departure, and almost fell when he made a big leap to avoid a new [carpet]. The man is [good] and one is good to him here. But you will be coming back soon, and that isn't bad either; I know people who look forward to it, among them Mlle. Anders. Oh yes, Felix—old love doesn't rust if it sits behind me in the alto section. To hear Fräulein Sydow speak of your *Hora,* you'd think she had something of an enthusiastic maenad in her. Oh well! Take good care. Beckchen, the little imp, wrote so much that out of necessity I must already begin to close, so that there will also be a little room for Mother and Father. My husband sends his best. He just started on Ludwig—what do you know!—and the picture is becoming nice.[3] You haven't responded to our breakfast invitation; don't stay too long, for otherwise the coffee will get cold and the [ ] cake old.[4] My man, we will have fun, and the little girl will also be here. Adieu, until we see you soon.

And I'm taking up another little line and only want to tell you how bittersweet every letter of yours is in which you say you're not going yet, you dear one! And how happy I am that the little lied has given you joy once again,[5] and how we love Klingemann, who traveled away for the first time, and how deeply we enjoy the entire dear German group.

[Abraham, Lea]

[1]The concert on 4 November 1829 included Carl Fasch's *Inclina* (first performed at the Singakademie in 1798) and Felix's *Hora est.* The *AMZ,* 16 Dec. 1829, col. 829, says of *Hora* that it is "a new 16-voice composition for four choruses . . . full of spirit and fire."

[2]Mühlenfels had been in England with Felix, as mentioned in Felix's letter of 3 July 1829 to Paul (NYPL). In a more recent letter, of 27 October 1829 (NYPL), Felix wrote that Mühlenfels, Klingemann, and Rosen had all spent time with him.

[3]Identity of Ludwig uncertain.

[4]Fanny had invited Felix in her letter of 9 October 1829 (GB I 101), although passing hints of the invitation appeared in the summer.

[5]Perhaps the lied mentioned in Felix's letter of 23 October 1829 (NYPL). Cramer came over and requested Felix's English lied in A major to present to someone as a Christmas gift, which would appear in print under the name "*Gem*, or *Album*, or *Apollo's Gift,* or *Nosegay*, or something else tender for the ladies." Presumably this is *Der Blumenkranz (The Garland)*, set to a poem of Thomas Moore.

35

n. d. [c. early November 1829][1]

My husband has given me the duty of going to the piano every morning immediately after breakfast, because interruption upon interruption occurs later on. He came over this morning and silently laid the paper on the piano, and five minutes later I called him over and sang it to him exactly as it appeared here on the paper fifteen minutes later. Teichmann thinks this letter will still arrive this month, so I'm sending it out, together with a little wedding brooch that Beckchen and Paul are always wearing.[2] I wish it and you a good trip. But if this letter arrives before the end of the month and still doesn't reach you, I'll be extremely delighted. Adieu. Take good care.

[1]Approximate date based on Fanny's statement at the end of the letter that she hopes this letter will reach him before the end of the month. Since Felix returned home in early December, Fanny probably hoped to reach him before he left London at the end of November.

[2]Fanny had mentioned the brooch earlier, in a letter to Felix of 4 October 1829 (GB I 99). He will receive a decorated gold brooch, presented to each of the siblings, when he arrives on the Continent.

36

Tuesday, 18 May 1830

When one has so many important things to do tomorrow, as I, one must write today, for otherwise one doesn't do it. First of all, Father came home from Leipzig at 8:30 yesterday—you'll hear about that later—because the horses must have been totally worn out.[1] But the short trip did him a great deal of good and we're happy to hear that yours has begun pleasantly. Last time you went immediately from the short introduction Hamburg into the great and full movement London. This time it's starting piano like a flute, continuing in Leipzig like a rasping oboe, passing through Weimar slowly, and then proceeding with a crescendo on the way to Munich. If only we were together now and speaking of those silly things instead of my writing them by myself, we would be in Mexico soon.—Fouqué has invited us to a musical event tomorrow at the concert hall in which two acts of his *Undine,* composed by Girschner, will be executed at the concert hall. Our WHOLE FAMILY is to attend the execution. Afterwards he'll help execute some soup and trimmings at our place along with Marx, who introduced Kapellmeister Guhr, and Kapellmeister Guhr, who was introduced by Marx.[2] Thus everyone is helped. Marx and Fouqué love each other, Guhr will say that he's seen a ghost, and actually a beautiful ghost, which Fouqué won't echo. We weren't able to invite Father, for he doesn't like 2 of the 3 guests. Beckchen and Paul have eaten out today, and I, as a soul of genuine Jewish descent, have projected a spiritual and operatic homeland between the poet and composer.

This letter is not proceeding well. The quill that you praise still hasn't learned anything from my mouth, but perhaps it will improve once you've written. But what weather you have! It's hardly permissible to experience such a May, but to travel in it at one's leisure is almost an arrogant stroke of fate. Good luck!

Beckchen will strangle me, but this letter validates its birthright by telling you that Devrient sang Orestes with success, but the following bizarre incident happened during the performance. When he fell into the arms of his Pylades with emotion, the latter fell down as a result of the added weight, and so Orestes became a rider. Fortunately the public didn't laugh and Therese wrote about it with good humor.[3]

I often [have] pleasant dreams in the daytime about your Symphony—please send a copy.[4] Today, the 19th, you are in Weimar, so please give Ulrike and Frau von Goethe my best wishes.[5] You'll have a very good time there. N.B.: Beckchen is standing next to me, waiting for the sheet of paper. She's wanted to write here but nothing is coming of it again. You see she hasn't changed very much yet, for she still wears only an openwork comb with a high gallery of pictures, and besides that she looks like the devil. It just rained and now it's clearing up again—the weather is

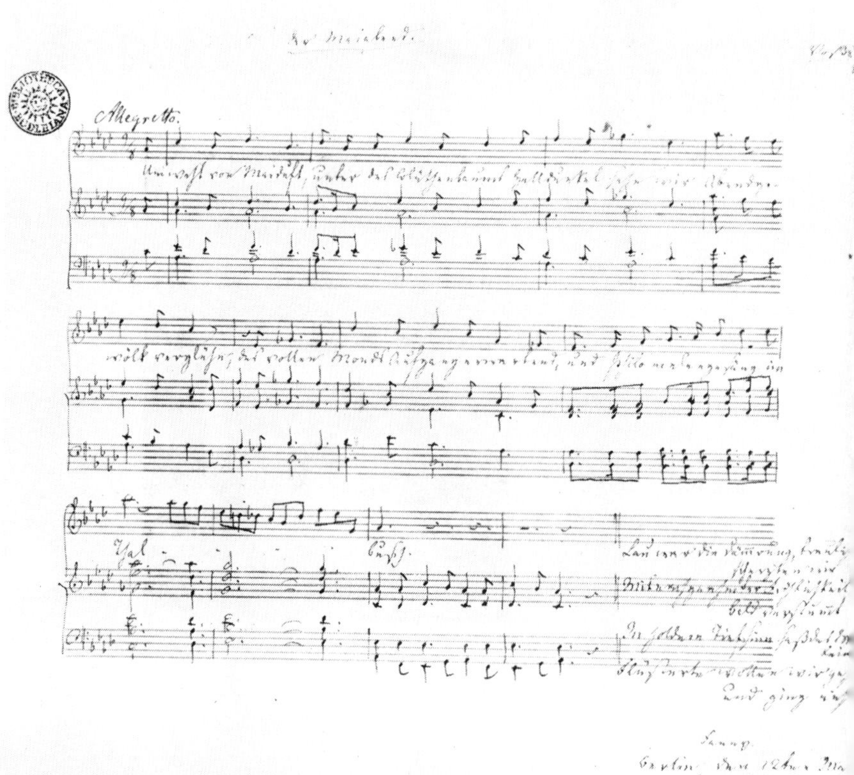

Illustration 6—Autograph fair copy of Fanny Hensel's lied, *Der Maiabend,* 12 May 1830 [Bodleian Library, Oxford: MS Margaret Deneke Mendelssohn d. 8, fol. 73].

the only perfect thing on earth this May. How horrible *Undine* is! Now I have to stop and get dressed and take care of many trivial tasks. Farewell, my dearest. Hensel sends his best. Perhaps we'll hear from you today?

[Paul]

[1]Fanny's Tagebuch entry of 13 May 1830: "Early this morning Felix left with Father, who will accompany him as far as Leipzig." ("Heut früh ist Felix mit Vater, der ihn bis Leipzig begleitet, abgereist.")
[2]Felix and Guhr became very good friends several years later. See Felix's letter to Fanny of 18 June 1839 (DB 7).
[3]Therese Devrient.
[4]Felix responds in a letter of 25 May 1830 from Weimar (Sutermeister, *Reise*, 20): "To you, dear Fanny, I'll send the copy of my Symphony soon; I'm having it copied here and will send it to Leipzig (where it might be performed) with the express order for it to be sent to you as soon as possible. By the way, I'll probably publish the parts and a 4-hand arrangement soon. But collect opinions on the title I should select: *Reformation* Symphony, *Confession* Symphony, *Symphony for a Church Holiday* (for the Pope), *Children's* Symphony, or whatever you wish. Write me about it, and a clever suggestion instead of all sorts of dumb ones. I also want to know the dumb ones, which will undoubtedly be devised for the occasion."
[5]Ulrike von Pogwisch.

37

n. d. [22 May (1830)]

[Rebecka]

The 22nd of May. Your lovely, first letter has just arrived and made us very happy.[1] You haven't unlearned how to write, and I think we should relearn the same during the time it's needed, but not for too long, as there is something much better.—The weather continues to be incredibly beautiful this year and every day I think how glad I am that it's accompanying your journey.

I will attend to your request to Klingemann the next post day.[2] By the way, I'm glad that the Leipzig music dealers are GENTEEL and that your Quartets are being issued.[3] I'm especially delighted with a Bach Cantata, *Es erhub sich ein Streit:* there the old man really liked to rage.[4] In one stroke 14 new cantatas, which our soul dared not dream of.[5] The old bear was prolific if nothing else. Can you imagine Sebastian Bach young? Incidentally, I've thought up a theme for this Cantata and will take it very hard if, as so often happens, it isn't suitable.—We, and not Rellstab, have acquired two youthful collections of music. I had one given to me and wrote in my household accounts book, *almost too pathetically*, "Lieder by Felix, 20 [gulden]." I shoved them down Schlesinger's throat.[6] We had a ROUT here yesterday: the Heydemanns, Droysen, Horn, Röstell, Ulrike, Lorn, and August Franck. The last is a very nice chap. He laughs "ha, ha," speaks just like Hermann—only more muted, which is no flaw—has a taste for all sorts of humor, and likes to listen to music attentively. The actual reason for yesterday's gathering was that Albert Heydemann wanted to hear the lieder that I wrote for you last year, which he still didn't know.[7] I wanted to incorporate that activity with drinking tea outside, but a gloomy sky and a cool wind prevented it. Then we sang a few of your lieder and afterwards Ulrike performed the beloved scene by Weber. She is in good voice, has actually cured her poor intonation, and looks very good. We're fond of each other. My lieder were sung next, and *In weite Ferne* last. That is a lied that must be sung only when you're away, for then it assumes additional meaning. But the best remains *Das Scheidende.*[8]—Horn only stayed a while as he had to go to the hospital because of a patient with typhus.—Hensel sketched a genre painting and is now occupied with the child and mother. He also made a charming drawing for my wedding organ pieces that he's presenting to his sister.[9] Except for a thick red nose, he's well and sends his best. The day before yesterday we went to see *Käthchen,* which he hadn't known before, and he enjoyed himself immensely.[10] As much as Lindner pleases me, I'm glad that you can't see her now, for she has aged considerably. She and Count Rebenstein were a very close couple.

Farewell. I think this letter will still be mailed today. Be well wherever you may be, which today is probably Weimar. Think of us when you're happy.

Your F.

[Rebecka]

[1]18 May 1830, from Leipzig (NYPL).
[2]Klingemann should ask the Taylors whether they agree with Felix's opinion to publish the three little pieces, and then Attwood should be asked how much Felix should request for them from the publishing firm of Cramer (18 May).
[3]Breitkopf & Härtel bought the a-minor String Quartet, which Marschner had heard and liked. Hofmeister bought his other Quartet (E-flat) and offered to publish all the piano pieces that Felix brought him (18 May). See Felix's letter to Hofmeister of 19 May 1830 in Mendelssohn, *Verleger*, 286.
[4]BWV 19.
[5]Felix mentioned some new Bach pieces that Breitkopf & Härtel had sent him, as well as an upcoming Leipzig auction of authentic Bach manuscripts (18 May).
[6]12 Lieder, Op. 9, published by Schlesinger (1830), of which three songs were composed by Fanny: *Sehnsucht* (No. 7), *Verlust* (No. 10), and *Die Nonne* (No. 12). Fanny's remarks may imply that they were forced upon Schlesinger, or merely be humorous.
[7]The song cycle *Lieder von Fanny für Felix, 1829,* which Fanny sent to Felix in England. See letter 20.
[8]Both from Op. 9: *Scheidend* (No. 6), *In weite Ferne* (No. 9).
[9]Presumably Minna, a member of the wedding party.
[10]*Käthchen von Heilbronn* by Kleist (1810).

38

30 May 1830

I know of no greater pleasure this Pentecost day than writing you a short note, since neither Hensel—who has a sitting—is here, nor Father—whose whereabouts I don't know, nor Paul—who busily runs about, nor Mother and Beckchen—who run away from me. In short, I'm alone. Each of your letters is a breath of fresh air that gives me immense pleasure. I'm glad about the score you've promised and the forthcoming publication of your Symphony, which, if it appeared with a name other than *Reformation* Symphony, would seem as strange to me as if you were suddenly called Petzold.[1] But when you publish the Symphony, will the *Midsummer Night's Dream* and the *Calm Sea* remain stuck in your pocket? My little arrangement here is very nice. The blue inkpot is on a small table next to my bed, a splendid sunny rose cutting is nearby, and the balcony doors are open and admitting glorious fresh air for the first time. I munch on strawberries every day, with which, according to Bertha, my very prudent husband spoils me.[2]

[Rebecka]

Farewell. I'm at my wits' end. I find it hard to believe that Beckchen finds Hensel's quills too hard, for I find them easy to write with. But the good child has complimented me and I find that very endearing. For the sake of DECORUM I lie in bed but would rather be up and around and whistling my own tune. Beckchen has slandered the weather; I just went for a walk and found that it couldn't be nicer. Farewell. My next letter will be to the point.

[Lea]

[1]See letter 36. The Symphony was published posthumously as Op. 107. Could Fanny's phraseology be an allusion to the section that begins "What's in a name?," from Act II scene 2 of *Romeo and Juliet*?
[2]Fanny is pregnant and in her lying-in period ("Wochen").

39

n. d. [PM 29 June (1830)]

[Rebecka]

My dearest brother, how often I think about you, your music, and a few individual pieces: the *Scotch* Symphony with its unforgettable opening,[1] the dear *Hebrides* Overture, and everything in the future and the past. My life is indescribably good.

The careless acts that I committed with my eyes consisted of reading through your lied twice and half your letter once.[2] I don't want to commit the third transgression so I'll close instead.

Your F.

[Rebecka]

[1]In Felix's letter from Edinburgh of 30 July 1829 (NYPL), he wrote that he found the start of his *Scotch* Symphony in the ruins of an old chapel, which contained the altar on which Queen Mary was murdered. See Todd, *Ossianic*.
[2]Felix sent Fanny a piano lied in his Munich letter of congratulations on the birth of Sebastian (26 June 1830; Schnapp, *Brief*, 85-91). The piece, in B-flat major, was later published as Op. 30 No. 2 (Book II of *Lieder ohne Worte*). Felix had sent Fanny another piano lied almost two weeks earlier, in a Munich letter of 14 June 1830 (facsimile in Sutermeister, *Reise*, between 24 and 25).

40

Berlin, 5 July [1830]

My dear Felix, recently I was so happy to write you a few lines by myself that I forgot everything that I actually wanted to write. Marx is to take this letter with him and before he leaves I'll be able to complete it in various spare moments. What I actually wanted to write recently was that I'm exceedingly happy how heaven has granted you such extraordinary honor and pleasant reception in each city, as in Munich, where you were instructed by respected teachers; such honors haven't yet been accorded you here.[1] I believe that in some upcoming city you will be called into a hospital to play patients back to health; I'll volunteer for it, but I'm not sick, praise God.

The 7th of July. You heard from us directly yesterday. I had an extremely happy day. We ate at Mother's at noon with Droysen, whose birthday fell on the same day as Hensel's, just as it did last year. Röstell was also there and we formed a merry group. After dinner the Heines, Heydemanns, and Mühlenfels came over. I remained in the hall until 9 and it did me a great deal of good, although the young ones were a bit rowdy and their noise reverberated in the hall. Sebastian, whose progress you must follow in great detail, was dressed for the first time today, but not with jacket and boots. Rather, he's grown into a regular child's outfit (vulgarly called "Stechkissen") from a little package that was bundled up and put into a tiny bed almost too pathetically. I've just received permission today to go walking in the garden because the weather is beautiful. Father is having a pleasant journey, you're having a pleasant stay. But remember that we who remain at home also need nice weather, and the bearer of this letter needs some sunshine as well so that he can carry out his duties successfully.

The 8th. Since this sentence was begun, a gentle rain has started, and it proves that one can't count on nice weather even this summer. When I stopped writing yesterday, I made use of the permission I had just received and took a walk to the front house, but Mother and Beckchen weren't there, and they, meanwhile, had gone towards the garden. I found only you, whom I also hadn't seen in a long time, and greeted with great enthusiasm.[2] Marx will see your nephew one more time today so that he can bring you the latest report. I want to say good-bye for today and convey a thousand greetings from Hensel. Marx will probably tell you all about Hensel's new painting. He's very taken with it, as are most people, including me. The canvas for Beckchen's painting is being ordered in the next few days.[3] Adieu, my dear man, be well and happy, and think of your loved ones.

Your F.

[1]In a letter to Fanny from Munich of 21 July 1830 (S. Hensel, *Familie I*, 295), Marx reports on Felix's reception: "Yet one can't help noticing how everywhere he goes he's the star attraction, how he's the focal point of every gathering." Marx also says how Felix continually receives invitations, and that people will attempt to accommodate his schedule so that he will accept.

[2]That is, Hensel's portrait of Felix.

[3]Felix looks forward to Hensel's upcoming portrait of Rebecka. He does not want anything unnaturally fancy, but a serene likeness (Felix to Fanny of 26 June 1830; S. Hensel, *Familie I*, 305).

41

n. d. [c. 9 July 1830][1]

A half hour ago Beckchen came over and said that letters to you would be mailed in a half hour. Since then, a half hour has passed, and as you see, I have no more time to write to you. In fact, I can't even include additional greetings from Hensel, as much as he asks me to do so. I ask you to send greetings to Marx in the same amount, although I'd really like to do so. I can't even tell you anything about Sebastian—neither that he drinks a lot, sleeps a little, nor looks around cheerfully with blue eyes. If I had the time I'd also complain that I'm not yet permitted to play the piano and fear that if the 19 days remaining in the 6 weeks don't pass soon, I won't be able to hear the Liederspiel again, for Mantius is leaving.[2] But you won't have the chance to hear more about that and many other cute things because, as I said before, I'm out of time. Auguste has been standing at the door for a half hour waiting for the letter,[3] and I am, was, and will remain yours as long as we live.

[1]See note 2.
[2]Sebastian was born on 16 June 1830, which places this letter c. 9 July. The Liederspiel is *Die Heimkehr aus der Fremde,* Op. 89, performed at the silver anniversary celebration in December 1829. Mantius was one of the performers. Fanny's retrospective Tagebuch entry of 6 August 1831 reports a very lovely performance of the Liederspiel on 31 July the year before.
[3]Perhaps a servant, although it could be either of her friends Auguste Wilmsen or Auguste von Le Fort.

42

n. d. [c. end of July 1830][1]

Since I've discovered in all honesty that I've missed out on my bad joke through dishonest means, I'll take heart and not make one any more.

Do you still remember how we used to call you Grelix? I just spoke with Beckchen about the wretched spot in which you used to sit between us on the sofa, but now I hope that you're romping in Marx's arms. By the way, I'm rained in at the front house and am using Gans' paper case at Beckchen's secretary. My husband and child are calling for me, but the former isn't here and the latter is undoubtedly calling out, but not for me. In the last three days the little imp was put in the sun and now he has red cheeks. Today he is confined indoors again, but I'm bathing him myself and thereby feel very maternal.

My dear Felix, I'll tell you about many things soon in a personal letter, but not anything new, for as Klingemann and I like to say, everything is the same, or rather I'm just the same. Meanwhile, I've returned to my usual routine and eat fresh potatoes and spend my evenings outdoors—in short, I'm thoroughly enjoying life. In addition, my little one is growing every day. I haven't composed anything yet; I had plenty of ideas when I wasn't permitted to compose, but now I'll probably undergo the familiar dearth of inspiration, which I pick up from the weather.[2]—It's a shame that Father didn't embark on his journey a few days earlier, for then he would have heard the news in Paris about the seizure of Algiers. It must have been a great sensation.—Incidentally, the desertions from the African armies can't be more numerous than those in Berlin now—there's not a soul to be found here. And at this moment I'm deserting the desk so that I can eat the eggs that Beckchen arranged to be cooked for me.—And now, on to a pretty tale: it's raining cats and dogs and I think perhaps I won't be able to return home the entire day. Hensel just arrived, made a big scene, and—alas—I received a scolding. Adieu, dear lamb. Ehrhardt is to take this letter and is champing at the bit; just stop and imagine Ehrhardt champing at the bit—isn't that a pretty picture? I'll take my leave until our possible reunion. Ehrhardt has one foot out the door and I want to scrawl in my little space completely. If you don't send me the organ piece in A major as soon as possible I'll be annoyed.[3] I think about it occasionally and would like to run through it before the baptism, as I will put on my wedding dress that day. We'll tell you more about the baptism. Should Zelter, perhaps, be your stand-in?

Sebastian just wanted to greet you himself, but the poor little tyke can't write his name yet. He spit up on himself and thus it didn't work. Who will baptize him? Wilmsen. Who will hold him? Beckchen. When? Around the middle of August. Who is to stand in for you? I've suggested Zelter; do you object?

But I can't give you any adequate estimate yet as to what we'll eat, since we haven't determined the time of day.[4] But you are to find out about every morsel.

I'm happy about your reunion with Marx. You will have a great deal to say to each other and that can be very nice. Send him our best. We received Father's second letter from Paris today, so on the basis of that I think he'll be back soon. I'd like that.

Farewell, my dear lamb. Before you turn around we will be there, lifesize.[5] I love you very much and therefore I'd like to be able to bring Beckchen along.

Hensel sends his best, and I remain

F.

Only please write soon and let me know that you don't think our trip is foolish and that you're glad to see us come; this is still necessary to make me truly happy.

[1]Since Fanny mentions in this letter that she is back to a regular routine, the date must be at least six weeks after Sebastian's birth (16 June); see letter 41.
[2]For comments by Felix about Fanny as a composer around this time, see Felix's praise when he compares Fanny very favorably to Delphine von Schauroth in a letter to Fanny of 11 June 1830 (NYPL), and also Felix's explanation to Fanny that she is now a mother and so should not be depressed about not being able to spend as much time on her compositions (16 November 1830; Sutermeister, *Reise*, 67-68).
[3]Probably the first movement of the third of the Six Sonatas, Op. 65, which was originally intended for Fanny's wedding.

[4]Felix asked these questions on 16 July 1830 (NYPL). In a congratulatory letter to Fanny after hearing of Sebastian's birth (23 June 1830; DB 3, 3), Felix said he wanted a "rascal" ("Rüpel") whom he likes, to stand in for him.
[5]On 23 July 1830 (GB II 61), Fanny wrote to Felix that "hopefully we'll be on our way to see you in a little over 2 months." (" . . . heut über 2 Monate sind wir hoffentlich auf dem Wege zu Dir.") Her Tagebuch entry of 4 March 1831 discusses the outcome of their plan: "Meanwhile, we were entertaining the idea, still under discussion, of spending the winter in Italy. A tangle of difficulties, only one of which was the frightful aversion of our parents, forced us to abandon the idea." ("Wir hatten indessen noch immer den Plan, nach welchem wir handelten, den Winter in Italien zuzubringen, eine Complication von Umständen, von denen die entsetzliche Abneigung der Eltern nur Einer war, nöthigten uns, den Plan aufzugeben.")

43

Berlin, 22 April 1833

[Abraham]

You will be very upset about this unfortunate turn of events, dear Felix, but certainly not more than we, who had such great expectations for Father on this trip. However, given the real possibility that he would have to stay there longer than he wanted, Father prefers not to go to London at all, and one can't blame him for that. We found out about your happy arrival in Düsseldorf from yesterday's *Staatszeitung*.[1] Our paper adds that you were very pleasantly surprised by the preparations for the festival.[2] I hope Paul will be able to confirm this statement. Sebastian says that he's not happy when you're not in your room. Recently he held me around and said, "Now I have my dear mother in my arms." He's learned something that's just like you, namely, "Heute hat es keine Noth." He added the second verse thus after much deliberation, "weisses Brodt, schwarzes Brodt," but that was already less like you. My sister-in-law arrived Thursday and I'm extremely fond of her.[3] It's really a shame that you haven't had the chance to know her better. The figure on your picture is already changed, but I can tell you that Hensel never had such a difficult decision in his entire life. But once he's started, it's much easier for him. Herr Girschner was at my house yesterday and returned some things you had lent him, and wanted some others. Should I give them to him? Farewell. May you repose in Klingemann's arms now and let yourself be sheathed in roses by Rosen.

Yours

[Rebecka, Lea, Abraham]

[1]Felix arrived in London on 25 April 1833, via Düsseldorf; he traveled to England to conduct the premiere of the *Italian* Symphony.
[2]Felix will conduct the Lower Rhenish Music Festival in Düsseldorf, 26 to 28 May 1833.
[3]Luise Hensel.

44

n. d. [c. 8 May 1833][1]

Only a greeting, for the weather is too beautiful to write inside, and the shadows still too deep to write outside. I also have nothing more to tell you than good luck in your Academic honor;[2] it's no fun that you came through with Rungenhagen.[3] Tomorrow *Orpheus* will make its debut in front of 60 people[4]—well, that day too will pass, says Herr von Rothschild.[5] I'll report to you later in detail. Despite all the rehearsals, the scene in Elysium hasn't been perfected. Thanks for the Englishman;[6] he just completed his tour of the garden hall.

[Rebecka, Lea, Abraham]

[1]The third section, by Lea, is dated 8 May [1833].
[2]Possibly wishing him good luck on his premiere of the *Italian* Symphony, which takes place on 13 May at the London Philharmonic, or on his upcoming direction of the Lower Rhenish Music Festival in Düsseldorf later in May.

[3]Reference to Felix and Rungenhagen having been the final two candidates for the directorship of the Singakademie, which chose Rungenhagen over Felix on 22 January 1833. See E. Werner, *Mendelssohn*, 227-33.
[4]By Gluck.
[5]Unclear which one of the Rothschilds, as none settled in Berlin; presumably the Frankfurt banker, Amschel Mayer Rothschild.
[6]Identity unknown.

45

Thursday, 16 May [1833]

[Rebecka]

Although modesty actually inhibits me, I'll nevertheless do as Sebastian does and say, "Oh tell us," and tell you that we tooted our horn successfully and that everybody, including Aunt Hiny and Uncle Joseph,[1] had a very good time; that Hähnel charmed all the evil spirits; that the weather was so nice that we could leave the garden doors open the entire evening; and that Gans has been asking everybody, "Were you at the Hensels? I wasn't invited. I'm angry." But he is angry in dead earnest, and I'm just waiting to run into him so that I can demonstrate to him why he hadn't been invited and will never be invited to our musical gatherings, and why I, on the contrary, am angry at him. Then he will say, "Give me your hand," and the matter will be settled. My congratulations on Father's trip![2] Would you send a copy of the new *Israel* back with him? Where did you come across this find?[3] My dear Felix, you possess great powers of judgment but good luck in no less measure: another stroke of fortune. Farewell. Duty calls in the form of a hairdresser.

[Lea]

[1]Henrietta Mendelssohn and her husband Joseph, at Fanny's performance of Gluck's *Orpheus* (see letter 44).
[2]Abraham attended the Lower Rhenish Music Festival in Düsseldorf, which began

on 26 May. See extracts of a series of letters from Abraham to Lea (22 May to 2 June 1833) in S. Hensel, *Familie I*, 315-29. Then Abraham accompanied Felix to London; see Abraham's letters to the family (early June to 9 August 1833) in S. Hensel, *Familie I*, 329-45.

[3]*Israel in Egypt,* with Handel's original instrumentation, was one of the works performed at the Festival. Felix wrote that he found Handel's original score to *Israel in Egypt,* and it contains all the arias, recitatives, etc. that were missing from their scores. He will perform almost the entire work in Düsseldorf and announce this new find in his opening remarks at the Festival. The piece was published after Handel's death with substantial omissions. One of the novelties is the fourteen consecutive choruses—"they should be surprised" (7 May 1833, NYPL). Fanny writes in her Tagebuch on 26 May 1833: "He had the skill and good fortune to find the original score of *Israel in Egypt,* which will probably be a sensation in Düsseldorf." ("Er hat das Glück u. das Geschick gehabt, die Originalpartitur von Israel in Egypten zu finden, womit er wohl Aufsehn in Düsseldorf machen wird.")

46

Berlin, 22 October 1833

I haven't written you in a long time, dear Felix, but I haven't forgotten, so I'm sitting down on the spur of the moment at 3:30 and still have a long morning, for today our winter season starts, with our meal at 5. But you're now going to soirées. We're still having your lovely fall weather, with the warm sun and hardly any leaves on the ground yet. I took a long walk with Sebastian and we ran into Paul on Unter den Linden. He gave me his arm and we didn't go far before we met up with Beckchen and Dirichlet. (This time Hensel brought me nothing but blotting paper.) I wish you could have been here last night. I had a spat with Beckchen which you would have loved—Mother and Father practically laughed themselves sick. It started over our husbands' waistlines and moved so far afield that I was reproaching her for her pregnant cook, but then we couldn't keep it up because we were laughing so hard. We're very merry and well. Father is feeling very good; he is actually eating a great deal of wheat (he is also drinking large quantities of it) and that is keeping his health stable. By the way, he's very charming and, in defiance of you, is making conquests of women. *À propos*, Immermann is here, but I haven't seen him because he's visiting Mother, not us.—Has somebody already written you that I recently accompanied Decker in *Oberon* on the dreadful dulcimer at her house? It was as bad as it could be under the circumstances, since Devrient, Mantius, and Hoffmann also sang with her. But I've finally convinced her to get a new instrument. We tried one out yesterday and it will be delivered today. Tomorrow *Semele* will be performed there and I will accompany. Taubert, who was her Kapellmeister last winter, hadn't even forced her to acquire a new instrument the entire time.[1] But it will be really horrible again; Sophie Ebers' singing extends below that level. Do you know *Semele* very well? There are some wonderful numbers in it, and with the proper cuts it would be highly appropriate for a concert. Do you know the score?[2] Schaum admits to many changes; I'd like to know, for example, whether the very loose text has more coherence in the original. Your Concerto is indeed splendid. But I favor Gluck and Beethoven, and even find those very lengthy before *Alexander's Feast.*[3] You Düsseldorfers must have good stomachs. I know whom I'd rather see in attendance at these concerts than all of you. Dear Felix, I'm now giving musical instruction to 4 young girls who play very well. But I yell at them as though inspired. Can you picture your sister as a witch? Sebastian is darling and has grown a great deal. The wagon you gave him is still the joy and envy of the young court personnel; no plaything has lasted so long. He remembers you quite well and mentions you every day. When we were at the Heyses' recently, I let him go to the table alone and he passed the test with flying colors. When you see him again, you will be astonished. His speaking is truly melodic, and everyone is struck by it. He gets his eyebrows from his Frau Mama Cantor, but [has] very blonde hair.—We had a fire in the house recently. We've been spending our evenings quietly at our parents' house, above which General Braun has been living for a while with his several booted sons, rumbling about. But that evening the noise suddenly became deafening, with great running in every which way and very loud talking. Then a noise sounded as if it were raining in that room, accompanied by a veritable rain of chalk dust and crashing at our door. We all jumped up and discovered that the hall above us was burning. The men ran upstairs, and we couldn't, because the old general was putting out a fire in the drapes with his shirt; he had ignited them earlier with a lamp. He withstood the smoke and vapor for over an hour and burned his hands. But there was a horrible smell of fire through the house as a result. Nevertheless, we were able to dismiss the disaster which, fortunately, didn't spread to the street, for otherwise our house would have been overrun by the rabble. Dear Felix, there you have a letter with practically nothing in it. Yours, however, was very nice, and the story of the mayor and the wine really amused us.[4] Farewell. It's getting dark, approaching dinner time, and I'm very hungry. We will have to introduce a more orderly system of correspondence—so far it's been helter-skelter.

Wilhelm and Luise send their best.

[1]"It's a commonplace that you're a better Kapellmeister than Taubert" (Felix to Rebecka, 26 October 1833, NYPL).
[2]"I'm familiar with *Semele* and wouldn't perform it. I find the choruses very weak as compared to other Handel choruses. This winter I'm thinking of presenting *Acis and Galatea, Du Hirte Israel,* and perhaps *Gottes Zeit,* not to mention the modern ones" (26 October).
[3]In Felix's letter to Abraham of 9 October (NYPL), he presents ideas for his first concert in his new position in Düsseldorf, on 22 November, and says: "What do you think, Fanny? Or make another suggestion so that your name day is celebrated in a fitting manner." Fanny's middle name is Caecilia, and 22 November is St. Caecilia's Day. The program for Felix's first concert is Handel's *Alexander's Feast,* Beethoven's *Egmont* Overture, and Beethoven's Concerto in c minor. Felix's Concerto is probably the g minor, Op. 25.
[4]As related in Felix's letter of 9 October.

47

Berlin, 2 November 1833

Dear Felix, your splendid letter is once again strong evidence that something good is worth waiting for. It made us tremendously happy. I have to answer it by heart since Mother has it upstairs, and therefore begin with the translation you requested.[1] The following should correspond fairly well with the original:

"Der Liebe Heil
Doch Kunst errang den Preis,"
or: "gewann den Kranz,"
or: "gewann den Preis,"
or: "errang den Sieg," etc. I rather prefer the first, because "Kunst" together with "Kranz" is harsh, and "Preis" is better to sing than "Sieg." Judge for yourself. Meanwhile, we had your poet Immermann here for a while and found him much friendlier than his reputation in that regard. But I don't believe he can ever make a good opera for you, as he is very tight-lipped and far too reflective. But he speaks very well. First he was at Mother's one evening at which, as we discovered, the giants of German education were gathered: Steffens, Gans, Rosen, Mühlenfels, Heyse, Devrient, and Immermann. The last served as the piper around whom everybody danced. You know how unhappy Gans is in such circumstances. He was very friendly towards Hensel and requested to be permitted to make a visit, and since there was no other convenient time, he came to our Sunday musicale. During the first piece he looked at the atelier and expressed his satisfaction, but during the rest of the music he conversed with Devrient and Steffens. Then he ate with us at our parents' *en famille*, since we really wanted to hear him talk again. And then he spoke profusely and gladly and very well. Sebastian was also at the table, and when the conversation turned to last year's *Musenalmanach*, and Rebecka, at Immermann's instigation, uttered Heine's epigram that ends "und ein Gedicht ausgespuckt," Sebastian lashed out, "Now listen, Mother! One doesn't spew out a poem, one recites a poem." Immermann was very

pleased by that and generally took a great interest in Sebastian.—Alas, we don't write on long sheets of paper any longer, where everyone reads the other's part, and that will have the unavoidable result that you will enjoy the same thing 20 times with slightly varied interpretations; I can't bear that. Your festival must have been wonderful—I wish I could have been there. And now truly *à propos*, thank you for your music that you sent me.[2] Although I haven't become well acquainted with it yet, I like it very much. Devrient recently sang the aria very beautifully; I'm having it copied and then I'll have it sung.—Tonight we are invited out to some people's home, where Herr Felix, if he were there, would flirt not just a little. A 15-year-old daughter who is gorgeous, yet still so childish as to play with dolls, and who sings very well—in short, a little angel, whose name is Rose. Speaking of attractive women, we were with a woman yesterday who is so beautiful that I couldn't take my eyes off her—such is Frau Blandine Wangen. Both nasty men understood art well enough to marry interesting women.[3] Dear Felix, I'm thinking of having a little party here on the 22nd of November to celebrate the start of your concerts. But so far everything is still up in the air, and I'll let you know as soon as the affair is more definite. Dear Felix, what should I play next Sunday? Last time I presented the Trio by Moscheles and I fear that Rey's Trio, a possibility, won't suffice for the winter.[4] You ought to have a firescreen, my dearest—by Christmas, if possible.[5] And now farewell, I have to leave. Say hello to Frau Bendemann and Frau Hübner. I'm very glad that Decker has stopped insulting your face.[6] Alexander was just here and sends his best [ ].[7] Sebastian had a formal dinner yesterday. You should have been there, for it was one of the funniest things I've ever seen. I'd covered a little table with small plates, knives, forks, and napkins. The little Heyse children ate here, then they became merry, and Paul Heyse, who really ate like a *pig*, started to sing the melody of the *Mantellied* with the words, "Ich habe so viel gefressen."[8] Then Sebastian exclaimed "Cheers!" as they clinked glasses on high and conducted a regular drinking bout.

Sebastian sends his best, as do Wilhelm and Luise. Farewell now for the second time.

[Abraham]

[1]In his letter of 26 October 1833 to Rebecka (NYPL; Mendelssohn, *Briefe II*, 10), Felix requested a translation of the following verses, which close Part I of *Alexander's Feast:* "So love was crown'd, but music won the cause." Felix cited Ramler's translation: "Heil Liebe Dir, der Tonkunst Ehr' und Dank," which Felix thinks does not make sense and is nothing more than a mere translation.
[2]Possibly Felix's Vespers, Op. 121, composed in 1833.
[3]Is one of these men Wilhelm Hensel?
[4]*NGD XV*, 782, lists a published collection of Trios by Rey for two violins and cello (no date).
[5]"Ho, ho, Beckchen—here comes the punchline.—Make me a firescreen" (26 October).
[6]Felix wrote of Decker: "This nice, dear person had Schmidt tell me that I might cut off my whiskers. To please her I did it 3 weeks ago" (26 October).
[7]Alexander Mendelssohn.
[8]A popular tune of the day. Felix notates a varied version of the *Mantellied* in his letter of 6 October 1834 (NYPL).

48

Berlin, [23 November 1833]

[Rebecka for Sebastian, Rebecka]

I wanted to tag along somewhere and was refused by Mother. First let me thank you for your lovely birthday letter with its many delights.[1] I'm looking forward to your *Melusine* Overture so please send it when you have a chance. Thanks also for the lovely landscape, but I haven't received it yet.[2] The wagon hasn't driven up yet.[3] But now I want to tell you how we celebrated St. Caecilia's Day and the start of your concerts yesterday.[4] We had a beautiful celebration, so—but I have to take a new sheet of paper now.

I composed a verset from the Mass of St. Caecilia in two days in such haste that the accompaniment hasn't been copied yet.[5] Mother will probably send you the text. The whole thing was arranged as a double surprise: first Decker appeared without singing, then she sang a few notes unseen, and last sang in full view, from memory of course. It is said to have made a magical, beautiful effect. This much is clear—her beauty so far exceeded her usual appearance that I could only place one person next to her, little Rose Behrend as an angel, who really, without exaggeration, looked heavenly. I've never seen such an angel's head on a person. I'm only sorry that Hensel has no need to paint an angel at present; whoever painted her now would create the most beautiful angel imaginable. It's too bad that you won't see her this year, for who knows whether she will be this beautiful next year—one really does have to be fifteen years old. In general, I would have wished that you, with your well-known lamblike sensibility, could have seen this little package of beauty. Decker's costume was modeled on Raphael's *Caecilia* and her hair was arranged accordingly, which was very becoming. The angels wore white. Little Rose Behrend wore a headdress made up of some of her long golden blonde hair, which hung down to her knees in abundance. She has the finest, most regular features, and deep brown eyes. Wings, diamonds on her forehead and shoulders, and flattering illumination didn't spoil anything either—in short, I wish you could have been there for you certainly would have fallen in love and composed some beautiful quartet, which would have been to our benefit.

Little Clara Jacques, a lovely 8-year-old with black locks, also made a pretty good angel. Little Therese Thürrschmidt, although by far not as beautiful as the other two, did very well in her role. It was a charming touch to have the two taller girls hold some music in their hands in the manner of the angels in the old paintings. By the way, the entire exhibition occurred without the help of a single craftsman—Wilhelm and his students did it all. They concocted the loveliest organ in the atelier. Now I want to tell you that there is one section in the piece that I consider good.[6] So farewell for now. I still have *des arrangements* to make and want to go out to congratulate Steffens on her birthday. *Dunque*, addio. Do you know that Hensel finished priming the large painting by my birthday?[7] Now he's working on a few other small works and then he will continue with it full speed.

[1]Felix to Fanny of 14 November 1833 (NYPL).

[2]Felix wrote that he just finished the *Melusine* Overture and would like it to be her birthday present today, but it will have to wait. He has prepared a landscape for her with the assistance of Schirmer (14 November).

[3]"Der Waagen" could mean a wagon, or a male person with that name; thus "der Waagen" could be a pun.

[4]22 November, the date of Felix's first concert in Düsseldorf.
[5]*Zum Fest der heiligen Cäcilia;* the autograph is dated 1833, and is in private possession (Elvers, *Quellen*, 216-17).
[6]Presumably Fanny's *Cäcilienfest;* see note 5.
[7]Presumably *Christ before Pilate.*

49

Berlin, 1 December 1833

A great deal of time has passed and we still haven't heard anything about your concert, about which we're very curious.[1] Your friend, the newspaper, dispenses with such reports and thus we don't know anything. Schrödter from Düsseldorf, who has probably seen you recently, was here yesterday but unfortunately we missed him. (Oh my, the renowned English ink has anemia also.)

We're having a little domestic upheaval now after a smooth period during the past several months. Luise is quite sick and is in bed today and I have the feeling that it will be a prolonged illness. May God forbid that. Actually I started writing you today to pour out my heart over the Zelter correspondence, which makes me seethe constantly with inner rage. Because Father can't read in the evening now, it's read aloud to him over there and of course meted out by the spoonful, like medicine, and as a result one derives more dubious enjoyment from this book than is proper. Father is also indignant, and thus we have a unique situation in which we all agree with each other and haven't even argued over one single passage. On Zelter's side, an unpleasantly awkward way of thinking predominates that we could presume him to have possessed, but which we always rationalized away. But here it's irrefutably expressed in the trappings of self-interest, egotism, a disgusting idolizing of Goethe without a true, reasoned appraisal, and the most indiscreet exposing of everyone else, which is permissible in such a personal correspondence, but which should be absolutely prevented from being published. All this and many more make this book despicable. One of the numerous instances of Zelter's unbelievable lack of knowledge is found when Zelter asks Goethe what Byzantium is and then receives his answer. And for that one corresponds with Goethe! The shallowness of the entire collection far surpasses all expectations. Theater gossip and trivia are the sole contents and it's also as clear as day that Goethe is usually unable to respond with something clever. Oh phooey! Here one still has the pleasure of hearing everyone talked about who feels insulted, with justification—people who find themselves censured, without their permission. There are people who are literally described there as though they were on a wanted poster. And now enough of this messy subject—for me this book has totally and forever spoiled the memory of a man whom I loved and would have liked to respect.[2]

Sebastian is really darling and always remembers his Uncle Felix fondly. You are assuming a meaningful place in his childish games and you are always the one who rides here as the postilion in his games. He often says without any special reason, "When is my dear Uncle Felix coming back?" He certainly thinks you're coming for Christmas. He just mentioned you again. Since I have no one to take care of him, I walk with him every day as well as take him on errands and visits. He can go almost anywhere. He is thinner but happier and livelier than ever, and his talking elicits astonishment from me even though I hear it daily. But his affinity for the ladies, dear Felix, is still the same. Hähnel will eat with us today, but Sebastian can't wait until she comes, and has already asked for her 20 times. Decker was just here, and *Don Juan* is scheduled for her place on Wednesday. I truly regret that my score was stolen and I'll try to replace it. Then, dear Felix, I'll show off and astound everyone by playing *The Magic Flute* from score and the *Opferfest* from manuscript.[3] I'm innocent, however, of the latter *renommège*, for it coincided with my Caecilia festival and thus I didn't have time to check the score in advance. In general I'm making a great deal of music this winter and am extremely happy with it. My Sunday musicales are still brilliant, except for the last one, which had a brilliant lack of cohesiveness. Farewell for today.

[1]In his letter of 28 November 1833 (NYPL), Felix wrote that in the concert of 22 November the *Egmont* Overture "went very well," the accompaniment to the Beethoven Concerto he performed never went better, and *Alexander's Feast,* except for the soprano solos, was also very good. Overall the concert was a great success.
[2]Felix wrote that Düsseldorf is "very short of books," and thus he would like the book sent to him when they are finished with it (28 November). In his letter of 11

December 1833 (NYPL), Felix states that he does not possess a copy of the correspondence yet; not only has Fanny written him about it, but people in Düsseldorf have read it and solicited his opinion. But in his letter to his father of 28 December (NYPL; Mendelssohn, *Briefe II*, 13), Felix airs his views: "Anyway, to return to the much-discussed correspondence of Goethe and Zelter, one thing strikes me. If one speaks ill of Beethoven or the like, in an unseemly way about my family, and in a tedious way about many things, it leaves me very cool and collected. But when the talk is of Reichardt and they both judge him so highly, then I can't contain myself from becoming angry, although I can't even explain it to myself." In February Felix writes to his mother: "I find Zelter's correspondence, whose 3rd volume Immermann just lent me, sad, and many passages truly insulting. Nevertheless I agree with Father that Riemer is the real culprit in the matter, and when I see him again I certainly will not refrain from giving him my CUTDEAD for it" (1 February [1834], NYPL). And a few days later to Devrient: "I truly dislike Zelter's and Goethe's correspondence. It's as though a gross misunderstanding runs through the whole thing. For me, the situation with books is like the situation with people—I support them and have reservations, or am at cross purposes with them. And for me this book belongs to the latter category, for I'm generally in a bad mood after I've read it a while" (5 February 1834, in Devrient, *Erinnerungen*, 172). Two years later, in a letter to Lea and Rebecka of 14 June 1836 (NYPL), Felix mentions how Riemer had so little tact and delicacy in comparison with Eckermann, *Gespräche*. For a summary of the impact of the Goethe/Zelter correspondence on the Mendelssohns, see E. Werner, *Mendelssohn*, 281-83. Fanny's views are echoed in the review by Miltiz in the *AMZ*, 9 July 1834, cols. 457-58, especially when he points out that one's reverence for Goethe can only diminish because of the correspondence, and he is appalled that Zelter asked Goethe, among other things, what Byzantium is.

[3]*Das unterbrochene Opferfest,* opera by Peter Winter (Vienna, 1796).

50

Berlin, 25 January 1834

I had intended to write you a long, detailed letter for your birthday, one that I would start a month in advance, but God knows how it is; you cannot imagine how the time has flown, and I've had so many loose ends to attend to that I can't do any one thing really completely. In addition, since you left, what's happened almost constantly is that I've been sending out my letter about an hour before yours arrives, and that is, with all due respect, absurd. But now I have one in front of me and have to tell you that I'm amused how certain small incidents, coincidental and otherwise, recur between us, even across the miles. When your letter in which you mention your rehearsals of *Don Juan* was passed around to me, I was sitting at the piano with the score of *Don Juan* before me, for it was to be sung at Decker's the other evening.[1] You write that you improvised on the cellos from *Fidelio* recently,[2] and there lay the piece in the *Fidelio* score directly in front of me, for tomorrow we're having a merry Sunday musicale and are singing a few of the principal pieces from the opera.

Recently I've been rehearsing and performing a great deal of music. If only once I could have as many rehearsals as I wanted! I really believe I have talent for working out pieces and making the interpretation clear to people. But oh, the dilettantes! If I were Jean Paul, I'd include an extra sheet on them alone—I'm certainly not lacking for material.[3] But with Decker it's glorious to make music—that's a real talent! She was here yesterday and casually mentioned that she had a tender affection towards you and I requested permission to tell you so for your birthday. You will receive a belated birthday gift of a firescreen from your *soeurs grises*, which will be something to see. You can invite Zick and Preger to scrutinize it. But Hensel and I especially request that you adopt the violinist who peers out from the box. I hope you don't have it yet; I have a great passion for that drawing and sent it to Father for Christmas, but we wanted you to partake of it also. I hope you will write us in advance where you will be spending it (namely your birthday) so that we can seek you there. *À propos*, why haven't you sent a sketch of your room, with the location of your sofa (No. 1), piano (No. 2), etc.? Please send a similar portrait of the dining table in your inn as well.

The 26th. My *Fidelio* has just ended, and given the circumstances, it was well received. The public, which has begun to increase again, as at that time, was delighted. Decker sang wonderfully and all the dilettantes reasonably well. To answer your question as to who sings tenor here, it's Herr von Dachröden, who is trying very hard and has a nice voice to sing with, and a nice face to draw from in the atelier. Jaquino was sung by a little student of 4 inches, named Jörg, who has a very nice voice and sounds like a parody of Mantius. Also Antonie Nölinchen, Busolt, and Riese. The poor clumsy man, who is an unbelievable musical fool, made only half the mistakes I expected him to make on account of his hard work. He even sang much of it quite well.—Do you know Frau Wangen? She is one of the most beautiful women in Berlin, just as Rose Behrend is the most beautiful girl, and today had her hair arranged in peculiar braids to please her husband. But when the music was over Rebecka and I took over and expressed our opinion that it should be somewhat different. So she had to sit down, I took a comb and dustcoat, and we fixed her hair. Then you really would have liked that hair: jet black, and long and silky as a coat. I can't get my fill of that woman.

The 28th. Yesterday Möser went all out for Mozart's birthday.[4] (You see how musical we are.) Old Fuchs liked it and so did the public. The Symphony in C major went very well and was exhilarating—what a splendid, lively, and youthful piece! The vocal pieces were not all well chosen, and Taubert played a not very beautiful Concerto not very beautifully. His playing sounds quite amateurish and immature and he doesn't know how to convey the beauty of a melody. Herr Robert Müller, dilettante from Scotland, stood at the door.—So you want a book about Sebastian and a book about Walter? Beckchen will write a book about Walter, which will begin, "a tooth, a tooth is out." I could write a very lengthy account of Sebastian for the little boy is darling. Yesterday he had eaten at Beckchen's and come down again when we were still at the table eating duck and turnips. After various unsuccessful attempts to eat another time, he started flattering us most tenderly and said, "Dearest Mother, do me a great favor and give me a little bone that has *nothing at all* on it, and then I will imagine that there is something on it." And then when he saw that we couldn't contain ourselves from laughing, he went on more boldly, "And then give me a turnip. Isn't that just like an added bayleaf?" This morning he said, "I love you the most of all; I don't love any stranger as much as you." When Hensel woke up he said that his eyes were still glued together with sleep, whereupon the little wiseguy started right in, "In Basedow is a hunter who puts glue into a container. The apes go there and glue their eyes shut." It's really too cute to hear him retell something that he's heard perhaps once, and to realize from the way he retells it that he clearly and correctly understood it.

Here he is himself.

[Fanny for Sebastian]

Yesterday he said to his father, "But Father, you always have the same colors, and yet paint such different pictures: Aunt Beckchen, and the Moor and the Jew. How can that really be?" (his expression). Recently he had spilled a glass of water in my petticoats, and later said, when I gave him the proper scolding for it, "But Mother, you love me. That was only clumsy, that wasn't naughty."

The fact that we're not totally behind more southern countries can be shown by our blooming crocus, green-leafed woodbine and finger-length, fast-growing hyacinthe, as well as the usual flooding in the garden, which you probably know about already. I personally am delighted with this very un-wintery weather, but I haven't been able to feel comfortable in my room yet with only one heating. Your firescreen will probably arrive as *moutarde après diner,* and you will have to salt it away over the summer. Meanwhile there will be more winter, and you will also not spurn it as an object merely languishing in your room. In England, have you read about the new railroad project that could take a person [ ][5] to Düsseldorf in 4 hours? O hypercivilization, when will you reach us? Hensel naturally procrastinated until today, and naturally has a sitting today. So permit me to be his substitute and tell you all. I must be content and not start the other page, and since Beckchen is standing here and watching me write, I can't continue anyway.

Adieu.

[1]Felix's rehearsals, mentioned in his letter to Abraham of 11 December 1833 (NYPL), culminated in the well-known scandal of the *Don Giovanni* performance, as described in another letter to his father (28 December 1833, NYPL).

[2]The number "Mir ist so wunderbar," from *Fidelio,* was performed with the cellos and was part of a long improvisation, in Barmen, using different pieces in succession that Felix concocted, based on a submitted poem. The start of the improvisation was very good, but the finale was a failure (16 January 1834, NYPL).

[3]In 1825, Fanny wrote a detailed essay on the sad state of dilettante music in Berlin (bound with her Tagebuch 1829-1834), in which she proposed the establishment of an instrumental society for dilettantes, to be made up entirely of men. If things

went well, then they could offer subscription concerts and join forces occasionally with the Singakademie, for example, in larger pieces. Eduard Rietz's Philharmonic Society, similar in function to Fanny's proposed group, and the basis of the later Berlin Philharmonic Orchestra, was founded in 1826 and provided the instrumental accompaniment in Felix's historic performance of the *St. Matthew* Passion (March 1829).

[4]The program consisted of the duet from *Titus,* the Symphony in C major, a trio from *Idomeneo,* the Quintet in g minor, an aria from *Idomeneo,* a Piano Concerto (performed by Taubert), and an aria and the finale from *Così* (see the *AMZ,* 5 March 1834, col. 157).

[5]The brackets encompass a few words in parentheses that clarify the grammar in German but are nonsensical in the English translation.

51

Berlin, 18 February 1834[1]

Many thanks for your *Schöne Melusine,* which is now beginning to be "schön" to me after its previous rough beauty.[2] Your scores are generally difficult (I recently triumphed when I read the entr'acte to *Egmont* very fluently), and I have to pay for some of my enjoyment by the effort expended to decipher the many puzzling passages. But, as I said before, I'm beginning to see the light, and very lovely light, but I don't know how I will manage to perform that piece for the enjoyment of others. I don't think you'll like the way Moscheles reworked your *Gypsy* Variations: it's not skilfully done, there's very little in it that I ascribe to you, and the added sections, such as the introduction, are dull.[3] The arrangement should have tried to bring out some of the immediacy of its character. I say *cependant*, you say phooey, and the matter is settled. *Der Hofer* pleases me very much and can't fail to make a splendid impression wherever it's performed.[4] Both *Lieder ohne Worte* are also very pretty. I will probably leave one of them, "intended for the young ladies who, etc.," unplayed. Young man, why do you always write such excruciatingly awkward music? Compared to you, one would consider Beethoven's music downright idiomatic for the fingers.[5] *À propos,* when I first received *Melusine,* I immediately took out the slip of paper that was inserted, and read: "The location of this marker designates my favorite passage." I don't dare decide—is it at G major? You must think us asses with your rebuses, for we've solved only half of them, and had great arguments about the texts of the last two: "saufen ungeheuer" and "Bettler ging am Segestade."[6] We've appealed to you and a half-dozen bets are riding on it. What's QUITE touching is that we were involved with similar artwork three days before your rebuses arrived and had decided to send you a whole batch. Now that would be a duplication. You still owe us an account of the ball on your birthday, *Egmont,* and your second concert, which Kortum told us took place. Don't be so taciturn. Write us in general about the families you know there and those to whom you've brought about misfortune; write me a personal letter sometime about *les amours de Jacques* in Düsseldorf—I won't repeat it to anybody—and when we conclude a contract for the publication of our letters, we'll decree that the names be omitted.

[S.]I.V.P.[7]

[Hensel, Fanny for Sebastian]

I'm supposed to remind you about the title of your Symphony for Schlesinger.[8] Hardly anybody can remember any event that has aroused such interest as Schleiermacher's death.[9] You will read the description of his funeral in the papers, which this time is not exaggerated, for there really must have been between 30,000 and 40,000 people on foot, and one hears of nothing else. In Schleiermacher you also lost a friend. On Thursday the Academy will perform the b-minor Mass, which will probably be dreadful; the second part, for instance, supposedly has not been rehearsed. Try to be well now. I'm getting hungry and must have breakfast. Let us know when you're coming to Berlin this year. You mentioned May recently, but would you prefer to take your vacation in the fall and be able to stay for a while and attend the exhibition? In any event, I hope that you will give our city first billing when you travel. I really doubt that we'll be able to take a trip this year. I hope that Hensel will be finished, but I can't conceal the fact from myself that he's playing for high stakes. The matter has already been set up for weeks, and the slightest serious obstacle tends to provoke an angry outburst from him. May God grant us good fortune. Don't respond to this. By the way, the picture will be superb.[10] You cannot believe how imposing all the painted sections look, and I believe that it, like everything genuine, cannot fail to have a great impact. Farewell.

[1]Crum, *Catalogue I*, 17, lists "15 Feb. 1834." The manuscript is not clear; it could be "18" or "15." The postmark is 18 Feb. I believe the reading is closer to "18" than "15."

[2]Felix intended it as a Christmas present for Fanny: "For Fanny is the *Melusine* Overture with all its scratching-out and ink blots. But she will prefer the old, familiar music paper to trombonist Schauheil's most tender Fraktur and stationery" (PM 20 Dec. [1833], NYPL). But it is not sent to Fanny until 1 Feb.: "the *Melusine* score is all the more speckled, and I'm curious whether Fanny will find her way through it successfully. It's splendid that she's now playing so much and so beautifully. . . ." (1 February [1834], NYPL).

[3]Moscheles's and Felix's joint authorship of Variations on a March from Weber's *La preciosa,* published as Moscheles's Op. 87b, for two pianos (originally with orchestra). In his letter of 1 February, Felix asks to be informed when the piece is issued. See Moscheles, *Letters,* 63-64, 88-89, 94, 97. In his letter of 7 March 1834 (NYPL), Felix responds that Fanny's and Rebecka's comments about the piece annoyed him.

[4]Presumably referring to some Felix piece, perhaps the *Gypsy* Variations. But there was a popular piece by Berger, *Andreas Hofer,* which was a lied for 4-part chorus (Op. 20 No. 5; published 1825). Felix may have set this same text, which was similar to that of a folksong.

[5]One of them is probably in b minor, dated [30] January 1834, and the other perhaps in D major, dated 12 December 1833 (Op. 30 No. 4 and No. 5; Bartlitz, *Works*, 153). The D major is marked *Andante grazioso,* but the left hand has fast etude-like thirty-second notes, and is marked *Il Basso sempre piano e leggierissimo.* Fanny probably found this writing awkward. To the piece that Fanny is leaving unplayed, it is likely that Felix appended a description that it is intended for the ladies.

[6]The four rebuses, consisting of individually-drawn objects, are found in Felix's letter of 1 February. Felix asserts that they are not easy and he is giving them a "little test" with these four. The solutions are given in his letter of 19 February 1834 (NYPL): No. 4 is "Junger Lisbeth ging am Seegestad," and No. 3 is "Einige Leute." The Hensels solved the other ones correctly, but Felix is having trouble with some of the rebuses the family sent him.

[7]The string of letters probably stands for "S'Il Vous Plaît"—"please" in French.

[8]It is the c-minor Symphony (composed 1824). Felix writes on 7 March: "Symphony for orchestra, composed by F. M. B. and dedicated to the Philharmonic Society of London, 10th (or 11th) work. *No higher number*!" Fanny did some of the corrections for the publisher; see the correspondence between Felix and Schlesinger in Mendelssohn, *Verleger*, 281-82.

[9]Felix's reactions to Schleiermacher's death appear in his letter of 19 February. He was not especially affected by the death at first, but later could not stop thinking about it.
[10]Hensel is working on the painting *Christ before Pilate*. It eventually became an altar-piece in Berlin's Garnisonkirche, but the Church burned down in 1908. The woman and son in the lower right were modeled on Fanny and Sebastian, and the work became one of Hensel's most famous paintings. See Alexander, *Letters*, opposite 32, for a copy of the sketch.

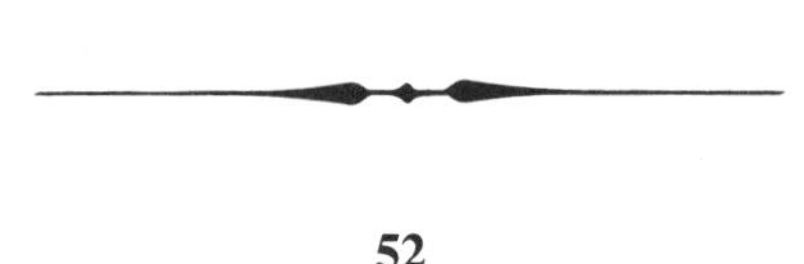

52

n. d. [c. 27 February 1834]

I've mastered your *Schöne Melusine* rather well now and am enjoying it thoroughly. The piece splashes around quite splendidly and you've given the waves a graceful variety. By the way, I'm not at all familiar with the story. What sort of a sea lion rumbles along so wickedly in f minor and afterwards is always calmed down by the friendly play of the waves? Like Sir George, I would like some written information about the Overture, or advice as to which fairy tale I should read.[1] (I wanted to write you a first-class letter and therefore took a pretty sheet of paper and a newly-cut quill. But unfortunately the quill is bad and is destroying my airy mood with pollen, as Bärmann would say.[2] Another of life's deceptions!) But you have no idea how the sun is shining in here. I just opened the window. But to return to your fish, it's really quite a different situation from when we used to sit together at home and you would show me a totally new musical idea without telling me its purpose. Then, on the second day, you would have another idea, and on the third day you would undergo the torment of working them out, and I would comfort you when you thought you couldn't write anything more. And in the end the piece would be completed and I used to feel that I had a share in the work as well. But those lovely times are of course a thing of the past. Thus, after several months, I receive a sheet of paper in which I rejoice first over your handwriting and the date of your birthday, but then comes the tedious process of working through the new score before I can derive any enjoyment from it, instead of experiencing pure joy immediately upon first acquaintance with the work. But now I'm also experiencing this with *Melusine*. I'm so far along that I'm discovering many things in the musical details that I like very much. I'm postponing mention of a few things I don't like because I don't feel like meting out criticism today.

The 28th of February. Meanwhile, your letter has arrived, in addition to one from Madame Moscheles, which reported on the favorable reception of your Overture in London. When will I get to hear it? Believe it or not, I haven't even heard your *Reformation* Symphony once. You're certainly planning to have the *Walpurgisnacht* performed in Düsseldorf; have you decided when? When you have a chance, please send me the score for a few weeks; that would please me very much. Return dispatches are always carried out from here by the well-known, good porter. Loewe is here again, and one of his short operas, based on a libretto by Raupach, was performed.[3] Devrient and I think all appearances point to him becoming the next Kapellmeister here. His habit of persistent rudeness bothered me at first but now amuses me. I'm certain that he knows me, for we will meet, stand next to each other, speak with the same person, but he won't acknowledge my presence. He was even more impolite with regard to Marx. A student told him about his club at the University, and Loewe said, "Who is Marx?" Marx is publishing two pieces for men's chorus that contain some very nice music.[4] I've given him my opinion many times on weaknesses and pitfalls, and he's revised almost everything in line with my suggestions.

I was just told that I could have the letter sent with the wax candles but would run the risk of the letter being burnt as well.[5] I fear that the great London festival will be a draw—not that London's appeal for you needs any strengthening. Or will you be loyal and come here? A few quiet months together once again would probably be needed. Devrient brought me your *Volkslieder*,[6] which please me enormously, particularly the second. I like the birds and the night winds in the last. The poems are very charming, and one realizes what Heine can do whenever he gives up the ironic conceit. But what I don't understand is why you set your dear little lieder for

4 voices, especially since I don't think the text warrants such a texture nor is it suited to your conception. Tell me, o good Ali.[7] To return to your *Melusine,* I want to mention the detail now that I don't like. It concerns the first modulation after the dominant, a passage that you yourself have often complained about. On the other hand, you returned to F major very nicely. The entire middle section with the lyrical passage in A-flat major is splendid. Then a passage occurs that I don't like, and I'd wager that it's given you a great deal of trouble. It starts at the end of the crescendo that leads into the forte:

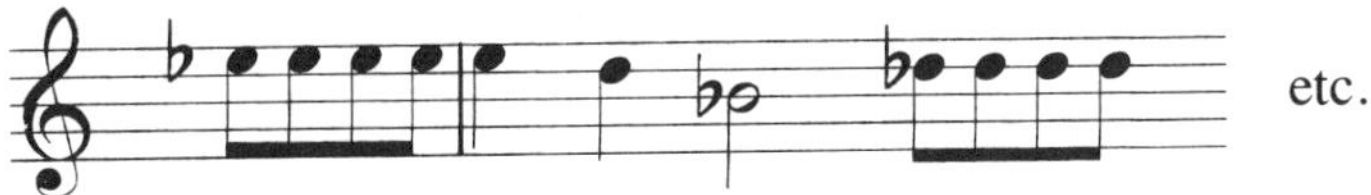

continues through the place where the crescendo turns around thus:

[8]

and then the following forte, until the volume diminishes and it goes into G major, where it is beautiful again. Nevertheless, I feel that the passage just discussed is an integral component of the piece. In the subsequent development, where I especially like the 7th over the g in C major,[9] one measure occurs that doesn't sit right with me—the one in C major before the beautiful A major. I don't like it because you were already in C major for a long time. A great favorite of mine is the passage with the ornamented clarinet line, then both violas below, and then the theme again with the lovely flute. The entire ending is wonderful. And now I'm finished.[10] You will find that I've profited greatly from Rellstab and J. P. Schmidt. It's crazy how every written opinion about anything immediately sounds so darned much like a review and so awful. Meanwhile, I've just reread this letter and would like to rip it up, but then you wouldn't have the pleasure of being illuminated by my wisdom—

only your wax candles would illuminate you. So I'll let it stand. But write me and tell me that I'm a blockhead, and I'll kiss your hand. Regarding your vocal Scena, you've written only that there's an obbligato violin part for Bériot, which leads us to infer a soprano part for Malibran.[11] Is the key suitable? I'm curious about your revisions of *Calm Sea*.[12] As a rule, contemporaries of a first edition are unappreciative of the second, and I have a nostalgic fondness for the old piece with its mistakes. Yesterday there was a concert at the Ganzes that we attended out of courtesy for our Sunday musicales. It consisted of nothing but modernisms. Among other things, Herren Arnold and Taubert hacked away at a new Double Concerto by Kalkbrenner whose compositional value was exceeded only by its rendition and whose rendition was exceeded only by its compositional value. Leopold Ganz had composed a *Pastorale* that was accompanied by the ringing of a bell (never performed here). But Moritz Ganz plays very well and had at least taken themes from *Don Juan,* as well as the Overture from Taubert's *Zigeuner.* He doodled around with your music a long time and shook up your themes like dice until he brought forth a nice one that sounded like a will-o-the-wisp, but he didn't use it to best advantage. Furthermore it's very long for an opera overture.[13] Dear Felix, I have no idea how I feel. The Zelter-Goethe scandal has been dormant the past month, and one has a respite until the 4th part comes out.[14] I hope Duncker's great losses in this *entreprise* will open the eyes of other publishers and we can be spared similar gifts that are on the way. Among others, rejoice over Bettina Arnim's correspondence with Goethe[15]—I can see your face from here!—and then Hegel's diary, etc. Adieu, be well. Sebastian harnessed up the goat and put a posthorn around his neck and is off for Düsseldorf. He eats alone these days since we have dinner after six. His dinner has just arrived. Farewell. I've just written you two letters in a row, and a fearfully long one today, so now you can write me a special one in return. Adieu.

[1]Felix responds emotionally, in a letter to Fanny of 7 April 1834 (Mendelssohn, *Briefe II*, 24): "O you! You ask me which fairy tale you are to read? How many are there? And how many do I know? And don't you know the story of the Schöne Melusine? And shouldn't one prefer to wrap himself up and seek refuge totally in instrumental music without a title when one's own sister (you black-hearted sister!) doesn't even like such a title? Or have you really never heard of the beautiful fish?

But when I recall how you could scold me when I scolded you in April over a letter in February, I'll say little and do the noble thing.--I wrote this Overture for an opera by Conradin Kreutzer that I heard around this time last year at the Königstadt Theater.''

[2]Presumably either Heinrich Joseph or Karl.

[3]*Die drei Wünsche,* premiered at the royal theater on 2 February 1834. A favorable review appears in the *AMZ,* 2 April 1834, cols. 227-29.

[4]Two Motets for 6-part Men's Chorus, Op. 4 (Berlin, 1834).

[5]Felix requested that the family send him wax candles, but he is uncertain whether they are capable of being sent (19 February 1834, NYPL).

[6]Drei Volkslieder, Nos. 2, 3, and 4 of Sechs Lieder, Op. 41.

[7]''You also want to take me to task for the four voices of my *Volkslieder,* but there I stand firm. I think this is the only way that one can write Volkslieder, because any piano accompaniment smacks immediately of the chamber or the music chest, and because 4 voices without an instrument can therefore most easily carry such a lied. And if the reason is too aesthetic, then accept the reason that I really wanted to write something of the sort for the Woringens, who sing such things in a charming manner. But seriously, I find that the four-voiced texture suits 'the text (as Volkslied) as well as it does my conception.' And so we are frightfully divided'' (to Fanny, 7 April; 24).

[8]Both passages perhaps near the location of rehearsal letter ''C'' in the final version.

[9]In the final version, beginning one measure after the change of key signature, where the horns have an F above the G in the bass.

[10]Felix thanks Fanny for her detailed reading of his *Melusine*, and he will write her a special letter soon (15 March 1834, NYPL). Felix adopts some of her suggestions: ''For Fanny I'm announcing that I will change and remove . . . the passage in A-flat major that she pointed out, as well as numerous other, important ones . . .'' (4 August 1834, NYPL). See also Mintz, *Melusine*, although this study does not take into consideration the letters of the Green Books or the NYPL collection.

[11]Presumably *Ah! ritorna, età del oro,* as identified in Foster, *History*, 128. ''My vocal scena for the Philharmonic will be completed in a few days. The words are the most beautiful nonsense of Metastasio—recitative, Adagio, and Allegro compiled from four different operas—but a solo violin accompanying the voice should make everything good again, and in that department I'm thinking of de Bériot'' (19 February). See also letter 58.

[12]First version composed 1828, the final version completed 1834; published as Op. 27. Felix wrote about the new version on 19 February: ''Then in the past few weeks I had to pull out *Calm Sea* again, whose score is to appear now, and felt very good that I previously was forced to change a great deal. Thus I finally ended up writing a completely new score, since the old one was stolen anyway, and revised the piece from the ground up. I believe it is now vastly improved, and had the pleasure of noting as I was working that I've become more skillful. The main change occurs from the first entrance of the piccolo to the timpani passage at the end. In between there is nothing left of the old version other than both lyrical

passages of the high cellos and the low clarinets. But the entire piccolo part, the chords, and the entire return of the theme have been changed, and are less indistinct. In orchestration and voice-leading in *Calm Sea* only details have been improved, and up to the piccolo entrance nothing has been changed, but tightened up. I would love to hear it sometime soon." And in a letter to Klingemann of 14 May 1834 (Klingemann, *Briefwechsel*, 131), Felix writes that the piece has been so extensively revised "that it's actually become a totally different piece." See the correspondence between Felix and Breitkopf & Härtel in Mendelssohn, *Verleger*, 32-39.

[13]The concert was reviewed in the *AMZ*, 9 April 1834, cols. 241-42. Probably the Kalkbrenner Concerto for 2 Pianos in C (Op. 125; published 1835). Uncertain which *Pastorale*. The German phrase "Glöckchen begläutet wurde" = a pun on "begleitet" and "gegläutet" ("accompanied" + "rung by a bell"). Taubert's opera *Der Zigeuner* (libretto by Devrient) was first performed in Berlin on 19 September 1834.

[14]See letter 49.

[15]*Goethes Briefwechsel mit einem Kinde* (1835).

53

Berlin, 12 April 1834

Thank you, oh moon, for your sunbeams![1] They have actually arrived in the nick of time to ward off my potential great rage towards you. Just now I'm thinking about you so much that my thoughts weigh on me, as the French newspapers recently said about Rossini because he hasn't written anything in such a long time. To begin, the Arconnatis will be doing us a great favor by taking the oft-mentioned firescreen with them today. In this regard, please clip out the following part of my letter and send it properly sealed to Frau Bendemann, but it would be even better if you yourself were to go there and read it to her aloud. (You can also read the above part first.)—"Dear noble and respected lady: May we be pardoned (Rebecka and I) for being so bold as to involve you in an extensive matter without prior inquiry. For since it concerns our brother, whom you have spoiled very much, and time is fleeting, we were of the opinion (considering Pauline's circumstances) that you were the only person in Düsseldorf whose well-known and beneficent kindness could encourage us to make such a request. You will therefore soon receive a long, thin package and also a large package, both wrapped in oil cloth. It looks like anything but a firescreen, but to be sure it is one. There is also a little piece of handwork that we have wrapped very nicely and that we hope will arrive in good condition, and also a little package of string. Would you then be so kind as to engage an upholsterer or carpenter to assemble the thing properly, and also tie up the piece of handwork, and then send the whole thing to Felix? And finally, we ask you to put us in the position of repaying our debt to you soon, although we are going to remain in your debt our entire lives."

Speak nicely to Madame Bendemann, and then await the things that will arrive there. I'm not telling you yet which part is from me, and which from Rebecka—you'll have to guess.

I received your letter this morning as I was drinking coffee with Sebastian, and whenever I laughed out loud, he asked what I was laughing about, and when I said over the letter, he laughed along with me and said, "What a merry letter." Wilhelm says hello from his ladder. He is now trimming the beards of the high priests.[2]

If I had written you yesterday or this morning, I would have been able to tell you via the Arconnatis, who are leaving today, how we have been angry, just like Berlin as a whole, for the past 3 weeks.[3] I've never seen the public so unanimous over anything. But today I'm more merry than angry and merely mention that you'll be happy to meet them. D'Epino is a good-natured, upstanding fellow, and she is a fine, pleasant woman. Everybody, including us, appreciated them very much,[4] and they will be able to tell you about our trio this past winter. The manner of their departure has now created a state of confusion and everybody is sorry about it. Now let's talk about music. I'll grant you your reasons for the 4-part setting, especially in regard to the Woringens.[5] If all four of us were together and had sung them, it probably never would have occurred to me to have anything against them. But who will sing tenor here if you are in Düsseldorf? This darned paper makes me look like a Philistine, totally lacking in verve. But now tell me, my dear silly boy, can you really picture your sister so forsaken by God and so addled in the brain that she didn't know any of the things that you told her about *Melusine?*[6] I know you can't abide long-winded discussions over old business, otherwise I would tell you how much

I know and have known about it for a long time, and also would scold you for your scolding, then you would scold me for the scolding of the scolding, and so on, with grace, *ad infinitum*. If you stood behind the door even once and heard me play it alone, *con amore e con espressione*, you would know immediately that I identified her as a fish. Send me the Trio for F. P. as soon as possible—that is indeed pure happiness for me.[7] Have I already told you that I had good success with Moscheles' Trio this winter?[8] Luise Dulcken sends her best and warmly asks you to send her your new Rondo.[9] She plays your Concerto truly remarkably,[10] and I never would have thought that anybody besides you could scold that much. Of course you play it much more freely, and your last performance of it here was particularly noteworthy. I don't agree at all with her interpretation in the singing passages, but her fingers behave as if energized by fire, and her power and speed are truly admirable. By the way, she is a woman who is intelligent, good, and charming over and above her talent, and she feels very comfortable with us. Rebecka and I have become so close with her again in the last few days that we feel we've been together with her for a long time. What a shame that she has such an abominable husband. I feel very sorry for her and unfortunately am convinced that the situation will never improve. Sebastian wants to write:

[Fanny for Sebastian]

Whereby my little man truly behaves like a young hero. You have no idea how dear and good the child is. Now he always goes to bed in the dark by himself, but previously he had insisted that the door be slightly ajar. But only recently he's gotten out of the habit and boasts about his heroic courage. Yesterday he had gone to bed rather dispirited from painful eyedrops that I had to press into his poor ailing little eye, and after the many kisses that I always have to give him when he goes to sleep, he said (*piangendo*): "Leave the door—(*fièrement vivace*) leave the door shut; I can't stand it open." That was really touching and funny. By the way, the doctor (now Dr. Stosch, since Bing has a long-term illness) promises me that it will be better soon and there's nothing to be concerned about. Felice, you must visit us for a few weeks in the fall, even if you do no other traveling, which would please me. You must see our exhibition this time—please, please!

I've just returned from the garden, where the most beautiful, yet horribly cold spring is blossoming forth. It's impossible for us to experience that pleasant feeling of spring given the impending sale of the beautiful park section of the garden. Next week we'll have the pleasure of seeing it cleared with axe and saw. But what annoys me almost more is that the cad of a gardener has distorted and spoiled the rest of the garden with impunity, but not quietly, and that all our counteractions fall back on our heads. Meanwhile, we constitute only one party against the holy Bremer. Therefore we intend to align ourselves seriously against him and see whether the combined efforts of 2 to 4 children and their spouses cannot achieve their aim against the obvious deceit of this rascal, towards whom I bear not a little malice. If only somebody else would agree with us! We want to take General Braun into our confidence. Can't Herr von Woringen do something for us? Since becoming the Director you've gained his confidence, but I'm not convinced that you could have Bremer or Carl tossed out.[11] Dear Felix, don't think that I would want to copy Taubert by copying you and first filling up the letter and then adding on to it. But I find the method very convenient and state openly that I want to imitate it and tell you quite a bit more. But don't rejoice over the fourth part of the correspondence, for I assure you that it's even more deplorable than the others, and I can hardly bring myself to finish it because of my disgust and boredom.[12] A copy of Marx's 6-part men's songs is here for you and I'll send it with the next royal dispatch.[13] He's very cheerful and plucky now. Everything is also going well in the atelier. An uncommonly charming picture by Burggraf (for which Rose Behrend posed) and a round landscape by Pohlke, which you've already seen, were sold from the easel. Many other things have been ordered and the young artists have some income from making portraits. A new student moved in last week who is named Hübner, strangely enough.[14] They are all eager, very fond of Wilhelm, and extraordinarily diligent. You'd like everything, but particularly Burggraf's darling little picture. It just occurred to me that he found the recent appearance and removal of Hähnel as the Druid priestess Norma extraordinary, but Luise Dulcken found this opera so abominable that I don't have the courage to see it. I only wanted to tell you that I haven't seen Hähnel in a long time, and a performance of *Semele* seems to drag on forever because of her. She's very busy and must now sing in Potsdam as well, where she receives rave reviews in the papers. Wilhelm has made superb drawings of her and Dulcken. Rebecka will probably write you about her birthday.[15] Do you know that I'm corresponding with Mary Alexander and like her very much? She recently asked me for an albumleaf and I composed three lieder on texts that she translated delightfully from German. I gave them a kind of unity, as much as possible, and Wilhelm drew a little arabesque for it, but unfortunately there wasn't much space on the paper she sent. I think she will like it. Her German letters are truly precious.[16] We just started a piece of needlework for her. Was that gossipy? But don't be so cruel again, and instead write soon.

Your F.

[1]Letter to Fanny of 7 April 1834 (Mendelssohn, *Briefe II*, 23-25).
[2]Painting, *Christ before Pilate.*
[3]Presumably over the fourth part of the Goethe/Zelter correspondence; see letter 52.
[4]In her Tagebuch entries from March and April 1834, Fanny mentions the Arconnatis attending her musical gatherings.
[5]See letter 52.
[6]See letter 52.
[7]The identity of this piece is unknown.
[8]Uncertain which Moscheles Trio.
[9]Fanny writes in her Tagebuch on 9 April 1834 how much she likes Luise Dulcken, who visited for a week. The piece is the Rondo *brillant,* Op. 29. Felix wrote about it on 1 February [1834] (NYPL): "The score of my Rondo, in front of me, is finished; Fanny should play it when it comes out. The thing pleases me very much, although it's too much like a concert piece. But I believe it has some good qualities." See Felix's correspondence with Breitkopf & Härtel in Mendelssohn, *Verleger*, 29-43.
[10]In g minor, Op. 25.
[11]Implication is that Bremer, as a Hanoverian official, was part of the embassy at Leipziger Strasse and was ordering modifications to their garden. Carl's identity is uncertain.
[12]The Goethe/Zelter correspondence.
[13]Two Motets for 6-part Men's Chorus, Op. 4.
[14]Hübner is also the name of a famous contemporary Düsseldorf painter and friend, Julius Hübner.
[15]On 11 April.

[16]See Alexander, *Letters*, 43-50. Fanny's correspondence with Mary began in 1833. For example, in a postscript to a letter from Abraham to Mary of 14 October 1833, Fanny writes that she has learned English only as an adult, which has evoked ridicule from her brother and sister; also, she hopes to visit England soon (44). Mary had sent her several Heine texts that she had translated into English and Fanny set three: *Once o'er my dark and troubled Life, I wander through the Wood and Weep,* and *What means the lonely Tear* (autograph of 10 March 1834, MA Ms 42, 10-14; fair copy with Hensel's drawings in private possession, but a facsimile of the first page appears in Alexander, *Letters*). Fanny sends the songs to Mary with a letter of 7 April 1834 (45-46), in which Fanny mentions that this is the first time she has ever set English texts. Felix writes about these songs in a letter of 9 May 1834 (NYPL): "Klingemann writes me about your lieder for Mary Alexander and says how much he likes them and how he is paying many visits so that he can receive a copy. Fanny, have one pay a visit, and send it along. You should have done it long ago to delight your brother, the music director."

54

Sunday, 27 April 1834
The Blue Room

Bulletin

The night was completely calm and now it's noon. Mother has consumed two oranges and is very cheerful. She has also received permission to get up when she wants. That was a warning shot, dear Felix, and whoever saw her in the evening the day before yesterday would not have believed that she would recover so well by yesterday. Thank God that she has. We've experienced a really great change this week. Our last letter was, I think, the craziest one that you've received in Düsseldorf.[1] We were really completely exultant with laughing, shrieking, and wonderment; 2 hours later Mother became ill. The agitation over Paul, for whom she's actually very happy, and over Marianne, whom she basically, like Varnhagen, holds dear, may well have contributed to it.[2] Incidentally, I can assure you that while the illness was at its worst, she used every free moment to speak about Marianne and to find out what this one and that one is saying about it. Paul, namely, has been totally drilled into the ground—nobody mentions him, including us.[3]

Mother wanted me to tell you that she sent Nathan to the Rabbi to find out exactly how old the bride is: 49 years old, the same age as Nathan.[4]

Mother's chief ailment still involves severe heartbeats, for which she puts ice on her chest. This remedy doesn't inconvenience her in the least and is doing her a great deal of good. She wants me to tell you that if you have a doctor, let him know that you also have a disposition towards strong heartbeats. Stosch says that one can and must do something about it early. We're exceptionally pleased with Stosch—he's very serious, attentive, thorough, and on top of everything else possesses the incomparable virtue of residing in the house. He was able to come down 5 times the day before yesterday, something that one could not, by any means, ask of anybody else.

Herr Bendemann, whom Mother had wanted to see for a moment, has just left. He delivered your things yesterday, for which we're very grateful. No, my little son, this time I didn't pull out your slip of paper like a silly goose, but I haven't been able to play the Sonata yet.[5] Mother had your slips of paper read aloud and is very grateful for the album.[6] They've made a fine abomination of Hensel's drawing;[7] since they missed all features of resemblance, I'm almost glad that they missed the name as well. But he's had especially bad luck with lithography. Anyway, the [GEM] contains a lot of trash. If "GEM" were derived from "[jämmer]lich" I'd find the title more appropriate.[8] Both of your pieces seem very pretty after a first reading, but perhaps your *Frühlingslied* bears as little resemblance as your picture.[9] Just think that I, such an unmodern person, have first of all, in this GEM, gotten to know a major piece, a Waltz by the renowned Hünten. I haven't composed anything in a long time. Drained! What is one to do? Is one to write a waltz for the GEM like Herr Hünten? Hensel's picture is proceeding nicely and will be splendid.[10] I hope that he, *à moins d'accident*, will be finished. A thousand greetings from Marianne and Varnhagen, who have just left. In general, Rebecka and I have been busy receiving visitors the entire day, while alternately staying with Mother. Be well, my dearest. I hope we'll have very good news to report tomorrow.

Your Fanny

Mother sends her very best and asks me to commend her wishes for your good health. Thus my permission to break a leg will serve only to reinforce hers.[11] Adieu. Father also sends his best.

[1]From Fanny and Rebecka, 20 April [1834] (GB III 114).
[2]The relationship between Marianne Saaling and Varnhagen.
[3]Possibly because of Paul's secret engagement to Albertine Heine; see Gilbert, *Bankiers*, 81n.
[4]Nathan Mendelssohn, but the identity of the bride is uncertain.
[5]Sonata *écossaise*, Op. 28. See Felix's correspondence with Simrock in Mendelssohn, *Verleger*, 184-88.
[6]The album is entitled *Gem*, and is apparently an anthology.
[7]Apparently included in the album.
[8]A pun on the similar appearance and sound of the two words.
[9]Probably the lied published later as part of Op. 34, on a text by Klingemann.
[10]*Christ before Pilate.*
[11]The German "ein Pferd zu halten" is probably an idiom roughly equivalent to a modern English colloquial expression for "good luck," such as "break a leg."

55

Berlin, 11 May [1834]

Mother is doing very well, dear Felix, and feels particularly good in the evening. Then we sit down to tea, as usual, and Mother is cheerful, as usual. As a rule she's somewhat weak in the morning and was especially fatigued yesterday and the day before on account of the humid weather. But yesterday afternoon it cooled off and today she's also much more cheerful. This morning weakness is a kind of weakness of the nerves that is readily explainable after blood-letting, and which we in the family, except for Mother, have known all too well. Much of it is also hypochondria, for she is, thank God, unaccustomed to illness, and you have no idea how apprehensive she is, but every diversion and every visit lifts her spirits. In the afternoon and evening, I repeat, she is almost completely normal: cheerful and involved, and merry and jocular, marching boldly around the garden and, like *everybody else*, continually making Marianne and Varnhagen the butt of her comments and jokes.[1] Your letters give her enormous pleasure, so please write faithfully. But I must reject your reproach that we didn't tell you everything. We didn't write you until the third day of the illness because we didn't want to worry you needlessly, and before then the situation was unclear and could have changed from one hour to the next. But Saturday morning it appeared certain that she would improve, and after that we wrote diligently every day until the reports weren't really necessary.

Your musical reports are very welcome—please send more—but I'm disturbed that your concert wasn't full.[2] You probably planned it too far into the lovely time of the year when your Rhenish rogues take walks and drink May wine. Drinking seems to play a large role there. Isn't Rahlès the young music director from Barmen? I thought he lives there.[3] I like your Sonata in f-sharp very much. I play it diligently for it is, *à la* Felix, very difficult. Many thanks for it.[4] Dear son, I haven't lacked opportunities and I wanted to send you your *Idomeneo,* but, like many other things, it seems to have gotten lost. I searched for it this winter so that Decker could sing the first aria, which I love so much,[5] but it was gone. I maintain that we must have a music thief in the house.—Please write whether the firescreen has really arrived in good shape, unbattered, clean, and uncrumpled, and tell us how it looks in your room.[6] I was constantly afraid that it would arrive at the same time as the first upsetting letters and thus would have given you no pleasure.

Farewell, my dearest. I want to spend a little time with Mother in the garden. Please send me something I can set to music, only don't make it the history of the world, the thirty years war, the era of the popes, or the island of Australia, but instead, find me something really useful and solid. *À propos*, have I ever written you that Elsholz gave us an opera text to read that he wants to send to you?—the greatest abomination I've ever read, a contest between bad taste and boredom, truly unbelievable. I just thought of it because yesterday we laughed at his new tragedy, *König Harold.* We told him in the most courteous way that you would hardly compose an opera in *this genre*, because, please note, he wanted to know our opinion of your opinion. When you receive it, it will be postage paid by us, not by him, because he's not only Elsholz, but also a miser.[7] Adies.

[Lea, Paul]

[1]Marianne Saaling and Varnhagen are engaged to be married. Fanny writes about them in her Tagebuch entry of 24 May 1834 and relates how their forthcoming marriage rests on shaky ground, and how Mme. Arconnati and Gans are spreading malicious gossip about the pair.
[2]Presumably of the premiere of *Calm Sea,* which took place at the Gewandhaus on 20 April (*AMZ,* 30 April 1834, cols. 302-03).
[3]It is Schornstein, not Rahlès (17 May 1834, NYPL).
[4]In a letter of 16 January 1834 (NYPL), Felix wrote that the piece is being published now and will appear presently. Presumably the piece is issued by Simrock on 15 April, the day agreed upon by Felix and the publisher. See the correspondence from March and April 1834 in Mendelssohn, *Verleger*, 186; see also letter 54.
[5]"Padre, germani, addio," for Ilia.
[6]In his letter of 9 May 1834 (NYPL), Felix stated that he has received it, it looks lovely, and he likes it very much. His letter of 17 May contains a thorough description of its appearance in his room.
[7]Play on words between "Elsholz" and "Geizhals" (= "miser").

56

Berlin, 4 June 1834

I actually have all kinds of things to write you: merry, businesslike, and respectable things, as well as the opposite. Where should I begin? With the business. I wrote to Henning, but still no answer.[1] Schlesinger recently wrote me a lovely letter and enclosed the corrections for your Symphony (4-handed version). I looked through them, but am so afraid of scolding that I would rather give you a little trouble than burden myself with pangs of conscience. Therefore I responded that I would send them to you first. Why? Because there are mistakes in the manuscript that are unique and so fatuous that I still can't grasp them all. Look at the scherzo.[2]—I've also sought out Marx's score and want to point out a few places that I like very much.[3] For example, in number 2 I like the close of the first section in its present form with the many e's, although I find it too long. But you should have heard how it sounded as it appeared in the original manuscript; there the basses and tenors sang together forte on the e. I told him that they wouldn't be able to sing because they would be laughing. I also find the following piece, number 2, good. On the other hand, I don't like "Wende dich Herr" at all, and told him so, and said that in general I object strenuously to 6-part men's vocal pieces. Everything lies much too close together for the harmonies to have enough space, and the resultant sound is murky and rattling. The same difficulty in his lieder. There are always so many totally unmusical qualities in his music. There are ideas all right, but they don't lend themselves to musical treatment, and so it's left to good will and chance whether one can guess his intentions, for they are not realized. But write him something about his church piece, because you know how sensitive he is and how he listens to you, and you alone.[4]—Now, one more word on this page, because the other will be visible to everyone. We're very happy that you want to visit Father in Baden, and we wanted to ask you to do it.[5] Mother, namely, will not go along, as she herself will probably write you. But don't infer any setback on her part from that statement. On the contrary, she's doing very well, but as incredible as it sounds, Father had persuaded her to go on this trip without consulting Stosch, who now says, with perfect sense, that she should protect herself from every change and scare and thus not embark on a journey. The carriage could overturn, she could be overexposed to the sun—in short, there are a thousand little things that can be avoided at home, but which are totally unpredictable on a trip. Now, on account of his eyes, Father can't stay in Baden alone; he can't meet anybody nor go anywhere because his nearsightedness makes him timid and anxious.[6] At any other time, we Hensels would have the greatest delight in accompanying him there, but in this particular year Hensel must stay here, and I am too necessary to his well-being and inspiration to work to leave him in the middle of his important project. Rebecka would travel with Walter if you couldn't, but since you've already tentatively offered to do it, as I had hoped, my suggestion for you to go to Baden and stay with him for a month won't be unexpected. He can make the trip quite adequately with Carl, but once there he needs somebody. It's your vacation time and you can work in Baden, but the offer must come from you, for if we make the suggestion he will grumble that you should be left in peace, *à la* royalty. Marianne Saaling just came over around noon for the purpose of emitting sighs, and we take turns with Albertine so that she doesn't drive Mother crazy. There's never been such a fuss! But keep your mouth shut. Our good father is pretty soft on the issue; that angers me the most. I'm disturbed that Mother wrote you such infamy in her last letter,[7] and just as I react to all defamation of character, so am I angry about this one. I want to pass my hand through fire to show that it's sheer slander and falsehood. Yesterday was *not* the founding day of the atelier, but rather a week ago yesterday. Because it was 10 degrees outside that day, the celebration in Charlottenburg was postponed until yesterday, so at 10:30 the entire atelier had a breakfast of broth and sauerbraten and many other things in the garden. Then they were seated in the Academy where Pohlke was awarded a prize, as were 6 other artists, among them Kaselowsky and Wagner, who were excluded because of a cabal. Then old Schadow proceeded to admit something ridiculous and untrue, namely that the exhibition would be meager because the best students had gone to Düsseldorf. Then they left and we traveled to Charlottenburg, where we saw the *Transfiguration*[8] and a large picture by Catel in the church. Rosa visited later and the day closed happily.[9] On top of everything, two of the young people celebrated birthdays. So, farewell. This sheet of paper was to become an envelope, and has actually become a real letter beyond all the chit-chat. I would love to hear Chopin.[10] But tell us about your *St. Paul* and send the lieder.[11] I've also composed some out of empathy but unfortunately nothing major. *Iphigenie* will be sung here next week, with Bader as Orestes. That's not bad, is it?

[1]Felix wrote to Rebecka and Fanny on 28 May 1834 (NYPL) and claimed that tuning is awful in Düsseldorf, especially of the wind instruments. He wants Fanny to write to Henning to obtain a tuning fork that reflects the tuning of orchestras in Berlin, then to have Calix test it, and then have it sent to Felix.

[2]Of the c-minor Symphony, Op. 11; see Mendelssohn, *Verleger*, 280-82. On 282, Elvers cites a pertinent letter from Felix to Fanny of 12 June, which presumably is located in the Staatsbibliothek. See also letter 60.

[3]Presumably Two Motets, Op. 4. See also letter 57.

[4]Felix discussed Marx's music in his letter of 28 May 1834: "You once wrote me that there were some lovely things in it, and to my great disappointment I didn't find anything that I liked, and quite a bit that I strongly disliked. If I found a passage that was good I'd write him about it, but I can't say anything like that, and

only await the next piece of his, which I hope will be otherwise. I find it extremely affected and dry, yet without any novelty or individuality."

[5]In letter of 28 May 1834.

[6]Abraham developed cataracts, which became progressively worse. He had been severely nearsighted, however, for many years (S. Hensel, *Familie I*, 357).

[7]Of 30 May [1834] (GB III 162).

[8]Presumably Hensel's earlier copy of Raphael's *Transfiguration.*

[9]Rosamunde Mendelssohn.

[10]Felix praised him as a pianist, and as a composer for the piano who brings out new effects, like Paganini for the violin (23 May 1834, NYPL; also in Mendelssohn, *Briefe II*, 26).

[11]In a letter of 17 May 1834 (NYPL), Felix wrote that he had not composed lieder in a while, but has recently written a few, including an "altdeutsches" lied in G major (*Minnelied,* Op. 34 No. 1), which he thinks will please Fanny.

57

n. d. [11 June 1834]

Although I'm busy arranging festive events, I must sit down and write you a commentary—which Mother is probably telling you this very minute—so that you won't think I'm completely dull or have turned into an idiot in your absence. By the way, it's been a very musical week. So—Mother has certainly told you about the Königstadt orchestra on Saturday and how I stood up there with a baton in my hand like a Jupiter *tonans*. That came about in the following way. Lecerf had his scholars play and smashed his finger to pieces in the process, then I went out and brought your white little baton and handed it to him. Later my Overture was played and I sat at the piano, then the devil in the form of Lecerf whispered to me to take the little baton in my hand. Had I not been so horribly shy, and embarrassed with every stroke, I would've been able to conduct reasonably well. It was great fun to hear the piece for the first time in 2 years, and find everything the way I had remembered. People seemed to like it—they were very kind, praised me, criticized a few impractical passages, and will return next Saturday. Thus I took part in an unexpected pleasure.[1] Tomorrow *Iphigenie* will be launched, with a respectable cast.

I will be receiving the tuning fork from Henning soon.[2]

Who is the wit who made up the lovely verses?[3]

I wish I could hear the Bach motets. Are you performing them uncut?[4]

I'm quite curious about *St. Paul.* In Potsdam, Marx performed the first of his two Motets at the School Teachers Music Festival and is quite pleased with the performance and the warm reception.[5]

Vale—Today is the rehearsal of *Iphigenie,* but probably few will show up for that.

The 13th. My little letter from the day before yesterday was not sent off, and now I can give you a direct report on *Iphigenie,* which was well performed. I wish you could have been here and heard how the three voices sounded and heightened each other, an effect not heard often. It was truly magnificent. I've never heard a stream of sound like that which Bader and Mantius produced in the duet. Decker was also in excellent voice and sang better and better as the piece progressed, but Bader was supreme. He had never sung the part and arrived at the rehearsal yesterday rather *maussade*; he also thought the part was too low for him. But after he sang the first act, he was a completely new person and later thanked me for having arranged for him to sing the part. To my great delight, I've won him over and he's offered to sing with me anytime—what I want, when I want, chorus, solo, etc. And he will sing, by gum. Probably the *Ave Maria* will be first, which appeared in the church diocese of the Archbishop of Cologne, was later performed in St. Petersburg, and about which I'm dying of curiosity.[6]

Incidentally, 100 people were here, Mother and Father took part in the *fête*, and many notables were invited. So it came to pass that I had the honor of seeing the Mayor Herr von Bärensprung, the Ölrichs family from Bremen, and many others. From our side, many Englishmen were here, including Lady Davy, a charming woman who knew a great deal about you. She said that she had never heard Cramer speak of anyone with such delight as he did about you. He usually prides himself on his high standards.

By the way, my choir was excellent: 8 sopranos, 4 altos with Thürrschmidt and Blano, and Bader and Mantius on tenor. It was splendid and a few things really surprised me. Devrient, who had taken the part of Thoas, canceled as usual at the last minute without any special reason, and Busolt was gracious enough to step in for him.[7]—Regarding everything else, the garden was splendid, the rosebushes were in full bloom, and the place never looked better.

Meanwhile, all traces from yesterday have vanished, and nothing is left except a few stray tones still ringing in my ears. Addio. Mother also wants to write and I want to correct parts, for tomorrow my Königstadters will return. Farewell, my little son, let us hear from you soon. Hensel sends his best. His picture advances by leaps and bounds and is gaining manifold and warm respect. Most likely, Mother has written you that the King has sent Humboldt and Bunsen here; but since that's only gossip within the family, keep it confidential.

[Abraham]

[1]The Königstadt orchestra was a major source of "pick-up" musicians in private performances. Felix had used the expression "Jupiter tonans" in a letter of 25 May 1830, in Sutermeister, *Reise*, 21. The autograph of Fanny's Overture is MA Ms 38, dated 29 March [ ]. Elvers has attributed a date of 1830 (*Verzeichnis*, 171), whereas Sirota erroneously claims spring 1834 (*Hensel*, 81). Because Fanny mentions two years ago, the work could not have been composed later than 1832. The work is in C major and scored for a large orchestra.

[2]See letter 56.

[3]In a letter of 6 June 1834 (NYPL), Felix wrote: "O Fanny, a wise guy who was passing through wrote the following verse in my album: 'Felix, if only you had bestowed these three to the world, / *Lustige Brunnen's Rand,* and *Die Nonne,* and *Wüsstens die Blumen,* / You'd appear worthy, so that the ruler of sunbeams / Would be eager to sprinkle you with laurel juice from your soles to the top of your head.' " The three lieder cited were composed by Fanny but published under Felix's name: Op. 8 No. 12, Op. 9 No. 12, and Op. 9 No. 10.

[4]The Bach Cantatas *Gottes Zeit* and *Du Hirte Israel* will be performed on 29 June in the church (6 June).

[5]Two Motets, Op. 4, performed on 5 and 6 June. See the *AMZ* report of 9 July 1834 written by Marx (cols. 469-71).

[6]Part of Felix's Op. 23.

[7]Fanny's Tagebuch entry of 3 July 1834 reiterates her statements about the success of the *Iphigenie* performance.

58

Berlin, 18 June 1834

My dear, poor little Felix, once again I want to report on business matters first. You will receive the tuning fork with the next royal dispatch.[1] I couldn't have it countersigned by Kalix because he's away and I didn't want to wait until he returned. Schulz, the instrument maker who tuned for me in the meantime, found it slightly higher than his tuning fork, and so I had it tested by Kubelius, who took it home and compared it with his own. By the way, Schulz tells me that Spontini utilizes an unreasonably high tuning because of personal preference, whereas in Paris, according to Henning, the pitch has been lowered by a full half-step. It would be interesting, however, if you could compare this tuning fork to one from Paris.—The two e-minor Fugues must be among your things in Düsseldorf, dear Felix; I sent you everything that you might find useful and didn't find them in the two remaining folders here that contain old items or unfinished pieces.[2] But if you write me that they are definitely not there, I'll turn the house upside down and dig them up. You'll also receive the Mary Alexander pieces with this dispatch. If you asked me for my opinion, I'd say no. 1 is not good at all, no. 2 is only slightly better, and no. 3 is poor. Marx, however, likes no. 2 very much and considers it one of my best lieder, something I find incomprehensible.[3]

On Sunday the Königstadt orchestra performed here again. It was a real hodgepodge; it lacked a second flute, but had trumpets, 4 horns, timpani, and other miscellaneous junk. Between them, the Ganz brothers acquitted themselves well. One of the gentlemen had brought a dreadful Overture along, which I nevertheless found quite suitable. I invited them to rehearse here whenever they wanted, and they offered me their collective services in deep appreciation. I'll have your *Melusine* performed when the occasion arises again. My Overture went very well last time and everybody seemed to like it.[4] In general I've made the pleasant discovery that people are warm and friendly towards me and that I probably can impose on them without fear. The theater will let me have as much music as I want anytime.

Hensel's picture is making great strides and I'm now convinced that he will finish on time unless any unforeseen hitches occur.[5] His brush really flies over the canvas. You will appreciate the wonderful, strong figures. The frame is ready, and you've probably heard that Uber won't take anything for it, but has requested Hensel to paint a half-length picture of him in return. That is a definite sign of appreciation comparable to Runge's supplies of lacquer. Unfortunately he can't place the picture in the frame in the atelier, so we'll see it assembled for the first time at the Academy.

Stosch is away now and Mother has taken on Becker in the interim. He's told her to get up early, drink mineral spring water with Father, go into the garden, and drink a glass of cold water. Thus far these measures seem to agree with her.

Dear Felix, it's 9 A.M. Sebastian hasn't gotten washed yet and my menu hasn't been ordered. I merely wanted to start the letter and instead the quill got carried away. Sebastian's birthday was the day before yesterday and the child was exuberant. He received a real-live lamb from Rebecka that is so wild that it tears all the ropes to shreds and won't allow itself to be brought under control; I believe it's a horse in disguise. He had invited the students to his party, just like last year, and Ratti is his favorite. In the evening we played blind man's buff, in which he concealed himself very nicely and skillfully and altered his voice as well as an adult, and didn't want to stop because of all the laughing and fun.— Marianne and Varnhagen are officially ex-engaged now: she in Freienwalde, he very gay, both acting as if *on ne peut pas plus mal*. The story is so disgusting that hardly anyone tries to figure it out—just imagine![6]

Adieu, my dearest.—Your letter just arrived.[7] I'll write to Rosa today in Charlottenburg.[8] I'm very glad that you like the Franck child—Hermann paints him as a delightful boy.[9] Between us, however, Hermann is tasteless and heavy handed, and it's not surprising that such a style of living has made him coarse and gruff, especially in his advanced years. You would undoubtedly find such aimless running around quite disagreeable.

Please write an overture to *Macbeth.*[10] Felix, I beseech you, send me immediately the theme of the Allegretto or the middle movement from your A-major Symphony—I'm trying desperately to remember it.[11] By the time you send it, I probably will have remembered it, but NEVER MIND. Adieu. Who sang your Scena? Malibran is in Italy.[12]

[Lea]

[1]Felix responds that it is tuned to "A" (5 July 1834, NYPL).
[2]One has the chorale (Op. 35 No. 1, composed 1827), and the other begins with a descending seventh (composed 1827, added to the Prelude of 1841, and published in *Album Notre Temps*).
[3]See letter 53. Felix mentioned receiving them in his letter of 5 July: "I've already played and replayed the lieder and then housed them in my red case. But my assessment is exactly the opposite of yours, dear Fanny, and doesn't coincide at all with Marx's. I like the first lied the best, especially the beginning, where the sound is very lovely. And I don't like the second at all, and it's perhaps the only one of your lieder that I can say that about. Between musicians and colleagues these things can be said, and therefore you certainly won't take my directness badly. I'm being this crude because you write me that Marx considers it one of your best lieder."
[4]See Fanny's Tagebuch entry of 3 July 1834. Her Overture, which was performed again, includes 4 horns, 2 trumpets, and timpani, and these were present that day.
[5]*Christ before Pilate.*
[6]Fanny reports at length in her Tagebuch entry of 3 July on the official dissolution of the engagement, and of the scandalous behavior of both parties—especially Marianne Saaling—after the breakup.
[7]Of 13 June 1834 (NYPL).
[8]Felix asked Fanny to copy the voice parts in Rosa Mendelssohn's piano score of his *Verleih uns Frieden,* which Felix made for her in Bonn, and to send that copy to him (13 June).
[9]According to Fanny's Tagebuch entry of 3 July, this young Franck is Hermann Franck's youngest brother, i. e. Eduard, whom he took to Düsseldorf to study with Felix.
[10]"I truly believe I must write an overture to a PLAY of Shakespeare if I go [to England] next year—I have the desire for it, but so far nothing else" (13 June).
[11]In his letter of 5 July, Felix writes: "Fanny, I'm sending you through the Prinzens a copied version of my Andante from the A-major Symphony, instead of merely the theme, which you requested. Oddly enough you wrote me just at the time when I was in the midst of copying it again, in order to play it for Franck. I hit hard at the passages that I improved, then I had greater interest in it, and I also appended a Minuet and last movement, or rather revised them. I want to do more work on the first sometime later; the three other movements, I believe, have turned out well."
[12]In his letter of 13 June, Felix mentioned having received word from Moscheles and Klingemann that the Philharmonic had performed many of his pieces, including the *Gesangscene.* The piece is *Ah! ritorna, età del oro,* composed for the Philhar-

monic, sung by Mme. Caradori-Allan at the concert on 19 May (Foster, *History*, 128), but written with Malibran in mind (see letter 52). The work is unpublished; as there is no listing in Bartlitz, *Worklist*, the manuscript may be lost.

59

Berlin, 1 July [1834]

[Lea]

Only 2 words, for this morning [ ] I've miscalculated, mislaid, mismanaged, mis-, mis-, mis-, etc. Devrient came the day before yesterday to ask me to go to *Euryanthe* to hear Grosser.[1] I then went about acquiring a ticket in an original way, but that is too lengthy to relate. She possesses the range for the role of Eglantine: from a-flat below to b or c above. A very nice top. The middle and deep notes seem weaker to me. (Two days ago Beckchen found them extremely strong.) She managed the scalar runs just barely, so that one could see her agility, but her delivery is still thoroughly uncultivated and her acting completely ordinary, so that, as you can imagine, she was a horrible Eglantine. Clear enunciation is totally lacking, she also didn't seem handsome, but her intonation is completely pure, and, *so I've heard*, she learned the part in one week and memorized it securely and perfectly—quite an accomplishment. To sum up, I believe you could probably make a singer out of her. I ask you, however, to consider that I heard her one time, in the large opera house, as Eglan, certainly the most disadvantageous circumstances for judging a newcomer. I consider Lenz far better. Meanwhile, she seems to have a foothold here. But I've also heard from Grosser that one is thinking of engaging her here.—Devrient wanted me to write you my opinion, and I've done it. Now farewell.

Today Amalie is also moving out of my house, as she is expecting her 4th child.

[1]Review in the *AMZ,* 23 July 1834, col. 501. The reviewer believes she needs further training, but acquitted herself well, especially in comparison with her co-singer, Schröder-Devrient.

60

n. d. [c. 1 August 1834]

I'm probably writing you for the last time before we see each other, please God, for if the quill notices that you're coming soon, it won't budge an inch. I hope you'll leave on the 18th and come here directly, for one can't plan around Mother's and Father's trip. You know first of all how undecided they are, how little enthusiasm for travel Mother has always had, and also how the present severe heat would make the trip even more uncomfortable. I consider it much more likely that Father or both of them will accompany you on your way back, which is by far a better plan because we aren't deprived of any part of your vacation. You could then spend the entire time here with us. *Audi, et vidi, et inclina aurem tuam.*

Aren't you amazed at my self-control that prevented me from opening up the package of *St. Paul* addressed to Fürst in order to read it first? How did Fürst get to move among the prophets?[1] And thank you for the Symphony movement that just arrived; it gives me great pleasure. I immediately played it through with Beckchen twice, but she couldn't continue because she's suffering from the extremely oppressive heat.[2] I tolerate it much better; I melt only a few hours each day and stay in the atelier most of the time, where it's reasonable. But Hensel endures it the best. He works on his ladder all day until he can't see any longer. The work is proceeding toward its conclusion and you will like it very much. It definitely is not lacking in strength. He's just painted his [candles][3] for Pilate. But I've digressed from your piece. I don't like the change in the first melody at all; why did you make it? Was it to avoid the many a's? But the melody was natural and lovely. I don't agree with the other changes as well; however, I'm still not familiar enough with the rest of the movement to be able to render a reasonable judgment. Overall I feel you are only too ready to change a successful piece later on merely because one thing or another pleases you more then. It's always tough, however, for someone to become accustomed to a new version once he knows the old one. Bring the old version along when you come and then we can argue about it.

Your *Vespers* were recently performed by Marx in a student concert.[4] But unfortunately it didn't go well, perhaps because it's too difficult for a completely volunteer choir, which, like those in other academies, does not contain eager female voices to lend cohesion to the ensemble. The solo movement with the lamenting bass can't help but make a splendid effect. The following 4-part passage after the individual entrances was very powerful:

If sung cleanly, the closing chorale should end magnificently and quietly, but the chorus went flat because of the heat, and since the church was empty, it echoed mightily on top of everything, which of course spoiled its clarity.

The 3rd of August.

First of all, let me announce that your manuscript was returned to me because Herr Fürst has taken a trip, and, unless you instruct me otherwise, I will keep it until I find out that he's returned.

The weather has cooled off considerably today. A strong storm alternately clutches and dispels thick thunderclouds, and I hope that the clouds will enjoy the pleasure of washing everyone's walking outfits free of charge on the King's birthday as well as on Sunday.—I had a bad day yesterday. Hensel had the most awful stomach cramps three times within 24 hours, which finally made us turn to homeopathy in desperation. Luise has used it with good results for a long time, and this time it worked well, most likely in conjunction with the natural weakening of the malady. Hereafter we will probably turn to the homeopathetic methods of Stüler on a regular basis, as we currently don't have a doctor that we trust. Stosch is moving far away and never comes on his own, which is certainly quite unacceptable for me.

Rebecka will probably have written you that Steffens has become rector. We're very happy about it.

Farewell.

[1]Felix wrote Fürst a letter on 20 July 1834, in Mendelssohn, *Briefe II*, 29-30, relating his progress on the oratorio, and his gratitude for the text. Felix compressed and simplified much of his text after he went back to the original Scriptural passages. Part I will probably be completed by next month, and the entire oratorio by January.
[2]It is the slow movement of the *Italian* Symphony. See letter 58. The item catalogued as DB 3, 43, dated 22 July 1834, is a note accompanying the items that were sent.
[3]A possible translation; the meaning of "Candillen" is unknown.
[4]Op. 121 (composed 1833).

61

4 November 1834

I definitely want to write you once again. You won't believe how busy I am doing nothing and how important it is to me that the exhibition not lack clever people. This great vehicle of pleasant leisure will soon disappear and then everything will probably be back on its old track. With the opening of the exhibition fast approaching, large boxes stand empty in the corridor of the Academy, as I've just discovered; nothing major, however, can be missing any longer, and the rooms are abundantly filled. Recently a picture by a Dutchman, Maass, made a big hit with the public and delighted all the experts and artists. It's a life-size, half figure of an Italian woman in familiar peasant costume who kneels before a chapel, carrying her sleeping child in her arms. She is illuminated by two sources—daylight and the altar lamp. The artists can hardly lavish enough praise on this lighting, its reflection on the figure, and the receding of the background, while I especially admire the splendid head and arms of the sleeping child and might only regret that everything else is hidden in the disproportionate, colorful wrappings. Bendemann's picture has been hanging for a few days but I like it even less here than in his atelier—it still looks rather grey and dull. The lack of content is even more striking since Sohn's painting on the same subject, but with a splendid figure, is next to it. We also can't appreciate the two sketches, and that makes me sad, because I'd so much like to agree with you. But I especially don't like the pastoral scene, and the family doesn't like it any better. Stilke's works are generally the best of the Düsseldorfers. Köhler's works, which, if I remember correctly, you couldn't stand, please me because of a certain cheerfulness and brightness that stand out favorably compared to the predominantly elegiac mood of the other pictures there. But one can't deny that there aren't any traces from the Old Testament and the Egyptian maiden who rescued Moses.—I don't know if anyone has written you that Kaselowsky's picture was very well received and sold in the first few hours after his exhibition. Yesterday Steffens and the landscape painter Dahl spent the evening here and Hensel sketched Dahl for his book. None of the Düsseldorf painters has visited Hensel. They apparently made an agreement among themselves, because, except for them, hardly any foreign painter passes up our house. One can't count Stilke, since he's an old friend. Gruppe continues to wage a little war against Hensel, but he's the only one, and I'm thoroughly satisfied with the reception that the master and his students have enjoyed this time.[1] I've finished my Quartet and incorporated your advice on the scherzo as best I could.[2] I'll have it tried out this week. We've read in the newspapers about the start of your concerts and theater performances, and are now very anxious to hear the details from you.

Gans is back, very taken with Italy. He gives very lively and picturesque accounts of the dangers in Switzerland, how they almost lost their lives through daredevil meandering on ruined streets. For now, adieu. I must go to the change at the exhibition.

The 5th. This evening Paul will host a large gala where he will break in the gifts that were presented to him for his birthday.[3] Yesterday we spoke to his lieutenant, who told us that the lower officer thought he was the best in the drills. By the way, he's still surly about his service and there are frequent arguments about it. Yesterday I heard from rather reliable sources that Dulcken has gone bankrupt again. He was in Berlin recently and took a number of things from a tapestry dealer here, a business friend of his, who now wants to regain those things, if possible, in Hamburg. There's no hope for the unfortunate Mme. Dulcken if she doesn't get a divorce from the good-for-nothing man, but she hasn't even contemplated such a step. Lafont, the sweet man who has brought us recent news from you, still cannot perform any concerts and I fear he won't line up many engagements.[4] When one looks at him, one can't help expecting his playing to be outmoded. He is so much *ci devant jeune homme*, and resembles Neukomm so closely,[5] that one has to be struck by the thought that since then, the art of violin playing has undergone a drastic change through Paganini. You will know from the papers that Crelinger and her daughters had guest roles in the Königstadt Theater, but only this private report will tell you that people physically fought for seats at the first performance. Phooey, that smacks of a letter by Zelter. I'm exceedingly disturbed about the sinking of the English steamship. Such an incredible event shakes one's well-founded confidence to the core. Brrr—I wouldn't want to travel by sea now because the mild, stormy weather is continuing. Doesn't Klingemann fear for his digestion? No word from him in your letter to Paul yesterday, in which you mentioned how both of you took on the *Templar and the Jewess.* That is truly one of the most difficult operas, and if you succeeded, you could probably venture anything.[6] I'm very glad that things are working out for Rietz, for it will probably be of inestimable advantage for him. How do you stand with him now with regard to the directorship? Are you conducting what and when you want, *à caprice*, or have you divided the duties as well?[7] And what did you perform in your first concert? Adieu, dear Felix. Write us a lengthy letter sometime. Your F.

[1]Felix responds that he disagrees with her artistic assessments, especially of Stilke's works (to Fanny, 14 November 1834; Mendelssohn, *Briefe-RE*, 174).
[2]Fanny's only extant String Quartet. Autograph MA Ms 43, dated 26 August 1834 to 23 October 1834. Perhaps Felix's advice had been verbal, as he was in Berlin with the family from the end of August to the beginning of October. A recent performance of this unpublished work, by the Concord String Quartet, took place at the Metropolitan Museum of Art in New York in March 1982.
[3]30 October.
[4]Felix had heard Lafont in Paris in 1825, perhaps for the first time: "But I recently heard Lafont; he plays very nicely, very finely, very elegantly, very coldly . . ." (18 April 1825, NYPL). Lafont performed in Berlin in late November 1834, as reported in the *AMZ,* 24 December 1834, col. 885, which notes his sweet tone.
[5]Felix had dubbed him "Altkomm" in a letter to the family from Paris, dated 23 March 1825 (*Briefe-RE*, 41).
[6]By Marschner, based on Scott's *Ivanhoe* (Leipzig, 22 December 1829).
[7]Julius Rietz has been engaged by Felix as an assistant conductor in Düsseldorf.

62

Berlin, 24 November [1834]

Many thanks, oh CLOWN, for your dear birthday letter.[1] The others have probably already written you about all the warm festivities, the present from the young ones, and other pretty things: tea in the magnificently decorated atelier, and the wonderfully performed charades. I think that such performances will still give me great delight when I'm an old woman. Yesterday was Frau Steffens' birthday, which she celebrated by a party in her new, charmingly furnished apartment. One always encounters the nicest people there, and I can't recall having met so many nice people as I did then. Among the sketches that you list and have in mind the Trio doesn't appear. Have you given up on it?[2] Please finish it for me because I eagerly look forward to it.

Wilhelm gave me a very beautiful drawing for my birthday: Miriam, the prophetess, with the timbrel in her hand, the women behind her, Moses on a mountain leading the migration, parts of the army in the background laden with the spoils, and the pyramids standing in the distant dawn. The composition is round, and very rich, lovely, and unusual. I hope he will paint it.[3] This drawing is the first page in a lovely book that we've designated as a family album.

The 27th.

You are now receiving the 6th and final volume of the Goethe-Zelter correspondence. The editor took the trouble of appending an alphabetical index, in which anyone who knows his ABC can easily find out where and how often he's been insulted or praised in the entire opus, which in this case amounts to the same thing.[4] (You were mentioned 58 times.) You would say "Figaro!" if you were here, but I can't help you; it offends me from start to finish to think that in a country without freedom of the press in which public officials hide from public criticism, harmless private persons are assailed as if by thieves hiding in a bush, and even talked about and defamed. And not only that, the ink sometimes flows in tainting their honor, depending upon the relationship of the persons to the thieves. They write that I play like a man, and I guess I have God or Zelter to thank that a blatant insult doesn't come next, for the book abounds in such slurs. You will find Father harshly criticized on several occasions for not having permitted you to travel to Sicily.[5] In England, such a book would not be read at all, since one is accustomed to personalities there, and that is its only interest. But I don't find it nice under any circumstances, but rather thoroughly rude, to publish things about private persons.

But I still have to argue with you—not about the paintings, for that is too far-reaching a topic for letters and we disagree about them too much. We can save that for another time.[6] But why do you bawl me out for saying that Paganini has changed violin playing?[7] Isn't that true? Is violin playing today the way it was in its infancy? Who brought about the changes if not great talents? And how, as you've said, can there be *drastic changes in people* if the people can't drastically change anything outside themselves? The French newspaper seems entirely right to me, even if it might express itself in a clumsy manner. What do you want other than advancing yourself and the art of music? You are extremely diligent for that very reason and not for the purpose of filling up reams of paper. I've said my piece and saved my soul, which actually was in no great danger with you, isn't that so?[8]

Yesterday we were—o wonder!—at the theater to see Crelinger's daughters in *Minna von Barnhelm.*[9] A pair of delightful girls: pretty, natural talents, and so accomplished that one might almost say it was too much for their age if one weren't compelled to believe that such fortunate natural endowments can be helpful in the future. Despite the most awful seats, we had a delightful time.[10]

The last vestige of Russian royalty slipped out today. Everybody is making a fuss about how both behaved like a pair of raggedy vagabonds. The Czar didn't contribute to any charitable institution, and the Czarina hasn't made a commitment, although perhaps she will. It almost seemed like a satire in that the immensely rich, silly Demidov contributed 1,000 talers to the poor in honor of her presence. She didn't even spend one taler for anything at the exhibition, which is especially appalling given that the exhibition was extended 2 weeks just for her. She only ordered a copy of a sketch of Blanc's picture. In general, people are full of praise for her coolness and her childish and graceless behavior. She definitely added to the exhibition's losses by wasting the King's money and time, so that neither he, nor the Crown Prince, nor anyone else at court bought anything—in short, a veritable outrage. The Czarina did inquire about pictures costing 20 louis d'or but she considered them too expensive.

I've just read your letter to Rebecka containing the complaints about being an Intendant, and I thank God that you are out.[11] Be well. I want to go and read aloud to Father from Ranke's *Popes*.[12]

[1]Of 14 November 1834 (Mendelssohn, *Briefe-RE*, 173-75).

[2]Felix is sketching the Overture to *St. Paul;* he plans to finish the oratorio by March, and to compose a new a-minor Symphony and a new Piano Concerto. See Felix's letter to Fanny of 14 November. Felix writes with regard to the Trio: "Unfortunately the Trio hasn't progressed much because I have too much to do on the oratorio, the second part of which I'm working on now. Please forgive me; it should, however, be finished sometime soon" (11 December 1834, NYPL). Felix had had plans to compose a trio earlier, in 1831-32, which also did not come to fruition. See Mendelssohn, *Verleger*, 8-10, 12, 177, and 291.

[3]The painting, *Miriam's Song of Praise after Crossing the Red Sea.*

[4]Riemer was the editor. See letter 49.

[5]"His father absolutely did not want him to see Sicily. He may have had his reasons, but a father of an obedient son should limit his power. I made the elder one aware of it" (letter to Goethe of 10-15 June 1831).

[6]See letter 61.

[7]"Thus I don't think you're justified in talking about the upheaval in violin playing since Paganini on the occasion of hearing Lafont, for I'm not familiar with such upheavals in art, only in people. I think you would have been similarly displeased with Lafont had you heard him before Paganini appeared, and therefore you shouldn't praise his good side any the less because you've heard the other. I just read a pair of new French musical newspapers here, in which they continually speak of a *révolution du goût* and a musical revolution that have been taking place over the past few years, and in which I'm also to play a pretty role—this upsets me very much. I continue to believe that one should be industrious and work, above all not hate anyone, and leave the future to God" (to Fanny, 14 November).

[8]Felix's response appears in a letter to Rebecka, 23 December 1834 (NYPL; Mendelssohn, *Briefe II*, 46): "By all means I must write again about 'upheavals.' Actually it's directed mainly at Fanny, but aren't you both the dear girls? And therefore couldn't it be shared by both of you and be answered by both if you wish? And haven't I reflected and plotted a great deal on the subject since your letter, which now compels me to write? But you must also tread properly, until every last detail about upheavals has been uttered. You see, o dear girl, I believe that there are great distinctions between reform, etc., the process of reforming, and revolution, etc. Reform is that which I desire and love in all things, in life, and in art and in politics and in street paving and in God knows what else, for a reform

by itself is only negative when used against abuse, and only takes *away* what is standing in the way. But an upheaval by which that which was previously good (really was good) is now no longer so is absolutely intolerable and is only responding to fashion. Therefore I didn't want to hear what Fanny said about how Lafont's playing was no longer interesting since the upheaval by Paganini, because if his playing was ever able to interest me, it will always do so—and even if the angel Gabriel plays the violin in the meantime. But those Frenchmen of whom I spoke had absolutely no idea of the fact that everything old remains good, yet nonetheless, what is to come must be different from the old, because it issues from new or different people. Inwardly they are the same everyday people as the others, but they have learned by rote to expect something new, and they work to find it. And if one is ever miserably applauded or stung, he immediately thinks that the *révolution du goût* has arrived. For that reason I have a very low opinion of myself when, as you say, they do me honor by placing me among the leaders of this movement—because I know very well that at least one person belongs to it to improve himself (often it doesn't suffice), because no Frenchman and no journal knows, and is to know, what the future will bring and offer, because above all one must himself be active in order to lead another movement, and because one looks backwards, not forwards, in such observations, and progresses only through work, not through talk that they don't believe. Thus I'm reacting as if you grabbed me by the throat. But that I, for God's sake, don't spurn movements and reform, and that I myself also hope to effect reforms in music, that you see because I'm a musician—nothing else says it for me. Now send me a good answer! And preach again! This subject is interesting because it is so universal, but it is different in politics because there the concept of right is always changing, which in art, however, is manifested only in the outermost form. If I were sitting on the sofa between both of you now, the matter would soon be settled.'' (N. B.: four of the last six sentences were omitted from the published version.)

[9]Comedy by Lessing (1767).

[10]The Czar and Czarina of Russia were present at this performance on 26 November 1834; see the *AMZ,* 26 Nov. 1834, cols. 816-17.

[11]Letter to Rebecka of 23 November 1834 (NYPL). Felix complains about being the Intendant. He lists the unfair division of duties between him and Immermann, and all the petty, bothersome details that have occupied his time. Felix was currently in the midst of negotiations with Leipzig; see E. Werner, *Mendelssohn*, 237-52.

[12]*Die römischen Päpste . . . im 16. u. 17. Jahrhundert* (3 vols., 1834-36).

63

30 November [1834]

I've just reread your translation of Byron's poem and find it much better than Theremin's except for the ending, which in Theremin is infinitely more beautiful—I might even say more beautiful than in Byron.[1] You must try to find a way to change it still, and close with "hell, aber ach! wie fern." Something wondrous resides in the poem—I've hardly ever known anything expressed more powerfully. It exerts a totally magnetic force on me and I can't stop thinking about it.—On the whole, I'm becoming familiar with him now in a way that is not to a poet's best advantage, for I'm reading his verses once a week with a teacher, but only understand them more or less with great effort. What clearly permeates his writing is the power of his rhythms, the wonderful sounds of his verse in this elusive language: the profoundly poetic essence of the poet himself.

His biography has fallen into my hands recently and I'm reading it with great interest. As you know, it always disturbs me if we can't agree, even over small matters. As you hold the opposite view, I've attempted to approach Loewe's setting of that Byron poem with a critical eye, but cannot, because it always moves me, even if I merely think about it.[2] Its beautiful dreamlike quality, its evocative remoteness—I cannot express it any other way—and its exhaustive word associations sweep me away as soon as I try to find fault with it.

The 10th. I started this page with the intention of writing you every now and then when I find the time, and so here goes. I've had all sorts of minor frustrations the entire day. This afternoon I played through two Trios by Reissiger and Onslow, which I had given myself in connection with the anticipated resumption of my Sunday musicales.[3] I really wanted to present something totally new, and that Onslow theme occurred to me in the store. But it was such a dull, stiff, thoroughly boring thing that I almost fell asleep playing through it and then turned to the litany and my favorite motet, *Gottes Zeit,* to recover. Ah!! How it makes a person feel good again! I know no preacher who is more insistent than old

Bach, especially when he ascends the pulpit in an aria and holds on to his theme until he has utterly moved, or edified and convinced his congregation. I know of almost nothing more beautiful than the fearful "Es ist der alte Bund," during which the sopranos so movingly intone, "Ja komm, Herr Jesu, komm."[4] Sebastian, not Bach, is now taking the quill from my hand.

[Fanny for Sebastian]

The 23rd of December. Since I'm only sending you my Quartet, I wanted to append a letter, and since I can't write anything sensible before Christmas, I'll let it sit until afterwards.

The 25th. So the letter hasn't been touched for two days. We had one of the merriest Christmases and only regret that you weren't here, for from my knowledge of your character, I think you would have died of laughter. For the time being, many thanks for your package and your dear picture—the latter gave us both great pleasure. My package will arrive *post festum*.

[Fanny for Sebastian]

Report: Rebecka and I have built something together once again, and the following description explains it. If one proceeded from the door of the grey room, one encountered alternate Christmas trees and tables. On the tables were the things that were distributed accordingly, and their contents indicated on a tablet with writing made out of raisins: "Chur" stood in front of the table with the artistic things, "Gamet" in front of the toys, etc.[5] Our artistic table was particularly brilliant: new, beautiful engravings for the young people in the atelier, a charming drawing by Hensel for Albertine of Paul as a soldier, little Walter portrayed by Moser as a present from Rebecka for Mother, a beautiful, large Swiss landscape by Lory from her for Dirichlet, and many engravings and books. The plaster table, on which Rebecka had decorated a colossal antique bust of Ariadne with Apollo feet and a Michelangelo hand, was also very lovely. There was a wealth of all kinds of beautiful things such as we've never had gathered together here. Both of the non-family guests, Lory and Lafont, received presents and had a wonderful time. After everything was duly examined (Mother will probably tell you about her delightful structure behind a screen), the things were cleared away, and *la chambre se constitua en théâtre*, whose stage was formed by the tables. The slip of paper tells you the rest. The first picture, in which they appeared together in costume with noses, was accompanied by the unison chorus, "Prinz Eugen."[6] This gave me the opportunity to become familiar with the song that probably has the craziest rhythms in all of music. Have you ever seen it notated?

Then came the marriage proposal from Paul to Albertine, with Hübner functioning as page. I had to miss that because of a costume change for the following number, in which I was arranged as Miriam in Hensel's drawing and had to beat the drum. Beckchen with the harp and Albertine with the piccolo followed me, and it is said to have been very well received. Next came a sensation. The curtain went up, and a large hurdy-gurdy was turned by Pohlke dressed in a fabulously tattered outfit, who sang the part of Dr. Eisenbart. But behind the hurdy-gurdy sat Kaselowsky, Paul, Hübner, Löwenstein, and Wagner unseen, and they imitated the hurdy-gurdy so remarkably with their gorgeous voices that at first no one laughed because they thought it was the real hurdy-gurdy. But afterwards we certainly laughed very hard over it. I recommend this piece to you for performances at the Academy.

Sebastian described the bear's dance to you.[7] It was wonderful, and the last one did honor to Paul's creativity and taste. The pyramid consisted of students, and Paul was the tip. Everybody held a light in one hand and a present in the other, and had a piece of paper hanging out of the mouth, which indicated the name of the recipient. Everything was selected by Paul, and very successfully; they were extremely useful and pretty.—The students gave me very lovely drawings based on their recent paintings. As our concluding activity, we fashioned a lottery for the atelier from all the remaining little items, which was fun for everyone. But you'll probably be most cheered to know that Mother and Father both were extremely well and delighted—I haven't seen Father laugh so heartily in a long time. My old mother-in-law was also very happy and cheerful, even though she is very weak now, and of course the children's cheerfulness goes without saying.

We also enjoyed our Christmas because the matter concerning the picture was virtually settled recently. It's been referred to the ministry and now travels a slow, but, as everyone assures us and we concur, certain path. That is one reason why I haven't written you in such a long time. Hensel was worried sick, and then disgruntled because of his illness, and had definitely decided to move out of Berlin permanently if his work were rejected. (But this, of course, is strictly between us.) You can imagine how this very real prospect, coupled with the complete uncertainty of our present situation, tormented me and put me in a sour mood. I'll tell you about our current plans another time. Düsseldorf is part of them.—Now in great haste: I believe I've already told you that I don't have your two e-minor Fugues.[8] You'll have to look for them among your things. Regarding your church music and your new pieces that I don't know yet, and many other things, next year.[9] It's now 11:30 and I'm sitting in a cold room. Meanwhile, since I foresee the impossibility of completing this letter tomorrow in the midst of all the wedding flurry, I'll end it now. Start to read it on the second page. Sebastian would like you to write him a separate letter as well sometime. Farewell. Your

F

[Hensel]

[1]The Byron poem is "Sun of the Sleepless." In his letter of 23 November 1834 (NYPL) to Rebecka, Felix found Theremin's translation of the first strophe incomprehensible, of the second strophe inaccurate. Felix offered his own translation:

"Schlafloser Augen Sonne, Heller Stern!
Der du mit thränenvollem Schein, unendlich fern,
Das Dunkel nicht erhellst, nur besser zeigst,
O wie du ganz des Glücks Erinn'rung gleichst!
So funkelt längstvergangner Freuden Licht,
Es scheint, doch wärmt sein matter Schimmer nicht,
Der wache Gram erspäht die Nachtgestalt
Hell, aber fern, klar—aber ach wie kalt."

Felix commented: "The poem is quite sentimental and thoroughly suited to me, as Moritz Veit would say, and I believe I would have already set it many times in g-sharp minor or B major (in short, with many sharps), but it always strikes me how you and Fanny like Loewe's music, and that pulls me away and nothing comes of it." But Felix does set this poem on 31 December 1834.

[2]Loewe's setting is No. 6 in the third book of *Hebräische* Gesänge, Op. 13 (Berlin,

1827), on poems of Byron. Here it is entitled *Die Sonne der Schlaflosen* and uses F. Theremin's translation.

[3]Through 1834, Reissiger had written eight Trios; therefore the intended one cannot be determined. Onslow wrote ten Trios, of which nine were probably composed through 1834; again, indeterminable.

[4]The Cantata *Gottes Zeit,* BWV 106. Abraham found the section "Es ist der alte Bund," as well as the bass aria "Bestelle dein Haus," edifying and impressive (to Felix, 10 March 1835; Mendelssohn, *Briefe II*, 53).

[5]Obscure terms to identify; "Chur" is the capital city of the Swiss canton, Garubünden, and "Gamet" are planting seeds.

[6]Identity unknown.

[7]The painter Franz Wagner was dressed up as a bear and Paul as an ape.

[8]See letter 58.

[9]In Felix's letter to Abraham of 11 December 1834 (NYPL), Felix asked Fanny to select two other sacred pieces to be published with *Verleih uns Frieden,* composed in 1831. The latter was published later, as a supplement in the *AMZ* of 5 June 1839.

64[1]

Berlin, 27 December 1834

I'm not functioning merely as a quill now, but rather as a part-time author.[2]

A certain misunderstanding has prevailed in our correspondence during the past several weeks, my dear Felix, and so I'm going to sit down immediately and clear it up once and for all. The letter that Rebecka wrote you in response to the one you wrote me, which was in response to the one I'd written you *au sujet de* Lafont, whom I then hadn't heard—all that is not from Rebecka's head, although from her pen. Rather, it was the first one that Father dictated.[3] Are you surprised? Read it again and the blinders will disappear from your eyes, and then you won't be able to understand how you didn't spot it immediately. However, I can well appreciate how one would assume that what one already knows will be readily apparent to someone else. Father thought that you would immediately recognize the point in the letter where he started to dictate. I didn't think you would. Nevertheless, that doesn't actually change anything. What *I* responded was from me, and since we started to get involved in a parliamentary discussion at one time, let us continue. *Je demande la parole*, which you certainly will send me without question from Düsseldorf.

One can't deny that times change, and with the times the taste, and with the taste of the times we also change. There is definitely also a positive Good in the arts. I don't believe that what we have recognized as the highest and always will recognize as such can be subject to fashion, and I hope you would never think me crazy enough to be capable of such beliefs. Little Hanna in the *Seasons* will age as little as Alceste or the evangelist Matthew. But now there appears an unbelievable number of grey areas within that Good. Since two times two don't always equal four in aesthetic matters, there will be a point (primarily regarding performance interpretation) where the outer world, or the changeability of time, or the *fashion* (get around the word as you wish) will exert its influence. You remember as well as I that there was a time when we were thoroughly charmed by Spohr's music. Now we no longer feel that way. His music hasn't changed and we are still the same people, but our relationship to him has changed. Let's take the case that we've considered before—violinists. Spohr certainly possesses infinite positive Good in his playing, which won't fade away, but he also has a certain sweetness that perhaps contributed to his fame at the time. Now along comes Paganini who plays in a wild, fantastic, and powerful way. All young violinists strive to imitate him and tear the G string. Then, after several years, I hear Spohr again and his sweetness is instinctively more noticeable than before because my ears are now exposed to a totally different style. The public at large is chiefly susceptible to this influence, individuals more or less, but no one is immune to it. It wouldn't be difficult for me to cite lots of other examples of things or people who were pleasing in the past and now seem dull and boring, or bizarre or unbearable. Such change naturally affects the highest and best of its kind, but I am convinced that even the Good will appear more or less good within the context of time. Respond to this, CLOWN! Should I register this entire correspondence in my journal of disputes?

By the way, it's amusing that this entire discussion got started over a silly, rash judgment that I pronounced on Lafont's wig, for at that time I didn't know anything else about him. Since then I've heard him in concert, where his clear, flowing, nice playing has pleased me very much, and particularly his charming interpretation of melodic passages. Then he played here once and I accompanied him in variations. I thereby ran the risk of falling back on my first judgment about his old style, because his compositions, variations with Herz and Kalkbrenner, etc., are such that not even the most extreme adherence to fashion could excuse them, and it disturbed me that the nice violin was playing nothing decent.[4] And now I've prattled on and on and lost time to rehearse your new lieder for a performance *in pleno* tomorrow.[5] I like them very much and without a *but*; I consider them among your best. The Fugues are excellent and the short one has a very nice flow.[6] In the long one, I'm not completely satisfied with the ending, for the texture becomes thin again after being thick for so long. There's also a place in the middle that seems flawed—I think it's a patch—after the piano crescendo forte, when the bass has the theme in octaves in C major and is then imitated by the upper voice, just like the following thematic area in f. Otherwise it's marvelous and I'd love to hear you play it first.[7] The character of the little one reminds me of a little piece of yours that's one of my favorites, and despite all *drastic changes* in taste, or reforms, or ecclesiastical revisions, will probably still remain so, or I would have to become a Turk, a true renegade. I'm referring to the Quartet Fugue, which affects me deeply if I merely think about it and the person who performed it so beautifully.[8]

The 27th of December[9] To return to said drastic changes of taste, I want to cite a case in which I totally agree with you. Last year I was still very opposed to homeopathy and especially to doctors dispensing their own medicine. Now Stüler is our physician, he gives me and everybody else here his little powders, I'm satisfied with them, and Hensel especially has responded favorably to his treatment for stomach cramps. But in spite of that, I can't stand the fact that so many homeopathy neophytes behave as if the heavens had suddenly been opened up to them and no human had ever been cured before. I'm certainly free of such prejudice and believe it's generally true.

Today I played your new pieces for my Sunday public, and the public was extremely delighted. You obviously wrote the first lied, in E-flat major, for piano solo because you didn't find any words for it.[10] Since that is indeed a true lied with lovely declamation, you should have approached the authors of your numerous lieder, for example Egon Ebert or Voss; they certainly would have written you a text according to your wishes. In the second lied, I ask your permission to change a note:

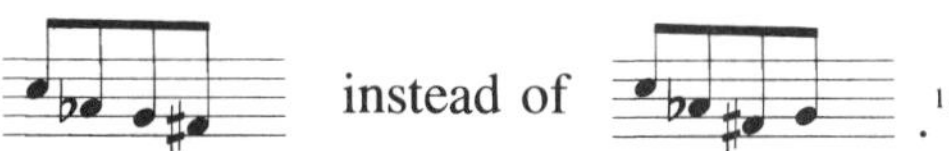

.[11]

There is a place in this lied that compels me to say every time, "very pretty!" It's at the return of the theme, which is enchanting.

Your nuns' pieces are to be copied immediately and sent to you.[12] With regard to the Fugues, I've already told you that I can't find them.[13] Upon your express wishes, I sent you everything then that you thought you might need. But now I'm stopping and won't write you anything until you write me a decent personal letter. My goodness—what do you think of me? You're treating me badly. Since you left, you've only written me once, which made me miserable on my birthday.[14] Is that right? No, Herr Cou——sin. Hensel intends to send you a personal letter with a nice sermon about your use of the color green in your pictures. In the meantime, treat this as a prescription. The Swiss painter Lory, who is here now, and painted more than 100 Swiss views in watercolor, would interest you. I will receive a picture from him, and Hensel will sketch him in return.

[1]According to Crum, *Catalogue I*, 28, Abraham dictated part of this letter to Fanny. But it is not evident where that section is located; perhaps it could be the third paragraph. Because of the uncertainty, I am treating the letter as though it were written entirely by Fanny.

[2]Fanny has acted as secretary for Abraham and written letters for him as he dictated to her.

[3]Of 27 [November 1834] (GB III 322).

[4]Felix responds in a letter to Rebecka of 2 January 1835 (NYPL): "I've scraped into a real scrape with the upheaval. Only don't take it amiss that I responded in such a professorial manner . . . but you are well aware that when I don't understand something I must take time to grasp it. By the way, it's really no misfortune that we occasionally argue in our letters. . . ."

[5]Felix wrote on 1 December 1834 (NYPL) that he has "three new *Lieder ohne Worte*, two with words, a pair of fugues, and an entire movement of *St. Paul.* He then discussed how there is no one in Düsseldorf to critique his pieces: "The cantor with the thick eyebrows and the criticism is missing."

[6]Presumably sent to Abraham as a Christmas gift. Identified through Felix's letter to Fanny of 29 November 1839 (DB 3 16) as the Fugues in D major and f minor, No. 2 and No. 5 respectively of Op. 35. The D major is the short one.
[7]Uncertain which measures; perhaps Felix changed these passages for the final version.
[8]Conceivably the quartet Fugue composed in 1827, which was posthumously joined with three other individual string-quartet movements to form Op. 81, Vier Sätze für Streichquartett. Felix also composed twelve Fugues for string quartet in 1821, but it is more likely that Fanny is referring to a more recent piece.
[9]Either the opening date or the second date of "27 December" is incorrect. Crum, *Catalogue I*, 37, lists the second half of this letter as a separate letter, dating from c. 27 Dec. 1835. Both external and internal evidence do not support the 1835 attribution, however.
[10]Both from Op. 38. Although it is conceivable that the E-flat lied could be No. 1 of the Op. 30 set, Fanny's description of the piece's lyricism applies more to Op. 38 No. 1.
[11]The notated example is m. 7 of Op. 38 No. 2, in c minor.
[12]Felix asked Fanny for them in his letter to Rebecka of 23 December 1834 (NYPL): Three Motets, Op. 39, originally composed in 1830, final version 1837.
[13]See letters 58 and 63.
[14]Felix had spent September 1834 in Berlin, and returned to Düsseldorf for the first concert of the season on 23 October. The only letter that Fanny received from Felix was the one dated 14 November 1834 (DB 3, 6).

65

Berlin, 16 January [1835][1]

That was really a tidy letter, and you are to be thanked.[2] Now I have a great deal to respond to again, and a great deal to tell you, and since the diary style of the last letter pleased you, I want to try again in all cases, even if the letter will then lie around a while longer. I'm not likely to avoid that, for the days fly by now. Herr von Sybel told us yesterday during the *Seasons* that you've had frustrations again. We're very eager for letters from you; I hope it's not so terrible, but undoubtedly unpleasant enough. You've already had to endure much frustration, and I fear the worst is that you won't remain in Düsseldorf beyond your contract. Leipzig would please me very much because of its proximity, and I'm always hoping that it will come to pass.[3] Now, just between us, I want to tell you our immediate plans. But you know how gossip flies between Berlin and Düsseldorf and can imagine how important it is to us not to let it be known there ahead of time too.[4] Therefore I entreat you to give the world the first example, as you're wont to say. We will visit you soon. Is that all right? We've written to Paris to inquire whether the exhibition will be there this year. If it is, and the negotiations don't proceed too slowly here, and the King permits it (you see, still many "ifs"), we'll go to Paris with the painting, via Düsseldorf, and visit you for a week—I look forward to it like a little child. If the arrangements concerning the picture don't work out, then it is still likely that we will go to Paris, only somewhat later—approximately in April—and stay in Weimar, Frankfurt, and Düsseldorf a few days.[5] If you are able and willing, you can meet us then in Frankfurt; we'll have a bit more time to spend with each other and can travel back together. Won't that be merry? We're then thinking of tacking on a seaside resort to our Paris trip, and so we will be away approximately 4 months in all.[6] You asked about the status of the matter concerning the picture, and here I want to tell you that the ministry demanded a recommendation from the Academy, and old Schadow said to Hensel that he would be satisfied. At the same time they had to put a value on the picture, and if they proceed honestly, Hensel will be very glad to have that burden out of the way.

The 2[0]th: It is impossible to describe the *furor* your lieder are creating here. I play them everywhere, and a pair of ladies regularly fall into a dead faint nearby. Our little artistic circle, made up entirely of irrational *fanatici parla*[ ] who love waltzes and Sebastian Bach, has, among other things, instructed me to kiss your hands in writing. Following your wishes, I want to suggest a change for that one place in your Fugue.[7]

The 22nd. When I recently wanted to start to write, Marx came over and stayed a very long time; when he had gone, I wrote the previous 3 lines. Then another visitor arrived, and then it was too late. Therefore: couldn't you transpose a line up so that they'll play *unisono* immediately after this passage?

A few notes would have to be changed then. I thought the ending could also sound a bit fuller without too much effort.[8]

Since then your last letter from Father has arrived.[9] Since I have few doubts that you will choose Leipzig, I look forward to our proximity very much. Then one can travel here for a concert a few times a year, act on a WHIM any time, and make the decision some evening and be there with you the next evening. And how venerable you (student of Plato) will look in the position and chair of old Sebastian Bach. Alas, if you'd ever made such music as I today! Let me not tear open the barely healed wound again; Blankensee played with me. ⚲ Alas—that's supposed to be a face when the young one cries out, but it's not recognizable.

[Fanny for Sebastian, with Sebastian's signature]

This is his own signature. You will be able to make out a few printed letters with some effort. One evening recently, without any instruction, he suddenly began to write, and actually much clearer and better than here above. The child possesses truly excellent capabilities, and it's doubly fortunate for him that he doesn't have parents who want to make a *Wunderkind* out of him, because I'm convinced that one would be able to do that with very little trouble.

Your birthday is fast approaching. When you live in Leipzig, the whole bunch of us will be able to bestow a whole table full of things on you. This time you're receiving an English engraving work, *Views of Granada*. These English volumes of engravings are a childish amusement of mine, although Hensel constantly reproaches me for their mere virtuosity. Nevertheless he himself enjoys them too.—We've discovered that the recommendation from the Academy was superb and unanimously authorized by everyone. We want to try to procure a copy of it.

Have you found out that a reconciliation with Droysen took place recently at a gathering at Rebecka's? To my great joy, because in part I like him personally very much, and in part because I can't stand splits with old friends in general. He will visit us again soon.

[1]Fanny mistakenly wrote 1834.
[2]Probably Felix to the family of 3 January 1835 (NYPL), or possibly a private letter I was not able to locate.
[3]See E. Werner, *Mendelssohn,* 239-54, for a summary and analysis of the transition from Düsseldorf to Leipzig; Felix's letter to Abraham of 15 January 1835 (NYPL) is also very revealing.
[4]Presumably referring to the political rivalry between the Berlin and Düsseldorf painters.
[5]Hensel's painting, *Christ before Pilate.*
[6]The Hensels did attend the exhibition in Paris and vacationed at Boulogne-sur-Mer on their return trip.
[7]In his letter of 3 January, Felix mentioned one of his recent piano lieder, and said that he composed another one, in E major (probably Op. 30 No. 3), at 12:30 the night before.
[8]The f-minor Fugue, Op. 35 No. 5; see letter 64. The passage could be an early version of mm. 77-78.
[9]Felix to Abraham of 15 January.

66

n. d. [PM 29 January (1835)]

Lafont and I have played quite a bit together recently. His playing is wondrously beautiful and seems genuine in an elegant, noble, simple manner that is dated but not outdated. But his pretensions with respect to singing are unbelievably ridiculous, and the entire man is and remains a ludicrous anachronism. He made music with Decker here yesterday. She sang his long bravura aria splendidly at sight, but then he sat down and wrote out a few romances for her and sang with her, high and low, including the runs and trills. I could hardly refrain from laughing, and I thought a hundred times of Pückler's lovely story about the English lady's trills.[1]

Farewell. I've become extremely dull and can no longer write a decent letter. In addition, I've become a lector and read the works of three different authors to three different people each day: the newspaper to Father in the morning, Shakespeare to Hensel in the afternoon, and Löhr to Sebastian in the evening. Now I want to go and fulfill one of my reader's duties.

The 27th. Since we've received a response from Paris, I can give you a more specific report on our traveling plans. Everything rests on our expenses being paid by the King, for otherwise we will be forced to remain at home and be left with our mouths watering. But that's hardly likely.

We aren't submitting anything to the exhibition in Paris this year. The pictures must be there by the 18th of February at the latest, and even if everything were in order here, that would be an impossibility. The exhibition lasts until the first of June. We're now thinking of leaving around the first of May so that we can travel leisurely with a decent stopover and still catch the end of the exhibition. Then directly to the sea resort, probably to Dieppe, and return to Paris, since, as you may know, they have a heartbreaking, nonsensical policy of exhibiting the new pictures in front of the old ones, which are kept from view during that [ ] time. We must therefore go back to view the museum, and then we're thinking about making a scenic return trip—exactly how, we ourselves don't know yet. I'm hoping now that you won't be prevented from expecting us in Düsseldorf around the beginning of May, or meeting us in Frankfurt.

[Rebecka]

[1]See letters 61, 62, and 64.

67

Berlin, 17 February 1835

I want to thank you for your 2 letters and answer the appropriate items first.[1] (Forgive me—I just saw that I started this letter on the wrong page but will nevertheless go ahead with it this way.)[2] I'm ready to send off both pieces that you want, but I haven't gotten one of them back from the copyist. With respect to publishing, I wanted to ask you whether you haven't forgotten *Wer nur den lieben Gott lässt walten,* which I like very much. And if I had to choose between the 2, I would pick *Christe du Lamm Gottes.* I especially like the first movement from *Ach Gott vom,* particularly from the unison passage to the very serious and lovely entrance into A major.[3] The aria is wonderul and beautiful, as is its text. But I must raise strong objections to the last movement—only please don't take it as a tit-for-tat action, for it certainly is not. It starts in f-sharp minor and ends in a minor, or rather C major, with few modulations in between, and yet I believe the words call for an extremely constant and steadfast musical setting in the hymn. If we were together, we could easily arrive at an understanding over it, but I'm asking you to respond to this point and tell me how much your views have changed since you wrote the piece a couple of years ago.

The aria from *Wer nur den lieben Gott* reminds me to mention that many of the solo numbers in your small sacred works exhibit a trait that I wouldn't want to label a mannerism, although I don't know exactly what to call it. The style is overly simple, which I don't find natural to you—the rhythms, for example, are short and seem somewhat childlike but also somewhat childish—with the result that the music falls short of the seriousness of the genre as well as your earnest manner in treating choruses. I mainly have the aria from the Christmas music in mind, where I can easily imagine how you arrived at your setting.[4] But the principle is applicable in many other instances. It would really be nice if we could make the selection together—if it could wait until we see each other—because

I'm not yet familiar enough with the music I don't possess to impart my wisdom to you.

Thanks for the tidy critique of my Quartet.[5] Will you have it performed sometime? You know, I find that we write each other very nice letters; perhaps they're not as merry as when Beckchen and I used to sit together and each grabbed the quill out of the hand of the other, but they're sensible, and concern everyday matters. It's fine with me if it stays this way. I wasn't able to write you last week because I was very busy practicing your Rondo *brillant*. Yesterday, Sunday morning, it was officially launched, using an accompaniment of double quartet and contrabass, with great success. Because of my enthusiasm for the piece, I was mad enough to play it twice in spite of a bad cough and a weak body.[6] I've composed a soprano aria that you would like better than my Quartet in terms of its form and modulations.[7] It's rather strictly handled, and in fact I had finished it before you wrote me about the Quartet. I've reflected how I, actually not an eccentric or overly sentimental person, came to write pieces in a tender style. I believe it derives from the fact that we were young during Beethoven's last years and absorbed his style to a considerable degree. But that style is exceedingly moving and emotional. You've gone through it from start to finish and progressed beyond it in your composing, and I've remained stuck in it, not possessing the strength, however, that is necessary to sustain that tenderness. Therefore I also believe that you haven't hit upon or voiced the crucial issue.[8] It's not so much a certain way of composing that is lacking as it is a certain approach to life, and as a result of this shortcoming, my lengthy things die in their youth of decrepitude; I lack the ability to sustain ideas properly and give them the needed consistency. Therefore lieder suit me best, in which, if need be, merely a pretty idea without much potential for development can suffice.

ich will mir al- le Mü- he ge- ben
9

Do you know *Eugene Aram*?[10] I haven't finished it yet and will give you my verdict in the next letter. Do the same and then we can see if our opinions match.—Listen, it would be a horrible blow to our plans if you weren't in Düsseldorf this spring, for you know you're one of the linchpins of our plans—*cela va sans dire*.[11] If you have to go to England, I can't object strongly (it wouldn't help anyway), but I thought you could visit Leipzig just as easily in June as in May, and if we go at all, we must be in Paris at a certain time. Only an unforeseen obstacle would prevent our trip. The only unforeseen obstacle would be the excessive delay in the business side, and that is certainly possible. Thus far three expert opinions have been demanded and given on account of the nature of the exhibition, but since things have turned out all right, the matter should be taken care of soon. Nevertheless, the ways of the cabinet are unfathomable.

But be in Düsseldorf!

Friday we will attend a *fête* at the Heydemanns, with whom we've made peace, just as with Droysen. What do you say to Louis' wedding, which the whole world is talking about? You certainly knew her before they knew each other. I find her very OUT OF THE WAY and not at all suited to Louis, for whom I would have imagined a very innocent 16-year-old *à la* Marie Mendheim. I want to advise the dear girl to consult Dr. Jüngken, but I fear that she is suffering from a total loss of vision and nothing will be able to change it. I like Louis very much. He possesses an uncommonly fine, thoroughly cultivated nature—so sensible without being cold, and proud without being offensive. On the contrary, he's gentle and charitable. There's only one thing I've never been able to understand in his thoroughly respectable soul—the supporting of relationships that are not *protégeable*, e.g. of Paul's, in which there was definitely no cause to conceal and support the concealment, and where he conducted a formal intrigue commensurate with the circumstances, but an intrigue nevertheless.[12] And now he has maneuvered himself into a relationship that I understand least of all.

I'm glad that you're enjoying *Granada*.[13] I hope to spend a fair amount of time with it in Düsseldorf. We didn't have time for it here and Hensel didn't even page through it. Your birthday must have been very nice.[14] Your concert is good, and I'm extremely glad that you're really pleased with Rietz.[15] He always seemed arrogant to me and I feared he might lead to frustration. We're doing *Gottes Zeit* and your *Ave Maria* next Sunday, if I can pull things together.[16] Should Herr Riechers or Herr Stümer have it? But just think, if I didn't get to hear your *St. Paul* on the trip! PRAY, please have both of the Caprices that you played here copied.[17] I've been performing your things continually this winter and they have been a huge success. Adieu, my dearest—the letter has once again become chatty and long. F

Hensel and Luise send their very best, and so does everyone. Beckchen is taking a lesson with Pohlke but will write soon. She is making very nice progress in drawing and is our pillar in English. To my great relief, the elevated one knows no more than I.

[1]One is to Fanny of 11 February 1835 (DB 3, 7); the other letter was not located.
[2]She began the letter on page 4 of the quarto.
[3]These are three Cantatas: *Wer nur den lieben Gott lässt walten* (May 1829 at latest; see Todd, *Review*, 447); *Christe du Lamm Gottes* (1827); and *Ach Gott vom Himmel sieh' darein* (1832). See also Pritchard, *Cantatas*.
[4]Possibly *Vom Himmel hoch* (1831), which contains two arias and one arioso.
[5]Fanny had sent it to Felix as a Christmas present. Felix's critique probably was contained in the second letter by Felix to which she is responding (not located).
[6]In a letter of 1 February 1834 (NYPL), Felix had stated that "Fanny should play it when it's published."
[7]Uncertain identity.
[8]Presumably expressed in the unavailable letter from Felix to Fanny.
[9]Uncertain identity.
[10]English novel by Edward George Bulwer-Lytton, which appeared in 1832.
[11]In his letter to Fanny of 11 February, Felix wrote that his travel plans for May and June are uncertain; he might, for instance, travel to England. But meanwhile he is determined to complete the oratorio, for which he needs at least eight weeks.
[12]Presumably in Paul's clandestine engagement to Albertine.
[13]A book of engravings Fanny and Rebecka gave Felix for his birthday. In his letter to Fanny of 11 February, Felix wrote that these engravings are the highlight of his birthday gifts this year, and he's even thinking of composing a companion piano piece.
[14]Felix described his nice birthday and mentioned how many different pieces were performed in his honor (11 February).
[15]Julius Rietz was engaged as assistant conductor in Düsseldorf. "I'm learning to value him greatly here; he is a perfectly cultivated, musical musician. The orchestra here, very raw and wild, kills itself for him, although he says stronger things to them than anyone else, and therefore he's already made vast improve-

ments in a few months through rehearsals and repetitions and scolding." ("Den lerne ich hier recht schätzen; er ist ein vollkommen durchgebildeter, musikalischer Musiker. . . . Das Orchester hier, so roh und wild es auch ist, läßt sich todt schlagen für ihn, obwohl er ihnen stärke[re] Sachen sagt, als irgend einer so daß er sie durch Probiren u. Repetiren u. Schelten seit den Paar Monaten schon ungemein verbessert hat.") This assessment appeared in Felix's letter to Fanny of 11 February, as did the program for Felix's concert the next evening.

[16]*Ave Maria* is from Drei Kirchenmusiken, Op. 23 (1830). Abraham writes to Felix on 10 March 1835 (Mendelssohn, *Briefe II*, 52-53), praising the Bach as a composition, and also the wonderful way that Fanny played the opening instrumental introduction. But he says that passages in both the middle and end of Felix's *Ave Maria* seemed too complex and thus not well suited to the Catholic spirit permeating the remainder of the piece. Rebecka had added that there were performance problems at those particular passages.

[17]Probably two of the three Piano Caprices, Op. 33: No. 1, composed 9 April 1834; and No. 3, composed 25 July 1833 (Bartlitz, *Works*, 154).

68

Berlin, 8 March 1835

I want to answer your main question without delay, dear Felix. In all likelihood Father will not be able to have an operation this year, although his condition has declined considerably in the past few months. Jüngken was with him a few days ago and expressed himself quite vaguely as to what he wouldn't do if he wanted to get temporary relief. But it's also as clear as day, and must be understood by every lamb, that Father is very far away from having an operation. Light still hurts him so that he can't stand it, but he can still find his way around the rooms and even read a few words, although with difficulty. Incidentally, the patience, kindness, and gentleness with which he tolerates this malady are indescribable: his excellent qualities come to the fore increasingly with each passing year and his character becomes more mellow and kind. We are naturally doing everything possible to help him pass the time, and one of us, with the assistance of our loyal husbands, is always at home with him in the evening.

The question of whether I will be at the music festival in

Cologne buzzes around my head constantly and I don't know how to answer it.[1] I think, however, that time will pass and advice will be forthcoming; in any case, I look forward to this trip like a child. I don't know whether I wrote you recently where Hensel's painting has gone, but, as Gans says, it is better to find out something twice than not at all. It's gone to the Garnison Church, above the choir, where a few windows have been bricked up. One will be able to view it from below at a distance, and nearby from above.[2] Hensel is very pleased with the site in every respect, and I'm glad that one of his works is finally available to the public.—I thoroughly concur in your instigation of a rule to be passed stating that no work by the conductor may be performed at music festivals. If that isn't formally stated, it would be impolite not to request some of his pieces, and not all directors are as modest as my brother, whom, out of modesty, I cannot name. Father is thinking of attending your *St. Paul* in Frankfurt, but please don't tell him that I chatted with you about it.[3] I continually hope that the piece will be performed closer to Berlin, for after we've both come home, it will be impossible for me to travel so far again. But if it were performed at Leipzig, it would be more feasible. If you come here sometime, you'll have to honor the pictures in the Garnison Church by making beautiful music. I hear that the Passion is to be given there this Easter.[4] It's a shame that you didn't select all the large Bach pieces with all the trimmings for them, because what the fools themselves have atttempted has once again sunk without a trace.

I accompanied *Don Juan* at Decker's yesterday, and both music director Grell and organist Schneider stood alongside and kept an eye on me. But I didn't give Grell any satisfaction by making a mistake. Dear God, how the man looks! And what a lout he is! When Elvira's aria started, he opened his wise mouth for the first time and said to his neighbor, "The aria has a very pretty orchestra."

Heydemann's bride, as the world puts it, is Frau von Siebold, the widow of the renowned MAN MIDWIFE. She's pretty, very flirtatious, and somewhat questionable. *Relata refero*. This much is certain: he's at her house every day, she's at his very often, and we have it on good authority that she's putting out every effort to ensnare him. She wouldn't be my choice, but that would be practically meaningless to him. We saw them here one evening, and

Albert and Minna, not he, courted her—certainly very suspicious.[5] There, you've just heard some gossip.—Dear Felix, I'm hanging myself, shooting myself, and killing myself. Your nun's pieces, which I had arranged to have copied for you about a month ago, aren't here, as if swept off the face of the earth.[6] If I sent them to you with the copies by mistake, please send them back from this excursion at your first opportunity. I now possess the nicest choir of 10 sopranos, 2 altos, 1 tenor, and 5 basses, who are supposed to sing them, *relaxa facinora*.

I just read in the *Spenersche Zeitung* about the contents of Halévy's *La Juive*.[7] Dear Felix, it's truly another remarkable step forward in artistic freedom when people can be fried in boiling oil on stage—Shakespeare never had such a new, sublime idea. When will you acquire a suitable text! Find one, for God's sake. Unfortunately, Cherubini has also suffered from Scribe's madness, particularly in the unbelievably bad ending (I'm speaking of *Ali Baba*).[8] It's really strange how opera has progressed in the last 50 years, and how, at least in my opinion, it now suffers from an excess of progress, which it totally lacked then. In *Ali Baba* the ensembles overwhelm each other. But the thickest ensemble pieces aren't even enough any more—they must all be fed with chorus as well. Its most charming quality, the driving vivaciousness, is not pleasant by the end because it hasn't been alleviated by any relaxed sections. That at least was my impression from a first hearing, but as soon as it is repeated, I'll go again and try to grasp the many sections of wonderful music. I thought it was very carefully and thoroughly rehearsed, and the orchestra sounded excellent.

Farewell, *mon ami*. The weather is so beautiful that I'll go out again for a moment.

[1]Felix is to conduct the Lower Rhenish Music Festival at Cologne between 7 and 9 June. In a letter to Fanny of 4 March 1835 (DB 3, 8), Felix wrote: "Living accommodations have been arranged, your name stands on the alto list in Cologne. Now you may not fail to appear—otherwise the entire Pentecost Committee will wring your neck." ("Dein Quartier ist bestellt, Dein Name steht auf den Altlisten in Cöln, nun darfst Du nicht mehr ausbleiben, sonst kommt Dir das ganze Pfingstcomité auf den Hals.") He then inquired into their departure date from Berlin and future plans, and hoped that Abraham would come along. The entire top floor of old Woringen's house is ready for their visit.

[2]The painting *Christ before Pilate*. It remained there until the Church burned down in 1908.

[3]*St. Paul* was originally intended for the Caecilienverein in Frankfurt.
[4]Unclear whether this is a reference to Graun's *Der Tod Jesu* or Bach's *St. Matthew* Passion, for the *AMZ* reports: "With regard to church music, we should mention the performance of Johann Sebastian Bach's Passion According to St. Matthew by the forces of the Singakademie, and Graun's Cantata, *Der Tod Jesu,* by Herr Hansmann in the Garnison Church, and on Good Friday in the hall of the Singakademie" (20 May 1835, col. 334).
[5]Albert and Minna Heydemann.
[6]See letter 64.
[7]First performed in Paris, 23 February 1835.
[8]Opera by Cherubini, first performed in Paris, July 1833; new version first performed in Berlin, 27 February 1835 (repeated 1 March 1835). See the *AMZ,* 18 March 1835, col. 183.

69

Berlin, 19 March 1835

Here's a brief piece of good news—it's highly probable that we will attend the music festival. Contrary to the reports from Paris, we found out from well-informed people here that the salon will be closed by the first of May, which makes a great deal of sense in a year-long exhibition. In that case we wouldn't make it without a terrible rush, but we could happily delay our departure a little while and spend time with you in Cologne. I wrote to Leo a few days ago and as soon as I receive his assurance, I will officially ask you to obtain living quarters for us in Cologne, and enroll me in the alto section.[1] It's a shame that we won't be able to live together, but 7 houses, defending the honor of seven cities, will quarrel over you and we might not have a place to stay. Now I'll ask you to tell me immediately when you'll travel to Cologne and begin the rehearsals; I'd like to participate as much as possible.[2] I'd also like to know whether it's probable that you'll return to Düsseldorf with us the day after the festival and spend a few quiet days with us. For there won't be much time for conversation in Cologne, but it would be nice if we could talk with each other. I must also hear *St. Paul.* I look forward to this trip just like a child, and thus can't quite verbalize the way I feel. The start with you and the Cologne festival, then to Paris, and last a seaside resort[3]—it surely won't be in the planning if the trip is a failure. May God bless this venture. It just occurred to me that we could make the return trip from Havre to Hamburg via the new steamboat. It's attractive because it takes less time, and one tends to long for home after traipsing around the world for a while. In the meantime, let's not talk about returning home before we've stepped out the door.

Your Overtures have arrived and I'm going to play through them immediately.[4] Please forgive this rather dull letter, but I literally can't think of anything except this trip and wanted to convey this news, which I believe will make you happy.

Everyone is well and sends his best.

Your Fanny

Only please don't think that I'm holding up the copy for the Crown Prince; it's at the binder's, but Breitkopf sent one to Mother and Father.[5]

[1]Felix has already done so; see letter 68.

[2]One of the principal works is Handel's *Solomon,* in which Fanny will sing in the alto section.

[3]The Hensels ended up at Boulogne on the northern coast of France.

[4]The orchestral scores to Op. 21 (*Midsummer Night's Dream* Overture), Op. 26 (*Hebrides* Overture), and Op. 27 (*Calm Sea* Overture) just issued by Breitkopf & Härtel. See Mendelssohn, *Verleger*, 40-45.

[5]Of the *Melusine* Overture; it is dedicated to the Crown Prince of Prussia, later King Wilhelm IV. See Mendelssohn, *Verleger*, 42, 44-45.

70

Berlin, 8 April 1835

Be it be at the gates of hell, let me enroll as an alto. We will arrive a few days before the music festival to participate in the last rehearsals, but I will be familiar with it already. To show how everything is in order, I was sitting at the piano yesterday and playing the first notes of the first chorus from *Solomon* when your letter arrived. You wrote how happy you are, and you can believe that I'm happy too. So obtain a place for us to stay, and although it's a nice idea to imagine us staying together, it won't work.[1] Sebastian and Minna will accompany us, but no servants.[2] It's an impossibility for us, numbering four-man strong, to approach complete strangers who are not innkeepers and say, "Kind sir, here we are." One would have to possess at least a certain degree of brashness, which unfortunately we don't possess. I consider it highly doubtful that you will placate me with your flowing herb sachet that you have honored with the poetic name of May wine, but which is in fact only a very poor copy of bishop.[3] If I finally decide I like it, however, I will own up to my mistake. But I want to tell you one thing—if you make a big fuss over me and make people there eager for my playing, I won't come. For I'm so unreasonably afraid of you anyway (and of no other person, except slightly of Father) that I actually never play particularly well in front of you, and I wouldn't even attempt to accompany in front of you, although I know I'm very good at it. I can already see how you will torment me in Düsseldorf, and how I'll worry, and blunder and miss notes, and make myself angry. Especially since people there have heard you play every piece that I could play. And now let's consider another subject carefully. Father told someone recently that he wanted to attend your oratorio performance in Frankfurt this October. If it's already certain that this performance will take place and you will remain in Düsseldorf during the preceding months of August and September, then you should invite Mother and Father to visit you and spend these months perhaps alternately in Düsseldorf and

Horchheim. I have various reasons for making this suggestion. In the first place, I believe Mother and Father will be able to enjoy themselves at their leisure. But secondly, I want to tell you in confidence that Beckchen is angry at us because we postponed our trip a bit on account of the music festival. She believes, or seems to believe as displayed by her bad mood, that this will disturb her travel plans. But since we both had the plan from the beginning to stay at a seaside resort, and one can only do that during a very limited time of the year, we had thus agreed to stay away approximately 4 weeks together. The fact that the 4 weeks have become perhaps 6 is really not of great enough import to warrant her giving up her trip. In addition, our absence falls in the summer when the days are long, the weather good, and Father can go outdoors a great deal and therefore be less disturbed by the absence of someone there to read to him. I find her complaints and mutterings directed at me so unpleasant and unjustified that they dampen my enthusiasm for the trip, as you can well appreciate. But if that particular plan comes to fruition, everything would be all right. As soon as I see [Stüler], I will speak to him about Mother, and I doubt that he will object to the journey. We hardly need to inquire about Father, because the doctors even suggested it last year, his foot is healed, and his eye condition has hardly changed. Think it over and write me soon. It's self-evident why you won't mention my second motive. We've modified our trip to the extent that we are thinking of first going to the seaside resort after Cologne and then traveling to Paris. If you have the time and inclination, then jump into the water with us.

Wagner and Pohlke will travel to Paris tomorrow for the exhibition, await us there, and return in the winter. Both young people have honorably earned the means to make this journey. In general things are very good at the atelier and *everything* has been sold from the last exhibition. Farewell, my dearest Felix. How happy I am.

[1]Felix wrote that he wanted everyone to stay together (to Rebecka, 31 March [1835], NYPL).
[2]Minna Hensel.
[3]In the same letter, Felix wrote that they will drink May wine ("Maitrank") together. Bishop is a type of mulled port spiced with orange, sugar, and cloves.

71

Berlin, 8 October 1835

I must drop a line, dear Felix, to justify myself with regard to the story of Baron Speck, for otherwise you'll curse me like the devil and consider me the worst gossip. But you know best of all from your own experience how certain things often make an unexpected impact. In the first five minutes after our arrival[1]—as you know, a period in which everybody starts to talk at once and is then interrupted in mid-sentence—I naturally started to give an account of you. I was pleased about the good things I could report, Father asked whether you had pleasant contacts and I answered in the affirmative, and he then asked whether you had been at Baron Speck's, and then your refusal note just rolled off my tongue. Later I was sorry and I asked Mother to let the matter rest and dispense with a reprimand. I didn't do the same with Father. But one week later, when I wrote down his letter to you and noticed what he was driving at,[2] I objected to what I had to put down, but as his secretary I couldn't avoid writing what was being dictated. He claimed you wouldn't notice it. Pardon! and please don't stop telling me stories any more, for in the future I'll be more careful.

Today we buried my mother-in-law. It was the first time in my life that I viewed death and all its ritual so closely.[3] There is a strong element of miraculous solemnity in seeing a life pass on and realizing that in an instant the thread is broken. But in this case there was absolutely nothing adverse or fearful; she died with full consciousness, very calmly, and desirous of release. How happy I am that we came back at the right time.

A letter from Rebecka just arrived; she will see you in 2 days. If she knew that she would miss Moscheles' concert because of it, she probably wouldn't do it.[4] But she's lucky because she can attend your concert, and I'm very sorry to have missed the Handel scores and Chopin by one day.[5] Although we may have agreed about him more readily if we had heard him together, I can't deny that his playing lacks one major component—namely power—which must be part of the total artist. His playing is not characterized by shades of grey, but rather by shades of rose, and I wish it would bite back sometimes! He is a charming man, however, and either you're mistaken or I expressed myself incorrectly if you think that his idylls haven't delighted me.[6]

Devrient asks me to tell you that he's withdrawing his order because of the Leipzig dramatic authors (what a shame!), but requests your signature.[7] The others have just come in. Say hello to Moscheles and tell him how sorry we are to have missed him.[8] Does Chopin really have a feeling for Handel's music or a *St. Paul* score?[9] Ha, ha, I don't think so.

Dear Rebecka, you will really be interested to know that I've just finished my travel stories and now you'll be coming with a fresh supply—that will be splendid. Only don't forget the reason why I look jet black, and don't let it frighten you.[10] If you see the lovely Mlle. Pensa, convey my very best wishes. I couldn't remember her name recently because I always had Herr Mecum in mind. Will you bring my laundry from Bonn?[11] Please bring the score that I left with Hauser and send my best to those dear people.

Adieu, you silly people—make sure you come home.

[1]The Hensels returned to Berlin on 27 September after their journey to the Cologne Music Festival in the spring, then to Paris for the art exhibition, then to Boulogne, and then back through various towns in Belgium. Rebecka, meanwhile, was in Ostend, but left before the Hensels passed through.
[2]Probably to Felix of 4 October 1835 (GB IV 109).
[3]She died on 4 October.
[4]The Dirichlets will stop in Leipzig and presumably miss a concert by Moscheles, which occurs on 9 October. See the *AMZ,* 21 Oct. 1835, col. 705.
[5]Before Chopin left Leipzig, Felix's scores of Handel's music had arrived; Chopin showed a genuine childlike joy in them. They consist of thirty-two large books bound in thick green leather. These volumes were a gift from the committee in charge of the 1835 Lower Rhenish Music Festival in Cologne (6 October 1835, NYPL; Mendelssohn, *Briefe II*, 63).
[6]Felix reported on Chopin in his letter of 6 October (62): "In particular, the day after I had accompanied the Hensels to Delitsch, Chopin was here. He wanted to stay only one day, and so we were together his entire stay and made music. I can't deny, dear Fanny, that I recently discovered that you don't give him enough credit in your judgments. Perhaps he wasn't really in the mood to play, which may often happen to him. But his playing delighted me anew, and I'm convinced that if you and Father as well would have heard a few of his better things, as he played them for me, you would have said the same. There is something very individualistic in his piano playing, and yet so much that is masterful, that one can call him a truly perfect virtuoso. And since I find all manner of perfection so noble and gratifying,

the day was extremely pleasant.'' Chopin performed some of his Etudes, a new Concerto, and a few Nocturnes. It is unclear which Concerto Felix means, as Chopin's works for piano and orchestra were composed well before 1835, although two were published as late as 1836.

[7]Unknown reference.

[8]Moscheles performed Felix's second collection of *Lieder ohne Worte* (Op. 30) for Felix and Schubring. Felix found his playing superb. Moscheles will stay through the second concert, when he and Felix will play Moscheles' piece for two pianos. This afternoon Felix, Clara Wieck, and Moscheles will play Bach's Triple Concerto in d minor (6 October).

[9]Felix played his oratorio for Chopin. The 32 Handel scores arrived before Chopin left and he was delighted with them (6 October).

[10]Presumably because she is in mourning for her mother-in-law.

[11]The Dirichlets were in Bonn when the Hensels met them there on 19 September; they were going to travel back to Berlin together, but the Hensels rushed to Berlin upon hearing of the serious illness of Hensel's mother. The Dirichlets stayed with Felix for a few days and then traveled to Berlin with him and Moscheles, arriving home on 14 October.

72

Berlin, 29 October 1835

My dear little Felix, day after day has passed since you left but I haven't been in the mood to write you.[1] Dear Leipzig is so close that it gives one the feeling that you might walk through the door any time, and we see people every day who have seen you, heard from you, etc. In short, it's all very nice. But it would really be wonderful if the railroad went there.[2]—Your Hauser is a dear man whom we are spoiling horribly; you know we can do that when we like a person. He will appear as *le diable* tomorrow and has to act in such a hellish manner that we are all scared with him.[3] Alas, it wasn't his choice, but we're happy for him, since it will be an explosive performance. Eichberger will appear with him; the senior Elslers, the King, and members of another court—our dear friends, the Russian officers—will attend. And may he be a great success, God willing. If only the theater were a room and the large opera a German lied: no one can sing that better than he, especially since his voice sounds magnificent with the piano. I've become totally entranced with a lied by Hauptmann, *Komm heraus, tritt aus dem Haus*. But I don't know how you can call me portly since you know Hauser, for he has consumed all the portliness in the world and left none of it for any other upstanding person.

We started a Tuesday circle here recently, which will alternate among us three siblings. The first one was very gay, and you can't imagine what crazy things they did. It was arranged that at 9 o'clock, with the tea, instructions are laid out as people dive into the refreshments. This was horribly ridiculed and criticized, everybody said they had no appetite, and it finally ended up that everybody ate everything and a few extras. Hauser laughed like an imp at all the pranks, and then we performed music, danced, etc. until midnight. Incidentally, no one was there besides parents and siblings, Hauser, a few students, and Franz Woringen, who began to loosen up and become merry.

Your music has been at the copyist a while, dear Felix.[4] I gave it to Koch, who always copied for me last year, and today a Herr Kowalsky came and said that Koch obtained a position and couldn't copy any longer, but that he had worked for you previously and I should give him the work. I followed his suggestion meanwhile and urged him to hurry as much as possible. I will send it to you as soon as I receive it.

The 30th. Today is Paul's birthday and we will go to Albertine's tonight and play children's music. We're giving him an *avant avant la lettre*, that is, a trial printing of the lovely *Tiriana* in our museum, beautifully engraved by Kaspar.[5] Hauser is thinking of coming after the theater. The poor man's depression is the worst I've ever seen. Send my best to Madame Hauser. Sebastian sends his best to Moritz and Joseph and asks them to come back soon.[6] I would love to see Moritz as a choir boy—he must look darling.

Adieu, my young man. I must go out and the weather is bad. You are truly a lazy correspondent now. Hauser pines for a letter from you as much as his portliness permits.

Your F.

[1]Felix's MS diary notebook for 1835 (MS MDM f. 6) lists the following: "15 October, Journey to Berlin; 17 October, Return . . ." ("Reise nach Berlin; . . . Zurück").

[2]See letter 74.
[3]In Meyerbeer's opera, *Robert le diable.*
[4]"And is *Medea* at the copyist, oh Fanny?" (18 October 1835, NYPL).
[5]Presumably a painting.
[6]Moritz and Joseph Hauser.

73

Berlin, 7 November [1835]

We all attended the performance of *Figaro* and I'm glad to be able to tell you that I was very pleased with Hauser. He not only far surpassed my expectations, which is nothing particularly complimentary, but performed much better than when we saw him last, in Leipzig. His voice amply fills the opera house and sounds very rich and beautiful, especially in the lower register. The high range from e-flat is not steady, however. Furthermore, he always sounds like the musically cultivated singer, particularly with accompaniment, for he superbly understands that combination and his voice is perfectly suited to it. Moreover, in my opinion they can't do without him, because then they would have to be prepared to do without opera, which they are getting ready to do, because they can't cast *Don Juan*—they have no Donna Anna. He was called to the Count yesterday but nothing was settled.[1] When he related the discussion to me, I had to laugh out loud, for it sounded so much like all your stories about him that one came out as the real thing and the other as the preparatory example. [ ].[2] Farewell. Dr. Reiter is bringing you [ ] of your things.[3] Since [ ] large library we will probably have to postpone [it] until [ ] because of the climate. Everything is organized.

[1]Count Redern.
[2]Two sentences are omitted because of numerous blotches that preclude a translation.
[3]See letter 74.

74

Berlin, 9 November 1835

I'm sorry I can't carry out all your requests right away, dear Felix. Despite all my pushing and exhortations to speed things up, I haven't been able to receive the Overture to *Medea* yet. But as soon as I obtain it I'll send it off.

Dr. Reiter will bring you the Haydn score and a piece from *Medea* with this letter. And here the passage from the A-flat major Sonata.[1]

The Overture to *Medea* was just promised to me definitely today. Should Dr. Reiter already be gone, I'll send it in the mail since I don't know whether I ought to wait for Herr Limburger. Are there many like him on your *comité*[2]?—The Steffens were here last evening. I'm delighted when people come here daily who saw you the day before. Hauser sang marvelously last evening—I've really never heard a smoother, I might say more touching, bass voice. This quality, whose sound really goes to one's heart, is much more likely to be heard in tenors. Have you ever heard his rendition of Mozart's aria, "Mentre ti lascio o figlia?"[3] This aria, as well as the lied by Hauptmann and the lied from the *Wasserträger,*[4] forms the favored repertoire. Hähnel dropped in to eat with us today. Hauser is also eating with us. When the railroad starts to go from Berlin to Leipzig, I'll invite you early in the day and you'll be here at noon to eat your favorite dish.[5] Hauser has a sweet tooth just like yours and can become ecstatic over jam. The Woringens have written about a rumor circulating in Düsseldorf that says that Immermann will go to Leipzig as director. I hope it isn't true, for it certainly would be very unpleasant for you. I can well imagine how malice would contribute to such a decision on his part.[6] Adieu, dear Felix. Reiter is coming at 11 to pick up your things, and I must still get dressed and go out. Addio. I will probably receive a letter from you this week.

[1]The A-flat Sonata could be Op. 26 of Beethoven. Grossmann-Vendrey, *Vergangenheit,* does not mention Felix performing any Haydn piece around this time. A

likely candidate, however, is *The Creation,* excerpts from which Felix would present in Leipzig during the first series of historic concerts at the Gewandhaus (1837-38; *Vergangenheit,* 161). He had also performed excerpts earlier, during his tenure at Düsseldorf. However, Felix performed other Haydn works during the 1830s, including *The Seasons,* the *Farewell* Symphony, and several Masses. See also letter 106.

[2]The board of directors of the Gewandhaus concerts in Leipzig, where Felix is now commencing his new duties.

[3]Aria for bass, K. 513.

[4]Perhaps Hauptmann's lied mentioned in letter 72, *Komm heraus, tritt aus dem Haus. Der Wasserträger* (= *Les deux Journées*) is an opera by Cherubini (Paris, 1800).

[5]The first German railroad went between Dresden and Leipzig (*ADB VII*, 235). The Leipzig-Berlin railroad was completed in September 1841 (Mendelssohn, *Briefe-L*, 157n).

[6]Felix and Immermann had not been on good terms when Felix resigned his post in Düsseldorf. See E. Werner, *Mendelssohn,* 240-43, which draws on both published and unpublished documents. Felix responds to this rumor in a letter to Fanny of 13 November 1835 (DB 3, 9): "The report that Immermann is to come here is a rumor. It's as if one claimed that Dirichlet was becoming an organist; there's no thought of it." ("Daß Immermann hieher kommen soll, ist ein Gerücht, als ob man sagte Dirichlet würde Organist; es ist kein Gedanke daran.")

75

Berlin, 18 November 1835

Thank you for your letter, dear CLOWN.[1] I'm sitting down on the piano stool, which I've placed in front of my desk, specifically to write you a good answer, and thinking warmly of you. Hauser is sitting on the sofa, has a headache, and hasn't uttered a word since yesterday. But don't tell his wife, for there is really nothing to say. At the same time, he is the foremost German hypochondriac. It's incredible what he drags along: mustard and horseradish remedies, a pinch of snuff, an egg cover on his infected nose, the egg yolk for his infected throat, apple juice in a pail, linseed tea and porridge, basins to wash his feet, and everything including the kitchen sink. One evening recently, he was bundled up to set forth with 3 bottles and pots, and I warned him not to fall into the clutches of anybody over there, for otherwise he would be teased constantly for a week. He took that to heart and had us scout the area to see whether the coast was clear. At night he falls asleep at 8 and then is either pinched or sent to bed. But when he can rouse himself from his laziness and hypochondria and is in good voice, he can sing magnificently. I started my musicales last Sunday and performed *Liebster Gott, wann werd ich sterben* and *Herr, gehe nicht ins Gericht.*[2] Hauser gave a beautiful rendition of the recitative from the Cantata, *Wohl aber dem,* to enthusiastic acclaim.[3] In general, it was very well cast, and I enjoyed it immensely. I think I'll have the audacity to play your Concerto next time and see whether it bites.[4] I certainly think that the E-flat Rondo is ten times better than the one in A; you have no power of judging the composer.[5] And now, changing the subject, I come to your list.[6] Its beauty must have dazzled you so much that you completely overlooked the following article that clearly appears on it: *8 bundles of letters*. But now I want to take the opportunity to report that there are 7 bundles of letters and an 8th is labeled "Portfolios and Miscellaneous," which we didn't want to inspect. I've locked them up in a closet where they won't see the light of day until you ask for them, but I have to confess that I rashly broke open the first of these bundles without seeing the label when I was unpacking the box. I give you my word that I didn't view any individual letters but only saw them from the outside, and immediately pushed the bundle away as if it were on fire. (Hauser is sleeping.) I still have to remark that almost no set of parts is complete among the numerous ones that we listed. Nevertheless, the list, which has no claims to beauty, is remarkable in being reasonably accurate: the Count may praise his servants. Now I find myself caught between two alternatives. When your Limburger architect or architect Limburger was here and I was supposed to play for him, I brought out the Etudes by Cramer, among others, and played a few.[7] He didn't like them, and Father even less, but I told him that if he didn't hear all of them you would kill me at Christmas. And he said that he would kill me before Christmas if I played all of them. Which death am I to die now? Sebastian recently said to Freistädtl, whom you probably still know as von Alters, "Let's have a Concerto now. Do we want one by Beethoven or Uncle Felix?"

The poor little fellow has been plagued by coughing for a long while and none of us sleeps the night undisturbed. Furthermore, hardly anybody is well now, which is probably attributable to the unusual weather.

If Pixis is in Leipzig,[8] then Mme. Camille Pleyel is here, and she interests me greatly both as a beautiful woman and a good pianist.[9] Good manners need not be learned from her, however. I'd love to come to Leipzig for your *Melusine,* if only, if only—if only there weren't so many "ifs."[10] But send me the score of your *Walpurgis.* I already have the parts here, and I'd love to have some of it performed. You also haven't sent me the pieces that I was allowed to select and you wanted to have copied for me. They are stuck away in the red case for a long time, once again, and I'll have to come to Leipzig to choose them once more because you won't remember which ones they are. Oh CLOWN, and not one word about receiving the Overture to *Medea,* which arrived one hour after Dr. Reiter's departure and followed him the day after into your arms. But say hello to Dr. Reiter.[11] He's a nice man and resembles Stengler so closely that I always run the danger of mixing them up in my head and taking one for the other when I see them. Hauser is continually taken for Hensel here; that scenario was just acted out. But he isn't sleeping any longer now because a visitor came and disturbed him; otherwise I'd be able to vouch for it.

Farewell, my dearest. Hensel sends his best. He sent me the color sketch of *Miriam* for my birthday and I'm extremely delighted with it.[12] Overall I received very lovely gifts, among others, a gorgeous F-major Andante by Beethoven that I didn't know.[13] You probably played it in Düsseldorf.

[1]To Fanny, 13 November 1835 (DB 3, 9).

[2]The Cantatas BWV 8, BWV 105.

[3]BWV 139.

[4]No. 1 in g minor, Op. 25.

[5]The E-flat is the Rondo *brillant,* Op. 29; perhaps the one in A is lost, or is a work by another composer.

[6]Fanny sent Felix an inventory of his books, music, and miscellaneous personal items (undated; GB IV 204). Felix wrote Fanny on 13 November: "The Catalogue made me laugh. . . . But is the Catalogue correct, Fenchel? Or is it more beautiful than accurate? Because, among other things, I don't see all my letters, organized in various packets, which were in the box. Didn't you find them there, and what have you done with them? Still water runs deep." ("Der Catalog hat mich noch zu lachen gemacht. . . . Ist denn aber der Catalog auch recht genau, Fenchel? Oder ist

er mehr schön, als wahr? Denn ich vermisse darin unter andern alle meine Briefschaften, in verschiednen Pakets geordnet, die in der Kiste waren. Habt Ihr die nicht darin gefunden, u. was habt Ihr damit gemacht? Tiefe Stille herrscht darüber im Wasser.")

[7]Limburger was in Leipzig with Felix for an hour (to Rebecka, 13 November 1835, NYPL). In Felix's letter to Fanny on the same day, Felix wrote that Limburger spoke about Fanny's piano playing: "He said you should be a touring artist, that you would play circles around the others."

[8]"Pixis is here now. . . . If I said that he made a good impression on me, I'd have to be lying. A true picture of a speculating, avaricious musician—therefore a sad one. One can only converse with him about financial matters, financial plans, and financial losses . . ." ("Pixis ist jetzt hier. . . . Wenn ich sagen sollte, daß er mir einen guten Eindruck gemacht hätte, so müßte ichs lügen. Ein rechtes Bild eines spekulirenden, geizigen Musikers—also ein trauriger. Er ist auf kein ander Gespräch zu bringen, als auf Geldsachen, auf Geldpläne, u. Geldverluste . . .") (to Fanny, 13 November).

[9]In 1835 she separated from her husband, after four years of marriage.

[10]On 23 November (16 November 1835, NYPL).

[11]Felix wrote that he arrived in Leipzig and was very enthusiastic about Father (to Fanny, 13 November).

[12]Wilhelm was working on the painting *Miriam's Song of Praise after Crossing the Red Sea,* completed in 1836. It hung in Buckingham Palace as of 1923.

[13]Perhaps the Andante in F published in Vienna in 1805, and later given the catalogue number WoO 57 (*NGD II*, 400).

76

Berlin, 11 December [1835]

We haven't heard a word from you, dear Felix! How are you, what are you doing? We're hoping for news through Hauser, who brought you the latest news about us, but we haven't found out anything.

Today will be difficult for you, as it is for us.[1] It's gone from a happy day of celebration to a solemn *memento mori*. We had nothing but happiness, and nothing can deprive us of those memories. "Honor my memory." We are indeed honoring his memory and will attempt to do it in such a way that we always hold his example before us, and that means conduct ourselves as he would have wished.

Rebecka is sleeping in front for the first time and is very busy with moving. Mother wants to write you a few lines herself. How did David's first appearance go?[2]

Farewell, dearest brother, and write soon. Paul will travel to Leipzig on Wednesday. If the cold weather persists, you will both suffer.

[Lea]

[1]It is Abraham's birthday; he died on 19 November.
[2]David will become the concertmaster of the Gewandhaus orchestra for the duration of a year; see letter 81.

77

Berlin, 5 January [1836]

Mother didn't take me along yesterday so I have to go out by myself and see whether I can pick up the mail.

The new year has started off badly for us: two changes in cooks (were you or had you a wife you would know what it means to have three cooks in three days), a sick husband (Hensel lay in bed on the 2nd), and general domestic chaos. May God grant us some peace now—we can use it.

I've diligently played through the *Te Deums* and made profound observations that are more readily understandable in light of the dates on each piece—how the earlier ones seem far more old-fashioned and formally awkward, the later ones freer and more Handelian, especially the *Dettingen*.[1] I very much like "TO THEE ALL ANGELS CRY ALOUD." But I don't know all the pieces yet and will write you about them later.

The 9th. When one of my letters lies around for 2 days, I usually find it so incredibly stupid that I don't send it off. However, when I think about it, I realize that I will hardly write a better letter on the 9th than on the 5th, and if it then lay around until the 11th, the whole cycle would start over again, and so on.

We're planning a get-together with the Devrients and

Woringens to sing *St. Paul* the day after tomorrow. Hauser is mired in hypochondria and dirt, and now I don't believe that his stay has been pleasant for us—he's too odd. Two months ago Father delighted in his singing. Do you like it also? Father's memory wafts over me so often, like that of someone who is on a trip, that I'll think to myself that I haven't seen him in a long time, and then the truth first sets in.

If only you were here! I become very melancholy when I think that we'll be apart indefinitely. I'd love to visit you in Leipzig but fear that it won't happen this winter. I'm going to break off this letter again and be annoyed at myself tomorrow all over again.

The 12th. Today I want to send off this piece of paper blindly, without reading it again. I'm not completing any decent letters, although Beckchen thinks everything around me looks like the home of an aesthetic woman. My living room is truly pretty with its lovely engravings, instrument, and desk. But it doesn't quite feel like home because you aren't familiar with it, and it's necessary for you to know everything in my life and approve of it. Therefore I'm also very sad, truly not out of vanity, that I haven't been able to be grateful to you in such a long time for liking my music. Did I really do it better in the old days, or were you merely easier to satisfy?[2]

Our *St. Paul* was postponed again until tomorrow. Of the three persons required, four couldn't come today. Since I've received it from the copyist, I play it with joy and edification. Father's presence is always nearby—as though I could play it for him. Addio. Be well, say hello to David, and write soon.

[1]It is uncertain how many pieces entitled *Te Deum* Fanny is discussing, but they are probably all by Handel. The *Dettingen Te Deum* was first performed in 1743; *NGD VIII*, 121, lists four earlier pieces by Handel entitled *Te Deum.*

[2]Felix's lengthy response appears in a letter to Fanny of 30 January 1836 (DB 3, 10; Mendelssohn, *Briefe II*, 71): "I deny everything and assure you that I have cause to be grateful for everything you create. When two or three successive things don't please me to the same degree as other works of yours, I think the reason lies no deeper than the fact that recently you've written less than in earlier times, when if one or two lieder, and then another, quickly made and hastily written down, might not have pleased me, we reflected little on why we liked them less, but rather just had a good laugh. Here I cite *In die Schönheit nicht, o Mädchen,* and many others in the *prima maniera* of our master that raised an uproar. Then came the beautiful ones again, and so it is now as well, only that they can't follow each other so quickly, because now you must often think of other things than creating

beautiful lieder.—And that is probably all to the good.—But if you think that your recent pieces are somehow inferior to your earlier ones, you are totally mistaken, and I know no better lied of yours than the English one in g minor, or the close of the *Liederkreis*, and so many other recent ones, and you also know that there used to be complete *books* of yours that I liked less than others of yours, because, true to my sign, I'm a Schuhu, and belong to the wild nation of brothers. But you know that I like *all* your things and especially those that have grown so close to my heart. You should write me promptly and say that you do me an injustice when you consider me a tasteless person, and that you won't do it again." In a letter to Madame Kiené of 1 June 1835 (LC), Felix wrote that Fanny was more prolific before her marriage. He praises her enormous musical talents, yet adds that it is good for her to be tending to domestic concerns.

78

Berlin, 26 January 1836

My dear Felix, I hope you won't be angry if your request for a prompt dispatch is exceeded by *one* day, because you will still have it in time and even a day early.[1] Tomorrow, Wednesday, I'm going to mail it, Friday it will be there, and Saturday you need it, as you've written. You're familiar with the kindness of our local copyist. He's had the score for 2 weeks and, upon repeated inquiries, always claims that it will be ready soon. But when I called for the music yesterday, I found out that he had just started. Due to my awful scolding and grumbling, he will work through the night and be finished early tomorrow, but ready or not, I will keep my promise and send it off tomorrow. Many thanks for *Melusine*—it will give us many hours of pleasure.[2] Your little winter scene is very pretty and shows great progress. Make one for me sometime. Rebecka is having great fun with floral painting and has made remarkable progress for so short a time. I'm reading English fluently, writing down words and memorizing them. I'm also trying to bolster my musical memory, which has fallen into abysmal decay, and am methodically learning music by heart. We want to celebrate your birthday with *St. Paul* and perhaps take something from *Nobis*.[3]

Sebastian, who must spend the entire winter indoors, has only gone out twice, but today the weather is so lovely that I want to take him out for his first walk. Thank God he's much better again. But since the sun doesn't wait, I'll say addio and write more next time.

I've just finished taking Mother and Sebastian for a walk. Since your edition will probably not be published for a long time, please be so good as to make a copy of whatever is finished and send it to me.[4] Mother wants to send it to us so that we may have the pleasure of hearing it earlier. And now farewell.

[Rebecka]

[1]In his family letter of 1 January 1836 (NYPL), Felix said he's working on the oratorio and wants to finish it soon, and therefore asks Fanny to have the piano version copied immediately, for he might need it right away. But she can still hold on to it for two more weeks.
[2]Probably the four-handed version soon to be published, which Felix mentioned in his letter of 20 January 1836 (NYPL). The arrangement was done by Czerny. See Mendelssohn, *Verleger*, 47-48.
[3]Felix's Psalm 115, *Non nobis Domine,* composed on 15 November 1830 for Fanny's birthday. It was just published by Simrock with German text as *Nicht unserm Namen, Herr* (Op. 31).
[4]Of *St. Paul,* whose completion was aimed at the piece's premiere on 22 May.

79

3 February [1836]

Dear Felix, may God keep you, and everything else we possess that's good, and bestow upon you His best blessing.[1] You know what I wish you the most now, and may you be successful, like so many things in your life; Father always wished it with all his heart.

You'll find Schiller in the Berlin package, and one is a memento from us. These one-volume editions are handy on trips. Of course you won't compose *Freude schöner Götterfunken* from it—at present I wouldn't know what else—but just as little would I have imagined that you would make such splendid music from the Druids as you did.[2] Thus I know very little of what slumbers in a volume of poetry.[3]

Do you know a Cantata by Bach in E major that Hauser has: *Wohl dem, der sich auf seinen Gott recht kindlich kann verlassen?* It is the old chorale of the blind hurdy-gurdy man on the New Promenade.[4] If you don't know it, I'll have the first chorus copied and sent as a belated birthday gift. I find it glorious; it is thus one of the [ ] in the country.

Hensel sends his greetings and best wishes, Sebastian likewise. He is now, thank God, completely well, as we all are. We haven't been able to say that much in a long time.

Farewell, and also write me sometime. Hensel made a drawing of me that Madame Kiené requested, which has provoked great partisan battles in the house again.[5] Dirichlet didn't recognize it, and Paul is very angry about it; everybody else, on the other hand, finds it very beautiful and a good likeness. Adieu for the second time.

Think of your

Fanny[6]

[1]Felix's birthday is 3 February.

[2]A reference to *Die erste Walpurgisnacht,* based on Goethe's poem of c. 1799.

[3]Felix thanks them for their gifts in a letter to Lea (undated; postmark blurred, but month is February; NYPL).

[4]It is the Cantata BWV 139. The chorale in the first movement is "Mach's mit mir, Gott, nach deiner Güt," in the sopranos.

[5]Presumably one of the ten listed in Lowenthal-Hensel, *W. Hensel*, 28-29.

[6]Approximately one-half of the last page is cut from the manuscript, possibly containing Lea's writing.

80

Berlin, 4 February 1836

I want to respond to your invitation to write you a real cantor letter abounding in fifths and nitpicking, but I won't.[1] Yesterday we sang the numbers that we have from *St. Paul* for the second time,[2] and entreat you to send some more right away, especially the beginning. Thus far it's gone very well. On the whole I wouldn't want to abandon anything: the pieces are well ordered and follow each other nicely and naturally. My criticisms only concern details. And in order for you to see immediately that the judgments are presented subjectively as mine and not, *à la* the reviewers, as *ours*, I'm telling you directly as an upstanding person how edifying it is that Devrient and I disagree diametrically over one passage. Whereas I can't stand it, Devrient says to himself with inner fervor, each time he hears it, "Exquisite!" Now guess which one it is. A few of the recitatives (in which the strength of the entire work resides) are really pointless or too modern. The first one and the following chorus, chorale and second recitative are grand and beautiful and I wouldn't want to omit any of them.[3] The entire first part of the aria in b minor, from "Herr, thue meine Lippen auf" through the *tempo primo*, is marvelous.[4] I find the return of the words weak. The ending is again very lovely. The start of the following recitative is very nice—so serene and cheerful and calm, and it's one of my favorite passages through "denn siehe, er betet."[5] I find the subsequent text through *tempo primo* too trivial and modern. Don't you think *Allegro con moto* too quick a tempo for this passage?[6] The next piece contains the passage about which Devrient and I disagree: the entrance of the altos with the text "denn der Herr hat es gesagt," with the sopranos in imitation 2 bars later.[7] Together with the accompaniment, this passage doesn't really seem stern, and I think you invented the theme merely to serve as a countermelody to the first. Later the theme sounds lovely with the accompaniment, as well as when it's alone and followed by the entrances of the other voices. Only this double entrance on the same notes doesn't sit well with me.

And finally, I still want to express my opposition to a passage in the last soprano recitative:[8] the musical treatment of "und ging hin und liess sich taufen" doesn't measure up to the importance of the text.

And now I'm finished.

Hauser and Paul also made a great fuss because they found the ending of the last fugue with the high a and the six-four chord too modern.[9] But I told them in no uncertain terms that it wouldn't be changed because it was so Felix-like. Moreover, the soloists have a high tessitura and the choruses are very light. We all take great pleasure in the work and are comforted that Father had the opportunity to hear some of it in Düsseldorf,[10] but I'll always be sorry that I didn't participate in it.

The 5th of February. Yesterday we went to a concert for the first time and heard *Israel in Egypt,* where I had to swallow my anger again. How this rogue has dragged down the Singakademie as well as some lovely talent![11] Not one single vocal entrance in the entire work was precise, and only someone who already knew the piece could have the vaguest idea of what was going on. I was constantly forced to think about the organ and the choruses in Cologne. And now we have the Rungenhagen trombone that is obbligato in every piece. He added 2 horns and timpani to Miriam's song. By the way, it's really terrible that Lenz, that delightful singer, has lost her voice entirely. You probably remember how she sang the Queen of the Night, yet now she reaches f-sharp with great effort and can't make g. I could hardly believe that it was the same singer.

Along similar lines, it just struck me: do you think Handel himself played the organ in his own pieces? Because the written-out organ parts are not there, an organist would probably have filled in notes based on the numbers, unless it were Handel himself.

I wish I could have heard your Mozart Concerto.[12] For the past 7 years—i.e. since you reached your artistic maturity—we haven't lived together and I've hardly ever heard you play in public. And if we hadn't visited you in Cologne last summer, I wouldn't have had a view of your public life. And meanwhile here sits an ape who spoils the 6 concerts he plays each year despite the best forces and an unlimited number of rehearsals.[13] Phooey!

Finally, I'd like to turn the conversation back to myself, even though it's unpleasant to act as one's own advocate. We are certainly not in the habit of beating around the bush. You said in Leipzig that I shouldn't compose sacred music any longer since my talents don't lie in that area. Since my return—or rather for the past week, to be exact—I've played through many of my old sacred pieces, and must say in advance that a person evaluating the fruits of his earlier labors is the harshest judge imaginable. Many of them, even most of them, bored me so much that I had to force myself to finish playing them. But many of them—for example, the aria "O dass ich tausend Zungen hätte,"[14] and a few choruses and recitatives from the so-called *Choleramusik*[15]—pleased me so much that, as foolish as it may sound, I felt exuberant. For I consider it a kind of test when one is satisfied with one's things again after a long time has passed and they have been totally forgotten. Meanwhile, what you've said has fallen on deaf ears, and I've become mistrustful, although I generally believe I have more skill for it now than previously, and would have undertaken the revision of a few pieces if your interdict hadn't deterred me.

On your birthday the day before yesterday, Hensel had a nice surprise for me: the figure of a lad in the background of the picture he's painting who is merrily blowing his horn and resembles you with his long brown hair. I believe the picture will be very lovely. He's utilized all of Father's suggestions.[16]

Adieu. This was another thoroughly trivial letter. Write me again soon.[17] Will you come here after the concerts are over?

[1]In his letter to Fanny of 30 January 1836 (DB 3, 10; Mendelssohn, *Briefe II*, 72), Felix asked her to critique *St. Paul:* "And then not a word about *St. Paul* and *Melusine* in this letter or the previous one, as one colleague should write to the other—i.e., observations on fifths, rhythm, and voice leading, on conception, counterpoint, *etc. animalia.* You should have done so, and should still do it, because you know how much it matters to me, and any possible reprimands concerning *St. Paul* would come at the right time." Felix had received detailed comments earlier from Abraham on the fashioning of the text—e.g. on the division of the text into two rather than three parts, and whether there existed the implicit understanding that Saul was present at the stoning of Stephen. Abraham's comments appeared in a letter of 17 December 1834 (GB III 334) as dictated in Fanny's hand. Felix's response to these points was contained in his letter to Rebecka of 23 December 1834 (NYPL; also excerpted in Mendelssohn, *Briefe II*, 46-47). Fanny, in a letter to Klingemann of 4 February 1836 (S. Hensel, *Familie*

II, 2), says how much Abraham liked the work, how he liked St. Stephen's sermon and the following pieces, and how he possessed the ability to critique music.

[2]From her comments, Fanny had the last half of Part I: Nos. 13-21 (Nos. 17-25 in the first version). For a detailed presentation of the various compositional stages of *St. Paul*, see Kurzhals-Reuter, *Oratorien*, 45-68, 97-114.

[3]Probably referring to "Und als er auf dem Wege war" (No. 17; No. 13 in the final version); the chorus "Mache dich auf, werde Licht" (No. 18; No. 14); the chorale "Wachet auf" (No. 19; No. 15); and the second recitative "Die Männer aber" (No. 20; No. 16).

[4]Part of the bass aria "Gott sei mir gnädig" (No. 21; No. 17). "Herr thue meine Lippen auf" in the final version is near the end of the *Allegro maestoso* section.

[5]"Es war aber ein Jünger" (No. 22; No. 18). Parts of this music omitted in the final version (Kurzhals-Reuter, *Oratorien,* 114). The passage through "denn siehe, er betet," at least in the final version, is for soprano.

[6]Probably referring to the last ten measures of this number, which in the final version are marked *Poco animato* = 84.

[7]Aria con coro—"Ich danke dir, Herr," bass solo; the chorus "Der Herr wird die Thränen" (No. 23; No. 19). "Denn der Herr hat es gesagt" occurs four bars after letter "C" in the final version: the altos begin, and 2 1/2 bars later the sopranos enter with the same text, but with a countermelody, while the basses entered in exact imitation two bars after the altos. Fanny implies that at least in the version she saw, the sopranos—not the basses—imitated the altos after two bars. Perhaps Fanny's comments contributed to the revision here.

[8]Part of No. 24 in the first version, and modified in No. 20 in the final version, where this text has been divided; No. 20 begins with "Und Ananias ging hin," continues with a tenor recitative, and goes into an *Allegro molto* orchestral section, and then the soprano recitative recurs and includes the text "und stand auf, und liess sich taufen. . . ."

[9]Probably referring to the final cadence, the third measure from the end of the chorus, "O welch eine Tiefe" (No. 25; No. 21), which ends Part I.

[10]Probably when Felix's parents returned with him to Düsseldorf after the Lower Rhenish Music Festival in Cologne from 7-9 June 1835. The Hensels attended the festival but went to Paris for the exhibition.

[11]Fanny lodges the same complaints about this performance and the lamentable decline in the Singakademie, in a letter to Klingemann of 8 February 1836 (S. Hensel, *Familie II*, 3).

[12]Felix performed the Mozart d-minor Concerto (K. 466) at a concert on 29 January 1836 at which he also conducted three pieces. In his letter of 30 January 1836 he notated and described the cadenza he used in the first movement.

[13]Presumably Möser.

[14]Aria in A major, No. 4 from her *Lobgesang,* text by Johann Mentzer. This aria is in a separate autograph, "dedicated to Karl Klingemann from Paul Mendelssohn Bartholdy, 24 July 1831," MA Ms 16, 3 pages (Sirota, *Hensel*, 313).

[15]Fanny had written in her Tagebuch on 1 January 1832: "I haven't spoken at all about Father's birthday [11 December], which we celebrated with my *Cholera* Music. It went very well, Schätzel sang magnificently, and the most delightful

result is that Father made up with Marx." ("Von Vaters Geburtstag habe ich noch gar nicht gesprochen, der bei uns durch meine Cholera Musik gefeiert wurde. Es fiel sehr gut aus, die Schätzel sang wunderhübsch, u. das erfreulichste Resultat war, daß Vater sich mit Marx versöhnte.") Parts for the Cantata, copied by Fanny and Rebecka, are in MS MDM c. 58.

[16]Presumably *Miriam's Song of Praise after Crossing the Red Sea.*

[17]"Dear Fanny, I'd like to have thanked you individually for your lovely letter of review, but I'm not in the mood to write and am inserting my thanks here" (18 February 1836, NYPL).

81

Berlin, 20 February 1836

I prefer to send you the music right away, dear Felix, since you've promised to send it back to me soon.[1] Two weeks are almost too short for the copying of parts, people coming together, etc. But keep your promise. And also ask for the Rondo in E major.[2] Has it been printed already in the Paris Album? Rebecka and I are playing the Overture to *Melusine* with much expression;[3] it would even be worth the trouble for you to come to Berlin to hear it. I'm sincerely happy over David's engagement, both for his sake and yours. I believe it will be an additional reason for you to continue in your position.[4] Send him my warmest regards and tell him that he is still the old favorite. A few days ago at the museum, I was moved when I saw the picture again that inspired the name "house-Turk" which we gave him many years ago. Ah, the past!

So will you go to Düsseldorf? If only I could go there! Your story of the Polish Jew is very good.[5] The rascal is truly a phenomenon—he's creating a furor here. If I could only comprehend how wood on wood can yield tone.[6] Take care.

[Lea]

[1]Felix wrote on 18 February 1836 (NYPL) concerning the music of *St. Paul:* "But don't be angry with me if I make a request here that bears similarity to the dog presented as a gift in Shakespeare's *As You Like It.* To wit, I'll need the entire first part of my piano version *here* in 2 weeks, and since my copy goes to Simrock the

day after tomorrow, I'll have no other one here but yours (I'll receive the first half of the first part tomorrow from the copyist). I therefore ask you to lend me yours, since I absolutely need it, and the question is now whether I should send you for 2 weeks the part of the copy I'll receive tomorrow and whether you then want to send everything back together, or whether you cannot use it for such a short time and would rather send me the second half (which you have there) now. You are to have everything back (and the second half as well) in a month. But please send me an immediate reply.'' See the correspondence between Felix and Simrock in Mendelssohn, *Verleger*, 199-201.

[2]Rondo *capriccioso,* Op. 14, published in 1827.

[3]See letter 78.

[4]Felix announced that David will be the concertmaster in Leipzig for a year; he is very happy about it and says that David has many friends there (18 February).

[5]''I'm curious if you all liked Gusikow as much as I. There was a splendid scene here at his concert. I went out to speak with Gusikow in the room where he was staying and to give him my compliments. Schleinitz and David wanted to go in also, and a whole troop of Polish Jews marched behind and wanted to hear the compliments. But when we came to the chamber all the Polish Jews pressed forward so quickly that David and Schleinitz remained last, and then the doors were closed in front of their noses, and they were completely still and awaited the compliments that Gusikow was to receive. But I could hardly keep from laughing at how the entire chamber was crammed full of the bearded fellows and how both were shut out. By the way, I haven't been so entertained at a concert in a long time, for he is a true genius'' (18 February; Mendelssohn, *Briefe II*, 76-77).

[6]He uses a folk-type instrument constructed with a wood bar.

82

Berlin, 1 June [1836]

[Rebecka]

Here we are, dear Felix! Back so soon that they thought we were our ghosts. We arrived on Monday, 2 nights ago, at 8:30 P.M.[1] I found Beckchen QUITE CHARMING, thank God, and she doesn't get tired listening to other people tell their news. How lovely it was in Düsseldorf and how I can still hear *St. Paul* ringing in my ears! As soon as Rebecka is well enough to participate, I'll have it performed, to the delight of everyone in the house. This letter will probably arrive simultaneously with you in Frankfurt.[2] Say hello to everyone we know, and write soon. Also, I'm very interested in hearing about the further progress of *St. Paul.*[3]

[1]After attending the premiere of *St. Paul* in Düsseldorf on 22 May 1836.
[2]Felix will travel to Frankfurt on Saturday, the 4th (1 June 1836, NYPL).
[3]Approximately 3/4 page after this is excised from the manuscript.

83

Berlin, 28 June 1836

I haven't gotten around to writing you in such a long time, dear Felix, that today, Tuesday the 25th of June, at 5 P.M., I'm sitting down in the garden expressly for that purpose, and with that will get started. Actually I don't have anything to write because it's fairly quiet here at home and will become even more so when Beckchen departs on her trip in a week. Your letter from Frankfurt was QUITE CHARMING and delightful.[1] Rossini, who heard the b-minor Mass, cuts an unforgettably comic figure for me.[2] A few days ago I wrote almost the same thing to Klingemann that you wrote me about Eckermann.[3] The book holds one's interest until the end, but I do find that Eckermann's personal, simplistic observations become more laughable each time they're repeated. It's inconceivable how anybody who had enough judgment to write this way about Goethe later didn't have enough intellect to understand the superficiality of these *raisonnements*. Hasn't it struck you how many things appear in the book that Father himself used to say? As I read each line I can't help thinking what Father would have said about it and how he would have enjoyed the numerous coincidences.

I recently held a performance of the first part of *St. Paul* and will undertake the 2nd part shortly. But let me know how things stand with respect to its publication, and when it will appear.[4] In addition, please send me the metronome markings for "siehe wir preisen selig,"[5] and Paul's aria, "Herr sey mir gnädig."[6] Paul and I have been arguing about the tempos. I'm truly sorry that I didn't know the entire oratorio before Düsseldorf. There exists a special charm in first becoming acquainted with a work when it's finished, but it's even more enjoyable if one knows every note in advance. But I wish you could hear Decker sing the soprano arias sometime—she did a splendid job.

Sebastian received a bird and a crossbow for his birthday and promptly did so well with the shooting that he [shot down] the bird the next day. So yesterday he played boccia with the adults for the first time and did quite well.[7] He exhibits considerable skill and grace in physical exercises now and thus we like to watch when he waters, hoes, and cultivates his little garden. The sweet little chubby one[8] is his faithful helper. The boy has a very nice disposition and it's really cute when he calls Sebastian "dear friend" or "dear brother." The weather is splendid today, one of the nicest days in a long time. We've been suffering from the most unpredictable moods of wind and weather. Klingemann, the traitor, hasn't written yet—have you heard anything about him? Certain Berlin joys await you and I must prepare you so that the surprise doesn't shock you: you will see Herr Rex in Frankfurt and Herr von Varnhagen in Scheveningen!

Send my best to Aunt Schlegel, the Veits, Hiller, and André,[9] whose good face I probably would love to see again. It's really peculiar that you found a resemblance to him, because you decidedly resemble Mother's side of the family rather than Father's.[10] I'm very glad that Sebastian inherited the shape of his skull. [ ] It often hits me deeply what a heavy responsibility one assumes in raising a child. In that regard I can do no better than closely emulate the model of our parents, although some things of course are not imitatable and the cases are different. May God help us—and He will, according to Father's proverb, if we help ourselves.

Farewell, dearest Felix, and write soon. What will you work on after the editing of *St. Paul*? Won't you take up the earlier Symphonies again?

This evening there will be a grand *fête* at Rebecka's.

[1]Letter postmarked 14 June 1836 (NYPL), but incorrectly dated 14 July 1836 by Felix at the head of the letter. The incorrect date of 14 July appears in Mendelssohn, *Briefe II*, 81-84.

[2]Felix saw Rossini at Hiller's house. Hiller has recently become fond of people like Auber, Bellini, and Meyerbeer (Mendelssohn, *Briefe II*, 83, substitutes Rossini for

Meyerbeer), and Felix was glad to have the opportunity of influencing him to change his views. Felix has promised Rossini to have the Bach b-minor Mass performed for him, and in general liked and admired him for his warmth and geniality (14 June).

[3]*Eckermanns Gespräche mit Goethe*. Felix expressed his views in his letter of 14 June. In a letter of 11 June 1836 (S. Hensel, *Familie II*, 11), Fanny wrote Klingemann that she just received the first volume of the Eckermann book. In a later letter, incorrectly dated 7 June in S. Hensel, *Familie II*, 11, Fanny wrote that she has read most of Volume I and is very pleased with it: the best view of Goethe thus far in print. "What I find particularly striking is the similarity with many opinions that Father used to utter. He would have been absolutely delighted with it had he known it. . . . The agreeable little book holds one's interest through the end."

[4]The first public performance had taken place on 22 May 1836 in Düsseldorf. Typically, Felix undertook extensive revisions after the premiere. The full score is published by Simrock in January 1837, and also by Novello. For Felix's correspondence with the former see Mendelssohn, *Verleger*, 190-211.

[5]Andante con moto, ♩ = 80 in the final version (No. 10).

[6]= "Gott sei mir gnädig" (No. 17 in the final version); Adagio, ♩ = 88. "Herr" is probably Fanny's error.

[7]A popular lawn game imported from Italy.

[8]Presumably referring to his cousin, little Walter Dirichlet. There is also the more remote possibility that "Der kleine gute Dicke" refers specifically to some boy with the last name of "Dicke."

[9]Most likely Johann Anton André, but could be one of his several sons.

[10]Perhaps Fanny means that Felix is taken to resemble Philipp Veit, although her phraseology implies that Felix resembles André. Felix discussed Veit at some length in his letter of 14 June, but did not mention any physical family resemblance.

84

Berlin, 30 July 1836

It doesn't occur to me to be angry or request a few personal letters, dear Felix. I certainly would have already replied to your previous letter,[1] but when I sat down earlier, took out some paper, picked up the quill, and considered what I should write, I didn't know anything, just like Humboldt's monkeys, who can't speak because they have nothing to say. But the manifold delights in your most recent letter[2] provide me with things to write about even though there's nothing to report here. Among other things, one of the most enjoyable turned out to be one of those little coincidences that occur more often as we get older and which I don't care to ascribe to chance. You are reading Goethe's biography for the first time since childhood, and I've been engaged in the same activity for several weeks.[3] Eckermann's book no doubt prompted this reading, but there may be several thousand people reading that book but not Goethe's biography afterwards. I was also thinking that if I ever return to Frankfurt, I must become acquainted with that city in connection with his life. I'm reading the 4th volume to Hensel now, just as I did with the Eckermann.

Furthermore, your lovely young lady from Frankfurt arouses my interest not inconsiderably.[4] You wouldn't believe how I wish for your marriage; I sincerely feel that it would be best for you. If I were Sancho[5] I'd cite an entire list of maxims to hasten a favorable decision: "nothing ventured, nothing gained"; "fortune favors the brave"; "grab the bull by the horns"; "strike while the iron is hot"; and many others that are not suitable here. It really sounds as though you're serious this time, and if you fall in love with Doris Zelter in the Hague now and nothing comes of it, I will be highly DISAPPOINTED. By the way, it just occurred to me that all your romances (see Rosalie Mendelssohn's unpublished works)[6] have taken place away from home, and so I've never seen you in the midst of a courtship, and yet I'm very curious about this area of your life. These are all bad jokes, but in all seriousness, I would very much like you to get married.

I held two very pleasant rehearsals of *St. Paul* while Decker was here. But now everybody is scattered in all directions and so I think the event will have to be postponed until the fall. I'm truly sorry that you've had such a tough time with the piano arrangement; had you given me even one part of the job, I would have gladly worked hard on it.[7] Furthermore, I am liking the oratorio more and more as I know it better. The weak passages, or those that appear so to me, which we have discussed, are few in number, and I'm very curious about the most recent changes.[8] For example, have you really omitted the first chorus as well?[9] I hope not "Der du die Menschen"—that aria has grown on me.[10]

The local music scene is more slovenly than ever. I'd love to know why they engaged Hauser, since he never performs. At Hensel's request I've started performing again on Sundays, but the Ganzes are not here, and I'm really too spoiled to let myself be accompanied by beginners.[11] As the strict taskmaster has ordered, I've continued to compose piano pieces, and for the first time have succeeded in completing one that sounds brilliant.[12] I don't know exactly what Goethe means by the demonic influence, which he mentioned very often near the end, but this much is clear: if it does exist, you exert it over me.[13] I believe that if you seriously suggested that I become a good mathematician, I wouldn't have any particular difficulty in doing so, and I could just as easily cease being a musician tomorrow if you thought I wasn't good at that any longer. Therefore treat me with great care.

Just as there is a Young Germany, there is also a boring Germany that Beckchen is finding in Eiger, and an odious Germany that you are discovering in Scheveningen. Madame Robert and Herr von Varnhagen can even make one detest palm trees and oysters.[14] But please don't lose this letter in the sea, for then one of them would be certain to find it and love me accordingly.

Adieu. Hensel sends his best. Dirichlet is leaving today and then Mother will be our dinner guest. She usually listens when I read to Hensel, and that gives me great joy because lovely memories are associated with that pastime.

Farewell, and remain fond of me.[15]

Your Fanny

[1]Presumably of 13 July 1836 (NYPL).

[2]Of 24 July 1836 (NYPL; Mendelssohn, *Briefe-RE*, 193-95).

[3]Felix wrote of his great joy in reading the first parts of *Dichtung und Wahrheit* recently, the first time since childhood (24 July 1836, 195; this passage had been incorrectly printed in Mendelssohn, *Briefe II*, 85-86, as part of his letter of 2 August 1836 to Rebecka).

[4]In the general family letters, Felix mentioned her only in passing, writing that he wants to see a beautiful young lady in Frankfurt again on his return to Leipzig in September (13 July). But in his letter to Rebecka of 24 July 1836 (NYPL; S. Hensel, *Familie II*, 25), Felix wrote: "I'm so horribly in love, as never before, and I don't know what I'm to do." In addition, he does not know how she feels about him; "so you have a secret, which you are to tell to no one" (26). Thus Rebecka, rather than Fanny, was his preferred confidante in this important personal matter.

[5]Sancho Panza, the servant in Cervantes' *Don Quixote*, who dispenses pat advice to

his master. Like many works of foreign literature, this classic had recently received an improved German translation. See, for example, Friedrich Schlegel's favorable review of Tieck's translation, in *Athenaeum,* II (1799), 324-27.

[6]Probably an invented name, as a joke.

[7]Issued by Simrock (Nov./Dec. 1836), and Novello (1836). See the correspondence between Felix and Simrock in Mendelssohn, *Verleger*, 199-207.

[8]Felix was making many changes in June and July 1836; see Mendelssohn, *Verleger*, 203-06.

[9]The first chorus was not omitted (Kurzhals-Reuter, *Oratorien*, 57).

[10]No. 11 in the first version, omitted in the final version. Simrock wanted to publish this separately but Felix could not reach a decision (Mendelssohn, *Verleger*, 210-11). It was issued posthumously by Simrock in 1868 along with another omitted piece from *St. Paul,* the arioso "Doch der Herr, er leitet die Irrenden nicht," as Zwei geistliche Lieder, Op. 112.

[11]The word "Alevin" is French for "fresh fish," which in this context can mean "beginners" or "neophytes." It is conceivable, of course, that Alevin is an actual person, although no evidence could be found to support that possibility. See also letter 123.

[12]According to Sirota, *Hensel*, 307-13, there is a spate of piano pieces from June to September 1836. Either the Prestissimo in C major, dated 17 June 1836 (MA Ms 44, 21-28), or the Allegro agitato in g minor, dated 8 July 1836 (MA Ms 44, 53-58), could be the "brilliant" piano piece that Fanny mentions she has completed recently.

[13]A substantial section in Goethe, *Dichtung*, 177 (Part IV, Book 20), discusses the demonic element and the result of its manifestation in an individual. A statement by Goethe on 11 March 1828, in Eckermann, *Gespräche*, 514, also touches on the demonic, claiming that it can rule Man just as divine providence does.

[14]The identity of Mme. Robert is unclear. Friederike Robert, a close friend of Fanny, had died in 1832.

[15]Felix thanks Fanny for this letter on 9 August 1836, from the Hague (NYPL).

85

Berlin, 19 October 1836

I have to thank you from the bottom of my heart, dear Felix, for an enchanting lied that has given me a great deal of pleasure.[1] But afterwards I plan to keep my mouth shut and not utter a word until you will have written everyone in the world and lastly me.[2] As the saying goes: that which is shouted into the forest will be echoed out of the forest.[3] But that's not the case with us—I shouted continually the entire summer without hearing a single echo. Now I actually don't take this badly in the least, for I know how busy you are. However, since writing exists in the place of conversation, it also bears a similarity to it: if one person alone always speaks, in the end he makes himself weary and the listener as well.

I'm really sorry that you weren't able to send me the completed score of *St. Paul*; I would have liked to have it performed here this fall in the garden hall, and now that's out of the question.[4] When the printed score appears, the parts that I have won't be suitable and must be notated again. Have you heard anything further about the performance in Liverpool?[5] Was Klingemann there? If he should write about it, please send us his letter.

I've received a darling letter from Cecile. If I were as unselfish as Mother I'd send it to you, but I'm protecting myself, because you probably wouldn't return it. I asked her to tell me how you became acquainted and engaged, and she wrote with an endearing naiveté and simplicity. Her praises have been sung so loudly that I really started to get tired of not knowing her myself, especially since Paul reminded me again that we had a letter from Emmeline for the Souchays.[6] We idiots—if only we had been able to deliver it; now we cannot.

I should write you about the exhibition,[7] but that will be somewhat difficult, since I have full confidence in my ability to be impartial, just like any other observer, but you hardly trust that confidence. You will probably have had your fill of French landscapes and seascapes. If one doesn't know such things, one can easily hear much too much about them. This much I can tell you: they are superb, and no less so than the historical paintings they sent, so that I'm fostering a French mania here and can easily imagine their works replacing those of the Düsseldorfers. With all their unbearable coldness, the Berliners have a sort of lucifer fire that burns one moment and reeks one hour later—they always do too much or too little. I don't want to say anything about Hensel's painting. It smacks of egotism if one praises his own works, and in the end no one, including you, would believe that I would find his painting truly beautiful even if he weren't my husband.[8] Sunday it will enter the exhibition in addition to a sketch and preliminary head for a dying Moses, and a few framed drawings—he's made some excellent ones recently. Mother has probably written you that Moser won the Beer Prize. Hensel sends his very best and asks me to tell you that it wouldn't be right if you didn't spend a few days with us and visit the exhibition. If you could it would be very nice; otherwise we won't see you at all as a betrothed man. I would also like to see Cecile as a betrothed girl with her mother and sister. She certainly won't be any the less lovely after the wedding, but she will be different, and I'd like to know her in every way.

Farewell. Send her my warmest wishes and tell her that I'll answer her after a polite interval of time has passed. If I followed my instincts I would sit down and answer her letter as soon as I received it.[9] But one doesn't do that, and I am well brought up.

Your Fanny

[1]It is a "*Duett ohne Worte,* which you wanted to have; may it please you" (11 October 1836, NYPL). It was also mentioned by Rebecka, who was in Leipzig with Felix, in a letter home to the family of 2 October 1836 (DB 38), in which she announces that she's bringing the piece home for Fanny. It is the *Lied ohne Worte,* Op. 38 No. 6, in A-flat major, entitled *Duette,* dated 27 June 1836.

[2]Felix responds individually to Fanny on 23 October 1836 (DB 3, 14): "My dear Fanny, it's truly wrong of me not to have written you a separate letter in such a long time, and therefore your letter that arrived the day before yesterday delighted me doubly. I was also on the verge of writing you that day. But it's not right of you to say, 'You won't take it badly,' and then say, 'But in the end you would make yourself and the listener weary.' It is probably even more unjust for you to judge me for not writing in such a long time. I'm sorry enough that Mother doesn't do otherwise—i.e., she sends me a letter only when I've answered the previous one. I mean, she must know me and know of my love for her during the almost 7 years that I've been away from home. And in that time I've also clearly shown that I've always been with you, everywhere. But that you, as well, could entertain doubts about it, which you only mention sometimes, probably hurt me much more. And thus your dear letter doubly calmed and delighted me. For of course I've reproached myself from time to time, thought that you probably knew that my letters to Mother, as usual, are also intended for you and Beckchen and Paul, and that it would be nice if I continually didn't have to call myself to mind through letters during a period in which I can barely find a spare minute until late in the evening." ("Meine liebe Fanny es ist wohl Unrecht, daß ich Dir so lange nicht einen eignen Brief geschrieben habe, und deshalb hat mich Dein vorgestern angekommener doppelt gefreut; auch war ich an dem Tag ohnedas im Begriff an Dich zu schreiben, aber es ist doch nicht Recht von Dir, daß Du erst noch sagst 'Du nähmest mirs nicht übel' und dann dazu setzest 'Du würdest doch am Ende Dich und den Hörer ermüden.' Das ist wohl noch mehr Unrecht, daß Du mit mir

so rechnest, als wenn ich so lange nicht schreibe; daß Mutter es nicht anders thut, und mir nur denn einen Brief schickt, wenn ich den vorigen beantwortet habe, thut mir leid genug, ich meine sie müsse mich u. meine Liebe zu ihr doch während der 7 Jahre, die ich nun fast vom Hause abwesend bin, wissen u. kennen, u. ich habe es in der Zeit auch wohl mit dem Correspondiren gezeigt, wie ich immer u. überall mit Euch war u. bin—aber daß auch Du daran irgend einen Zweifel hegen konntest, der nur irgend darüber sprichst, ist mir wohl noch mehr leid gewesen, und so hat mich Dein lieber Brief doppelt beruhigt u. erfreut. Denn freilich machte ich mir selbst zuweilen Vorwürfe. Aber dann dachte ich, daß Du doch wohl wissest, daß nach wie vor meine Briefe an Mutter eigentlich an Dich u. Beckchen u. Paul mit sind, u. daß es schön wäre, wenn ich mich nicht eben immer durch Briefe ins Gedächtniß zu rufen brauchte in einer Zeit, wo ich wirklich kaum zu einer richtigen Minute bis spät auf den Abend kommen kann.") Felix then says that he has to write separate letters to Cecile and members of her family, and that he has not been writing to his closest friends.

[3]There is no comparable English proverb that contains the sylvan imagery. Fanny's point is that one reaps like rewards from one's labors, with a hint of "Do unto others."

[4]In his letter of 11 October, Felix wrote that he is sorry that the piano score of *St. Paul* is not ready to send to Fanny. For one thing, he does not want her to read through an inaccurate score. He then wrote: "I'm very curious what you will say about the new passage in *St. Paul* after the heathen's chorus." In his letter to her of 23 October Felix explains further: "I've brought along the corrections of the first part (score) of *St. Paul* from Frankfurt and haven't been able to look through them. Beckchen will certainly have related how things are going here, and yet they don't seem to want to let up. The piano arrangement must arrive in 2 weeks at the latest; it goes without saying that then you'll receive it immediately, *in addition* [to a copy of printed] choral parts." ("Die Correctur des ersten Theiles (Partitur) von Paulus habe ich von Frankfurt mitgebracht u. sie noch immer nicht durchsehen können; Beckchen wird ja erzählt haben, wie es hier hergeht, u. noch scheint es nicht nachlassen zu wollen. Der Clavierauszug muß eben spätestens in 14 [Tag] en kommen, u. dann erhältst Du ihn gleich, *nebst* [einem Exemplar gedruckten] Chorstimmen, das versteht sich.")

[5]The first performance in England took place on 7 October in Liverpool, under the direction of Sir George Smart.

[6]Emmeline is possibly a Souchay.

[7]Felix inquired about the exhibition (11 October).

[8]*Miriam's Song of Praise after the Crossing of the Red Sea.*

[9]In Felix's letter to Fanny of 23 October, he writes that he is glad Fanny has answered Cecile, but he finds it "*not at all* nice" ("*gar nicht* hübsch") that Fanny will not send him the letter in which Cecile relates how they became engaged.

86

Berlin, 28 October 1836

Many thanks, dearest Felix, for your dear letter.[1] But to apologize on three pages is something you shouldn't have done—that wasn't my intention—and it should not and probably will not lead to misunderstandings between us.[2] And since you're such a trustworthy person and return letters, you are also to have both dear letters of Cecile. Herr Schunck will deliver them to you and you can send them back with Paul. You can expect him for *Israel*; the Alexanders[3] are coming on Sunday and then he will make preparations as soon as he's handed over everything. *Israel* will be splendid; organ and church together in a Handel work haven't been heard since time immemorial. I wish I could hear it.[4] We could also use some nice autumn weather. Since Hensel's picture has been at the exhibition,[5] we haven't had one hour of sunshine, but it could certainly use some. For since they built 12 new halls, there naturally isn't enough room to hang a painting properly. This is due to the fact that the best spaces near the windows are occupied by wide doors, so therefore three-quarters of the space is totally unusable and the other quarter is fairly dark. I dare not get started on the story of the new section, which old Schadow perpetrated surreptitiously with the architect of the royal stables, for otherwise I'll fly into a rage, and you will say, "An enraged girl." But it's the most terrible thing that's been completed here in a long time, and that says a lot. In general, however, we're very happy with the reception of the painting.

You ask what I've composed, and I answer, a half-dozen piano pieces, as per your instructions.[6] I'll send them to you with Paul. If you have time, play them through sometime or have one of your students play them, and let me know what you think. I bear such a great similarity to your students that I always find it most profitable if you tell me to do this or that. In the recent past, I've been frequently asked, once again, about publishing something; should I do it?[7]

Next week we have to give a formal musical party that promises to be a sticky business, and it's already put me in a lousy (pardon) mood today. To be specific, an Italian female singer was recommended to us, whose beauty and voice are said to be truly astonishing. I'll want to ask the Deckers to it, and Curschmann and dear Rose,[8] who currently sing everywhere, and then they might do some trills. I'll insert a tender lied—as tender as Curschmann, if possible; or should I perform Beethoven's 33 Variations?[9] The opera performances are also being resumed at the Deckers'.

But I must turn to the exhibition one more time. I've never seen one in which there are so many diverse focal points. The exclusive supremacy of the Düsseldorf regime has come to an end. They rightfully have their public, and will retain it, and Hildebrandt is their most prominent representative this time. The French are enjoying great success, and a few of their most significant works are also here: splendid landscapes of Rome, many paintings by Germans who are studying in Paris, a splendid landscape by Konckonck that I wish you could have seen, a forest in winter, Robert's *Harvest*, and a superb picture of his brother. In all, there is a wealth of beautiful and interesting works here from diverse origins, and one cannot assert that the exhibition has any one focal point. But perhaps that makes it all the more interesting. Farewell, oh Felix, and don't work so hard.[10] Are you composing anything now? what? Will your Symphonies never see the light of day?[11] When will the decision be made whether or not you remain in Leipzig?[12] Give my best to Cecile. I will write her soon.

Your F.

[1]To Fanny, of 23 October 1836 (DB 3, 14).

[2]The apology for not having written personally to Fanny in a long time occupies the first two pages of this letter; see letter 85.

[3]Alexander and Marianne Mendelssohn.

[4]Felix described the large number of singers (200, comprised of all the local Gesangvereine) and how it will be performed with organ, and how he is looking forward to a good performance (11 October 1836, NYPL). In his letter to Fanny of 23 October, he stated that the performance date will be 7 November. The organ part is ready, and "it will, I believe, make a splendid effect" ("sie wird glaube ich einen herrlichen Effect machen").

[5]*Miriam's Song of Praise after Crossing the Red Sea.*

[6]"Have you really composed nothing new? You don't say anything about it, and Beckchen also had little to announce on the subject." ("Hast Du denn gar nicht neues componirt? Du sagst mir nichts davon, u. auch Beckchen wußte wenig darüber zu melden"; 23 October). The piano pieces are among the group of at least seven piano pieces composed between June and October 1836 (in MA Ms 44); see Sirota, *Hensel,* 307-12.

[7]Thus far, she has had six lieder (three each) in Felix's Opp. 8 and 9, under his authorship, but nothing under her own name. Felix apparently gave a negative response, for in letter 88, Fanny states that he is opposed to the publication of her music. Nevertheless, Fanny has a lied, *Die Schiffende,* published in an *Album* issued by Schlesinger in early 1837. Fanny contributes a fair copy of this song to Cecile's Christmas album (MS MDM b. 2). According to Crum, *Catalogue II*, 85, this album is dated 24 December 1844, which is curious given that the album was apparently presented to Cecile in 1836 (see note 2 to letter 90).

[8]Presumably Rose Behrend.

[9]The *Diabelli* Variations, Op. 120.

[10]Felix related his musical activities: the performance of Lachner's *Preissymphonie,* his performance of Beethoven's G-major Concerto one week later, and the upcoming rehearsal of *St. Paul* after the new year (23 October).

[11]Probably in reference to the *Scotch* Symphony (Op. 56; published 1843), and the *Italian* Symphony (Op. 90).

[12]"The decision as to whether I'll remain in Leipzig will hopefully be made before the New Year. I fervently wish and hope that it will turn out that way. You really have no concept of the musical forces of this city. . . ." ("Ob ich in Leipzig bleibe, das entscheidet sich hoffentlich noch vor Neujahr, ich wünsche sehr sehnlich, u. hoffe auch, daß sichs so machen wird. Du hast von den musikalischen Mitteln dieser Stadt wirklich keinen Begriff . . ."; to Fanny, 14 November 1836; DB 3, 15).

87

Berlin, 16 November 1836

Dear Felix, many thanks for your dear letter, which I enjoyed very much.[1] At this stage in my life, I actually think that a person between the ages of 16 and 61 doesn't need a birthday (although I like to celebrate everybody else's birthday), and so I've given up the customary ritual of cake and accessories for a long time. But a letter, a friendly face (that should replace this), or a dear drawing by Sebastian—anyone who would not be pleased by all these would have to be older than old.—I'm very sad that you can't tear yourself away from your rushed existence, for I know and can see how it often affects Hensel and attacks his nerves. I hope that your marriage will do a great deal for that.[2] You won't save time through eating together at home, but it will be very pleasant. In any case, you'll want to be at home so much that you'll find the means to do it, and that will do you a lot of good.—I find it a real shame, by the way, that *Israel* won't be repeated; it would be a double treat for the same amount of effort.[3] And I can't comprehend how it would hurt the directors in the spring—I would have thought the opposite.

I've gotten an idea of how *Solomon* will sound, but it might sound quite different with a competent church organ. Franck told me that his brother wrote out the entire organ registration. Is that true, or did the younger Franck make up a story?[4] You have no idea how I react to all the music here that I don't prepare myself. I literally hear no tone, and what am I to hear, after all? How Möser never lets the same symphonies be scratched out year after year in the same order, or how Ries rather cleanly but very monotonously plays one quartet after the other?[5] I even hold a subscription to the latter but never attend. We don't have operas. I'll probably hear Handel's *Joseph in Egypt* at the Academy concerts because I don't know that work and therefore won't be so upset when they ruin it.[6] As a result of such a lack of stimulation, I've become so apathetic about music that I haven't made any real music in a year and a day. I'm resolved, however, to pull myself out of it, and will perform your Psalm and the three nuns' pieces, which I can cast very nicely, when I resume my concerts at the end of the month.[7] Decker is still extremely warm towards me. And last week we also held a very successful performance of Marschner's *Templar* at her house.[8]—You can therefore imagine how happy I am that you're pleased with my piano pieces, for it leads me to believe that I haven't gone totally downhill in music. Only please return them; I will have them copied for you, and for that, send the one in c minor, *à la* Thalberg.[9] The exhibition will close on Sunday, which explains why we're using today's cloudy weather to go again—we can't wait for nice weather any longer.[10] We certainly have good cause to be extremely satisfied with the results, dear Felix, but what holds us here is really much more than that, as you well know and can imagine. However, we must start to plan and think seriously about spending a year in Italy in a few more years. It's a necessity for Hensel, and of course I concur. I have a few thoughts with regard to the present school situation, which have been confirmed at this exhibition. In order to establish a real school, it's necessary for both master and students to work together on a project for a long time, as in the Middle Ages and only in Munich at present. But how is it possible for 300 or 400 young painters to paint one picture each and every year? Their artistic prowess, weak to begin with, will be diluted, they will repeat the same subjects endlessly, and finally, as in Düsseldorf, a leader will leap forward and 100 others will attempt to imitate that leap. But Hensel is not like that. He runs his studio without flattery and exclusively in the best interest of his students. Therefore he lets them go after they can stand on their own feet, with the result that he is always dealing with new students who can't exert influence on him artistically or personally. This time, however, he had the pleasure of seeing his atelier capture the only 2 prizes that are awarded by this country in this category. Kaselowsky has already gone, Moser will leave in the course of the winter, and then the entire first generation, who were our principal colleagues, will be scattered. And you can probably appreciate that Hensel doesn't want to perpetuate this trend *ad infinitum*.

I always have the following thought in the back of mind: why shouldn't it be possible for all of us to work out a plan to spend a summer together in a lovely place, such as the Rhine, Baden, or Dresden? What do you think? Shouldn't that be possible and very nice? Or on Lake Geneva? You also haven't assured us yet that you will bring Cecile here as soon as she is yours. We all hope for that very much and would love to hear it soon. And we really would like to see her first as a girl.[11] Marianne and her children were here on my birthday,[12] and once again we spoke about [her] a great deal. Everybody seems to know her [well] except us—that's dreadful. Send her my very best wishes and tell her we think of her fondly. Her letters are truly lovely. How did she describe the engagement incorrectly? Refute it. She wrote another enchanting note to Mother recently. Mother, Beckchen, Hensel, and everyone send their best. Everything is fine here except for the fact that I caught a cold that was making the [rounds] and now has a hold on me, and Hensel suffered a toothache that led to an extraction and is continually plagued by his stomach in spite of all the [gallbladder] capsules.

His previous large picture has been very successfully lithographed in great dimensions. The stone just arrived at the exhibition, and we hope to send you a print for Christmas. But I beg you, please keep this strictly between us. [ ] Farewell and remain as always.

Your F.

[1]To Fanny, of 14 November 1836 (DB 3, 15).

[2]Felix and Cecile Jeanrenaud are engaged.

[3]In his letter to Fanny of 14 November, Felix wrote: "Of all the performances in which I've participated, *Israel* is the best. At the same time the effect on the public so decisive that it showed how much musical feeling is present there. Apart from the fact that 2,000 listeners thronged in the church with the cold weather, they seemed to want a repeat, and the directors won't do it so that they can be even more certain of their situation in the spring. But the effect of the work in its correct form was striking and far surpassed my expectations; the organ at the end fearful." ("Der Israel war von allen Aufführungen bei denen ich gewesen bin, die allerbeste, zugleich eben auch die Wirkung aufs Publicum so entschieden, daß sie zeigte, wie viel musikalisches Gefühl auch dort vorhanden ist. Abgesehen davon daß bei der Kälte sich an 2000 Zuhörer in die Kirche drängten, so schienen sie jetzt von allen Seiten um eine Wiederholung u. die Directoren thuns nicht, um im Frühjahr ihrer Sache desto gewisser zu sein. Die Wirkung des Werks in seiner rechten Gestalt war aber schlagend u. über meine eigne Erwartung groß, die Orgel gegen das Ende furchtbar.")

[4]Younger Franck is presumably Eduard Franck, described by his older brother Hermann Franck.

[5]Pieter Hubert Ries.

[6]The oratorio *Joseph and his Brethren* (1744), given its first performance in Germany on 15 December 1836; review by J. P. Schmidt in the *AMZ*, 8 Feb. 1837, cols. 81-85.

[7]Psalm may be *Non nobis Domine*, Op. 31, published in late 1835; nuns' pieces are Op. 39, published in 1837.

[8]Opera *Der Templer und die Jüdin*.

[9]"To my great joy I see that clearly again in the piano pieces that you sent me through Paul and Albertine. There are indeed some excellent qualities about them and I thank you very much for the great joy I've derived from them. It is so rare that new music pleases one so thoroughly, and the impression is so much the greater when one meets up with the Right—as if one were staring it in the face—and is forced to say 'There it is.' I experienced such feelings with many of your pieces, immediately upon the first playing, but in particular at the close of the first in B-flat major, which is extremely endearing, and then at the slow one in G major, which pleases me exceedingly. However, I've only been able to play through them

Illustration 7—Autograph fair copy of Fanny Hensel's lied, *Suleika,* 1836, with Wilhelm Hensel's drawings (first page) [Bodleian Library, Oxford: MS Margaret Deneke Mendelssohn b. 2, fol. 10].

once and want to write you something in detail when I'm better acquainted with them and will have gained more pleasure from them." ("Ich sehe das jetzt zu meiner größten Freude wieder so recht an den Clavierstücken, die Du mir durch Paul u. Albertine geschickt; es sind da gar vortreffliche dabei u. ich danke Dir sehr viel mal für die große Freude, die ich daran gehabt habe. Es kommt so selten, daß einem neue Musik so durch u. durch gefällt, u. desto lieber wird einem solch ein Eindruck, wenn man so dem Rechten, Getroffenen sich gegenüber fühlt, als ob man ihm ins Gesicht sähe—und sich sagen muß, da steht's. Solche Empfindung habe ich bei mehreren von den Stücken gehabt, gleich als ich sie das erstemal spielte, namentlich aber beim Schluß des ersten in b dur, der höchst liebenswürdig ist, u. dann bei dem langsamen in g dur, das mir überaus gefällt. Doch habe ich sie alle erst einmal durchspielen können, und will Dir gern etwas ausführliches schreiben, wenn ich sie besser kenne u. mich mehr daran erfreut habe"; 14 November). The two pieces Felix mentioned are in MA Ms 44; the second one was later published as Fanny's Op. 2 No. 1. Based on the list of works in Sirota, *Hensel,* 107-12, it is uncertain which piece is "à la Thalberg." It is not part of MA Ms 44, but it may be in private possession or lost.

[10]Felix wrote to Fanny on 14 November about the deserved reputation and respect Hensel is gaining through the exhibition.

[11]That is, as a virgin.

[12]Marianne Mendelssohn.

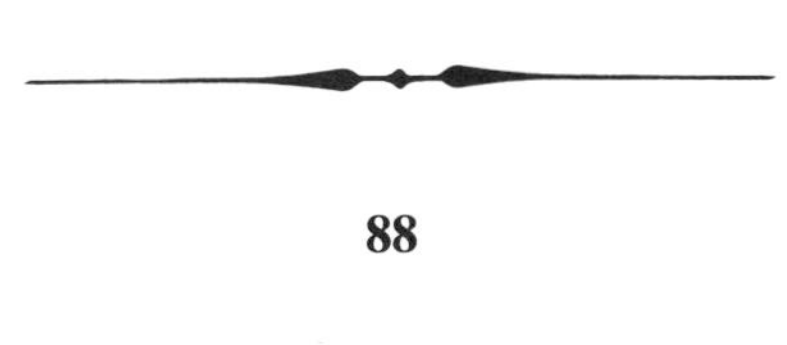

88

[Lea]

Berlin, 22 November [1836]
St. Caecilia's Day

Best wishes on this festive day!
Actually, I wanted to write you immediately after the receipt of Paul and Albertine's letter from Leipzig, which conveyed so many wonderful tidings: how much progress your orchestra has made, how happy and more complete you've become, and how pleasant your present situation is. With regard to the latter, we're also very glad that the prospects for the retention of your position look very favorable, for the fact that one *can* visit you in 8 hours is very comforting and gratifying. It's very nice that you're making an album for Cecile and requesting my lieder for it, and Hensel, of

course, will be pleased [ ] to contribute a few vignettes.[1] Just let us know soon exactly what you would like, for there's always much to do before Christmas. Can I use paper, as I'd prefer, or am I to write directly into the album?[2]

With regard to my publishing I stand like the donkey between two bales of hay.[3] I have to admit honestly that I'm rather neutral about it, and Hensel, on the one hand, is for it, and you, on the other, are against it. I would of course comply totally with the wishes of my husband in any other matter, yet on this issue alone it's crucial to have your consent, for without it I might not undertake anything of the kind.[4]

Yesterday I heard an Italian improviser named Bindocci here. Those who heard him for the first time were enchanted. Given that I don't understand enough Italian, or that I'm unfamiliar with the entire method and approach, I found his *sung* poems ridiculous and disagreeably tiresome. I liked his spoken improvisations much more, and I think his real talent lies in the completion of rhymes submitted to him, especially those with comic themes. Furthermore, I believe the whole business is easier than it looks. He avoids many of the suggested themes, especially the more arcane ones, and instead concentrates on generalities that he's probably had in his repertoire for a long time. But above all, one must possess enormous facility in making rhymes, as well as quick presence of mind.

Mother, the Dirichlets, Julie Schunck, and Marianne Saaling are eating here today. I'm going with Julie to the exhibition earlier. I think the poor child is rather bored here. The Benecke girl is always ailing and almost never goes out, and it's also very quiet at their house.

Farewell, my dear Felix. Give my best to dear ones in Leipzig and Frankfurt and remain as always.

Your Fanny

[1]Felix made these requests in his letter of 18 November 1836 (NYPL).

[2]"Therefore, dear Fanny, please notate the lieder, which you've promised me, on separate leaves (since I can't send you the book), the same size as this whole piece of paper, if you give another 1 1/2" to the long sides (these below), so that it assumes the usual shape of small manuscript paper. This is the shape of the album. Now I'd like to have you delicately write the following lieder: 1) the duet (*Suleika)*, although it's published, as one of the Jeanrenauds' favorites; 2) *Die Schif-*

fende; 3) a truly melancholy, short one; 4) one of your favorites.—These are my wishes. And now to you, dear Hensel, the request for a few strokes—the longer the better, and the more the better. Whether it's to be vignettes for the lieder or a separate drawing, or whatever, that I leave entirely to your judgment and generosity, and now respectfully request as many as possible'' (26 November 1836, NYPL). The four lieder Fanny included are: *Suleika u. Hatem* (duet), earlier published as No. 12 of Felix's Op. 8; *Suleika* (solo version; see Illustration 7); *Die Schiffende* (undated), to be published in early 1837 in a Schlesinger *Album*; and *Nacht liegt auf den fremden Wegen* (undated).

[3]This imagery is based on the ''Buridan's Ass'' fable, supposedly taken up by the fourteenth-century French philosopher, Jean Buridan. In this fable, an ass stands between two piles of hay that are exactly alike, and because he cannot decide which one to choose, he ends up starving to death.

[4]Fanny publishes a lied, *Die Schiffende*, in a Schlesinger *Album* in early 1837.

89

[11 December (1836)]

I wanted to write you in great detail about *St. Paul* again and express my gratitude, dear Felix,[1] but since I've just heard that this note will reach you *at the earliest* just as you are leaving, I'll merely wish you a good trip. More will reach you in Frankfurt, where, God willing, you will have a wonderful time.[2]

As for me, I very much look forward to performing *St. Paul* on Christmas, as well as my talents will permit.[3] But I still don't know whether we will have a merry holiday. Hensel has begun the little pictures for Cecile's lieder, and we will send them to you in Frankfurt. We hope she will like them.

We will be angry if you don't send us definite confirmation from Frankfurt as to *when* you'll visit us. You must stay with us; the blue and yellow rooms are at your disposal this summer. If you could persuade the Jeanrenauds to travel to Leipzig before the wedding, we would go too. I really want to see Cecile while she's still a girl.

I've had the great pleasure of hearing Döhler several times, especially in a moderate-sized room. Since it's so rare that one has the opportunity of learning anything new here, I'm overjoyed if it occurs even once. He modestly gave his concert in the Hôtel de Russie, which was full, however, and I hope he will perform more often.

And for now, addio. Good luck and much happiness in Frankfurt, and give my best to Cecile, her mother and sister, the Veits, and Aunt Schlegel. Think of us when you're happy.

Your Fanny

A very unpleasant matter: Herr von Schramm, who pretends to play the violin, is traveling to Leipzig and wanted to be recommended to you. Fortunately your departure gives me a legitimate pretext for a refusal. But I did have to promise to announce his arrival to you, which I've done herewith, and can live at peace with my conscience.

Today is the 11th of December.[4]

[Lea]

[1]To Fanny on 29 November 1836 (DB 3, 16): "Just when I want to send Elsholz's package to Mother, the package with the piano arrangement of *St. Paul* arrives, and since it's on pretty white vellum, I must deposit it in the Bibliothèque Imperiale—I mean, send it to *you*—and request that you play through it sometime. May it give you pleasure and remind you of good days." ("Eben als ich das Elsholtzische Packet an Mutter abschicken will, kommt das Packet mit dem Clavierauszug des Paulus, und da es gerade auf schönen weißen Velinpapier ist, so muß ich es deponiren in der bibliothèque imperiale, ich meine *Dir* schicken u. Dich bitten, es zuweilen durchzuspielen. Magst Du Freude daran haben, und es Dich an gute Tage erinnern.")

[2]Felix is spending Christmas with Cecile and her family.

[3]Most likely performed for a relatively small gathering.

[4]Abraham's birthday.

90

Berlin, 19 December 1836[1]

Here is our contribution to the album, dear Felix.[2] Please note that the very beautiful drawing that is being sent will serve as an apology for the other, which is merely an outline. But I insisted that they be mailed, for otherwise you wouldn't have received them in time. Luise created the ornamental drawing for the third sheet with her usual individual grace.[3] I hope you'll be pleased. Now my only hope is that you also didn't choose *Feuchte Schwingen* from the *Divan* for Cecile, for otherwise I'll kill myself.[4] Also explain to Cecile why she is receiving a printed lied, because otherwise she will think that I haven't written any others.[5] For your gift, dear Felix, you have to assemble the enclosed gatherings of steel engravings, which contain sharp points. And may God grant both of you and everyone there a merry Christmas, and see that we spend it together next year.

I held a very nice rehearsal of the first part of *St. Paul* yesterday. Bader was there and sang a few pieces gloriously, obviously very taken with the music. Bötticher, a young bass from the theater with a wonderful voice, will sing the part of Paul; I hope he does a good job. My chorus rejoiced; I can't tell you how happy that made me. Berger, whom I ran into at Döhler's concert recently and became acquainted with again, was here and sat next to me while I played. It was just like old times, as if he would say any minute, "Stand up, Faniska, I want to play for you."[6] He derived extraordinary pleasure from the music, and I can't express how touched I was by his sickly appearance, and how quiet he's become.

I agree with most of your changes but not all of them.[7] I would have gladly taken a slap on the face rather than the change in one of my favorite passages, "welcher gemacht hat Himmel und Erde und das Meer."[8] Furthermore, I can't understand why you've excluded the soprano aria that I like so much.[9] I could have done without the one in F major or the alto aria.[10]

On the other hand, I'm glad that you've distributed the dialogue between bass and tenor at the epiphany,[11] and am especially grateful for the change at "denn der Herr hat es gesagt."[12] Why haven't you inserted a lively chorus at the end, as you intended?[13]

Today Madame Schunck will return with Julie.[14] They are certain that Madame Jeanrenaud, Cecile, and Julie[15] will travel to Leipzig. Follow through on this matter, and then we will also be able to see each other, which otherwise would be almost impossible this winter.

I've persuaded Mother to insert a page for Cecile, which will make her happy.[16] Rebecka unfortunately isn't ready and consequently very upset.

We still don't know how we will spend our Christmas, nor even where—whether here or over there. But that's to be settled today. We always turn up with such an army—12 students alone this time—that we really can't expect anybody to include us.

Farewell, my dearest. Send my heartfelt wishes to Cecile and her family, and rejoice in your good fortune. Hensel sends his best.

Your Fanny

[1]Crum, *Catalogue I,* 43, erroneously lists "19 Nov. 1836."

[2]Felix's thanks are expressed to Fanny and Wilhelm in a letter of 31 December 1836 (DB 3, 17). See also letter 88.

[3]Luise Hensel did the silhouette for the third lied, *Die Schiffende.*

[4]*Feuchte Schwingen* = the lied *Suleika,* from Goethe's *Divan.* See Illustration 7. Felix had also composed a *Suleika,* Op. 34 No. 4. Fanny's lied, her second setting of this poem, was composed on 4 December 1836, presumably specifically for this album (autograph MA Ms 45, 24-26; fair copy MS MDM b. 2, f. 10-11).

[5]Either the duet *Suleika und Hatem,* No. 12 of Felix's Op. 8; or *Die Schiffende,* which is shortly to be published by Schlesinger in an *Album.*

[6]Fanny and Felix had studied piano with Ludwig Berger.

[7]Fanny most likely had the version that was published in January/February 1837 by Simrock.

[8]Words similar to these occur many times in the first chorus, but the exact text is "Herr der du bist der Gott, der Himmel und Erde und das Meer gemacht hat." This is the opening text, through letter "A." Fanny sometimes tended to be loose in her citing of text.

[9]No. 11 from the first version, "Der du die Menschen," published posthumously as Op. 112 No. 2. Felix's reluctance to have the piece published separately in 1837 is expressed in letters to Simrock of April and May (Mendelssohn, *Verleger*, 210-11).

[10]Presumably No. 26, an arioso for soprano, "Lasst uns singen von der Gnade des Herrn." The alto aria is presumably part of No. 12, "Doch der Herr vergisst der Seinen nicht."
[11]Part of No. 13; Saul is the bass, the narrator is the tenor, and a four-part women's chorus speaks as Jesus.
[12]Part of No. 19. See Fanny's criticism of an earlier version of this passage in letter 80.
[13]Presumably a lively section for chorus at the end of No. 19.
[14]Julie Schunck.
[15]Julie Jeanrenaud.
[16]This page is no longer present with this letter.

91

Berlin, 20 January 1837

Above all, my congratulations on Cecile's decision to travel to Leipzig. Her mother writes that she will be there at least three weeks, so therefore you won't be alone for much of the remaining time. The 23rd.

Admire how much I've written in the past three days. In part I wasn't feeling well, in part *St. Paul* was launched yesterday.[1] Friday evening there was a rehearsal, Saturday the room had to be turned upside-down, and then I couldn't get back to it. By the way, I'll let Mother tell you how much she enjoyed it. I was especially glad to see Berger so warm and engaging once again, and he attended all the rehearsals with great interest. All the singers derived great pleasure from it, especially Bader, who sang splendidly. Even Stümer, with what little voice he has left, sounded very nice. Decker excellent, and Bötticher exerted every possible effort. He has a wonderful, rich voice and is uncommonly musical, but his singing is still somewhat crude and stiff, and consequently nothing is more difficult for him than a piano. He could really sing out in the theater, but he's being retained here, given a larger annual salary, and never used—what incredible nonsense![2]

I've had a rather unpleasant winter inasmuch as Hensel is almost continually ill and doesn't sleep at night. As soon as spring arrives I'll drive him out; it's still questionable whether I'll go along. Incidentally, we've been spared the flu, which otherwise has spread like wildfire.

Send my best to Cecile; I'll write her soon. Herr von Liphart took the aria again, and I hope he'll make the correct delivery this time.[3] I see that my tempi were correct, for the first part took just 10 minutes less than in Düsseldorf, which figures up exactly considering the 2 excluded arias here. I didn't include the soprano aria, which is being copied for another time, and the alto aria, on account of Thürrschmidt's illness.[4] Decker is with child and whines, but nevertheless acquitted herself quite well in the main choruses.[5]

Farewell.

[Lea]

[1]"Her orchestra consisted of members of the Royal Opera or the Königstadt Theater." This performance at Fanny's Sunday musicales was the first performance of the final version in Germany. But Kurzhals-Reuter incorrectly states that 20 January 1837 was the date of the performance (*Oratorien*, 148-49).

[2]Presumably Bötticher is engaged at the royal opera rather than the royal theater. Fanny's statement that he is never used is an exaggeration, as can be seen by his roles from this period as listed in Ledebur, *Lexicon*, 69-70.

[3]Felix asked Fanny to send the aria from *St. Paul* to him directly after her performance (8 January 1837, NYPL). But it is uncertain which aria is intended here.

[4]The excluded soprano aria could be "Der du die Menschen," discarded by Felix in the revising process after the Düsseldorf premiere, or "Jerusalem" (No. 6). The alto aria is presumably "Doch der Herr vergisst" (No. 12).

[5]Felix thanks Fanny on 28 January 1837 (NYPL) for her account of the performance.

92

Berlin, 27 January 1837

I think I wrote you a rather stupid and confusing letter last Monday because I was so tired.[1] Hensel had been ill the entire night and I couldn't sleep off the excitement from *St. Paul.* But now, Wednesday, I've received your dear letter and thank you for it. I'm so glad that your only care in the world now concerns when the Jeanrenauds will come. We're emitting a long sigh once again for the railroad, for then there wouldn't be any question of you visiting us here. But unfortunately that isn't even a question. It's patently absurd that we're separated by only one day of heavy traveling and yet never see each other. Mother is planning to travel to Leipzig for *St. Paul,* and so is Aunt Levy; I think they will probably travel together.[2] My trip looks highly improbable in the interim, dear Felix, and I'm pressing Hensel to travel alone. But the question is whether he wants to wait for a greener time of year. But I beseech you—reserve a great deal of time for us this summer so that we can say more than merely hello and good-bye! Paul and Albertine are coming at the end of April and will, I think, stay here indefinitely, and then we will spend a nice life together. Paul is extremely happy over your happiness, and what particularly pleases me is how he's proud of your love to a certain extent—as if he had discovered it himself. Your news about the Davids makes me very happy. That's truly one of the stories that one can only judge after the fact, and if it turns out well, then they did the right thing.[3]—My authorship, consisting of one published lied, has not given me any enjoyment, dear Felix. On the contrary, I've found all the hoopla with which the Schlesingers have surrounded this quite pitiful bit of an album quite repugnant. In particular, they couldn't be any happier about its wonderful exterior appearance, but one need only look at the worst French or English work in a similar vein to know how wretched the local one is.[4] Incidentally, something funny happened with respect to the Leipzig Album. I had intended to compose Byron's *There be none of* for Cecile, but then dropped the idea when Rebecka told me that she didn't know any English. Afterwards when I read that you had contributed something to the Leipzig Album, I went to a music store to find out what. On the way, I thought about my English lied again and finished it in my head, then I enter the store, order the Album, open it, and see your piece, *There be none.* I want to acquire it soon and have it copied.[5] But it was very funny. This winter, punch is very fashionable here, as is checkers, which you probably already know. Minna has mastered the art of making punch so well that Mother is even tempted to take a half glass now and then (you can tease her about it). The Devrients were here two nights ago after a considerable passage of time, and we spent a very nice evening together. The poor people can't extricate themselves from domestic chaos and continual illness and distress. (Pardon the ink blot. I just saw it when I turned over the page but don't have the energy to write another letter.) Ries has announced your *Melusine* for a concert on the 4th, and it will be another good performance.

Send my best to Hiller again. When I was at his house I mischievously installed myself as the music director of the Music of the Spheres, but I probably won't be so rash again.[6] How is Schelble? Will Hiller still continue with the Caecilienverein?[7] And won't they stifle him?[8] Might one write the Jeanrenauds that one is happy over the escape of the Frankfurt students, or are they aristocratic? The jury in Strasbourg has provoked great arguments between Dirichlet and everyone else. What is your opinion? Farewell. Everyone sends his best.

Your Fanny

[1]Letter 91.

[2]Felix said *St. Paul* will be performed on 13 March in the church in Leipzig (14 Jan. 1837, NYPL). Grove, *Mendelssohn,* 133, states that it took place on 16 March.

[3]Presumably the decision to stay on as concertmaster in Leipzig. Felix wrote that David is happy about it (to Fanny, 24 January 1837; DB 3, 18).

[4]The lied is *Die Schiffende,* and the Album was just issued by Schlesinger. Felix wrote to Fanny on 24 January (S. Hensel, *Familie II*, 35): "Do you know, Fenchel, that your A-major lied in Schlesinger's Album is creating a furor here? That the new *Musikalische Zeitung* (I mean its editor . . .) raves about you? That everybody says it's the best in the Album—a bad compliment, for is there anything else good? That they really like it? Are you now a real author, and does that make you

happy?'' Felix writes on 4 March (NYPL) that ''probably it's not possible for you to hear about Grabau's concert on Monday. Among other things, she's singing *Die Schiffende* by Fanny, which is enjoying great success here.'' After the concert, Felix writes how much he liked that song when it was performed, and that ''I, for my part, give thanks in the name of the public in Leipzig and other places that you published against my wishes'' (to Fanny, 7 March 1837, DB 3, 19; S. Hensel, *Familie II*, 34). There is an autograph letter from Fanny to Schlesinger in the Library of Congress, thanking him for his kindness. Although the letter is undated, it may well originate from January or February 1837.

[5]Fanny's setting is dated 29 December 1836, autograph MA Ms 45, 27-30 (copy in MA Ms 31, 44-47). Felix's setting dates from c. 1834. The Leipzig Album = *Album musical,* published by Breitkopf & Härtel, late 1836, containing Felix's Zwei Romanzen von Lord Byron: *There be none* and *Sun of the Sleepless* (no opus number). They were also published in an *Album musical* of 1837, with piano pieces by others, including Chopin and Hünten (Mendelssohn, *Verleger*, 51, 74).

[6]Possibly a private joke between Fanny and Felix.

[7]Hiller stood in for Schelble as conductor of the Caecilienverein in Frankfurt, and began a postponed trip to Italy in the summer of 1837.

[8]Felix alludes to the political feuds within the Caecilienverein in his letter to Hiller of 13 July 1837 (Hiller, *Mendelssohn,* 97).

93

Berlin, 13 April 1837

I want to show you a sign of life so that you'll know that I still exist and, what's more, am feeling well.[1] The repeated accidents were not my fault, and I felt so good up to the last moment that I became very optimistic. I've recovered very quickly and now, after less than 2 weeks, feel as if nothing ever happened.[2] My head, at least, feels completely clear, even if my legs still cannot carry me along. I look dreadful, but I hope that will change when the weather improves, *if* it ever does. We were very anxious to find out where you had endured the great snow catastrophe, and the letter we received today from Strasbourg informed us about it.[3] We feel bad that you didn't consult us in forming your plans or lack of plans, and I've already given up any hope of seeing Cecile this year. I won't leave Berlin. As soon as everything turns green, I'm driving

Hensel out of the house and directing him to Dresden, and from there he can travel on foot to Saxon Switzerland to paint. If you were in Leipzig I'd go with him and visit you, but instead I'll remain in *min Hus*. That goes without saying for the others as well. How I rejoice in your happiness, and how zestfully Hensel and I relish your unplanned roaming around—very nice for newlyweds. I also look forward to your honeymoon preludes;[4] of all the times when one can exist, the time of the honeymoon is indisputably the most pleasant.[5] My very good husband nursed me so attentively in my sickroom that it's the least I can do not to begrudge him a trip to the great outdoors. For now, farewell—there is nothing else to tell you. You know we love you, and that will never change. Wilhelm and my sisters-in-law send their best.

Your Fanny

[1]Fanny addressed the envelope: "To the newlyweds in seventh heaven." Felix and Cecile were married in Frankfurt on 28 March.

[2]The exact nature of these accidents is not known. Felix writes Fanny the next day from Freiburg (DB 3, 20) that he just found out about them that morning in a letter from Rebecka and Mother.

[3]Letter of 9 April 1837 (NYPL). Felix reported very cold weather and a thick snowstorm, which forced them to change their itinerary and travel from Speyer to Strasbourg.

[4]In his letter of 9 April, Felix mentioned that he has composed three Organ Preludes in Speyer, to be published soon. He hoped Fanny will like perhaps one or two of them. They are the Drei Präludien u. Fugen, Op. 37 (Bartlitz, *Works*, 154, lists the early part of April as their date of composition); see also his letter to Fanny of 14 April 1837 (DB 3, 20).

[5]The German is untranslatable into English, for it has a multiple pun centering on "Wochen." It means "weeks," it is the second half of the word for "honeymoon" ("Flitterwochen"), and also designates the very last weeks of a pregnancy. The expression "in die Wochen kommen" means "to be near one's time" at the end of a pregnancy. Thus it seems that Fanny was making a humorous allusion to pregnancy as she wrote to the newlyweds on their honeymoon.

94

Berlin, 2 June 1837
Rain, thunderstorms,
and cold weather

Your letter from yesterday, dear Felix, has loosened my tongue, which was somewhat frozen—how can it be otherwise with this weather?—and I will now clatter on like a mill-wheel so that you may have to stop me at the end.[1] First, I have to say immediately that Alexander,[2] and Madame Schunck, and whoever else may have told you that we or I take offense at your English trip are totally mistaken. I wouldn't dream of anything like that, for I understand the importance and advantages of this trip only too well.[3] Since I'd love to make that trip myself with my husband, I certainly wouldn't begrudge any deserving person that pleasure, least of all you. Also, we are far from the point of pretending that you ought to give up anything that could be helpful or pleasant to you so that you could visit us.[4] But now that the subject has come up, I want to tell you candidly what's behind it. I actually was not angry that you and Cecile didn't come from Leipzig, although you could have accomplished the visit without any kind of sacrifice had you followed the plan I sketched out for you at the start. Rather than being angry I felt hurt, and probably said so here and there. Madame Jeanrenaud's reasons for her quick return trip have never been clear to me and the result has shown that apparently I was justified, since the wedding came off remarkably well without her having been there three weeks earlier, and Madame Souchay was also not so irreconcilable.[5] If your business affairs prevented you from staying here longer than a few days, this still would have sufficed to bring Cecile here. And it was never promised that you would stay more than a few days. However, those are nothing but "ifs" and "woulds" that cannot change what is already past. It's just a shame that the loss is irreplaceable for us, because it is no longer possible to see Cecile as a girl. If we could have traveled, we naturally would have gone to Leipzig, although you didn't seem too kindly disposed to that possibility as well in the beginning, and so that was eliminated. I thank

God that I didn't jeopardize my health by venturing the journey, because otherwise I would have reproached myself endlessly on account of my accident.[6] I therefore believe, dear brother, that you won't hold it against me, but instead consider it a sign of love, that I felt bad because the visit didn't materialize. If you think back to the time when we were constantly together, when I immediately discovered every thought that went through your mind and knew your new things by heart even before they were notated, and if you remember that our relationship was a particularly rare one among siblings, in part because of our common musical pursuits, then I think you'll admit that it's been an odd deprivation for me the past year and a day to know that you're happy in a way I've always wished for you, and yet not meet your beloved, now your wife, even one time. No descriptions help—they only confuse matters. In addition, it now appears that I'll have little chance of seeing her in the near future, because a winter journey here will probably—and so easily—be impossible for one reason or another, and so another year and a day will pass before we see each other. Three years have already passed since we visited on the run for a few days. Unfortunately, my husband has as little official reason to go to Leipzig as you do to Berlin, so my wish to spend some time together with you probably belongs to that category of human endeavors in which one must deny oneself in the quest for its fulfillment. One gets wiser with time. In short, it seemed as if this alienation, which certainly will have no effect on me, was not leaving you completely unchanged, if not with regard to me personally then with regard to my family. I can't remember the last time you inquired about Hensel's work or Sebastian's progress, and thus I've gradually stopped talking about them because such topics call for reactions, and I have nothing more important to report. Just tell me that I'm mistaken—I very much want to think so.[7]

Those are more or less the reasons for the recent silence, dear Felix. You see that it concerns everything except even a shadow of disapproval for your English trip. I really didn't have anything to write that would have been worth the effort. And forgive me if this first letter that I write you now troubles you deeply; I would rather return to the old, silly tone which so often made you laugh, if only I could. Above all, don't show this letter to Cecile, for she will, as we say here, stand in terror of her grouchy sister-in-law. You always used to call me Grimmhild and must permit me to keep as much of my wrath as I'm capable of retaining with great personal effort.[8]

The musical eccentricity that you mocked[9] stems from the fact that hardly any musical activities took place this winter, and then three virtuosos—Döhler, Wieck, and Henselt—appeared in a row.[10] You know that I generally let myself get run down, and at that time I had frayed nerves and felt quite antiquated. But since then my health has improved, I've acquired the Chopin Etudes, and I'm practicing a few of them diligently. Henselt played a pair of Chopin Etudes in his concert, as well as a very nice pair of his own. These two were played very delicately and quickly and were the best things on the program. He also performed the somewhat boring Trio by Hummel in the same manner that we used to perform it in the old days—the one we had dubbed "Schmöckerio."[11] I believe that this style of performance will generally become fashionable again, for since music is as subject to fashion as porcelain, clothing, and lithography, it must keep pace with them. Thus music will probably seek out the rococo style, for in art Louis XIV wigs are the current rage, at least in England and France.[12]

Henselt played some of his own Variations at the end of the concert.[13] In spite of their difficulties, there was so little that was brilliant, yet so much that was ugly, that I became disgusted, as I generally am with this type of concert.[14] Not one of these three pianists had a regular concert; none played with accompaniment, but only solo Etudes, Variations, etc. Next they will go before the public and give a lesson.—If I can pull everything together, I want to perform some music again this summer. But I'm skeptical, since my friends, the Ganzes, are in Baden and I know far too few musicians. I attended the opera a few times and thoroughly enjoyed *Armide,* despite the uneven performance.[15] Fassmann's vocal equipment doesn't match the requirements of this role, but her complete sacrifice of all her vocal powers and her total commitment to the part compensate for her shortcomings. One gladly overlooks a great deal because she is singing good music, and, to all appearances, sings it with respect. Spontini's conducting also amused me. Although I would have preferred some things differently, the interpretation was lively and the orchestra sounded good. In any case, 8 or 10 performances of *Armide* were sickly, and the *Nachtwandlerin,* in which I saw Löwe, was all right.[16] Now one could still claim that the public doesn't like to hear good things when they are presented to them, but the public here doesn't have the energy to demand good things.

I'm pleased with your Fugues.[17] I've only had the chance to look through your lieder for an hour because I knew we'd be receiving them, but I'll give you my impressions when I'm more familiar with them.[18] I like *Sonntagslied* and *Auf Flügeln des Gesanges* among the old ones, and Heine's *Reiselied* the best among the new. The beginning is magnificent, but I don't like the passage where the sixteenths stop. Incidentally, I'm finding it very odd to see your things first in published form, when I immediately form an opinion of these pieces by Mendelssohn, as though they were not by Felix. I set Byron's *Farewell* yesterday, and before your letter arrived, I thought of sending that to you instead of a letter because I'm fond of it.[19]—What kind of a Psalm have you composed?[20] And is it German or Latin? Let me know about your subsequent composition plans.[21] Will you be writing soon the comic opera that I've been awaiting for such a long time? I'd love to write a Liederspiel some time if I only had the right text.

Today the weather is so bad that one wouldn't want to turn a dog out into it. It's been pouring buckets the entire day, with cold temperatures and thunderstorms. I'm convinced that we won't have any summer this year. The entire garden stands in indescribable splendor, and we've had scarcely three days to enjoy it.—Mother, whose last letter pleased you so much, is, thank God, miraculously bright, happy, and healthy. May God keep her so. Farewell. A thousand greetings to Cecile.

Please convey my sincere thanks to Madame Jeanrenaud for her kind, warm letter, which I definitely will answer soon. The Woringens, whom you've asked about, are well—we've had letters from them recently. You'll probably find out that Ferdinand became a Councillor in Liegnitz,[22] and that Louis Heydemann did brilliantly on his examination and will get married now.

[1]Fanny is responding mainly to a personal letter from Felix dated 29 May 1837. The original was unavailable or perhaps lost, although a brief excerpt, discussing non-personal issues, is published in Mendelssohn, *Briefe II*, 87-88. Felix mentions in his letter to Rebecka of 29 May 1837 (NYPL) that "I've written Fanny today in

detail about the trip to England." Fanny is also responding to the letter to Rebecka, and to a letter addressed to Lea of 29 May 1837 (NYPL). It was very unusual for Felix to write three separate letters to members of the family on the same day; no doubt his concern over possible bad feelings on the part of Fanny and Rebecka towards him prompted this multiple response. In his letter to Lea, Felix wrote that Fanny and Rebecka have not written him in a long time, and he fears the reason is their anger over his absence from Berlin this summer.

[2]Alexander Mendelssohn.

[3]Felix and Cecile were invited to visit the family in Berlin during the summer of 1837. This trip meant a great deal to the family, as they had not met Cecile.

[4]Felix wrote to Rebecka on 29 May: "I couldn't have declined the invitation without making a grave error. On such occasions it always strikes me how sorry I am that I'm just not able to live my life in Berlin with all of you. But then I must convince myself that I've certainly done everything in my power to make it possible, that circumstances have made it totally impossible, and therefore that it's no one's fault—things are the way they are. And yet I often come back to the disagreeable 'if.' Particularly when I'm alone with Cecile and see how kind and good she is, I'm often struck by the fact that all of you ought to know her, and then I really wish that Birmingham would go to the devil. But, as I said, I couldn't and shouldn't turn it down, and have to be glad that it's come to pass. All my connections with England seem to be getting even stronger. Hardly any weeks go by in London when they don't present my music . . . and from all that I realize that I'm doing the right thing by going there again."

[5]Cecile and her mother visited Felix in Leipzig in early February and had firm plans for a trip to Berlin for a few days, but on the morning they were to travel there (either 17 or 18 February), Madame Jeanrenaud came down with a bad sore throat and flu. She improved over the week, and then when it seemed possible that there would still be time to go to Berlin, she decided she wanted to return to Frankfurt so that she could be there for at least three weeks before the wedding (28 March). These events are explained in Felix's letters of 13, 18, and 25 February 1837 (NYPL). See also Fanny's letter to Felix of 20 February [1837] (GB VI 18).

[6]See letter 93.

[7]Felix responds that the letters of Fanny and Rebecka show "that for some reason they both think or thought me changed." Let it finally be said "that we will never change the way we feel about each other. Fanny says that I might say that she's mistaken, [and] she'd like to believe that—but is it a happy feeling for me to first say that she's mistaken regarding a matter in which I would have to misjudge and despise myself if it were true? And I want to answer her myself regarding the individual points she writes me, for none of them is really justified. But today I'd like to ask all of you not to believe in changes any more; they make life bitter and petty" (8 June 1837, NYPL).

[8]The creation of the nickname "Grimmhild" reflects Fanny's "Grimm" ("wrath"), but is also a modest transformation of "Kriemhild," the leading female figure in the Nibelung saga.

[9]Presumably mentioned in the unavailable letter from Felix to Fanny of 29 May.

[10]For Döhler see the *AMZ,* 21 Dec. 1836, col. 848, and 1 Feb. 1837, col. 76; for

Wieck see the *AMZ,* 22 March 1837, cols. 193-94; and for Henselt see the *AMZ,* 14 June 1837, cols. 388-89.
[11]Trio in E, Op. 83 (*AMZ,* 14 June 1837, col. 388). The word "Schmöker" carried the connotation of a trashy, old book.
[12]Fanny was fond of neither rococo style nor porcelain, as S. Hensel relates in *Lebensbild,* 48: "To the prejudices to which she subscribed and which I grew up with belongs, among others, the revulsion for the Rococo—in architecture, pictures, porcelain, furniture. It was an inviolate article of faith that the charming Charlottenburg Palace was horrible; one tolerated Sans Souci at best out of historical reverence; Meissen porcelain was a childish plaything, not to be discussed in artistic language; the pictures from the 'era of the braids' were not worthy of a glance."
[13]Variations on Meyberbeer's *Robert le diable* (*AMZ,* 14 June 1837, col. 388).
[14]"What you write about Henselt sounds sad—but what I could write about the musicians here wouldn't be any more cheerful." ("Was Du von Henselt schreibst klingt traurig— was ich Dir aber von den hiesigen Musikern schreiben könnte wäre eben nicht lustiger") (to Fanny, 24 June 1837; DB 3, 21).
[15]Opera by Gluck.
[16]Sophie Löwe sang the role of Amine in Bellini's *Nachtwandlerin* (= *La Sonnanbula;* Milan, 1831).
[17]Presumably the Sechs Präludien u. Fugen, Op. 35, published in the spring, 1837.
[18]Sechs Gesänge, Op. 34, published in the spring, 1837.
[19]Autograph dated 1 June 1837, in MA Ms 45, 36-37 (copy in MA Ms 31, 48-49).
[20]*Wie der Hirsch schreit,* Psalm 42, Op. 42.
[21]In his letter to Fanny of 24 June, Felix mentions a Quartet he has finished (probably e minor, Op. 44 No. 2), and another one he will start (probably E-flat major, Op. 44 No. 3); large piano pieces; and his difficulty with the Concerto (d minor, Op. 40).
[22]Presumably Ferdinand Woringen.

95

n. d. [PM 19 June (1837)]

I am herewith sending the said ram, to which I have added neither a red stroke nor any other stroke.[1] In this regard, it occurs to me that a report in the *Spenersche Zeitung* on the animal show in Stargard included the following: "Count von Itzenplitz, the senior civil servant, won, as usual, the prize offered for the best ram." That reminds me that Dorn told me yesterday that he saw the following placard in the park in Mannheim: "Whoever damages this notice risks prosecution to the full extent of the laws of this country."

Yesterday I held a brilliant rehearsal of *St. Paul* in the garden hall, with a chorus of 40 that will swell to about 50 next Sunday.[2] That probably seems rather ridiculous to you, but we're very happy about it. So think of us, dear Cecile, between 11 and 2 next Sunday. After that I don't need to tell you that everybody is fine here. Unfortunately Decker won't be able to perform all her solos because she's very close to her delivery date and ailing.[3]

Adieu, dearest children, I must go out. Write soon. Cecile is well, I hope? I assume that is the case, since Felix hasn't written anything to the contrary.

Your Fanny

[1]"Ram" could be figurative for "item."
[2]Felix writes that he would love to hear the performance "and also see my dear cantor at the piano; that will sound fuller than many of the renowned public performances that the newspapers drivel about." Felix had claimed that a performance of *St. Paul* in Berlin had been ridiculous, for it included only eleven numbers, presented out of order (24 June 1837, NYPL). Felix thanks Fanny for her efforts on behalf of his oratorio (to Fanny, 24 June 1837; DB 3, 21).
[3]Felix asks Lea: "Please also write me sometime whether Fanny gets exhausted from her large gatherings and the music making. They always made me very tired, and since Fanny suffers from weak nerves, [ ] I think she must be very careful." He then suggests that a "sea journey" would do her good (24 June, NYPL).

96

n. d. [after c. 10 July 1837][1]

I'm hereby retracting my recent condolences and pity, dear Cecile, because I can't commiserate with a *pauvre homme* like you who's living in Bingen on the Rhine with all possible comforts.[2] I was there with Paul and Albertine for a day last year, and it's marvelous. Are you staying in a guest house that one reaches by going through a small garden with 2 belvederes in both corners?[3] I've forgotten its name, but we stayed there. The summer is passing extremely fast here and our days are fairly uniform, but the Woringens will probably inject some change into our routine. Last week we spent 2 days in the country, 4 miles from here, to pick up Sebastian; he had traveled there with Luise a few days earlier.[4] It was actually the first time that I had been in the country in this area. If only the roads weren't so dreary as soon as they leave the stagecoach highways. Our stay there was very pleasant, for the people are very friendly and hospitable, and the wealthier gentry do almost as much visiting and socializing with their neighbors as people in happier countries.

Meanwhile, we did our part in spreading the rumor perpetrated by M. J. Herz about Felix's departure for England. Dear Felix, I could only read with nothing but disapproval that you count Meyerbeer, who is leaving his wife, among those musicians who lead a bad life, since you too are about to leave your wife so wickedly.[5] In her position, I would consider this just cause for the breakup of the marriage. Anyway, she's always complaining in her letters that she can't stand you. I have very few objections to the Prelude and Fugue that you want to play in London—why not?[6]

Do you know that Gluck's operas are being given here once again? Even though Eichberger appears as a veritable butcher in the role of Admetus, and Blume is an ox as Hercules, I still can't deny that I thoroughly enjoyed hearing the opera again.[7] Fassmann, whose vocal means are by far inadequate, sings and acts with such a sacrifice of all her available powers that she doesn't merely carry it off, but instead is a smashing success. Of course, one can't think of Milder, whose voice alone, apart from her musicianship, made such a wonderful effect in many passages. Nevertheless, one is happy to hear the notes again and see the same public after the passage of 10 or 20 years, when no Gluck opera was left unheard. The first tier in the opera house was empty, as previously, but the rest of the house completely full. The younger generation in particular, who didn't have the chance to hear Milder in her prime, was thoroughly delighted. There is a story about Milder being asked whether she had heard Fassmann in *Alceste,* to which she replied, "No, I've only heard the role done once by Milder and don't ever want to hear it again." Fassmann's appearance is reminiscent of Flaxman's figures, as Hensel very astutely perceived.[8]

Dear Felix, give me an idea of your Psalm, *Wie der Hirsch schreit.* Does he pant in 4 voices or 8, *a cappella* or accompanied?[9] And I'd like to find out about your Concerto.[10] I'm glad that you're thinking of writing another oratorio,[11] although one can't fashion a comic opera around the Bible. I would love to hear that you were writing one.

My musicales must now manage without Decker. Compared to her, the man who pulls out geese intestines is merely a string, and I've always claimed that she would give birth to a house rather than a baby. I'm sorry that the Woringens aren't able to see her more mobile. Be well. It's noon now and I'm still in my sleeping gown, and the doorbell just rang. Alas! Isn't it always the case that when one is behind in one's schedule, everyone comes to visit, but when one is dressed and looking nice, nobody comes. Please be well, and give my best regards to Madame Jeanrenaud.

Your Fanny

[Rebecka]

[1]See note 2.

[2]In a separate letter to Cecile, of 10 July 1837, Fanny offered Cecile her sympathy because Cecile was all by herself, as her husband went off somewhere. Crum, *Catalogue I*, 46, does not split these two letters. But the fact that the first one is addressed and directed only to Cecile, and the second one directed to both, points strongly to two separate letters. The earlier one, to Cecile only, is not included in this edition.

[3]Felix writes that it is the same place that Fanny and Paul stayed (22 July 1837, NYPL).

[4]Luise Hensel.

[5]Felix grumbled about having to leave his bride of four months (to Fanny, 24 June 1837; DB 3, 21).

[6]Felix asked Fanny what she thinks of him playing the Bach Organ Prelude in E-flat major and the Fugue at the end of the same collection, in Birmingham: "I believe she'll scold me, but I believe I'm right" (13 July 1837, NYPL; also in Mendelssohn, *Briefe II*, 91).

[7]*Alceste,* by Gluck.

[8]Ledebur writes of Fassmann that "at that time she filled a lacuna, which had originated when Milder left the Royal stage" (*Lexicon*, 149).
[9]Psalm 42. It is scored for five-part chorus and full orchestra: No. 1 is a chorus in F major of "Wie der Hirsch"; No. 2 a soprano aria in d minor; No. 3 a quintet in B-flat major for 4 men's voices and soprano; and No. 4 the final chorus in F major. "You would certainly like the first chorus and the quintet—I know it" (22 July). The final version has two additional middle movements. The compositional genesis of this Psalm is investigated in Seaton, *Sketches*, 136-79.
[10]The d-minor Piano Concerto, later published as Op. 40. Felix writes that it is not anything special as a composition, but the last movement "has so many fireworks that I often have to laugh when I go to play it properly. Again there will be three continuous movements—the first in d minor, Adagio in G major, the last in D major" (22 July).
[11]Recently he has definitely decided to write a new oratorio for the next Düsseldorf Music Festival, in two years. He will tell them all about the text as soon as that is determined (13 July 1837, NYPL). Felix requested Schubring's advice on a subject for this oratorio; he is thinking of St. Peter (14 July 1837, in Mendelssohn, *Briefe II*, 92-94).

97

31 July 1837

Today I only want to ask whether I've solved both canons correctly. Here is the first:

And here is number 2:

I'm not sure about the latter; the last measure sounds so base and not at all the way such a harmonious (I almost wrote "fragrant")[3] master such as you would create it. In the meantime, if a better solution strikes me, I'll telegraph you in Koblenz with the news—after all, this news is as important as anything else sent by telegraph. Today I cheered for the Chamber in Baden, which issued a unanimous petition of protest against the government's letters patent. Incidentally, this is discussed here more infrequently than one might imagine, for nobody wants to find himself in the position of defending this clumsy fool who so crudely plopped himself into his new kingdom. The most ardent legitimists don't even risk it, and if one has an opinion, the conversation soon comes to an end.[4] Unfortunately, we don't know anything yet about the Woringens and hope that nothing has happened in the interim—that would be a real shame. Meanwhile, everyone who had remained is now leaving the city, and only our good wishes will sustain them.

Does anyone know about Klingemann? We haven't received any word from you about him. Various letters from various members of this household have been left unanswered by the ingrate. Ompteda has arrived in Hanover and the legation is dissolved. What will happen to him now?[5]

Adieu, farewell. Enjoy yourself while you can. Think of me from time to time.

Please send my regards to your mother, dear Cecile.

[1]Published in Moscheles, *Letters*, 225. My thanks to Douglass Seaton for the following list of autograph sources: "Canone a 3," 16 December 1835, Leipzig, for Carl Kunzel (apparently listed in a 1960 catalogue by Hans Schneider); "Canone a 3," May 1836, Düsseldorf, with an engraved portrait of Theodor Hildebrandt (owned by William Sterndale Bennett's heirs in England); "[Canone] a 3," 17 September 1837, Birmingham, for Charles Woolloton (now at Staatsbibliothek in West Berlin); and "Canone a 3 unis.," 11 July 1842, London, to Felix Moscheles (published in the letters volume; autograph apparently auctioned by J. A. Stargardt, 15 May 1960).

[2]Identification unknown.

[3]An untranslatable German pun; refer to the original.

[4]As Baden had joined the Prussian Zollverein in 1836, perhaps this petition of protest was directed at the Prussian monarch, Friedrich Wilhelm III. Fanny, although generally apolitical, held liberal sympathies, in contrast to her royalist husband. See S. Hensel, *Lebensbild,* 14.

[5]Victoria's coronation took place in 1837, but under Hanoverian law no woman could serve as monarch. Thus the thread between these two countries was broken. Although the Hanoverian legation in London was officially dissolved, Klingemann was given another diplomatic position in London.

98

Berlin, 29 August 1837

We hasten to send you the news you request, dear Felix, which is, thank God, very reassuring about all of us. Previously we didn't know when you would arrive in England and where to address any letters.[1] As you've probably read in the newspaper, cholera has been rampant here, but we are cautious, unafraid, and, even better, exceedingly delighted with our dear guests.[2] I'm convinced that they have stayed with us longer than originally planned because of the cholera epidemic, and that makes them strangers no longer. This is their 4th week with us and they seem to like it here. Since Rebecka is rather inert and Mother doesn't go out in such heat, the *honneurs* of Berlin have largely fallen to me, and my dear husband and I have dispatched them with the greatest of style. We've made music or done silly things in the evening and laughed more in these few weeks than in several years. Franz paraded his comic talents, always praised by his sisters, after a 4-year silence, which far surpassed our expectations, and I can assure you that he is an extremely talented comic actor. They also performed improvisations in the Rhenish dialect, in which he portrays a stock figure, *dat* Hännesche. I'm sure that if you saw it you'd die laughing. The old man hasn't changed—he's still as kind and cheerful as ever—and it's been a real pleasure to live with such wonderful people.

Yesterday a letter from Ferdinand Woringen to his father arrived simultaneously with the letter from you and Cecile, and it contained a great deal of news about both of you. We're very happy to hear even more about him through word of mouth.—A few days ago poor Decker gave birth to a dead child after a great deal of suffering; fortunately, she herself is well. She really looked terrible in the final days of her pregnancy.

Tell Klingemann that I sincerely do not send my greetings. No one here sends his greetings, because the man is a traitor.[3] There are a few English songs here for him and his little MISS,[4] but he won't receive them soon. One of the things we don't know is in what capacity he will remain in England.

Adieu, farewell. I'm handing over the quill to Mother now. I have unlearned how to write. Did you take your lovely score of *St. Paul* to England?[5]

[Rebecka, Lea]

[1]Felix requested information on the cholera outbreak in Berlin and the health of the family, as he had not heard from them in a long time (24 August [1837], NYPL). Felix traveled to London on 25 August.
[2]The Woringen family, including Franz, Rosa, and Elise, and their father Otto.
[3]Klingemann writes a lengthy section at the end of Felix's first letter from London (29 August 1837, NYPL).
[4]Identity unknown.
[5]Felix will conduct *St. Paul* and other pieces in Birmingham.

99

Berlin, 12 December 1837

[Luise Hensel, with signatures of Sebastian, Margarethe Mendelssohn, Marie Mendelssohn]

I'm sitting down immediately to add something to the foregoing statement, signed by honorable witnesses, attesting to my innocence and to the slander on the part of the Singakademie. I've heard what you've been saying about me in Leipzig: "Fanny always has to meddle in my affairs," or "Who asked Fanny to answer for me or say anything for me?'' In short, I'd wager you're angry, but I protest.[1]

I'm looking forward to Clara Novello very much and plan to do everything possible to make her stay pleasant and useful.[2] I've heard Vieuxtemps, who plays wonderfully. A week ago Sunday he performed here: Variations by Bériot, and then Beethoven's Trio in D major with Ganz and me.[3] Then came *Davidde penitente* in which Decker sang the soprano part splendidly. The aria in B-flat major was unbelievably brilliant, and the long cadenza that I composed for her created a furor.[4] There were between 120 and 130 people here, and it was one of our most brilliant morning musicales. Little Vieuxtemps pleases me in several respects. He is unassuming and obliging, traits that are very admirable in someone who, since the age of seven, has been dragged around the world as a *Wunderkind*. Here they create enormous difficulties and intrigues against him, i.e. Möser and company, and unfortunately the cards are stacked here against a foreigner who wants to give a concert. But don't tell that to Novello.—Incidentally, congratulations on your new residence—may you live there in the best of health. I look forward to seeing you both in the spring; then you will be our guests. Dear Cecile, everybody here falls in love with the drawing of you, even more than the painting. But I am still exceedingly fond of that likeness.

Your meetings with Privy Councillor Keil must have been very interesting, but I also know why Felix doesn't want to miss them.[5] Or is such teasing no longer proper? Farewell. I wish Cecile the best news from Frankfurt.

Your Fanny

[1]The alleged meddling concerns the Singakademie's upcoming performance of *St. Paul* in January. Felix writes to Fanny on 13 January 1838 (DB 2) and pens a tongue-in-cheek, gently chiding response to her utilization of minors to sign her legalistic affidavit. ''You, meanwhile, are sentenced to attend the rehearsals of the Singakademie as punishment, which to be sure must be hard for you, since I know from experience what an unspeakable feeling it is to sit there, champing at the bit, but nonetheless being unable to help at all with the nicest words, because only the stick can help (I mean, of course, only the conductor's stick).'' (''Du indeß zur Strafe verurtheilt bist den Proben der Singe Akademie beizuwohnen, was allerdings für Dich hart sein muß, da ich aus Erfahrung weiß welch unsägliches Gefühl das ist, so dazusitzen, Jucken in allen Fingerspitzen zu fühlen, dennoch gar nichts

helfen zu können mit den schönsten Worten hinterher, weil nur der Stock hilft (ich meine ja nur den Dirigirstock).") Then, in all seriousness, he goes on to thank her for her help; he has heard from Lea, for example, how Fanny is trying to tell them their tempi are too slow. See also letter 100.

[2]On 13 November 1837 (NYPL), Felix reported on Clara Novello's great sensation in Leipzig. Two months later, Felix writes that she is to arrive in Berlin in January (13 January).

[3]Vieuxtemps performed in Leipzig (letter of 13 November). Felix wrote a formal letter of introduction for Vieuxtemps to the family (20 November 1837, NYPL). On 10 December 1837, Felix asked Fanny for her opinion of Vieuxtemps (DB 3, 22). He performed concerts in Berlin on 9 and 18 December; see the *AMZ,* 17 Jan. 1838, cols. 47-48.

[4]Mozart's K. 469. The only B-flat aria is "A te, fra tanti affani," for tenor. Another aria, "Fra l'oscure ombre funeste," is in MA Ms 71, with the soprano part written in Hensel's hand (undated).

[5]Felix told of boring social gatherings at Hofrath Keil's house (10 December).

100

Berlin, 15 January 1838

You've written such a lovely, merry letter, dear Felix, in spite of your painful ears and the bitter cold, that I can't refrain from sitting down immediately to answer it.[1] Oh, if one only knew if letters to you were being received, whether they elicited a joyous cry when received. May God render their journey short and sweet. If it's sometime, then that's short enough in this case. The assurance that I sent you recently and to which you responded in your last letter should validate once and for all the fact that I don't meddle freely in your affairs. If, for example, Adolph Martin Schlesinger tells you that I've allowed him to publish your copy, then he is lying. Or if the archivist Werner (husband of a bad actress) sends you a text with the remark that I've accepted it in your name and promised that you'll give him 1,000 talers for it, then be assured that I would politely have given him to believe that you probably wouldn't like any of his texts, for you are very peculiar and often critical and dangerous, and therefore one can't second-guess your opinions. Also, you live in Leipzig, and so a letter sent to you in the mail would arrive 2 days later. This is how I speak, so please call to mind these fruits of my wisdom when someone writes you to the contrary. Usually I add that it's not easy to count on an answer from you since you are a very busy man, your spelling is not the best, and your secretary is sick. By the way, the story concerning *St. Paul* is really fascinating. If nothing else, in my role as advisor I was able to avert great disaster for the noble apostle. Mother seems to have written you that Rungenhagen asked me in writing to attend the rehearsals and enlighten him with my opinions. So I went there last Tuesday and was quite appalled, just as you have described it.[2] I was suffering and champing at the bit, just like you, as I heard the whining and Grell's dirty fingers on the piano. I thought to myself, "If you were only up there, everything would be fine." Lichtenstein sat next to me and heard my sighs. They started "Mache dich auf" at half the right tempo,[3] and then I instinctively called out, "My God, it must go twice as fast!" Lichtenstein invited me to show them the way but told me that Schneider, the music director, had assured them that one cannot be ruled by a metronome marking. Then I assured them that they could be ruled by my word, and they had better do it, for God's sake. I went back on Friday, this time to the small hall in the Academy. I hadn't been there since Zelter's death and encountered all sorts of living and deceased ghosts. Then Rungenhagen came up to me after each chorus and asked me whether it was correct, and I told him honestly yes or no. But, overall, I was pleasantly surprised to find such an improvement, and started to become hopeful. On Saturday Rungenhagen was here for over an hour and had me listen to all the solo numbers. Friday I also spoke to Ries, who asked, among other things, how I would feel about adding a tuba to the organ part, as has been done in churches.[4] Now, said tuba is a monstrosity; it transforms all passages in which it appears into drunken beer brewers. Thus I fell on my knees and asked them to spare me and leave the tuba at home. Rungenhagen lifted me up and granted my plea.[5] Yesterday was the first large rehearsal, which far exceeded my expectations. To my great satisfaction, I can tell you that I was totally delighted with everything. The choruses, now taken with the correct tempo (a few perhaps too fast), were performed with fire and power, and enunciated as well as one could wish. The good old blockhead really went all out, and everyone was astonished at his liveliness. Many people realized from which direction the wind was blowing. But I've calmly restrained myself so as not to seem like the Don Quixote of your *St. Paul,* and I hope I haven't made any enemies—unless you count the tuba player. Ries was here again today, and I dispensed all the good advice that I had in my arsenal. Now I'm silent. First I must get together with you and learn some more. It's a shame, however, that you aren't conducting this performance; it would have been splendid and required only a minimum of effort on your part.[6] Tomorrow is the dress rehearsal—I'm very curious about it.—I'm looking forward to Novello very much. I've arranged to put on *Titus*[7] this Sunday, with your suggestion that she should sing from "Più di fiori" if she's so inclined.[8] Decker is singing Vitellia, and Fassmann, who came forth voluntarily and offered her services for everything, is singing Sextus, I think. It should be lovely. We've put a bee in Mother's bonnet that she should give a *Fête* for Novello. We and the Dirichlets have no money (I'm terribly hard up this winter), for otherwise we would do it.

This morning I discovered Mother sitting at her desk, deep at work, gluing in 10 to 12 new, ridiculous announcements into that certain book of hers. It's really nice for someone who is 61 to still have such a craving for fun.

The 16th. But tell me how far along you are with Planché, for of course I'm very interested.[9] Anyway, we will have so much to chat about in the spring, and how I look forward to that.[10] Among the Cantatas of Bach that you mentioned, please have a few of your choosing copied for me and sent as soon as possible.[11] I've presented many Mozart works this winter; a few new Bach pieces wouldn't hurt as a contrast. The Singakademie just sent 6 tickets with an invitation to honor them with my presence at *St. Paul.*[12] They're becoming very GENTEEL.

Adieu, my dearest. Commend me to Madame Schunck and Madame Jeanrenaud, and greet a certain Cecile from me. When you find this letter in the night light, you will think I sent it, but actually I didn't. I can nonetheless recommend it highly, for I have one just like it, and Cecile will delight in the nice glow it makes on the ceiling during her lying-in time.

Farewell, dearest people; my husband sends his best.

[1]To Fanny of 13 January 1838 (DB 2). In his various letters to the family of early

January 1838 (including in NYPL), Felix complains of ear trouble, a malady he had contracted many times.

[2]See note 1 to letter 99.

[3]Number 14 in the final version.

[4]Pieter Hubert Ries.

[5]Felix would agree with Fanny, as he never utilized the tuba in his orchestral works. Since beer was considered a vulgar drink, Fanny's imagery is especially pointed (see S. Hensel, *Lebensbild,* 7).

[6]Felix wrote on 13 November 1837 (NYPL): "It's curious with regard to the Berlin performance of my *St. Paul* in January. From all sides people ask me whether I'd accept the invitation. It's even in print, I've heard, that I'm to conduct. But no one has written me about it, and furthermore it would be in vain, because I couldn't go away even if I wanted to, as there are 4 subscription concerts and several additional concerts that month—and yet that's the least important reason holding me at home in January." The invitation from the Singakademie to Felix to conduct this performance is dated 20 November 1837 (GB VI 119). Six months earlier, Felix had clearly sounded negative about the Singakademie performing *St. Paul:* "When one really thinks about it, one has to become angry. They will certainly also perform my *St. Paul* for the public, but then I'll already have something else completed and no longer need their recognition and criticism" (24 June 1837, NYPL).

[7]= *La Clemenza di Tito.*

[8]In his letter to Fanny of 13 January, Felix mentioned Novello coming to Berlin on Tuesday or Wednesday, bringing letters from Felix. He advised that Novello should sing "Non più di fiori" (aria for Vitellia from *Titus*) and some works by Handel. He also described a concert she gave in Leipzig. Fanny had met Novello previously, in Leipzig (see Felix to Fanny of 14 January 1838; DB 3, 23).

[9]Felix has ordered an English opera text from Planché, since Holtei did not respond. "And yet I have so little interest in setting English! And yet I must." ("Und doch habe ich so wenig Lust Englisch zu componiren! Und doch muß ich") (13 January). Although Planché completes a libretto, based on the siege of Calais in the fourteenth century, Felix becomes disenchanted and withdraws from the project. The librettist recounts the events of the collaboration and his bitter disappointment at its outcome in his *Recollections*, 200-29.

[10]Felix is planning to come to Berlin and spend most of the summer of 1838 with the family (S. Hensel, *Familie II*, 44).

[11]Hauser has sent Felix a half-dozen Bach pieces for the Cologne Music Festival, of which two or three are really excellent. Felix offered to have some of them copied for Fanny, and he mentioned the 8-part *Nun ist das Heil und die Kraft*, BWV 50, as a work that will dazzle at her Sunday concerts (13 January).

[12]Performed on 18 January.

101[1]

Berlin, 19 January 1838

I want to send you a summary report on *St. Paul,* dear Felix, because since I was satisfied overall, you won't ask me to go into details and mention the mistakes. It was by far the best performance that has taken place here since Zelter's death. Every possible effort was expended, and one couldn't ask for more from anyone. It would have become a historic performance had you been here. The public was delighted, and here I'm declaring that I'm more satisfied after the fact than I had been, because such good impressions shouldn't be weakened by blame, even if justified.[2] I never heard the soprano part sung as beautifully as Fassmann did on this occasion. She is perfectly suited to this music, with a simple, noble, clear interpretation, transmitted by a beautiful, bright voice. I know you would like her. Clara Novello was there with Mother (we were all scattered) and enjoyed herself very much. On Sunday she will sing Vitellia's two arias here, Decker the remaining Vitellia and another *parto* as well, and Fassmann the remaining Sextus.[3]

I sent off the packet inserted in the Concerto yesterday, since it didn't occur to me in my wisdom the day before to check whether something else was there. I don't know Herr Dr. Meysenburg, have never even heard his illustrious name, and will not mention him again.[4]

But every Leipziger I've spoken with recently complains that you're overtaxing yourself, dearest Felix—you rehearse too much, etc.—and I've also seen how you don't have any rest. Cecile! I call on you to exert all your influence and, above all, to give us a daily report on the status of Felix's ears, as there are many people at your house who can drop us a line.

Now that Ries is dead, the Caecilienverein is without a director once again.[5] But don't take the position—I wouldn't like that at all.

What do you think about the London stock exchange?[6] Fire is voraciously consuming a great deal this winter.

20

Berlin, 19ten Jan.
1838.

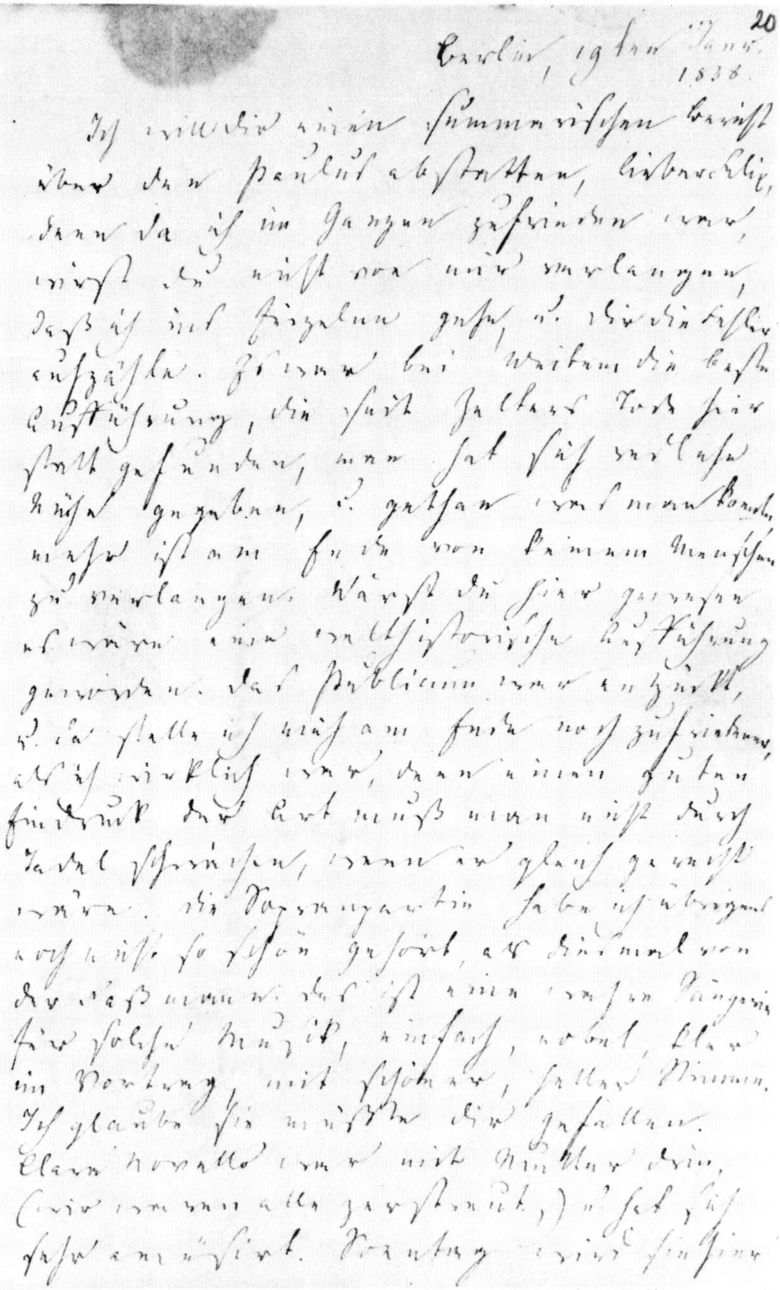

Illustration 8—Autograph letter from Fanny Hensel to Felix Mendelssohn, 19 January 1838 (first page) [Bodleian Library, Oxford: MS Margaret Deneke Mendelssohn d. 33, letter 20].

Tell me about your current pieces. Will the nuns' pieces and the new Psalm be issued soon?[7] It's fitting for you to perform Bach at the Rhenish music festivals, and I find *Du Hirte Israel* highly appropriate. He could hardly have created anything more cheerful. Or should it be something unpublished?[8] Don't forget to send me a pair of Cantatas.[9]

Adieu. Write soon about Felix's ears. Especially details. How things are in general.[10] I've heard, unfortunately, that in spite of the combined wisdom of Clarus and me, your residence is damp. Does it affect the bedroom also? Where do you eat? Where does Madame Jeanrenaud live? Adieu.

Your Fanny

My husband and sisters-in-law send their best.

Have you seen the lieder of Madame Matthieux? Two of them are quite lovely.[11]

[1]See Illustration 8 showing the first page of the autograph.

[2]"Your report on *St. Paul* in the Singakademie was also very gratifying, but forgive me if I attribute your pleasure more to your feelings for me and my music than to the performance." ("Dein Bericht über Paulus in der Sing Akademie war auch sehr erfreulich, aber verzeih mir, wenn ich Dein Vergnügen dabei mehr Deiner Gesinnung für mich u. meine Musik, als der Aufführung beimessen kann") (to Fanny, 3 February 1838; DB 3, 24). See the review in the *AMZ,* 21 Feb. 1838, col. 131.

[3]"If only I'd been at Fanny's *Titus* with Decker, Novello, and Fassmann! That must have sounded quite good . . ." (23 January 1838, NYPL).

[4]Felix asked Fanny if she knew him (to Fanny, 13 January 1838; DB 2).

[5]Ferdinand Ries.

[6]The second royal stock exchange was destroyed by fire in early 1838.

[7]Nuns' pieces = Drei Motetten, Op. 39, issued by Simrock c. March 1838; Psalm 42, Op. 42, issued by Breitkopf & Härtel c. November 1838.

[8]Felix wrote to the Committee for the Lower Rhenish Music Festival on 18 January 1838 and said that he wishes to introduce Bach into the festival. His suggestion is to perform a short Bach Psalm (c. 20 minutes to 1/2 hour) on the first day, and if the Committee is afraid to introduce Bach on the second day as well, then Felix suggests doing a Handel oratorio instead (Mendelssohn, *Briefe II*, 104).

[9]"You are to have a pair of Bach Cantatas very soon." ("Von den Bachschen Cantaten sollst Du recht bald ein Paar haben") (3 February).

[10]Felix writes that his ears feel much better (23 January).

[11]Ledebur, *Lexicon*, 355, lists many collections. Opp. 7 and 8 were issued in 1838 (Berlin), but Fanny could be referring to an earlier collection.

102

Berlin, 2 February 1838

Best wishes on your birthday tomorrow, dear Felix. But the greatest gift that a person can be given is another person who belongs to him. May your dear wife deliver that to you, and may the baby be washed, bathed, and wrapped up for you. By the way, I'm happy to be able to announce that the negative reception you so greatly feared for Novello didn't really materialize, and they seem to like her here as much as she likes them. You already know that she sang to a sold-out opera house, and at her concert in the large hall yesterday, the most elegant people attended—the entire court and everybody *comme il faut*—and showered her with applause. In the opera house her stance was a bit timid, as she stood motionless and looked slightly underdressed without anything in her hands. Since it was quite obvious, we told her about it and dressed her to best advantage for yesterday's concert. She held a fan of Rebecka's and a bouquet from Paul, wore a wreath that I gave her, and all our jewelry—she looked glorious. I'm curious to speak with her now, for she must be thoroughly satisfied; such a concert hasn't been given here since Sonntag and Paganini. But tell me whether her style of performing Handel—for example, using a quick tempo, much to my liking—is common in England. She is such a marvelous concert vocalist that her plan to go on the stage in Italy seems risky: she lacks mobility and fire, both necessary dramatic qualities. What do you think? Don't you agree?[1] We were with her at a very brilliant gathering recently, where Jews and actors were in attendance, and the finale from *Don Juan,* among others, was magnificently performed.[2] I've never heard the so-called masked trio, sung by Fassmann, Novello, and Mantius, rendered so well. Bader, who was ill, heard it that evening for the first time and was thoroughly charmed. Moreover, she seems to have turned the heads of the Leipzig gentlemen who followed her here—your cousin Schunck and Dr. Weber—and they stand next to her on either side and hang on to her every word. There will be a big bash at Paul's on Monday to which just about everybody is invited. We won't be able to give any parties this winter because we're too hard up.

Tomorrow Hensel will celebrate the silver anniversary of his campaigns of 1813.[3] One grows old, and before one turns around, a part of one's life is over. Adieu. This dreadful observation shouldn't appear at the end of a birthday letter, so let me say instead, rejoice in your happiness. Give Cecile my warmest wishes. Have a delightful day, but a quiet one, for Cecile might be in bed and the little one might bring you a serenade. Adieu, you dear ones.

Fanny

Hensel sends his very best wishes.

[Sebastian]

[1]"It completely surprised me that Novello is doing so well there. I actually recommended her more out of feelings of duty than friendship, because for me personally her coldness is too cold, and remains so. But everything is lovely and musical, and thus better than most of what we hear. I don't want to predict whether she is suited for the theater. She will warm me as little on the stage as in the concert hall, but she will therefore also be fine and irreproachable, and such a quality usually pleases people more than clumsy ardor, which they encounter all the time, and which distorts the text." ("Das hat mich ganz erstaunt, daß die Novello bei Euch so viel Glück macht; ich habe sie eigentlich immer mehr aus Pflichtgefühl als aus Freundschaft empfohlen, denn mir persönlich ist diese Kälte wie zu kalt, u. bleibts. Aber nett u. musikalisch ist alles, u. somit besser als das meiste, was wir hören. Ob sie zum Theater taugt, oder nicht möchte ich doch nicht voraus sagen; mich wird sie auf der Bühne eben so wenig erwärmen, als im Concertsaal, aber sie wird drum auch da fein u. untadelig sein, u. den Leuten gefällt dergleichen meist besser, als die unbeholfene Wärme, die ihnen immer in die Queer kommt, u. den Text verdreht.") Then he thanks everyone for their kind reception of Novello (to Fanny, 3 February 1838; DB 3, 24). See the *AMZ,* 21 Feb. 1838, cols. 131-32; and 21 March 1838, cols. 194-96.

[2]Part of the Finale to Act I, sung by Donna Anna, Donna Elvira, and Don Ottavio.

[3]He was wounded three times, in the battles of Lützen, Bautzen, and Leipzig, in the so-called Wars of Liberation fought against Napoleon's forces.

103

Berlin, 14 February 1838[1]

Although I really have nothing to write except my very best wishes, I want to thank you on my behalf for the numerous, timely, and excellent bulletins.[2] I haven't read any as interesting since those issued with respect to the sleep and happy mood of the Archduke of Austria in Venice. Cecile seems very adept in her wifely *métier*, and may God preserve her. We have great fun with the big boys' mischief (the eldest one is now taking a lesson in writing and arithmetic with another boy in the room).[3] May Paul have a girl! He will attend the baptism with Albertine and looks forward to it very much. Have you already decided on the baby's name? Cecile will certainly recover her beauty—her shape, color, and everything else—when she gets up and around. According to local practice, she should be leaving her bed tomorrow. By the way, it seems that women there are also subjected to a humiliating hunger, when otherwise Cecile is not a glutton. Her complaint moves me very much, since I know how I always feel about bland soup.[4]

Ries spoke with Paul 2 hours after his arrival, but he hasn't been here yet.[5] Almost a year has passed since you were such abominable correspondents last April, but I hope you will make up for it soon. Send me your Psalm in advance so that I'll have something to sing at my Sunday musicales. I really didn't know that you had composed even more movements for it.[6] Oh, the dilettante concert! If I had a sense of humor, I'd tell you stories about it. They make great fun of me in the house because I always stick up for Curschmann. Beckchen claims I do it so that I can speak well of *one* local musician, whereas I claim he's the only one who regularly displays any manners and doesn't eat soup with his fingers.____But how important are manners if he uses the first opportunity in which he appears as a conductor to arrange a despicable, terrible concert such as the world has never seen? It's as if one were to arrange a dinner in the following way: soup—sugar water; steak—a piece of candy;

vegetables—a meringue; fish (I interrupt with a reasonable item, for I by no means acceded to his will in all respects—he also wanted a piece played totaling a dozen measures); roast—a piece of sugar; and for dessert—all of the above, and may the—!

By the way, I'm not fearful now and hope that state of mind will continue.[7] Novello is still wracking up successes and one can take it for granted at present that the house will be full wherever she sings.[8] At the Ganzes' recent concert, she sang, on my advice, a few lieder to her own accompaniment (we had already gone, because we had to remain in the anteroom in the back), and is said to have made a hit with the Berliners. Now we see her rarely because she is becoming depressed, a feeling you know only too well. Farewell. Hensel sends his very best, especially to Cecile. He delivered a very lovely drawing of Marianne's three daughters yesterday, which, to our great delight, received unanimous praise.[9] Now he's reworking one out of gratitude to the King of Saxony. Farewell, dearest people. Commend me to Madame Jeanrenaud, dear Felix, and give my very best to Madame Schunck and Julie.[10]

Your Fanny

[1]Incorrectly dated 13 February 1838 in Crum, *Catalogue I*, 52.

[2]Felix's letters to Fanny of 9 February (DB 3, 25) and 12 February 1838 (DB 3, 26) reported on the progress of the newborn baby, Carl. Fanny sent congratulations in a letter of c. 7 February 1838 (GB VII 178).

[3]Presumably Sebastian and his younger cousin, Walter Dirichlet.

[4]See letter of 13 February 1838 (NYPL).

[5]Pieter Hubert Ries had been in Leipzig to participate in a benefit concert (to Fanny, 3 Feb. 1838; DB 3, 24).

[6]"My Psalm *Wie der Hirsch* is and remains my favorite piece of church music, and pleased me very much yesterday at a concert . But you know that I've composed 4 additional numbers for it (the entire Psalm); you'll receive the piano version soon." ("Mein Psalm 'wie der Hirsch' ist u. bleibt mir mein liebstes Kirchenstück, u. gefiel mir gestern wieder gar zu gut. Du weißt doch, daß ich noch 4 Nummern dazu componirt habe (den ganzen Psalm) nächstens kommt der Clavierauszug für Dich") (to Fanny, 9 February). See Seaton, *Sketches*, 136-79.

[7]Regarding her piano playing in the forthcoming public charity concert. See letter 104.

[8]See letter 102.

[9]Marianne Mendelssohn's three daughters: Marie, Margarethe, and Alexandrine.

[10]Presumably Julie Schunck.

104

Berlin, 21 February 1838

In the hope that your good health will permit you to read a letter yourself now, and with the intention of preparing you for a healthy boredom, I'm addressing this letter to you, dear Cecile. I want to tell you how happy we are over your exemplary lying-in period and all your wifely virtues. Certainly you must derive infinite joy from holding your infant at your breast and nourishing him yourself; how I look forward to seeing you this way! Your admirable calmness is also one of the indispensable qualities for nursing. How fortunate that Felix doesn't have a child to nurse! In general, Mother Nature knew very well what she was doing when she left the entire department of childbearing to us—I would love to see a man take it on even once! I want to leave this topic, however, because, who knows, in the end your mother may not allow you to read a letter yourself, and she will read it to you, and then I'll be embarrassed in front of her. I have a terrible fear of your mother anyway—

Our much-discussed dilettante concert was launched with dazzling success the day before yesterday. It took in 2,300 talers and cost practically nothing. But you wouldn't believe what a wealth of trivial vanities, grand claims, and considerable unpleasantness came to the fore in the process. Such dilettantes are wilder than a pack of horses once they unleash their bestiality. Mother will have written you how comically the little, sweet-voiced Novello let herself go with her hands, feet, and lungs to portray a *prima donna*. It was certainly poetic license to count her among the dilettantes. Today she's giving her last concert. I wanted to be the one to tell you that I surprised myself and played without fear and inhibitions. I'm very glad to have made this discovery on one occasion.[1] It's a shame that the arrangement of the entire concert was so ludicrously bad; it could have been really wonderful for the same expenditure of money. If Novello grants me another day as a favor—she actually wants to travel on Saturday—then I think I'll have the thrice-performed *Don Juan* given one last time on Sunday. I'll tell you more about it later. Ries told me many nice things about both of you, including Felix's new Psalm, which, according to what he told me, must have received an entirely new shape.[2] How I look forward to it. He also told me about the new Quartet.[3] It's actually unnecessary for me to write—Mother writes so often and so well that I'm just a 5th wheel and never have anything new to say. But I do it anyway for my own pleasure. When you're here, we will have a merry time together. Regarding the city, I think that even Felix in the midst of his furious anger against us poor Berliners cannot deny that it won't be the best time of the year to visit—sometime earlier would have been best for the cultural attractions, and sometime later for the garden. So you will be forced to be fond of being alone with us. But let's get along with each other—my great quarrel with Felix last time still sears my soul.

Dear Felix, I received a note from the good Mme. Kiené yesterday. She still lives as always, is quite fond of you and everyone here, and sends you her heartfelt wishes. When you have the time, drop a line to the dear old woman—she will be very grateful. I will also answer her right away. Farewell. I must give Sebastian a lesson. He's feeling fit as a fiddle this winter, thank God. What will you name your little man, who will eventually be a big man? Have you had great debates over it? Farewell, you dear ones!

Your Fanny

[1]A review appears in the *AMZ,* 28 March 1838, col. 209, which mentions Fanny briefly: "Then a sister of the composer performed the Concerto for Piano in g minor by F. Mendelssohn-Bartholdy rapidly and securely." Felix wrote Fanny before the event: "You are indeed playing in concert! *Bravisississisimo.* That is lovely and splendid; if only I could hear it!" ("Du spielst ja im Concert! bravisississisimo. Das ist nett u. prächtig; könnte ichs hören!") (12 February 1838; DB 3, 26). In the general family letter a few days later, Felix asked someone to write and tell him about Fanny's performance, "which truly enlightens the Berliners" (14 February 1838, NYPL). Fanny also writes to Klingemann about the event, on 27 February 1838 (S. Hensel, *Familie II*, 43).

[2]Psalm 42.

[3]An E-flat String Quartet, dated 6 February 1838 (Bartlitz, *Works,* 153), and published as Op. 44 No. 3.

105

Berlin, 7 September 1838

You dear angel, you sweet lamb, it's awful that you have the measles and your lovely clear face is full of spots.[1] People like you who were born under a lucky star should never have such misfortune. If I didn't have my child to care for and weren't expecting my husband, that is, if my duties to my immediate family weren't holding me here, I would have come immediately to pamper you and help pass the time when Felix had to go out.[2] It was my first instinct, but unfortunately I couldn't follow it. If I were in control, I'd proclaim that the illness is over, and tomorrow you would be permitted to get up and have clear soup. Now we're sitting back with a little smile on our faces to see who will be infected by this second round of measles—Mother, Madame Dirichlet, Minna or I, or any others. It would be a very unfortunate time for me to contract the disease now because my husband is expected home next week; I wouldn't be so concerned at any other time. If little Carl held his ears stiff, it would be miraculous. Furthermore, I can assure you, dearest Cecile, that children are a real joy. Sebastian had a fever for two days and was burning up and hallucinating as easily as Felix. But then he immediately became cheerful again, regained his appetite, and was in a wonderful mood. By the way, he comes up with the funniest ideas when he's feverish, and one can't help laughing. At the moment, he's walking around in a long sleeping gown and lacks only a pipe in his mouth to be a total Philistine.

Rebecka really liked the oysters that I gave her yesterday. She first got out of bed the day before yesterday, had a strong migraine attack yesterday that passed fairly quickly, and will go down to Walter the day after tomorrow. He will be out of bed tomorrow. Now we can finally see the light at the end of the tunnel. But this was truly an unfortunate time after the good times this summer.[3] If only the nice weather would last a while longer to help you recover from the measles! Of course, it would also be beneficial to my husband's crossing. Last week, just when Sebastian was ill, the most sinister storms roared; oh Cecile, I became frightened when I thought of the crossing and then of the feverish child. Hensel wrote that Bunsen had a terrible sea journey. It took some 50 hours from Rotterdam to London; during 10 of those hours the ship was aground on a rock, in the worst of danger, and everyone was seasick.

We've made such an improvement to our garden that I'm angry at myself that I didn't suggest it for your visit. But it didn't occur to me earlier, so I suppose it's nobody's fault. Half of the thick lilac bush that ran the entire length of our house was cut down, and now the little yew tree stands alone, hardly reaching our balcony. This enables us to have a clear view of the lawn. A large section of the other lilac bush was also cleared, permitting air and light to stream into our house. It also looks much nicer.

Dear Felix, when text is removed from sung lieder so that they can be used as concert pieces, it is contrary to the experiment of adding a text to your instrumental lieder—the other half of the topsy-turvy world. I'm old enough to find many things utterly tasteless in the world at present: that may well fall into that category. But shouldn't a person think a lot of himself (no, he shouldn't) when he sees how the jokes that we, as mere children, contrived to pass the time have now been adopted by the great talents and used as fodder for the public? From time to time the public is indescribably undemanding, and then another time totally severe. In short, the public is just like a man. Since you left, I've dragged Mother to the theater twice. We've seen *Correggio,*[4] and Löwe in *Hamlet.* We had to stand at *Correggio,* and it was dazzling. At a 2nd performance, Gern was ill, and—Seydelmann took his place and played the landlord. Mother didn't want to go at first, but later enjoyed herself immensely.[5]

Now farewell, dearest children. It's the afternoon, and I must put Sebastian to bed for a nap, since he's been up a long time. Mother, the Dirichlets, and Minna send their best and wish you a speedy recovery.[6]

[1]Fanny is addressing Cecile; Felix reported her measles in a letter of 4 September 1838 (NYPL).

[2]Hensel is returning from a trip to London, which had begun in late May. His experiences there are described in S. Hensel, *Familie II*, 44-49.

[3]The Felicians had spent a lovely summer with the family in Berlin, but hastened home sooner than planned because of the measles epidemic (*ibid*, 49-50).

[4]Play by Oehlenschläger.
[5]Felix also saw Seydelmann, who makes a strong impression, "but not as great as in Berlin, where his environment is completely different" (to Fanny, 11 October 1838, DB 3, 28; S. Hensel, *Familie II*, 52).
[6]Almost one month later, Felix is still weak from the measles (fourth week), but Cecile is totally recovered (11 October).

106

Berlin, 14 December 1838

Dear Felix, Schulz was here yesterday and today to discuss the matter with me. She is very desirous of having her daughter reach an agreement with you, but stated that the contents of the letter from the directors were totally different from your letter.[1] She noted specifically that everyone would know that her daughter was already engaged as a singer for half the season, whereas you stipulated only one concert. I don't know how she answered your letter, but she asked me to tell you that she didn't want any honorarium for these engagements, but only travel and lodging expenses for herself, her daughter, and a maid. I am ordering as per her instructions. Furthermore, I believe that if you do reach an agreement, you will have acquired a fine property in Hedwig Schulz. She really sang beautifully as Gabriel in the *Creation* yesterday. Her voice is lovely and rich, and she has already made considerable progress. Of course, there are still flaws. For example, she does a trill in which she risks being thrown off a half-step at the end, just like Fräulein Schlegel. But that doesn't constitute a risk if you forbid her to do it, because she is a very agreeable and teachable girl. In addition, when she holds a note, the pitch wobbles excessively because she hasn't mastered her control yet. But she is still in the process of learning and will improve rather than get worse, and if you take her on, which you've done for many undeserving people, and she disciplines herself a little, I believe she will meet the standards that the Leipzigers have come to expect in their female singers. I'm actually acting contrary to my best interests in concluding this contract, because I could certainly use her in my musicales now that Decker will be absent, which is very likely after the New Year. Herr von Dachröden also expressed an interest in her yesterday. It would be extremely difficult for anyone to find two dilettantes anywhere who could sing the soprano roles in the *Creation* as well as Schulz and Curschmann did yesterday.

Everything is fine here, thank God. Rebecka went out yesterday and she's been feeling well since that emergency with her tooth. May God grant that it stays this way. If only we could spend some Christmas together again! But unfortunately this holiday has the nasty habit of falling in the winter, when traveling with children is extremely arduous. We won't be very cheerful this year but will make the best of things. The poor Woringens will have a sad holiday. I'm very curious to know what they will decide for the future.

Recently we took Sebastian and Walter to the theater for the first time and they were a delight to watch. We saw *The Magic Flute.* During the entire first act they sat with their mouths open in dead seriousness, but later they gathered the courage to laugh and have a good time.

Adieu, my dearest. Darling Cecile, you could also write me sometime. Kiss little Carl for me and tell him about his ridiculous aunt. Oh, how nice it was when both our dear children were taken into the garden together.

Farewell.

Your Fanny

[1]Hedwig Schulz and her mother, Mme. Schulz. Felix wrote on 10 December 1838 (NYPL): "Herein is a letter from our concert directors to the daughter of Mme. Schulz. I'm requesting Fanny to have it brought to her as soon as possible, and to send me her answer as soon as possible. If the women would like to have more information verbally, then would Fanny be so good as to give it to them. We would like her to sing here once in February or March (i.e., an aria and a cavatina—the former, if possible, with recitative), would naturally take care of all the costs of the trip, also (if she wants it) an honorarium, although of course not a large one, and if she'd like, we'd love an engagement for all of next winter to grow out of it." Felix sends a preliminary response to Fanny on 29 December 1838 (DB 1; S. Hensel, *Familie II,* 53): "Herein is once again a letter to Mme. Schulz on behalf of the directors. I want to tell you, dear Talleyrand, that the gentlemen are offering her the enclosed 60-taler honorarium for the concert—the costs incurred on the trip, etc., seem too uncertain—and suggesting the 31st of January. I am divulging this

to you so that you can assure her, in case it comes up, that we cannot pay any more; for presumably she will want to negotiate, but I'm against it, and I'm glad that the gentlemen immediately settled on a sum, which they've never given before, because our Englishwomen receive less. I also thought one can be satisfied with it.''

107

Berlin, 6 January 1839

Dear Felix, I've been a very poor foreign minister and fear that your chamber will ask for my resignation, no matter what the address on this letter may turn out to be.[1] Schulz will appear as the Countess in *Figaro* next week. She will be of little value to the local stage because I don't think her voice is capable of filling the opera house, although she would have been fine for your hall. And so, as often happens, she's not putting herself in a situation where she can shine. I'm sorry on your account, and hers and mine as well, that I wasn't able to help you. Your big shot, Thalberg, is also here now. He was at Mother's, who kept him for herself. Tomorrow we will eat with him at Alexander's,[2] but I hear, unfortunately, that he doesn't play at private gatherings, and one won't be able to learn much from the pair of concerts. One must really view these wizards as they play. I'll acquire the things ahead of time that he will play in order to get the most out of them. These gentlemen approach the difficulties in an incredibly casual way, and don't even need a rehearsal because they perform everything without accompaniment, resulting in more money in less time. I'm well aware that you are the gentlest of the gentle, and am convinced that Thalberg plays magnificently, but I just cannot praise this style of playing—that makes me the Charivari.[3] We had a great delight two nights ago when Seydelmann read to us again. He had selected Antonio in *Tasso* because it will be his next role.[4] But because he wasn't in optimum voice to read an entire play, the rest of us, with a sacrifice worthy of praise, were prepared to rattle off the other roles, although we confined ourselves mainly to the scenes in which Antonio appears. What refinement, charm, irony and dignity he brings to this role—one can hardly conceive it even when one knows it. It is truly a masterpiece. Later we requested *The Cranes of Ibicus,* and then he suggested the *Battle with the Dragon.*[5] He was so pleased with our delight that he's volunteered to read whatever and whenever we ask him, and we will certainly not hesitate to take up his offer. Seventeen people were here, about the maximum number that can fit comfortably in our living room, and the evening was thoroughly enjoyable.[6] But now to Franck! We had already heard it rumored that after all of Europe had *taken to him*, he would take to Leipzig in the end. That's wonderful for you. If the women like each other he will be an invaluable improvement to your little circle.[7] Give him my heartfelt wishes. I would love to see this old friend once again. But please tell him for me that if he wants to buy furniture here, he should do it in person. I want to run around with him and first take him to the worst stores so that he will have to stay longer, and then in the end make sure he's satisfied. Around the same time that your letters made me think about him, I came across his splendid Etude with the caption, "Gentle and somewhat sentimental, but not too slow." If he wants to publish it himself, I'll send it to him, and since he knows the composer well, he could order the remainder of the dozen and include a description of himself as a preface, instead of a portrait, which I, another famous author, made of him. Does he still intend to have his first child nursed by a lioness? And is his wife in agreement with this choice of a wetnurse?

I'm very glad that you're publishing your Psalm in E-flat.[8] I like many parts of it very much, especially the beginning and end. Where can the reviews by Goethe from 1772 and 1773 be read? Have you read the letters to Countess Stolberg in *Urania* 39?[9] They are truly strange. On the whole, Goethe's estate confirms the general rule of estates: there are usually good reasons why a clever man withdraws certain items from public view, and as a result the public hardly loses out. However, one can still become angry at his publishers, his correspondents, and his heirs, and even the person himself. But then one need only read a scene from *Tasso* and a song from *Hermann und Dorothea* to belong to him heart and soul, or possibly more deeply than that. We're fortunate to have had him. I believe he would have been pleased with Seydelmann in the role of

Antonio.—Since then, we've eaten with Mother and squabbled over everything again. I think I hear you laughing when we argue so seriously about the King's beard. But Cecile, my dear Cecile—you haven't sent me even the tiniest letter since you left. Is that right? Remember that there are hardly any people who love you as much as I.

The 7th

Yesterday evening the big shot drank tea at Mother's.[10] You know that our gatherings are the most boring when a great man is there. This discovery was confirmed yesterday as well. Among those whom he is accused of resembling, I mention only Lord Wellington, the lovely Victoria, and Lida Bendemann. Select one from this group. I have *à peine* made his acquaintance. Earlier I had intended to ask him to give me the opportunity of hearing him play in a room, but then I found him so virtuoso-like, so posh and self-satisfied that I preferred to let it go, and, as always in such situations, let my eloquence carry me along. He will meet Paul in Russia, who disclosed yesterday that he has to travel to this hellish place in a week. He's leaving Albertine here, which I find very sensible considering the time of the year, and therefore he will, I hope, return soon.

The Woringens are having great difficulties, and life in their house seems to be becoming totally unbearable. Ferdinand, as you know, is still there, Franz intends to fetch the girls at Easter, and yesterday Rebecka made the very sensible suggestion that they ought to travel with her to the seacoast—a health measure long prescribed for Elise. If this plan comes to fruition, it will be very beneficial for both sides. Ferdinand will come through here in approximately one week, and we'll probably hear many more details from him. I hope they will remain here in the future.

But I must praise you once again for your light screen and your little picture for Rebecka, which both turned out quite lovely.[11] Make a round light screen sometime, which can be placed on the lamp—they look so pretty. You could also paint another little picture for me sometime, and Cecile owes me a little something too. Today, I think, the little picture for Mother should arrive.[12] Adieu, dear people. Felix, a more unjust accusation has never been brought before a tribunal than this, which says that I write you short epistles for long ones: 3 long and short for one, *à la bonne heure*.[13] Thalberg related something about Dreyschock—it's really fantastic: he plays the [18]th Etude of Chopin with octaves in the bass.[14] Thalberg says, looking all the while like honey cooked with sugar and a little drop of rum, "If the man had taste, he would play us all dead." The Prunelle woman has spread the rumor here that little Carl has 3 tiny teeth. If it's true, how can you, hard-hearted Mother, write us nothing about it? But in all seriousness, be well. Writing goes well for me today, as you can see. Do you know that Henselt is giving lessons in Russia for 3 ducats?

Adieu, my husband sends his best. If you gave a landscape to the exhibition sometime, the public would certainly not say your wife was unfortunate, for two reasons.

Your Fanny

[1]Regarding the Hedwig Schulz negotiations; see letter 106.
[2]Alexander Mendelssohn.
[3]Charivari = someone with an unpopular point of view or a fussy attitude. Both Fanny and Felix applied the appellation to Fanny. Thalberg had given a concert in Leipzig on 28 December, and Felix wrote to Fanny on 29 December 1838 (DB 1; S. Hensel, *Familie II*, 54) that Thalberg "gave me extraordinarily great pleasure. See that you get to hear him a lot, for he, like everything perfect, gives one the desire to play and study again. One can only be astonished at such a fantasy by him (namely, that on *Donna del Lago*): a compendium of the most desirable, finest effects, and an intensification of difficulties and delicacies. Everything so worked out and refined, and with such sureness and skill, and replete with the finest taste. In addition, the man possesses unbelievable power in his fist, and further such experienced, light fingers—unique. As I said, hear him very often; one cannot find anything more exquisite in virtuoso music."
[4]Play by Goethe (1790).
[5]Ballads by Schiller.
[6]Sebastian held fond memories of Seydelmann's excellent readings (S. Hensel, *Lebensbild*, 18).
[7]Hermann Franck, who appeared rather suddenly at Felix's house and announced he will be living in Leipzig for a while. They have visited many times and get along famously (28 December 1838, NYPL). In 1839 and 1840 Franck edited the *Deutsche Allgemeine Zeitung* in Leipzig.
[8]Psalm 95, *Kommt, lasst uns anbeten,* to be published as Op. 46. "I'm now preparing my Eb-major Psalm for publication; you'll be surprised at the new things in it. On 24 February is a charity concert; we want to perform this Psalm and the previous one, *Wie der Hirsch,* . . . then." ("Ich mache jetzt meinen es dur Psalm zur Herausgabe fertig, Du wirst Dich über die Neuigkeiten drin wundern. Am 24

Februar ist Armenconcert, da wollen wir diesen Psalm u. den vorigen 'wie der Hirsch schreit' . . . aufführen'') (29 December). See also Felix's correspondence with Kistner in Mendelssohn, *Verleger*, 303-17.
[9]= *Urania*, a literary annual, for the year 1839.
[10]Thalberg.
[11]Both Christmas gifts from Felix (22 December 1838, NYPL).
[12]A view from Felix's window, painted by Cecile (28 December).
[13]The accusation appeared in a letter to Fanny of 29 December.
[14]Felix heard Dreyschock on 27 December and wrote that he ''plays both ears off the devil'' (28 December).

108

n. d. [c. 3 February 1839]

Best wishes on this third of February, dear Felix and dear Cecile! May you preserve everything you have—it doesn't come any better —and thank God we can all express our good wishes. Unfortunately I have little prospect of seeing you this year, but I do think that Rebecka will come as soon as the weather turns warmer.[1] Above all, I hope she will relax and be able to recover. How long it's been since we've spent any of our birthdays together. What a blot on our personal history that we don't live in the same city. But let's at least come together as often as possible, for life is short!

From Paul we've had daily reports of snow; he's traveled from Tilsit to Schlitten. Albertine is eating with different members of the family each day.

We experienced a gruesome pleasure yesterday evening: Seydelmann read *Richard III* to us.[2] Each time one hears him, one thinks he's never read before, but when he gets warmed up and excited, he turns into a veritable tiger, and that is really magnificent.

I've had particularly bad luck with music making this winter. I still haven't succeeded in getting started, and if it doesn't happen soon it will be too late; then I'll give it up.

Won't Shaw be coming here? Please send her![3] Today I read that Garcia has been engaged for the Philharmonic's season in

London. I'd really love to see her there. Tomorrow Thalberg will present his 4th concert, in addition to a charity benefit he performed at the opera house. His third was already billed as his farewell concert, this one his last. I don't know whether he will follow up with an absolute last, but this much is clear: he scorns no virtuosic trick.[4]

Dear Felix, you will find a small alabaster bust of Shakespeare in this box; please use it to adorn your room. My husband joins me in conveying our very best wishes. Sebastian wants to congratulate you himself in his stiff style. Farewell, dearest brother. May God grant you a long and happy life. The more virtuosos I know, the more I thank God with self-righteous pride that you didn't become one of them, so empty and so vain.

Rebecka recently claimed that Mother has always sent packages to you on the sly, since we usually find out about them after the fact. Farewell, dearest children, and think of us in your happiness.

Your Fanny

[1]Felix had invited Fanny for a visit (to Fanny, 29 December 1838; DB 1).

[2]Sebastian later described this event: "In *Richard III* before the great battle scene, when Richard calls, 'A horse, a horse, my kingdom for a horse,' he stopped, because, he said, it must be screamed in a terrifying way, which is impossible in a room" (S. Hensel, *Lebensbild* 18). Felix had seen Seydelmann for the first time in 1834 and thought him wonderful (19 February 1834, NYPL). His popularity in Berlin reaches back a few years; Fanny wrote in 1835 about the Seydelmania ("Seydelmannie") rampant there (to Felix, c. May 1835; GB IV 47).

[3]Felix is sending her to Berlin from Leipzig with a letter for the family, which includes a formal introduction. He also described her demeanor, her style of singing, and her favored repertoire. Fanny will truly enjoy making music with her (29 January 1839, NYPL).

[4]For extensive reviews of his five Berlin performances in January, see the *AMZ,* 20 Feb. 1839, cols. 141-44.

109

n. d. [c. 4 February 1839]

First of all, dearest Felix, I'm sending my best wishes once again, this time on a later date than appears within the little box.[1] And secondly, on to the main item. I can't deny that the report of your impending trip to England, which would lie very close to ours and yet fall at a different time, has stirred us considerably.[2] Wouldn't it be possible for your plans and interests to coincide if you traveled directly from Düsseldorf after the music festival? If I may ask, why are you going to England? Is it on account of your opera? Naturally, you must not sacrifice anything for it, since human affairs are never certain, and if you did sacrifice to meet us there and then we couldn't make the trip after all, I'd be extremely distressed. But if only it could work out! Then we would be happy for several reasons and derive great advantage from the situation, something not inconsiderable in England—for example, stay together IF IT WILL SUIT YOU, etc. Please send me your opinion soon. You can imagine how it would help overcome my gruesome fear of London if I knew I were going to meet you there.[3] Hensel's paintings are now in the BRITISH INSTITUTION . . .[4]

Shaw is here now and is truly a nice, lively person. I went shopping with her yesterday, and it goes without saying that we will do everything possible for her. But unfortunately we're not holding a musicale this Sunday, which possibly could have been to her advantage, but next Sunday.

Farewell, you dear people.

Your Fanny

[1]Referring to the package of the bust she is sending him for his birthday. The opposite side of this letter says "An extra goody" ("Eine Rosine im Kuchen"), indicating that this letter was probably included as an afterthought.

[2]Felix responds that his trip looks doubtful, and he certainly could not do it before the end of March (to Fanny, 6 February 1839; DB 3). A few weeks later he writes more negatively: "It's definite now that I won't go to England this year. Therefore Count Reuss also sent me an English newspaper yesterday which said that I definitely would be going to England this year. But I don't know whether we can come

to Berlin after the trip to Düsseldorf. We probably have to spend some time in Frankfurt as well. . . ." He also has a great deal of work to do before the autumn (19 February 1839, NYPL).
[3]Felix gives the following advice: "But if I may be permitted to give you advice as an old Englishman, dear cantor, it is this: don't let yourself become too agitated by the trip and the stay there. . . ." ("Wenn ich Dir aber als alter Engländer einen Rath geben darf, lieber Cantor, so ists der: laß Dich durch die Reise u. den Aufenthalt dort ja nicht zu sehr agitiren. . . .") Her great fears will ruin her trip, and she should go around and see the sights and enjoy herself (6 February).
[4]Approximately one-half of the next page is cut away in the autograph.

110

Berlin, 26 February 1839

Dear Felix! You bawled me out with the rest of Berlin so harshly in your last letter that I still haven't fully recovered from the shock.[1] But I must risk showing my face one more time, if only to report that I passed on your instructions with all due dispatch in regard to the Doberan music for wind instruments.[2] It actually wasn't executed in the refined manner you envisioned, for Herr von Dachröden, the chamberlain and theater intendant, lives in Strelitz and knows nothing about Schwerin, but the Herr Hofmusikus P. Lappe in Schwerin was instructed to send the music directly to you in Leipzig. If you've already received it, then please let me know, and if you haven't in a short while, then ditto. Then Lappe won't be able to slip through our fingers.[3]

I think that Rebecka will visit you, but perfect health and good weather must coincide, and that hasn't happened yet. I'm only persuading her gently because it's a real responsibility to urge her to take this trip, and furthermore, she hardly has any enthusiasm for it. Overall she's still very LOW SPIRITED.[4]—Yesterday Mme. Shaw gave a concert in the theater. The parquet and first loge were full and the other sections were not. Unfortunately she's not as successful as Novello nor as she deserves to be. She is warmly applauded and has numerous admirers, but she doesn't handle her reception well, and one must repeat with all due respect that she doesn't understand the concert-giving business very well. Her performance coincided with Ole Bull, who knows more about people and pocketbooks, and the Lewy family, who are under age and therefore great hits. Her noble, simple singing and her natural manner can't compete with such tricks.[5] But at the same time, she seems content, and that's the main thing. I like her very much, as does everyone here. She's sung at two Sunday musicales and delighted everyone, especially in the aria from *St. Paul.*—Speaking of which, I just thought of Paul, who's written very lovely, amusing letters from Petersburg and painted a graphic picture of life there, which is truly unpleasant. Albertine thinks he will return soon, but I believe he will stay for quite a while. Fassmann was with us today. She's leaving Berlin and considering the Woringens' offer in Düsseldorf. But she tells me that she doesn't know anything more about it yet. Do you know how the matter stands and whether they're counting on her? She's visited Shaw many times to work on her English in *Messiah;* one can't ask for more modesty in a singer.[6]

Will Cecile attend the music festival this year? I thought she would.[7] Your Psalm will sound splendid with the choir, and I'd love to hear it.[8] Will your new Psalm be issued soon?[9] I'd still like to perform it.

Who in the world did Liphart marry? That family makes foolish marriages—suddenly he's sitting there at the concert and has a wife! How are the Francks? Do they like Leipzig? Have they added to the world's population with a little Franck?

Say hello to Carl, runner and chatterbox. Also say hello to Cecile, whom I don't like very much at the moment and fear I may never learn to like. However, she is my sister-in-law, and I must get along with her. What should I do? Adieu, you dear people. Everyone sends his best.

Your Fanny

I received letters from Klingemann and Fanny Horsley last week. The one from Klingemann was his first long, cheerful letter in a long time. Meanwhile, you're certainly right about my concern over the trip to England.[10] I feel that way myself, but what am I to do? I don't believe I'd be doing my husband a favor by going along; on the contrary, I think I'll hinder him more than support him. That upsets me even more. Incidentally, both of the above correspondents—only one of whom I know personally—wrote me so warmly and confidingly that it should justly overcome my fears. As soon as we know more about the trip I'll let you know. But it's better for me not to talk about it here. Matthieux will be passing through Leipzig any day.[11] She wants to travel to Bonn to divorce her husband, but the foolish man doesn't want to do it. Has anything like that already happened to you? Don't let this letter fall into the wastepaper basket, for then she might find it and read it. So this entire 4th side has been a postscript—what female foolishness.

[1]"I find it more annoying than I can say that you must let my *St. Paul* be spelled out to you by the Singakademie, and that Mother writes with a kind of pleasure that she has just received 5 seats for it. It affects me, as it were, very much. The pack of louses is not even worth the anger, and yet I can't help myself. What have the shabby, unmusical rascals in common with my *St. Paul* and my family? . . . Those fools! that solid pack of lunkheads!" ("Daß Ihr Euch meinen Paulus müßt von der Sing Akademie vorbuchstabiren lassen, und daß Mutter mir mit einer Art Vergnügen schreibt, sie habe noch 5 Plätze dazu bekommen, das ist mir doch tiefer verdrießlich, als ich sagen kann, u. rührt mich gewißermassen sehr. Das Lausepack ist nicht einmal den Aerger werth, u. doch kann ichs mir nicht abgewöhnen; was haben auch die schäbigen, unmusikalischen Kerls mit meinem Paulus u. mit meiner Familie gemein? . . . Das halbe Pack! das solide Lumpenpack!") (to Fanny, 6 February 1839; DB 3). He apologizes for the diatribe in his next letter to Fanny (2 March 1839; DB 4).

[2]Overture for Wind Instruments, Op. 24. Simrock is going to publish a revised version for a larger wind orchestra, but also wants to publish the original version (1826) and Felix does not have any of the music to the original. Therefore he wants Fanny to hunt it up, and suggests that she go to Dachröden (6 February). See also Mendelssohn, *Verleger,* 221-26.

[3]Lappe's response to Felix is dated 4 March 1839 (GB IX 81).

[4]In late 1838, Rebecka's second child, Felix, died at the age of thirteen months, and Rebecka also suffered severe neuralgia in the face and intense bodily pain (see Fanny's letter to Klingemann of 30 November 1838, in S. Hensel, *Familie II*, 55-56). Rebecka did not make the trip.

[5]For reviews see the *AMZ,* 13 March 1839, cols. 216-17.

[6]Felix wrote how well Shaw sings Handel arias, especially "He shall feed his flock" from *Messiah* (29 January 1839, NYPL).

[7]Cecile will attend the festival in Düsseldorf (2 March).

[8]Psalm 42, performed at the Gewandhaus on 21 March 1839.

[9]Psalm 95. He tells Fanny that he's a real dolt if he doesn't do a piano arrangement right away and send it to her, and that he's inserted new choruses (2 March).

[10]As conveyed to Fanny in a letter of 6 February; see letter 109.

[11]Felix reports on Matthieux's arrival and how she sang her lieder for a small gath-

ering at Felix's. She has an awful voice, but sings musically (2 March 1839, NYPL). She had married Matthieux in 1832, and they had separated after a few months.

111

Berlin, 4 March 1839

Dear Felix! One hour after reading your letter, I visited La Fass and want to disclose my wisdom.[1] La Fass wants nothing more than to play Alceste opposite a Hercules who could also play the high priest. That might not be possible because Bötticher is already engaged. If you still need a tenor from Berlin, then take Eichberger. He plays Admetus and can always travel when Fassmann travels, because he only plays together with her. I inquired with respect to her terms, and she didn't know, and thought and thought, and then I asked what she received in other middle-sized cities. And then she answered, "Twenty-five to 30 French louis d'or for a large role." I believe that if you insert your dialogue in *Alceste,* you will be able to get her for less. Furthermore, I think you can negotiate with her if you think that sum is too high.

Concerning her other demands, she wants no fee but only travel expenses. She's only now returning from her present trip and therefore allowing herself to figure out her expenses later. When I shyly asked, "How will you travel?" and was answered, "With the express coach," I exerted every effort on behalf of the Düsseldorf music society to describe with great eloquence the beauties of nature around the Rhine. I assured her that if she traveled with the fast coach to Mainz and from there glided down the river on the steamboat, her soul would delight in the emerald flowing waters, which inspired me to become even more poetic. Then she responded that since Bötticher was also traveling there, she could take him and three EXTRA persons along for the same price as three persons traveling with the fast coach. "That is RATHER true," and since I felt that my powers were AT AN END here, I closed with a refrain in praise of the Rhine and went home to give you my report. Since then, I've lingered over a large package from Luise containing charming gifts and letters. And now you know everything, except this: letters to Fassmann should be sent to Bremen until Easter, and to Hanover afterwards. She will be back here in about 5 weeks. By the way, she's so pretty with her beautiful blonde curls that she will certainly be well liked in Düsseldorf.

Beckchen has referred you to me and instructed me to tell you that among the things that Shaw sings well are a pair of arias from *Orpheus* that constitute truly FIRST RATE MUSIC. They will dine with us tomorrow, after she will have given her last concert here tonight. I feared almost no one would come, for something was in the air, but I haven't heard many rumors to that effect. Tomorrow I'll also invite Miss Forrester, a very nice English lady who's giving us lessons.—I laughed for three hours, not for 3 measures, over the abominable [ ][2] sounds in the symphony, which I heard from here. Everyone laughed except the singer, who did well to refrain. Dear nettle, next time you will receive a separate letter from me and then we can argue again.[3] I agree with you completely about Matthieux, however.[4] Regarding Fräulein Franck ripping up little Carl's diapers, she doesn't need to be half a princess to do that.[5]

Felix, I'm as melancholy as if I had a bad hangover, but champagne is not the cause. How much one torments oneself needlessly! Farewell. I must begin to close, and that usually means one more page. I hear that the Beneckes are traveling to Leipzig. When you see them, please send them my compliments and inquire as to what we've done to offend them. I'd truly like to find out, for at a recent soirée at Marianne's,[6] we received a snub and therefore had a difficult time. But say hello to MISS Schunck anyway—I mean Julie and her mother; she is actually the nicest lady in the family. But the world is stupid, the world is bad, and growing more insipid every day.

Herr Lappe will get a tongue lashing from me soon—the rascal hasn't even responded.[7] Now I'll turn serious. Adieu, farewell. Think of me when you eat soup and I'll do likewise.

Your Fanny

[1]Felix asked Fanny to go to Fassmann and inquire whether she would do a performance of *Alceste* for the music festival (in Düsseldorf, 19-21 May), and a Berlin

tenor is part of the deal. Fanny may also inquire about Fassmann's terms for such a performance (to Fanny, 2 March 1839; DB 4). The letter from the Committee of the Lower Rhenish Music Festival to Felix requesting Fassmann in the opera is dated 17 February 1839 (GB IX 62).
[2]Omitted words concern varied spellings in German.
[3]The subject of their argument is unknown.
[4]In a letter of 2 March 1839 (NYPL), Felix stated that he likes Matthieux's lieder. See letter 110.
[5]Presumably Hermann Franck's baby girl.
[6]Marianne Mendelssohn. "Sauree" in the German is an invented word by Fanny that combines the meanings of "Soirée," "sauer" (sour), and "Sau" (sow). Thus the soirée at Marianne's must have turned quite sour.
[7]See letter 110.

112

Berlin, 28 April 1839

Dear Felix, I'm very grateful for your lovely little letter that Drouet brought me.[1] Mother, who is the best and most diligent reporter of events, and whom I trust more than Rellstab (so there about her eavesdropping), will write you how much I tried to help him. In fact, I did something that I'd never done before, namely, wrote a letter on his behalf to Count Redern, as he didn't have a letter of introduction to him. This proved highly successful, because three days later he performed in the opera house to great acclaim. At one of our morning musicales, to which the public had been invited, things went well for me but not for him, and in his interest I thought it best for him to perform in the theater and not give a separate concert, for the time and the circumstances didn't seem favorable. But now I have to pass along some gossip and apologize for it in advance—you are of course well aware that I usually don't do that—but NEVER MIND. I'm apologizing for gossiping because I'm ashamed. Frau von Fassmann was here this morning to tell me that Novello had gone to her daughter and told her that *she* was engaged for the Düsseldorf Music Festival but wanted to divide the arias from *Messiah* with Fassmann.[2] Also, that she was invited to sing the role of Alceste but didn't know yet whether she would accept, since she hadn't appeared on the stage yet and wasn't strong enough in German. Upon Frau von Fassmann's wish to view the letters of the *comité*, she naturally didn't think to bring them along, and so Frau von Fassmann came to inquire whether I knew anything about this supposed engagement of Novello. *C'est du pack* would be said by one of the leading composers of our day.[3] I didn't want to refrain from conveying the above to spare you the fat—which in any case couldn't damage a lean person like you—as Fassmann is a *protégée* or a *protectrice* of mine, which accords with your wishes.

But please do tell me when your three Quartets will be issued.[4] Your Cello Sonata is the quintessence of an elegant edition.[5] Are the lieder that are appearing now to be sung or played?[6] You've again done good damage with your *Lieder ohne Worte.* In this respect, they remind me of the innkeeper who dispenses all wines from the same barrel. Lieder, etudes, *refrain with chorus*, nocturnes, caprices, duets, liebeslieder—but everything dispensed from the same old piano barrel. Henselt invented the art of making instrumental music vulgar, and he could take out a patent on it. Through his headings he's happily remedied the evil of one not being able to choose lewd texts for mere etudes. Liszt invented the art of happily confusing and disfiguring musical orthography, which I thought existed to make music *readable*, to such an extent that he's succeeded in making his compositions, which were already nonsensical and formless, even more nonsensical and more formless with the help of his notation. If chaos hadn't already been invented by the good Lord before the creation of the world, Liszt could have disputed His right to it. But now I think I'll stop reviewing the rest, for otherwise Cecile will say again that I'm having a mild fit. I have no such feelings towards her but only warm thoughts, or rather a rich wealth of love, which I hereby instruct you to lay at her feet, wrap around her neck, or place on her mouth. In an ascending line of respect, please send my best to Madame Jeanrenaud, Madame Souchay, and Aunt Schlegel, whom I shall write shortly. My husband sends his best. Remain my faithful brother

Felix Mendelssohn Bartholdy

[Rebecka, Lea]

[1]Dated 17 April 1839 (DB 5). Drouet also carried a letter to Lea that listed his many musical talents and asked the family to assist him in his attempts to have successful concerts in Berlin (17 April 1839, NYPL).
[2]An interesting incident in light of letter 111, in which Fanny relates how she was acting on behalf of Felix to engage Fassmann for the Düsseldorf Music Festival.
[3]The expression, whose first two words are French but last one German, is perhaps equivalent to "What a rogue!" or "What nerve," or "What else can one expect."
[4]The three String Quartets of Op. 44. "My 3 Quartets, dedicated to the Crown Prince of Sweden, will also be out soon . . ." (to Paul, 30 December 1838, NYPL). They appeared in the summer of 1839. See Mendelssohn, *Verleger*, 78-96.
[5]Op. 45, issued by Kistner in early 1839. See Mendelssohn, *Verleger*, 303, and Felix to Paul of 30 December.
[6]Sechs Gesänge, Op. 47, published by Breitkopf & Härtel. "The lieder volume contains 3 new ones and 3 old . . ." (23 April 1839, NYPL). It was issued in early November 1839 (Mendelssohn, *Verleger*, 92).

113

Berlin, 8 May 1839

I don't want to go any longer without giving you a report, dear Felix. Everyone is fine, thank God. Rebecka has held up well and this exceedingly sad week has at least not damaged her health.[1] We just came back from Gans' burial. Students carried him the entire way, and a boundless sea of people—the entire university and everyone who knew him—followed on foot. He was buried in the Oranienburg churchyard near Hegel and Fichte.[2] I hadn't seen such a sensation since Schleiermacher's death. The loss to each of his friends cannot be assessed, nor can his importance be gauged with regard to his rare frankness and unflagging zeal, which knew how to make itself felt wherever it was right and necessary. But he was also a very fortunate man, as we've mentioned several times in the past few days. He practically never experienced adversity, and only one instance of serious misfortune. Everything— acceptance as well as opposition—was a potential source of delight for him, and he enjoyed a rich life. Indisputably, his powers began to fade, and thus it can be considered a blessing that he died before this decline became noticeable and painful to him. If a person has filled his life with meaning, then he's lived a long life regardless of his number of years.

Farewell, dearest Felix. May these emotional days not exhaust you and Cecile too much. I keep thinking of how you were still sleepy even after a week's rest three years ago. I hope we'll hear from you soon. We've received a letter from Frankfurt. Farewell, and say hello to the Woringens.

Your Fanny

[Rebecka]

[1]See note 4 to letter 110.
[2]A town north of Berlin.

114

Munich, 23 September 1839

Before our departure tomorrow,[1] I must thank you again for your nice recipe for an Italian journey, dearest Felix. I will make every attempt to follow it.[2] With regard to the portrait gallery in Florence, I've only read your observations once because I intend to make my own and then compare them with yours. But there are a few that made such a deep impression on me because of their obvious truth that I'll probably jot them down. For who would dispute that Raphael is a master and Carlo Dolci a fool? I also want to tell you that I met Delphine Handley and was delighted with her—a charming person and an extraordinary talent.[3] With the exception of you, I've never heard your first Concerto performed as well. We visited her and found her so exceedingly warm that it's difficult to put into words. We immediately played some music and she invited us for tea on another evening, when she played that Concerto superbly for us. It's utterly indescribable how fondly they remember you in this house. They know every word you spoke and every movement you made. But what I especially liked about her playing is her inspired improvisations, a rare talent in women. I tell you, she pleased me a thousand times more than the wheezing Dreyschock. My husband sketched her and she was delighted with the result.

I've remembered your favorites in the Pinakothek and gone to see them, but you wouldn't recognize them in their present form.[4] There can scarcely be any place more splendid than the two rooms housing 95 paintings by Rubens. One has to stand in awe of this monumental talent. Do you remember the portrait of Frau von Vandyk with her child? The woman looks so noble and fine and slightly sad, and even a tiny bit boring. And what about his portrait of an Antwerp organist? That is an extremely good likeness of all tenors, for one can imagine him singing "Dies Bildnis ist bezaubernd schön" in reference to himself.[5] And the young, blonde Vandyk is quite good too. Munich is an interesting city. We've been here two weeks and only scratched the surface. We could easily use twice as much time, because what is happening here in new art and the acquisition of art is very significant and meaningful on the highest level. Glass painting, fresco technique, encaustic painting, architecture, carved and cast sculpture, and porcelain are all new and important in their own right. You can imagine how much my husband has enjoyed seeing so many new ideas in his field, as well as artists he's known since his days in Rome.[6] I knew no one here and therefore my head was stuffed full of new things and new people. It's always heartening to discover that people who are away from home are welcome and treated with great hospitality. We've only made a cursory visit to the Glyptothek. But autumn impels us over the mountains and we're planning to make the highest mountain journey in the express coach; we want to go over the Stelvio Ridge. You know that I've had the burning desire to see such a pass since I was young,[7] and now I'm to have my chance. My husband will thereby become acquainted with an entirely new section of Italy. I hope we'll be away from the very severe Munich autumn air in 5 or 6 days and then pass into spring. We'll journey over the lakes into Milan, and if we encounter nice weather, the trip will be particularly magnificent. If either of you writes to Berlin soon, please tell them that they shouldn't worry if they don't hear from us for a while. It will be about a week before we'll be able to write, and since we're starting out with very full traveling days, the letter will take even longer. It's a peculiar feeling, however, to leave the fatherland by going over the Alps, but it must be a similar feeling when traveling by sea. On the other hand, a flat, arbitrary border is nothing. When you see Franck, dear Felix, thank him for his letter. Unfortunately we weren't able to lay our hands on a *lascia passare*,[8] and so we'll become the property of the Austrian customs agents—a good way to practice patience. Dear Cecile, Hebaba, Tata[r], and [Orja][9] kiss the dear little Carl. Stay well, my dearest, and let us hear from you soon. Until *circa* the 20th of October, write us in Venice *poste restante*. Adieu, dear Felix and Cecile!

Your Fanny

[1]To Italy.
[2]The recommended sights and things to do in various Italian cities were listed by Felix in a letter to Fanny of 14 September 1839 (Mendelssohn, *Briefe II,* 128-31).
[3]Felix praised her playing in a letter to Fanny of 11 June 1830 (NYPL).
[4]Does not appear in Mendelssohn, *Reisebriefe* or in Sutermeister, *Reise*. It is probably from the two omitted Munich letters, of 7 and 18 October 1831. All fifty-nine journey letters are found in MS MDM d.13.
[5]An aria from *The Magic Flute*.
[6]The artists Schwanthaler, Hess, Schnorr, Cornelius, and Kaulbach (S. Hensel, *Familie II,* 69).
[7]When she was on the Swiss side of the St. Gotthard Pass in 1822, but did not travel over it into Italy (Fanny to Marianne Mendelssohn, in S. Hensel, *Familie I,* 126).
[8]A visa.
[9]Either children's-story characters, or else the manner in which Carl pronounces the names of the members of the Hensel family.

115

Rome, 1 January 1840

My first order of business in the new year is to write you again, my dear Felix and Cecile. I couldn't hold out any longer after not hearing from you in such a long time.[1] I still haven't received even the tiniest little letter from Cecile since her lying-in period, and nothing from Felix since Venice. May God bless you this year and in the years to come, and may He bring us all happily together soon. But let me know, dear Felix, whether we can look forward to meeting you in Berlin when we return, or in Leipzig, or in Frankfurt, or anywhere else. For we *must* see each other this year, and I must see the dear little Carl and become acquainted with my first niece.— We're enjoying a pleasant life here. We have a comfortable, sunny apartment and thus far have enjoyed the nicest weather almost continuously. And since we're in no particular hurry, we've been viewing the attractions of Rome at our leisure, little by little. It's only in the realm of music, however, that I haven't experienced anything edifying since I've been in Italy. I heard the Papal singers 3 times— once in the Sistine Chapel on the first Sunday in Advent, once in the same place on Christmas Eve, and once in St. Peter's basilica on Christmas day—and have to report that I was astounded that the performances were far from perfect. Right now they seem to lack good voices and sing completely out of tune. Unfortunately, I never had the opportunity to find out in advance what they would be performing (which I certainly won't fail to do for Easter), and by whom. Then I only heard the sound and didn't like it very much. One can't part with one's trained conceptions so easily. Church music in Germany, performed with a chorus consisting of a few hundred singers and a suitably large orchestra, assaults both the ear and the memory in such a way that, in comparison, the pair of singers here seemed quite thin in the wide expanses of St. Peter's. With respect to the music, a few passages stood out as particularly beautiful. On Christmas Eve, for instance, after the parts had dragged on separately for a long time, there was a lively, 4-part fugal passage in a minor that was very nice. I later discovered that it began precisely at the moment when the Pope entered the chapel, and I didn't know it at the time because women, unfortunately, are placed in a section behind a grille from which they cannot see anything. This section is far away and in addition, the air is darkened by the smoke from candles and incense. On the other hand, I could at least occasionally see the officials on Christmas day in St. Peter's very well, and found them quite splendid and amusing. We naturally had a Christmas tree, because of Sebastian, and constructed it out of cypress, myrtle, and orange branches. The branches were very lovely, but it wasn't the best-looking tree, and Sebastian and I attempted to outdo each other the entire day in feeling homesick. My husband, dear Cecile, gave me a very beautiful small wardrobe inlaid with ivory, and I gave him a sketch by Paul Veronese, which he liked very much. He's thinking of giving it some well-needed restoration. One sees far too many beautiful things here, especially pieces from antiquity, but I'm also very attracted to the marble works and the carved shells. If only everything were not so frightfully expensive. In this respect, Rome has declined considerably, especially since last year, when everything was overflowing, and the Romans demanded the most outlandish prices and received them. This year it's supposed to be the same in Naples. We're spending a lot of time with the Schadows. He looks quite ill but is gradually recovering here, and complains less than he did at first. I'm happy to be able to tell you that they were friendly towards us, and you can easily imagine how we were glad to reciprocate. Schadow is happy when I play for him and says that it reminds him of you in some respects. He is your very dear friend. Old Santini sends his best and would like you to send him a short piece in manuscript. The kind old man visits us more often and talks about his pride and joy, his library. Every conceivable woman has spoken of you with delight, and proudly mentioned that you had visited them and played for them. Undoubtedly you no longer know them by name. In addition, I don't want to hurt Cecile by discussing Luise Nitschmann. But I must have your advice now. Since you didn't travel to Vienna and thus were unable to select an instrument for me, please tell me how I should proceed in procuring one. I played on one at Landsberg's that I particularly liked the first time, made by Felix Gross in Vienna. It has a full, lovely tone. Its action is good, although not very precise, like all Viennese instruments. But now I haven't played or heard anything in months except that wretched rattletrap, and therefore I cannot fairly assess how much of my satisfaction results from my dissatisfaction with my present instrument. Are you familiar with Gross' instruments? Can you advise me on them? And do you know anybody in Vienna whom you can trust to make the selection? I must confess that I didn't like Schunck's instrument at all, which, if I remember correctly, was chosen by Hauser.[2] What do you say to that? Please send me a sensible, business-like response to all these points, because I don't want to make a decision without your advice. Please forgive me for adding to your already considerable duties and interruptions. Should you not have the time, then please tell Cecile what she should write me. I have less sympathy for her time and she should be able to write me once. But please do it soon. If possible, I'd really like to find an instrument when we return to Berlin. Otherwise, much of the time left on our journey will be spent writing back and forth on this matter. If you think I should write to Vienna directly from here, I will gladly save you the trouble of sending a letter there.—Have you found, as I have, that Rome looks magnificent from every viewpoint, even from the lowest prominence? I was thoroughly delighted with the view from the tower of Cecilia Metella, and find this entire area exceedingly lovely and attractive in general. We were there on a gorgeous day, just like the weather when we visited the Villa Mills recently. Everything was in bloom—millions of roses and other flowers, between them the splendid evergreen trees—and an enchanting view emerged on all sides. I relish the climate and I can't tell you how good I feel. Sebastian is also responding very well and looks better than ever. We're exceedingly pleased with him. The child is really darling, which is typical for his age. I believe that once a person has tasted such a winter, he will always have regrets. I truly would not want to be an Italian, nor anything else but a German, but it wouldn't be so bad if we could move our dear fatherland a little farther south. Mother wrote me yesterday that it was 12 degrees in Berlin on the 19th, and we're still living here without coats and practically without a fire. That's one of life's material comforts that ranks at the top of the list. And such vegetation the entire year! Although I see it every day, it astonishes and delights me anew.

Farewell, dear Felix. Kiss Cecile and your dear children for me. What are you working on now? Let me know. My husband and Sebastian send their best.[3]

Your Fanny

[1]Felix's next letter is dated 4 January 1840 (Mendelssohn, *Briefe II*, 136-38), but is not a direct response to this letter.

[2]According to Felix's letter to Breitkopf & Härtel of 10 December 1839, it is a Viennese piano, and the owner is presumably Philipp Daniel Schunck (Mendelssohn, *Verleger*, 98-99).

[3]Many of the items mentioned in this letter also appear in letters to the family in Berlin. See Fanny's letters of 16 and 30 December 1839 (S. Hensel, *Familie II*, 92-97).

116

Rome, 4 March 1840

Dear, dear *pater, peccavi*! It is by no means my fault, however, because while I was scolding you in my letters to Berlin, the nicest letter was salted away here at the post office for six—I repeat—six weeks.[1] *Oimé!* My husband went there often before he got sick even though we were no longer expecting any letters *poste restante*. Instead, we were expecting your letters through Valentini. But even then they must have withheld the letter from him—the *asinacci*!—which is comparable to our having heard about Cecile's delivery one week late in Venice.[2] Just recently we gave Kaselowsky a letter to take to the post office and asked him if he might casually inquire whether there was any mail for us. And then back he came with the most marvelous letter. I read it six times in a row and died laughing over it six-hundred times. But, as you can see, I'm still alive. You rob me of my health when you don't write more often, because you have no idea how healthy it is to laugh myself sick. And now I'll respond to your excellent questions and advice. What have I been doing in Rome? Going around by myself the first two months. We made a respectable *giro* and are still far from finished. I took care of my husband the 3rd month and thus didn't get any farther than Monte Pincio, which I often approached in tears because I was *supposed* to walk and yet was so worried and upset.[3] Then Carnival time arrived, and since my husband began to regain some of his strength, we took him along with great pleasure, and I had a better time than I ever thought possible. Last night we had the *moccoli* ceremony and now it's over.[4] We'll start to travel around the city once again, because our precious time is unfortunately coming to an end here, and we still have a great deal to do before Easter. We are living on the Via del Tritone, which runs into the Piazza Barbarini. If we turn 2 corners we arrive at the *passeggiate* to Monte Pincio, and we often took advantage of the proximity of this pleasant, sunny walk with its decent view, especially when Hensel was recovering. I haven't had broccoli in a salad yet, even though you've told me twice that I'm obliged to do so.[5] Excuse the oversight. But I've just ordered it for tomorrow. My God—I'm crazy about Madame Titian who is hanging in the Sciarra Palace,[6] and I've been fascinated with her since Florence. There she was in the Uffizi—unfortunately not in the Gallery—under the name of *Flora,* with a white blouse and a handful of flowers, looking as much like a goddess as a scamp. She can also be seen in the Barbarini Palace sporting a wig *à la* Bellini,[7] a dress completely sprinkled with color (my husband says it was painted with his blood), a thick hanging chain (my husband says it made Titian her prisoner), and a marvelously fresh face. But the gorgeous little minx looks naughty, and surely must have made his life both wonderful and miserable. How would I, a nobody, have made the acquaintance of all the Cardinals?[8] I'm definitely near-sighted, never get into the Sistine Chapel, and am very far from the holiness of the caps and tails in St. Peter's. Therefore, I only see these men when they loosen their tails, and then they look nothing less than beautiful. [The 6th] I already received a clear impression of Papal fifths at Christmas.[9] This is the perpetual refrain:

And if those aren't fifths, then I don't know what fifths are. I've only heard other church music in Sta. Maria Maggiore, on one occasion, when the *Vera cella* sounded merry. But I've had enough. Out of sisterly love I wanted to hear the nuns at Trinità,[10] but it's very difficult to gain entry now and I would've been forced to hide myself behind one of my devout cousins.—The day before yesterday there was a festival here which, in terms of local standards, was probably unique: a ball at the capitol square for the benefit of the cholera orphans. One climbed up through the Forum, illuminated with countless torches, and in whose glow the old figures on the columns looked eerie and fantastic. The capitol square itself, with its statues of Marcus Aurelius and the Dioscuri, also looked splendid in the torchlight. Unfortunately it was pouring cats and dogs, and one can imagine how much more wonderful the place would have looked on a moonlit evening. In general, the Carnival was not favored by good weather. The first days we had awful *tramontane*,[11] and then rain. Even the *moccoli* evening had to be celebrated with umbrellas, but nonetheless I had a wonderful time. The event is so mad that it truly approaches the poetic: the countless moving lights, the mad merry shrieking, the masked costumes illuminated in numerous ways, the continual assaults that one must try to repel, and the attempts to reignite the torches that have been extinguished. All this is so bewildering that one no longer knows if his head is on straight. The Italians possess a very special virtuosity in their expression *senza moccolo*, which rings out from all sides if someone has no light or his torch has gone out, for it conjures up the complex images of mockery, astonishment, pity, deepest regret, questioning, and triumph. One can die laughing when one is thus shouted at on all sides. On the other hand, the expression *sia ammazzato*, which Goethe heard, is no longer in vogue.[12]

Hiller's decision to work hard in Leipzig does him honor.[13] Send him my very best and tell him how sorry we were not to have met him in Milan. But in general we've had bad luck with people on this trip. It's really a shame to spend an entire season in Rome and not meet up with one single person of distinction. Liszt was here for four months last year—how I would have loved to hear the Hungarian magnet! Have you ever heard anything more ludicrous than this boastful tale? Lablache also could have let himself be heard by me, and I very much fear that he, or rather I, will become acquainted with everyone else before I become acquainted with him. Stop! Which Psalm of yours is being performed now? Is it *Kommt, lasst uns anbeten* or *Als Israel aus Egypten zog*?[14] Just be careful that the European Congress doesn't think that you intended Abraham to strike at the Battle of Nisib when he left Egypt.[15] But send me a serious response to this question, and also to the matter concerning the piano, i.e. should I buy one from Felix Gross, citizen of Vienna?[16] I don't want one from Graf because they are too light, and I've just seen a sobering example, in the person of one Frau Hensel, of how one can become spoiled. The woman has had an old, light, played-out rattletrap for three months and received another, ordinary Viennese instrument. I heard her yesterday and can assure you that she cannot continue this way. Should she come to

Leipzig soon, you would see that she can't play any longer. Every new start *is difficult*. Oh, and composing! I've already complained in a letter to Berlin that no ideas strike me any more—nothing good and nothing bad. *Dio mio!* Abraham is getting old![17] But now I'll switch from your terrain and speak to Cecile. Good day, my dearest! If I had enough room I would scold you and make you blush, for you should write me often, very often. You know very well that your letters cheer me and I find them very interesting. I am thus forced to hear the most darling stories of little Carl in letters from Berlin. Aunt Hund delighted me very much.[18] And congratulations on the pianino.[19] When I visit you again, let's make some soft music together. That is truly a lovely present! I've also been given wonderful presents here: a very beautiful oil sketch and a splendid ink drawing from Elsasser, and a forthcoming painting from Catel. In addition, we've given many presents ourselves, and you'll probably like the gifts we're giving you very much. But I hope we'll find you in Berlin, and if God grants us good health when we meet, our joy will be complete. With this devout wish, I want to close, and ask you to commend us to the Schuncks and other Leipzig friends. And please, please—write soon. You have no idea how happy your letters make us. My husband and little man send their best. Your Fanny.

Kaselowsky sends his warmest regards to you, dear Felix.[20]

[1]Presumably of 4 January 1840, in Mendelssohn, *Briefe II*, 136-38.
[2]Their second child, Marie, was born in late 1839.
[3]The Casa Bartholdy, where Lea's brother Jacob lived and worked for several years, is on Monte Pincio.
[4]A special candle-procession ceremony that is part of Carnival.
[5]As in his letter of 4 January (136).
[6]Felix wrote that Fanny must think of him when she views it (137).
[7]Uncertain which Bellini, but probably Giovanni.
[8]Felix asked if Fanny knows the names of the Cardinals yet (137).
[9]"Pay attention to the horrendous fifths the Papal singers make when all 4 voices are ornamented with coloratura at the same time" (137).
[10]Felix composed three motets for the nuns of Trinità dei Monti. They were written when Felix was in Rome in December 1830, revised in 1837, and published as Op. 39.
[11]A severe northern wind in Italy that comes from the Alps.
[12]Within Goethe's lengthy description of Carnival in Rome, in Part III (1788) of Goethe, *Reise,* 306, under the subsection "Moccoli": "Now it becomes everyone's duty to carry a blazing candle in the hand, and one hears the favorite wish of the

Romans—'Sia ammazzato!!'—repeated everywhere. 'Sia ammazzato chi non porta moccolo!'' *Death be to him who doesn't carry a blazing candle!* cries one to the other, while he tries to extinguish his light. Igniting and extinguishing, and a furious cry, 'Sia ammazzato,' stir up life and movement and multifarious interest within the huge crowd.''

[13]Hiller is remaining in Leipzig the entire winter to complete his oratorio *Jeremiah,* which will be performed there in March (4 January; 136).

[14]Psalm 95, Op. 46; Psalm 114, Op. 51.

[15]The Battle of Nisib took place in 1839, in Egypt.

[16]See letter 115, and also Fanny's next letter to Felix (7 March 1840; GB XI 83).

[17]Felix wrote to Fanny: ''Compose a great deal; work goes splendidly in Rome'' (4 January; 137).

[18]Felix wrote of Carl's make-believe game in which the aunt is called ''Tante Hund'' (4 January, NYPL).

[19]Felix wrote of Cecile's joy in receiving a pianino as a present and how she played on it continually while she suffered from severe toothaches (4 January, NYPL).

[20]Many of the topics in this letter, especially concerning Carnival, are also featured in Fanny's letter to the family in Berlin of 14 March 1840, in S. Hensel, *Familie II*, 101-02.

117

Rome, 10 May 1840

Dearest Felix, thank you for your dear, humorous letter from the 7th of April.[1] I much preferred hearing about your journey to Berlin from you than receiving the letter from Berlin, which let me know that you did indeed arrive there without incident. This letter took almost 3 weeks to arrive, which is almost impossible to believe, and thus I started to become worried. You went to Berlin at just the right time (not for us, of course), because in light of the fact that the Woringens just left, and considering Beckchen's little condition, we were afraid that it might become a little too quiet at home before we, as fresh arrivals, could bring back some new life and new stories. If only I could predict when we can see each other and where! I've had my eye on Frankfurt, which we will pass through in any case and which you probably won't want to miss either. Of course, I'd prefer if we were to meet in Leipzig, at your house, and then our trip would come full circle and you could give us lodging again for a few days.[2] I really want to see you and tell you all about our trip. I can't find words to tell you how happy we are here, and how much we like everything. We've extended our stay until the end of the month, and I see with sadness how time is slipping through our fingers. We couldn't tear ourselves away, and even now I become very sad whenever I think about our departure. Fortunately Naples is ahead of us, and I look forward to it very much. We're now thinking of spending only a very short time in the city itself and of making excursions from Castellamare, as a number of people have advised us. Perhaps there will be some time left for a few seaside resorts. We've had such marvelous weather for the past few weeks that it's been a joy to be outside and drink in the air. We were very busy making excursions into the Campagna, which I couldn't love more if I were an artist, and recently spent a delightful day at Tivoli. The Alban hills are still ahead of us. These are the mountains I've seen the entire winter in their incredible beauty. I often made detours and scaled heights in order to see them when I hadn't seen them for a few days, and yet I don't feel the urge to go there now. All in all, I've been in Rome long enough so that my original travel fever has subsided. I even agree with Zelter—I'm too young to see everything, and only when you've come to that realization can true enjoyment begin. There are certainly many things I will not have seen when we leave Rome, but I will have visited my favorite spots over and over again and enjoyed them immensely. Three weeks from today we will be in Naples, please God, and undoubtedly will have a wonderful time there as well.

I would have liked to experience Liszt in Leipzig.[3] Here he is talked about to an astonishing degree. He was here for 4 months last year and became friendly with Ingres and the musicians on a pension, just as we have, and they always tell me about him. I'm very sorry that I didn't come upon him, because he must have been especially humane here. He didn't give any concerts but only played at his own residence and Ingres', whatever and as much as people requested. He's dedicated 2 of his arrangements of Beethoven Symphonies to Ingres and sent them to him recently.[4] If the wild rain that's poured down almost incessantly since two nights ago would be so kind as to abate, we'll go there tonight and I'll look at the crazy things for myself. Here they are entranced with the way he plays Beethoven Symphonies, whereas you seem less taken with it. I'm curious to hear you describe the experience. I'd love to have heard the Bach Concerto from you three.[5] Just think—I'm also performing it this week, with a Danish and an Italian woman, both very good pianists.[6] But no doubt there will be considerable difference between the performances. I tell you, the French now admire nothing except *Bacque*—it's really too funny! I've had to play the Concerto in d minor at least a dozen times and they're always wild with delight over it. They're also very appreciative of your music, and one has to give them credit for their attentiveness and their ability to retain so much after only 1 hearing. You can't expect more than that. Whenever old Santini sees me, he pesters me to have you send him some music. I'll have to give him one of the pieces I brought with me; I can see that he won't let me leave otherwise. But he's a dear old man, by far the most agreeable person among the wealth of boring ones here. Because that is the other side of Rome: the countless unbearably boring people, especially among the official dignitaries, which include the Germans as well. God, what awful people! But quiet—I've promised my husband not to criticize anybody in letters. I won't, however, gag my mouth against verbal expression, and since Beckchen isn't here with us, I must function as both Charivari and Figaro in the guise of a single person. But here I walk around with rose-colored glasses and thus let many things pass that I wouldn't at home. Perhaps the air has imparted some of its inexhaustible gentleness to me.—

The 11th. The rain eased up yesterday, so we went to the Academy and I viewed the Liszt-Beethoven-Ingres Symphonies. It's very good that he states in the preface that he wishes to help popularize the works through this edition. If the musical populace or rabble would ever play that, then string me up! For all their technical apparatus, I don't doubt for one moment that you could play them ten times more beautifully. Congratulations on the success of Hiller's oratorio.[7] If you ever worked that hard with me some time, I would also compose one. I'm truly sorry that I won't be able to experience the celebration of printing somewhere in Germany.[8] That will be a beautiful celebration if ever there was one, and I'd be intrigued to see the actual printing done in the street. I'd love to see how the monks here would celebrate such an occasion: with a Requiem, no doubt. Have you ever heard an Armenian high mass? It's the most ghastly caterwauling that I've ever heard, and meow is the only word that could be clearly understood. The people, of all things, have such beautiful, earnest heads, and the bishop is such an honorable old man, that one doesn't know whether one should be surprised or feel sorry for these people who grunt at their God in such a cannibalistic manner. The Greeks, on the other hand, sing very well. They have 3-part men's choirs, and decently-composed music with a pure, strong, self-assured style of performance that is firmer by far than the Papal singers, who began the *Miserere* in b minor both times and ended in g minor once and f minor the other time. We'll also have to discuss that at length. If Spontini hadn't already made suggestions for the improvement of church music, I'd submit a report to His Holiness, for an improvement is really necessary. And since Magnus,[9] the heretic, is painting a Cardinal, one can't really tell for sure. I hear that Otto Nicolai was planning to become the director of the Papal chapel, and even willing to become a Catholic and a priest—necessary conditions for the position—since it didn't matter to him. But since the plan failed, he's thrown himself into the arms of opera and is now in Turin. If Hiller returns to Lake Como in June, it's quite possible that we'll see him there in July. We were at Lake Como only one day, a rainy day at that. It's so heavenly beautiful there that we might well go from Milan to the town of Como, a place we haven't seen yet, if things work out. It's absolutely impossible, however, to see everything on *one* trip to Italy, even if you criss-cross about as much as we did. We'll probably have to give up Parma and Perugia as well, places my husband has never visited. It's too *fatiguant* to travel through all of Italy in the middle of summer—it took 6 days alone from Rome to Florence—and therefore, if Sebastian and I can endure it, we'll board a steamship from Naples to Livorno.—Dear little Cecile, many thanks for your dear note from Berlin. They write me such dreadful things about you, and you're reputed to look so ugly now, that I'm downright impatient to see you so that I can ascertain whether all that is true. Furthermore, no one at home can stand your children and that must have been particularly unpleasant for you. In my absence little Carl has developed his talent for singing and undoubtedly is a sweet little charmer by now. I'm very eager to meet my first little niece.[10] What kind of children will there be in Berlin this year? Every letter I've received has given notice of new hopes, and next year something will be crawling and wobbling wherever you look. Farewell for now, dearest people! I do so hope that snow won't fall before we see each other again. After this trip I need it more urgently than ever. My husband sends his best. He's busy with preliminary sketches and is bringing back a few very beautiful heads. We're all well now, thank God, and I'm enjoying my life ever so much. You know, dear Felix, how crazy I am about fresh air, and therefore you can appreciate how happy I am to drink in this heavenly air. The weather has cleared up after a few rainy days, and we can look forward to the most glorious weather once again. For us now it's a time in which every moment is experienced to the utmost, and every hour has a pulse that one can feel. It's the same for me when we're together with you dear ones. May it happen again soon!

Your Fanny

[1]This letter was unavailable; however, E. Werner, *Mendelssohn*, 315, presents a substantial excerpt.
[2]Felix discusses his summer plans in a letter to Fanny of 13 July 1840 (Mendelssohn, *Briefe-RE,* 209-10).
[3]Felix wrote the family about Liszt on 30 March 1840 (NYPL), and stated that he considers Liszt and Thalberg in the first rank of pianists, but does not like Liszt's behavior at concerts. Felix wrote extensively to Fanny about him on 7 April 1840 (E. Werner, *Mendelssohn*, 315).
[4]Symphony No. 5 and Symphony No. 6, both arranged in 1837 (*NGD* XI, 68).
[5]Performed by Hiller, Liszt, and Mendelssohn; see Hiller, *Mendelssohn*, 166, and Felix's letter to Fanny in E. Werner, *Mendelssohn*, 315.
[6]With Charlotte Thygeson (Dane) and an Italian woman amateur (S. Hensel, *Familie II,* 123). Performed at Landsberg's.
[7]Hiller conducted his oratorio *Jeremiah* in Leipzig on 2 April 1840. Hiller describes how much Felix helped him with both the libretto and the music (Hiller, *Mendelssohn*, 166-67).
[8]Festival will take place in Leipzig on 25 June 1840.
[9]Eduard Magnus.
[10]Marie.

118

Berlin, 28 September 1840

Dear Felix! This letter should reach you when you return from England, and in order to prevent you from rushing unduly to read it, let me quickly add that there's nothing especially important in it, only a little chit-chat. I want to give you some good advice, just as you gave me numerous times in Rome. If you ever want to travel to Italy again, you should try to acquire a work about Italy that I just read with great interest, for it's the best treatment I've come across of this oft-described subject. But it's very difficult to acquire, for it is, to my knowledge, much RARER than Decker's *Nibelungs*, which exists in only 106 copies, and the editions of English greats, which exist in only 3 or 4 copies. For there is only one single copy of it, in manuscript, and in this regard we are no better off than before the invention of printing (a timely observation). In a word, it is the letters of a traveling musician, who incidentally happens to be my elder brother.[1] I can't tell you how much these letters have interested me, now when my fresh memories of Italy can be stirred by your moving impressions ten years ago. Whoever might doubt that ten years is a long time need only read letters that were written then. It's dreadful how few of the people and relationships mentioned in them still remain: everybody either dead, ruined, or separated. One must thank God when people who belong together actually stick together and don't part from each other unless death steps in. And, come to think of it, it is this I want to mention—namely, to tell you again how much your life and activities please me, and how happy I am that we happen to be siblings. My God, I'd love to be proud of my brother, with all my satisfaction and pleasure, if only I could get around to it. I mean inwardly, because it's obvious that I'm proud of you among strangers. It's truly a terrible mistake in our lives that for the past ten years we haven't spent time together with the exception of a few days per year at best, which seem stolen in haste. This will very likely continue for the rest of our lives as well. It wouldn't hurt us to be together. And this appears to be the most tolerable thing about Berlin—at least it's only one day's journey from Leipzig. Of course, Dresden would please me much more because it's much closer. When I think back on Rome, as I often do, and recall how gloriously we lived there and how much I'd like to return there sometime for a longer stay, I must immediately keep in mind that then I wouldn't be able to see you any longer. And so, you can't have your cake and eat it too. But I must tell you in confidence, since I like telling you everything, how little we still like Berlin since our return. Rome made the same impression on you that it did on us—it's a mixture of serenity and excitement. We also found the serenity very striking and refreshing, and I can't tell you how severe the sharp Berlin character seemed, and still seems, in comparison, with its hard, dry criticism of everything. Perhaps this perception could at least serve to rid me of my share—I'm very conscious of it—and I have every intention to do so. But that's a sore subject![2] I'm very glad that we agree about so many things with regard to Italy. In particular, our impressions of Rome were quite similar, as were our comparisons between Rome and Naples. But I think you do it an injustice on the whole, for its beauty is truly divine. We're also unanimous about Florence and especially the Gallery, and you echo my thoughts about Raphael's portrait, only you express them better. But we disagree over two paintings in the Gallery—you didn't like Raphael's portrait of a woman, *Fornerina,* for you thought it ordinary, whereas you were enraptured to the point of piety with the beauty of Titian's *Venus.* With me it was completely the opposite: Titian's *Venus* is a little too wild for me, whereas Raphael's portrait so far exceeds all measure of beauty that I can't get my fill of it. Wilhelm holds another opinion: he claims that both paintings are superb. And in the end he is right.

When one experiences the past in old letters and sees how many fears and anxieties one had that ruined so many beautiful, precious hours, and how the feared thing never came about, and also how so much that was unexpected ensued; and when one goes on to consider how that trait tends to persist, for instance, how I wasn't able to enjoy the 5 recent days in Leipzig at all because I ate my heart out with worry over your trip to England, and now this trip is happily behind you for the most part, and brought you joy and good fortune instead of disaster; and if one is convinced that

that is what *living* is all about, then one should really aspire to some frivolity so that one can more cheerfully enjoy what one has at present and be unconcerned about the future, which in any case almost always turns out differently from our expectations, because one cannot and should not fathom it. To be able to overcome this shortcoming is a gift like all others, but he who possesses it should not cultivate it, for if he does, he will become just like the Backhausens, who are here now, and will travel to Mexico in 2 weeks, and speak of it as if it were a trip to Charlottenburg, whereas we consider a trip to Potsdam much more seriously. They want to attach their wild children to long ropes as they run around, so that they won't fall overboard. And besides that, they are always laughing. It is truly fortunate to be able to take life so lightly.[3]

Furthermore, I must tell you how it amused me that everybody expressed himself like Jean Paul around the time you left on your grand tour, and how you gradually developed a totally personal, Felix-like style in your writing from Rome. I firmly believe that this letter smacks a little of the old days, since I am reading about them with such delight. What is there to make a person happier than having the chance to enjoy his loved ones and boast about them, and I'm happy whether it's my husband or my parents or all of my brothers and sisters who come to mind. Cecile also belongs to this group in no small way, dear Felix, and every time I see her I can't thank God enough for the kindness He has shown you. For among all the women that exist, you found the one that suits you the best and can make you the happiest. And it is with great confidence that we can also look ahead; your little Carl is a dear angel, and our boys here are also very good, marvelous children. I wish you could see them together now—it's really a pleasure. They couldn't be closer if they were brothers. They're inseparable and haven't squabbled even once. Next week they'll start school together—of course not in the same class—but they look forward to it very much. It's really a joy to see them go into the garden arm in arm.

I've taken up your Trio now and am practicing it, but it's very difficult.[4] If I resume the musicales, it's to be the first piece performed. But thus far I haven't felt like doing it. I was very spoiled on the trip by an exceedingly grateful public that continually urged and invited me to play this and that, and always kept me on my toes. One becomes accustomed to that only too quickly. But it's not fair of me to expect that now, and I'll really make an effort to get over it. But it's disturbing that there's nobody here with whom to make decent music—perhaps when the Woringens come.

But now it's really impossible for me to send off a letter that contains nothing of consequence, so therefore I'll at least tell you that Albertine has moved into the city, is in good spirits, and Beckchen is waiting. The printers held a slovenly, belated celebration here, and also had an exhibition that included a Gutenberg Bible.[5] Our art exhibition arouses much talk, but unfortunately it's not very much, and I'll tell you about it in my next dispatch. I assure you that if one participates or has to participate in art for whatever reasons, and thereby experiences more of the aggravations than pleasures of life, one could shoot oneself to death after such an exhibition. Unfortunately, I've never seen so much artifice, imitation, sameness, and unpleasantness drawn together here. There are many reasons for this, but the main one is that everyone is hounded to death in Germany, and now every city with three inhabitants wants to have at least one exhibition of four pictures.[6]—But I don't want to close with such ranting and raving, and instead will ask Cecile to send us a few details about your stay in Birmingham, since you yourself will probably be overwhelmed with business matters right away. Farewell, you dear people. Dear Felix, don't judge this long letter that contains nothing important to be too dumb, for I just had to chat with you again and show you my black heart. Have both Julies returned?[7] How are Cecile's sister and mother? My husband sends his best, and I am your

Fanny

I have to tell you quickly who was Sebastian's partner in a game of boccia yesterday and who lost a match against him: none other than Böckh. Isn't that very funny? Dirichlet is also a fierce boccia player now and challenges everyone to a game.

[1]Felix's letters from his journey to Italy 1830-31, part of the *Reisebriefe*. The original letters are catalogued as MS MDM d. 13.

[2]"For I consider the only sour note in it—that you can't acclimate yourself to Berlin after Rome—merely temporary. How can anything be pleasing after a year-long stay in Italy?" (to Fanny, 24 October 1840, DB 9; Mendelssohn, *Briefe II*, 155).

[3]Felix discusses how he and Cecile fretted and worried before the trip, and yet how everything turned out all right (24 October).
[4]In d minor, Op. 49.
[5]Leipzig had had its celebration in June, in which Felix participated.
[6]Felix compares Fanny's frustrations with his own over the Leipzig Liedertafel upon his return from England (24 October).
[7]The Schuncks are not back yet because an uncle in Manchester is very ill, but Julie Jeanrenaud Schunck returned in good spirits from her journey (24 October).

119

Berlin, 9 December 1840

Dear Felix, I want to give you an immediate report on the execution of your very difficult task.[1] First of all, I looked in the address book for Rungenhagen's conference hours (Heinrich Beer has them also) and found he was available between 7 and 8 in the morning, and 4 in the afternoon. So then I had to try and see if he could confer at different hours, because 7 to 8 is my time to sleep and 4 my time to eat. Thus I confidently went to see him this morning after my coffee, adorned with the accouterments offered this time of year: item—a red nose; item—an icicle hanging from it, etc. I threw my request at dear little Herr Rungenhagen and he agreed to listen to me and was very gracious, saying that he and everything he possessed was at our service. But don't become irate now in the belief that I think these scores belong to him, for I know better. I said this only in a manner of speaking; they don't belong to Zelter either, but to the Academy. As I then heard the little female pupils squealing in the next room, I said I would like him to send me the list of the things, because I didn't want to disturb him further (I possess manners, to wit). But he said, "I won't let you do that; just write down the titles here." Thereupon, in all politeness, I tossed him out to his pupils after he had allocated some paper and a quill. But what a quill, I tell you—it was so coarse that Zelter in his coarsest hours was courtly in comparison. If absolutely necessary, one could write with it using pressure but not at all lightly. There was a blue cloth on the table with which I cleaned it. It had never been cleaned previously, and I also believe it had not been sharpened since plucked from the goose. In short, I wrote down everything with the quill. *Brennus* is there and probably a Flute Concerto as well,[2] and I hope you'll receive all of it at the right time. I can't, however, give you a definite promise since I'm not the copyist, and if I were it would definitely take *much* longer. When I left I saw your *Lieder ohne Worte*, dedicated to Fräulein von Woringen, [and] *Sehet, welch eine Liebe* on the piano.[3] When I read the name Nitschmann in your letter, I was very happy because I gathered you wanted to give the poor little Luise a chance to earn something. I'm still in contact with her and will definitely let her scrawl some music again shortly, because she's just as dreadful, but also as wretched, as ever—soup rations and a wool jacket WONT DO.[4]

I heard that Paul just had time to write you that he must travel to Hamburg suddenly today. It's really a sad tale to think that we haven't been together once since we've been back. When will we be able to be together sometime—that means with you too? I might even say that I long to see you once when there's more time available than merely saying hello and good-bye, and for the past three years it hasn't been otherwise. You want *aperçus*? Signs of recognition? Glances?[5] The hunt with Siegfried's death provides a splendid finale to the 2nd act. The third act must begin with Chriemhild and her women as she steps out of her door and finds the dead Siegfried there. You can fashion a polonaise with chorus from that.[6] Incidentally, should you be uneasy over the success of the opera, I would suggest that you let a double chorus of Huns and Nibelungs, as a *captatio benevolentiae*, sing "sie sollen ihn nicht haben"[7] to the melody of *Ei du lieber Augustin:*

sie
sollen
ihn
nicht
haben

Isn't it wonderful that the Hanover censor is prohibiting the lied and the Crown Prince composed it?[8] Adieu! I wrote you on Saturday—why didn't you receive the letter on Monday? Farewell.

Give my best to Cecile and that dear little angel, Carl. My husband sends his best.

Your Fanny.

[1]"I need copies of a few things, which must be within Zelter's Bach manuscripts or elsewhere in his library, which now are located in the Singakademie. Therefore do me a favor: have Rungenhagen open the said library while you visit him and cajole him, take the scores [ ] out, don't give them to my pretty Luise Nitschmann, but rather to a much more correct rascal of a copyist, and see to it that I have the stuff in my hands, if possible, in 2 weeks, in 3 weeks at the latest—clean, correct, and not post-paid. I want to reimburse you shortly as an honest man for the copying, and if you want to figure in a little profit for your trouble, I'll naturally consider that totally in order, and will be in agreement with every provision that you, etc., etc., etc. Am I not a regular businessman?" ("Ich brauche ein Paar Sachen hier in Abschrift, die sich unter Zelters Bachschen Manuscripten oder sonst in seiner Bibliothek befinden müssen, die sich jetzt in der Sing-Akademie befindet. Thu mir also den Gefallen, laß die besagte Bibliothek von Rungenhagen aufschließen, indem Du ihn besuchst u. um den Bart gehst, nimm die Partituren quasst. heraus, gieb sie meiner niedlichen Luise Nitschmann nicht sondern einem viel correcteren Kerl von Abschreiber, und mach daß ich wo möglich in 14 Tagen höchstens 3 Wochen die Scharteken in meinen Händen habe, sauber, correct u. unfrankirt. Ich will Dir die Copielien als ehrlicher Kerl augenblicklich erstatten, u. willst Du ein Profitchen für die Mühe rechnen, so finde ich das natürlich ganz in der Ordnung, u. werde mit jeder Provision einverstanden sein, welche Du etc. etc. etc. Bin ich nicht ein ordentlicher Geschäftsmann?") Felix wants Bach manuscripts, but only scores: 1) of Orchestral Suites, but he already has those in b minor and D major; 2) the Concerto grosso in G major; 3) the Concerto for 3 Claviers (in C or D; it exists in both keys); 4) the Concerto for 2 Claviers in c minor; and 5) the Concerto for Violin in a minor. He also requests the score of the Overture to *Brennus* by Reichardt, and any pieces she can find by Frederick the Great, especially a Flute Concerto (Felix already has Frederick's Overture to *Re Pastore*) (to Fanny, 7 December 1840; DB 10).

[2]= *Brenno,* opera by Reichardt (Berlin, 1789); a Flute Concerto by Frederick the Great.

[3]Unclear whether it is the second collection (Op. 30) or the third (Op. 38). *Sehet, welch eine Liebe* is a Cantata by Bach (BWV 64).

[4]In his letter of 18 October 1840 (NYPL), Felix wrote that Fanny should give Luise as much copying of music on Felix's behalf as possible so that Luise can earn some money. Yet in his letter to Fanny of 7 December, Felix wrote that Luise should not copy the Bach manuscripts (see note 1 above).

[5]"You also owe me another Nibelung letter, dear girl, with opinions and *aperçus*. Don't have me wait too long for it." ("Du bist mir auch noch einen Nibelungenbrief schuldig, Gere, mit Anschichten und aperçus. Laß mich nicht zu lang darauf warten") (7 December).

[6]In a letter to Fanny of 14 November 1840 (Mendelssohn, *Briefe II*, 159-60), Felix

asked for additional comments on the dramatic possibilities of the saga. Fanny replied that she had worked out a text sketch of the Nibelung saga herself, but Felix's is more advanced (5 December 1840, in S. Hensel, *Familie II*, 179).
[7]= the *Rheinlied,* popular as a patriotic protest song in the Rhine area against a French takover of their territory. See Felix to Klingemann, 18 November 1840, in Mendelssohn, *Briefe II*, 163. Felix wrote that many composers are setting melodies to this text, but Felix abhors the lied and refuses to do it (to Paul, 20 November 1840, in Mendelssohn, *Briefe II*, 164-65).
[8]Presumably of Hanover, Crown Prince George.

120

n. d. [after 9 December 1840]

My signature below attests to the fact that Rungenhagen is a fat ass and a horned one at that, for he can't retain even 3 names in his dumb head. I still want to go to the Academy today to search for the other things you've requested and which aren't supposed to be in their library.[1] I flew into an indescribable wild rage against him yesterday. Your Psalm is splendid!—the most expansive you've ever composed.[2] Farewell! The dear God suffers all sorts of creatures in His patience, and the leaders of the Singakademie are some of the most useless among them. The mail won't wait. Adieu.

[1]See letter 119.
[2]Presumably Psalm 114, *Da Israel aus Ägypten zog,* for 8-part chorus and orchestra, composed in August 1839, and later published as Op. 51.

121

Berlin, 13 January 1841

Dear Felix! I would have preferred not to write you again until I was able to send you the things you ordered.[1] Have you, however, received three scores through Professor Puchte? I feel it's taking too long and my conscience impels me at least to ask your forgiveness. But don't think badly of me! I started poorly and stupidly this time, but don't retract your tasks from me, because I want to try again another time and complete the job more to your satisfaction. If only you don't become more embarrassed through this unfortunate delay —then I would be inconsolable. Please write and tell me that you're not angry, and let me know whether I can send you separately what I have, which thus far consists of the Violin Concerto.[2] I've had my instrument for 2 weeks and it passed its test with flying colors on Sunday morning. Naturally I've found fault with this and that. The middle range is noticeably weaker than the rest, namely the very beautiful and rich bass. It also possesses the same defect as your first English piano:

an unpleasant additional sound is present when one is playing at a piano dynamic level. But in spite of this, I must admit that it's a good instrument, better than the local ones, which I've concluded once and for all I don't like, and better than the Graf pianos. Paul's Graf, for instance, sounds unbelievably rickety and bad after such short use. It's not as good as the *best* Streicher but far better than the one he sent Schunck. And what other option did I have, since we couldn't spend 1,000 talers for an English instrument? Decker's is magnificent and everything else pales in comparison; she's very happy with it.[3]—I wish I could show you around our apartment sometime—it's very pretty. The entire blue room is adorned with old and new paintings that we brought with us, not to mention the warm travel mementos in every corner. Everyone who sees it likes it very much.

The 14th of January. Your wonderful letter with the parcel arrived last night. You vindictive person! You can't forget that I forgot one time! I certainly won't let your splendid suggestions concerning tempi and interpretation get lost, and I'll try to perform it next Sunday. Many thanks. I also see from your letter that the others have already written about our decorating, and that I've once again harped on a familiar string. I'll definitely play the Beethoven Sonata with Eckert.[4] Thanks for the cadenza—it's very interesting. Would you also permit me to insert it in my musical newspaper?[5] Sebastian received *Die Musikschule* by Moscheles and Fétis as a Christmas present from Henry Schlesinger (Beckchen claims that any decent thing we have comes from Henry), and then, with delight, I found an old acquaintance composed *express* for this method.[6] I'm thus sending you what I have now with our next dispatch. I still haven't been able to hunt up Fritz's flute solo,[7] and I've been sent from Pontius to Pilate to find it. But I hope to succeed soon.

So farewell. Say hello to Cecile—may God send her a happy hour—and kiss the English crooners, whose concert I might prefer to hear to many others.[8]

Addio

If you don't need your Symphony Cantata any longer this winter, could you send me the score and *circa* 20 parts through the mail or personal envoy?[9] I also want to ask Grell about the tempi.

[1]See letters 119 and 120.
[2]Bach Violin Concerto in a minor, BWV 1041.
[3]Felix bought the piano for the Deckers, an Erard, in England, for he paid in guineas. Discussed in his letter to Fanny of 24 October 1840 (DB 9).
[4]On 9 January 1841 (NYPL), Felix wrote that Eckert is traveling to Berlin tomorrow. Fanny should accompany Eckert once in the c-minor Beethoven Violin Sonata, for she would be astounded how wonderfully he plays.
[5]It is unclear what Fanny means by her musical newspaper.
[6]*Die Musikschule* = two studies published as Moscheles' Op. 98 (1840).
[7]= Frederick the Great. Even today, Berliners affectionately dub him "der alte

Fritz." Felix asks Fanny on 18 January 1841 (NYPL): "Please let me know *right away* whether I can receive the Flute Concerto of Frederick the Great, and when? If I don't have a definite yes or no in a few days, I'll be in an embarrassing situation." See letter 119.

[8]The identity of the English crooners is unknown, but it seems to be a family joke. Felix's letter of 28 March 1841 (NYPL) constitutes a mock invitation to Leipzig musical events, which feature the bass-singer "Balzer" (= "crooner").

[9]*Lobgesang*, Op. 52 (composed 1840).

122

Berlin, 29 January 1841

Dear Felix! First let me report that Rebecka had another tooth extracted and is well now, thank God. Yesterday was a dreadful day, however! I want to tell you now about Eckert's oratorio, which surprised me very much, for it's a very beautiful work considering his age.[1] To get to *le moral* first, as the French say: The hall was approximately half full and he will barely cover his costs. However, when we talked with him later, he seemed quite pleased. The choruses went magnificently, in an extremely brilliant and lively manner, the orchestra only so-so. Of the soloists, Mantius and Bötticher were very good, all the others weak, and unfortunately the main role really pitiful. It's known here that Fassmann embodies all the tragic, comic, brilliant, and solid qualities of sopranos, but poor Eckert was referred to Hofkunz. She did what she could, but unfortunately she can't do much. Eckert just will not deny his training. His conducting amused us very much. He didn't exactly copy you, but instead very deftly adopted your style. He did everything rather decently, looked nice doing it, and was full of life, and I never would have thought he possessed these capabilities. Perhaps you blew some divine breath into his nose. As to the music itself, one meets you every step of the way, but I find that all right since it rarely descends to mechanical imitation, is clothed in original features, and is not lacking in good, solid workmanship. I find his immaturity the greatest weakness, but I sincerely believe he's on the right path, thanks to you, whom he verily adores. I believe he'll blossom into a fine conductor eventually.[2]

As you already know from Mother, I had your Psalm performed on Sunday, and it went surprisingly well after only 2 rehearsals.[3] The choir consisted of 25 members, an imposing group for the blue room. And at present it is so well constituted that the piece really sounded powerful. We placed it at the beginning and had to repeat it at the end. How I look forward to rehearsing your *Lobgesang*! Will I receive it soon?[4] I want you to know how sensitive I am about having done so poorly in the execution of your task. I'll keep whatever I receive since you can't need it immediately any longer, [5] only please don't punish me with your anger and rest assured that I've learned through my mistakes and will do much better next time.

I've given Luise Nitschmann a taler in your name for wood rations, hoping Cecile's jealousy won't be aroused again at the mention of her name, and will do it again if you're not opposed.[6] She's receiving soup rations and work from us so that she can at least subsist, and if we succeed in restoring a human shape to this miserable skeleton, we can truly say that we've done a good deed. Farewell, dear Felix. Give my best to Cecile and the dear children.

Yours FOREVER,
Fanny

[1]Eckert's oratorio *Judith,* in three acts, premiered at the Singakademie on 28 January 1841 under the composer's direction; see the *AMZ* review of 24 Feb. 1841, cols. 173-74.
[2]Felix praises Eckert as a good musician (to Fanny, 14 February 1841; DB 11).
[3]Presumably Psalm 114. In his letter to Fanny of 14 February, Felix wishes he could attend her Sunday musicales, especially to have heard the lovely performance of his Psalm. "You certainly topped Grell with it!" ("Du hast gewiß Grell dabei übergangen!")
[4]"The *Lobgesang* should be calling on you soon." ("Der Lobgesang soll mit nächsten seine Aufwartung machen" (14 February).
[5]Felix wrote on 22 January 1841 (NYPL): "You, dear Fanny, I thank many times over for your efforts on behalf of the music manuscripts I wanted. Please have copies made of whatever hasn't yet been copied. They served mainly as fodder for our historical concerts. But since one of these has already taken place, and in the next, this coming Thursday, the way is cleared back through Haydn, I therefore can no longer use the other things, namely the Frederick the Great piece . . ." He

thanks her again for all her efforts, especially since she has had to deal with such Philistines. See also letters 119, 120, and 121, and Fanny's letter to Felix of 20 January 1841 (GB XIII 27).
[6]See letter 119.

123

Berlin, 2 March 1841

In the annals of our correspondence it's probably never taken me three weeks to answer one of your letters, dear Felix.[1] But everything here is topsy-turvy, or rather, as Humboldt would say, horizontal. When your letter arrived, both my husband and I were sick in bed. I recovered fairly quickly but my husband remained quite ill. Then it was Beckchen's turn and then my poor Bax's, who was laid up for ten days with open frostbite on his feet and first permitted to stand a limited amount the day before yesterday. His extreme diligence caused the severity of the injury, for he was already limping with difficulty on his way to school for a period of two weeks, yet refused to be absent even one day. Now he had to forfeit 8 *first* places, and when you think back on your school days and realize what that means to a young boy, you won't be surprised that it cost many bitter tears before we finally forced him to stay home. But this winter has been very long and severe, and I assure you that the piles of snow everpresent in the garden over the last four months wear on my soul much more than my eyes. Every night frozen windows still, during the day slight melting in the sun—you probably have the same complaints and may well have viewed a similar mess from your windows. A so-called dilettante concert will take place the day after tomorrow, rather as *moutarde après diner*, because this time, I hope, there isn't such a great need for it any longer. I'll perform your Trio.[2] Actually, I should have selected the Serenade for the concert hall, but it doesn't lie well in my fingers and I haven't been able to learn it yet.[3] The Trio, however, although perhaps no less difficult, lies more comfortably, and since I'm not accustomed to playing in public, I must choose something that won't worry me. This concern will be laid aside the day after tomorrow and then I'll be busy with another important matter. I don't know whether one of our siblings has already told you that we're planning a *fête monstre* for Mother's birthday and hope to bring three families together for the occasion. Now it's common knowledge that nothing is more difficult than arranging such an event to everyone's satisfaction when everyone has a say, and just between us, I fear we will start tearing each other's hair out before the 16th of March.[4]

But what about you? Are you coming? When are you coming? The garden apartment above us, which Paul rented for the summer, is at your disposal whenever you want it.—If you regret not being able to hear our Sunday musicales, then I regret with probably greater justification not being able to hear your concerts.[5] I would especially love to have heard your *Lobgesang* once with orchestra. By the way, when you visit, you will be presented with the best Sunday musicale I'm capable of giving, although I can already feel myself becoming anxious and not knowing where to begin. I want to ask your advice, although I'm perfectly capable of making such decisions when I'm alone. So do you know of any new pieces for my Sunday concerts? Sometime soon I want to bring Spohr's *Lieder* with clarinet to light,[6] for my orchestra, whose concertmaster position threatens to be filled by some beginner,[7] has increased with the addition of the young Herr Gareis, clarinettist and eldest son of the old Herr Gareis. If only there were a decent dilettante violinist here! As far as your bills are concerned, there's time until you get here.

And now, farewell! Carl tells the nicest children's stories possible; I'll never forget that he admonished the preacher to be quiet. Say hello to Cecile. How I look forward to spending some time with her, because we're all assuming with certainty that you'll visit us, and then we'll have a wonderful time. May everyone be well!

Your Fanny

[1]To Fanny, of 14 February 1841 (DB 11).

[2]In d minor, Op. 49.

[3]The Serenade and Allegro gioioso for Piano and Orchestra, Op. 43 (composed 1838).

[4]Felix is sorry he cannot attend (to Fanny, 13 March 1841; DB 12). Fanny describes the event to Felix in a letter of 7 March 1841 (GB XIII 130).

[5]"Yes, only don't write me anything more about your Sunday musicales. It's truly

a sin and a shame that I haven't heard them!—But if I get upset over that, it's also upsetting that you aren't hearing any of our really brilliant subscription concerts. I tell you, we create fantastic sparkle—like Bengalese fire'' (14 February; Mendelssohn, *Briefe II*, 180-81).

[6]Six German Songs, Op. 103 (Leipzig, 1838), for clarinet and piano.

[7]''Alevin'' in the original. See note 10 to letter 84.

124

Berlin, 13 July 1841

If one is a member of the people walking in darkness who don't know when they will see you, the Great Light, in person, then one probably had best proceed with the help of quill, ink and paper, standard accouterments of absence, in extending one's thanks and congratulations. I had actually thought that it wouldn't be necessary to write for a while, but that isn't the case yet.—I therefore congratulate you, Herr Music Director, upon attaining the highest human office next to Privy Councillor and Pope. Kapellmeister is a proper title, insofar as it shows what sort of a person one is, whereas Doctor could just as easily refer to a tooth puller or midwife, God be with us![1]—As to gratitude, I express my sincere thanks for your bittersweet—or sweet and sour (as indeed journeys are)—exquisite *Reiselied,* parts of which you had already played for me here.[2] Odd things have happened again involving Lang's lieder. Several days ago Trautwein had sent me a package of new pieces. And JUST the day before Paul returns, I play them through and discover, after encountering many novelties that prevent me from proceeding beyond the first ten measures, that they're by Lang. I like them so much that I play them, and play them again—I can't tear myself away—and then finally put them aside. I've been singing them all day so that I'll remember them, especially the one alto lied, and I've also been telling everybody about them. Then Paul comes the other morning, and brings them from you. I was really glad that this time fate had protected me from becoming a parrot; if I know your opinion about something, I'm always uncertain whether I'm only imitating you or actually feel the same way. I'm enjoying these pieces immensely: they're extremely musical and heartfelt, and the modulations often quite ingenious and original. Had I met her in Munich, I'd definitely write her now to tell her so.[3]—Pasta is here now. To begin with, she's a very charming, friendly, modest, truly agreeable woman. I saw her onstage in *Norma* and a few scenes from *Otello* and *Semiramide. Norma,* performed in its entirety, was by far the most significant—I can't tell you how joyful and mournful I felt. Her mastery is truly extraordinary: the nuances in her voice, particularly a powerful crescendo; her style of performing recitative, which you probably remember; and the most noble and tasteful ornaments (I can still remember those from *Otello* that you notated once in Paris, and recognize now as unchanged). But now, problems in intonation, which supposedly she's always had, are so severe that she almost continually sings between an eighth- and a quarter-tone flat, especially in her lower register. Such torment cannot be described! It's so bad that one becomes totally confused from time to time and thus cannot discern what one is hearing. At that point, one must rise above one's misery if one is to marvel at her greatness, and you can appreciate how no real enjoyment can be derived in such circumstances. And yet she had moments in *Norma* that I will never forget. In addition, her high trills are much cleaner, and the longer she sings, the greater the clarity of her voice. Therefore ("therefore" doesn't fit here at all—substitute another word), her greatest fans are non-musicians, for instance my husband, who dutifully becomes angry if her poor singing disturbs me.[4]—We received another letter from Beckchen in Heringsdorf yesterday. She seems to be well and enjoying herself there, likewise her mother.[5] I accompanied the Woringens to the coach office yesterday morning; they're going to Liegnitz for a few months. It seems that almost every day someone from our circle is going away, yet we don't have the least desire to travel this summer. Our recollections of Italy are still strong and will remain so for a long time to come.

I've heard about a new Psalm of yours, which is reputed to be lovely,[6] and of serious variations, which have aroused my curiosity.[7] Adieu, dear Felix. Be well. Send my best to Cecile and the sweet little brood. Farewell!

Your Fanny

[1]To the King of Saxony (see the *AMZ,* 14 July 1841, col. 550).
[2]Presumably the *Wanderlied,* Op. 57 No. 6, composed 29 April 1841 (Bartlitz, *Works*, 156).
[3]Conceivably this was an unpublished set of pieces. Trautwein was not the original publisher of any of her lieder collections. Opp. 10, 16, and 40 are all Lang collections for alto, and they all have songs dating prior to July 1841 (Köstlin, *Lang*). Felix's enthusiasm for Lang's lieder is communicated in a letter to Lang's fiancé, Köstlin, dated 15 December 1841 (Mendelssohn, *Briefe II*, 205-07).
[4]Felix first heard her in Paris in 1825. Although he recognized her dramatic talents, he criticized her raw tone quality and poor intonation (6 April, in Mendelssohn, *Briefe-RE*, 44). Sixteen years later Felix reports on Pasta again, this time from Berlin: "I recently heard Pasta in *Semiramide.* She sings so fearfully out of tune now, especially in the middle register, that it's really a torment. At the same time, the splendid traces of her great talent, the features that betray a singer in the first rank, are of course often unmistakable." In another city they would not tolerate the bad intonation, but they do in Berlin, and even praise her to the hilt (to Verkenius in Cologne, 23 August 1841, in Mendelssohn, *Briefe II*, 201-02). See the lengthy review in the *AMZ,* 11 Aug. 1841, cols. 634-37.
[5]Madame Dirichlet.
[6]Either Psalm 114, or the revised version of Psalm 95.
[7]In his letter of 5 June 1841 (NYPL), Felix mentioned "15 Variations sérieuses pour le piano," in d minor (Op. 54).

125

Berlin, 5 December 1842

I've neglected to thank you for a long time, dear Felix, for your dear birthday letter[1] and the very welcome *Lodoiska.*[2] I can only attribute my tardiness to the numerous wars waged by everyone in the house over the past few weeks against coughs, sore throats, toothaches, nosebleeds, et al.—enemies of the worst kind. And my share prevented me from dashing off a letter, as you like to put it—I'm quite satisfied if the quill merely creeps along the paper. But this time my nosebleed wasn't as bad as last year; a very solid cold is helping out now. In addition, we've had a true English fog since yesterday that simultaneously darkens the atmosphere and turns into precipitation during the night, and furthermore gives a lift to the shortest days now. *À propos* of English, what do you say to the historical events that are taking place there again? China and Kabul with the same mail system—that's patently absurd. Their proportions are so colossal that everything else pales in comparison. I find that if one has just been thinking about the English position in the world (excuse that expression, but a comparable, less pretentious word doesn't come to mind immediately), one need only think about everyday concerns, such as today's lunch, to get anything done. I must continually visualize how the King of the Empire in the Center of the World and his quilted army must have been incredibly frightened and surprised by the barbaric breastplates that crowded in on them, and how difficult it may have been to pronounce the word that kills a civilization that has existed for several thousand years.[3] The English ambassador, who asks me to send his heartiest greetings every time he sees me, personally accepted all the good wishes I conveyed to him recently on behalf of the British success, since one had named a regiment after him; for the moment he thought that much more important than Kabul and Tischin-Kiang-Fu.—Mrs. Austin is here and will stay through the winter. I really hope she takes to Berlin, for I like her very much. She is indeed a blue stocking in the very best sense.—You've heard Lachner's opera.[4] Write me your impressions and also what you've heard about *Rienzi.*[5] Lachner's opera seems incapable of retaining its vigor. Halévy's piano score of his opera displeases me very much—very common motives clothed in lofty pretensions and infinite length.[6] Meyerbeer is also here again. Why is his *Prophet* never *une vérité*?[7] Oh well. I've also seen Fanny Elsler and can't detect much progress there. Please note, however, that I didn't see any national dances other than one character ballet, *Bluebeard,* in which I found her original interpretation quite mannered and unattractive (her costume was also horrible), but her dances very light, graceful, and secure, just like her earlier style. She's a greater virtuoso than the others, but in the same tradition. It's also rather unlikely for a dancer between the ages of 30 and 40 to make such progress.[8]—Since we're on the subject of modern productions, let me recommend *Thomas Thyrnau* to you, Cecile—keep in mind that it's for you, not for Felix, as it's not suitable fare for men.[9] But you must stay home sometime for three days, on account of a cold or some other reason, and read it. Procure a copy and you'll enjoy yourself, just as we women have here.—I think it's a fine idea that the erection of the Bach Monument be delayed until his birthday[10] and the advent of spring. I hope I can attend the dedication ceremony and at the same time catch your Symphony and any other good work being offered.[11] You want to leave a good taste behind in Leipzig, and I don't begrudge it to you or to them, although now they can boast that you're staying there through the winter. Send them my best—i.e. those with the names of Schunck, Schleinitz, David, etc. And kiss those who are children of yours there, probably no sacrifice on your part. Please tell Carl and Marie that I have a pretty little canary that sits on the window under the flowers, and two stuffed birds next to it, and when they come again they are also to receive a new train. My family send their best, and if I can no longer see well enough to sign my name because of the fog, you will probably recognize me anyway.

[1]Of 16 November 1842 (DB 13).
[2]Opera by Cherubini (Paris, 1791). He sent her the piano score, but wanted to give her the full score. Unfortunately it was not available in Germany (16 November).
[3]Part of the Opium War.
[4]Could be *Alidia* (Munich, 1839) or *Catarina Cornaro* (Munich, 1841).
[5]Felix probably heard the Lachner opera, and may have heard Wagner's *Rienzi* while in Dresden in November 1842.
[6]Identity uncertain. Perhaps Halévy's most recent opera, *La reine de Chypre* (Paris, 1841).
[7]*Le prophète,* first performed in 1849 (Paris). The score had been completed in 1840 but laid aside for various reasons (*NGD* XII, 250).
[8]See the *AMZ,* 18 Jan. 1843, cols. 42-43.
[9]Presumably a contemporary novel fashioned for women.
[10]21 March.
[11]The ceremony actually occurs on 23 April 1843. Fanny is presumably referring to the *Scotch* Symphony.

126

Berlin, 17 January [1843][1]

Many thanks, my dearest Felix, for your lovely letter and your warm invitation, which we gratefully accept.[2] But first of all a question: have you received the scores? I had them sent as per your letter.[3] With regard to your visit, we should hardly expect you this month, since you've written nothing about it yet. But with respect to our visit to you, we place ourselves entirely at your disposal. Sebastian has fulfilled all his requirements thus far, so that I can even take him along in all good conscience, since we can't wait for his next vacation shortly before Easter. Therefore Hensel will request, if it's possible, a few days of vacation for him from his director when our plans are more definite. With regard to Hensel himself, I ought to ask you whether you'd be willing and able to pose for a painting, for then he would be overjoyed to come. But if he doesn't have a specific project to work on there, I can't guarantee anything. So write us when you want us and when Cecile can use us, and if no special problems arise, we will come—either two of us or three. My husband's foot still hasn't recovered completely, but he's able to walk on it. In short, I hope it will get better.

Like you, we are living a quiet life: week after week at the Dirichlets during the day, our house in the evening. It's always a bitter moment when we cross the courtyard past the steps we clambered up every day for so many years. It's also painful to see the dark windows of the hall, which always were illuminated. We had good times and a happy childhood as few have experienced, and not one hour passes in which I don't think back on it with warmth and gratitude.[4]

Incidentally, Berlin is incredibly horrible this winter. Burglaries are commonplace, and one hears the most dreadful details in that connection. For instance, Herr von Weber tangled with 2 villains in his room one night. At the same time, our house is so lonesome now—we're the sole inhabitants of the garden house—that we take extra measures to lock ourselves in. And yet I can't shake an eerie feeling that sometimes comes over me when it storms, and everything starts clinking, clattering, and rattling as if the entire place were about to crash down on us any minute.

I was very interested to read what you wrote about the Danish composer. He'll be pleased by your letter.[5] It's high time for another great talent to appear on the horizon; there's a dearth of new blood. I'm very curious about your revisions of the *Walpurgisnacht.* You know how difficult it is for me to adjust to revisions, but I'll try my best. If only you've retained my lovely alto solo—that gave me great pleasure as a young woman and an old woman. The memory of such triumphs doesn't disappear.[6]—I had no idea that you had enough things of mine to fill 2 volumes. As per your request, I'll send more material, and I have a fairly good idea of what you like.—Dear Cecile, I've heard to my great delight that your sister Julie is feeling much better. Send her my very best wishes and tell her how *very* dear she is to me. Should I not have the opportunity to see her soon, I'll send her a letter, but I probably will see her. I've just written to your mother in the past few days. Kiss the dear children for me. Carl should write and tell me what I should bring him and dear little Marie. Paul's gift will just appear. Adieu, you dearest, be well, and remain fond of us.

Your Fanny

[1]Fanny mistakenly wrote 1842.

[2]To Fanny, 13 January 1843 (DB 14). The invitation was to visit Felix, which the Hensels did between c. 20 and 28 February.

[3]To send as soon as possible the copies of the scores of the Beethoven Concertos in E-flat and G major that Eduard Rietz had made (13 January).

[4]Lea Mendelssohn had died on 12 December 1842.

[5]Felix wrote to Fanny regarding Niels Gade on 13 January. They tried out a Symphony by him and will perform it soon [on 2 March]. Felix praised the work highly, and wrote the same to Gade himself (13 January 1843, in Mendelssohn, *Breife-RE*, 222-23). After the performance, Felix thanks Gade for dedicating this c-minor Symphony to him (3 March 1843, in Mendelssohn, *Briefe II*, 245-47).

[6]"Fortunately, as I wrote you previously, I had rewritten the entire *Walpurgisnacht,* but barely the 4-part chorus, because it was to be sung in a week and the rehearsals had already begun. Then the entire orchestra had to be written up, and the mass of small details, which had to accompany it, were the first and only things, as I said before, that really occupied me, not just apparently. It's been finished for a long time and I believe that even you, who knew the earlier version better than anyone

but me, will be surprised how unbelievably better the whole thing has become. I can't stand the thought now that anyone knows it in its first version; for everything that was good in it, and remained, only now receives its true meaning, while what was lacking and flawed has been deleted and replaced." ("Ich hatte, wie ich Dir schon früher schrieb, zum Glück die ganze Walpurgisnacht umgeschrieben, aber blos den 4stimmigen Chor, weil es in 8 Tagen gesungen werden sollte, und die Proben schon angefangen hatten; nun war noch das ganze Orchester aufzuschreiben, und die Masse kleiner Details, die da hineinkommen mußte, waren das erste u. einzige wie gesagt, was mich wirklich beschäftigte, nicht blos scheinbar. Sie ist jetzt längst fertig, und ich glaube, selbst Du, die das Frühere so genau kannte, wie keine Seele außer mir, wirst Du Dich wundern, wie unglaublich das Ganze nun besser geworden ist. Ich kann jetzt den Gedanken gar nicht leiden, daß irgend jemand es in der ersten Bearbeitung kennt; denn alles was gut drin war, und geblieben ist, bekommt erst seine rechte Bedeutung indem das Mangelhafte und Verfehlte weggefallen und ersetzt ist.") The piece will be finished shortly, and then Felix wants Fanny and Paul to critique it (13 January). Fanny may be referring to the alto solo in No. 2. The revised version was performed in Leipzig on 2 February 1843.

127

Berlin, 2 March 1843

We arrived safely from a pleasant and well-nourished journey,[1] thanks to Cecile, who provided for us handsomely. But to our shame I must confess that we've consumed almost all of it, and Sebastian especially performed miracles. The letter, dear Felix, went out two nights ago around 11. It was very nice to spend a few days in your dear company. Having the chance to see the dear children for such an extended period is the greatest joy that one can experience, and I think of each and every one of them with extreme tenderness. Many thanks for your hospitality and every kindness you showed us, and especially for the mere fact that you were there. It was very nice of you.[2]—Rebecka is swamped with things to do and so only sends her greetings today. Dear Carl, Sebastian had such a good time with you that yesterday he was quite afraid to go to school again. Everyone sends his best and I do the same, since this note is only a telegraphic dispatch. Farewell. Dear Cecile, take good care of yourself.

Your Fanny

Felix, write your memoirs!

[1]The visit with the Felicians, from c. 20 to 28 February.
[2]According to her diary, Fanny heard a great deal of music, including Gade's C-major Symphony, met Berlioz, and was enchanted with Clara Schumann's playing (S. Hensel, *Familie II*, 210).

128

Berlin, 28 March 1843

I haven't heard from you in such a long time that I must knock on the door again. Actually, we're awaiting news of Cecile daily, and you've probably postponed a letter until there was some definite news.[1] If it continues much longer, you'll find yourself in the end in a difficult situation with respect to Palm Sunday. Everything is the same here.

Seydelmann is dead, as you probably already know, so therefore the theater is presently out of the picture for me. I won't have the desire to attend for a long time, unless I want to partake of Berlioz's success, which is impossible to predict. In Hauptmann's *Musikalische Zeitung*,[2] there was a very nice essay about him that was too musical for a philosopher and too philosophical for a musician. Who could have written it?[3] Since we're on musical subjects, let me take care of a task I agreed to undertake, although reluctantly. Music Director Lecerf is presently traveling from Berlin to Dresden and wanted to know whether you thought it likely that there would be something for him in Leipzig. Perhaps I myself am the unfortunate, innocent cause of this request, because I made him aware of the death of Music Director Pohlenz.[4] That was a *frappant* sad case at the time, coming directly after the beautiful Jubilee Concert.[5] One must give the Leipzigers credit for knowing how to do such things. How long will your Bach Monument remain covered?[6] The two busts, for whose care I'm very thankful, have been placed on my two large music chests and look very solemn. I particularly like the one of Bach; Handel's wig is a little too wide.—A lovely work was exhibited here recently: an equestrian statue of Frederick the Great by Kiss, known for his *Amazon* statue, cast in bronze for the city of Breslau. I found the head especially beautiful, ingenious, and nobler than I would have thought possible given Frederick's ugliness. He was represented as a young man, victorious over Silesia.—Spring this year is no different from the past 3 years, with east winds, a dry climate, and days that are sunny and cold—in short, weather I dislike the most. In addition, everybody in the house, and everybody in the city, is coughing and sniffling. Dear Cecile, Margarethe's wedding is to take place next Wednesday, assuming everybody is well enough.[7] Little Clara has scarlet fever, which explains why we haven't seen each other,[8] and many more of the Oppenheims are ill. Does little Marie still like to eat "hunte hute Nute?"[9] Thank you for the excellent chocolate that you sent via Albertine. Say hello to the dear children from me. When I visit Leipzig again, Carl must tell me about his trip—it was too beautiful that morning! Adieu, dearest Cecile—may you do as well this time as in the past, and remain fond of me. Adieu, dearest Felix and loveliest children. My husband and Sebastian cough and send their best.

Fanny

[1]Regarding the birth of Felix's fourth child.
[2]= *AMZ.*
[3]*AMZ,* 15 March 1843, cols. 217-21.
[4]Felix responds that he had seen Lecerf before her letter arrived, and Lecerf had already inquired about the position. Felix told Lecerf that there are many applicants; furthermore, Lecerf is not a very good organist (to Fanny, 4 April 1843; DB 16).
[5]Concert of 9 March commemorating the one-hundredth anniversary of the first Gewandhaus subscription concert in 1743.
[6]The Bach Monument is to be unveiled on Sunday, 30 April. Felix intends to have a large concert the night before, as well as some music in the morning before the ceremony (4 April).

[7]Margarethe Mendelssohn's marriage to Otto Georg Oppenheim.
[8]Perhaps Clara Jacques, or maybe a member of the Oppenheim family.
[9] Probably baby talk.

129

Berlin, 17 April 1843

That was a great disappointment! I didn't know how I would rip open your letter fast enough and unfold it fast enough so that I could see whether I had another niece or nephew to love—and then I find a score! Cecile, you are vacillating! Don't you feel the time is long enough? You poor thing, you have to spend the nicest part of the year indoors! The score, dear Felix, is herewith enclosed; is the chorus to be sung at the dedication?[1]

Last week Beckchen and I were completely alone, without our husbands. Dirichlet is still away but Hensel returned on Saturday from a very pleasant, short trip to Brunswick, where they like to see him and where, as a result, he likes to visit. Please send me sometime the name of your peculiar friend in Brunswick, dear Felix, for I'd like to know if he happened to run into him. Hensel sends his very best and requests Cecile to show him some consideration so that he can become a godfather before his trip to England.[2] Dirichlet wrote that Jacoby's situation is serious and unfortunately he won't live much longer.[3] Dirichlet is therefore paying special attention to every word that this eminent man utters. He also attended a lecture by Walesrode, became acquainted with the other Jacoby,[4] and will have the opportunity to meet Schön. If we could still read the dear Leipzig newspaper we would certainly be presented with an analysis of this trip to Königsberg.

Coincidentally, Böckh was also away last week, and so we were a totally female group. The Woringens will be with us a few more days before they move away. They don't have any furniture with them. Their move will be one of the greatest social losses we've ever sustained.—You should be here now, my children. The garden looks splendid already—a melancholy sight for us—the peach trees and almond trees are in full bloom, the shrubs are totally green, and everything else is on the verge of becoming magnificent—for me the most beautiful of all.

Farewell, dearest ones. Write us some good news soon and kiss the dear children. Beny is here now.[5] Whenever we see each other we talk about dear Carl, whom he also finds darling.

Your Fanny

[1]The identity of the score is unknown. The dedication is the unveiling of the Bach Monument, to take place on 23 April. For an excellent compilation of documentary material, see Grossmann-Vendrey, *Vergangenheit*, 154-56.
[2]His second trip to England; in September 1843 he paints a portrait in Buckingham Palace of the Prince of Wales (the future Edward VII).
[3]Gustav Jacoby, who fell seriously ill at the time.
[4]Dr. C. S. Johann Jacoby.
[5]Benjamin Mendelssohn.

130

Berlin, 2 May 1843

Dear Felix! You will receive this letter through Herr Gounod, our friend in Rome and Hauser's in Vienna.[1] I'm very sorry that he will be going to Leipzig just at the moment when you have your hands full and he won't be able to see Cecile. But since he's returning to Paris directly and really wanted to see you before he went, I arranged matters this way. Please give him as warm a reception as possible under the prevailing circumstances. He's had a nice time with us and is a talented man. Also, belated thanks for the invitation to the Bach commemoration, which I certainly would love to have attended. But since I was there recently and am thinking of returning this spring, I feared I would wear out my welcome. Pauline just told us about the festival and your case of the flu, and how you thus weren't able to enjoy yourself at the festival.[2]

[Rebecka]

The last month witnessed a massive influx and exodus of people that one doesn't encounter every day. We won't be able to get over the Woringens so easily because we miss them very much! We released Kaselowsky with a clean bill of health and it wasn't easy to part from him either. I'm truly glad that the first expenditure of our blessed father's endowment has borne such fruit—a good omen for the future.[3] Then Hensel left and returned, Dirichlet left and returned, Marie and Margarethe went to Italy with their husbands,[4] and Hauser and Gounod, among others, passed through. Now we'll probably settle down to a peaceful existence.

Dear Felix, I'm afraid I have to burden you again with a request. The Leipzig supplier of beetles has really sent a substantial package for Sebastian, and we're keeping the main things for the young man. Gounod will take the rest back with our payment. Would you therefore be so kind as to send both to him and ask for a receipt?[5]—Is it really true, dear Cecile, that you've received a gorgeous Rococo porcelain watch from the King of Saxony? At least that's what we heard. Alas, my dear ones, one hears absolutely nothing from you, and it's terrible that you write so infrequently. We also thought you would be coming to Berlin this month—may we still dare to hope? How happy that would make us!—For an hour I've been sitting here like a fool, checking the bill for Sebastian's beetles, and writing down our name and address in Berlin. It just doesn't sit right with me for him to receive another beetle, and a few less gulden back than he ought to according to the bill. The old man probably made a mistake. But he can feel satisfied—we decided to take half his things. Dohrn, who is here, admired a few of the main things, and also took him to the zoo and showed him beetles that cost 200 talers. If only Herr Franck wouldn't send such things here![6] I entreat him ([although it's probably a waste of time])[7] not to send anything here at present; we will look in on him when we visit Leipzig. Farewell, dearest Felix! My dearest Cecile, I think about you a thousand times a day and wonder whether you're screaming in agony now. Give the children my best and kiss them for me.

Your F.

The 3rd. [Rebecka]

May God bless you a thousand times and grant you much happiness, my dear Felix and Cecile![8] How happy I am that poor Cecile is finally free of her burden! Once again she brought off her task with such great mastery that she must certainly be working for all of us too.—Gounod was supposed to deliver this letter to you today, but since he became ill yesterday and will probably have to remain here a few days, I'm taking it out of the envelope again (. . .)[9] and mailing it by itself. If he (. . .)[10] follows in a few days, he will bring the beetles and money mentioned in this letter, and it can also serve as his letter of introduction. Farewell. Let us hear from you every day. What have the children said about their new little brother? Carl no doubt has made very cute observations. And now, may God bless you all. Your F.

My husband and Minna send their very best wishes.[11]

[1]The Hensels met Gounod in Rome. Fanny's diary and letters from late April through July 1840 mentioned him frequently (S. Hensel, *Familie II*, 114-61).
[2]Presumably Pauline Bendemann Hübner.
[3]The specifics of this endowment are unknown. They are not, for instance, mentioned in the NYPL collection. Perhaps the endowment was being used to assist gifted musicians, such as at the newly-founded Leipzig Conservatory, whose establishment was instigated by Felix.
[4]Marie and Margarethe Mendelssohn; Marie was married to Robert Warschauer, and Margarethe to Otto Georg Oppenheim.
[5]Sebastian is an avid collector of beetles; see S. Hensel, *Lebensbild,* 32-34.
[6]Presumably the supplier of beetles rather than one of their friends named Franck.
[7]Inferred translation; "das wird wol Gristel oder Fette bestellen" probably an obsolete colloquial expression.
[8]Felix and Cecile's fourth child, Felix, born on 1 May, announced in a letter of 2 May 1843 (DB 17).
[9]The omitted passage only makes sense in German. Fanny is noting that there is confusion in meaning by use of her word "den," which can refer either to a person (Gounod) or to an object (the letter). In English, however, this confusion is absent.
[10]See note 9.
[11]Minna Hensel.

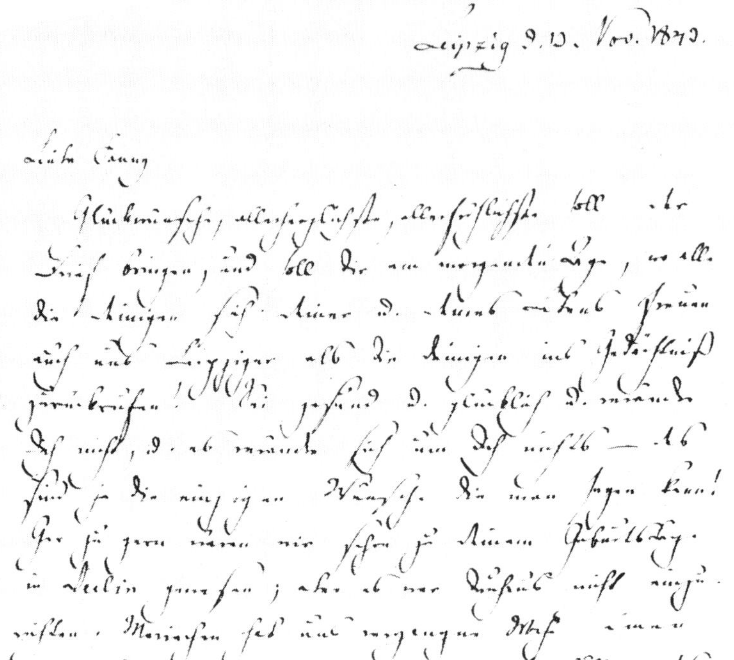

Illustration 9—Autograph letter from Felix Mendelssohn to Fanny Hensel, 13 November 1843 (first page) [Staatsbibliothek Preussischer Kulturbesitz, Musikabteilung, Berlin (West): Depositum Berlin 19].

131

Berlin, 14 May 1843

This time Gounod is really traveling to Leipzig, laden with beetles, money to pay for them, and the burning desire to meet you. I hope he'll also be able to see Cecile for a moment. I don't want to write any further, since we will, I hope, be seeing each other in a few days, if you still come here on the 20th as promised. Your violinist hasn't called on us yet.[1] Since the advent of the railroad, people always need a few weeks to travel from Leipzig to Berlin so that they can get off at every little whistle stop to give a concert. Is your weather as awful as ours—cold and sunny days, a cutting east wind, and abominable dust?[2] There will be a dilettante concert today (I have no connection with this one), in which the lovely Pomowitz will declaim the melodrama from *Antigone.* Adies. An interruption prevents me from continuing.

Your F.

[1]Presumably the twelve-year-old Joseph Joachim. In a letter of 18 October 1843 to Rebecka, Fanny describes the enchanting violinist Joachim, who traveled to Berlin alone and lives by himself in a hotel (S. Hensel, *Famile II*, 244).

[2]Dust on the streets was an everpresent problem in Berlin; see S. Hensel, *Lebensbild,* 4.

132

Berlin, 4 June 1844

Dear Felix, I must continuously burden you with my infamous hand (royal words) to give you news of Beckchen that will cheer you. To my great surprise I received a blissful letter from Palermo,[1] after she had last written dubiously from Naples about the journey. The crossing was accompanied by beautiful weather and she was thoroughly delighted with it. I'm really happy that she's having the pleasure of seeing Sicily, and there's no better proof of her well-being than the quick execution of this plan. Since I assumed that you both wouldn't find out anything from her directly by mail, I didn't want to withhold this news.—What an interesting time you're having in OLD England once again! We'll find out O'Connell's sentence today. No novel is as tense as this serious piece of non-fiction. If O'Connell posts bond he will be signing his death sentence. Klingemann should write me privately about it, because I'd love to know what *he* thinks and also what the *general public* thinks.

Here we are occupied with other political questions: the vase for Devrient and the memorial for Thorwaldsen. Regarding the former, if you want to honor him by adding your name, then make your wishes known soon, for the porcelain artist is standing poised with his dipped brush, awaiting only your instructions.[2] With regard to the latter, the Thorwaldsen memorial has distinguished itself from all others like it in that many more blunders were made than usual.[3] Among others, the King and the entire court were not invited *by mistake*, and furthermore a few other little things were forgotten, namely Beuth and Humboldt. You can well imagine the great consternation when the ceremony started off so rudely. Kopisch had penned a cantata text that paraded around on such high platform shoes that it almost resembled a pair of stilts. You'll hear about Taubert's music for it over there. The introduction was the funeral march from *Antigone,*[4] which he had, of course, cloaked in a short coat and a thin mask. But the old boy could be recognized right away. In order to lighten the work, he used only men's chorus almost continually through the first piece. They played ball with each other with half verses, and the women merely sat there. But had he started out immediately with mixed chorus, the biographical resemblance would not have been so obvious. Then there was a transition from mourning into the joy of eternal glory. It was marked by brilliant sounds—"tut, tut, tut, tut," 4 chords from the *Midsummer Night's Dream,*[5] done with trombones and women's voices. The overall effect was truly very beautiful and brilliant. It is a curious talent that Taubert possesses. He makes decent, well-crafted music sound good and does it totally with borrowed devices, but when that happens to me, I attribute it to family kinship. But he really has no right to it—darn it!

I only wanted to write you a few lines, so please excuse me. Cecile wrote that the dear little children are feeling better, thank God. Albertine and her tender offspring are likewise coming along quite nicely.[6] Farewell. Everybody sends their best. Write soon.

Fanny

[1]Possibly the letter from Palermo in S. Hensel, *Familie II*, 305-08.
[2]The Devrients are moving to Dresden, where he is taking up a position as director of the royal Saxon theater. This is a gift presented at a farewell celebration. See the letter from Fanny to Rebecka in S. Hensel, *Famile II*, 317.
[3]The memorial took place on 1 June at the Singakademie. Thorwaldsen had just died; Taubert's piece was the Cantata, *Klage zur Ehrenfeier Thorwaldsens,* on a text by Kopisch. The opening piece was a "Festhymne" by Rungenhagen (also Kopisch). See the *AMZ,* 26 June 1844, col. 445.
[4]Reference to No. 7 of Felix's *Antigone,* Op. 55.
[5]Possibly in reference to the four opening chords of Felix's Overture, Op. 21.
[6]This child died before reaching maturity.

133

Berlin, 30 July 1844

Dear Felix, I must immediately answer your wistful letter from Soden, in which you so beautifully and perceptively described your relationship to oak trees and their inhabitants, and also took me to task—something I certainly don't deserve.[1] I've never received the piece that you intended for my wedding (I've now passed half the anniversaries on my way to the silver) but never finished on account of your injured knee, so therefore I can't send it to you.[2] Here I can see a smile and an *Ave Maria* forming on your lips now, and instead I can produce a drawing that had disappeared for years but recently surfaced in a meaningful Roman letters patent. In short: I don't have the piece, I've never had the piece, and you must fashion it anew by heart, even though it will probably be quite different. But your life in Soden must be idyllic. If I saw you thus it would seem that I didn't quite know you, because I've never seen you when you've had any time. You will no doubt reply that you've never seen me when I've had none. In fact, I'd like to take a trip with you sometime to a *country tract* and get to know you as you lie around in the grass with nothing to do. But have no fear, I won't tag along—you know me too well for that. By the way, you must be having totally different weather than we poor dogs here—we wouldn't want to lie around in the grass. It's even out of the question this summer to sit on a bench under a tree. All sorts of bad weather have taken turns with each other; we haven't had a single nice day in two-and-a-half months. Yesterday, together with yours, we received a letter from Rebecka from Sorrento.[3] The mail doesn't do as well very often. They're living in the lap of luxury and requested that the answer be sent to Zurich, but intend to return no earlier than the end of September. I hope they will be at least half as enchanted with their residence as I.[4] I spend most of my waking hours here and arrange and rearrange everything until I'm satisfied that things couldn't be better. On one day I squabble with the landlord, on another with the landlady. They both don't want me to open the windows for fear of the sun damaging the mahogany doors, but since I won't let my family damage themselves through a lack of air, I go ahead and open them anyway. In truth I'm feeling very philosophical and nearly old this year. Since I've been here, living my peaceful life, I see and hear of everybody taking trips and yet hardly possess any desire to do so myself. But the fact is I do, and take consolation in my secret hope for the year after next, when we can spend a merry time with our *grown* son during his vacation. He'll write you from his residence at Interbock, where he arrived yesterday with Matusch for a 3-day stay. In this way, I'll be following your instructions not to read his letter.[5] Among all the nice things you wrote, however, you didn't say a word about a visit. If I weren't here in Berlin I wouldn't be offended that you find Berlin so rotten. But I very much look forward to seeing you and your darling children, who really would be missing out on so many interesting things here, even more than their parents: young goats, young chicks, and young storks. *À propos*—Andersen sends his best wishes to you and especially Cecile. I know that you've heard him recite fairy tales, for I remember that Carl once cried over them (he was justified). But have you ever heard him deliver these children's tales in an incredibly ingenuous manner to nobody but adults, as I last night? That's beyond the bounds of nature and must be seen to be believed. I felt so much like a child again that I was on the verge of believing in the stork and demanding mushy food.—Paul received a splendid letter from Klingemann that contained a wealth of good news about you. I'd truly love to see that marvelous person again! He's promised to visit us in October, but then probably won't come. In your letter you said that you're composing a great deal, but didn't mention what, and I don't think you'll be content with merely a commissioned collection of organ pieces once you get busy. I think that since you have so much time in Soden (otherwise you shouldn't have said so), you ought to write me another wonderful, spirited letter and tell me more about them.[6] And then I'd tell you that I'm busy, in my fashion, composing lieder for a short novel that my husband wrote for me while taking the waters. For you, this is or would be a snap—you write as many notes in three-quarters of an hour as I do in three-quarters of a year. But I plan to give it my best effort, and the result should be another small collection with vignettes.[7]

Now to you, dear Cecile, my thanks for your dear lines, in which you said you're feeling better—the best news you could have written. I think perhaps you'll be able to continue your milk treatment here with our goats. We possess a complete drinking establishment in our garden this summer, the 3 goats can provide milk for many people, and the fountains promenade is lively in spite of the bad weather. Perhaps the fresh milk will also prove beneficial to little Felix. Give my best to your dear mother and thank her for her warm letter. I haven't written to her today but intend to respond shortly. You probably know that we saw the London Beneckes here, but unfortunately only in passing. Nevertheless, it's always pleasant to have at least seen someone whom one has heard so much about, even if the encounter proceeds no further.

My husband sends his best. He's feeling better than ever, which is probably due to his taking of the waters. This is to occur one more time in the fall. Marianne has traveled with Marie to Ostend,[8] and the Charlottenburgers send their best.

Your Fanny

[1]To Fanny of 25 July 1844, in Mendelssohn, *Briefe II*, 272-74.
[2]Felix requested the organ piece in A major that he composed for her wedding (see letter 31). He wants to revise it for inclusion in a collection of his organ pieces that an English publisher wants to issue (Op. 65).
[3]Perhaps the letter of 6 July from Rebecka to Fanny, in S. Hensel, *Familie II*, 325-27.
[4]The Dirichlets were moving from Leipziger Strasse 3 into an apartment at nearby Leipzigerplatz 18.
[5]In his letter of 25 July, Felix stated that Sebastian should write him a letter, and insisted that no one should look at it, for that would inhibit him (274).
[6]Felix responds in a letter to Fanny of 15 August 1844 (Soden), in Mendelssohn, *Briefe II*, 274-78: "But I should enumerate my works for you—so far there's been little to say: besides five large organ pieces and three small lieder nothing is finished; the Symphony proceeds slowly; I've also resumed work on a Psalm. . . ." The Symphony could be the incomplete C-major Symphony discussed in Todd, *Symphony*. The new Psalm is probably Psalm 22, *Mein Gott, warum hast du mich verlassen* (Op. 78 No. 3).
[7]This collection may be lost, or in private possession.
[8]Marianne Mendelssohn and her daughter, Marie.

134

Berlin, 21 December 1844

Thank God, dear Felix, that things are going so much better there—may they continue to do so and improve each day.[1] I don't know if Cecile would like to hear about similar cases, but I can't help telling her that Bertha Friedheim has a very pretty 5-year-old child who had the exact same illnesses—measles and whooping cough—with the same resultant abdominal problems and then completely recovered. Many thanks for your 2 dear letters,[2] for hardly had I sent off mine when your first arrived. I've given your organ pieces to the copyist, because although I trust you completely, even with regard to my wedding piece, I'd still like to take the collection with me, and therefore can't send it to you in its original form.[3] Keep the other ones ready for me—I'll pick them up from you this summer. But, alas, those are only plans. And if we hadn't already known that man proposes but God disposes, we certainly would have learned it this fall. We still don't know definitely if we'll make the trip, for we haven't heard anything from Florence in the past 2 weeks, and who knows what the next letter may bring.[4] The weather is marvelous now, and if it continues this way the entire matter won't be so hazardous. I'm anxious to view the situation with my own eyes, and then you could depend upon complete and honest reports. But I'm very calm, dear Felix, and feel neither *furioso ma non tanto*, nor *agitato ma con* I don't know what. A veritable attack of nosebleeds, which I contracted soon after you left, may well have contributed to that feeling.[5] I honestly haven't had the time to grieve *con amore* over your departure,[6] for during the first few days after you left, I was so weary from all the recent events that I just barely vegetated, and then new problems arose. All this can make one's head throb. Everybody likes your picture very much, especially me.[7] I would have been quite disturbed if it were destined for Russia, if I didn't know from the beginning in my heart of hearts that it probably would never leave. Paul had also announced when you were still here that he didn't want it to go, but he didn't want us to tell you—I don't know why. Hensel is attempting to complete it in every spare moment, but he runs into difficulties because there are so many visitors who come to see it, as well as the Elsasser picture, and they take up a great deal of his time. So today he finally had to close his doors (only not to Humboldt, who was thoroughly delighted with it), because he wants to hand it over to Paul at Christmas. Well now, my dear Felix: when, how, and where will we see each other? I wish that someone would issue me a bill of exchange valid for such a visit, which the good Lord would honor at the right time!

Am I in the mood to tell you, and are you in the mood to hear, that I enjoyed seeing Lind as Norma at the opera house yesterday? Unfortunately she probably won't sing any other role while I'm still here. Her voice is of the sharpest purity, which is very pleasing to hear, and exquisitely beautiful in her high register through b-flat. Her dexterity is not exactly overwhelming but certainly adequate for every large role, her trills very good, and her interpretation and expression, as much as one can tell in such a mawkish work, quite strong and lovely, as is also her acting. I can't say much about the power of her voice since we had miserable seats, and have to assume that we lost half the sound.[8] But now turning to the interior of the theater,[9] I, like Mephistopheles, have had enough of academic arguments,[10] and must once again act like a true Berliner. All the gold, red, silver, white, velvet, plaster, gas, stucco, finery, and splendor of every description are not capable of pasting over the spirit of the paperhanger and bookbinder that lies at the core of all its proportions and forms. Hiltl's spirit infuses every loge! Oddly enough, the previous theater, built smack in the age of wigs and braids, had the simplest, noblest, and most beautiful lines that I've ever seen in any theater in the world. The present one, built during our eclectic architectural age that loves all styles from Ptolemy through Semper, has opted to crawl under the most beautiful reactionary style.

May you have a joyous holiday and not a care about your children. We will spend Christmas Eve at Paul's. What a comfort it must have been for Cecile to have her mother close at hand during this sad time. Give my best to the good Madame Jeanrenaud and commend me to Frau Souchay. Hensel sends his best to everybody. Sebastian received a very favorable report from school and was also praised when we spoke to his school director at the time of his trip. Poor, dear Carl must already study so much! Dear Cecile, I found a little shirt of his among Beckchen's children's laundry that I will send you some other time.—Farewell, my dearest! May heaven grant that we meet again happy and healthy.

Your Fanny

The delightful travel expenses book that you gave me three years ago concludes its vignettes with Florence, where it says "to be continued." Isn't that sentimental? I'll make use of it now.

[1]Little Felix was quite ill. Felix writes to Fanny that the doctors say his illness could last a long time (21 December 1844; DB 24).

[2]Personal letters from Frankfurt of 10 December 1844 (DB 22) and 15 December 1844 (DB 23).

[3]"Please have the 4 organ pieces, which I wrote for you for the 14th of November, copied more fully for me, or send them to me here *in natura* for a few days. If you do the latter, I can write up the rest on the same sheet and have the copying taken care of here. But if you don't trust me, then do the former—just as you please." ("Bitte laß mir die 4 Orgelstücke, die ich Dir zum 14te November schrieb, [vollen]der abschreiben, oder schick sie mir in natura auf einige Tage hieher; wenn Du letzteres thust so kann ich gleich die übrigen auf demselben Blatt weiterschreiben, u. mir selbst die Copie hier besorgen lassen. Traust Du mir aber nicht, so thue das erstere—ganz wie Du willst") (15 December).

[4]Rebecka has been very ill with a severe case of jaundice, and might be pregnant, although the doctors are not certain. But finally, in a letter to Fanny of 25 November 1844 (S. Hensel, *Familie II*, 343-44), Rebecka informed Fanny of her condition, and then Fanny decided to make the trip.

[5]A recurrent condition.

[6]Felix spent the autumn in Berlin and lived with the Hensels.

[7]Hensel did a portrait of Felix during his last two weeks in Berlin. It was originally intended for a Russian, Colonel Lvov (S. Hensel, *Familie II*, 338). Perhaps it is the portrait printed in Worbs, *FMB*, 85.

[8]See the review of her performances of 15 and 20 December in the *AMZ*, 1 Jan. 1845, cols. 12-13. Jenny Lind has Berlin engagements through the end of February 1846.

[9]The Royal Opera burned down in August 1843. Fanny wrote to Rebecka about it on 19 August 1843 (S. Hensel, *Familie II*, 224-26). The architect of the new building was Langhans the younger.

[10]The expression comes from Goethe's *Faust*, Part I, "Studierzimmer," line 2009.

135

Florence, 4 March 1845

My dear brother and *musicus*! Unfortunately we've had to write so many letters regarding illness and, thank God, good health, that it's probably high time to think of one's own daily work again. My God, do I know whether you've finished your 7th transcription from *Robert le diable?* Or which opera by Verdi (Donizetti is obsolete in Italy) is now the main focus of your genius? Or whether you performed the fantasy from *Lucia* or the waltz based on the chorale from the *Huguenots,* this most inspired creation of Meyerbeer, in your concerts this winter? When I'm enlightened about everything, particularly whether you'll compose a new trio some time, I'll permit you to use the theme of the Berlin Academy for it.[1] But if you should prefer to try your hand at an original creation, I'll tell you about my own progress in music for your edification and emulation. I still haven't been to the opera—you can't believe what one learns there! I intend to lead art, which has strayed much too far from nature, back to its original path, and to this end am studying with great enthusiasm the utterances of my youngest niece as the mood strikes me.[2] A certain degree of confusion and bad craftsmanship predominates, a mezzoforte muttering that promises very interesting effects in its transferral to the orchestra. When Berlioz will have placed the 50 pianos that he considers necessary, I would advise him to place a wet nurse with a nursing child who hasn't been fed for a few hours next to each. I'm convinced that the public, especially the mothers of the children, would be very moved. With regard to my technical training, it's really quite vast. I froze my right index finger in the mild climate prevalent here. I say "ouch" each time I use it because the injury is located exactly at the tip. This is a totally new and useful effect that I can recommend to you.

In this regard, it just struck me that I actually have something to write you about: if you somehow thought that the christening was taking place on the 6th, then think twice, because it will take place on the 12th.[3] That date is definite, God willing, and my departure for Rome is set for the 15th. If it weren't for the fact that I know how fond you are of precise knowledge, it would almost be unnecessary, after all the above, to assure you that mother and child are doing exceedingly well. Both are in excellent health, respectable humor, and are recovering; both are growing appreciably paler—one is losing her redness, the other her brownness; and both take to eating and drinking and are gaining weight. I'm extremely satisfied with both of them. I hope your next letter will sound a note of confidence—in your first, which arrived the day before yesterday, one could read the anxiety between the lines. Dear Cecile, your description of little Franck in a woolen jacket made us laugh a lot because of its similarity to the manner in which our poor *bambino* entered the world.[4] It was clothed in one of Dirichlet's woolen jackets without any special amenities, with one sleeve drawn over the head and dragging along below. But the next morning I was able to wrap it up halfway decently and take it to Beckchen. And now, just when we've used up our temporary dowry, the package from Berlin arrives, and the seven lean years are over. Regarding future letters that you dear ones want to write me, please send them via Beckchen in Florence, for she will, of course, know the date through which letters will be able to reach us in Rome. I do want to stay there through Easter, because I have to flirt with my musical education this time. A Frenchman who lives here in the same house has made significant contributions to that education with his inspired, stimulating conversation. By profession he's a language teacher, by inclination a Lutheran propagandist, who in the process rides a very lame musical hobbyhorse. Whenever he hears me in the corridor he sings:

[5]

And when he comes to tea, he asks whether I like *Don Juan,* to which I respond, "My dear Monsieur, one doesn't ask such questions." But in all seriousness, please write me a nice musical letter and let me know what's new, so that, as Jacoby says, I won't become totally thick.[6] That can easily happen to somebody who, like me, has the good fortune of being able to spend a half-year in Italy. Farewell for now. The best of health to you and your dear other half and 4 little quarters. Commend me to the dear Madame Jeanrenaud, whom I very much look forward to seeing again, and remain fond of me.

[Rebecka]

[1]"In her last, merry letter, Fanny requests musical news, but I honestly know no more than she." He has begun a Trio (Op. 66), of which the first movement is complete; finished six organ pieces (Op. 65); completed the entire music to *Oedipus* (Op. 93); and has several other things in mind. He then mentions playing late Beethoven Sonatas at private gatherings, seeing a new opera by Aloys Schmitt, and being involved with some rehearsals of choral pieces, including Cherubini's Requiem and Bach's Passion (to sisters, 16 March 1845, NYPL).
[2]Rebecka's new baby, Flora.
[3]Felix is the godfather of Florentine (16 March).
[4]Possibly a baby of Hermann Franck.
[5]Identity unknown.
[6]Probably Gustav Jacoby.

136

Rome, 3 April 1845

Dear Felix, in order for the wheel to remain round,[1] our correspondence should travel back and forth via Florence while we're here. But that won't last very long. You've probably already heard through Beckchen and Paul what a difficult time we had here at first, so therefore it makes me especially happy to be able to report good news. Hensel is recovering nicely, although he's still a bit weak, and every precaution will be taken to insure his good health and prevent a relapse or mishap.[2] Sebastian and I are also being cautious, although I've never felt any negative effects from the climate. On the contrary, I possibly feel more like the *pont neuf* here than at home. (Rebecka will write "knock on wood" if I don't do it myself.) And so now I can turn to a more pleasant subject, namely your suggestions for a family gathering, which we gladly accept. But you probably won't move to the country so soon after the fearfully hard and long winter, so if we follow Beckchen's and our very first plan to depart from Florence in the middle of June (we wouldn't like to do it earlier), we could arrive in Soden in the first half of July, and that's probably the right time for you and Paul. Since you'll be settled there for the summer, it won't hurt anything if one of us waits for the others at your house, since it's virtually impossible for travelers from Florence and Berlin to arrive exactly the same day. As the time approaches, we can discuss whether you brothers can't push things up a little and perhaps meet us in Freiburg, where we'll be staying with the Woringens in any case. When we're in Soden, do you think Hensel should take the waters? Is there Marienbad water in Frankfurt? Assuredly there must be. And one more thing—can one procure a room in Soden that's suitable for painting? Cecile, you certainly know what I mean: windows that are not too low, and perhaps a wall beyond them. If you would be so good as to make an excursion to Soden when you have a chance and inquire on our behalf whether there is a residence with such features, I can promise you that we'll want to stay in Soden until you show us the door.[3] And now if God insures good health to all, then we can look forward to a happy, peaceful time after so many upheavals. It was very nice, dear Felix, to receive your answers to my musical questions 2 days after my letter had gone out.[4] I particularly look forward to the Trio and hope I'll be able to play it.[5] You can't imagine how much I feel I've regressed in this department and also how weak my hands have become. If I hadn't had so many other things on my mind and so little music since time immemorial, I would truly be upset. I'm very glad that you are looking for an opera, for, as it is written, "seek and you shall find." And you shall indeed find one.[6] Regarding the answer to your question, I want to tell you first that Ritter Landsberg, that rogue whom you don't want to know anything about, has rented an Erard piano to a Russian for *one* month for 35 scudi. Also, you're unjustified in our eyes for disliking Mme. Sabatier so much—we've found her quite pleasant, warm, and obliging. Of course we didn't see your confidante, Marchese Martellini, in Florence because he hadn't returned there yet.[7] But we'll probably see him in Munich on our return trip, and his wife and daughters, who have moved into my good graces through their highly developed musical taste, in Florence. When I first visited there, I went past a room in which the b-minor Quartet by Mendelssohn was receiving a fine performance.[8] They know everything by this inspired *compositeur* and adore him, and made me describe him from head to toe. They were so excited about the entr'acte of the *Midsummer Night's Dream,*[9] which I played for the first time since Berlin, that I, as mentioned previously, formed a very favorable impression of the family. Eckert is no longer in Rome,[10] but little Franck is still there, for I saw him yesterday. He's really metamorphosed from a little squirt into an unattractive but very decent young man.[11] The director of the Papal chapel is NOBODY (Abbate Garombo),[12] the eldest bass beats time, and they think that this is all you need to know. I hope to live to see the day when the Papal music will simply run out. They balk at the reform concerning boys' voices, just as they do at every other reform in the world, and the old ways will eventually become so antiquated that everything will grind to a halt. I celebrated Palm Sunday in Rome in the coach on the country road and so have no opinion about it. We eat *broccoli all' insalata* every day, dear Felix, much like a toast to your health.[13] Yesterday Charlotte Thygeson sent me some from her villa, and our excellent Francesco—who is cook, waiter, maid, and general servant rolled into one, and whose attire consists of cut-off dressing gowns that some old English woman forgot here, and whose kitchen speaks nothing but Italian—prepares it well. Are you familiar with *riso di Germania*? It's a type of coarse pearl barley that we want to try for a change, because otherwise the Italians know only of *riso di pasta* and *pasta di riso*. Farewell for today. I don't want to restrict Beckchen's space unduly. Say hello to Cecile and the dear children. I hope you're finally having some good weather, although it can't be as good as ours, and little Felix is losing the last traces of his nasty illness. May God preserve him and all of you.

Your Fanny

Herr Schmitz is very friendly and obliging and served me well when I left. Thank Herr Bernus for the reference when you see him.

Dear Felix, Beckchen just wrote that she sent you one of my letters. You will find that I am an expensive sister with respect to postage—please forgive me!

[Sebastian, Rebecka][14]

[1]"Now the letter is wending its way in today's mail to all of you, yours to Paul in Berlin, and when he receives one, he'll send it to me—that is also a kind of wheel." ("Nun wandert der Brief mit der heutigen Post zu Euch, der Eure nach Berlin zu Paul, u. wenn der einen bekommt, schickt er ihn mir—das ist wieder eine Art Rad") (to Fanny, 12 February 1845; DB 25).
[2]Fanny found Hensel quite ill after she left Rebecka in Florence and rejoined him in Rome.
[3]Felix answers these questions in a letter of 20 April 1845, in S. Hensel, *Familie II*, 359-61. The sisters' departure in mid June is fine, and there are suitable rooms for the Hensels in Soden.
[4]See letter 135.
[5]The c-minor Trio, Op. 66. "The Trio is a bit disagreeable to play, but difficult it is not. 'Seek and ye shall find' " (20 April; 361).
[6]"I'm reading novels and history books to death in search of an opera (but so far I haven't found anything)" (to sisters, 16 March 1845, NYPL).
[7]Felix mentioned these three people in his letter of 16 March.
[8]Probably the Piano Quartet, Op. 3 (composed 1824/25).
[9]Part of the Incidental Music, Op. 61 (1842).
[10]Felix inquired in his letter of 16 March.
[11]Eduard Franck.
[12]Felix asked his name (16 March).
[13]"Eat *broccoli all' insalata* with ham, dear Fanny" (16 March).
[14]Presumably added when the letter went via Florence to Germany.

137

Berlin, 4 August 1845

Dear Felix, we arrived here safely the day before yesterday with the second coach as according to plan,[1] after a morning in which things could have really gone awry. The mail coach that Rebecka had boarded because of the rain overturned 15 minutes outside Halle—at the last minute, one might say—and the wheel flew off, just as at

Kronthal. Rebecka herself sustained a severe bump to the forehead and a small contusion of the hand. Everybody else was totally unharmed, including Walter, who fell off the box seat. The main reason I'm writing you about this little accident is for you to make sure that Johann pays great attention to the wheels.[2] By the way, she's feeling very well and went about her business today, which included a shopping trip. She's also very pleased with her apartment. We were away for such a long time that we have to adjust to being at home. For two evenings, the garden was brilliantly illuminated in our honor, and this celebration was "favored by the nicest weather." The Pauls are both fine and still living in our house; Beckchen is preparing rooms for you at her house. That's really the only thing to report. I just picked up the first *Spenersche Zeitung*, and it abounds with talk of Hersky and Ronge, Illuminati and Jesuits,[3] Jews, Protestants and New Catholics to such a degree that it puts me in the mood for a religious war—I smell nothing but fire and brimstone. In Italy one moves so easily between art and the enjoyment of life that it's really quite difficult to become adjusted to hearing so many unpleasant things again. This laxness is just like Italian music: one's ears become so soft after hearing a lot of it that every reasonable modulation begins to sound like a presumption. Now you'll think that the reunion with Heinrich lifted my spirits over every one of life's privations, but it didn't—or, as we used to say, "not at all."[4]

Farewell. If the Thirty Years War breaks out in Germany, I will go to Italy again. Cecile, have a pleasant journey with your little brood. Dear Madame Jeanrenaud, remember us fondly.

Fanny

[1]The Hensels and Rebecka journeyed from Italy on 15 June, met their brothers in Freiburg, and then spent a few weeks together. See letter 136.
[2]Johann Krebs.
[3]"Illuminati" = a secret society in Germany in the late eighteenth century whose members were freethinkers and republicans.
[4]The identity of Heinrich is uncertain.

138

Berlin, 20 September 1845

Dear Felix! Why do blunders exist in this world if not to be committed? I've made a truly stupid one, for I rejected the arrangement with the piano that you offered me, and now I'm on the verge of making another stupid one again. "One shouldn't set a bad example"—oh no, that isn't applicable in this situation at all; "prosperity spoils a person"—but that isn't a proverb. I, poor *rat de campagne*, was quite satisfied with my rural Viennese piano until the proud *rat de ville* invited me to his banquet once and confronted me with a taste for plain fare. To put it in a nutshell, I'm so thoroughly disgusted that I may not want to play any longer. And if anything is to prevent me from totally throwing in the towel now with respect to making music, it is a full, heavy, really tough piano. Is such an instrument available? Have you already looked around for one? I must have it. If the deficit is too large at the end of the year I'll sell my pearls—my swan-like neck can exist without them.

We were very happy to learn from Cecile's letter to Rebecka that she's so well and cheerful and likes the new apartment. Our resolve to sell the house always begins to waver, even though I hoped the decision would be firm. Of course, we have the greatest personal interest in the matter, since we have many requirements for the living areas, the atelier, and the garden. We have no idea how all these features could be combined. I'm still leaning towards the construction of a new house.

On the day you left we received news of the death of our dear Elsasser and Hallmann, the architect, with whom we were also very friendly and had seen almost daily during our last trip to Rome. Today I received news from Rosa and Elise in Liegnitz.[1] Both have contracted typhoid fever and have been in bed for approximately the past six or seven weeks. Their letter was written in pencil from their sickbeds. The greatest danger is actually past, but Elise in particular is still supposed to be very weak. And so, troubles never cease!

Illustration 10—Oil portrait of Felix Mendelssohn by Eduard Magnus, c. 1845 [Staatsbibliothek Preussischer Kulturbesitz, Musikabteilung, Berlin (West)].

Farewell. May God keep you and insure that Cecile will feel better soon.

Antigone was performed at the New Palace the day before yesterday.[2] Hensel had been sent a ticket and attended. It was supposed to be a very good performance. Best regards to Madame Jeanrenaud, Fräulein Jung, and the children.

Fanny.

Please let me hear from you soon about a piano.

[1]Rosa and Elise Woringen.
[2]Op. 55. In Potsdam.

139

Berlin, 2 February 1846

Anything that's mailed here on the 2nd will reach you in Leipzig on the 3rd, with its congratulations— actually my warmest congratulations. You're indeed a venerable head of the family when all five offspring appear at a birthday. May God preserve them and grant you everything good. Amen.—Everyone is fine here. Paul will make his first trip the day after tomorrow. All the children are well and little Florentina acquired a totally new face after the measles.[1]

This week there is an overflow of musical treats: today Leonard with your Concerto;[2] tomorrow Lind in *Feldlager,* for which fate tossed us two tickets (a worthy celebration of your birthday);[3] at the end of the week the theater; a charity concert with Lind; on Wednesday *A Midsummer Night's Dream*—where do I begin? where do I end? You've also had Lind in Leipzig again. What did she do there?[4] I haven't been able to see her again because she's not easy to see, so I don't know how we'll manage to get together, especially since I'm not the pushy type. I've continued to be pleased with my piano, and everyone who hears it likes it. It's amazing how brilliant it sounds. I played on a small Pleyel recently and wasn't able to extract any tone from it, whereas I can produce the most beautiful fortissimo with my stiff arms on my piano.[5]

But I don't want to allow this letter to be sent without passing along a suggestion that's been on the tip of my tongue for a long time. I can't deny that we haven't thought it very nice that the only picture by Hensel hanging in your house is old and unsuitable, and, to put it another way, not a worthy representative of his art, especially since you had Magnus paint Carl and Cecile.[6] That seems contrary to the spirit of a family as well as patently unfriendly. Therefore Hensel is making the following suggestion, which I support. You can give Rebecka's picture back to him, and in exchange he'll make a copy of yours for Cecile, which pleased you and all the relatives here, especially Paul. It would certainly not be a bad exchange for you, and you would be doing us a favor. Therefore I would think you'd be amenable to this suggestion. Please let us know.

Dear Cecile, I'll send you a little package tomorrow with miscellaneous items for the children. I haven't been able to finish the shoes for my dear little Felix because I don't know his measurements. Please have the work done before the others receive their gifts, for otherwise the dear child won't be completely clothed. Everything is my own work. Now farewell, you dear ones. Have the most wonderful day tomorrow and then nothing but the same thereafter. Hensel sends his warmest wishes on your birthday. Your Fanny.

[Sebastian]

[1]Flora Dirichlet.

[2]Violin Concerto in e minor, Op. 64.

[3]*Ein Feldlager in Schlesien*, Singspiel by Meyerbeer (Berlin, December 1844).

[4]Lind sang on 4 December 1845 at a Gewandhaus concert (*AMZ*, 10 Dec. 1845, col. 891).

[5]In a recent letter to Felix, Fanny expressed her satisfaction with the instrument: "Now I want to tell you that I'm extremely satisfied with my piano. It pleases me here much more than in Leipzig, and I'm very happy with it. Now I want to see whether I can effect a revival in my piano playing. When alone I manage to master it quite well; with instruments, I believe, it will be a bit more difficult." ("Nun will ich Dir sagen, daß ich mit meinem Flügel ganz außerordentlich zufrieden bin, er gefällt mir hier noch weit besser, als in Leipzig u. ich bin ganz glücklich damit. Nun will ich einmal sehn, ob ich noch einen alten Weibersommer für mein Clavierspiel zu Stande bringen kann. Allein zwinge ich ihn schon ganz gut, mit Instrumen-

ten glaube ich wird es mir ein bischen schwer werden'') (c. end of January; GB XXIII 188).

[6]Eduard Magnus. His portrait of Cecile, presently exhibited at the Staatsbibliothek in West Berlin, is probably her most famous likeness. See Illustration 10 for a portrait of Felix by Magnus, c. 1845.

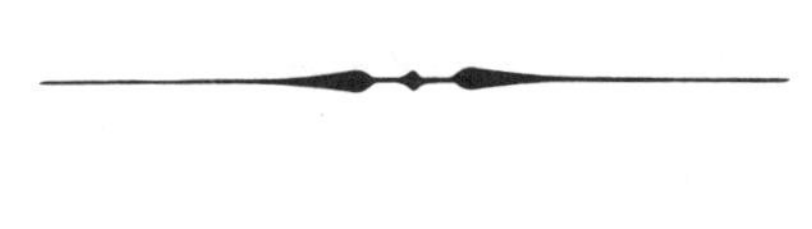

140

n. d. [before 11 April 1846][1]

Jenny Lind is traveling to Leipzig and wants me to give her a letter of introduction to you in the hope that she might also give me one when I travel to see you some time. I don't want to refuse her request. How are you? We're all ill, sickly, and unwell. Hensel has been ailing for almost a month and isn't back on his feet yet. I was sick for 2 weeks, and Mama Dirichlet and Beckchen's younger children have the flu. Sebastian was confirmed yesterday. Those are the current events. But as to events that haven't happened yet belongs *Athalie,* which you didn't send via Taubert. Please send it, for I'd like to hold a musicale 2 weeks from tomorrow.[2] How beautiful the weather is already— the almond blossoms have fallen from the trees, the peach tree and apricot trees are about to shed their blossoms, and the other fruit trees will bloom in a few days. Does one have a hint of this on the Königstrasse?[3] I sent Cecile a certain little male animal a while ago, which won't, I fear, earn the children's gratitude. But I hope she hasn't mentioned it to them. I just read in today's newspaper that you'll conduct a singing society in Cologne and have promised them a new piece. Don't you already have enough to do? Will you be performing your new oratorio in England?[4] Please fill us in on some of your busy plans and thereby enliven our stagnant life. *À propos*, would you be so kind as to have the lied[5] copied and sent back with *Athalie?*

 [6]

If you should think of it, when you see Dr. Härtel, thank him for his friendly note and the package containing the strings. They helped, and I'm on the verge of showing Berlin its first example of how one can live without Kalix. I've fallen out with the old one and don't like the young one, but there's still someone here who can tighten a string and tune it with a minimum of fuss.

Farewell, you dear trees; shake your branches loudly enough for them to be heard here. What is my friend Marie doing? Is she still thinking about coffee and cake? The Cléments have a cow again—she would like it. Why in the world have I none of the children here! I'm by myself much too often and as a result become moody.

Farewell!

Your Fanny.

[1]The internal evidence regarding the parts for *Athalie* suggests a date prior to that of letter 141, which also discusses them.
[2]Op. 74, completed 12 November 1845; first performance in Charlottenburg, 1 December 1845.
[3]Felix lived at Königstrasse 3 in Leipzig.
[4]*Elijah*, first performance in England (Birmingham) on 26 August 1846.
[5]See letter 142.
[6]Identity unknown.

141

n. d. [11 April 1846]

Dear Cecile, I received your letter recently, just as I sent off a few lines to Felix via Lind. Many thanks. I've also heard direct news from the Devrients. Won't Felix be coming here for a few days before he takes his trip? And is he composing his oratorio for England?[1] The series of music festivals on the Rhine will be very nice; if I weren't as poor as a church mouse this year I'd gladly attend.[2]

Say hello to all the dear children. Will you remain totally inactive while *he* runs around? Farewell!

Dear Felix,

I've promised to preface, etc., the enclosed letter, and am doing so.[3] I think that Friedheim went along to select a Leipzig piano so that she could have the pleasure of writing you a letter. Please give Walter the parts to *Athalie*—please don't forget. He will feel his worth as a traveler and won't let them lie in Köthen. I really look forward to performing the piece—it gives me much pleasure. But *Peri*—that is *impossibile*. I just can't acquire a taste for this Schumann.[4] Cecile, give me your hand. Farewell. Today is a birthday,[5] and Walter will provide you with more details. If he doesn't act too silly.

Adieu! F.

[1]*Elijah*.
[2]At Aachen, the Lower Rhenish Festival, 31 May to 2 June; at Düsseldorf, a soirée; at Liège on Corpus Christi (11 June), the newly-composed hymn, *Lauda Sion;* and at Cologne, the first festival of the German-Flemish Association, for which Felix composed a Festgesang on Schiller's *An die Künstler* (Op. 68).
[3]A letter of introduction attesting to the musical credentials of Dr. Ritter, possessor of the choral parts to *Athalie*.
[4]Schumann's *Das Paradis und die Peri*, Op. 50; composed 1843, published 1845; first performance, Leipzig, 4 December 1843. In the Library of Congress, a letter from Felix to the English publisher Buxton of 27 January 1844 praises the work, laying the groundwork for Schumann himself to write to Buxton regarding its publication. The letter, in English, appears in full in E. Werner, *Mendelssohn*, 440-41.
[5]Rebecka's birthday.

142

n. d. [after 11 April 1846]

Dear Felix, I can't let this beautiful black pigeon fly away without placing a sheet of paper in its beak. This time it could have easily become a blank piece of green paper, exactly the type of correspondence you like, if I didn't have a few things to tell you. First of all,

I'm delighted with your choice of text for the Cologne music society, and it once again shows that you have a good grasp of things and are able to pick out a text that already contains the essence of the entire work.[1] I wish I could participate in this lovely series of concerts.[2] Secondly, many thanks for the lied, which I like very much. If I perform it here I'll have to change the title, for otherwise people will make fun of the table on which there's nothing to eat.[3] Thirdly, [I think] you didn't send me enough parts for *Athalie*. Please send double the amount with Paul. What do you think of my chorus?[4] Everyone wants to participate in it. They're all looking forward to the piece, but not as much as I. Therefore, please don't forget both of them—I'm asking Marie to remind you.

May you all be well. I wish you everything good, you dear people.

Fanny

[1]Schiller's *An die Künstler*.
[2]See letter 141.
[3]Possibly *Abschiedstafel* for male chorus, dating from 1844 (Op. 75 No. 4). But unless Fanny had it performed SATB, it is curious that she would want to perform it, as she did not like settings for male chorus.
[4]According to the list in Sirota, *Hensel*, 326-28, Fanny composed many choral works in 1846. But since this letter is undated, the particular chorus cannot be identified with certainty. It is not one of the six dated choruses from 1846 later published as Op. 3 (*Gartenlieder*), because Fanny writes Felix later in the year that he has not seen these pieces (see letter 145). Two possibilities, undated but presumably from 1846, are *Nacht ruht auf den fremden Wegen* and *Schon kehren die Vögel wieder ein* (MA Ms 49, 108 and 89-92).

143

Berlin, 22 June 1846

My dear Felix, be kind and merciful towards me sometime, and after you will have delighted Europe and neighboring countries, delight and gladden your own family once again. Either come here for a few days *incognito* and tell us, tell us absolutely everything over an entire day, or if that's not possible, bestow upon us at least an hour's worth in the form of a long, detailed letter. This time I won't consider all your activities valid excuses and will even make a claim on your time—I think I don't do it too often. Just imagine that some idiot were sitting there an extra hour—wouldn't you throw him out the door then? In short, let us share the many wonderful things you've experienced. It must have been truly magnificent in Cologne, and give me an idea of how 2,000 men's voices sound—I know very well how 10 sound. I must also hear that sometime.[1] And what happened in Liège? I can hardly believe that you didn't want to conduct because the music went so badly, for I remember the incident in Zweibrücken in which you held the baton under the singer's nose. You probably should have confessed beforehand, or something of the sort.[2] In short, let us hear from you, for I'm dying of curiosity.[3] All those events lie within the grand style of living, but our little pocket edition is also enjoying a very pleasant and delightful summer. I'm quite busy with my music and am enjoying it immensely. I had thought that such pleasure was only a thing of the past and am truly very happy with my life. I don't know whether redoubled efforts are necessary after living through a particularly difficult time, but I haven't enjoyed myself as much as this summer since I was a child; we've been blessed with a peaceful time, thank God. I wish I could say the same of Rebecka, but her depression seems to have gained such a foothold that I can't foresee an end to it. Sometimes I think I'm not being fair when I numb myself to it to a certain extent, and instead rejoice in my own good fortune, which I certainly wasn't able to do for a long time. But my husband has the chief claim on me, and if I made his life miserable in the process of pursuing my own happiness, that wouldn't be good in the end. She's living with her mother-in-law and small children on the floor above us now, the place you stayed during your last visit. The children are so marvelous and cute that they alone should suffice to make her feel cheerful, happy, and grateful. I assure you, dear Felix, it's an awful tribulation to witness such a state day in and day out, and I thank God many times over that I'm now in a position to withstand it and spread a little happiness and cheer in the house. I wasn't capable of doing it in the winter—I was almost always in an incredibly bad mood then.—Paul and his family are living in the Tiergarten and unfortunately we don't see each other often. They sit in their garden, we sit in our garden, and each family receives visitors. It is only on Sundays that we come together with regularity. Their children are also very darling; our family's legacy to the future makes us extremely proud. Of course, one must not look out beyond one's four walls, because there is too much unpleasantness out there. Have you heard, among other things, that they've retracted the travel award to young artists here and decreased the purse? Everywhere else such programs are being expanded and made more accessible, but here it seems as if they haven't even considered the possibility of helping our local artists stand on their own two feet. I'm curious about the new statute of the Academy—that should be something! Farewell. The conversation is drawing to a close again and is actually old hat, but even if it is, tell us in person or write.

Say hello to Cecile and the children from me and everyone here.

Your Fanny.

[1]It is compared to the difference between thirty violins and ten violins (to Fanny, 27 June 1846, in S. Hensel, *Familie II*, 373).

[2]In the same letter (373): "My not conducting came about quite naturally. I arrived a quarter of an hour before the dress rehearsal and had never thought of taking up the baton. Then they all rushed in on me, but I had come to listen and stayed with my plan. Moreover, the means that the Bishops had employed were extremely deficient, and nothing much could have been done in one rehearsal. Instead I enjoyed listening very much. . . ." This was the *Lauda Sion,* composed expressly for this concert. Felix had conducted at the Zweibrücken Music Festival on 31 July and 1 August 1844. The incident about the baton may be one of the mishaps that Felix alluded to in his letter to Fanny of 15 August 1844 (Mendelssohn, *Briefe II*, 278).

[3]Felix's letter to Fanny of 27 June.

144[1]

Berlin, 9 July 1846

My dear Felice, thank you for your letter with the nicest news, which positioned your mention of the rice pudding at the top, naturally.[2] I could have tolerated more news, for if you imagine that Cecile wrote a great deal, you are, as they say here, under a false illusion.[3] Cecile is too stolid to write details. I gratefully acknowledge, however, that I was the idiot upon whom you bestowed a half hour.[4] And why not? Am I to imagine that I'm not as worthy in your eyes as Spohr?[5] I definitely won't be such a modest rogue. In fact, we could conclude a contract with each other stating that you would write a long letter after every music festival and every important event so that one could find out about them. Whenever we get together after a long separation, too many of the details are lost, and, as Gans said, it is better to hear some things twice than not at all.[6] Now an entire oratorio of yours is being introduced to the world again, and I don't know a note of it. When will we hear it?[7] Actually I wouldn't expect you to read this rubbish now, busy as you are, if I didn't have to tell you something. But since I know from the start that you won't like it, it's a bit awkward to get under way. So laugh at me or not, as you wish: I'm afraid of my brothers at age 40, as I was of Father at age 14—or, more aptly expressed, desirous of pleasing you and everyone I've loved throughout my life. And when I now know in advance that it won't be the case, I thus feel RATHER uncomfortable. In a word, I'm beginning to publish. I have Herr Bock's sincere offer for my lieder and have finally turned a receptive ear to his favorable terms.[8] And if I've done it of my own free will and cannot blame anyone in my family if aggravation results from it (friends and acquaintances have indeed been urging me for a long time), then I can console myself, on the other hand, with the knowledge that I in no way sought out or induced the type of musical reputation that might have elicited such offers. I hope I won't disgrace all of you through my publishing, as I'm no *femme libre* and unfortunately not even an adherent of the

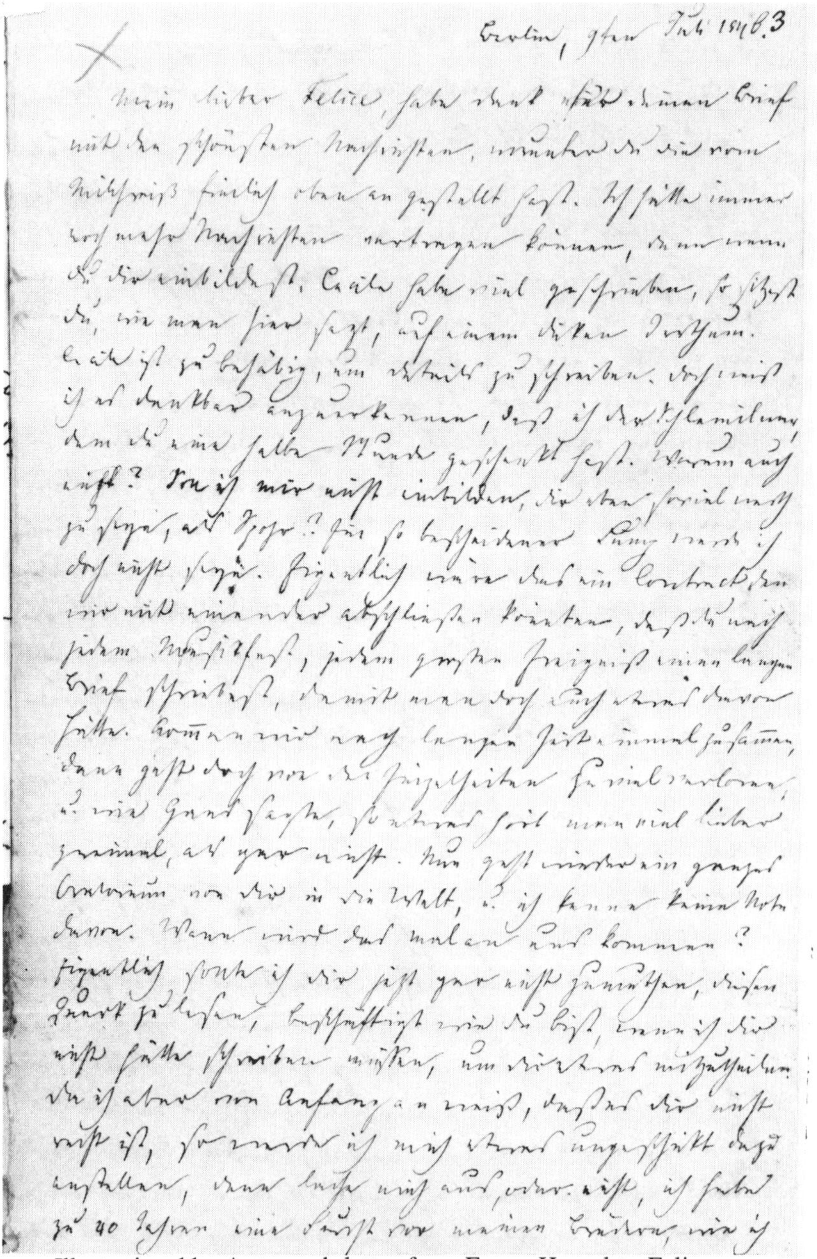

Illustration 11—Autograph letter from Fanny Hensel to Felix Mendelssohn, 9 July 1846 (first page) [Bodleian Library, Oxford: MS Margaret Deneke Mendelssohn d. 50, letter 3].

Young Germany movement. I trust *you* will in no way be bothered by it, since, as you can see, I've proceeded completely on my own in order to spare you any possible unpleasant moment, and I hope you won't think badly of me. If it succeeds—that is, if the pieces are well liked and I receive additional offers—I know it will be a great stimulus to me, something I've always needed in order to create. If not, I'll be as indifferent as I've always been and not be upset, and then if I work less or stop completely, nothing will have been lost by that either.[9] "That is the true basis of our existence and salvation."

Would it be possible to borrow the music of the dervish chorus from Leipzig sometime?[10] I don't need it now, in any case, because the next Sunday will be the last musicale for the summer.[11] You will be receiving my chief bass, Behr, in Leipzig. I believe he'll become a very good comic singer, but he must tone down his excessive buffoonery a bit. He certainly has a talent for comedy. What do you think of this heavenly summer? I'm truly sorry that you have to spend it in the Königstrasse.[12] I'm enjoying the garden more than ever and love it more tenderly than ever—perhaps a premonition that we will lose it soon. All kinds of plans regarding selling the house, and horrible plans about tearing it down and breaking through the street are spooked again, but Pourtalès would be a real fool if he didn't buy it.[13]

Farewell, you dear ones. Say hello to dear Cecile and all five children. Hensel also sends his best.

Your Fanny.

Just one more request. If Herr von Keudell, whom you certainly know, drops by to see you within the next 2 weeks, and perhaps at a time when you're very busy, receive him warmly nevertheless, for he's here with us very often and is a close musical pal. He has the finest feeling for music and a memory that I've seen in no one except you. Works such as Schubert's Op. 150, Beethoven's Op. 130, a few numbers from Mendelssohn's Op. 60,[14] and many other trifles he knows by heart; he also plays very well.[15]

The above-signed

[1]See Illustration 11 showing the first page of the autograph.
[2]To Fanny, 27 June 1846, in S. Hensel, *Familie II*, 370-74.
[3]Felix said in his letter (371) that he did not write her every detail because he knows that Cecile wrote Paul a letter about most of the events, and that letter crossed with Fanny's (letter 143).
[4]See letter 143.
[5]Spohr was a guest at Felix's and Cecile's house for a while (370).
[6]An expression Fanny used previously. See letter 68.
[7]*Elijah.*
[8]Of Bote & Bock, Berlin music publishers. S. Hensel claims that two Berlin publishers were vying to publish her music (*Familie II*, 365-66).
[9]Fanny writes to her friend Angelica von Woringen on 26 November 1846 about the publishing venture: "I'm glad that you, dear Angela, are interested in the publication of my lieder. I was always afraid of being disparaged by my dearest friends, since I've always expressed myself against it. In addition, I can truthfully say that I let it happen more than made it happen, and it is this in particular that cheers me. . . . If they want more from me, it should act as a stimulus to achieve, if possible, more. If the matter comes to an end then, I also won't grieve, for I'm not ambitious, and so I haven't yet had the occasion to regret my decision. . . ." ("Daß Du, liebe Angelica, Dich für die Herausgabe meiner Lieder interessirst, freut mich, ich hatte eigentlich immer Angst, von meinen liebsten Freunden gemißbilligt zu werden, da ich mich mein Lebenlang u., bis in meine jetzigen Jahre entgegengesetzt ausgesprochen habe. Auch kann ich mit Wahrheit sagen, ich habe es mehr geschehn lassen, als gethan, u. das ist es, was mich eigentlich freut. . . . Wird mehr von mir verlangt, so soll es mir ein Sporn seyn, wo möglich mehr zu leisten, hat die Sache damit ein Ende, so werde ich mich auch nicht grämen, denn ich bin nicht ehrgeizig, u. so habe ich bis jetzt noch nicht Gelegenheit gehabt, meinen Entschluß zu bereuen . . .") (MS MDM c. 36, f. 19-20). Fanny mentioned the significance of encouragement and support from others in earlier letters. She wrote to Rebecka on 22 August 1841 (NYPL): "I also thank you for giving my lieder to Mme. Frege—she should really sing this type very beautifully. If you didn't look after my reputation, who would?" And to Klingemann on 15 July 1836: "Felix, for whom it would be an easy matter to take the place of a public, can only encourage me a little, since we're hardly ever together, and so I'm rather alone with my music. My own and Hensel's joy in the thing doesn't allow me to drop it completely, and I consider it a sign of talent that I stick with it despite such a total lack of stimulation from outside" (S. Hensel, *Familie II*, 35-36). See letters 84 and 86 for Fanny's statements to Felix on the importance of his support and opinion of her as a musician.
[10]No. 3 after the overture in Beethoven's Incidental Music to Kotzebue's Festspiel, *Ruins of Athens* (Op. 113).
[11]Felix offers suggestions for Fanny's musicales—for example, a piece with wind accompaniment, such as a quintet by Mozart, Spohr, or Beethoven (to Fanny, 12 August 1846, in S. Hensel, *Familie II*, 367).
[12]Felix lived at Königstrasse 3 in Leipzig.
[13]See Cullen, *Baubiographie*, 53-55.

[14]Schubert's Gradual, *Benedictus es, Domine*; Beethoven's String Quartet in B-flat major; and Felix's *Die erste Walpurgisnacht*.
[15]Fanny writes about Keudell in her diary near the end of July 1846 (S. Hensel, *Familie II*, 365): "With regard to music-making, Keudell is the foundation supporting my continued activity, as Gounod did earlier. He looks with the greatest of interest at anything new I write, and makes me aware of shortcomings. And as a rule he's right." And then, after not having seen him because he was ill, Fanny writes, "I can truly say that I've missed him, as well as his musical company, very much. One cannot be a more benevolent and yet more disciplined, observant critic; he has continually given me the very best advice." Felix writes to Fanny on 12 August that he has seen Keudell and likes him very much (367).

145

n. d. [after 26 August 1846][1]

My dear Felix, the grapes and figs are here again and since they are such excellent advocates, and you're so idle, I want to answer your letter—it looms before me.[2] If your letter were my only pleasure from the publishing of my lieder, I wouldn't be sorry.[3] It's very kind and has made me happy the last three days, even if I weren't so already.[4] Why didn't I address my lieder to you? In part I know why, in part I don't. I wanted to enlist Cecile as a go-between because I had a sort of guilty conscience towards you.[5] To be sure, when I consider that 10 years ago I thought it too late[6] and now is the latest possible time, the situation seems rather ridiculous, as does my long-standing outrage at the idea of starting Op. 1 in my old age. But since you're so amenable to the project now, I also want to admit how terribly uppity I've been, and announce that 6 4-part lieder, which you really don't know, are coming out next.[7] I gladly would have shown them to you, but you didn't come, and sending them to you is hardly feasible.[8] My Friday singers have enjoyed singing them, and supported by the good advice that's here at my disposal, I've made every effort to make them as good as possible. I will take the liberty of sending Dr. Mendelssohn a copy.

But now, my thanks many times over! The Beethoven has given me great pleasure and arrived just at the right time, since I'll

Illustration 12—Autograph fair copy of Fanny Hensel's lied, *Warum?*, 18 August 1838 (first page) [Bodleian Library, Oxford: MS Margaret Deneke Mendelssohn c. 21, fol. 133].

perform some music next Sunday.[9] One hour before your letter arrived I asked Taubert whether there was nothing new he could recommend and whether he knew anything about the *Ruins of Athens*. Now I can have the things written out and rehearsed. I had a wonderful time with it yesterday morning. How kind and humane he is in this music; it is only in the dervish chorus that he assumes the old grouchy role only too well. The only thing I didn't like in your letter is the uncertainty of your visit here, and the fact that I don't know anything yet about your new oratorio whose *name*, to be sure, I've discovered (I also have pet topics for teasing).[10] The entire Birmingham public, however, among whom there may be a few who enjoy your music as much as I, is wise to the piece—the chorus and orchestra even wiser. "AND A TREMENDOUS AFFAIR IT IS," said the report in the *Morning Chronicle* about one of the encored numbers, which my friend, Lord Oxenpantoffel, sent me directly. In short, I'm very impatient. Do I have to wait until everything is published? That can really take a long time, and a person ages considerably during that period. Come soon! It's been ages since we've seen each other, and everything is fine here, thank God. Beckchen is still living here but will move over there next week. She and Hensel make use of a kind of grape cure in the garden. Sebastian was promoted to the first level with very good grades and is diligently studying watercolor painting with Biermann during his vacation. Franck will live here for a while—actually on the Leipziger Platz—and we're very happy about it; our social activities will thereby be considerably enlivened this winter.[11] Everyone sends his best. Mama Dirichlet wants me to tell you how touched she is by your good wishes. Beckchen wants me to ask whether Behr delivered the horses from Walter intended for Carl. How is everything there with my friend Behr? Are the Leipzigers taken with him? A tragic event occurred in connection with a box of grapes that was packed up and ready to go the day before yesterday, which unfortunately prevented it from being sent. The present grapes are a bit rained on and you'll find, unfortunately, that they're past their peak. Wasp nests, sparrows, and a long dry spell also took their toll. Please send the container back, however; perhaps we'll find some more that are worthy of you. Farewell, farewell, you dear ones. It's all very nice that we can reach Leipzig in 7 hours, provided that seven months and longer don't go by before we see each other, as the records indicate.

F.

Hensel sends his best.

[1]So dated because Fanny implies in the letter that *Elijah* has been premiered, which took place on 26 August.
[2]To Fanny, 12 August 1846 (S. Hensel, *Familie II*, 366-67).
[3]Sechs Lieder für eine Singstimme mit Begleitung des Pianoforte (Berlin: Bote & Bock, [1846]).
[4]"My dearest Fenchel, only today, shortly before my departure, do I, nasty brother, step forward to thank you for your dear letter and bestow upon you my professional blessing for your decision to enter our guild. I herewith confer it upon you, Fenchel, and may you derive pleasure and joy from it, . . . and may you become acquainted with only the pleasures of authorship, not the miseries, and may the public pelt you only with roses and never with sand, and may the black lines of the printer never seem oppressive and black to you—I actually believe there's no doubt about it" (12 August; 366).
[5]Cecile thanks Fanny for these lieder in an undated letter to her (DB 31): "Heartfelt thanks for the lovely lieder, which gave me great joy, especially when Felix sang them to us quite nicely with his wonderful voice. I actually did let myself pick up the *blassen Rosen* [No. 3 of Op. 1]. Although I haven't sung for over a year, I view this as *my* lied, but Felix sang the others and continually swore in between that he wanted to avenge himself. Mother also wants me to tell you that she is really delighted, and not at all as egotistical as Felix, who wanted to begrudge the world something so beautiful." ("Herzlichen Dank für die schöne Lieder, die mir große Freude gemacht haben, besonders als sie uns Felix mit seiner wunderlichen Stimme sehr angenehm vorsang. Die blassen Rosen habe ich mir zwar nicht nehmen lassen, obgleich ich über ein Jahr nicht gesungen hatte, so betrachte ich das als *mein* Lied, aber die anderen sang Felix und schwor immer dazwischen er wollte sich rächen. Auch Mutter läßt Dir sagen, sie sei ganz entzückt, und gar nicht so egoistisch wie Felix, der der Welt so etwas schönes nicht gönnen wollte.") *Warum* was composed in January 1837 (MA Ms. 45), and presented to Cecile, probably in August 1838, as a later addition to her Christmas Album of 1836 (MS MDM c. 21). See Illustration 12.
[6]One lied, *Die Schiffende,* was published ten years ago. See letters 86 and 92. Two years later, another lied, *Schloss Liebeneck,* appeared in a collection entitled *Rhein-Sagen und Lieder* (Cologne and Bonn: J. M. Dunst, 1839). It is curious that no mention of the latter publication occurs in her correspondence with Felix.
[7]*Gartenlieder:* 6 Gesänge für S.A.T.B. (Berlin: Bote & Bock, [1846]). They are recorded on Northeastern 213 (1984).
[8]Unless there was an urgent time consideration with regard to publication, this statement is surprising, as sending music to each other in different cities was com-

mon practice over the course of at least seventeen years. Did resentment guide her statement?
[9]Presumably some movement other than the dervish chorus from the *Ruins of Athens*.
[10]*Elijah,* first performed on 26 August 1846, in Birmingham.
[11]Presumably Hermann Franck.

146

n. d. [between c. 27 August and 25 October 1846][1]

My dear Felix, I'm sending along a letter with this box that is just the way you like it: a green sheet of paper or a blue grape.[2] You, who avoids correspondence, are not to have anything else to read; I, on the other hand, like letters that are in black and white. I'd love to receive the latest chapter and upcoming volume of your biography: when you're thinking of visiting, what you're performing (approximately), and whether Cecile is coming with you. Agreed? What do you think of this incredibly wonderful year? We're enjoying ourselves thoroughly and can't snap up our fill of fresh air. I'm only sorry that dear Cecile hasn't had the chance to enjoy it. The garden was gorgeous and we've never had such fun with the grapes. The trellises broke under the heavy load. Cecile, be so kind as to return the box so that it can be filled again next week. Adieu, my dearest brother. I really look forward to seeing you soon, for it's been a long time since we've been together. Beckchen is still living here and is well.

Eigendorff is coming. Farewell!

Your F.

[1]Dating based on internal evidence and its chronological position relative to letters 145 and 147.
[2]Cecile thanks Fanny for the grapes and looks forward to the next batch (undated letter to Fanny, DB 31).

147

26 October 1846

I must write you a note today that is neither a sheet of paper nor a grape,[1] and in fact concerns the affairs of other people. Madame Hildebrandt, the daughter of Bernhard Romberg, was here a few days ago to ask when and where she could see you, and whether you would receive her warmly if she came to you with her son to ask for your assessment of his musical talent. I thought I could promise her the latter, and such cases always remind me of how Father traveled with you to Cherubini.[2] Regarding the former, I promised myself to inquire, and perhaps I'll also find out through personal envoy. The woman is living in Hamburg now and wants to travel to Leipzig or preferably Berlin with her son. Meanwhile, I understand that it's not at all certain that you'll be visiting us as we thought, and that grieves me. Oh, if only life didn't proceed inexorably to its end in this fashion, year after year, with so few visits. Almost another 9 months have gone by without our seeing each other. It's sad!

Thank you very much for *Comala.*[3] *Peri*[4] and Ossian—nothing but descendants of the *Walpurgisnacht.* To the extent to which you turned this short, simple ballad into a most interesting work (sung here again last Sunday with enthusiasm—my little choir knows it by heart and came in *tutti* when a new soloist was missing at the rehearsal), the others are coming up with bland imitations, which, I greatly fear, will be carried to their graves from boredom. Please forgive me if I make rash judgments. I've played through Gade's piece only once and was predisposed to mistrust the Ossian text, which I find much too monotonous. Only the chorus of spirits provides a contrast to the perpetual lament. I can't perform anything else from it for my Sunday concerts, and in any case, this is the last concert of the season. But I'll have the entire work sung in the spring and thereby throw myself with full force into the opposition, i.e. modern German music, even if one doesn't always like it. One must forge ahead with good pieces here, where they have an unbelievably bad, haughty attitude towards everything new. I tell you, if some employee or customer put in as much effort for the thing as I and a pair of dilettantes do, it would be a totally different situation. I persuaded Taubert to agree to Gade's Symphony and it received a fine performance at the first soirée.[5] I found it extremely delightful once again, especially the Andante, whose sweet, charming simplicity is my favorite.—What are you doing now? What are you working on?

Hensel still has to guard the house; his wound hasn't healed yet. Mama Dirichlet twisted her ankle about the same time and had to stay off her feet a few days. Both lame ones held a touching reunion the day before yesterday. It's a shame, however, that you won't have the opportunity to see the exhibition. It's very interesting, and I consider it a plus that no single picture has grabbed the limelight, for Berliners are completely insufferable when they're wild about something. This time their love and hate can distribute themselves, and one can live with that. There's certainly no shortage of controversial material, but it won't lead to murder.

You'll find Beckchen greatly improved if you visit her soon and winter doesn't weaken her in the meantime. When I recall the miserable, sad time that we experienced with her, I can't thank God enough that the situation has improved far beyond our expectations. Farewell, my dear, dear Felix. The only thing that saddens me from time to time is that we live so far apart and hardly hear from you. Give my best to Cecile and the dear children. Everyone here sends his regards. Is Madame Jeanrenaud still there?

F.

[1]See the beginning of letter 146.

[2]During Felix's and Abraham's trip to Paris in 1825.

[3]By Niels Gade, on a text of Ossian.

[4]By Schumann; see letter 141.

[5]Presumably the c-minor Symphony that Felix had performed in 1843; see letter 126.

148

n. d. [c. 1 December 1846][1]

My dear Felix, your Frankfurt friends are herewith delivering a portion of the things you wanted. Unfortunately I wasn't able to dig up everything. To be specific: first of all, I wasn't able to find your geography book, but I think you took those sorts of things that were still here a few years ago. Secondly, I'm ashamed of myself and will go around in long, white penitents' robes for a week because I wasn't able to find the *Gartenzeitung*.[2] Since it's so easy to put the blame on other people, I'll point the finger at Albertine, who must bear the guilt for everything that's been misplaced over the past ten years. She lived here when we were in Italy last time and moved everything out except my desk. But I'll find it and send it to you as soon as the first corner decides to show itself. On the other hand, you're receiving the letters of our dear, late father, the poetic creations of Klingemann that were divided between Rebecka and me, and my new goodies. I'd like to have seen both parts of the collection appear simultaneously, or rather not be divided, but it won't help if I delay sending you the first half.[3] Perhaps you've seen it before I. You poor Felix, of all the things that could happen to you—you had to give a Berliner a letter of introduction to me. I received the little Würst mentioned in the letter quite properly and thereupon invited him the other day to my Trio performance.[4] This winter we are to celebrate every third Sunday if violins are present —I'm in a jolly mood and want to live life to its fullest. The Bernuses attended a small party here the day before yesterday, a small party at Paul's yesterday, and both small parties turned out to be exactly the same. Paul, who went away the day before yesterday and therefore missed our party, discovered this to his great and very comical dismay. But no harm was done.

Hensel's foot still isn't better, and the condition has been lingering for 5 weeks. But today it seems to be making some progress. Beckchen is quite well this winter, thank God—*speriamo* that it keeps up, for then life can be truly pleasant. Our little daily circle has rounded out quite nicely. Franck is a great improvement;[5] one couldn't ask for better company in such a close-knit group.

Farewell for now, you dear ones. I sigh, and sigh again, that your visit has been postponed once again into the distant future.[6] May God rectify the situation. Give my best to Cecile and the dear children. I haven't heard detailed news about them in a long time and would especially like to hear about Felix and Lili. Farewell. I'm very sorry about poor Johann and sympathize with you.[7]

Your Fanny

[1]See note 7 below. Date based on Fanny's expression of sympathy at the end of the letter for poor Johann, who died on 23 November 1846.
[2]A newspaper compiled by Felix and Fanny from 1825 to c. 1828 at Leipziger Strasse 3, in which brief stories, reviews, and poems would appear.
[3]Of Fanny's Vier Lieder für das Pianoforte, Op. 2; the first half appeared in 1846 and the second in 1847 (Berlin, Bote & Bock).
[4]Felix introduced Herr Würst to Fanny in his letter of 5 November 1846 (DB 26), saying that he's a fine Berlin musician who would like to participate in her musical gatherings. Fanny may have made a pun on Würst's name; in modern German, at least, it is a colloquial term meaning "squirt."
[5]Presumably Hermann Franck.
[6]Felix makes the trip later in the month. A slight hitch develops, however, for on his way to Berlin the train gets stuck in the snow, and so the trip is delayed a few days (to Fanny, 11 December 1846; DB 27).
[7]Johann Krebs, Felix's servant for many years, died on 23 November 1846. See, for example, Felix's letter to Klingemann of 6 December 1846 (Klingemann, *Briefwechsel*, 316).

149

Berlin, 2 January 1847

I must start my day's work with the green sheet of paper, otherwise I won't succeed in writing to you, dear Felix and Cecile. First of all, many thanks for the good-tasting package and the good news. Dear Cecile, I can't tell you how much I enjoyed Felix's visit. It wasn't as turbulent as it usually is when he's around. He stayed at home the entire morning, played *Elijah* for me, and said that it was a splendid week. He actually froze at our house, but the knowledge that he was making me so happy must keep him warm afterwards. The winter is severe and we've suffered a great deal in our thin little summer palace. As compensation, the greater part of the year was that much more beautiful. Everyone was at our house Christmas Eve and we had a very lovely decoration: the large orange tree was a Christmas tree (this statement is intended for Marie) illuminated by hollowed-out lemons in the branches, there was a garland of lights around the pail, the earth had moss, the moss was covered with colorful candies, the doors were draped with yew-tree boughs, and everything was full of flowers, lights, and plaster objects that make beautiful decorations. We gave them away as presents. Afterwards we played 3 children's Symphonies together, which were repeated on New Year's Eve "with the cooperation of the famous virtuoso, Herr Ernst." I don't know whether you remember, Felix, how you placed an *agnolo* on the same thing, which Paul carried away on a little white poodle to great applause.

Everything would be fine now if the Heidelberg affair were decided—we're all quite anxious about it.[1] If it came to naught because of a delay here it would really be abominable; yet deep down everybody hopes, and he not least of all, that he will remain. His friends have done everything in their power for him—they can't be faulted. And except for this awful surprise at the end, the year was generally good; I hope to experience many more. Of course, it was the richest for Paul—two children in one year.[2] That's really something. Albertine is a bit exhausted this time and is recovering more slowly, but she is well.

Now farewell, you dear people. Have a good year with all your children, and may we come together often. I wish it more than I dare to hope it will come true.

Hensel sends his best and likewise wishes you a happy new year.

Your Fanny

[1]Dirichlet is considering a position in Heidelberg. Felix presents his objections to the move in a letter to Dirichlet of 4 January 1847 (Mendelssohn, *Briefe II*, 309-11).

[2]Ernst and Katherine. Katherine died in childhood.

150

Berlin, 1 February [1847]

On the day in which all the people approach the throne of your eternal musical majesty through delegations, I venture to offer my sincere congratulations as well, Herr Brother, and furthermore wish you as much happiness as you, thank God, now have and deserve and are able to tolerate. In fact, one would have to stand in line behind your wife and all your children to wish you a happy birthday, and then it would only occur every 7 years. I just fear that little Felix and Lili are as little served by a letter as you, and as a punishment you should merely read that you started out in Hamburg 30-odd years ago. You should let chocolate and cake crumbs fall on it and throw it on the table amid all serenades and flowers, and ladies' needlework, and the poem by Herr von Webern, and a volume of other poems, and all the visits, and all the signs of joy that everyone is expressing.[1] With that, everyone is of course well served. Unfortunately, the only thing I'm sending you is my 4-part lieder.[2] Please play them for dear Cecile, who's always a good audience for me. A copy for Mme. Frege will be coming shortly with Eigendorff. I spent some very pleasant time on these pieces and therefore they mean more to me than other of my goodies.

I recently received a letter from Vienna that essentially contained nothing but an inquiry as to whether I was the author of *Auf Flügeln des Gesanges.*[3] In general, I'd like to send a list of my pieces that are floating around the world concealed. It seems they're not even clever enough to separate the wheat from the chaff. I'll have to sharpen my wits for the task, for I find it RATHER trivial to respond merely, "Alas, gentlemen—unfortunately not!" And I also don't want to be so dull as to point to my few little things with my finger, for I have more respect for the matter. But I also don't want to be impertinent. So, in short, I am almost forced to leave things in a state of darkness similar to the situation on our streets after the magistrate took over the job of illuminating them.[4] On Sunday there will be a christening at Albertine's.[5] I hope her brother

Illustration 13 - Autograph fair copy of Fanny Hensel's lied, *Bergeslust,* 13 May 1847 (first page) [Bodleian Library, Oxford: MS Margaret Deneke Mendelssohn c. 47, Fol. 35].

doesn't do something odd; he is unfortunately in the last stages of his illness.[6] The child is really darling and resembles little Katherine very much,[7] and since they both had the same wet nurse, the resemblance will probably grow stronger. Oh, if only I could see your children some time—all of them have grown so tall during the past year. I believe, dear Cecile, that I was a very ungrateful rogue recently and didn't thank dear little Marie for her pretty needlework. Please do it for me and tell her I enjoyed it very much. And I'd like to thank you, dear Felix, for your Trio and your lieder collection,[8] both of which have been used several times, and for the Beethoven letter that appeared in the newspaper, which is very interesting.[9] The Härtels should publish such things more often. Lind's affairs in London have really become tangled in a nasty fashion, and it seems as if she might not be able to travel there.[10] In that case, who will sing the part in your new opera that the newspapers have been telling us about?[11] How far along is *Elijah*?[12] Naturally it won't be performed here this winter, then it will be presented everywhere else this summer, and we will be left out in the cold again. So what good is it to live at the forefront of civilization?

Unfortunately, the situation with Dirichlet has not budged an inch.[13] He hasn't heard anything from Heidelberg or here and is starting to become very depressed. I only fear that the Minister here is glad to see him go, because otherwise he could have stirred himself long ago in accordance with the steps the faculty had taken, and which the King supports. You probably know that they decorated him with a ribbon.

As for the rest, we are extremely happy. Everyone is involved in his own activities, and we see many people. Just imagine, dear Cecile—Sebastian is a veritable young man and a popular dancer. Of course he's not permitted to neglect his studies in the least. Today he'll attend a ball given by the elder Madame Magnus. Oh Felix, we're growing old, for we also danced there in previous centuries. I'm glad that he doesn't show a trace of stupidity or affectation, although he has other faults. But in general we're very happy with him. Hensel has applied the first coat of paint to his large picture[14] and is working on several things simultaneously. He sends heartfelt birthday greetings, as does Sebastian. I can't wait for him to come home from school before sending this green sheet of paper, which is actually blue, to the train. I still want to thank you again for freezing here for one week before Christmas—it was a lovely time. And if the truth be known, I've been freezing here for the past 17 years, except for the summer months, and feel very good nonetheless.

Farewell. Let's hear from you soon.

Your F

[1]"Program 'For the Birthday Celebration' ('Zur Geburtsfeier') Leipzig, 3 Feb. 1847. Anon." is catalogued as GB XXV 87a.
[2]Published as Op. 3.
[3]From Felix's Op. 34 lieder.
[4]See S. Hensel, *Lebensbild*, 6.
[5]Of Ernst.
[6]Presumably Eduard Simon Heine.
[7]His sister, Katherine.
[8]Uncertain which lieder collection is mentioned; the Trio could be Op. 66.
[9]Presumably in a Leipzig newspaper.
[10]Whatever difficulties she may have had were cleared up by 4 May 1847, when she made a huge success in her London debut in *Robert le diable*.
[11]In a letter to Lind of 31 October 1846, Felix wrote that he wants to compose a good opera especially for her, and if he does not accomplish it now, he will never do it (excerpts quoted in E. Werner, *Mendelssohn*, 442-43). Since October 1846 he was corresponding with Lumley in England about an opera on *The Tempest* (libretto by Scribe). It was even announced in London for the 1847 season. But Felix was dissatisfied and rejected it. For a summary of these two operatic ventures, see E. Werner, *Mendelssohn*, 442-46.
[12]Typically, Felix was revising *Elijah* after its premiere (26 August 1846).
[13]See letter 149.
[14]Perhaps the painting that was left unfinished after Fanny's death in May, originally intended for the Duke of Brunswick's coronation room.

The Letters in German

1

28 Oktober

[Paul, Rebecka, Boucher]

Weißt Du wohl noch die Worte zu diesem Liede Mozarts junior? Dann wirst Du Dir leicht erklären können, warum ich meinen Brief damit anfange. Du fehlst einem spät u. früh, lieber Sohn! u. die Musik besonders will gar nicht rutschen ohne Dich. Doppelt u. dreifach danke ich es nun Freund Begasse, daß er uns die liebe Fratze so natürlich auf die Leinwand gepinselt, als stünde sie lebendig vor uns. Es ist ordentlich, als sollte ich keinen Akademietag vor Dir voraus haben, denn seit gestern bin ich so unwohl, daß ich nicht an Singen denken kann, ich huste wie eine alte Spittelfrau. Mutter ist auch nicht so ganz wohl heut, sie ist ein bischen erkältet, aber ganz unbedeutend.

Wie ist Deine jetzige Minerva, Prof. Mentor, mit Dir zufrieden? Ich hoffe, (um recht hofmeisterlich zu reden) daß Du Dich recht *vernünftig* aufführst, u. der Erziehung Deiner *Hausminerva* Ehre machst. Wenn Du zu Goethe kommst, sperre Augen u. Ohren auf, ich rathe es Dir, und kannst Du bei Deiner Rückkehr mir nicht jedes Wort aus seinem Munde wiedererzählen, so sind wir Freunde gewesen. Bitte, vergiß nicht, sein Haus zu zeichnen, es wird mir Freude machen. Wenn es ähnlich u. hübsch wird, mußt Du es mir recht sauber in mein musikalisches Stammbuch kopiren. H. Berger war gestern Abend hier, ich habe ihn aber nicht gesehn, weil ich mich schon um 7 legen mußte.—Von Lipinskis Conzert, u. dem Schicksale des Stralower Fischzuges bist Du durch Vater unterrichtet. Ich weiß nicht ob er Dir geschrieben hat, daß er heut eine Viertelstunde lang aus war.—Vom Freischützen ist noch nichts zu sehn und zu hören, vielleicht kommt er morgen in die Zeitung.

Heut stehn zwei allenlange Rezensionen des Fischzuges in der Zeitung, Vater vermuthet, die eine sei von Caspar, mir ist es auch sehr wahrscheinlich, daß er nie lernen kann, die Dinte halten![a] Dem armen Lipinski haben sie einen Nachruf in die Zeitung gesetzt, der ihm gar wenig hilft. Es erscheint jetzt fast keine Kritik, die nicht einen mehr oder weniger feinen Stich auf Boucher enthielte. Am Ende der Enden behalte ich noch Recht, u. alle seine Freunde bekommen ihn satt.—Du schreibst uns nicht, was Goethe für ein Instrument hat. Merke Dir sein Zimmer recht, Du mußt mir eine genaue Beschreibung davon machen.—Der liebe treffliche Rösel ist zurückgekommen, u. hat sich durch ein allerliebstes, sehr komisches Billett gemeldet, das mit den Worten anfängt: Petz ist wieder da! Sonderbar genug, daß Koreff, der vor einigen Tagen hereintrat, denselben Scherz machte.—Des Abends, wenn um die Theestunde die Treppenthüre geöffnet wird, rufen wir oft wie aus einem Munde: das klingt, als ob Felix käme. Bleibe aber immer noch eine Zeitlang weg, es ist besser wir entbehren Dich etwas länger, u. Du sammelst Dir in dieser Zeit die schönsten Erinnerungen für Dein künftiges Leben. Dienstag kommt wieder ein Brief, die Zeit bis dahin scheint mir so ungeheuer lang, als ob ein Monat dazwischen läge.—Ritz läßt Dir grüßen, er freue sich, daß Du die Symphonie gehört, und das Thema so gut behalten habest. Ich werde wol während Deiner ganzen Abwesenheit nicht auf die Academie kommen, denn trotz meines Pochens hält mich der Doktor noch immer zu Hause. Meine Freunde oben werden glauben, ich sei incognito mitgereist, u. Fanny war sogar neulich hier, um sich durch den Augenschein von meiner Anwesenheit zu überzeugen.

Adieu, mein Hamletschen! Gedenke meiner, wenn ich 16 Jahr alt werde. Noch eins, Du mußt auf meine Gesundheit ganz im Stillen einen Schluck Wein trinken, das bind ich Dir auf die Seele. Das Kupfer, welches daraus entstehn möchte, überneh[ ] ich ganz und gar. Adieu, vergiß nicht, daß Du meine rechte Hand und mein Augapfel dazu bist, daß es also ohne Dich auf keine Art mit der Musik rutschen will.

Deine treuste, hustendste Fanny. Marianne hat mir aufgetragen, Dich angelegentlichst zu grüßen.

---

[a]Fanny omitted "zu" before "halten."

2

Ueber Rietz kann ich Dir nichts sagen, ich habe ihn seit Deiner Abreise nicht gesehn. Der junge Ernst Fürster läßt Dich grüßen, ich sah ihn gestern bei Fräzkels, wo ich Elisen[a] gesessen habe. Morgen ist Pauls Geburtstag, Du wirst wohl daran denken, u. nun kann ich Dir erzählen, daß Du ihm eine sehr schöne Menagerie schenkst, in Gemeinschaft mit Beckchen u. mir, so daß auf eines Jeden Theil 8 gl. kommen. Er hat sich eine ganz Hetze Jungen gebeten, das schöne Geschlecht aber von seinem Feste ausgeschlossen. In 10 Jahren wollen wir einmal wieder nachfragen.—Das erste Stück von meiner f dur Sonate ist abgeschrieben, mit der Correktur ist es so eine Sache, sie geht mir nicht von der Hand. Indessen hoffe ich, wenn Du zurückkommst, soll Alles gethan sein.—Wie gefällt Dir Bouchers Brief? Caspar las uns gestern sein Bouchers Selbstbiographie vor, die höchst merkwürdig ist. Ich versichere Dich, er stellt sich über Bonaparte, u. neben Shakespeare, Corneille, Molière, u. die größten Männer aller Zeiten und Nationen. Dazwischen aber erzählt er, seine Gegner haben ihn Don Galimathias du violon genannt. Ich finde diese Benennung äußerst treffend. Indessen besitzt er unläugbar viel Gutmüthigkeit, er hat gestern im Concert des armen Lipinski gespielt, u. in der Probe war er das einzige Violoncell. Die Lithanderchen habe ich noch nicht gesehn, weil unser sehr unmusikalischer Husten uns bis jetzt verhindert hat die ganze Schaar der fremden Virtuosen bei uns zu sehn. Ich kann es auch gar ruhig erwarten, nur Lipinski möchte ich gern noch einmal hören.

Adieu mon fils! Ich muß aufhören, denn die Augen thun mir weh, u. der Kopf brummt mir. Vielleicht setze ich morgen noch einige Zeilen hinzu.

den 30. Paul hat einen vergnügten Tag. Er hat viele schöne Geschenke bekommen.—Aus der heutigen Zeitung sehen wir, daß Gugels in Hannover sind, und in einem dortigen Conzerte gespielt haben. Es wäre sehr hübsch, wenn sie durch Berlin kämen. Nun sage ich Dir zum zweiten Male Lebewohl, u. bitte Dich, alter Junge, den guten, lieben H. Professor, und seine dito Tochter aufs Allerherzlichste von mir zu grüßen. Will sich der freundliche, treuherzige Hummel noch meiner erinnern, so habe die Gefälligkeit, mich ihm ehrfurchtsvoll zu empfehlen. Du bist recht glücklich, wieder bei ihm Unterricht nehmen zu können.—Die

Deinigste Fanny

[Lea]

---

[a]Fanny omitted a word before "Elisen" (probably "neben").

3

3 Nov. 1821

[Dr. Caspar, Marianne Mendelssohn]

Es war mein Vorsatz gewesen, Dir, mein lieber Sohn, heute recht lang u. ausführlich zu schreiben, aber wie Vater gestern sagte, der Mensch denkt und der Husten lenkt. Dieser unwillkommne Gast hat mich mehrere Tage lang so gequält, daß ich ganz angegriffen davon bin, u. mich gar nicht viel beschäftigen darf. Denke Dir, daß ich sogar in drei Tagen nicht Clavier gespielt habe. Indessen kann ich doch nicht unterlassen, Dich wegen Deiner beiden lieben Briefe recht zu loben. Sie waren eben so hübsch gedacht, als gut ausgedrückt, (das Letztere ist sonst nicht sehr Deine Sache) u. uns daher auf jede Weise willkommen und angenehm. Wie gut ist es, daß ihr, statt die Feier in Wittenberg abzuwarten, gleich nach Weimar gegangen seid, diese Zeit ist rein gewonnen, u. Du wirst sie schon zu benutzen wissen. Es freut mich sehr, daß Du mit Deiner Oper so weit vorgerückt bist; schreibe mir doch, ob die mir unbekannten Nummern gut gelungen sind? Vergiß auch nicht, mir jedesmal zu melden, was Du vorgespielt hast, u. was am meisten Beifall gefunden, Du weißt, dergleichen Dinge können nicht zu umständlich erzählt werden, wenn sie an eine *Schwester* gerichtet sind. Von Hummels Unterricht muß mir auch durch Dich etwas zufließen, aber mündlich, bei Deiner Zurückkunft.—Die Geschichte von Hn. Professors Traum ist sehr rührend, sieh welche Sorgfalt der herrliche Mann für Dich trägt. Wie aber aus dem Briefe selbst hervorgeht, bist Du auch recht aufmerksam u. gut gegen ihn. Da aber im Goethe steht, Lob und Tadel muß ja sein, so kann ich auch nicht umhin, zweierlei an Deinem Briefe auszusetzen, aber sehr unwichtige Sachen. Erstlich, mein lieber Sohn, hättest Du in Deinem Kalender nachsehn können, Du hast ihn ja vor der Abreise gestellt, u. da würdest Du gefunden haben, daß es nie einen *32 Okt.* giebt noch gegeben hat, diesen Datum hast Du vor das Ende Deines Briefes gesetzt. Zweitens mußt Du bei der Aufschrift Deiner Briefe, den Ort *rechts* setzen, u. nicht links, wie Du es bis jetzt gethan. Das sind nun an sich sehr unwichtige Bemerkungen, Du wirst sie aber von mir nicht übel aufnehmen, denn Du weißt ja, daß sie wohl gemeint sind.

Als ich neulich eben meinen Brief geschlossen hatte, kam der Freischütz an, worüber ich vor Freude nicht schrie, denn das konnte ich nicht, aber krähte. Wenn Du da gewesen wärest, hätten wir eine sehr angenehme

Stunde gehabt, so aber war ich ganz allein u. unvermögend einen Ton zu singen, genoß also nur die Hälfte des Vergnügens. Die Arie der Seidler habe ich ziemlich eine, sie ist gar schön. Gestern haben sie den Freischützen wieder gegeben, die Vorstellung soll herrlich gewesen sein. Eine funkelnagelneue Nachricht (von Heinrich) ist daß Spontini seiner Macht wieder beraubt worden, u. Alles ins alte Geleis gebracht sei. Man schreibt dem Kronprinzen diese gute Handlung zu. Was sagst Du nun, Fl[ ]sch?[a]

Der arme Lipinski war neulich hier, Abschied zu nehmen. Er ist ohne zweites Conzert abgereist, u. war so gütig, sehr mit den Berlinern zufrieden zu sein. Heut ist Hartknochs Conzert, ich fürchte es wird ihm sehr schlecht gehn. Dienstag sollst Du Nachricht darüber haben.—Ich bin sehr neugierig auf den Text aus Wien, den Dir Mutter ankündigt; eine sentimental-naive Oper wäre so übel nicht, wenn sie sonst nur hübsch gemacht ist. Da giebt es gewiß allerliebste Cavatinen, Chöre mit obligatem Viehgebrüll, und dergl. Raritäten. Spaß aparte aber ist das eine Art die ich, hübsch bearbeitet, sehr liebe. Schweizerzöpfchen, Milcheimer, Mettenglöckchen, Gletscher in der Abendsonne, Heimweh, alles dieses sind musikalische, u. gar allerliebste Dinge, u. werden sich gewiß die Hülle und Fülle in Deinem neuen Texte finden. Und wie hübsch wird Mme. Robert die schmachtende Hirtin singen. Ich sage Dir, ich freue mich unbündig darauf. Rechne dazu, daß Caspar, durch Nachricht angespannt, sich gewiß beeifern wird, Dir auch einen neuen, recht schönen Text zu liefern. Dann bist Du für lange Zeit außer Sorgen. Adieu, lieber Bursche, freue Dich daß Du in Weimar bist, u. athme die poetische Luft ein, die um Dich herum weht. Deinem Finale muß man seine Vaterstadt anmerken. Erkenne, wie glücklich Du bist, eine Zeitlang in Goethes Hause zu leben, u. ihn im vertraulichen Umgange mit seinem Freunde zu sehn, grüße diesen und die gute Doris, u. den gutissimo Hummel, u. behalte lieb Deine Fanny.

---

[a]Resembles "Flesch," but this is not a standard word. Perhaps it is a special nickname for Felix.

4

Berlin 6 Nov. 21

[Abraham, Lea, Beckchen]

Was man nicht Alles in der Welt erlebt! Hätte ich es mir je träumen lassen, daß aus meinem Felix noch ein *schreibseliger* Reisender werden würde! Und doch ist es so, das beweisen uns Deine vielen, langen u. umständlichen Briefe. Die Ankunft dieser Briefe ist jetzt die einzige Begebenheit in unserm Hause, worin es warlich gar still und alltäglich hergeht; es fällt gar nichts vor; mein Felix ist nicht da, Marianne habe ich in 10 Tagen niemal gesehn, wenn das lange so dauerte, wäre es am Ende sehr langweilig. Sage Herrn Professor, daß ich ihn sehr ungetreu finde. Er schreibt nur seinem Straßenengel, ohne seiner ernsthaften Besten[n] auch nur einen Gruß zu senden. Ich will es ihn aber nicht entgelten lassen, sondern grüße ihn von ganzem Herzen. Diese Woche muß ich die Academie auch noch versäumen, aber in 8 Tagen soll mich kein Doktor mehr zu Hause halten.— Ihr müßt eine wunderliche Art von Ungeduld und Erwartung gehabt haben während Goethes Abwesenheit, schreibe uns nur, was seine erste Erscheinung für einen Eindruck auf Dich gemacht hat, er soll eine sehr imposante Figur haben. Du bist sehr glücklich so in seiner Nähe zu leben. Du weißt, ich war beschäftigt, Muttern sein Leben vorzulesen, als mich der häßliche Husten überfiel. Jetzt liest uns Rebecka alle Abende einige Seiten daraus vor, aber dieser Schneckengang ist meiner Ungeduld sehr zuwider. Alle Freunde grüßen Dich, namentlich Fr. Bing.

Will die junge Frau v. Goethe sehr meiner noch freundlich erinnern, so empfiehl mich ihr bestens. Vergiß mich auch nicht bei Hrn. Prof., Doris, und Hummel. Behalte lieb. Deine Fanny.

5

Ich muß nach einer bittern Klage über die Brieflosigkeit in dieser Woche, Dir lieber Felix, in aller Eile das neuste Berliner bon mot mittheilen, welches Alcidor, *Allzudoll* nennt. Deine scharfe Artikulation wird Dir, beim Aussprechen dieses Witzes, wohl zu Statten kommen. Du würdest

Dich gefreut haben, Deine Altscene v. der allerliebsten Mme. Müller singen zu hören. Sie hat sehr viel richtiges Gefühl, und ist ein *liebes Wesen,* um mit unserm, nun wieder eingerückten Rösel zu reden. Ihr seyd gewiß überall zugleich, u. Vater übermüdet sich, das wäre sehr unrecht denn er soll uns gestärkt, und nicht fatigirt, zurückkommen. Du kannst schon einen Puff vertragen. Deine Aenderung in der Sonate ist acceptirt, mein Generalstab, u. der hinzugekommene Medicinalrath haben entschieden, u. gespielt gefällt es mir auch wirklich besser, als schwarz auf weiß. Ich empfehle mich Ihnen ergebenst.

FMB

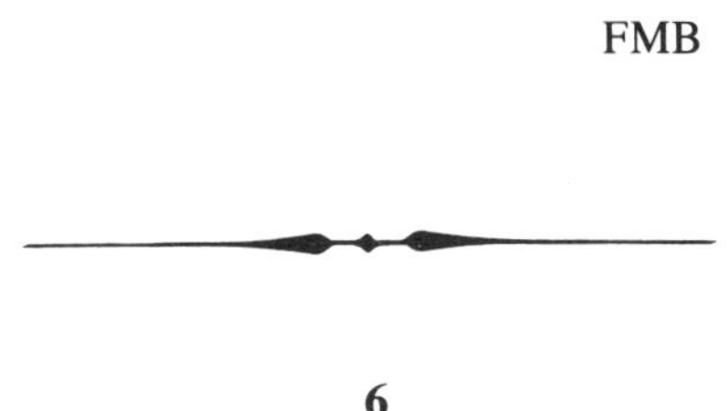

6

Montag d. 11ten April.

Du wirst Dich wundern, daß ich aus meiner holden Ruhe das Wort Unruhe als Echo aus Deiner rauschenden bewegten Welt wiederhole, u. doch ist es so, hundertmal unterbrochen, gestört, ist es mir nicht möglich, drei zusammenhängende Worte zu schreiben, darum fang ich einmal früh am Tage an, u. frage gleich los, was mir zuerst einfällt. Kennt Onslow, (nicht Onzlow) u. Schuhu Reihe Beethovens 33 Veränderungen über einen Walzer? Sonst solltest Du Dir eine Ehre daraus machen, da Du diese Herren allein auf ihrem Studierzimmer triffst, unsern grasnen Landsmann auch als Gelehrten und Theoretiker bei ihnen einzuführen. Du nennst Drouet noch nicht, ist er abwesend? Es scheint mir beinah, als ob Du vor lauter Hören gar nicht zum Sehen kämest. Du hast noch keine Sylbe v. den Thuillerien, Museum, v. der Stadt u. Deinen Promenaden gesagt. Indessen hoffe ich das in Deinem Tagebuche zu finden. Und zwar hast Du bis jetzt fast nur soireemusik gehört, ich sehe das ist tout comme chez nous, u. die Talente werden dort eben so gut abgeleiert, wie hier. Ueber italiän. Oper u. concert spirituel hast Du geschwiegen, bis auf einige Worte übers Orchester, die Ritz sehr verwundert haben, dem[a] er sagt eben diese Blaseinstrumente, wären immer Rodes Entzücken gewesen. Ueber diesen Rd. kann ich nicht genug, u. nicht zuviel hören. Wird er denn gar nicht die Geige in die Hand nehmen?—Eben kommt Vaters Brief v. 2ten u. 3ten, lieber Felix, es ist uns recht ängstlich, daß Vater so unwohl, u. verstimmt scheint. Ist er es so sehr, wie seine Briefe? Tante J. findet ihn munter, u. wohler, als vor einigen Jahren.—Boucher rührt mich, trotz seiner tollsten Tollheit. Wie erträgt er, mit seinem Eigendünkel, die allgemeine Geringschätzung in Paris? Also die vieille Muse habt Ihr auch wieder gesehn. Vater erzählt v. Bigotschen Hause, aber gar nichts v. Adelen, die mich sehr interessiren. Ich möchte Väterchen jetzt auch einmal freundlich u. bescheiden an Mme. Deloi vormals Emilie Riedel, u. an Mlle. Milan erinnern, welche ich beide herzlich grüße. Es ist schade, daß Ihr die allerliebste Müller nicht getroffen habt. Sie hat in dieser Woche fast jeden Vormittag mit uns zugebracht. Wir ließen sie ruhen, und das war ihr grade recht, da sie überall sonst zerrissen wurde. Sie machte viel Musik mit mir u. ließ sich gern v. mir begleiten. Sie hat sich Deine Altscene u. povero cor abschreiben lassen, obgleich letzteres zu hoch für sie ist. Auch mein Spinnerlied, welches ihr nicht in die Stimme lag, sang sie mit Mühe, aber sehr niedlich, nachdem ich ihr einige Stellen verändert, u. mich ihr zu Liebe erboten hatte, u. zu transponiren, was sie jedoch nich leiden wollte. Gestern früh kam sie mit ihrem Manne, um ein Quartett v. Dir zu hören. Franck aber blieb aus, u. wir beredeten Julius Ritz, die Stimme v. Blatt zu spielen, obgleich es Eduard nicht gern wollte. Er machte seine Sachen über alle Erwartung gut, hat einen guten Ton, festen Bogenstrich, u. fehlte im Takt nicht ein einziges Mal, u. in den Noten sehr wenig. Er hätte also Deinem *Professor* bei Trémont Unterricht geben können.—Nach Tisch spielte ich ihr noch Deine f moll Sonata, mit Ritz, dem diesmal das Adagio ganz ausnehmend gelang, dann schieden die lieben Leutchen, u. wir machten noch einen Haufen Musik. Wirst Du niemanden[b] Deine Oper zeigen?

Heut ist unsers Backfisch Geburtstag. Wir werden eine niedliche junge Gesellschaft haben, u. der Improvisatore wird hier seyn. Seit ich gehört habe, wie er die eroica abschlachten will, bin ich ihm sehr gram. Heut vorm Jahr hatten wir einen großen Ball, weißt Du noch, Lindenau nahm die Geige in die Hand, u. wir sprangen. Du hast einen Brief von Lindenau, der hier bleibt, weil er sehr dick ist. Mit der schnellen Expedition Deines 2ten Doppelkonz. wirst Du sehr zufrieden seyn. Ich hoffe Du wirst Gelegenheit finden, es mit einem der 10000 Virtuosen zu spielen, u. wünsche daß Du an einen kommst, der das letzte Stück besser bemeistern kann als Deine Dich liebende. Wie sehr würde ich mich freuen, wenn Du Gelegenheit hättest, Deine Symphonie zu hören.—Der Baron Trémont hat uns Allen, so wie wir den Brief lasen, an den Baron Bagge erinnert. Alles läßt tausendmal grüßen, u. ich empfehle mich für heut zu gnaden. Noch eins, ich habe einen Briefe v. Friederike Robert gehabt, die sehr grüßen, u. sagen läßt, sie habe ein Lied für Dich fertig. Robert hat es sehr übel genommen daß Du lieber Vater, dem Briefe der Varnhagen keinen Gruß beigefügt hast, die Varnhagen aber sagte, es ist ein Unsinn! ein Wahnsinn! Weil H. Mendelssohn so gut ist, den Brief mitzunehmen, soll er noch dazu schreiben, etc. Paul war gestern, bei dem Debüt des kleinen Ritz, sehr niedlich. Seine Augen glänzten vor Freude, er stand hinter ihm, u. nickte immer den Andern zu, um sie aufmerksam zu machen, u. nach jedem Stück, lief er herum, lobte ihn bei allen, u. war ganz entzückt.

den 12ten April. Die kleine Gesellschaft ist, trotz unserm Vorsatze, zum kleinen Balle

---

[a]Fanny mistakenly wrote "dem" instead of "denn."
[b]She used the accusative ending instead of the dative "niemandem."

7

den 25sten April 25

Etsch! Reist nach Paris, u. bekömmt keinen vernünftigen Ton zu hören, oder doch nicht viele, u. wir sind ruhig zu Hause geblieben, u. müssen alle Ohren aussperren. In einer Woche: Jessonda, Alceste, Samson u. die Pastoralsymphonie, denn die beiden letzteren Sachen giebt Sapupi übermorgen am Bußtage zu seinem Konzert. Was meinst Du? So viel scheint mir gewiß, daß Deine Anlage zum Schuhuhismus sich glänzend in P. entwickelt. Mein Sohn, Deine Briefe sind ja ganz aus Kritik zusammengenäht. Marx wird Freude an Dir erleben. Ich hoffe, in der Erinnerung wird noch Manches ein rosenfarben Kleidchen anziehn, was jetzt noch vom Staube der Befangenheit u. Vorurtheile graut, denn wenn Alles wirklich so arg wäre, wie Ihr es jetzt anseht, so wäre es ja Schade um die Reise. Kalkbr. karakterisirst Du sehr gut, u. rufst mir den liebenswürdigen Claviernagel wieder recht lebhaft ins Gedächtniß zurück. Ich wollte ihn einmal wieder über die Tasten blitzen hören. Rodes Ausdruck mit der execution foudroyante ist sehr gut. Hat denn K. noch gar nicht *jettlich* gesagt? Grüße ihn doch ja, ich bin sehr erfreut, daß er sich meiner erinnert. Du armer Tantalus! Rode täglich zu sehn, u. keine Harmonie aus diesen Sphären zu vernehmen! Doch muß ich gestehn, finde ich es recht tröstlich, ihn in P. zu wissen, wo doch ein Wiedersehn eher möglich ist, als in dem Winckel Bordeaux.—Ach was habt ihr für schöne Bilder gesehn! Warum schreibst Du davon kein Wort? Nichts von öffentlichen Gärten, der Stadt, den Gebäuden? Es scheint mir fast, als tödtete die leidige Soireemusik jeden Genuß in Dir. Nun, die unsrige, kräftige wird Dir schmecken, wenn wir erst in unserm großen, gewölbten Gartensaal Deine Symphonie streichen. Ach wie freue ich mich darauf! Deine Geschichte mit den Sechsen, die immer den Siebenten applaudiren, ist sehr gut. Was hat sich das alles zusammengefunden, u. schöne Dinge gesagt, Rossini u. Meyerbeer, Hummel, Moscheles u. Kalkbrenner, die sich doch wahrscheinlich einer den Andern ins Pfefferland wünschen. Jetzt haben wir den schönsten, heitersten Frühlingshimmel, u. grüne Bäume. Sonntag Nachmittag waren wir in unserm Garten, mit der jungen Garde, zu der sich ein Rekrut eingefunden hat, ein junger H. Schubring aus Dessau, der uns freundliche Briefe v. Wilhelm Müllers gebracht. Wir Alle huckten auf der Erde, u. suchten Veilchen, Klingem. mit; uns parodirend; wir behaupteten, er *buddele* Veilchen. Dazu hatte er seinen Brill aufgesetzt, u. dann ließ er sich auf einem abgehauenen Baumstamm nieder, die in sein Schnupftuch gesammelten Blumen, Erde u. Gras, zu ordnen. Kannst Du Dir diese grandiose Figur recht lebhaft denken? Unser Garten ist schon wunderschön; wie wird er nicht erst im Mai seyn, wenn der Flieder blüht. Du bist aber ein Stückchen Vandale, hast keinen Sinn für grüne Bäumen. A propos, hab ich, oder hab ich nicht erzählt, daß Klingem. schon 3 Violinstunden bei Ritz genommen? Er hat wirklich einen lobenswerthen Eifer. Wir haben ihm eingeredet, er müsse die Hauptsäule des Symphonienvereins werden, u. er glaubt es, u. mißhandelt nun tapfer R.s armen Aegidius Klotz. R. hat auch 3 Schülerinnen bekommen. Unsre kleine geschickte Nachbarin Eda Benda, die er von armen Lauska geerbt, u. die beiden kleinen Blancs. Gestern wurde für Lauska das Requiem v. M. gegeben. Ich konnte, wegen eines starken Hustens, der mich quält, nicht hingehn. Auf der Academie war das v. Zelter, u. bei diesem werden wir nächsten Freitag wahrscheinlich das von Hasse singen. Schade, daß Seb. Bach keins geschrieben hat. Ist denn Reißiger nicht in P., oder wie kömmts, daß ihr ihn noch nirgend angetroffen? Und Drouet?

Ist es nicht eine ungemein glückliche Idee, die Pastoralsymphonie vor dem Samson zu geben? Samson war just so ein Landmann, mit Dudelsack, Wachtel u. Nachtigall. Und doch, so verkehrt es ist, freue ich mich auf Beides. Und nun Adieu, eben ist die ersten Bratschenkorrektur gekommen. Wenn wir nur erst Antwort v. Weimar haben, ist die ganze Geschichte in 14 Tagen abgemacht.

Ich grüße Väterchen tausendmal, u. Tante J., u. Rode, über dessen Zeilen wir eine außerordentliche Freude gehabt haben. Lebt wohl. Wenn wir Euch doch bis Potsdam entgegen fahren könnten.

Fanny.

[Lea]

8

den 29sten April.

Ja ja, mein Sohn, die Pastoralsymphonie (zu Deutsch Hirtensymphonie) ist sehr schön, u. wenn Dus nicht glauben willst, so rufe ich Dir zu, schweige, u. höre, u. dann urtheile. Ich kann Dir *nicht* mehr sagen, als daß Mutter entzückt davon war, u. mich, als es aus war, frug, was nun käme? Klarheit u. Wahrheit, Reichthum u. Einheit v. einem Ende bis zum Andern. Die Scene am Bach ist wirklich ein Ideal v. Anmuth, das ganze Stück in heitrer, heller Farbe gehalten, nur das schwere Gewitter bildet den nöthigen Schatten in der Landschaft. Schade, daß mein Lieblingssatz, die Bachscene vollkommen verdorben ward durch das Tempo, welches unvernünftig, noch viel schneller war, als in Mösers Concert. Das Orchester fühlte das Tempo weit besser, als Möser, u. wollte nicht mit, dadurch entstanden denn böse Rückungen. Es ist der höchste Reiz, die lieblichste Anmuth der Instrumente, die ich kenne. Von Sapupis holder Ruhe hat gewiß Mutter schon erzählt. Samson ging, bis auf einige arge Placker, ziemlich gut. Die Milder war unübertrefflich.

Heut habt ihr uns vergebens schmachten lassen, haltet uns nur morgen schadlos. In 14-18 Tagen hoffe ich haben wir Euch wieder, u. vielleicht sind dies unsre letzten Briefe. Den v. Ritz erhielst Du lieber Felix so spät, weil er ihn neulich eine Stunde nach Abgang der unsrigen erst brachte. Ich wünsche Väterchen Glück zur angenehmen u. erwünschten Vermiethung der mittleren Etage. Es geht mit Pauken u. Trompeten. A propos v. Pauken u. Tr., wie ist es möglich, daß Dich außerordentlicher Wunderjüngling, vielgeliebte Bebe, 6 Wochen leben kannst, ohne eine einzige Note zu schreiben? Es kommt mir unwahrscheinlich vor.

[Rebecka, Caspar, Klingemann, Rebecka]

den 30sten.

Da Klingemann und Beckchen ausgerast haben, will ich einmal wieder die Feder ergreifen, um Dir für Deinen sehr gescheuten Brief v. 20sten zu danken. Ich bin nur froh, daß Du endlich einmal mit vernünftiger Begleitung gespielt hast, bis jetzt hab ich Dich doch darbend gewußt mitten im Lande wo Milch u. Honig fließt. Ehe ich es wieder vergesse, will ich Dir nur gleich eine Frage thun, die mir schon lange aus dem Herzen lag, die ich aber immer vergaß, wenn ich die Feder in die Hand nahm, nämlich warum Du aus alle den matinées, diners, soupers, u. was noch für art sind, noch gar nicht Dein Sextett gespielt hast? Giebt es in Paris in jener Gesellschaft nur Einen, der Bratschenschlüssel liest? Lieber F. ich möchte wol Ihr hättet Eure geliebte Mutter, Frau, Töchter, u. Du Deine vielgeliebte Schwester dort. Wenn ich von Euren *vernünftigen* Plaisirs lese, läuft mir der Mund voll Wasser. Doch glaube nicht, daß wir gar nichts vornehmen, wir haben gestern Abend Plaisir ausgestanden, so gut, wie ihr, wir waren auf einer Soiree. Da war es so heiß, so heiß, wie es nur in Paris hätte seyn können. Wir waren da mit Ivan Müller u. dem Improvisator Wolff zusammen. Mit ersterem ließ ich mich in eine lange Discussion ein, um mir seine Verbesserung der Clarinette u. Altoclarinette erklären zu lassen. Er behauptet, vermöge seiner Erfindung, mit mehreren Klappen, u. einem etwas veränderten Bau des Instruments, alle Tonarten auf demselben blasen zu können, u. alle Töne zu binden. Er schreibt daher auch jede Tonart in ihrer natürlichen Lage u. im ehrlichen Tenorschlüssel. Denke Dir meine Seligkeit bei der bloßen Hoffnung, meist alle Partituren so geschrieben zu sehn. Kommt dann noch irgend ein Müller v. Himmel, u. verbessert die Horne dergestalt, daß sie alle im Baßschlüssel geschrieben werden, dann lese ich Dir Partituren, wie Wasser. Kannst Du Dich bei Gelegenheit nach Müllers Clarinette erkundigen, so thue es doch, er behauptet, seine Verbesserung sey in P. durchgängig angenommen, u. auch hier haben schon mehrere Clarinetten angefangen, unter seine Leitung solche Instrumente anfertigen zu lassen. Du mußt gestehn, es wäre ein großer Vortheil, alle Tonarten auf einer Clarinette zu blasen. Sein Spiel gefällt mir übrigens nicht. Sein Ton ist zwar sehr schön, aber sein Vortrag so geschmacklos, daß man sich sehr davon verstimmt fühlt. Mitten in seinen albernen-trillerchen Läufchen u. Cadenzen hält er dann einmal einen Ton mit so abwechselnder Stärke u. so lange aus, daß einem der Athem vergeht, da soll man sich denn geschwind hineinfühlen, um augenblicklich wieder ins Laufwerk zurück zu fallen. So rasch fühle ich nicht, u. daher fühle ich wenn er spielt, gar nichts auf Kopfweh, welches mir dies durchdringende Blasinstrument im Zimmer unfehlbar erregt. Wolff improvisirte trotz tropischer Hitze, jostyschem Eise, Kuchen, u. einer ihm auf dem Halse lastende Menschenmasse, recht schön, und ich war so glücklich, daß er ein Thema wählte, welches ich ihm aufgeschrieben hatte. Dorn begleitete ihn viel besser als graulich. Er hatte einige musikal. aus dem Gedicht hervorgehende Ideen, die mich wirklich überraschten.

Ein dann folgendes Tyrolerlied war auf der Guitarre begleitet, welche sich meiner Idee nach weit besser dazu eignet, schon weil ihr dünner Ton die Stimme nicht zu sehr bedeckt.—Ich komme eben aus Vaters Stube, wo ich Ritz der kleinen Benda habe Unterricht geben hören. Sie spielt Etüden von Cramer u. muß brav wiederholen.—Rodes Wunsch, mit uns zusammenzuwohnen, wiederhole ich als tausendfaches Echo. Käme er nur her, es ist eine allerliebste Wohnung für ihn u. Frau u. Kinder da, dann wollten wir jubeln:

Wenn das Gewölbe wiederhallt

Fühlt man erst recht der *Geige* Grundgewalt. Und unser ganzes Haus sollte wiedertönen. Aber daran ist leider nicht zu denken. Was sagst Du denn, daß der große Geiger Klingem. unser Miethsmann wird, obgleich Ritz sehr vor ihm gewarnt hat. Es sey zwar gefährlich den Leu zu wecken, etc. allein das schrecklichste der Schrecken sey Klingemann in seinem Wahn, nämlich in seinem Geigenwahn—oder Wahnsinn, wodurch er als umgekehrter Amphion, Thiere Menschen u. Götter verscheuchen würde. Er hat gestern unter tausend Possen Abschied genommen, u. ist heut zur Hochzeit gereist.—Du kannst denken, wie froh wir waren, eben zu vernehmen, daß Z. einen eigenhändigen Brief von Goethe erhalten habe, u. wie sehr uns Gerücht seiner Krankheit, u. sogar seines Todes, geängstigt hatte. Gott erhalte uns dies Paar noch recht lange. Amen.—Und somit leb wohl, ich lobe Dich, ich liebe Dich, ich lobe Deine Briefe, u. hoffe, daß wir euch liebe Dreieinigkeit bald wieder haben werden. Könnte ich nur so viel gescheute Antworten geben, als die Leute immer die selben Fragen nach Euch thun. Adies.

[Rebecka, Lea]

9

Berlin, den 16 Februar

Motto: Ach! wie kalt!

Ich hätte nicht gedacht, daß ich, noch während Deiner Anwesenheit, eine Dich betreffende Nachricht erhalten würde. Der Zufall—doch den giebts ja nicht im Menschenleben—also die Vorherbestimmung führte mich gestern Abend in Cortez neben H. Simons Schwester, eine Leipziger Dame, welche Deine Symphonie gehört und mir versichert hat, sie wäre sehr gut gegangen, und mit ausgezeichnetem Beifall aufgenommen worden, auch sey das Concert eins der vollsten in L. gewesen. Außerdem wird Webers Jubelouvertüre gegeben, u. eine Webersche Cantate, Du warst also in guter Gesellschaft. Da ich Dir zu Liebe in der warmen Stube schneidermäßig friere, kann ich mir denken, wie Du mir zu Liebe auf der Landstraße frieren magst, u. es dauert doch noch einige Stunden, ehe ich Dich nach Stettin hineinbegleiten kann. Uebrigens aber wiederhole ich Dir zum letztenmal, daß Cortez die langweiligste Suppe ist, so ich je genossen. Und eine Aufführung! Sie führten sich alle schlecht auf, bis auf meinen Homili, welcher schön ist, beim Himmel! Deine Korrektur ist parat, u. ein rührendes Billett an Ad. Mt. dazu, von wegen Titel. Hätt ich einen Deiner Freunde gesehn, so würde ich sagen, er ließe Dich grüßen, so aber wird nichts draus. Das beste Lied in der Sammlung ist offenbar, laß dich nur nichts nicht dauern, ich versichere Dich, wenn mir nicht der dritte Vers in der ersten Strophe imponirt hätte, würde ich Fehler hineinkorrigirt haben, damit doch etwas drin wäre. Dies und noch mehreres anders dumme Zeug habe ich Dir zu wissen thun wollen, und nun laß mich in Ruhe, grüß den Löwen, der ein Lamm von mir ist, was Du ihm nicht zu bestellen brauchst, freue Dich Deiner Jugend, hüte Dich pebelhaft Cour zu machen, erfriere nicht die Nase, habe ein volles Concert, heiter lasse einem guten Ruf in Stettin. Trink nicht zu viel Bier u. noch weniger Wein, und denke meiner in Fährlichkeiten.

Deine 

Eben verlangte Mutter Deinen Pilgerspruch zu hören, ich schämte mir.

[Rebecka]

Welch ein Treffer, daß ich heut dies Billett bekomme.

10

Die Kälte steigt, u. ich weiß Dich mit Behagen in Stettin, und mit Unbehagen fern von Berlin. Wir haben gestern ein lustig Leben geführt, u. Abends eine Unmasse v. Liedern gesungen, näml. Therese Devrient u. Rebecka. Wenn ich das Duett Suleika einmal v. Löwen u. Theresen hören könnte, wollte ich es meine Lebtage nicht vergessen, sie singt es unverbesserlich. Franck, welcher die 12te Partie wirklich verloren, grüßt bestens. Allen andere dito. Guillon, der gestern bei Schlesinger gespielt hat, führt fort, nicht zu gefallen, zu meiner größten Verwunderung. Kohlreif begleitete ihn, Einbrot, David, Dein Steinbeck, die Sisen, etc. waren hier. Dein Schnitter kam auch vor. Röselchen ist eben einpassirt, Du weißt also genau, daß es Montag 5 Minuten nach 12 ist. Heut Abend frier ich Dir zu Liebe entsetzlich auf der Academie, weil ich auf Dein Te Deum hoffe. Es wird aber gewiß sehr leer seyn, u. sehr schlecht gehn.

[S. Rösel, Rebecka]

11

Es freut uns, liebes Lamm, daß Du so wohl bist, und so vergnügt, aber in Wahrheit, ich möchte einmal mit Dir in eine kleine Stadt, und Dich so viel spielen hören, als ich nur wollte, denn hier wird aus guten Gründen nichts draus, u. es wird mir manchmal ganz verzweifelt kribbelig nach Dir, so gestern Abend, wo ich Dir gewiß noch geschrieben hätte, wenn ich nicht vor sentimental Furcht gehabt hätte. Was Du von der Choralphantasie sagst, die ich auswendig wüßte, das ist sehr schön, ich hätte sie aber doch hören mögen, denn ich habe Dich in 7 Jahren nicht auf der Orgel phantasiren hören, also gar nicht.

Ulrike war gestern nicht hier, sie kömmt heute, auch Marianne Mendelssohn Abends. Vorgestern aß M. Saaling hier, u. blieb bis 9, dann kamen Ritz, David, Heydemann aus dem Symphonienverein, wo David ein Concert von Spohr sehr schön gespielt haben soll, später noch Gans, über den wir uns wirklich halb krank lachten, er erzählte Studentengeschichten, u. machte Wittgenstein nach. Gestern bei Zelter Messe aus g dur. Es gab großen Scandal, denn der Contrabaß war verlegt, u. Zelter suchte ihn wie eine Stecknadel. Nach Tisch gingen wir ein wenig zu Tante Meyer, Abends kamen Roberts, Varnhagens, u. Hensel, u. man war recht lustig. Ich bin so tolerant jetzt, die orribelsten dictus (oder tas oder sonst) der Varnhagen, brachten mich nicht auf, ich saß neben Beckchen, u. wir machten schlechten, nur uns zugänglichen Witz, u. sprachen vom Cluricaun. Unter andern war von nichts als von der Ausstellung die Rede, man sprach, Roberts beleuchteten die Sachen philosophisch, Varnhagens technisch, H. saß dabei mit jenem Schafsgesicht, das Du kennst, u. wir suchten unsre Füße unter unsern respect. Stühlen. Es war nicht übel. Zuweilen giebt es auch hier solche Musikkunstgespräche, wobei *wir* den Mund aufsperren, u. mit der Nase hören. Ich habe eben eine Fuge angefangen, auf ein Thema, sie ist ernsthaft, u. es soll Gegensätze darin geben. Was nimmt man sich nicht Alles vor. Bitte den alten Steinbeck, mir einen Canon für mein Stammbuch zu komponiren, auf die Worte: ach was soll der Mensch verlangen?—Du kannst auch die Worte weglassen. Ich glaube, der Alte thuts. Warum hast Du denn noch gar nichts von der Braut geschrieben?

Heut Abend sind lebende Bilder im Theater, under Andern Rinald u. Armide, nach Sohn.

[sentences divided between Rebecka and Fanny] [a]

[Rebecka]

Lebe wohl, o Mensch! bedenke kein Ende (nein kein Ende) aber das Ende Deiner [ ]sehaft.

ich meine Freundschaft für das intime Brautpaar so recht zu Herzen nehme u. erwäge. Beckchen steht neben mir, u. es zappelt ihr irgend ein dummer Einfall in den Fingern, denn sie zuckt nach meiner Feder. Daß Eine von uns gutwillig das letzte Wort behält, ist ein Ding der Unmöglichkeit . . .

[Rebecka]

Unsre Briefe lauten eigentlich neben einander her, wie Schlegels Conversation mit irgend Jemand, keiner antwortet dem Andern.

[Rebecka and Fanny mixed]

Wenn ich ein Steinbeck wär, u. auch 2 Flügel hätt, spielt ich was vor.
Ich wünschte aber, Du hättest Carl gestern Abend um Mitternacht durch die Geisterstunde zwitschern hören. Herr Felix ließen sich das Trio aus d dur ausbitten.

[Rebecka, then Rebecka & Fanny mixed]

Adieu Menschenherze! Cluricaun mußt schon wieder Porto bezahlen, wie schon damals nicht, denn nu geht kein Mensch mehr nach die Post, ausgenommen Ausnahmen, d. h. Stadtpost scriptum.

[Rebecka and Fanny mixed]

---

[a]Passage is indecipherable, as their handwritings are practically superimposed on each other.

12

Berlin, den 18 April 29

Ich hätte gern diesen ersten Brief, der Dich in London trifft, mit dem dreistimmigen Trompetenstoß angefangen, allein zur Stunde bist Du noch nicht hinüber, das Wetter ist hier schlecht, u. ich will nicht Gott versuchen. Glaube ich Dich erst hinüber, so ziehe ich alle Register meines Herzens, stoße in alle Trompeten meiner Lunge, u. erhebe eine Musik, daß Du sie in der Insel hören mußt. Just am Tage Deiner Abreise ging die Emancipationsacte durch, man kann sich also keinen interessanteren Zeitpunkt zu einer Reise nach England ersinnen. Ich will Dir jetzt von dem Gegenstande erzählen, der Dich vor der Hand noch mehr berühren wird als Emancipation, Departementalgesetz u. spanisches Erdbeben, ich meine unsre gestrige Passion. Hier von der Hand der Resultat: die Aufführung war weit über meine Erwartung, u. weit hinter den Deinigen zurück. Von den Montags u. Dienstags Proben wollte ich Dir gar nichts schreiben, um nicht dem Jammer in Dir zu erwecken, von dem meine Seele voll war. Zelter spielte selbst, u. was er, mit seinen zwei Fingern, u. seiner *völligen Unkenntniß* der Partitur, herausbrachte, kannst Du Dir denken. Mißstimmung u. Angst verbreitete sich im ganzen Chor, u. Deine Name ward vielfach genannt. Die Donnerstagsprobe war nicht geeignet, jene Besorgnisse zu vermindern. Z. taktirte nicht bei den accompagnirten Rezit. u. bei den Chören nur, wenn er es nicht vergaß. Stümer that Wunder, u. hielt sich, bei Z.s fast fortwährend falschene-Accompagnement, stets richtig. Um einige Einzelheiten zu nennen, so war Devrient so verwirrt, daß er unter andern nur das halbe Abendmahl einsetzte, u. gleich in f dur anfing: trinket Alle daraus. Die Milder warf das Duett wie gewöhnl. um, die Schätzel plack[erte] stark in ihrer Arie, die kleinen Chöre: der rufet dem Elias, u. halt laß sehen, ging drunter u. d[runter] , etc. Z. fuhr entsetzlich drein, war sehr böse, verwirrte sich immer beim Umwenden der aus golg. Scene Stücke, wodurch große Pausen entstanden, u. wobei ihn Stümer, mit mehr Discretion u. Haltung, als ich ihm zugetraut hätte, still zurecht wies, Devrient saß da, als ein vollendetes Ecce homo. Um 1/4 5 schloß die Probe, u. außer uns vor Ermüdung, Anstrengung u. Angst kamen wir nach Haus, nachdem ich noch mit Devrient, Ritz u. David einen kleinen Rath gehalten hatte, u. übereingekommen war, daß Ritz ganz durch taktiren, David aber pausiren solle, als hinge sein Leben davon ab, denn der 2te Chor war bei späteren Eintritten ganz auf sich allein angewiesen. Nach diesen Aspekten ging es denn außerordentlich. Deinen Vorschlag mit den 4 Clarinetten hatte Ritz in der Probe versucht, u. ich hatte den Chor angehört, wir fanden es aber nicht zweckmäßig, es klang zu spitz, u. verlor den Orgelcharacter, u. so blieb es beim Alten in der Aufführung. Eda Benda, die ich gesehn habe, sagte, der Choral habe wunderschön geklungen. Der erste Chor ging übrigens gut. Ritz taktirte, u. bei den Worten Jesu kamen die Instrumente fast immer präcis, was sehr zu verwundern. Die Milder sang die Arie sehr schön, schluckte zwar ein ganze Achtel lang, aber die Flöten gaben nach.—Abendmahl sehr schön. "O Schmerz", zu geschwind, u. das pp im Chor verschwunden. "Siehe er ist da, der mich verräth," sang Devrient laut Befehl. Duett wider Erwarten, vortrefflich, Chor schwach. Daß Z. endlich seine Lust büßte, u. die Fermate durchtaktirte, begreifst Du. Auch kamen sie nicht ganz präcis. Schlußchoral ohne Piano, Flöten vortrefflich. Alt Arie gut unter den Choreintritten, waren durchweg die Tenoren am Schwächsten. Die kleinen Chöre gut. Bei "Wahrlich du bist auch Einer" fehlten zu Anfang die Flöten. Je "Erbarme dich" machte die Schätzel denselben Fehler wie in der Probe, aber so geschickt, daß es wol nur wenige gehört haben. "Was gehet uns das an" war der einzige Chor, der anfangs sehr wackelte, "Der du durch Tempelgottes" viel zu geschwind, Ritz hielt an, aber der Anfang war weg. Nun kam der große Scandal, der nicht fehlen kann: "Ach Golgotha," fing statt auf dem 4, auf dem 8ten

Achtel an, u. mit ihrer gewohnten Consequenz blieb die Milder, *durch das ganze Rezit.* ihren halben Takt zurück, obgleich Zelter ihr mit aller Macht des Claviers rightig vorspielte. Ritz ging zu den Bassethörnern hin, u. brachte sie auch richtig in Ordnung, aber erst in den letzten Takten, u. solcher Jammer ward selten erhört. Sie hat mit wunderbarer Symmetrie das erstenmal der erste Stück verdorben, das 2temal das 2te, u. gestern das dritte. Als es aus war, umringten mich Viele, u. jammerten nach Dir. Bader u. Stümer an der Spitze. Stümer ward ganz weich und sagte, es muß Ihnen doch heut komisch zu Muth gewesen seyn. Dafür machte ich ihm die größten Komplimente, denn er war wirklich zum Bewundern, da Z. oft so falsch begleitete, so ganz andre Harmonien, daß ich noch nicht begreife, wie er sich hat halten können. Ritz hat auch Wunder gethan, denn Z. taktirte nur wenn es ihm einfiel, konnte er den Taktstock nicht schnell genug fassen, so nahm er die Hand, u. wenn er auch das vergaß, kamen die Chöre von selbst. Im Ganzen genommen, war es für das Publicum eine gute Aufführung, auf dem Orchester aber fühlte ein Jeder wo es fehlte. Mir stand der Kopf den ganzen Abend nach dem Dampfschiff. Es war übrigens sehr voll, der König von Anfang zu Ende da, u. eine [ ]. Noch muß ich bemerken, daß Devrient die Partitur nach der Probe aufgenommen u. die ausgebliebenen Stücke mit Mundleim sauber verklebt hatte. Er nimmt es wieder fort, u. außerdem ist Deine Partitur durchaus nicht verumreinigt worden. Ritz hat göttlich gespielt. Und nun glaube ich fertig zu seyn. Einige Theateranecdoten, die ich schon für Dich gesammelt habe, schreibe ich Dir das näch[st]emal durch Legationspost, wo ich mich besser ausbreiten kann. Du armer Junge, wie seekrank magst Du jetzt seyn! aber welchen göttlichen Hunger wirst Du nach Deiner Ankunft haben. Wir leben stillissimo. Heut Abend wird die Milder fertig gezeichnet, da habe ich ihr denn noch geschwind Deine Arie punktirt.

[Lea, F. Rosen]

Noch eins: Dein Oktett lasse ich ausschreiben, willst Du auch das Doppelconzert as dur ausgeschrieben haben, so erbitte ich mir umgehend Eilordre darüber, so lange warte ich damit. Tausend Grüße von Mosevius, der eben hier war, von Breslau zur Passion gekommen ist, mit 3 andern Breslauern die denselben Zweck hatten, u. vortrefflich gehört hat. Er brachte mir ein niedliches Briefchen v. Frank. Adieu, o Mensch, Nächstens ein Mehreres. Dies Blatt denke ich, haben wir beschrieben als sollte es auf die engl. Post.

13

Berlin, den 24sten April 29.

Heut erwarten wir unsre Leutchen zurück, mein Felix, u. ich freue mich nicht wenig darauf, mit Beckchen recht clownen zu können, mit Variat. auf das Thema: Schatz verloren etc. Eigentlich genommen, lebe ich erst recht wieder auf, seit Du von Hamburg fort bist, denn die Eifersucht, Beckchen allein mit Dir zu wissen, ließ mir wenig Ruhe, was hat das Kind nun für ein Uebergewicht mitgenommen! So acht Tage allein. Sie hat zwar viele Details Eurer letzten Tage schon geschrieben, ich werde mir aber die Details noch einmal detailliren lassen, u. fürchte sehr, den Neid über diese acht Tage werde ich sobald nicht los, wenigstens kannst Du allein ihn mir wieder nehmen. Ich freue, u. sehne mich nach einem ruhigen Briefe von Dir, in Hamburg warnt Ihr Alle etwas verdreht, Du, Wichtiges im Auge, ernsthaft zerstreut, das tolle Mädchen nicht wenig ausgelassen. Sie mögen ihr schon die Cour gemacht haben, das sah man jeder Zeile ihrer Briefe an, die von Uebermuth schäumten.

Wir haben so so gelebt. Den ersten Feiertag, während Deiner Schwimmfahrt, waren Abends einige Getreue hier, Marx, der fleißig kommt, u. von Mutter mit vieler Auszeichnung behandelt wird, Heydemanns, Droysen ist noch nicht wieder von seiner Reise zurück. Den zweiten Feiertag bekamen wir von Hamburg die Nachricht Deiner Einschiffung, u. waren Abends, horribile dictu, bei Fränkels, Rosa war aber da, u. so gings an. Dienstag zogen wir nach dem Garten, wo wir bis jetzt fürs Vaterland frieren. Wenn Dir der April so saure Gesichter schneidet, wie uns, so ist das wenig Lebensart, einen Fremden so aufzunehmen. Mittwoch Mittag aßen Caroline u. Auguste hier, tête à tête mit Mutter u. mir, nach Tisch kamen Märckers zum Kaffee, die gingen dann wieder fort, u. nun hätte ich Dich hergewünscht, um zu sehn, wie im Zwielicht Onkel zwischen Caroline u. Auguste auf dem Sopha saß, u. gräulich Cour schnitt, als ich mich über heiße Ohren u. kalte Hände beklagte, nahm er die Mädchen erst bei den Händen, u. dann bei den Ohren, um zu versuchen, obs ihnen auch so wäre, nachher zeichnete an Beiden. Ich emancipirte mich den Abend gleich den Katholiken, u. hatte für Mosevius einige Musik arrangirt, leider war Ritz etwas unwohl, u. hatte mir absagen lassen, David erbot sich freundlich, Dein Quartett, wie ich wünschte, zu spielen, u. brachte Landsberg u. Kudelsky mit. Es ging weit über meine Erwartung, namentlich spielte David (ohne Vergleich mit Ritz) wirklich sehr schön. Marx war auch ganz von ihm eingenommen. Vorher hatte ich das Trio von Beeth. d dur gespielt, u. war außerordentlich mit dem Instrument zufrieden, es klang prächtig voll u. stark, das ungemein zarte piano, das man hervorbringen kann, setzte mich in besten Humor, u. es gelang mir gut. Dann sang Devrient noch einige beliebte Lieder, unter denen besonders das "Glutverlangen" Ulrike zum höchsten Entzücken hinriß. Außer den Genannten waren noch Heydemanns hier, dem Albert trug ich auf, beim zweiten Tisch Bruderstelle zu vertreten, da Paul den Tag so viel zu thun hatte, daß er gar nicht herüber kam, er entledigte sich seines Amtes auch sehr gut, u. würde es noch besser gethan haben, wenn nicht Caroline dos à dos mit ihm gesessen hätte, u. so sein Herz zwischen Wirth u. Courpflichten getheilt, u. sein Hals oft umgedreht gewesen wäre.

Marx hat Paganini gehört, u. ist ganz hingerissen von ihm. Er fand Hensels Zeichnung nicht zureichend, u. hatte ein langes Gespräch mit ihm deshalb. Er giebt Concerte auf Concerte, jetzt im Opernhause zu hohen Preisen, alle brechend voll, dazu ist jetzt der junge Praun hier, der mit ungeheuren Prätensionen auftritt, zu denselben Bedingungen die Pag. spielt, u. geäußert haben soll, er wolle ihm überall nachreisen. Gestern hat er gespielt, ich weiß noch nicht mit welchem Erfolge, da wir gestern auf einem Ball bei Bendemanns waren, wo so viel Menschen von der andern Welt waren, wie ich noch nie in ordentlicher Gesellschaft gesehn habe. Rosa gewesene Kleider in Fülle, abgeblühte Blumen zu abgewelkten Gesichtern, u. August Oetzel war der einzige gute Tänzer, die hübschsten Mädchen Anna, Luise Oetzel u. Victoire. Hensel hatte erst Pauline, u. dann Victoire zum zweiten Walzer aufgefordert, u. letztere vergessen, sie tanzte dann mit dem Maler Remy, aber nahm es sehr übel. Martin ist noch immer nicht recht wohl, Alexander auch nicht, ich glaube die polnische Anleihe ist ihnen Beiden in die Glieder gefahren.—Paul hat jetzt bis zu seiner Einsegnung wirklich zu viel zu thun; gestern u. vorgestern Abend hat er bis 2 u. 3 gearbeitet, nachdem er bis um 9 auf dem comptoir war, sein Prinzipal hat den Versorger des Waarenlagers weggejagt, u. da ist Paul in seine Stelle gerückt, u. da er noch gar nichts davon versteht, u. bei jeder Gelegenheit fragen muß, so nimmt er ihm viel Zeit, er muß schon um 7 dort seyn. Ich hoffe, es soll nicht so arg bleiben.

Die neueste Theatergeschichte ist die, daß Spontini, nachdem er zehnmal Alcidor angekündigt, u. wieder absagen müssen, sich endlich entschlossen hat, einen förmlichen Abbittebrief an Bader gerichtet, an die Direction addresirt zu schreiben, den Redern dem versammelten Committee vorlas, u. B. nachher frug, ob er sich dabei beruhigen würde? Er war nicht sehr geneigt dazu, bis ihm Redern vorhielt, nun sey es genug, was er eigentlich noch verlange? Eben jetzt bekommen wir die Zeitung, worin Alcidor zum zwanzigsten Mal abgesagt, u. Oberon angesetzt ist, angeblich wegen Krankheit der Mme. Schulz.

Sonnabend. Gestern ist unser Volk eingetroffen. Vater ist ungemein heiter und aufgekratzt, Beckchen das versteht sich am Rande. Wir haben schon viel zu plaudern gehabt. Ach Felix, jetzt wird erst die Lücke fühlbar werden, bis jetzt war es mir noch immer, als kämest Du etwa mit den Andern wieder, die Gardinen an Deinen Fenstern sind hängengeblieben, u. am Tage sah ich fleißig herüber, ob Du wol zu Hause bist, aber am Abend ists finster. Ueberhaupt, wie wir wol in tiefster Stille so im Innern etwas wie Musik hören, so habe ich umgekehrt bei jedem Geräusch, mitten im Gespräch, u. bei allen hohen u. niedern Geschäften des Lebens eine große Stille in mir, den Gedanke an Dich, der mich in keinem Moment verläßt. Lebe sehr wohl, und laß es Dir in Londons großem Lärm zuweilen heimlich und stille seyn. Das gefällt mir gar zu gut an der Reise, daß man früher in London ankommt, als in England, u. daß man ohne Vorzimmer gleich mitten in der größten Hauptstadt der Welt absteigt. Lebe wohl. Postw[ ] erhältst Du wöchentlich Nachrichten von uns, die Plauder[n]briefe später durch Redens.

14

1sten Mai 29

O Felix, könnt ich jetzt schriftlich innig blöken, anders wüßt ich nichts zu sagen, was Dir meine Freude ausdrückte: Gestern kamen Deine beiden lieben Briefe, u. heut kam der, den Du direct nach Berlin geschickt hast, u. der blos mit der Post gegangen, am längsten unterwegs blieb, u. Du kannst Dir gar nicht denken, wie wohl mir der that, ich habe den ganzen Morgen die schönste Schimpflaune gehabt, (warum, kommt nachher) und nun bin ich so butterweich, daß man mich auf jedes Brodt streichen kann. Du Armer, was mußt Du ausgestanden haben, am Ostermontag verfolgte ich Dich beständig mit Tönen und Gedanken, u. stieß, wie ich nun sehe, viel zu früh in die drei Trompeten. In der Kirche, während der ganzen Predigt hörte ich nichts, als das Einströmen in die Themse, u. eilte gewaltig zum Schluß.

Daß Paul den 29sten eingesegnet worden, hast Du schon vielfaltig erfahren, es ist davon nichts Besonders zu berichten, Wilmsen sprach gut, aber die Handlung dauerte erschrecklich lange, was bei der Kälte in der Kirche besonders beschwerlich war. Ich freue mich Dir sagen zu können, daß wir jetzt Alle ausgezeichnet zufrieden mit Paul sind, die angestrengte

Arbeit, u. die gezwungene Entfernung von uns thut ihm sehr wohl, und Abends, wenn er zu Hause kommt, ist er zwar sehr ermüdet, aber auch so weich u. gut, daß wir uns herzlich darüber freuen. Sein Prinzipal ist sehr mit ihm zufrieden, u. die plötzliche Entfernung eines Commis, hat ihm Gelegenheit gegeben, rasch zu avanciren. Da wir neulich in der Kirche so unser letztes Geschwisterchen in die Welt schickten, traten mir die großen Veränderungen des letzten Jahres wieder recht lebendig vor, was sich da Alles auseinander- u. zusammen geschoben hat!

Heut ist der erste Mai, u. unser Zimmer ist nach zweimaligem Heizen erträglich warm geworden. Die Bäume sind genau so weit, wie vor 14 Tagen, in der ganzen Natur scheint sich nichts zu rühren als der Sturm.

O Felix, großer Censor! Wirst Du mich für hier u. dort verloren, für ganz aus der Art geschlagen, für aus meinem Character u. meiner Natur gegangen erklären, wenn ich Dir freimüthig das Bekenntniß ablege, daß ich heut Abend bei Redens zum Thee bin? Und daß das der Grund meiner übeln Laune auf der ersten Seite ist. Sage lieber, u. Du wirst es besser treffen, daß ich (in diesem Falle) so klug und so gut bin, wie Du, u. die ganze Sache lieber von der leichten Seite nehmen, als tagelangen Verdruß darüber erregen will, mit welchem Herzen ich herauf gehe, und wie gemein ich mir vorkomme, das—

Hier wurde ich gestern durch Hensel unterbrochen, der kam. So schwer ist es mir noch nie geworden, das Lachen halt zu verhalten, als da gestern, nach stundenlangen Vorbereitungen, Frau v. Stosch in b dur präludirt, u. mir eine süße Ahndung von per valli per boschi durch die Seele fliegt, u. nun wirklich die Leyer gequäkt wird, auf unbegreifliche Weise, etc. Aber ich dachte den ganzen Abend an Deinen Brief, u. ich versichere Dich, ich wäre überall hingegangen, u. wenn mir einer einen Backenstreich gegeben hätte, hätte ich ihm die andre Seite hingehalten. Du schreibst so ausführlich, daß ich Dich nicht genug bewundern kann, wo Du die Zeit dazu hernimmst, wenn Du nur halb so fortfährst, brauchst Du kein Tagebuch, u. noch dazu haben wir die Freude, Alles mitzuerleben. Mutter, die noch im Bett liegt, (es ist noch früh, und wir müssen gleich abschicken) trägt mir auf, Dir für Deine Punktlichkeit u. Ausführlichkeit sehr zu danken, Dir zu sagen, daß sie sich gestern mit einem schimmeligen englischen Ehepaar vortrefflich unterhalten habe, Familienverhältnisse mit England wegen, u. Dir in Ihrem Namen zu erzählen, wie herrlich gestern das erste Duett aus matrimonio v. Frl. Reden u. H. v. Röder executirt worden. Vater, der hinter meinem Stuhl stand, sang aus Herzensangst ganz laut mit, Frl. Elise war sehr heiser (wenn die Heiserkeit heiser ist, was ist das?) Mutter und ich sahen uns einmal an, aber dann nicht wieder, es wäre gefährlich gewesen.

Marx hat einen sehr hübschen Aufsatz über Paganini geschrieben.

Daß Paganinis Concert für die Danziger überfüllt war, u. daß er darin neue 4stimmige Variat. über God Save vortrug, sage ich Dir wie Rellst. von Hörensagen, denn es war Pauls Einsegnungstag, u. wir ruhig zu Hause. Heut Abend hören wir ihn bei Heinr. Beer.

Schreibe uns öfter Einladungen auf lange hinaus, die Du erhältst, heut Abend bist Du im Messias, es ist so angenehm, sich einmal vorstellen zu können, wo Du gern bist.

Ich habe den Klopstock: willkommen o silberne Mond, auf Marx's Veranlassung für Instrumente, näml: Contrabaß, 2 Celli, Bratsche gesetzt. Was! die Contrab. gehen nur bis a? Du mußt ihrer Tiefe eine f Anzusetzen. Was machst Du sonst mit der Meeresstille? Leb wohl, geliebter Schatz. Viele Grüßen von Hensel, der heut mit Deinem Bilde fertig wird. Er hätte uns etwas Unangenehmeres erweisen können als dies Bild.

Grüß Klingem., grüß Rosen, grüß Moscheles, grüß sie, u. nimm Dich in Acht, nicht sowohl, daß Du nicht unter die Wagen, als daß Du nicht zu oft ins Cabriolet kommst, er möchte wieder eifersüchtig werden. Sie scheint Dich zu achten. Aber was will das sagen? Ich mache mir wenig aus Dir.

Die ältere Fischotter.

15

Au au, liebes Lamm, der Sommer ist da. Von nun an schreibe Du alle Straßen, Plätze und Squares in denen Leute wohnen, an die Du Empfehlungsschreiben hast, denn wir besitzen einen Plan von London, ein Geschenk des Hofmalers, und wissen Manches. Wir wüßten aber gern, an welcher Queerstr. der great Portland place Du wohnst, denn Nummern führt der Plan nicht.

Dieser Brief wird Dir überreicht durch H. Werner, einen Neffen von Werner u. Neffen, ich bitte Dich, alles anzuwenden, um ihm seine Aufenthalt in Deiner Stadt angenehm u. ersprießlich zu machen, u. werde jeden ihm erwiesenen Dienst als mir selbst zugefügt, erkennen, stehe auch in ähnlichem Falle zu jedem Gegendienst bereit.

Wenn nun jetzt der Briefträger herumträte, und brächte Deinen Brief, so könnten wir noch heut darauf antworten, und es wäre nett, ich ahnde aber, er bringt nichts. Alle Briefe, die Du heut empfängst, werden von Paganini widerhallen, was soll ich noch hinzufügen? Dies: daß ihm nämlich Beckchen bei Betty gräulich die Cour gemacht hat. Nachdem sie mehremal zu ihm gegangen war, u. ihn angeredet hatte, auch Apfelsinen die er gemantscht, gegessen hatte, gingen wir zu Tisch. Bei uns war ein Platz leer, und als der große Heinrich in Triumph seinen Minister Paganini hereinführte, sprang das Töpfchen auf, lief ihm entgegen, und bat ihn, sich uns zu setzen.[a] Er nickte, folgte, u. als sie sich eben wieder gesetzt hatte, drehte er sich um, u. ging an einen andern Tisch, wo die übrigen jungen Damen, Hofräthin Herz, Mme. Beer, Mme. Henning etc saßen. Wuth u. Eifersucht bemächtigten sich das Töpfchen, u. schallendes Gelächter erhöhte die Empfindungen. Ja, sie hat in ihrem Zorn geschworen, ihn heut (er ißt bei uns) nicht wieder zu Tisch zu führen. Hegel war auch da, u. raspelte stark, Anna u. so fort, und Beckchen u. dergl. Ach lieber Felix, seit Du fort bist erfindet u. wiederholt kein Mensch dumme Redensarten, wir bleiben immer bei den Alten, u. Du wirst uns bei Deiner Rückkehr in dieser Hinsicht wie die Oesterreicher finden, stagnirend u. dumm.

Eben kommt Dein Brief an Paul, Du bester Felix, und Vater meint, daß wir heut noch Einer vom Freitag bekommen. Gewiß schreiben wir Dir alle Woche durch die Post, Vater hat schon sehr große Bogen angeschafft, die Gesandschaftsbriefe erhältst Du so als Zugabe. Und dan[n] ist die Gelegenheit sehr angenehm, wenn Du einmal irgend etwas geschickt haben willst. Wir wollten Dir so gern durch H. Werner Kuchen schicken, aber in dem Augenblick, wo ich ihn fragen lassen wollte, bebte ich zurück vor der Unbescheidenheit, und es unterblieb.

Am Montag wollten wir ein wenig aus der 2ten Passion singen, ich hatte mir allerhand Leute dazu bestellt, da aber ein fürchterlicher Regen war den ganzen Tag, kam Niemand als Ritzens, u. Marx, der Weg und Wetter nicht gescheut hatte, u. nach seiner Reise ohne Mantel u. in Schuhen gegangen war. Und wir sangen wirklich aus der Passion. Ein Paarmal mußte ich aber über Ritz, der neben mir Alt brüllte, fast laut lachen. Ich treffe ganz mit Marx überein wegen der Johannispassion, wenn ich sie erst noch genauer kennen werde, rückte ich damit heraus.

Gestern hatte Paganini ganz den Teufel im Leibe. Er spielte einen sogenannten Canto appassionato es moll, das Orchester in abgebrochenen tremolando dazu, plötzlich fährt er mit der ganzen Masse in es dur hinein, um sogleich wieder ins Moll zurück zu fallen, es war sehr schön, u. wirklich als wolle er sich seine ganze Seele ausspielen, u. zugleich der armen Violinen das Herz ausreißen. Die Hexenvariationen sind eklich, da macht der das Gequäck heiserer alter Weiber nach. Er schloß sehr unbrillant, das war schade.

Beni u. Rosa lassen grüßen, sie sind abgereist. Wenn man das Betragen der Beiden sah so, mußte man glauben, sie gehöre erst ursprünglich zur Familie, u. er sey nur so hinzugekommen, denn sie war immer die

Freundliche, u. er hielt sie möglicher Weise von Allem zurück. Er hat wirklich den gewissen Familienfehler im höchsten Grade. Bei uns ist er jetzt eben nicht Mode, es giebt wenig Unglück in Familien, ich habe so zuweilen mein Kleines privatim, aber das ist eine Sache für sich. (welches wiederum ein Pleonasmus ist.)

Lebe wohl, der Kerl steht und wartet auf den Brief, wir können also nicht auf Deinen etwaigen warten. Lebe sehr wohl, mein Lamm.

---

[a]Fanny omitted "neben" after "sich." Since this construction appeared in letter 2 as well, perhaps it was stylistic.

16

den 7ten Mai. 29.

Mein einziger Felix, obgleich dieser Brief erst mit denen vom nächsten Mittwoch zugleich ankommt, schicke ich ihn doch zu meiner eignen Beruhigung morgen. Ich kann Dir nicht beschreiben, wie mich die Sache mit den Stimmen quält, und wie ich mir hier Vorwürfe mache über den Verdruß, den ich Dir dort bereitet habe, durch meine Unachtsamkeit. Du hast mir gewiß gesagt, wo Du die Stimmen hingethan hast, gewiß Auftrag gegeben, sie zu mir zu nehmen, und ich Dumme weiß u. kann sie nicht finden. Sie sind, wie von der Erde vertilgt, ich habe Alles durchsucht, habe noch Ritz mitgenommen, weil ich meiner eignen Sorgfalt nicht traute, und nichts und wieder nichts. Und nun wirst Du am Montag Dich ärgern über die dumme Schwester, die Dir bis nach London hin Verdruß macht, und über den klugen Rath, den sie Dir von hier ausgiebt, und den Du Dir gewiß längst selbst gegeben hättest, wenn es nur anginge, aber Gott weiß, wo die Notenschreiber wohnen, und wo Du sie auftreiben kannst, und am Ende bin ich Schuld, daß der Sommernachtstraum nicht gegeben wird, dann kann ich mich nicht trösten. Bester Felix, das dauert nun bis Mittwoch über 8 Tage, ehe Deine Antwort kommt, bis dahin ängstige ich mich unaufhörlich. Ich versichere Dich, Du hättest Deine Ermahnung an Hensel, [m]ich zum Suchen aufzumuntern, gar nicht nöthig gehabt, er [hat] von Tisch aufstehn lassen, und war gar nicht zu beruhigen, als ich fortwährend [ ] behauptete, die Stimmen nicht finden zu können. Uebrigens will ich Dir doch sagen, daß Deine 3 Briefe, vom 28sten, 30sten

u. ersten, an demselben Tage, Mittwoch den 6ten angekommen sind, so begreife ich nicht, daß Du keine Nachrichten von uns hast, wir haben jeden Posttag geschrieben, ach! lieber Felix, wir könnens ja gar nicht lassen, und Du bekommst gewiß auch eine Masse Briefe auf einmal von uns. Wie das lange dauert, und breit und umständlich wird, was wir so gegen einander über mit fünf Minuten Brummen abthun, und mit dem Allen habe ich Dir doch nicht halb gesagt, wie leid es mir ist, daß ich Deine Stimmen nicht gefunden habe. Ach mein Alter!

Ich verwahre mir lieber das Plätzchen auf morgen, denn heut bringe ich doch nichts heraus, als Stimmen, Stimmen, und bin über all die Stimmen in solche Stimme auch gekommen, daß ich lieber aufhöre.

Sonnabend. Gestern, als ich zu Zelter ging, und auf dem Hof Dein Fenster grüßte, sah ich etwas Weißes davor, es war als hättest Du eben ein Papier weggeworfen, oder Dein Schnupftuch verloren, als ich näher kam, flog die Taube fort. Es war eine kurze, hübsche Täuschung.—Hensel hat mir neulich Morgens, nach einem kleinen Streit, den wir miteinander hatten, eine Zeichnung geschickt, die ich Dir mitschicken würde, wäre sie nicht so gräulich. Es steht darüber "Mißverständniß" und Du bists, im *Verständniß* mit einer *Miss,* die Du nach Hause führst. Morgen hat er die ganze Familie zu einem Frühstück bei sich eingeladen, um Dein fertiges Bild zu sehn, welches nachher zu uns gebracht wird. Du wirst über dem Kamin wohnen, mir im Rücken, wenn ich Clavier spiele, aber sonst aus der ganzen Stube prächtig zu übersehn. Zelter, der oft hier ißt, läßt Dich sehr grüßen, überhaupt alle Deine Freunde, die sich fleißig nach Dir erkundigen. Leb wohl.

[Rebecka, Lea]

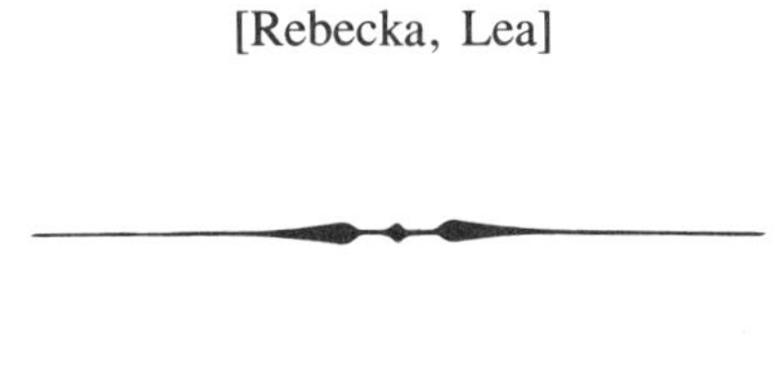

17

den 20sten Mai 29.

Deine Fischottern kommen so eben wieder von einem Gartengang, walk genannt, den sie in unmäßigem Wohlseyn über Deinen sehr frohen Brief gethan haben, da sie eben nichts anders thun mochten. Die Kastanien leuchten, der Flieder duftet, die Maiblümchen stehn, steif u. frisch, wie überhaupt die erste Jugend, aus der Erde heraus, u. diese angenehme Sommerszeit wurde von uns gewählt, diese Tageblättchen an Dich anzufangen, die wir, Eins ums Andre fortsetzen wollen, u. sie Dir wöchentlich, gesandschaftlich oder gelegentlich zu schicken zu denken.—Heut früh weckte mich der Schornsteinfeger um 6, sonst stehe ich so früh nicht auf, die Frucht meiner Ueberwindung war ein gutes Lied, des Du dich freuen wirst, an der Wendung dieser Phrase kannst Du nicht zweifeln, daß es von Droysen ist.—

[Rebecka]

Sonnabend 23sten April[a]

Das Kind ist so humoristisch, daß der alte Kantor mit seinen schwerfälligen Augenbraunen nicht nachkommt. Laß sehn, ob Du folgende Geschichte goutirst: als ich gestern, meiner Vicedirectorschaft gemäß, vor 12 zu Zelter kam, kehlte die Goroncy im untern Saal, ich trat ein, u. sie sang Grell ein Schweizerlied vor, darauf beurlaubte sich der, ich blieb noch einen Augenblick unten, u. als ich darauf die Treppe steige, höre ich oben dasselbe Lied mit rührendem Vortrag klingen, ich trete ein, Grell sitzt am Clavier, und ergötzt sich an Nacherinnerung. Wir feierten übrigens unsern Freitag durch ein Bachsches Concert, e dur, Herr gehe nicht ins Gericht, u. den ersten Chor aus der Johannispassion. Hellwig, der nicht Bescheid wußte, tanzte immerfort ums Clavier herum, vor dem Anfang, u. wunderte sich über meine Unverschämtheit, daß ich dabei stehn blieb. Am Ende frug er denn, ob nicht Rungenhagen an dem Flügel sollte, da meinte ich, ich hätte Auftrag, und die Sache war abgethan.

Vorgestern kam wol Ritz mit der Geige aber die Cotta kam auch, u. der alte Onkel auch, u. so ward nichts, als die Cotta fertig gezeichnet.

Gestern Abend kam der älteste Lewenhagen, der auf 1/4 Jahr verreist. H. v. Boguslawsky u. Märcker.

[Rebecka]

Mittwoch 27sten. Von diesen Tagen ist nichts zu sagen, also sollte ich billig still schweigen, aber nun fange ich erst recht an. Gestern erfuhr ich Hensels allerliebste Idee, mir den Stuhl von Deinem Bilde machen zu lassen, aber nicht, wie er es wünschte, sondern bei der Gelegenheit, daß Mme. Robert, die hier eingezogen ist, u. natürlich nichts weniger als die Idee hatte, uns dadurch zu stören, diesen Platz für sich wählte; ich bin heut zu ihr gegangen, u. habe sie gebeten, einen andern zu wählen, aber natürlich ist ihm die Freude verdorben. Ueberhaupt geht es mit Kleinigkeiten, wie es gegangen ist. Für mich bin ich wenig reizbar, wie ich aber früher für Dich an solchen Dingen litt, so jetzt für Hensel, den es fast so wie Dich affizirt. Mutter hat noch immer nicht gelernt, zu irgend einer Sache ja zu sagen, u. das giebt nach wie vor die unangenehmsten Momente. Noch neulich hatte ich wegen meiner Heirath eine der schlimmsten Scenen mit ihr. Uebersieht man frelich die Sache im Ganzen und Großen, so ist sie schön und gut, und unverbesserlich, u. die kleinen Ecken und Flecken fallen weg. Aber so gut u. so klug wie Du ist keiner von uns, u. darum erlangt keiner was von Mutter. Du bist unser Alpha U. Omega u. alles was dazwischen liegte. Du bist unsre Seele, u. unser Herz u. der Kopf dazu, der Rest mag sich hängen lassen. Wir sind Alle recht gut, so lange Du nicht da bist, aber von da an taugen wir wenig. Du bist eine Gattung Haupthahn, an der ist was, an uns schon wenig[er]. Das Stück spielt jetzt oft, wir nehmen die kleine Titania in die Hand, u. sagen, gesegnete Malzeit, aber wir sagen ein O davor. Für mich giebt es eigentlich zwei Gattungen von Menschen, Du, u. dann die Andere. Beckchen wird das lesen, aber das genirt mich wenig, sie weiß doch, daß sie da ist, u. Hensel, u. noch Stücker drei oder vier, u. sie kann es auch schreiben. So, nun habe ich Dir was vorgeklönt, und Dir vielleicht die Stunde verdorben, in der Dus liest, nun bin ich zufrieden. Nur noch eins, was macht denn die d moll Symphonie, denkst Du an sie? Deine schottische Sonate spiel ich oft.

[Rebecka]

---

[a]Fanny mistakenly wrote "23 April" instead of "23 Mai."

18

Berlin, 27sten Mai 29

Seit wir Beckchen und ich, das Tagebuchen eingeführt haben, werden wir Dir wenig mehr mit den Briefen zu schreiben haben. Die erste livraison erhältst Du durch H. Deetz, der mit dem nächsten Dampfboot nach diesem abgeht. Diese ganze Woche haben wir uns an Deinen Bällen gefreut, die Du unterdessen über zehn neue wieder vergessen hast. Heut wird nun wol die Beschreibung von Sir Alexanders eintreffen. Ich denke es mir sehr reizend, wenn aus dem tobenden Wirrwarr, worin doch gewiß nichts, als eben der in Gedanken zu fassen ist, Du Abends nach Hause zurückkehrend, so nach und nach Dein Inneres wiederfindest, und so Einer nach dem Andern von uns auftaucht, und um sich greift, und Dir denn am Ende kurz vor dem Einschlafen die ganze Heimath stark und lebendig vortritt, bis sich wieder alles in Nebel u. Wirrwarr auflöst, aber in einen stilleren. Wer vollbringt denn am Morgen die große That des Weckens? Heut giebt die Milder ihr danziger Concert, sie singt Dein Maris stella. Wir waren sehr verwundert, nicht zum Mitsingen aufgefordert worden zu seyn, bis wir erfuhren, daß Bach die Einladungen besorgt habe. Da ward uns Manches klar. Grell klagt sehr über ihn, er hat sein Stück nicht einmal probieren können, da Jener ihm die Orgel vor der Nase zuschloß. Ein Tonkünstler. Devrient war gestern einen Augenblick hier, er will Dir den längsten Brief schreiben, seine Frau ist aber immer unwohl, u. den ganzen Vormittag muß er in der Stadt zubringen, Agnes! Die Milder schimpft wie ein Rohrsperling, wir sind erschrecklich liirt, und sie hat sich auf morgen zum Essen gemeldet, wozu sie Hensel abholt, wie findest Du das?

[Rebecka]

Ich gab dem Kinde die Feder in die Hand, da die Friseurin kam, u. nehme sie nun wieder, nur um Dir noch zu melden, daß Ritz jetzt Niemand weiter umflattert, nur Eda Benda, u. uns ihretwegen komplett aufgiebt.

[Lea, Abraham]

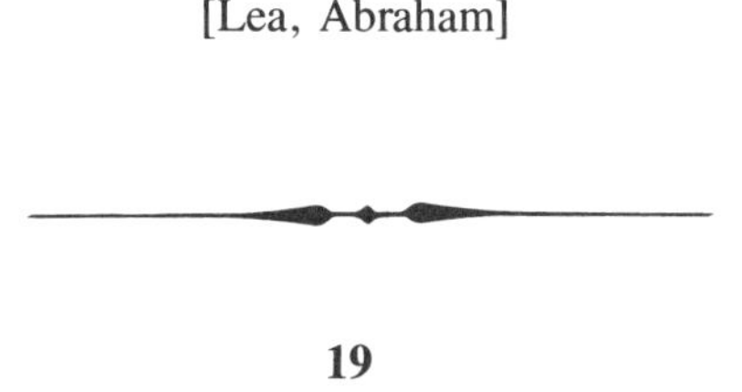

19

3ten Juni 29

Am Sonnabend trafen Deine Briefe mit der Gesandschaft ein, mein Sohn, u. Du thust sehr recht, in besondern Fällen diesen Canal zu benutzen, nur mußt Du so gütig seyn, mit Deinem nächsten Postbrief dann eine solche Sendung abzuzeigen, dann warten wir nicht darauf, u. sind geduldig wie die Lämmer. Auch wir haben vorigen Sonnabend einen Brief für Dich auf dem Wege abgehn lassen, u. morgen erhältst Du Schreiben von Zelter, der Milder u. Devrient. Zelter kam gleich Sonnabend zu Tisch u. theilte Deinen ganzen Brief mit, Devrient kam nach Tisch, u. las uns Stückchen daraus vor. Ritz kam den andern Tag, u. erzählte blos einiges, Marx war noch gar nicht hier, er ist sehr beschäftigt, denn trotz der Schwachfüßigkeit des Theaters wird sein Festspiel zur Vermählung gegeben, und er hat Sonntag allein drei verschiedene Proben davon gehabt. Die Welt denkt und träumt jetzt nichts, (Dein Vater, der Stadtrath an der Spitze) als Kaiserinn. Diese Person kommt am Freitag an, und eine macht ihretwegen unsägliche Anstalten. Der gesammte Magistrat nicht nur empfängt sie, sondern er hat auch wieder 76 weiße Mädchen gestellt, wir Beide habens refüsirt, weil uns das Wetter zu zweifelhaft war, (es pladdert schon vier Tage unausgesetzt). Vater hatte den Auftrag für Gedichte zu sorgen, er war bei Rellstab, Förster u. Fouqué, dann warb er Anne Fränkel für die Mädchenschaar, u. führt sie heut hin, ihr das Musterkleid zu zeigen, will auch in Vorschlag bringen, daß sie eine von den Vortretenden seyn solle, opponirt sich gegen Frl. Büschleg, weil die klein u. häßlich ist, kurz Du erlebst Wunderdinge.—Heut hoffen wir auf einen langen Brief von Dir, da wir zweimal nur wenig erhalten haben, ach, liebster Felix, bleibe ja bei Deiner guten Gewohnheit, Du wüßtest gar nicht, Du ahndest nicht, wie Noth es uns thut. Du bist aber wirklich ein Phönix, denn wer uns auch frägt, ob wir oft Nachricht von Dir haben, u. die Antwort erzählt, alle Woche wenigstens einmal, ist erstaunt, u. kanns nicht begreifen. Du bist eine Gattung Engel, bleibe es um Gotteswillen. Ach und bitte, schreibe einmal bei Gelegenheit einen kleinen Privatbrief an die Fischottern, u. sehne Dich nach ihnen, u. schicke das Lied, woran Du Dir vorige Woche Deine liebe Seele ausgesungen hast, u. das aus a dur, das Carolinische, welches ich gestern Abend Wilmsens vorspielen mußte. Es war eine rührende Naivetät wie Wilmsens, die sich den Tag vorher gemeldet hatten, um halb 8 kamen, u. wie Baur, der seit Deiner Abreise noch nicht hier war, um 8 kam, u. wie wir alle lachten, Auguste auch, und wie die drei munter um 11 abtrabten, als ob das so seyn müßte, versuche einmal das auf andre Leute zu transponiren, es geht gar nicht, diese unbeschreibliche Kindlichkeit gehört nur in die Wilmsesche Familie. Heynens sind in Charlottenburg, und haben da Alle das Fieber wiederbekommen, bei Marianne haben es auch ein Paar Kinder, Tante Meyer ist noch gar nicht heraus nach Charlottenb., sie läßt Dich tausendmal aufs herzlichste grüßen, ich war neulich bei ihr, und theilte ihr Einiges aus Deinen Briefen mit, worüber sie eine unsägliche Freude hatte. Auch Gustav Magnus war neulich hier, u. läßt Dich eigens grüßen, wir baten ihn wiederkommen, wenn er es bei Leuten mit kleinen Spiegeln aushalten könne, stehen aber im besten Vernehmen mit ihm.—Hensel hat jetzt ein Local für sein Studium im Luisenstift gefunden, zu meiner großen Freude also ziemlich in unsrer Nähe, u. erwartet nur die Bestätigung vom Könige. Ich nehme mich seiner Sachen an, u. treibe ihn ein wenig, u. denke, daß ich ihn wol von diesem Fehler nach u. nach befreien werde, da er mir zu Liebe schon so Manches abgelegt u. angenommen hat. Uebrigens sage ich Dir, Du magst es nun glauben oder nicht, daß, wenn wir beisammen sind, Du, u. wieder Du, allezeit der Gegenstand unsrer Gespräche bist. Du schreibst zuletzt von Lord Sandon, hast Du denn Tante Mine Bute noch immer nicht gesehn? Tante Mine heißt jetzt hier Tante Marianne, welche eine von Edas Tanten ist. Ich sage Dir, die Sache mit Eda ist nicht so ganz ohne Bedenklichkeit, er ist verliebt, wie er es nur jemals war, u. sagt immer von ihr, die Kleine, bei uns fährt er aber jämmerlich schlecht damit.—Die Academie stagnirt, es ist nicht auszuhalten vor Langeweile. Die Milder hat die Bestätigung ihrer Pension, ohne die gewünschte Vermehrung erhalten, u. wüthet, das Theater ist einzig mit Agnes beschäftigt, in der Königstadt gefällt Mlle. Vio, die ich noch nicht gehört habe, das ist Alles. A propos, aus einer Stelle Deines Briefes an Devrient, wo Du ihm schreibst, es sey Dir leid, daß die Eindrücke der Passion verwischt oder verdorben seyn, haben wir geschlossen, was er Dir für einen Todtengräberbrief muß geschrieben haben. Glaube ihm doch jetzt nicht, er ist schon wieder nicht zurechnungsfähig, seit den Proben von Agnes ist jedes Ecce homo ein Seiltänzer gegen ihn. Im Gegentheil, frage Ritz, der sagt, wenn Schubring Abends zu Haus geht, singt er aus der Passion, frage Baur, der geht Sonntags nicht in die Kirche, u. spielt aus der Passion, frage uns, wir singen u. spielen aus der Passion.—Eben kommt Dein prächtiger Brief mit der c moll Symphonie: Du armer Schelm, was haben sie Dich gehudelt, u. wie froh bin ich, daß Du nun über Alles fort bist. Ich habe nie an Deinem Erfolge gezweifelt, die Nachricht davon hat mich nicht überrascht, aber angenehm und leicht ist einem doch zu Muth. Mit dem Sommernachtstraum wirst Du furorissimo [machen]. Die Geschichte mit der Malibran ist nicht so übel. Nun muß ich Dir auch erzählen, da [ ] [n]eulich eine Wette verlor, weil er die Ouvertüre aus Figaro, die Du in einer Gesellschaft [ ] gespielt hast, auf die Malibran bezog. Eben zanke ich mich mit Beckchen, u. sage, ein andermal wolle ich schreiben, wenn Dein Brief angekommen ist, u. die Andern könnten anfangen, u. sie sagt, es finge immer [ ] sagte Alles von Alles was zu sagen ist, so daß sie nachher nichts zu schreiben hätte.

[Rebecka]

Alle unsere Leute grüßen Dich, u. freuen sich über Deinen Ruhm, sie sind stolz auf Dich. Sage mir nur das Eine, ob Moscheles ganz rein aus diesen Intriguen gegen Dich hervorgegangen ist? Aus dem Briefe erscheint es mir wenigstens nicht unzweifelhaft. Leb tausendmal wohl.

[Rebecka, Abraham, Lea]

20

[Rebecka]

4ten Juni

Als gestern Dein 2ter Brief kam, war ich aus u. als ich zu Haus kam, es zu spät, ihn noch zu beantworten. Und jetzt ist schon der 6te Juni, u. nicht mehr der 4te, u. es regnet noch immer, u. wir sitzen, horribile dictu! in der warm geheizten Stube. Und eben habe ich mein 6tes Lied an Dich fertig geschrieben, u. will es nun gleich auf das gelbe Löschpapier abschreiben, mit gräulichen Verwünschungen gegen H. Schwarz, der mich so fürchterlich hintergangen hat mit besagtem Fließpapier.

7ten Juni Pfingstsonntag. Ein grauer, regnigter kalter Pfingsttag, an dem wirklich nichts zu holen ist, für uns einsam u. unbedeutend. Zwei Korn Blumenkränze hängen drin am Spiegel, und wir sind noch uneins, ob wir sie nicht aufsetzen wollen, weil Du nicht da bist, oder aufsetzen, weil wir sie tragen würden, wenn Du da wärst, es wird wol beim ersten bleiben, denn es ist doch auch gar kein Blumenwetter. Eben habe ich meine Lieder fertig geschrieben u. bitte Dich, verfahre damit, nicht als seyen sie aus der Ferne an Dich gerichtet, denn das giebt der Sache nur einen relativen Werth, sondern als hätte ich Lieder mit den u. den Fehlern gemacht, u. bäte Dich um eine kritische Rücksicht darauf. Eins ist darunter, welches ich für eins meiner besten Lieder halte, ich will einmal sehn, ob Du auch der Meinung seyn wirst, Du wirst es sehr schön singen. Und so siehst Du auch, daß Hensel, obwohl der faulste Schreiber, dennoch für Dich u. mit Dir beschäftigt ist. Ob Dir Mutters Zeichnung gefallen wird, bin ich noch nicht gewiß, sie wollte anfangs nicht recht gelingen, jetzt aber, sey es, daß wir uns hinein gesehn haben, oder daß, durch viele Mühe, u. vieles Andere wirklich das Böse heraus, u. das Gute hineingekommen ist, wir finden es sehr gut.

Wir wollen gern die dummsten Possen für Dich schreiben, aber ach! die Possen sind uns ausgefallen wie die Haare. Zuweilen amüsire ich das kleine Töpfchen damit, daß ich ihr nach der Reihe die verschiedenen Urtheile der Menschen über sie vorführe, als da sind: Ideal der Weiblichkeit—drolliges Gesichtchen—tragisches Gesicht—altes Testament—wie sich die verschiedenen Personen—Marx, Rauch, Heyne, die Milder über sie geäußert haben.

[Rebecka]

Ja, Du bist der Klügste, ich setzte mich neulich ans Clavier, u. spielte das Ottett scherzo durch, u. versuchte mir vorzustellen, wo wol die luftigen d Trompeten kommen möchten, erzähle uns noch etwas vom lieben Scherzo, u. wie Dus angeputzt hast? Im Uebrigen kann ich die Ehre haben, Dir zu versichern, daß Du der vernünftigste aller Sterblichen bist, nicht als ob *ich* jemals daran gezweifelt hätte, aber glaube nur nicht, daß andre Leute daran zweifeln, ich war ziemlich ärgerlich, aus Deinem Briefe zu erfahren, was man Dir Alles geschrieben habe, aber das ist nur, damit Du dort nicht verzogen werdest, hier sind sie seelencontent, u. Vater wundert sich alle Tage, daß Du noch, u. immer noch kein Geld genommen hast. Weißt Du, wie ich einmal wüthete, da Zelter meinte, Deine Meeresstille sollte mit einem Contraste anfangen? Und Du mich beruhigtest, nu, nu, wüthe nur sich so sehr, liebe Gere.

[Rebecka]

den 10ten. Allwo Du in London Deine Symphonie zum 2tenmal vorreiten[a] thust. Wie beneide ich irgend einen John-Bull oder Ochs, der sich ennüyirt, um Dein Scherzo. Wahrlich, Deine Gegenwart thut Noth, denn Ritz schlägt ganz aus der Art, ja ich sehe voraus, daß ich Zeit Deiner Abwesenheit nicht [Dein] Quartett hören werde, wonach mir der Mund voll Wasser läuft, denn dreimal habe ich ihn sehr vergebens darum gebeten, u. mehr als dreimal bitte ich nicht.—Nun muß ich Bettys Börse noch ein wenig mehr erläutern, als Beckchen auf der vorigen Seite. Sie arbeitete sie für einen der vielen Damenvereine, welche für die Danziger verkauft haben, u. wir nahmen uns sogleich vor, sie für Dich zu acquiriren, in edlem Wettkampf mit kleinem u. großem Fritz, u. wirklich war ich in der ersten Stunde des Verkaufs mit Betty da, u. kaperte die Börse. Die Fritze hatten das Nachsehn.

Nun soll ich den Rand erläutern, Du lieber Himmel, u. schon sind die Lieder eingepackt, u. ich muß aus dem Gedächtniß bänkelsängern. Erstlich bittet Hensel wegen seines Briefs um Verzeihung; er schrieb ihn gestern Abend am runden Tisch, während Marx u. wir ein großes Geschrei dabei verübten. Zweitens schickt er Dir seine liebste Zeichnung, die von Beckchen, u. hat nur eine Durchzeichnung davon behalten, nach der er sie raconstruieren will, von der meinigen erhältst Du mit Nächstem eine Kopie. Ist es nicht ein ungeheuerer Beweis von Selbstverläugnung, u. Mangel an Neid, daß ich Beckchens Zeichnung allein abgehn lasse, da ich es doch, durch Connexion mit dem Maler, leicht hätte aus Intrigue hintertreiben können? Belohne mich dafür, gieb mir den rothen Adlerorden dritter Classe mit oder ohne Eichenlaub, und mache mich zum Hofrath. Aber der Rand: hear! hear! Vorne an sitzen wir als Kinder, u. spielen, Hensel behauptet, durchaus meine Grimassen getroffen zu haben, wenn ich einzelne Bässe dazwischen pauke. Daß der gute Pegasus ein Violinzeichen zum Schwanz hat, wird Dir wol nicht entgehn. Wir rücken weiter, u. gehn ins erste Lied ein, Du wirst geweckt. Hier weiß ich nicht, ob es dem Künstler gelungen ist, die herculische Arbeit, die besonders erforderliche Kraftanstrengung auf dem Gesicht der Weckenden gehörig auszudrücken. Der Hahn sitzt traurig auf der Säule, an die der Wanderstab gelehnt ist. Von dem Dache des Haupthauses (in welchem der Titel wohnt) sehn zwei wohlbekannte Thiere, die guten Störche, hinab in die Schlafstube. Der Sommer kommt, u. man schreibt Dir im Garten. (Dichtung) *Tulpen* u. *blaue Winden,* u. das *Vöglein in der Linden* sind zugegen. Das Mädchen sitzt an einer Weinwand, deren Früchtchen Dir bekannt seyn werden. Ist es wahr, daß Du einmal ein Lied, u. aus dem Lied ein Quartett machtest, u. daß Andre aus dem Quartett viel Wesens, u. Dir unaufhörliche Anspielungen darauf machen? Sieh ihren Fuß, er steht zwar nicht in Ungewittern, aber doch auf einem Sechszehntheit, sahst Du eine graziösere Fußbank? Nun ist die Welt mit Cypressen vernagelt, Meer u. Schiff, sechs Lieder flattern herüber; Hochland. Der Schotte aus jener Gesellschaft sieht sich verwundert um, wie Du mit Deiner andern Musik angestiegen kommst, nun ihr werdet euch schon vertragen.

Die unterste Zeichnung versteht sich ziemlich von selbst. Lache nur nicht über meine Naivetät des dreistimmigen Liedes, ich weiß recht gut wo ich es her habe, u. Du weißt es auch, aber das ist ja eben der Spaß. Was kann ich dafür, daß Du den Einfall schon voriges Jahr gehabt hast? Daß wir da in der Zeichnung aus grauer Vergangenheit in goldne Zukunft schiffen, wird schwerlich jemand verstehn, so verständlich ist es.

Lebe nun wohl, ich beende wieder einen Fetzen Tagebuch, möge Dir unsre Sendung so viel Vergnügen machen, als wir sammt u. sonders davon gehabt haben. Amen.

[Wilhelm]

---

[a]In this context, "vorreiten" does not make sense, but "vorbereiten" is reasonable. Perhaps Fanny mistakenly wrote "vorreiten," or else it may have been a contraction for "vorbereiten." In any case, "vorbereiten" is assumed for the translation.

21

Donnerstag, den 11ten.

[Rebecka]

Jucheysa, der erste Sommertag ist da, u. zwar heut, den 13ten Juni allwo man endlich im Freien sitzt, u. Dir schreibt. Der Schaute, der wie Beckchen auf der vorigen Seite schreibt, noch immer in Potsdam ist, war aber hier, u. sprach des dümmsten Zeuges viel, ich ärgerte mich über ihn, u. besonders deshalb, weil ich noch so gar nicht mit ihm aufs Reine kommen kann, denn ein Dichter ist er nun doch einmal, u. in ihm kann ich nichts Wahres finden, nicht einmal seine Eitelkeit ist wahr, u. damit meine ers doch am Redlichsten. Löse mir dies Räthsel, mein liebes Evangelium, wie Hensel Dich heut in Bezug auf mich nannte. Daß er mich liebt, sehe ich hauptsächlich, u. am liebsten aus der Art wie er meine Liebe für Dich respectirt, u. ihr gewissermaßen gern den Vortritt läßt, ich versichere Dich mir ist wohl in meiner Haut, ich bin gut gefahren, einmal mit Dir, dann mit ihm, schließlich u. sechstens mit Euch Allen, u. mit Euch Volk ist was aufzustellen, ihr stellt der Kunst ein Bein, u. kniet ihr auf den Hals, u. sagt dann was ihr von ihr wollt. Bleibt dabei. Dein Keix nach d dur gefällt mir schon nicht übel, u. ich kann mir allerlei dabei denken, aber raconstruieren das würde mir sehr schwer werden, vielleicht gehts. Weißt Du was wir Geren jetzt lesen? Die Kleine ohne meinen Consens: La nouvelle Héloise. Ich lese eigentlich das ganze Buch um der einen Stelle willen, die Dir einmal gefiel: vivre et mourir sans elle! vivre sans elle! Die italiän. Verse, die fast in jedem Briefe vorkommen, gefallen mir durchaus nicht. Eigentlich sollte man keine Romane lesen, wenn man welche—erlebt, aber da wir And[ ] die wir mit Verstande gesegnet sind, doch einmal ein eigentliches Küchenschürzenleben haben, so müßten wir diese Pflanzen ungelesen lassen, u. das wäre doch schade.—

[Rebecka]

Dienstag 16 Juni Seit vorgestern ist Dein liebes Bild hier, Sonntag bracht' es Hensel zur Supp[e] mit dem hübsche Gartenstuhl dabei, dem ich ein mal Plätzchen im Garten ausgefunden habe, da die Laube für uns verloren ist, eine Sache über die Hensel gar nicht abgewöhnen kann, zu wüthen, sprich nicht davon, es gehört zu dem Dingen, die eingehetzte Leute nicht berühren. Aber was hilft das Alles, Dein Bild ist gut, u. wir sitzen, Beckchen u. ich, Deine Geren, stundenlang davor, u. erwarten, daß es sich rühren möge, u. es rührt auch, wenn nicht sich doch uns, u. thut seine Schuldigkeit. Gestern früh besuchte ich Zelter, er läßt Dich sehr grüßen, u. kommt sehr oft her, sich Nachrichten von Dir zu haben. Die Medemsche Familie war gestern Abend hier, Auguste liebt noch immer ihre alten Freunden, Felix u. Klingemann, u. läßt ihnen sagen, daß ihre Hochzeit am 6ten Juli (ich füge hierzu, an Hensels Geburtstag) ist, u. daß sie einige Tage darauf nach Meklenburg abgeht. Trinkt also Montag, den 6ten Juli auf alle gebornen, u. verehlichten Kinder, ich will Augustes Grüße hiermit ebenfalls für Klingemann bestellt haben. Marx war auch gestern hier, der gern mit Augusten philosophirt, u. für Jettchenu. Constanze hatten wir Droysen u. Albert bestellt. Seit vorgestern haben wir uns angewöhnt, eine *feine Seele* zu sagen, u. so behaupten wir manchmal aus dem Stegreif von Dir, Du habest eine feine Seele. Es ist so eine kleine Herzenserleichterung. Adieu.

[Rebecka]

den andern Morgen. Das Gewitter kam herauf, u. zwar ein so furchtbares, sturmflüthendes, donnerbrüllendes, nachteinhüllendes, hagelzerschmetterndes, regengießendes, wie in hiesigen Landen noch nie erlebt worden. Wenig Fensterscheiben in der guten Stadt Berlin haben dem heftigen Eindruck widerstehen können, den der Hagel auf sie machte, auf einer kleinen Inspectionsreise die ich nach überstandenem Sturm mit Hensel durch den Garten that, fanden wir alle Wege mit Akazienblütchen bestreut, mit kleinen u. großen Zweigen u. Aesten obendrein verziert, u. aus unsern 200 Mistbeetfenstern waren wenigstens 2000 geworden. Was folgt aus dem Allen? Wir sind nicht fashionable, u. fahren nicht nach Epsom Steglitz, Vater aber reitet eben hin. Nun eine lächerliche Sache: Gestern im Feuer des ersten dreimaligen Lesen Deines Briefs, glaubten wir, das Concert mit Sommernacht. u. es dur Tageswären sey gestern, u. fingen dem zu Folge sogleich an zu schwärmen. (Unser Schwärmen besteht jetzt oft darin, daß wir Geren uns um den Hals fallen, u. uns reciproc. beißen, hernach aber vor Dein Bild laufen, u. ihm Männerchen vormachen.) Plötzlich aber fiel mir aus den Wolken in die Seele der Gedanke, das Concert sey wol gar nicht gestern, u. ich holte Deinen Brief, u. siehe da, ich hatte richtig gedacht. Also nächsten Mittwoch werde ich das es dur Concert von Beethoven in—Charlottenburg bei Heynes spielen müssen, wenn ich es überhaupt spiele. Gestern war ich grade beim Sommernachtstraum, als Zelter, u. nachher Dein Brief kam. Daß Deine Schreiben zuweilen verspätet werden, kann Dich nicht wundern, wenn Du siehst, daß es Dir mit den unsrigen auch zuweilen so geht, u. wir schicken doch höchst regelmäßig jeden Mittwoch Nachmittag unsern kleinen Brief auf die Post. Unsre ganze Familie wohnt jetzt wieder in Charlottenburg im Kamekeschen Hause zusammen. Tante Jette, die die letzte war, wurde durch eine von Tante Meyer angestiftete Feyerlichkeit empfangen, H. Tilenius nämlich u. H. Wigand waren als weiße Mädchen gekleidet, u. declamirten Zeile um Zeile ein Gedicht von Tante Meyers Fabrik, die Andere hatten sich als Ehrenpforte aufgestellt. Tante Jette soll Thränen gelacht haben.

[Rebecka]

Sonnabend, 20 Juni So eben geht Militiz von hier fort, der uns berichtet hat, daß zwei seiner Diebe, u. ein ihm der gestohlene Sachen entdeckt sind, u. daß der Bedienter unschuldig ist. Daß diese ihm sehr unvortheilhafte Geschichte ihn in sehr vortheilhaftes Licht gesetzt hat, werde ich bestätigen, Du wirst unglaubig lächelnd den Kopf schütteln, und es sey darum, er ist seitdem l'enfant chéri de toute la maison. Heut Abend wollten wir in die Oper gehn, die Schechner als Vestalin zu sehn, indeß leider Gottlob haben wir keine Plätze bekommen, nun wird heut Abend die Zeichnung beendet, die Hensel von mir für Dich macht. Trotz meiner Protestationen hat er mir wieder einen Kranz aufgesetzt, die Leute müssen glauben, ich sey mit einem solchen Möbel geboren. Weißt Du wer jetzt der angesehenste Mann unsres ganzen Kreises ist? Auf wen bei allen Gelegenheit die zartesten Rücksichten genommen werden? M[ ]. Du würdest Dich freuen, wenn Du es sähest, Du würdest Dich ebenfalls freuen, wenn Du erlebtest wie hübsch, liebenswürdig, u. durchaus gut Hensel mit ihm steht. Morgen ist Blumenausstellung, da hat er unser einziges disponibles Billet bekommen. Dienstag ist Blumenacademie, voriges Jahr war Dein Te Deum. Ich muß jetzt anfangen zu schließen, denn mit dem Ende dieses Blattes ist das Tagebuch mauseaus, u. muß gleich herauf zu H. Klingemann Substituten. Grüß mir den Mann, u. sage ihm, man wäre ihm hier Einiges gut. Schreib doch gelegentlich etwas Näheres über Deine Covent Garden affair, weißt Du schon etwas über den Text? Lebe wohl o Schatz, Lamm. Korrespondirst Du mit Wilhelm Horn? Ich würde einen unendlichen haut gout darin finden, wenn Du auf Deiner französ. Nordküstenreise ausglittest, u. auf 24 St. incognito nach Paris reistest. Ich weiß wol, ich könnte nicht widerstehn.

22

Berlin 29sten Juni 29

Zuerst mein lieber Felix, den Besten Dank für die unsre Heirath betreffende Supplik. Uns hat sie soviel Freude gemacht, als wenn sie von Wirkung gewesen wäre. Von Deiner Rückkehr übrigens war nie in der Beziehung die Rede, auf den Sept. oder Oktob. ist u. bleibt es festgesetzt. Paul sagte gestern zu Hensel, daß er Dich zu dieser Bitte veranlaßt habe, da aber Dein letzter Brief noch gar keine Antwort auf seinen enthalten kann, so ist es ein Zusammentreffen, welches mich von beiden Brüdern sehr freut. Ich bin so begierig, was Dein Tagebuch für Privatmittheilungen an uns enthalten wird, daß ich es kaum erwarten kann. Ich brauche durchaus einmal wieder die Versicherung von Dir daß Du zufrieden bist. Sie ist mir zuweilen so nöthig, wie die Luft zum Leben, dann hält es wieder eine Weile vor. Wir haben gestern u. heut die angenehmsten Morgen gehabt, indem Hensel gestern den ganzen Sonntag, u. heut früh von 6 bis 8 am Hintergrunde Deines Bildes, größtentheils im Freien, malte. Dabei kampirten wir sehr nett auf dem Turnplatz, u. es war hübsch, heut setzte er Dein Bild in die volle Sonne, wo es prächtig aussah, von einer ungläublichen Lebendigkeit. Neulich gab er mir einmal ein Gedicht, wovon er glaubte daß es im Garten gesungen werden könnte, dazu ist es nun freilich zu ausgedehnt, ich redete ihm aus daß es komponirbar wäre, u. schreibe es nun zu seinem Geburtstage, ich hoffe, damit fertig zu werden. Es wird 8 stimmig, Frauenchor u. Männerchor opponirend, dann beide zusammen.

Irgend einen Abend.

Dein Hora ist aber gar zu schön. Wie ich jetzt dazu komme? Ich bin seit 2 Stunden allein, u. sitze am Clavier, das heut grade besonders nett klingt, u. spiele das Hora, u. stehe vom Clavier auf, trete vor Dein Bild u. küsse es, u. vertiefe mich so ganz in Deine Gegenwart, daß ich—Dir nun schreiben muß. Aber mir ist unendlich wohl, u. ich habe Dich unendlich lieb. Unendlich lieb.

2ten Jul. So eben erhielten wir Deinen lieben Brief vom 25sten, um 24 St. verspätet, freuen uns des Sommernachtstraumerfolges, ärgern uns über die vorhergegangenen Verdrüsse, u. betrüben uns, daß die Gesandschaftssachen so langsam gehn, denn von wenigstens 4 an Dich abgesandten Tagebuchpartien hast Du erst eine einzige erhalten, u. wirklich schreiben wir eben so regelmäßig einmal wöchentlich mit der Gesandschaft, als mit der Post. Hier erhältst Du die verlangten kleinen Kupferstich, einen etwas größeren müssen wir zurücklassen. Wir haben einen für Dich beigelegt, der eine Rad-u. Lämmergegend vorstellt, leider war das eigentliche Lämmerhaus nicht sichtbar. Vorne an der Brücke findet ein rendezvous oder eine Begegnung statt, die deute Dir, wie Du magst, u. nun kaufe der karrenden Hökerfrau eine Metze Kirschen ab, statte einen der wandelnden Herrn mit einer langen Nase, einen andern mit einer Brille u. pommerschen Dialekt aus, nenne den dritten, der eine Dame führt Louis, u. die Dame Minna, u. ich wette, Du setzest Dich hinter die Scene in eine Droschke, u. fährst zu Hause, Leipziger Str. No 3 u. bittest um eine Marke.

Das Stück soll bald wieder spielen, u. manches andre dazu. Unter andern nehme ich mir vor, daß in der winterlichen Gartenwohnung Manches aufgeführt werden soll, u. daß der gentleman Jemand jeden Morgen bei mir Caffee trinken soll, sonst möchte ich ihn doch zuweilen nicht zu sehn bekommen, ehe er aus geht. Es wird eine gute Zeit werden, so Gott will, so hübsch, daß ich dahinter nichts mehr sehn mag u. kann vor der Hand. Leb wohl, tausend Grüße von Mutter. Ich schicke jetzt alles mit Mißtrauen, weil ich nicht weiß, wie lange es gehn kann, u. ob es Dich überhaupt noch in London trifft.

[Rebecka]

Du kannst den kleinen Einbrodt auch von mir grüßen, ich erlaube es. Wie ist die ganze Gesellschaft in die die[a] allervierwindesten Winde gestoben!

---

[a]Fanny mistakenly wrote "die" twice.

23

1 Juli 29.

Heut war Dein Brief mit mehr Ungeduld erwartet, weil [die] Relation vom Sommernachtstraum, u. wahrscheinlich Antwort auf die Lieder u. Zeichnungen drin steht, mit Mühe sammle ich mich soweit, um Dir jetzt zu schreiben, da ich später ausgehn muß, u. dieser Brief dann die Reihe herum geht. Am vorigen Mittwoch waren wir sehr vergnügt. Die Radgesellschaft bestand aus Minna u. Albert Heydemann, Louis [kam] erst nach Hegel [ ], Auguste Wilmsen, Droysen, u. uns. Mälchen Märcker war hinzugekommen[,] das Rad nahm die eine Seite des Tisches ein, u. viel Unsinn rollte hin u. her. Nach Tisch setzten wir uns auf den erhohten Platz einer Straße den Du kennst, u. nun ward der schöne Brief fabrizirt, den Du noch immer nicht hast, u. so gelacht, namentlich über Hensel, der sehr aufgekratzt war, daß besonders Droysen u. Heydemann wirklich den Athem verloren, u. in Gefahr zu ersticken geriethen. Später gingen wir in den Garten hinter dem Hause, um 8, der mutmaßlichen Anfangsstunde Deines Concerts, wurden wir feierlich, die Mädchen zogen Jede eine Kornblume aus ihrem Kranz, u. bewarfen Dich damit, Alle empfingen Dich mit Händeklatschen und Bravo, Beckchen u. ich wir intonirten die beiden Flöten, die Clarinetten blieben leider aus, u. während aller dieser Vorfälle saßen Albert u. Louis auf einem Baum, wie Katzen. Der Tag war äußerst angenehm, die kleine Gesellschaft hatte Stimmung u. Farbe, jeder Scherz griff u. keiner blieb. Als wir Abends die Eltern von Marianne abholten, begleitete das ganze Rad, Louis Heydemann trug Mäntel u. Regenschirm (es war eine trockne Hitze, u. keine Idee vom Regen) u. als wir uns eben trennen wollten, wählte das Rad, von Begeisterung ergriffen, auf offner Straße Hensel zu ihrem Mitgliede, welches durch einen feierlichen ringe[ ] Rosenkranz, u. Ueberhalten des aufgespannten Regenschirms geschah. Montag waren wir wieder in Charlottenburg bei Fanny Magnus, wo wir uns auch sehr wohl amüsirten. Martin und Gustav baten mich, Dich bei dieser Gelegenheit recht herzlich zu grüßen.

[Rebecka]

Ueber Agnes v. Hohenstaufen zirculiren die schlechtesten Witze, der beste unter ihnen ist, daß der Theaterdiener Blumen zu der letzten Probe aus Versehen die Partie aus Alcidor brachte, u. daß der Irrthum nicht sonderlich bemerkt ward, sondern die Partie bis zu Ende durchgesungen. Rellstab hat eine maliziöse Rezension abgefaßt, an der besonders kränkend für Sp. seyn wird, daß er bemerkt, wie die dritte Vorstellung schon leer gewesen sey, u. wie trotz der nämlichen ungünstigen Umstände von Hitze u. dergl. die 20ste der Stummen überfüllt war. Laissons là ce monde.

An dem Tage, wo Du diesen Brief erhältst, feiern wir Hensels u. Droysens Geburtstag. Ich habe noch vorgestern eine musikal. Arbeit für Hensel unternommen, die 8stimmige Composition eines Gedichtes von ihm. Es wird nicht viel, aber es wird doch etwas, u. es fehlt nur noch das letzte Stück, woraus ich eine Art Fuge zu machen denke. Du weißt, wie ängstlich ich immer bin, daß mir die Imagination davon läuft, daher freue ich mich immer, wenn es mir nur gelingt, Noten zu schreiben, u. sehe im

Anfang wenig danach, wie es wird. Nachher freilich ärgre ich mich, wenn es schlecht ist. Adieu, mein liebster Felix, ich verlasse Dich um Abschied von Fränkels zu nehmen, die morgen nach der Schweiz u. Italien abreisen. Anna raspelte neulich gewaltig vor Deinem Bilde, ich versichere Dich, Deine Erziehung war gut.

[Lea, Abraham]

24

[Hensel, Droysen, Rebecka]

Um Gotteswillen, was schreibt das Mädchen für Gottvergeßnes Zeug. Wirklich, wenn sie zuweilen ihren Schnabel laufen läßt, sollte man meinen, man müsse die ganze Person an den Fußblock legen, oder sie sey— Beatrice. Wirklich hat noch kein Sterblicher, außer Shakespeare, solche Possen geahndet. Aber nun bitte ich Jeder männiglich, diesen folgenden Brief wirklich nicht zu lesen, da er große Geheimnisse enthält. Die Mittheilungen im Tagebuch hören nun auf, da Du fortreist, u. die Gesandschaft leider so sehr langsam befördert. Also von der silbernen Hochzeit. Große Plane[a] haben wir wol auch, aber sie liegen so ziemlich im Dunkel, Du mußt sie erst ans Tageslicht fördern. So viel ist gewiß, daß, so Gott will, der Polterabend am 25sten Dec. bei uns, Hensels, im Gartenhause gefeiert wird, mit kleiner, junger, lustiger Gesellschaft, u. so vielen Possen, als im Reiche des Humors nur irgend aufzutreiben sind. Der Tag geht vorüber, am Hochzeittage selbst werden Vormittags die verschiedenen gratulirenden Behörden empfangen, u. Mittags speißt die könig. Familie unter uns u. bei uns, denn man muß sich nicht zu sehr fatigiren, weil Abends bei Euch große Musik ist, die [neue] Hochlandssymphonie kommt vor, das Scherzo mit den luftigen d Trompeten muß [ ] dreinklingen, u. Sommernachtstraum u. Meeresstille unvergessen bleiben. Was die älteste Otter betrifft, so möchte sie ihr kleines Laternchen lieber am Polterabend unter Wenigen leuchten lassen, denn erstens ist sie dumm, u. zweitens blöde, u. drittens kann sie nischt. Sie würde sich aber von ihrem Gemahl etwas dichten lassen, u. es auf Noten setzen. Auch der junge Hofdichter Droysen hat seine Dienste angeboten. Je mehr, desto besser. Du, o Bruder, mußt wieder eine [kindliche] Symphonie kneten, eine von denen, wo Mutter sich schon bei den Vorbereitungen todtlacht, u. die muß den Anfang des Ganzen machen. Ein Ball findet etwa in der Woche darauf beim silbernen Ehepaare statt, das Londoner Kind wird wol keinen Wunsch vergebens äußern. Das soll ein Leben werden, Felix, ein Leben! Ich versichere Dich, ich kann mir nichts darüber, u. nichts danach denken, jede Minute ein Feiertag, nicht jeder soll ein Lump. Und das versichere ich Dich, bei mir sollst Du ungestört spielen, keine Maus darf sich rühren, alle Rührung geschieht innerlich. Hensel ist gut, Felix, u. ich bin im weitesten Sinne des Worts, zufrieden, glücklicher als ich je es zu werden dachte, denn ich träumte, u. fürchtete, eine solche Verbindung würde mich von Dir losreißen, oder doch entfernen, u. es ist, *wo möglich,* grade das Gegentheil, ich habe mehr Bewußtseyn gewonnen, als früher, u. daher bin ich Dir näher, ich denke mehr, daher denke ich mehr an Dich, u. je mehr ich habe, je mehr ich haben werde, desto mehr werde ich Dich brauchen u. haben. Es ist nicht möglich, daß Du mir je von Deiner Liebe etwas entziehst, denn Du mußt es wissen, wie ich, daß ich nicht den kleinsten Theil davon entbehren kann. Ich werde Dir an meinem Hochzeittage dasselbe wiederholen, denn bis jetzt habe ich noch keine Empfindung u. keine Stellung kennengelernt, in der ich nicht dasselbe gedacht u. gesagt hätte. Zu dem [Allem] sieht Dein Bild sehr freundlich u. lieblich aus, es ist gestern, an Hensels Geburtstage, viel daran gemalt worden, u. heut kommt er wieder, er will an der einen Hand noch ein Weniges retouchiren, u. dazu soll ich sitzen. Die Angelegenheit mit dem Atelier ist nun auch so gut, als beendet, zu meiner großer Freude, dies Luisenstift ist so nah, u. der Weg durch die Gärten (falls ihm das Durchbrechen der Thür gestatten wird) so angenehm, daß wir es uns wirklich nicht besser hätten wünschen können. Dies Plätzchen hebe ich mir für morgen auf, doch noch eins, die Mädchen sind so toll nach dem kleinen Vater, daß Du wirklich von London aus Ordnung machen mußt, es ist zu toll, wenn Caroline und Beckchen nicht neben ihm sitzen, würden sie eben so gern gar nicht essen. Sie machen ihn eitel, u. dann muß wieder erzogen werden.

Mittwoch. Ich habe Dir nun weiter nichts mehr zu berichten, als von einer miserablen Aufführung der Iphigenie, Mlle. Schechner wurde vor dem Anfang als plötzlich unpäßlich, des Publicums Nachsicht empfohlen, u. bedurfte derselben auch gar sehr. Außerdem ist es wirklich schrecklich, wenn man solch ein Stück so kennt, u. es dann hört, daß auch nicht ein einziger Takt entsprechend dargestellt wird. Adieu, mein Felix, ich schreibe gern noch sofort, dann fällt mir aber immer ein, was Du immer gesagt hast, u. was immer falsch ist, daß man von Zu Hause nicht schreiben könne, ich glaube aber, es ist so, Männer müssen von Reisen schreiben, u. Frauen von zu Hause, die bringen dann jeden wohlbekannten Sandkorn aufs Tapet, u. das erfreut in der Fremde. Heut Abend kommen Devrients her, er wird uns wohl Deinen Brief mitbringen, der ihm außerordentlich viel Freude gemacht hat. Hier fällt mir endlich einmal zu rechten Zeit ein Auftrag ein, den mir Zelter vor sehr langer Zeit gegeben hat, u. der ich immer vergaß, ob Dir nämlich in London nicht deutsche Motetten von Händel vorgekommen seyen, dann möchte er gern die Titel, u. sonst einiges Nähere davon wissen. Leb wohl. Deine Fanny.

[Lea, Rebecka]

Zelter schickt so eben einen Brief an Dich, ich werde ihn auch mit nächster Gesandschaft befördern, glaube aber nicht, daß er Dich noch trifft. Ach lieber Felix, ich möchte Dir noch so Vieles sagen, u. immer wenn ich aufhören soll, kommt mir alles Gesagte so unzulänglich vor, aber alles geht auf in dem einzigen Wort, wir lieben Dich, u. Du bist so der Klügste u. der Beste, daß Du unsern Rath u. unser Besserwissen noch nicht bedurft hast. Aber wir meinens eben so gut, u. Du nimmst es eben so gut hin. Adieu. Das Wetter ist hunde, eben jetzt läßt sichs die Sonne einfallen, ein wenig zu scheinen, u. da will ich einen Augenblick in den Garten springen. In Klingemanns prächtigem Brief hat uns die Urlaubsschwierigkeit erschreckt, ich hoffe, zur Stunde ist sie überwunden, u. ihr werdet auch kostbar amüsiren. Wäre doch Deine Küstenreise zu Stande gekommen.

[Lea]

Nun Gott sey Dank, war mein imseitiges,[b] geheimes Schreiben eines von den drei Dingen, die es seyn konnte,[c] nämlich überflüßig, nach dem Schönen, was Dir Mutter schreibt. Auch versichere ich Dich, ich hätte, um Dir zu schreiben, Deinen Brief erst abwarten sollen, denn nun ist der Katzenjammer vorbei. Du kannst Dir nicht leicht etwas Lächerlicheres denken, als wir am Mittwoch, ehe Dein Brief kommt, u. wenn er da ist. Heut unter Andern saßen wir sentimental in der Küche, Schoten pelend, weil—der Briefträger über den Hof kommt. Und er kam, der Gute, u. wir sprangen auf, (von hier an ist alles Lüge bis zum Segno) die armen Schoten rollten behend in der Küche umher, die trägeren Schaalen hinter drein, u. der Küchenteller hatte Mühe, sich vor unsrer Hast zu retten. Wir fielen dem Manne in den Arm, rissen ihm den Brief ent—*Mutter öffnete ihn, u. während sie die 2te las ich die erste Seite flüchtig, dann konnte ich nicht weiter, denn ich heulte, u. schämte mich vor Vater. So habe ich denn Deine Freude noch gar nicht recht schwarz auf weiß gesehn, denn Vater, der sich freilich wenig ungeduldig anstellt als wir, riß uns dennoch den Brief aus der Hand, u. vermittelst Rechtes des Stärkeren, trug er ihn in der Droschke davon, u. bringt ihn erst zu Mittag wieder. Mutter hat mir indessen mündlich über eine Wette berichtet die über irgend einen 21te Takt schwebe, das Lied hatte sie vergessen, ich habe indessen nachgezählt, u. gefunden, daß es im dritten seyn müsse, wo die Stimme auf das Wort "leiden" h, a, g hat, u. in der Begl. beider Hände f vorkommt, fa, wie könnte es anders seyn? Habe ich mich verschrieben an der Stelle? In Eil berichte ich Dir noch, daß Dein Bild an Deinem Geburtstage 2 Küsse erhalten hat, von den beiden lieben Mädchen, die sich zu Anfange dieses Briefs unterschrieben haben. Mutter läßt Dich bitten, nichts auf den Schluß ihres Briefs zu antworten, u. nun zum 6000 mal Lebewohl.

[Rebecka, Lea]

---

[a]Fanny omitted the umlaut; perhaps this was an accepted spelling.
[b]Fanny may have meant to write "umseitiges," or else this was an earlier form of the word.
[c]Fanny omitted the umlaut.

25

So eben habe ich meinen großen Generalbrief an Dich beendet, lieber Felix, u. muß man diese kleine Privatdepesche hinzufügen, deren Inhalt folgender ist: Es ist Vater plötzlich aufgefallen, daß in mehreren englischen Blättern Dein Name blos Felix Mendelssohn genannt worden, u. er glaubt eine Absicht darin zu erkennen, u. will Dir heut darüber schreiben, wie uns Mutter gestern sagte, die es ihm auszureden versucht hat. Ob er es nun noch ausführen wird, oder nicht, weiß ich nicht, bin aber gestern Abend mit Hensel übereingekommen, Dir in jedem Fall diesen Brief zu schreiben, ist er unnütz, so schadet er auch nicht, möglicher Weise kann er Dir lieb seyn, u. ist er Dir unangenehm, so verzeihst Du ihn mir.—Ich kenne u. billige Deine Absicht, diesen Namen, den wir alle nicht lieben, einst wieder abzulegen, aber jetzt kannst Du es noch nicht, da Du minorenn bist, u. ich habe nicht nöthig, Dich auf die unangenehmen Folgen aufmerksam zu machen, die es für Dich haben könnte, es wird Dir genug seyn, zu wissen, daß Du Vater dadurch betrübst. Du kannst es jetzt leicht, auf Befragen, für ein Versehn gelten lassen, u. Deinen Vorsatz zu gelegnerer Zeit ausführen.—Die eigentliche Absicht dieses Briefs ist, Dich einiger Maßen über die Sorge der Zeit u. Entfernung hinwegzuheben, die

Dir Vaters Schreiben machen möchte. Wie Du selbst noch neulich schriebst, die Buchstaben sind so kalt, u. todt, u. es ist so leicht, den richtigen Vortrag zu verfehlen, Vater namentlich schreibt immer weniger angenehm als er denkt, so daß wir Dir gern über diesen Gegenstand noch einige freundlichere Worte wollten zukommen lassen. Es kann seyn, daß es Dich herzlich verdrießt, wenn Du hier zum drittenmal lesen sollst, was Dir Vater auf eine, u. vielleicht Mutter auf eine andre Weise schreibt, aber dann, wie gesagt, verzeihst Du uns eine übel ausgeführte gute Absicht, wir kennen uns, denke ich, u. Alles bleibt beim Alten. Es macht mir wenig Spaß, daß Du, der Du uns nur Gutes zukommen läßt, so oft von hier aus Unangenehmes zu erfahren hast, u. daß sich Dir grade in dieser Beziehung das häusliche Leben in der Fremde fortsetzt, ich wollte stark, es wäre anders, es ist nun aber einmal so, u. Gottlob, es geht in vielem Guten auf.—Wie wird es nun auf Deiner bevorstehenden Reise werden? Werden wir Briefe erhalten, so regelmäßig, wie bis jetzt? Ich denke mit Schrecken an den ersten Mittwoch, wo einer aus bleibt, denn wenn Mittag heran kommt, u. noch keiner da ist, fangen wir an, uns sehr ungebärdig zu betragen. Nun Du wirst schon sorgen. Adieu mein Felix, ich schicke diesen Brief an Hensel, der noch einige Zeilen dazu setzen, u. ihn selbst auf die Post bringen will. Du weißt, wie es Dich immer verdroß, wenn die Eltern Dir ihre Zufriedenheit verbargen, denselben Verdruß setzt uns Vater fort, indem er gleichgültig u. stoisch thut, u. wir ihn dann drüber ertappen, wie er Deine Briefe zu drei-viermal liest, u. wie alle Leute wissen u. sehn, wie er sich über Dich u. Alles was Dir begegnet, freut, nur wir sollen es nicht wissen. Wir wissen es aber doch. Und so lebe wohl, u. froh u. glücklich. Es sind mir während ich hier schrieb, zwei Augenwimpern aus u. aufs Papier gefallen, wenn die bis nach London kämen, würdest Du wissen, von wem der Brief ist.

[Wilhelm]

26

Montag, den 13 Juli
Während Deines Concerts.

Ich fange diesmal recht früh mit Schreiben an, weil ich Dir, mein liebster Felix, gern recht viel sagen möchte. Erstlich möchte ich Dir gern so danken, wie mich Dein Brief beglückt hat, u. da hat schon die Sache ein Ende. Gelesen u. wieder gelesen habe ich Deinen Brief, wie Du meine Lieder, u. weiß ihn eben so gut auswendig, u. wenn ich damit zu Ende bin, denke ich immer noch eine kleine Coda dazu, die heißt: wie bin ich armes Schaf doch so glücklich, daß ich Dir solche Freude habe machen können, u. dann singe ich mir den Schluß des 2ten Liedes, das mir allerdings auch immer am Besten gefallen hat, u. finde ihn gar nicht übel. Ich bin doch begierig, mit wem Du über die falschen Noten gewettet hast, da es noch niemand, als Sir George gesehn hatte, u. mit dem wirst Du doch kein Diner wetten. Was Dein Brief nächstdem für eine vortreffliche Wirkung auf Paul gethan hat, das kannst Du kaum glauben, ich finde ihn wesentlich verändert seit dem Tage, u. muß mit tausend Freuden wieder einmal bekennen, daß Du überall, u. immerfort das belebende, bessernde, reinigende, durch Liebe erziehende Prinzip bist. Was ich an Paul immer geschätzt habe, so lange er bei Besinnung ist, ist daß er keine Spur von Neid, sondern nur Liebe für Dich hat, obgleich er sehr wohl weiß, daß Ihr verschieden begabt seyd. Er ist jetzt fleißig u. brav, u. wenn ihm seine Sachen zuweilen etwas schwer wird,[a] so bedenke ich gern, daß H. Vonhalle kein angenehmer Mann ist, u. daß Lehrjahre überhaupt nicht rosenfarb aussehn, es müßten denn Wilhelm Meister seine seyn, u. da möchte ich denn doch, daß Paul mehr darin lernte. Der Kerl ist mir verhaßt, nicht wie alle schlechte Gesellschaft, denn Shakespeare hat bessere schlechte Gesellschaft. Wie leid war es mir, daß ich Dich nicht schon vor 8 T. Wilhelm Horns Adresse konnte wissen lassen, der Brief kam zu spät, Du brauchst nur an den Baron Delmar zu adressiren, bei dem Horn jetzt zu meinem größten Erstaunen, [ ]remistisich Beckers Stelle vertritt, da dieser nach Deutschland zurückgegangen ist. Horn hat zu gleicher Zeit hier sich nach Deiner Adresse erkundigt, Deine Briefe müssen ihm also nicht zugekommen seyn. Was triffst Du für Einrichtungen für Deine schottische Reise, werden wir fortwährend an Doxat schicken? Es ist hübsch, wie wir jetzt Beide nach unsrer Bestimmung leben, Du so frisch in der Welt umhersiehst, u. Dir in den drei Königreichen Platz siehst, weil Dir etwa das Eine zu eng ist, u. ich so still u. zufrieden meiner neuen

Existenz entgegen sehn u. gehn, die sich ganz ruhig u. langsam nach grade aufbaut. Nun einmal denke ich auch noch umherzuschauen, denn Hensel hält den Gedanken sehr fest, mich nach Italien zu führen, wenn Du da bist, u. so unausführbar mir der Plan auch noch immer scheint, so lieb habe ich ihn doch. Du ziehst uns nach, wir die Eltern u. das Kind, das nicht allein hier bleiben darf. Für Paul ist mir weniger bange, ihn wird sein Weg schon allein in die Welt führen, u. weiter vielleicht, als uns. So wäre denn mancherlei ganz hübsch eingefädelt, wie viel sich davon erfüllen mag, werden wir erleben. *Dienstag* Eben geht Betty Pistor fort, wir haben ihr die Lieder vorgeführt, nachdem wir einen langen Prolog von Dir gesprochen hatten. Wir führten uns alte Zeiten u. viele Spatziergänge vor, u. namentlich den Einen, als Gans u. ein gewisser Pole uns verlassen hatten, u. wir nun in den Straßen umher zogen, u. von den gegenwärtigen Zeiten als von zukünftigen sprächen. Dann kamen die Lieder, u. dann ward ein langer Epilog vor Deinem Bilde gehalten. Du mußt Dir nämlich die Sache so vorstellen. Das Bild steht auf einer Staffelei im Saal, vor dem großen Secretär, gegen das Fenster, im Fenster steht, wenn Du Dich erinnerst, eine Reihe Stühle, auf diesen saßen wir, man hat da das Bild hübsch bequem zur Seite, kann nicht aufs[t]ehn, ohne es anzusehn, u. das ist Einem grade recht. Wenn man sichs nur abgewöhnen könnte, den ganzen Mittwoch Vormittag im Fieber zu sitzen, u. die längsten u. abgeschmacktesten Gesichter zu schneiden, bis der schöne Mann kommt, der Briefträger, u. den schöneren Mann bringt, den Brief. Dieser "schöne Mann" hat eine Geschichte erlebt, er ist erst, wegen Mißbrauchs, von der Censur des Redes selbst, gestrichen worden, aber seitdem nur mit desto größerer Lebhaftigkeit wieder aufgelebt.—Tausend Grüße für Dich u. Klingemann von Auguste [v.] Le Fort, die gestern abgereist ist, u. uns einen langen Abschiedsbesuch gemacht hat. Sie ist überglückselig, u. unstreitig eine liebenswürdige Person. Sage nur Klingemann, wir erinnerten uns ganz wohl, daß voriges Jahr ganz Europa sich verschworen habe, ihm keine Brieftasche zur Reise zu schenken, da wir aber dies Jahr zu Schottland ein ähnliches Complott vermutheten, haben wir ihm vorgebeugt, u. eine besorgt, leider können wir sie ihm nicht mehr zu rechter Zeit zukommen lassen, u. er wird sie wohl bei seiner Rückkunft von Schottland finden. So auch Du die Musik von Marx, liebster Felix. Ich habe sie ihm bis jetzt noch immer nicht abdringen können, nun hoffe ich sie aber nächstens zu erhalten (die veränderte Ouvert. zur Ondine nämlich,) u. werde dann Alles mit nächster Gelegenheit absenden, bisher [. . .]

[Rebecka, Lea, Abraham, Rebecka, Lea]

Es ist Mittwoch Vormittag, u. d. h. so viel, als, eben empfingen wir

Deinen Brief, worin Du leider wieder klagst, den unsrigen nicht erhalten zu haben, da wir doch jedesmal pünktlich auf die Post schicken. Der Gedanke, daß fortan die Korrespondenz unregelmäßiger werden wird, fällt mir recht schwer, aber wie wir uns auf Mühlenfels freuen, das ist unbeschreiblich, ich fürchte stark, wir fallen ihm um den Hals. Ja, mein Kind, wir wollen ihn verziehn, wir wollen ihm Lieblingsgerichte machen lassen, wir wollen ihn achten, u. von ihm geachtet werden, kurz, es soll ihm wohl ergehn. Dein Cadenzbrei ist prächtig, sobald ich hier fertig bin mit Schreiben, werde ich mich besinnen, wo er hingehört. Also Moscheles spielt meinen Part, so dachte ich mirs auch. Fanny Magnus u. Victoire haben sich gestern stark nach Dir erkundigt, wir waren in Charlottenburg zu Tante Meyers Geburtstag.—Wie gefällt Dir ein Mainzer Jude, der wegen Betrügereien eingesteckt wurde, u.: "Judemann Beer Doctor" heißt? Ich habs gesperrt geschrieben, sonst glaubts keine Christenseele. Adieu Leben, ich nehme gewissermaßen Abschied von England, dieser Brief trifft Dich ja auch nicht mehr da. Möge es Dir immerdar gut gehn, in England bist Du zwar ein Engel, sey aber in Schottland kein Schote u. in Irland kein Irrender, sondern gut. Leb wohl.

[Rebecka]

---

[a]Fanny incorrectly wrote "wird" instead of "werden."

27

Berlin, den 15sten August 29.

Das Rad.

Was ist das Rad? Es erklärt nur sich selber, versteht auch nur sich allein, u. ist eine moralische Person. Beigehendes Aktenstück schrieb es Dir bei einer fröhlichen Zusammenkunft in Charlottenburg, am Johannistage, und sein Abgang ward verzögert, weil das folgende Aktenstück, eine bildliche Darstellung, an jenem Tage in freien, großen Bleistiftskizzen entworfen worden war, u. nachher theilweis zur Vollendung gedieh.

Bedarf es einer Erklärung? Kennst Du nicht den Jüngling in der Mitte, die Axe des Rades in englischem Frack und schottischen Zubehör? Sieht er nicht hier aus wie ein Regimentshoboist? Aber nach seiner Pfeife tanzt und dreht sich die ganze feine Gesellschaft. Fische schneiden ihn vom Continent ab, und ein neugieriger Delphin nascht ihm die frischgeschriebene Musik aus der Tasche. Die ihm auf den Kopf tritt, ist unverkennbar die Behörde im blauen Mantel, sie hing ihn um an jenem Tage, obwohl es sehr heiß war, u. die Fausthandschuh schützten ihre Hände gegen die Mücken. Das C über ihrem Kopfe, der Mond mit dem Mann im Monde, wird Dir verrathen, was Du noch nicht weißt. Die zierliche Gestalt neben ihr tanzt Galopp mit Deinem Schatten, da Du nicht bei der Hand bist. Das A stellt einem Fruchtbäumchen dar, an dem ein Männchen auf einer Leiter heranklettert. Das F ist ein Wegweiser, mit der Inschrift Berlin. Der freundlich Gebückte, der mit der einen Hand den Knäuel der Nachbarin hält, und mit der anderen eine silberne Schüssel präsentirt (Klara Ponsin) trägt Dir Dein Lieblingsgericht entgegen, einen Mohrenkopf. Einheit der Zeit u. des Orts ist wie Du siehst, recht beobachtet, denn dieser Handlung nach müßte die Scene diesen Sonntag Abends in der Leipziger Str. seyn, aber eine des D spielt auf eine Radgeschichte ein, in der bekanntlich zwar kein Jude, aber doch ein Oberlehrer ins Wasser fiel. Er steht mit ausgestreckten Armen u. man sieht ihn schreien, während eine Nixe nach seinem Füße schnappt. Der Knäuel führt uns auf dem nächsten Wege zum Strickstrumpf, u. seiner Herrin. Ich denke Du wirst Nasens Schwester nicht verkennen. Ihr M schreitet, als ehrbare Menuett einher. Der sich da kühnen Schwunges ins Rad wälzt, u. sich zugleich ungerechter Weise als Hemmschuh behandelt hat, denn er ist wahrlich kein Hemmschuh an diesem Rade, der hat keinen Anspruch von mir gelobt, oder nur einge[führt] zu werden, denn was geht er mich an? Ich habe zwar die Kette, an der er liegt, in Händen, aber was will das sagen? (Ich wurde auch einmal angebetet.) Ueber die zwei dummen, zusammengewachsenen Fischottern will ich weiter kein Wort verlieren, denn daß das B aus zwei seltsam gruppirten Böckchen besteht, u. das F. durch ein Fernrohr nach London kuckt, kann Dir nicht entgehn. Als es so gezeichnet wurde, war es wahr, u. wenn Dus eröffnest, ist es wieder wahr. Der nun folgende schöne Mann schnitt, als er konter[feit] wurde, gerade Silhouetten aus Lindenblättern und kuckte mit der Nase recht emsig auf sein Geschäft. Das Blättergesicht ist nur zum Silbermond geworden, u. sonst ist er tale quale abgeschrieben. Sein H zeigt Dir zwei moderne Balletttänzer. Das Andre verschweig ich, doch weiß es die Welt. Uebrigens ist diese Ueberschrift auch nicht ohne Beziehung, denn der schöne Mann trug an jenem Tage schwarze Strümpfe u. Schuh mit langen Schleifen zu weißen Unaussprechlichen, was sich absonderlich gut ausnahm. Die kleine Person mit den großen Mamelucks, die nun kömmt, knüpft sich den Ermel zu, Du wirst wol noch wissen, warum, (ich aber weiß nicht, warum über ihrem Kopfe sich zwei Personen zu einem freundschaftlichen *A* die Hände reichen?) sie hält eine Blume, welche dem Herrn Bruder bis an die Nase wächst, der dankbar einen Thautropfen in der Kelch der Blume legt. Ich behauptete immer es sey ein Silbergroschen, der kleine Kerl oben bläst ins Alphorn, u. ruft: Hule hule Gänsechen, kommt zu Haus.

Von weiteren Dingen, u. näheren Beziehungen nichts in diesem Briefe, der Dir zu spät zu Handen kommt.

28

Berlin den 21sten August 29

Ich will mich eben hinsetzen, um einen Brief zu schreiben, einen andern Brief, aber ich kann den Tag nicht anfangen, ohne die Antwort. Felix, Bruder, Engel, was soll ich Dir sagen? Noch ist nichts überlegt, nichts besprochen, aber Beckchen hat mir Deinen Brief vorgelesen, u. ich bin froh, Dir sagen zu können, daß ichs mit Hensel schon lange so ausgemacht, wie Dus geschrieben. Noch weiß ich nicht recht, wie? aber es soll, es muß werden. An mir liegt es, mir hat Hensel die Entscheidung anheimgestellt, was mich zurückhielt, war eines Theils die Sorgen um einen zu langen Aufenthalt, anderseits Beckchen, die ich mich nicht entschließen konnte, so zurück zu lassen, denn ich bin ihr Vieufelix,[a] das hör ich gern, u. es macht mich froh, nun für diese Sorge beruf ich mich auf Dich, u. die andre—ich weiß nicht, es ist mir heut alles so hell u. klar vor den Augen, als ob es gar keine Schwierigkeit in der Welt gäbe. Was Du Beckchen Liebes geschrieben, davon nehm' ich mir meine Hälfte, wie ich sie ihr auch immer gegeben habe. Denn wir sind u. bleiben die Geren, u. bist der Clown, u. wenn Du je aufhörst, Dich zwischen uns auf den Sopha zu setzen! Zwischen uns, hörst Du? Aber das wird nicht aufhören, denk ich, u. wir werdens einmal in einer andern Zone probiren. Denn Hensel u. ich wir habens so ausgemalt: Wenn wir Alle zusammen bis Neapel gereist sind, u. die Eltern dann Furcht haben vor der Seereise, so steigen wir vier ins Schiff, u. fahren nach Sicilien, u. wenn wir uns die Sache da angesehn haben, so steigen wir wieder ins Schiff, u. fahren nach Malta; u. wenns da sehr heiß ist, u. sehr blau, u. einem die Orangen über den Kopf hängen, u. man bei heiterm Tage die weiße Küste von Africa sieht, so erzählst Du uns von Staffa u. den Hebriden.—Ich denke wir haben uns unser Leben gut eingerichtet, u. wenn der liebe Gott ja sagt, u. alles gelingen läßt, so können wir einige leidliche Jahre erleben. Und nun nach alle dem das ruhige

Zusammenfinden in Berlin, wo wir, ich meine Du u. Hensel, von der leipziger Straße aus ziemlich weit ausgreifen werden, es wird passabel seyn.

[Rebecka]

den 25sten August. Du kennst selbst aus Erfahrung so gewisse Knoten von Begebenheiten, Tage und Wochen, wo so viel zusammen kommt, daß man gern an Jedes allein denken möchte. So waren für mich die Tage, in denen Dein Brief ankam, es drängte und wälzte sich Alles übereinander. Ein Theil ist nun schon aufgelöst, und das Andre geht langsam vorwärts. Mit der Bestimmung unsrer Hochzeit ist es noch, wie es war, das letzte Aufgebot am 20sten da Vater noch in Hamburg, und die ganze Wohnung noch einzurichten ist, nebst Töpfen und Schüsseln, Dir Deine Lieblingsgerichte zu bereiten, so ist der Tag noch nicht genau zu bestimmen. Bestimme Du aber, o Felix, um was ich Dich gebeten habe. Ich habe meinen Orgelausgang schon ziemlich im Kopfe. G dur, Pedal fängt an. Ueberhaupt bin ich recht froh, zu der Ueberzeugung gelangt zu seyn, daß der Brautstand meiner Musik nicht geschadet hat. Habe ich nun erst ein gutes Stück im Ehestande gemacht, dann bin ich durch, und glaube an ein ferneres Fortschreiten. Aber, nicht wahr? Besseres wie die Lieder für Dich habe ich noch nicht gemacht, und das Stück von und für Hensel ist auch nicht übel. Was ich aber jetzt für große u. größte Rosinen im Kopf habe, das möchte ich Dir eigentlich gar nicht sagen, aus Furcht, bei Nummer 1 stecken zu bleiben—ei was, ich wills Dir erzählen, hör zu. Joh. Gust. Droysen, sagte mir mal vor einiger Zeit, er fände es gar nicht übel, wenn die Lieder, die man so machte, einen gewissen innerlichen Zusammenhang hätten, so einen Faden, u. ob ich wol erlaubte, daß er so 'nen Faden suchte, u. da Lieder dran aufzöge. Ich erlaubte. Da kam er wieder nach einiger Zeit u. frug, ob mir die Sage von Loreley gefiele? Ich genehmigte, da brachte er mir seinen Plan. Aber das Ding war zu undramatisch für ein Stück, zu dramatisirt für eine Sage, kurz nicht recht Fisch u. Fleisch. Zu gleicher Zeit da ich sah, daß es ernst, u. groß wurde, wünschte ich doch sehr, daß mein gekünftiger Eheherr Theil an der Arbeit nähme, u. so versprach mir dieser auf mein Bitten, einen 2ten Theil zu schreiben, wenn Droysen seinen ersten dramatischer machen könne. Kurz, die Sache wuchs u. dehnte sich aus, bis ich nun ein großes Stück in drei Theilen vor mir habe, das heißt, den [Entwurf] dazu, an den wir noch immer herum schustern u. schneidern, u. ihn Droysen in dies[en] Tagen zu überliefern denken.—Deinen Auftrag haben wir ihm ausgerichtet. Wir gingen am Sonntag mit ihm aus der Gesellschaft, die im Saal versammelt war, nach der blauen Stube, u. führten uns die Sache lebendig vor Augen. Er wird schreiben.—Und nun laß mich noch einen Augenblick mich freuen, über heut und morgen. Hensel wird mir jeden Tag lieber, und dem Himmel sey Dank, ich glaube, daß er immer glücklicher wird. Und wenn er nun zurückkommt aus den Niederlanden da wollen wir Familie ein sehr nettes Leben führen. Du bringst viel Neues mit, findest viel Neues vor, u. ich stehe Dir dafür, die Zeit soll uns nicht lang werden. Hör mal, Deine Hebriden sind passabel, und die beiden Geigen sagen nicht umsonst so lange fis. Mir wurde seltsam dabei zu Muthe, wie Dir. Adieu Felix, nun bekommt Hensel den Brief. Wir sind die Alten noch geblieben.

[Hensel]

---

[a]Fanny omitted the "x" of "vieux."

29

[Rebecka]

31 August. Du hast einen Freund, der heißt Eda, u. spielt passabel die Geige. Gestern war die letzte Quartettversammlung vor Davids Abreise. Sie haben unglaublich gespielt. c dur von Beethoven, a moll von Felix u. die Wanderfuge. O Jeses o Jeses o Jeses wie haben sie gespielt. Donnerstag reist David, er war gestern gerührt, u. ich weiß nicht, Eduard hat jetzt eine Zeit, wo er so ganz, so ganz wunderbar schön spielt, wie etwa den letzten Abend vor Deiner Abreise. Freitag hatten wir auch 4tett, da spielten sie (David) einen Haydn, dann Ritz a moll u. f moll von Beethoven. So schön gings nicht wie gestern. Nun höre eine große Neuigkeit, eine Neuigkeit über die das Rad in Thränen zerfließt. Du findest Albert Heydemann nicht mehr hier, er geht zum ersten Okt. nach Stettin, auf dem dortigen Gymnasium sein Jahr als Oberlehrer abzudienen. Wo kann Nase sonst hin als auf ein Gym*nas*ium? Er ist sehr gutes Muthes dabei, u. freut sich sehr, Berlin einmal von Ferne zu besehen, uns ists schon weniger lieb. Aber Louis meint auch, es sey ihm außerordentlich wünschenswerth, und so muß man schon damit zufrieden seyn. Es ist jetzt wieder so eine Zeit, wo Mehreres abfällt, u. nichts Neues hinzukommt. Wir müssen sehn, den Rest zusammen zu halten. Im Ganzen genommen, wirst Du bei Deiner Rückkehr mehr eingeschränkt, als verändert finden. David u. Heydemann gehn fort, Gans kommt seltner, mehrere Unbedeutende haben sich auch weggezogen, u. kein Neuer ist hinzugekommen, dagegen in der letzten Zeit viele Fremde, Dir als Zugvögel ein vorübergehendes Leben mitgebracht haben, u. deren Spuren Du in Hensels Büchern finden wirst.

Hensel hat Frl. v. Heister angefangen zu malen, ich weiß nicht, ob ich es Dir schon geschrieben habe, im Hofkleide u. großer Pracht. Jetzt hat er eine Gliederpuppe mit ihren Kleidern angezogen, u. führt sie danach aus, u. ärgert sich, daß das Ding so schrecklich ruhig sitzt, u. meint, dafür hätte er lieber eine Sitzung von Gans. Daß Beckchen bis auf mein Zahnweh lächerlich machen will, ist doch sehr grausam, findest Du es wol sehr komisch, daß ich seit 14 Tagen rechts u. links leide, mir vergebens einem Zahn habe ausreißen lassen, u. einen sehr verbundenen Kopf trage? Ich wette, Du würdest, wenn Du hier wärest, meinen Kopf zwischen Deine beiden Hände nehmen, u. ihn schütteln, u. mich sehr bedauern. Ich sagte gestern einmal zu Ritz, ich hoffte, Du würdest ihn in Holywell gehört haben, ich meinte das hohe c im e dur 4tett, u. nachher spielte er noch ähnliche Töne in Deinem Quartett u. dem Schluß der Reisefuge. Mr. Thomson sagte, Du habest das Quartett bei Mr. Hogarth gespielt. Er verlangte eine Handschrift von Dir, ich habe ihm das Lied gegeben: laß dich nur nichts nicht dauern. Es war das einzige Entbehrliche.

[Rebecka, F. David]

2ten Sept. Obenunterschriebener David hat jetzt einen beträchtlichen Katzenjammer, was Abreise betrifft, er geht ungern, u. ich habe ihn auf alle Instrumente u. Seligkeiten versprechen müssen, ihn Dein Quartett aus B.P. dur, wie Klingemann sagt, zu schicken.—Marx hat mir die ersten Sätze aus dem russischen Festspiel mitgetheilt, u. ich habe ihm meine Meinung darüber gesagt. Das was ich ihm vorwarf, daß nämlich viele Sätze nicht gehörig abgeschlossen, u. ins Gespräch geworfen, zu kurz seyen, fand er ganz wahr, warf aber die Schuld auf Droysen zurück. Uebrigens kennst Du ja seine Musik, weißt also, was u. wie viel schön darin ist. Der Sept. hat nun auch ohne schön Wetter begonnen, nun muß man wol alle Hoffnung für dies Jahr aufgeben. Wie ich vermuthe, wird dieser Brief Dich schon wieder in London treffen, ich freue mich, Dich bald auf [d]em Festlande zu wissen, da der Herbst [ ] Stürme dies Jahr gewiß sehr früh eintreten, oder vielmehr gar nicht aufgehört haben. Der Rest ist schnell abgethan, u. ehe wirs uns versehn, klopft der December an die Thür, u. mit ihm ein Reisender, der nicht an die Thür zu klopfen braucht. Wir werden denn singen, o angenehme Winterszeit. Vater schreibt uns die allerlustigsten Briefe nach Berlin mit allen möglichen Neuigkeiten, nur kein Wort von seinem Wiederkommen oder Weiterreisen. Weißt Du uns nichts Näheres darüber zu berichten? Du weißt doch sonst die Dinge lange ehe sie entschieden sind. Jetzt läugne noch einmal Einer, daß Pauline Bendemann Hübner geheirathet hat. Du hasts lange gesagt, John Thomson u. ich, wir haben uns mit Musik beworfen. Er hat eine Menge gedrückte Sachen, u. einen geschriebenen Rondo hier gelassen, dafür habe ich ihn auf Verlangen ein manuscript of mine gegeben, wenn Dus je zu sehn kriegst, lachst Du Dich todt.

[J. Thomson]

Dieser Obenunterschriebene trat eben ein, als ich schrieb, vor 2 Stunden, u. da er hier eingeregnet ist, u. ich also nicht das Ende des Abschiedsbesuches absehe, ergreife ich die Partie in seiner Gegenwart weiter zu schreiben, der Mittwoch ist immer ein geschäftvoller Tag, u. wenn gar die Briefe kommen, ist es wie bei einem Finale, dann drängt u. treibt Alles durch einander, u. macht einen gräulichen Lärm. Seit Vater fort ist, schlafen wir Beide bei Mutter im Zimmer, u. machen immer sehr viel dummes Zeug. Heut früh lachten Mutter u. Beckchen sehr, weil ich sagte, als wir noch im Bette lagen: heut kommt ein Brief u. die Malon. Die Malon ist da, u. der Esel steht mit nachahmenswerther Ruhe auf dem Hof, während es Keulen regnet, aber der Brief ist noch nicht da. Es schreibt sich doch nicht gut, während einer engl. Conversation, die nebenbei geführt wird. Lebe so wohl, ich bin von nun an unzurechnungsfähig. Hensel grüßt Dich siebenhunderttausendmal, u. hat es mit heut noch schriftlich aufgetragen. Adieu Seele, grüß Klingemann vielmals. Er soll uns bald auf unsern letzten Brief antworten, u. Gutes, er weiß schon. Ich weiß nicht warum, ich schreibe schon so lange nichts, u. kann kein Ende finden; ich stehe etwa bei Dir oben auf der Stube, mit der Klinke in der Hand, während Du recht viel zu thun hast, u. störe Dich, u. kann nicht fort. Jetzt hast Du wol schon die gewisse komische Zeichnung, die ich nicht nenne, im Fall Du sie nicht hast, ich hoffe, sie hat Dir Spaß gemacht. Daß Du alle Personen erkennst, zweifle ich nicht. Adieu denn, zum tausendstenmal.

[Rebecka, Lea]

30

Leipziger Straße No 3
den 21sten Sept.

[Rebecka]

Dienstag den 22 Sept. Sitzt Deine älteste Gere wieder mit verbundenem Gesicht, weil sie sich einen 3ten Zahn hat müssen ausziehn lassen. Glaube aber nicht, daß dieser abwesende Zahn, oder diese anwesende dicke Backe mir menschenfeindliche Gesinnungen einflößen, oder irgend unsre Polterabendsconferenzen beeinträchtigen könnten. Ich stehe über mir selbst, und kenne mich u. die Welt (patetico) zur Sache. Abgesetzt, von meinem Posten verwiesen, meiner jüngeren Schwester untergeordnet, hab ich mich mit Größe in die Stille, des Privatlebens zurückgezogen, und wirke da ungesehn. Felix. Nicht Eigennutz, nicht Habsucht, nicht Ehrgier, nicht manches Andre ließ mich die Anordnung treffen, den Polterabend in einer gewissen Familie zuzubringen, sondern alle die Gründe, die mein Chef auf der vorigen Seite anführt. Indessen, im Voraus überzeugt, daß Du irgend einen zweckmäßigen Vorschlag in der Tasche hast, bereiten wir uns vor, auf Deine Plane einzugehn, Hensel will 3 Hochzeiten bringen, die erste, die silberne, u. die goldne. Hast Du aber auch nicht zu viel für den Polterabend berechnet? Drei Stücke, und was denkst Du mit dem zu machen, das Du bei Droysen bestellt hast? Es kommt gar nicht vor in Deinem Plan. Wir wissen nicht wo wir mit unserm Reichthum hin sollen, denn Deinen Plan von der ersten Oper finde ich so allerliebst, daß ich ungern davon abstrahiren würde, wenn ich mich gleich jetzt als Zerbino wunderlich gestalten werde. Es ist ein Einfall der so in Deinem Character liegt, daß ihn gar kein andrer Mensch in der Welt hätte haben können. Außerdem aber, glaube nicht, daß ich von einem Instrumentalabend ablassen werde. Was Kuckuck! Wir müssen doch Deine neuen Sachen hören! Das können wir aber später thun. Wäge alles, bringe den heil. Abend in Anschlag, berechne die Probenzeit, bedenke unser Bedenklichkeiten, u. schicke uns Dein ultimatum, wir schreiben dann los. Daß Du Vater nicht triffst, darüber kann ich mich noch nicht recht zufrieden geben, Du wirst nun die vielen Anspielungen in unsern letzten Briefen verstehn, wir hatten uns fest und steif in den Kopf gesetzt, daß Du mit ihm herkommen würdest, u. so hat mich Dein Brief an Vater (er hat ihn uns hergeschickt) fast geschmerzt, nicht nur in Deine u. Vaters. sondern auch in meine Seele. Bei dieser Gelegenheit will ich Dir denn auch vertrauen, was ich zwar nicht beschwören kann, aber was in mir feststeht, u. was ich mit zierlicher Gewißheit weiß, daß nämlich, Vater die Reise fast allein Deinetwegen, u. in der Hoffnung, Dich zu sehn, unternommen hat, er konnte es nicht länger aushalten. Das Gute dabei ist aber, daß nun die Reise einen Theil dessen thut, was Du hast thun sollen, u. daß Vater ermuntert u. in bester Laune zurückkommt. Wir haben heut einen sehr komischen Brief von ihm aus Amsterdam. Nun noch ein Wort über unsre Reiseprojekte. Das Einzige, was uns, Hensels, zurückhalten könnte, wären finanzielle Gründe. Da es in Deinem Plan liegt, daß wir nicht mit den Eltern davon reden, erwähnen wir natürlich [?] unsers Vorsatzes nicht, der dadurch noch unmotivirter erscheinen würde. Nun habe ich immer noch die Angst, die ich nicht zu überwinden vermag, erstlich ob wir genug erübrigen, um die Reise zu machen, zweitens, ob die Eltern es nicht vielleicht mit Recht mißbilligen würden, wenn wir, statt uns im Anfang unsrer Verheirathung einzuschränken, u. ruhig zu leben, u. unsre Pflichten hier zu erfüllen, uns gleich ein so kostspieliges Göttervergnügen machten, wobei, im besten Fall, der ganze Erwerb des Jahres darauf ginge. Wollten wir es anders einrichte, wie Du weißt, daß Hensel die Idee hatte, eine Anstellung dort zu suchen, so würde das einen sehr langen Aufenthalt dort zur Folge haben, was wieder seine sehr zu bedenkenden Seiten hat. Kurz, lieber Clown, sage mir mal ein vernünftiges Wort darüber, Du kannst Dir denken, wenn wir Euch alle so einsteigen sähen, u. müßten das Haus hüten, so würde uns das wenig amüsiren. Ein Umstand, der sonst unangenehm wäre, uns aber bei unsern vorhandenen Plane[a] zum Vortheil gereichen kann, ist, daß Henseln das Attelier im Luisenstift abgeschlagen worden ist, weil das Palais für Prinz Albrecht eingerichtet wird, u. Begas u. Ternite auch ausziehn müssen, u. daß er sich nun um die 400 rh bewirbt, die als Ersatz für ein königl. Attelier gegeben werden. Sieh, lieber Felix, da hast Du unsre ganzen häuslichen Angelegenheiten. Wie viel ich brauchen werde, u. mithin erübrigen kann, werde ich [erst] nach einigen Monaten beurtheilen können. Wenn wir uns nun (und Hensel hat gewiß die meiste Lust dazu) auch entschlössen, burschikos zu handeln, [allein], [ ] verjubeln, u. nachher von vorn angefangen, so fürchte ich doch, die Eltern würden mit einem solchen Plane wenig zufrieden seyn, u. ohne ihre Beistimmung (dies hat gewiß die Deinige), wollen wir beide nichts beschließen. Im Fall aber die Reise doch noch zu Stande käme, muß Hensel eine historische Bestellung beim Könige, u. eine andre, über die er schon in Unterhandlung steht, beim Großherzog v. Weimar sicher machen, zum Motiv würde er dann eben nehmen, die Skizzen u. Entwürfe zu diesen Bildern in Italien zu machen. Du siehst aber wie langsam dergl. hier geht, da er die Antwort auf die Atteliersache erst nach Monaten erhalten hat, u. da ein königl. Rescoipt 4 Tage v. Potsdam hierher geht, beinah so lange, wie ein Brief nach London.

Es ist daher sehr zu wünschen, daß Du Deine Rückkehr her beschleunigst, und aufschiebst, damit wir erst unter einander, dann mit den Eltern, u. zuletzt mit der Regierung einig werden. Sage uns Deine Meinung, rathe, sprich, u. laß uns bald wieder so ein theilbares Privatschreiben zukommen. Es ist immer göttlich, wenn die Briefe so durchgerissen werden, das mußt Du dann aber an den Hofmaler Hensel, Leipziger Str. No. 3 adressiren, denn der Mann zieht den 3ten Oktbr. aus. Sieh, mein Junge, die habe ich Dir nun einmal wieder Alles exponirt, mir ist gar zu wohl, wenn ich so eine weiße Seite vor mir sehe, u. Humor genug fühle, mich 24 Stunden lang mit Dir zu besprechen, u. wenn ich nur vom Schreibtisch aufzusehn brauche, um Dein Gesicht zu treffen, u. wenn Du Deine Geren so sehr lieb hast. Wenn nur eine Deiner Geren mit Dir ginge, u. die Andre bliebe hier, das wäre wol.

[Hensel]

---

[a]Fanny omitted the umlaut.

31

Berlin, den 28sten September 29.

Mein bester Felix, ich will versuchen Dir zu schreiben, obschon mir der Kopf wirklich etwas wüst ist. Man mag so viel vorher besorgt u. gethan haben, als man will, in den letzten Tagen häuft es sich dennoch ungemein, u. ich kann nicht recht unterscheiden, was mich mehr mürbe macht, ob die Ermüdungen der letzten Woche, oder das Bevorstehende, oder das viele Zahnweh, was ich zeither gehabt, aber nun Gottlob verloren habe. Vater ist Sonnabend Abend angekommen, sehr wohl u. ungemein erfreut von seiner Reise, er wußte schon Deinen Unfall, da er Einbrodt in Rotterdam gesprochen hatte, aber der gute Vater sagte uns nichts davon, da wir Deinen Brief noch nicht hatten. Der kam Sonntag früh, u. obgleich wir uns nicht eigentlich deshalb ängstigen, erwarten wir doch mit einiger Ungeduld den Mittwochsbrief, von dem ich, besonders da es der letzte vor meiner Hochzeit ist, wirklich mit Sehnsucht gute Nachrichten hoffe. Denn der gute Schooßhund mit der verbundenen Pote gehört noch auf andre Weise zum Thierreich, er ist erstens ein Lamm, zweitens ein Haupthahn, etc. Es scheint, daß man nicht ungezeichnet aus London kommt. Vater frug Einbrodt erstens selbst auf sein Ehrenwort, ob er hinüberreisen solle, u. schickte ihm dann noch Moritz Levy u. Carl zu, die ihm die Ehrenfrage wiederholen mußten, er blieb aber dabei, es sey nicht nöthig, u. daß Gott sey Dank keine Spur von Gefahr dabei ist, wiederholt ja auch Klingemann mit Nachdruck. Wie der mit der Kanzlei bei Dir sitzt, das ist sehr nett, u. seine Treue wird über den Canal nachempfunden. Gott gebe mir nur zum Mittwoch gute Nachrichten, mit welchen Herzen könnte ich sonst Sonnabend in die Kirche gehen? Doch lieber Felix, ich will mich nicht rühren, u. lieber historisch seyn, wie Du es wünschest. Zuerst die Scene: Beckchen hat eben angefangen, Werther zu lesen, u. sogleich wieder aufgehört, da Hensel kam, und stickt nun, Hensel zeichnet, Mutter liest die Zeitung, 2 Lampen stehn auf dem Tische, es ist 7 Uhr, aber ich schreibe weiter, weil ich am Tage nicht dazu komme, u. wir zufällig eine Minute allein sind. Unsre Einrichtung ist fertig, und ganz allerliebst, vollkommen geschmackvoll, passend u. hübsch. Vater war durchaus mit Allem zufrieden, meine Aussteuer ist noch fertig, u. ich glaube, die Kleider die ich trage werden Dir gefallen, auch erscheine ich diesen Winter als Behörde mit einem *blauen* Mantel, grade, wie gewisse andre Leute ihn tragen. Mittwoch wird eine kleine Ausstellung von meiner Aussteuer gemacht, u. die Mädchen strömen herbei, sie zu sehn. Donnerstag wird besagte Aussteuer in meine neuen Schränke geräumt, Freitag kommt Hensel mit seinen Sachen an, u. zieht ein, Sonnabend wird es denn bunt hergehn, allein ich rechne auf eine ruhige Viertelstunde, um Dir wo möglich eine Zeile zu schreiben. Die Krone fängt um 1 an, Betty Pistor kommt früher, denn, o Plaisir! Mine Stetzer heirathet an demselben Tage, u. so kann sie, die ich zur Brauthjungfer gewählt hatte, nicht kommen. Betty schimpft wie ein Rohrsperling auf die liebe Familie, u. wir haben ausgemacht, daß wenn Beckchen einmal Hochzeit macht, gewiß Tante Alberti auf denselben Tag zum 2tenmal heirathet, damit sie ja nicht kommen kann. Eine andre Brautjungfer ist mir sehr erfreulicher Weise zugewachsen, Hensels Schwester Minna, die wir in diesen Tagen erwarten. Daß meine Krone eine neue Braut zählt, kann ich Dir nicht verhehlen, lieber Felix, vor 2 Jahren hätte ich Anstand genommen, Dir mit einer kleinen Fußwunde, diese Nachricht mitzutheilen, aus Furcht, Dein Fieber zu vermehren, aber seit der ganze Sacrower See nebst dazu gehörigem Hause, Garten, Weinwand, Heliotropduft, Vanillathee, u. Volk in ein Quartett versenkt u. gefahren ist, kannst Du ja wohl mit Pomade anhören, daß ich—wage nicht—o Ritz!—daß—Victoire—mit—Rudolph—(nicht Gustav) Decker—nicht Magnus—o weh nun ist es heraus, u. Du fällst am Ende in Ohnmacht.

[Lea]

29sten Sept. um 2 ist man wieder todtmüde, wenn man den ganzen Vormittag mit Kleiderprobieren zugebracht hat. Felix, ich bin nicht so frivol, wie ich klinge, ich versichere Dich, meine Gedanken reichen über meine Toilette, u. wenn der kranke Schooßhund jetzt hier, u. der Gig eine Droschke gewesen wäre, 2 Geren hätten Zeit gefunden, an Deinem Bette zu sitzen, u. zu pflegen, bis die Freunde gekommen wären, u. sie vertrieben hätten. Da dem aber nicht so ist. Mein Orgelstück ist fertig, u. als ich gestern Abend aufhörte an Dich zu schreiben, schrieb ich es noch für Grell ab, wenn ich nur Deins bekomme. Ich fahre fort, wo ich gestern stehn blieb. Um 1 also ist die Krone, um 1/2 4 die Trauung angesetzt, zu der die Familie sich in der Kirche versammelt. Nachher fahren *wir* noch einen Augenblick zu Tante Meyer, die nicht nach der Kirche kommen kann, und uns doch gern begrüßen möchte, dann zu Hause, wo wir den Rest des Tages ruhig verbringen werden. Es ist mir sehr unangenehm, daß ich Dir, wie ich glaube, nicht die Stunde angezeigt habe. Was ich Dir aber unmöglich beschreiben kann, ist Mutters Thätigkeit, Munterkeit, Plaisir an Allem, u. unendlichen Güte für mich, sie kann gar kein Ende finden mit Kaufen, Besorgen, u. Einrichten, u. eine so komplett fertige Wirtschaft ist mir noch nicht vorgekommen. Vater hat im Ganzen Anordnungen gemacht, mit denen wir, wie Du denken kannst, ebenfalls einigen Grund zur Zufriedenheit haben, kurz—was soll ich Dir weiter sagen, Du kennst die Eltern, u. das ist genug. Ich schicke Dir wol noch ein Lied, was ich noch vor meiner Hochzeit zu machen gedenke, es wird das letzte Stück seyn, u. das erste denk ich, eine Sonate. Eben war Mühlenfels hier, Abschied nehmend, vielleicht kommt er noch zum Essen wieder, da er Vater u. Rebecka nicht getroffen hat, ich glaube es aber doch nicht. Rosen läßt Dir noch sagen, ob Du ihm nicht zwischen dem 20 und 2[3]sten irgendwo zwischen Brüssel u. Ostende treffen könntest? Adieu für heut.

[Rebecka]

Noch ein Paar Worte in einer hellen Zwischenminute. Eben kam Dein Brief, u. ist schön, aber daß ich kein Orgelstück bekomme, ist nicht schön, wer soll mich denn nun zur Kirche heraus begleiten? Der alte Bach, oder ich mich selbst? Wo soll ich denn die Zeit hernehmen? Hättest Du man[a] eins bestimmt, so wollte ich mich schon zufrieden geben. Aber daß Du in 8 Wochen kommen willst, ist schön. Die Geschichte von der Marmolade ist auch schön, u. alles gefällt mir, nur nicht der Gig. Der ist ein dummer Teufel. Die Hebriden sind sehr schön, u. werden mir noch ganz besonders gefallen. Aufs Quartett freue ich mich, u. Klingemann danke ich, bei erster ehelicher Muße schreibe ich ihm. Felix mein Brautkleid ist sehr schön, und wir werden alle gentleman aussehn, da ich aber glaube, daß Dir jetzt die Hochzeit *hier* sitzen wird (ich halte die Hand am Halse) so nehme ich Abschied von Dir, außerdem auch noch aus dem Grunde, Vatern diesen übrigen Platz zu reservieren. Leb wohl lieber Felix, ich freue mich, daß wir nun noch einen Brief zu erwarten haben. *Nachmittags.* Deine beiden andern Briefe haben wir nun auch, lieber Felix, u. wenn ich mich gehn ließe, könnte ich recht affizirt davon seyn, daß der letzte, den ich vor meiner Hochzeit erhalte, so verstimmt, u. leidend ist. Ich *will* aber nicht, sondern sage mir mit eben Nachdruck, dessen ich fähig bin, daß nun schon wieder 14 Tage drüber hingegangen sind, in denen Du Dich, mit Gottes Hülfe, von Unfall und Aderlaß erholt haben wirst, u. daß ich hoffen darf, Du werdest den 3ten Oktbr. frei u. froh u. gesund mit Klingemann zubringen. Ich hoffe es fest, u. habe den Muth mich zu freuen. Tausend herzliche Grüße von Hensel, der jetzt den ganzen Tag angestrengt malt, um das Bild der Gräfin Arnim noch in diesen Tagen zu vollenden. Tausend Grüße ferner von Mutter, Alle haben wir nicht mehr Zeit Dir zu schreiben, ich bin von Tische aufgestanden deshalb, sie läßt Dir alle mögliche Sorgfalt empfehlen, Gehorsam gegen Dr. Kind, Ruhe u. was Dir sonst nützlich seyn kann. Der Himmel gebe mir zuerst im Ehestande einen gesunden, frohen Brief, u. somit lebe wohl. Es bleibt Alles beim Alten ich auch.

[Rebecka, Abraham]

---

[a]Fanny probably meant "mal" instead of "man."

32

Mein liebster Felix! Heut ist der dritte Oktober, und mein Hochzeittag; und meine erste Freude an diesem Tage, daß ich die ruhige Viertelstunde finde, die ich mir längst wünschte, um grade heut an Dich zu schreiben, und Dir Alles noch einmal zu sagen, was Du längst weißt. Ich bin ganz ruhig, lieber Felix, und Dein Bild steht neben mir, aber indem, ich Deinen Namen wiederschreibe, und Du mir dabei so ganz vor leiblichen Augen stehst, weine ich, wie Du mit dem Magen, aber ich weine. Ich habe zwar immer gewußt, daß nichts kommen könnte, daß ich nichts Neues lernen würde, was Dich auch nur für den zehnten Theil eines Augenblick[a] aus meinem Gedächtniß entfernen könnte, ich freue mich aber, es nun erlebt zu haben, und ich werde Dir morgen, und in jedem Moment meines Lebens dasselbe wiederholen können, und glaube nicht, Hensel da mit Unrecht zu thun. Und daß Du mich soliebst, das hat mir einen großen innern Werth gegeben, und ich werde nie aufhören sehr viel auf mich zu halten, so lange Du mich so liebst. Sechs Wochen noch, und ich denke, Du wirst zufrieden seyn, wie Du die Sachen findest, es hat alle Anlage sehr niedlich zu werden, und wenn Du es gesehn haben wirst, werde ich erst wissen, ob es überhaupt was taugt, denn so wie meine Stube gestern lebendig wurde, als Bilder hineinkamen, (die Skizze Deines Bildes hängt über meinem Schreibtisch) so werden die Bilder lebendig werden, wenn Du hinein kömmst, u. Dich auf dem blauen Sopha in Gerenarme wälzest, u. Dich sehr kannibalisch wohl fühlst.

Die Scene mußt Du wissen, ich am Schreibtisch, wo es sehr bunt aussieht, und wo Dinte und eau de Cologne in holder Eintracht leben, Beckchen am Fenster, Blumensträußchen für meine Kronemädchen verfertigend, denn Du weißt doch, daß ich Blumen vertheile, daß in dreien Sträußen sich Myrthe befindet, und daß die Inhaberinnen der Myrthe die nächsten Bräute sind. Das Wetter ist schön, und alle kleinen Zufälligkeiten sind bis hieher gut gelungen. Gestern hatte ich einen sehr hübschen Tag, Vormittags war eine Zusammenkunft mit Grell in der Parochialkirche verabredet, wo er mir mein Stück vorspielte, ich war zum letzten mal auf der Orgel gewesen, als Du darauf spieltest, und amüsirte mich, das Stück klang gut, und ich hatte die äußerste Lust, Orgel zu spielen, was aber doch, Zeitmangels wegen, unterbleiben mußte, der Rest des Tages verging mit Laufereien, ich mußte mit Hensels Schwester deren ganze Toilette besorgen, Besuche, Geschenke annehmen, Hensels Sachen einräumen, etc. Um 8 war die Familie zum Thee und stillen Polterabend versammelt, Louis Heydemann kam noch dazu, und verdarb nichts, als Ausgangsstück hatte Vater die Pastorella vorgeschlagen, ich konnte sie aber nicht mehr auftreiben, und Grell kannte sie nicht, da meinte Hensel um 9, ich sollte mir doch noch selbst eins machen, und ich hatte die Unverschämtheit noch anzufangen, in Gegenwart sämmtlicher Zeugen, und bin um 1/2 1 fertig damit geworden, und ich glaube, es ist nicht schlecht. Ich habe es heut früh an Grell geschickt, und hoffe, er spielt es noch. Der Polterabend war sehr hübsch. Es geht aus g dur, das wußte ich schon, weil ich, ehe Du eine zu schicken versprachst, mir schon eins ausgesonnen hatte, aber die Ausführung ist ganz von gestern. Nun fängt es an bunt um mich her zu werden, es ist bald 11, um eins fängt meine Krone an, nach 3 die Trauung. Ich denke fort an Dich, so ruhig wie sonst, Hensel, der eben hier war, läßt Dir Manches sagen, und ich bin über Alles ruhig, weil ich weiß, daß er Dich liebt.

Von aller Liebe und Freundlichkeit die uns widerfahren, spricht der gewöhnliche Hamburger Mittwochsbericht, ich denke, ich werde mein Recht der Mitarbeiterschaft an diesem Blatte nicht einbüßen. Adieu. Ich grüße am heutigen Tage herzlichst unsern Klingemann, der sich durch sein Krankenwarten neue Kronen und Thronen erworben hat. Daß Du heut frisch und munter und vergnügt bist, leidet bei mir keinen Zweifel, wie könnte ichs sonst seyn? Nun leb wohl, und bleibe der Alte, hier findest Du Alles beim Alten, auch das Neue. Zum letztenmal

Fanny Mendelssohn Bartholdy

Beckchen grüßt tausendmal, sie hat eine schlimme Nase, und einen sehr grotesken Schmerz darüber. Eben kommt mein Kranz, und ist wunderschön; sehr dick, und sehr frisch und grün, und viele, viele Blüthen. Beckchen hat ihn mir geschenkt.

---

[a]Fanny omitted the genitive "s" ending.

33

Berlin den 8ten Okt.

[Rebecka]

Lieb Lamm, ich schreibe eine Gastrolle bei meiner Mama, mein Gemahl sitzt am Tisch u. zeichnet, es ist Abend, ich bin froh und vergnügt, u. sehr, sehr bei Dir. O wie ich mich darauf freue, Dich drüben bei mir zu sehn, zu haben, wenn es doch bald wäre, recht bald, mein einziger Felix! Ach, wenn ich mir Dich nur nicht liegend u. leidend denken müßte! Wir leben sehr angenehm, unser Mittagsessen nach 5 würde, oder wird Dir behagen, u. es gefällt Jedermann bei uns. Louis Heydemann läßt Dich grüßen, er hat uns heut besucht, u. aus der Tasche einen Pompadour seiner Schwester mitgebracht, voll Kartoffeln, zur Probe, da er uns die seinigen so sehr empfohlen hatte. Er reist auf 14 Tage nach Brandenburg, zu Steinbeck, u. wenn er zurückkommt, macht er sein Examen.—Ich mußte gestern aufhören, es war zu viel Lärm am Tisch, u. fahre nun in meiner eignen Behausung fort. Es ist sonderbar, aber mir ist, als wären wir weiter auseinander gerückt, seitdem Du meine Umgebungen nicht mehr so genau kennst, u. seit ich nicht mehr gewiß weiß, Dich im Londoner Strudel umhertreibend zu treffen, u. doch rückt die liebe Zeit immer näher, u. wir ihr näher, und es wird hübsch. O mein liebster Felix! Heut essen Rebecka u. Minna hier, zum erstenmal, worauf ich mich unaussprechlich freue, Mutter will noch nicht hier essen, sie hat es mir rund abgeschlagen, sondern erst einmal Thee hier trinken, was hoffentlich auch noch einmal diese Woche seyn wird, u. worauf ich mich sehr freue, Gans liest dies Semester Donnerstags um 4, Vater will ihn hören, u. wird dann bei uns essen. Vielleicht hörst Du ihn auch?

Weiter fällt gar nichts vor, wir bekommen Besuche die Fülle, Hensel malt, ich fange an wieder etwas zu arbeiten, bis jetzt konnte ichs noch nicht, gestern habe ich ein komisch Stück Arbeit gemacht, morgen ist Betty Beers Geburtstag, Hensel hat ihr eine Zeichnung auf ein Kästchen gemacht, u. wünschte, daß ich ein Rähmchen von Musik darum machen sollte, ich fand die Idee zu hübsch für den Zweck, aber er meinte, wir hätten eben nicht nöthig, uns hübsche Einfälle aufzuheben, so machte ich denn ein Stück welches gerade 4 Zeilen rund ums Bild her fällt. Meine Sonate fange ich vielleicht heut noch an.

Nach der Meeresstille habe ich eine unaussprechliche Sehnsucht, wie so gern möchte ich sie einmal wieder spielen! Ritz hat mich noch nicht besucht, ich erwarte ihn mit großer Ungeduld, denn wenn er nicht käme, wäre es mir erstlich an u. für sich sehr leid, u. dann müßte ich, zwar nicht die Musik, aber doch das Musikmachen gewissermaßen an den Nagel hängen. Ich bin außer Schuld, ich habe keine Freundlichkeit jemals gegen ihn außer Augen gesetzt, u. Julius hat mir auch eine dicke Visite gemacht. Der wird sehr gut, er ist munter, bengelhaft, tüchtig u. spielt sehr schön. Vorigen Sonntag war es brillant bei uns, Mendelssohns, Betty Beer, die Ridderstolpe, eine sehr schön gewesene Frau, Engländer, u. viele Fremde, Felix ich muß Dir sagen, daß mir seit meiner Verheirathung sehr geraspelt wird, ich habe eine Haube, die macht Glück, ich will sie gern aufheben, bis Du kommst, sie trägt grünes Band, u. kein abgewelktes Gesicht, u. ist ein schöner Mann. Gestern hat mich Mme. Heyne mit Carolinen besucht, eine außerordentliche Freundlichkeit von der Frau. Und nun lebe wohl, theurer Schatz, u. behalte mich in gutem Andenken, für heut.

[Lea, Abraham, S. Rösel]

34

[Rebecka]

Lieber Junge, ich nehme diesen Brief mit ganz besondrem Plaisir in die Hand, in der festen Hoffnung, daß er einer der Letzten ist. Gestern auf der Academie, hielt ich eine Stimme vom Inclina in Händen, das Singen wurde aber schwer, weil ich mir Deine Rückkunft ausmalte, aber mit einem Mal entschloß ich mich, legte die Stimme weg, setzte mich, u. dachte nun ungestört weiter. Kein Mensch hat Dir noch erzählt, daß heut ein Concert ist, zum Besten der Schlesier, worin Dein Hora vorkommt, daß dies, dank Grells Sorgfalt, recht gut geht, u. in einer Reihe von Proben ein lion der Academie geworden ist (ach nein, es heißt ein dear [ ]). Grell läßt Dich sehr grüßen, Zelter, u. Rungenhägelchen, u. die ganze Academie, man fragt unglaublich viel nach Deinem Beinechen. Beckchen hat Dir nicht erzählt, wie wir plötzlich einmal in einen Tanz ausbrechen, mit obligatem Kneifen begleitet, u. durch es den Clown haben wollen. Ich soll Dir Hensels Ganswitz erzählen? Als er seinen Namen auf das Bild setzen wollte, u. sich mit uns über eine Stelle berieth (Droysen war auch da), sagte er plötzlich, er wolle ihn in den Hut schreiben, das sey ein Zug der Aehnlichkeit, dann als dann habe Gans seinen mitgenommen, er hatte nämlich erst den Tag vorher unsern Drücker mitgenommen, u. erst denselben Morgen wiedergeschickt. Hensel malt ein Bildchen für mich, ich darf es aber nicht sehn, bis es fertig ist. Gestern waren wir einen Monat verheirathet, ich habe allen Grund zu hoffen, daß wir nach einem Jahre eben so zufrieden seyn werden. Es ist hübsch genug, daß Du Mühlenfels nun a[uch] wiedergesehn hast, der uns gesehn hat. Ich hätte wol dabei seyn mögen, wie er Dir erzählte, oder nicht erzählte, sondern alles sehr brockenweis herausbrachte. Wenn Du mit ihm von uns sprichst, bin ich ruhig. Grüß ihn mir u. Rosen u. Klingemann herzlich. Rosen hat noch den Tag seiner Abreise unsre Wohnung besehn, u. wäre beinah gefallen, da er einen großen Sprung that, um eine neue Decke nicht zu betreten. Der Mann ist g[ ] und man ist ihm hier gut. Aber nun kommst Du bald wieder, u. das ist auch nicht übel, ich weiß Leute, die sich darauf freuen, unter Andern Mlle. Anders. Ja, ja, Felix, alte Lie[be] rostet nicht, wenn sie hinter mir im Alt sitzt, damit Frl. Sydow vom Hora spricht, hat sie Einiges von einer begeisterten Mänade an sich. Nebbich! Lebe sehr wohl, Beckchen das Stückchen hat soviel geschrieben, daß ich nothwendig schon anfangen muß, aufzuhören, damit für die Eltern auch ein Plätzchen bleibt.

Mein Mann grüßt schön, er nimmt eben jetzt den Ludwig vor, potz Kukkuck, das Bild wird hübsch. Du hast uns nicht auf unser Frühstücksantrag geantwortet, bleib nicht zu lange, sonst wird der Kaffee kalt, u. der [ ]kuchen alt. Mann, wir wollen uns amüsiren u. die kleine Gere ist auch dabei. Adieu, auf baldiges Wiedersehen.

Und ich nehme mir noch eine kleine Zeile, u. will Dir nur sagen, wie sauersüß uns jeder Brief ist, worin Du noch nicht gehst, Du Einziger! Und wie mich freut, daß Dir das Liedchen wieder Freude gemacht, u. wie wir Klingemann lieben, der sein erstenmal ausgefahren, u. wie herzlich wir die ganze liebe, deutsche Gesellschaft genießen.

[Abraham, Lea]

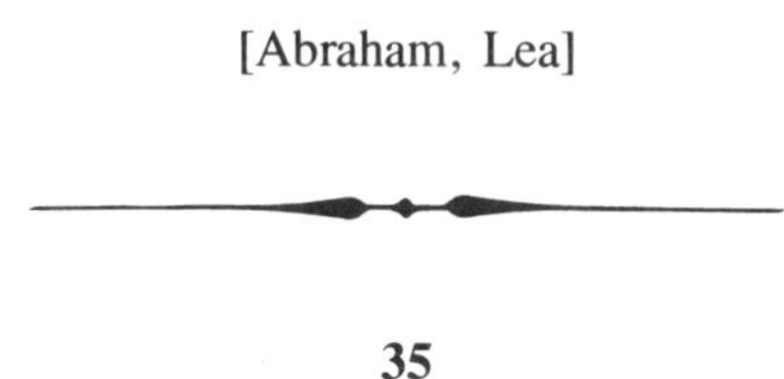

35

Mein Mann hat es mir zur Pflicht gemacht, jeden Morgen gleich nach dem Frühstück ans Clavier zu gehen, weil nachher Störung auf Störung folgt, heut früh kam er, u. legte mir stillschweigend das Blättchen aufs Clavier, u. 5 Minuten darauf rief ich ihn wieder herum, u. sang es ihm so vor, wie es eine Viertelstunde später hier auf dem Papier stand, u. Teichmann meint, es käme noch in diesem Monat an. Hier die kleine Hochzeitnadel, die Geschwister hier tragen sie immer. Ich wünsche ihr u. Dir eine glückliche Reise, u. wenn der Brief vor Ende des Monats ankäme, u. Dich nicht mehr träfe, so könnte mir nichts Angenehmeres begegnen. Adieu. Leb sehr wohl.

36

Dienstag 18ten Mai 30.

Wenn man morgen so wichtige Geschäfte hat, wie ich, muß man heut schreiben, denn sonst kommt man gar nichts dazu. Vorerst, daß Vater gestern 1/2 9 von Leipzig gekommen ist, wovon man reden wird in spätsten Zeiten, denn die Pferde müssen sich wieder einmal die Beine abgelaufen haben. Aber die kleine Reise ist ihm sehr wohl bekommen, u. wir haben uns gefreut, zu vernehmen, daß die Deinige angenehm begonnen hat. Voriges Mal kamst Du nach der kurzen Introduction Hamburg gleich in den tollen u. vollen Hauptsatz London. Diesmal fängt es piano an, dessen, eine Flöte, dann tritt Leipzig auf, etwa eine schnarrende Hoboe, so gehts über Weimar langsam crescendo nach München, etc. Wären wir jetzt zusammen, u. sprächen gemeinsam das dumme Zeug, statt daß ichs jetzt einsam schreibe, wir wären bald in Mexico.—Morgen also hat uns Fouqué zu einer Musikpartie eingeladen, 2 Akte seiner Undine, v. Girschner komponirt, werden im Concertsaal, executirt, u. dieser Hinrichtung sollen wir whole family beiwohnen. Dafür wird er nachher bei uns eine Suppe u. Zubehör hinrichten helfen, mit Marx, der den Kapellmeister Guhr eingeführt hat, u. dem Kapellmeister Guhr, der durch Marx eingeführt worden. Damit ist Allen geholfen. Marx u. Fouqué lieben sich, Guhr wird sagen, er habe einen Geist gesehn, u. zwar einen schönen, was Fouqué eben nicht als Echo wiederholen wird, Vater, der 2 von den 3 Gästen nicht liebt, haben wir also gar nicht dazu einladen können, Beckchen u. Paul haben heut ausgegessen, u. ich als eine Seele von ächt jüdischer Abstammung, habe eine Geistes-und Opernheimath zwischen dem Dichter u. dem Componisten projektirt.

Mit dem Schreiben will es noch gar nicht recht fort. Die von Dir belobte Feder hat dem Munde noch nichts wieder abgelernt, vielleicht wirds besser, wenn Du einmal geschrieben hast. Aber was für Wetter hast Du! Es ist kaum erlaubt, solch einen Mai zu erleben, aber ihn in schönster Muße zu verreisen, ist fast übermüthig angelegt vom Schicksal. Glück auf!

Beckchen wird mich stranguliren, aber dieser Brief macht sein Erstgeburtsrecht geltend, u. erzählt Dir, daß Devrient Orest gesungen u. damit gefallen hat, daß ihm aber nachstehendes groteske Unglück dabei begegnete, als er seinem Pylades mit Affekt in die Arme fiel, bekam dieser das Uebergewicht, und stürzte hin, so daß Orest auf ihn zu Reiten kam. Das Publicum aber lachte nicht, u. Therese hat es mit gutem Humor geschrieben.

Deine Symphonie [ ]ht mir oft in Tag Nachtträumen, u. macht mir Freude, schicke mir aber die Abschrift. Heut 19ten bist Du nun in Weimar, u. ich bitte Dich, Ulrike u. Frau v. Goethe aufs Beste zu grüßen, Du wirst viel Freude da haben. N.B.: Beckchen steht bei mir u. wartet auf den Bogen, sie hat wollen hier schreiben, nun wird wieder nichts daraus, Du siehst sie hat sich noch nicht sehr verändert, nur einen durchbrochenen Kamm mit einer hohen Gallerie trägt sie, außerdem der alte Mephistophel. Eben hats geregnet, u. nun wirds wieder klar, das Wetter ist wirklich das einzige vollkommene Ding auf Erden diesen Mai. Wie mies ist mir vor Undine! Nun muß ich aufhören, u. mich anziehn, u. lauter dummes Zeug vollführen. Leb wohl, geliebter Schatz, Hensel läßt sehr grüßen. Heut werden wir doch wohl etwas von Dir hören?

[Paul]

37

[Rebecka]

22sten Mai: Eben ist Dein lieber, erster Brief gekommen, und hat uns herzliche Freude gemacht. Du hast das Schreiben nicht verlernt, u. ich denke wir sollens auch für die nöthige Zeit wieder lernen, aber nicht auf zu lange, denn es giebt etwas viel Besseres.—Das Jahr läßt sich wirklich unvergleichlich schön an, u. jeden Tag freue ich mich von Neuem, daß Du es verreisest.

Deinen Auftrag an Klingemann werde ich nächsten Posttag besorgen, freue mich übrigens, daß die Leipziger Musikhändler genteel sind, u. daß Deine Quartetten erscheinen. Auf eine Bachsche Cantate freue ich mich besonders, es ist die: Es erhub sich ein Streit, da mag der alte Herr gewüthet haben. Mit einem Mal 14 neue Cantaten, von denen unsre Seelen sich nichts haben träumen lassen, fruchtbar ist der alte Bär gewesen, wenn auch sonst nichts. Kannst Du Dir Sebastian Bach jung denken? Ich habe mir übrigens zu dieser Cantate ein Thema in Kopf gesetzt, u. werde sehr aufs Maul geschlagen seyn, wenn es, wie natürlich, nicht paßt.—Nicht Rellstab hat die 2 Jünglinghefte bekommen, sondern wir, ich habe mir Eins davon geben lassen, u. nun steht in meinem Wirthschaftsbuch, *fast zu jämmerlich*: Lieder von Felix, 20sgl. Ich habe sie Schlesingern in den Rachen gejagt. Gestern war bei uns ein rout, Heydemanns, Droysen, Horn, Röstell, Ulrike, Lorn, August Frank. Letzterer ist einen sehr netten Kerl, lacht hä, hä, spricht genau wie Hermann, nur mit dem Dämpfer, was eben kein Fehler ist, goutirt guten u. schlechten Witz, u. hört gern u. gut Musik. Der Zweck der gestrigen Zusammenkunft war eigentlich, daß Albert Heydemann, die vorjährigen Lieder für Dich hören wollte, die er noch nicht kannte. Ich wollte damit denjenigen verbinden, Thee im Freien trinken zu lassen, was ein grauer Himmel u. kühle Abendluft aber so frei waren, zu verbieten. Nun wurden einige Lieder von Dir gesungen, dann sang Ulrike die beliebte Scene von Weber, sie ist sehr gut bei Stimme, u. hat sich das Detoniren schon merklich abgewöhnt, sieht außerdem sehr gut aus, u. wir lieben uns. Hierauf wurden meine Lieder gesungen, und zuletzt: in weite Ferne. Das ist ein Lied, was eigentlich auch nur gesungen werden muß, wenn Du fort bist, es gewinnt einige Bedeutung. Aber das beste bleibt doch das Scheidende.—Horn blieb nur kurze Zeit weil er zu einem Nervenfieberkranken auf dem Spittelmarkt mußte.—Hensel hat ein genre Bildchen aufgezeichnet, u. ist jetzt bei dem Kinde mit der Mutter, hat auch eine allerliebste Zeichnung zu meinen Hochzeitorgelstücken für seine Schwester gemacht. Bis auf eine dicke rothe Nase befindet er sich wohl u. läßt Dich sehr grüßen. Vorgestern waren wir im Käthchen, das er noch gar nicht kannte u. das ihm außerordentlich viel Freude machte. So sehr mir auch die Lindner gefällt, so ist mirs doch lieb, daß Du sie jetzt nicht zuerst siehst. Sie hat im Aeußern sehr gealtert, u. sie u. Graf Rebenstein waren ein dickes Liebespaar.

Leb wohl, ich glaube, der Brief soll heut noch abgehn. Laß Dirs wohl ergehn, wo Du auch seyn magst, für heut wohl in Weimar, u. ergeht Dirs wohl, so denk an uns. Deine F.

[Rebecka]

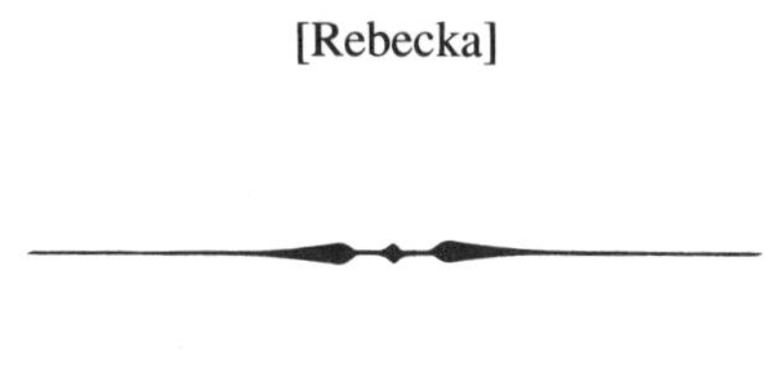

38

30sten Mai 30

Ich weiß mir kein besseres Pfingstplaisir zu machen, als Dir ein wenig zu schreiben, da nämlich jetzt weder Hensel, der Sitzung hat, noch Vater, von dem ich nicht weiß, wo er ist, noch Paul, der sich geschäftsmäßig umhertreibt, noch Mutter u. Beckchen, die mir entlaufen, sich bei mir, sogleich ich mich allein befinde. Jeder Deiner Briefe ist ein frisch Stück Leben, über das man sich freuen muß. Ich freue mich über die Verheißene Partitur über die angekündigte Herausgabe der Symphonie, die mich, unter einem andern Namen, als dem der Reformationssymphonie, ebenso fremd angucken würde, als wenn Du mit einem Mal Petzold hießest. Wenn Du aber die Symphonie herausgiebst, bleiben doch Sommernachtstraum und Meeresstille nicht im Sack? Meine kleine Anstalt hier ist ganz nett, neben meinem Bette habe ich das blaue Dintefaß auf einem Tischchen, einen prächtigen sonnigen Rosenstock dabei, die Balconthüre offen, wo zum ersten Mal wieder frische schöne Luft herein kommt, u. alle Tage nasche ich Erdbeeren, womit mich mein, wie Bertha sagt, sehr sorgfältiger Mann verzieht.

[Rebecka]

Lebe wohl, mein Latein ist auch zu Ende. Daß Beckchen Hensels Federn zu hart findet, finde ich hart, ich finde, daß sich sehr gut damit schreiben läßt. Das gute Kind hat mir aber geraspelt, u. das finde ich sehr artig. Ich liege blos des Decorums wegen zu Bette, u. werde ehestens aufgestanden seyn, u. mein Stückchen munter pfeifen. Beckchen hat das Wetter verläumdet, ich war eben spatzieren, u. finde, Du brauchst es gar nicht schöner. Gehab Dich wohl, mein nächster Brief wird sitzen.

[Lea]

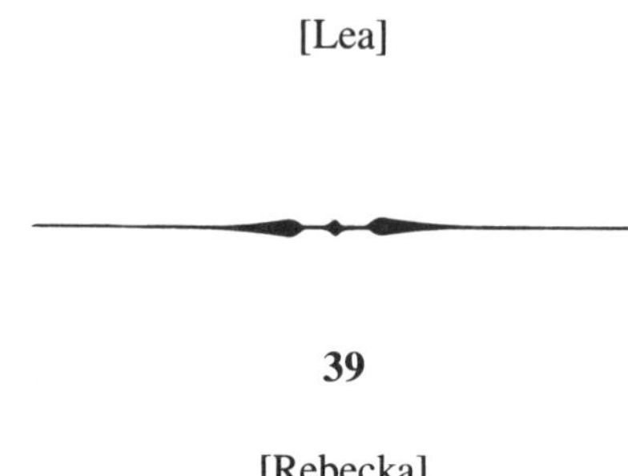

39

[Rebecka]

Mein liebstes Brüderchen, wie denke ich an Dich, an Deine ganze Musik, u. auch an einiges Einzelne, an die schottische Symphonie, mit dem unvergeßlichen Anfang, an die liebe Hebridenouvertüre, an alle Zukunft u. Vergangenheit. Mir ist unaussprechlich wohl im Leben.

Die Unvorsichtigkeiten, die ich mit den Augen beging, waren, daß ich 2mal Dein Lied, u. einmal einen halben Brief von Dir las, ich will jetzt nicht die dritte begehn sondern schließen.

Deine F.

[Rebecka]

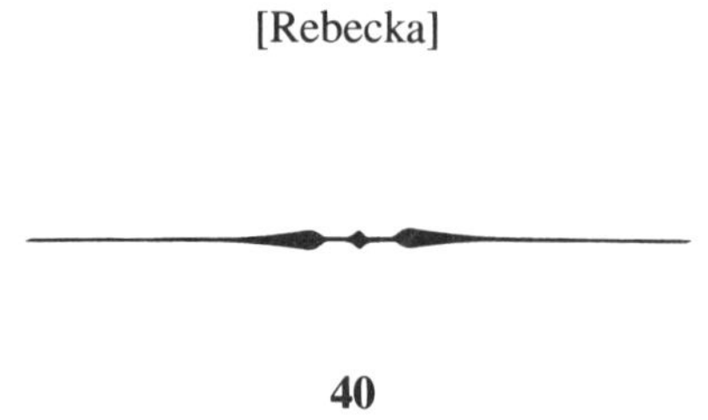

40

Berlin 5ten Juli

Mein liebes Felixchen, neulich war ich so voller Freude, einige selbständige Zeilen zu schreiben, daß ich darüber alles vergaß, was ich eigentlich schreiben wollte, diesen Brief nun soll Freund Marx mitnehmen, u. bis zu seiner Abreise kann ich schon in verschiedenen Absätzen etwas zu Stande bringen. Was ich neulich eigentlich sagen wollte, war, daß ich mich so unendlich freue, wie Dir der liebe Himmel in jeder Stadt so was Absonderliches von Ehre und angenehmem Wirken aufbewahrt, so in München das Unterrichten angesehener Lehrer, so was ist wieder noch nicht für Dich da gewesen. Ich glaube, in irgend einer nächsten Stadt wirst Du in ein Hospital gerufen, um die kranken Leute gesund zu spielen. Ich melde mich dazu, bin aber Gottlob nicht krank.

7ten Juli Gestern hast Du direkt von uns gehört. Ich habe einen äußerst frohen Tag gehabt. Mittags aßen wir bei Mutter, mit Droysen, dessen Geburtstag dies Jahr, grade wie das Vorige, mit Hensel auf einen Tag fiel, u. Röstell, u. waren sehr lustig, nach Tisch kamen Heynes, Heydemanns, Mühlenfels, ich blieb bis 9 im Saal, und es ist mir sehr gut bekommen, obgleich die Jugend etwas wild war, u. es im Saal sehr schallt. Heut ist Sebastian, dessen Fortschritte Du ja Alle wissen mußt, zum erstenmal angezogen worden, d. h. nicht mit Frack u. Stiefeln, sondern er ist aus einem Päckchen Mensch, das fast zu jämmerlich in ein Stück Bett gebunden war, in ein ordentliches Kindercostüm, vulg. Stechkissen genannt, hineingewachsen. Eben habe ich auch Erlaubniß erhalten, heut im Garten spatzieren zu gehn, denn das Wetter ist schön, Vater hat eine angenehme Reise, Du einen angenehmen Aufenthalt, für Uns, die wir zu Hause bleiben, ist es auch zu brauchen, u. Ueberbringer dieses kann auch einmal Sonnenschein zu einem Unternehmen brauchen.

8ten. Seit Anfangs dieser Phrase hat es schon wieder angenehm gepladdert, auf bleibend schönes Wetter kann man nun einmal in diesem Sommer nicht rechnen. Als ich gestern aufhörte zu schreiben, benutzte ich die eben erhaltene Erlaubniß spatzieren zu gehn, zu einem Besuch im Vorderhause, verfehlte aber Mutter u. Beckchen, die einstweilen nach dem Garten gegangen waren, u. fand nur Dich, den ich auch sehr lange nicht gesehn hatte, u. mit vieler Freude wieder begrüßte. Marx wird sich nun heut Deinen Neffen noch einmal ansehn, um Dir die neuesten Nachrichten von ihm zu bringen, u. ich will Dir für heut Lebewohl sagen. Von Hensel tausend [Grüße], sein neues Bild wird Dir wohl Marx auch erzählen, er ist sehr davon eingenommen, überhaupt gefällt es allen Leuten, u. mir nicht zuletzt. Die Leinwand zu Beckchens Bilde wird aber dieser Tage bestellt. Adieu, mein lieber Mensch, lebe wohl und froh, u. denke der Deinigen.

Deine F.

41

Vor einer halben Stunde kam Beckchen, u. sagte, in einer halben Stunde ginge der Brief an Dich ab, seitdem ist eine halbe Stunde vergangen, u. wie Du siehst, habe ich keine Zeit mehr an Dich zu schreiben, ja ich kann nicht einmal mehr von Hensel grüßen, so sehr er mich auch darum bittet, eben so wenig bitte ich Dich Marx zu grüßen, obgleich ich das wol möchte, ja sogar von Sebastian kann ich Dir nichts erzählen, weder daß er viel trinkt, noch daß er wenig schläft, noch daß er sehr munter u. blau umherblickt: hätte ich Zeit, so würde ich Dir auch klagen, daß ich noch nicht Clavier spielen darf, u. daß ich fürchte, wenn die 19 Tage die noch an meinen 6 Wochen fehlen, nicht bald verlaufen, das Liederspiel nicht mehr zu hören, weil Mantius sich verläuft, das Alles, u. noch viel andre schöne Dinge erfährst Du nun aber nicht, denn wie gesagt, ich habe keine Zeit, Auguste steht schon eine halbe Stunde in der Thür, wartend auf den Zettel, u. ich bin, war, u. werde in Zukunft bleiben so lange als am Leben die sehr Deinige.

42

Da ich auf ehrliche Weise erfahre, daß ich auf unehrliche Weise um meinen schlechten Witz gekommen, so fasse ich mir ein Herz, u. mache ihn nicht.

Weißt Du noch, wie wir Dich sonst Grelix nannten? Eben sprach ich mit Beckchen von der Kabuse, in der Du sonst zwischen uns auf dem Sopha saßest, aber jetzt hoffe ich, wälzest Du Dich in Marxi Armen; übrigens bin ich im Vorderhause eingeregnet, u. schreibe an Beckchens Secretair in der Gansischen Mappe, Mann u. Kind schreien nach mir, aber Ersterer ist nicht zu Hause, u. Letzteres schreit wol wahrscheinlich, aber nicht nach mir. Diese drei Tage hindurch hat sichs das kleine Brätchen in der Sonne sehr wohl seyn lassen, u. rothe Bäckchen erlangt, heut ists wieder in die Stube gebannt, aber ich bade es jetzt selbst, u. nehme mich dabei sehr mütterlich aus.

Mein lieber Felix, ich werde Dir nächstens in einem Privatbriefe auch Manches vortragen, aber nichts Neues, denn das ist, nach mir u. Klingemann, das Alte, sondern eben dies Alte. Einstweilen bin ich wieder eine Frischekartoffelnessende, Abends- im freien bleibende, überhaupt genußfähige u. genießende Person, u. mein Kleines wird alle Tage größer. Komponirt habe ich noch nicht, als ichs nicht durfte, hatte ich Ideen genug, jetzt wird wohl wieder die bekannte Dürre eintreten, die ich dem Wetter alle weg nehme.—Da Vater reiste, ist es sehr schade, daß er nicht einige Tage früher gereist ist, um die Nachricht der Einnahme v. Algier in Paris zu haben, die Sensation muß groß gewesen seyn.—Die Desertion kann übrigens beim Africanischen Heere nicht stärker seyn, als jetzt in Berlin, keine Seele ist hier, u. in dem Augenblick desertire ich auch vom Schreibtisch, um die Eier zu essen, die mir Beckchen hat machen lassen.— So, nun ists geschehn, u. eine schöne Geschichte, es regnet Keulen, u. ich kann vielleicht den ganzen Tag nicht wieder zu Haus, Hensel war eben hier, u. hat einen gewaltigen Spektakel gemacht, o weh, ich habe Schelte gekriegt. Adieu, liebes Lamm, Ehrhardt soll diesen Brief mitnehmen, u. steht auf dem Sprunge, stelle Dir einmal Ehrhardt auf dem Sprunge recht deutlich vor, ist das nicht ein schönes Bild? Ich empfehle mich Dir, bis auf etwaniges Wiedersehn. Ehrhardt ist fortgesprungen, u. so will ich mein Plätzchen voll kliern. Wenn Du mir nicht ehestens das Orgelstück aus a dur schickst, so nenne ich Dich ein Pferd, ich denke zuweilen daran, u. möchte es mir etwa vor der Taufe vorspielen, wie ich an dem Tage mein Hochzeitkleid anziehn werde. Die Taufe werden wir Dir noch näher anzeigen, soll etwa Zelter Dein Stellvertreter seyn?

Sebastian wollte eben eigenhändig grüßen, aber der dumme Junge kann noch nicht seinen Namen schreiben, er hat sich bespuckt, u. es ging nicht. Wer ihn tauft? Wilmsen. Wer ihn hält? Beckchen. Wann? Um die Mitte Augusts. Wer Dich repräsentiren soll? Ich habe vorgeschlagen Zelter, hast Du was dagegen?

Was wir aber essen werden, darüber kann ich noch nicht hinlängliche Rechenschaft ablegen, da die Tageszeit noch nicht ganz bestimmt ist. Du sollst aber jede Semmel erfahren.

Ich freue mich über Dein Zusammentreffen mit Marx, ihr werdet Euch manches Kluge zu sagen haben, u. es kann hübsch werden. Grüß ihn bestens von uns. Von Vater haben wir heut den 2ten Brief aus Paris erhalten, demnach ich glaube, daß er bald wieder hier seyn wird, es wäre mir sehr lieb.

Lebe wohl, mein liebes Lamm, ehe Du Dichs versiehst, sind wir da, in Lebensgröße. Ich habe Dich sehr lieb, darum möchte ich wol, wir könnten Beckchen mitbringen.

Hensel grüßt u. ich bin u. bleibe F.

Schreibe nur bald, u. sage mir, daß Du unsre Reise nicht für eine Thorheit hältst, u. uns gern wirst kommen sehn, das ist mir noch nöthig, um mich recht zu freuen.

43

Berlin 22 April 1833

[Abraham]

Du wirst recht verdrießlich über diesen fatalen Zufall seyn, lieber Felix, aber gewiß nicht mehr, als wir es sind, die wir uns sehr viel von dieser Reise für Vater versprochen hatten, indessen, in der möglichen Voraussetzung, länger dort bleiben zu müssen, als ihm lieb wäre, will Vater lieber gar nicht nach London, u. das kann mann[a] ihm nicht übel nehmen. Wir haben gestern aus der Staatszeitung Deine glückliche Ankunft in Düss. erfahren. Unsre Zeitung setzt hinzu, Du seist sehr angenehm überrascht gewesen, durch die Vorbereitungen zum Feste. Hoffentlich werden wir durch Paul die Bestätigung dieser Angabe erhalten. Sebastian sagt, es freue ihn nicht, wenn Du nicht auf Deine Stube bist. Neulich nahm er mich in seinen Arm, und sagte: nun habe ich mein Elterchen im Arm, er hat etwas gelernt, das sehr in Deinem Geist ist, erstens nämlich: Heute hat es keine Noth, den 2ten Vers fügte er aber nach einiger Ueberlegung so zu: weißes Brodt, schwarzes Brodt, u. das war schon weniger in Deinem Geiste. Meine Schwägerin ist Donnerstag angekommen, u. gefällt mir außerordentlich; es thut mir recht leid, daß Du sie nicht mehr hast kennen lernen. Die Figur auf Dein Bild ist bereits geändert, aber das kann ich Dir sagen, daß H. sich in seinem Leben nicht so schwer zu etwas entschlossen hat. Jetzt, wo er erst dabei ist, wird es ihm schon leichter. H. Girschner war gestern bei mir, u. brachte Sachen wieder, die Du ihm geliehen hast, u. verlangte andre. Soll ich sie ihm geben? Leb wohl, mögest Du jetzt in Klingemanns Armen ruhen, u. Dich von Rosen mit Rosen kränzen lassen.

Deine.

[Rebecka, Lea, Abraham]

---

[a]Fanny mistakenly wrote "mann" for "man."

44

Nur einen Gruß, denn das Wetter ist zu schön, um in der Stube zu schreiben, und der Schatten noch zu jung, um im Freien zu schreiben, auch habe ich Dir nichts als einen Glückwunsch zu Deiner academischen Ehre zu sagen, kein Spaß, daß Du mit Rungenhagen durchgekommen bist. Morgen debütirt Orpheus vor 60 Personen, na der Tag wird doch auch vorübergehn, sagt Herr von Rothschild. Ich werde Dir nachher ausführlich berichten. Die Scene in Elysium habe ich trotz alles Studirens nicht superfein herausgekriegt. Danke für den Engländer, er hat eben die Reise in den Gartensaal glücklich zurückgelegt.

[Rebecka, Lea, Abraham]

45

Donnerstag den 16ten Mai

[Rebecka]

Meine Bescheidenheit verbietet mir zwar, ich mach es aber wie Sebastian, und sage: doch erzählen, u. erzähle, daß unsre Flüte sehr schön geflötet hat, u. daß sich alle Leute, inclusive Tante Hiny u. Onkel Joseph sehr amüsirt haben, daß die Hähnel sämmtliche Höllengeister entzückt hat, daß das Wetter so schön genug war, um die Gartenthüren den ganzen Abend offen zu lassen, u. daß Gans alle Leute fragt: waren Sie bei Hensels? Ich bin nicht eingeladen. Ich bin böse. Er ist aber böse im völligen Ernst, u. ich erwarte nur eine Zusammenkunft mit ihm, um ihm zu demonstriren, warum er nicht eingeladen war, u. nie zu einer Musik eingeladen werden wird, u. warum ich im Gegentheil böse auf ihn bin. Drauf wird er sagen: geben Sie mir die Hand, u. die Sache ist abgemacht. Ich gratulire zu Vaters Reise. Kannst Du mir nicht durch ihn die Abschriften des neuen Israel schicken? Wo hast Du denn diesen Fund gethan? mein lieber Felix, Du hast sehr viel Verstand, aber nicht weniger Glück, dies ist wieder eins vom

Geschlecht der Säue. Leb wohl, mich ruft die Pflicht, in Gestalt einer Friseurin.

[Lea]

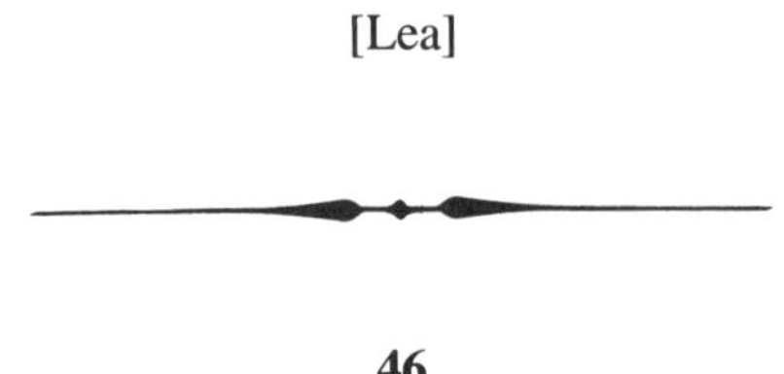

46

Berlin, 22sten Oktbr. 33

Ich habe Dir sehr lange nicht geschrieben, lieber Felix, u. es soll doch nicht in Vergessenheit gerathen, da setze ich mich aus dem Stegreif um 1/2 4 Uhr hin, u. habe noch einen langen Vormittag, denn heut fängt unsre Wintersaison an, mit um 5 Uhr essen, ihr aber geht jetzt in Soireen. Wir haben noch den allerschönsten fast blätterlosen Herbst mit warmer Sonne, u. ich habe eben weite Wege mit Sebastian gemacht, unter den Linden begegnete uns Paul, u. gab mir den Arm, u. wir gingen noch nicht lange zusammen, so kamen Beckchen u. Dirichlet. (Hensel hat mir diesmal lauter Löschpapier mitgebracht.) Gestern Abend hatte ich Dich hergewünscht. Ich hatte einen Zank mit Beckchen, der wäre was für Dich gewesen, die Eltern haben sich halb toll gelacht. Er fing an über die Taillen unsrer Männer, u. zuletzt kam es so weit, daß ich ihr ihre schwangere Kochin vorwarf, aber da konnten wir auch Beide nicht mehr vor Lachen. Wir sind ganz lustig u. gesund, Vater geht es sehr gut, er ißt zwar sehr viel Weiz, trinkt aber auch welchen, u. das hält sich das Gleichgewicht. Er ist übrigens sehr liebenswürdig, u. macht Dir zum Trotz, Dameneroberungen. À propos, Immermann ist hier, ich habe ihn aber noch nicht gesehn, er war heut bei Mutter, hat uns aber nicht besucht.—Hat es Dir schon ein Andrer geschrieben, daß ich neulich bei der Decker, auf ihrem gräulichen Hackebrett, Oberon begleitet habe? Es war so schlecht wie es unter den gegebenen Umständen nur irgend möglich war, da sie, Devrient, Mantius, u. die Hoffmann mitsangen. Dafür aber hat ichs doch nun durchgesetzt, daß sie sich ein neues Instrument angeschafft hat, gestern habe ichs mit ihr probirt, u. heut wird es hingebracht, morgen nämlich ist Semele da, wo ich wieder begleite. Taubert, der vorigen Winter ihr Capellmeister war, hat es doch in der ganzen Zeit nicht zu einem neuen Flügel gebracht. Es wird aber wieder sehr häßlich werden, Sophie Ebers s[in]gt[a] über die Möglichkeit hinaus. Kennst Du Semele genau? Es sind wunderschöne Sachen drin, ich glaube, mit gehörigen Auslassungen, müßte es sich sehr zum Concert eignen. Kennst Du die Partitur? Schaum bekennt sich zu vielen Aenderungen, ich möchte wohl wissen, ob z. B. der sehr lose Text im Original mehr Zusammenhang hat. Dein Concert ist ja prächtig komponirt. Ich bin aber für Gluck u. Beethoven, u. finde schon das sehr lang vor dem Alexanderfest. Ihr Düsseldorfer müßt gute Mägen haben. Ich weiß, wem ich diese Concerte lieber gönnte, als Euch. Lieber Felix, ich habe jetzt 4 junge Mädchen, die sich Alle musikalisch Raths bei mir erholen, u. recht gut spielen. Ich schnauze sie aber geistig an. Kannst Du Dir Deine Schwester Drude dabei denken? Sebastian ist allerliebst u. sehr gewachsen. Der Wagen von Dir ist noch immer das Glück u. der Neid des jungen Hofpersonals. So lange hat noch kein Spielzeug vorgehalten. Dein Gedächtniß sitzt ihm aber auch sehr fest, u. er spricht tagtäglich von Dir. Neulich habe ich ihn sehr emancipirt, u. ihn bei Heysens, wo ich mit ihm hingegangen war, allein zu Tisch gelassen, er hat aber die Probe vortrefflich bestanden. Der Junge wird Dich reuen, wenn Du ihn einmal wieder siehst, seine Sprache ist wirklich melodisch, u. fällt allen Leuten auf. Augenbraunen kriegt er, wie seine Frau Mama Cantor, aber blondestes Haar.—Neulich haben wir Feuer im Hause gehabt. Wir saßen des Abends ganz ruhig bei den Eltern, über denen seit kurzem der General Braun, mit vielen gestiefelten Söhnen wohnt u. schrecklich rumort. An dem Abend aber ward der Lärm plötzlich sehr arg, Hin-u. Herrennen, sehr lautes Sprechen, dann ein Lärm als ob es in die Stube regnete, begleitet von einem wirklichen Kalkstaubregen, Poltern an unsrer Thür, wir sprangen Alle auf, u. erfuhren nun, daß es in dem Saal über uns brenne, die Männer rannten hierauf, wir konnten nicht mit, denn der alte General löschte im Hemde sämmtliche Gardinen, die er vorher mit einer Lampe angesteckt hatte. Ueber eine Stunde hielt er in Rauch u. Dampf aus, u. verbrannte sich die Hände, damit, u. mit einem schrecklich[en] Brandgeruch durch Haus u. Hof, war aber auch das Unheil abgethan, welches zum Glück nicht auf die Straße drang, sonst wäre unser Haus gleich von Pöbel überschwemmt gewesen. Lieber Felix, da hast Du einen Brief mit lauter Nichts. Deiner aber war sehr schön, u. die Geschichte mit dem Bürgermeister u. dem Wein haben wir herzlich goutirt. Lebe nun wohl, es wird dunkel u. Essenszeit, u. ich bin sehr hungrig. Wir müssen hier mit dem Schreiben auch noch eine Art von besserer Ordnung einführen, bis jetzt geht es noch wie Kraut u. Rüben.

Wilhelm u. Luise grüßen bestens.

---

[a]Could be "singt," "siegt," or "seigt." None is completely suitable. A reading of "singt" conceivably derives from a pun in German on "singt" and "sinkt."

47

Berlin, 2ten Novemb. 33

Liebes Felixchen, was lange währt, wird gut, davon ist Dein prächtiger Brief wieder ein starker Beweis, der uns unendlich erfreut hat. Ich muß ihn auswendig beantworten, da Mutter ihn drüben hat, u. fange also an bei Deiner verlangten Uebersetzung. Sollte nicht Folgendes dem Original so ziemlich entsprechen:

Der Liebe Heil
Doch Kunst errang den Preis

oder: gewann den Kranz
oder: gewann den Preis
oder: errang den Sieg etc. Mir scheint aber die erste Lesart vorzuziehn, denn Kunst u. Kranz ist hart, u. Sieg nicht so gut zu singen, als Preis. Urtheile selbst. Euren Dichter Immermann haben wir einstweilen hier gehabt, u. ihn viel freundlicher gefunden, als seinen Ruf in der Hinsicht. Aber, daß er Dir eine gute Oper machen wird, glaube ich nimmermehr, dazu hat er einen viel zu fest verschlossenen Mund, u. viel zu viel Reflexion. Er spricht aber sehr gut. Erst war er an einem Abend bei Mutter, wo, wie wir dann ausmachten, die Höhen der Bildung deutsch versammelt waren, Steffens, Gans, Rosen, Mühlenfels, Heyse, Devrient, u. Immermann als Mittelpunkt, um den sie alle hertanzten. Wie unglücklich Gans sich in solchen Fällen fühlt, weißt Du. Er kam Hensel sehr freundlich entgegen, u. bat ihn besuchen zu dürfen, u. da sich dazu keine andre Zeit fand, kam er Sonntags zur Musik, wo er während des ersten Stücks das Attelier besah, u. sich sehr zufrieden äußerte, während der übrigen Musik aber sich von Devrient u. Steffens unterhalten ließ. Dann aß er bei den Eltern mit uns en famille, da wir ihn auch gern einmal wollten sprechen hören, u. da sprach er viel u. süßlich gern, sehr gut. Sebastian war auch bei Tisch, u. als das Gespräch auf den vorjährigen Musenalmanach kam, u. Rebecka auf Immermanns Veranlassung Heynes Epigramm sagte, welches schließt: u. ein Gedicht ausgespuckt, fing Sebastian ganz böse an: Hör mal Mutter! Ein Gedicht spuckt man ja nicht aus, ein Gedicht erzählt man. Das gefiel I. sehr, der sich überhaupt mit Seb. einließ.—O weh, wir schreiben nun keine großen Bogen mehr, wo jeder den Andern liest, u. das wird zur unausweichlichen Folge haben, daß Du dieselben Sachen 20mal mit etwas verschiedenen Saucen genießen wirst, das kann ich nicht ausstehn. Euer Fest muß wunderschön gewesen seyn, ich wollt ich wär dabei gewesen. Und nun redlich à propos, habe Dank für Deine Musik, die Du

mir geschickt hast, u. die mir, so oberflächlich ich sie bis jetzt kenne, sehr gefällt, Devrient hat neulich die Arie recht schön gesungen, ich lasse es ausschreiben, u. nächstens singen.—Heut Abend sind wir zu Leuten gebeten, da würde Herr Felix nicht wenig die Cour machen. Eine 15jährige Tochter, wunderhübsch, noch so kindisch, daß sie mit der Puppe spielt, dabei soll sie sehr gut singen, kurz ein Engelchen, heißt Rose. Dafür waren wir auch gestern mit einer Frau zusammen, die ich in einem Fort ansehn mußte, so schön finde ich sie, das ist die Frau Blandine Wangen. Die beiden garstigen Männer haben die Kunst verstanden, interessante Frauen zu heirathen. Lieber Felix, zum 22sten Nvbr. habe ich, um Deinen Concertanfang zu feiern, auch eine kleine Feier vor, bis jetzt aber ruht noch Alles in der Zukunft Schooß, sobald die Sache näher bestimmt ist, melde ich sie Dir. Lieber Felix, was soll ich nächsten Sonntag spielen? Das vorige Mal hatte ich das Trio v. Moscheles, ich fürchte sehr, das mögliche Reyertrio wird den Winter hindurch nicht ausreichen. Einen Ofenschirm sollst Du haben, lieber Schatz, wo möglich zu Weihnachten. Und nun leb wohl, ich muß von hinnen ziehn. Grüß Frau Bendemann u. Frau Hübner. Ich freue mich sehr, daß die Decker sich der Abstellung des Mißbrauchs in Deinem Gesichte angenommen hat. Alexander war eben hier, u. läßt Dich sehr grüßen u. [ ]. Gestern hatte Seb. ein Herrendiner, das hätte ich Dir zu sehn gewünscht. Komischeres habe ich nicht gesehn. Die kleinen Heysens aßen hier, u. ich hatte für die Kinder ein kleines Tischchen, mit kleinen Tellern, Messern u. Gabeln u. Servietten gedeckt. Nun wurden sie lustig u. Paul Heyse, der sich wirklich *befressen* hatte, fing an, auf die Melodie des Mantelliedes zu singen: ich habe so viel gefressen. Darauf Sebastian: lebe hoch! hob sein Glas auf, u. sie stießen an, u. hielten einen förmlichen Commersch.

Sebastian grüßt, auch Wilhelm u. Luise. Leb nun zum 2tenmal, wohl.

[Abraham]

48

[Rebecka for Sebastian, Rebecka]

Ich wollte mich gern irgendwo anhängen, und habe von Mutter einen Korb bekommen. Vors Erste muß ich Dir für Deinen lieben Brief an meinem Geburtstage danken, u. das viele Angenehme, was er enthielt. Auf die Melusinenouvertüre freue ich mich sehr, laß sie mir aber auch bei Gelegenheit zukommen. Auch für die Landschaft schönen Dank, ich habe sie aber noch nicht erhalten. Der Waagen ist noch nicht vorgefahren. Nun will ich Dir aber erzählen wie wir gestern den Cäcilientag u. Anfang Deiner Concerte gefeiert haben, wir haben eine schöne Fete gegeben: also—aber ich muß doch einen neuen Bogen nehmen:

Ich habe einen Versett aus der Messe der heiligen Cäcilia, von dem Dir Mutter wahrscheinlich ein Textblatt mitschickt, in 2 Tagen componirt, in solcher Eil, daß die Begleitungsstimme bis heut noch nicht aufgeschrieben ist. Das Ganze war als doppelte Ueberraschung eingerichtet, denn erst sah man die Decker, ohne, daß sie sang, dann sang sie einige Töne ungesehn, u. zuletzt sang sie als wirklich lebendes Bild, natürlich auswendig, was eine zauberisch schöne Wirkung gemacht haben soll. Soviel ist gewiß, daß sie so weit über ihr gewöhnliches Aussehn hin schön war, daß ich ihr nur eins an die Seite zu setzen weiß, u. das war Röschen Behrend als Engel, die wirklich ohne Uebertreibung himmlisch aussah, einen solchen lebendigen Engelskopf habe ich noch nie gesehn, u. es thut mir nur leid, daß Hensel jetzt keinen Engel zu malen hat, wer sie nur recht träfe, würde den schönsten möglichen Engel malen. Es jammert mich, daß Du sie dies Jahr nicht siehst, wer weiß ob sie übers Jahr noch so schön ist, dazu muß man eigentlich 15 Jahr seyn. Ueberhaupt hätte ich Dir mit Deinem bekannten Lämmersinn gewünscht dies Häufchen Schönheit zu sehn. Die Decker hatte sich ihr Kostüm nach dem der Rafaelschen Cäcilie machen lassen, u. auch ihr Haar so geordnet, was ihr wundervoll stand. Die Engel waren weiß, Röschen Behrend hatte einen Kopfputz aus eignen, hängenden hellblonden Haaren, die ihr in Fülle bis ans Knie hingen, dazu die feinsten regelmäßigen Züge, u. tiefe dunkle Augen. Flügel, Brillanten auf Stirn u. Schultern u. die vortheilhafte Beleuchtung verdarben auch nichts,—kurz—ich wollte Du wärst dabei gewesen, Du hättest Dich gewiß verliebt, u. irgend ein schönes Quartett gemacht, was uns dann zu Gute gekommen wäre.

Clärchen Jacques, ein schönes 8 jähriges, schwarzlockiges Kind, war auch kein übler Engel, u. die kleine Therese Thürrschmidt, obwohl lange nicht so schön als die beiden Andere, machte sich auch an ihrem Platz ganz gut. Daß die beiden größern Mädchen nach Art der älteren Bilderengel ihre Notenblätter in der Hand hielten, machte sich allerliebst. Uebrigens war die ganze Aufstellung ohne Hülfe eines einzigen Handwerkers nur durch Wilhelm u. seine Schüler geschehn, u. die schönste Orgel im Attelier fabrizirt worden. Nun will ich Dir noch sagen, daß ein Satz in der Musik ist, den ich für gut halte, u. nun lebe wohl, ich habe noch des arrangements zu machen, u. will dann ausgehn, der Steffens zu ihrem Geburtstage gratuliren. Dunque, addio. Weißt Du, daß das große Bild an meinem Geburtstage fertig untermalt war? Jetzt macht er einige Zwischenarbeiten, u. dann gehts wieder drauf los.

49

Berlin, 1sten Decemb. 33

Es vergeht recht lange Zeit, ehe wir von dem Verlauf Deines Concerts etwas erfahren, liebster Felix, u. wir sind recht neugierig darauf. Deine Freundinn, die Zeitung läßt sich auch Zeit mit solchen Berichten, und so wissen wir noch nichts. Gestern war der Düsseldorfer Schrödter hier, den wir aber leider verfehlt haben, wahrscheinlich hat er Dich doch in letzter Zeit gesehn. (O weh, die gerühmte englische Dinte hat auch die Bleichsucht.)

Wir haben, nachdem ich dankbar anerkennen muß, daß alles, viele Monate lang, ganz glatt gegangen ist, wieder ein kleines Hauskreuz. Luise ist sehr unwohl, u. seit heute bettlägerig, u. mir ist zu Muthe, als würde es ein langwieriges Krankenlager werden. Gott verhüte es. Eigentlich habe ich heut angefangen Dir zu schreiben, um einmal mein Herz über den Zelterschen Briefwechsel auszuschütten, über den ich in einer fortwährenden stillen Empörung bin. Er wird uns freilich sehr löffelweis eingegeben, denn da Vater jetzt nicht Abends lesen kann, wird er drüben vorgelesen, u. da genießt man dies Buch mehr als billig. Vater ist übrigens auch sehr unwillig darüber, u. es tritt hier der seltene Fall ein, daß wir Alle einstimmig derselben Meinung sind, und auch noch nicht einmal über eine einzelne Stelle gestritten haben. Es thut mir wirklich Zelters wegen leid, der sich selbst hier auf eine so schlechte Art auf die Nachwelt bringt. Goethes Ruf kann erstlich schon eher einen Puff vertragen, u. dann sind seine Briefe unendlich besser als Zelters, obwohl Beide durch diese Veröffentlichung nur verlieren können. Von Zelters Seite herrscht darin eine unangenehme fatale Gesinnung, die wir zwar immer bei ihm vermuthen konnten, die wir uns aber auch immer wegraisonnirt haben, hier ist sie aber unabweislich ausgesprochen. Eigennutz, Selbsucht, eine ekelhafte Vergötterung Goethes, ohne eigentliche verständige Würdigung, die indiscreteste Blosstellung aller Andere die zwar in einem vertraulichen Briefwechsel zu entschuldigen ist, aber die Bekanntmachung hätte unmöglich machen müssen, alles dies u. noch manches Andre macht mir dies Buch ordentlich verächtlich. Ein Beispiel unter Vielen von unglaublicher Unwissenheit findet sich auch drin, Zelter frägt Goethe, was Byzanz eigentlich ist, u. erhält von ihm die gewünschte Auskunft. Dazu korrespondirt man mit Goethe! Die Leerheit der ganzen Sammlung übertrifft wahrhaftig jede Erwartung. Theatergeschwätz u. Klatschereien sind der einzige Inhalt, u. daß Goethe darauf auch nicht viel Gescheutes antworten kann, liege am Tage. Pfui baba! Nun hat man hier noch die Freude, es natürlich von Jedem durchsprechen zu hören, der mit Recht beleidigt ist, sich ohne seine Zustimmung darin durchgehechelt zu finden, es giebt Leute, die ordentlich steckbriefmäßig drin geschildert sind. Und nun genug von diesem unsaubern Gegenstande, mir hat dies Buch das Andenken an einen Mann, den ich lieb gehabt habe, u. gern geachtet hätte, ganz u. für immer getrübt.

Sebastian ist ganz allerliebst, u. von dem Andenken an Onkel Felix immerfort erfüllt. Du nimmst einen bedeutenden Platz in seinen Spielen ein, u. bist immer derjenige, den er als Postill[i]on herfährt. Oft sagt er auch so ganz ohne Veranlassung: Wann kommt denn endlich mein guter Onkel Felix wieder? Er meint auch gewiß, Du kämest zu Weihnachten. Eben spricht er wieder von Dir. Da ich jetzt niemand mit ihm auszuschicken habe, so gehe ich jeden Tag selbst mit ihm spatzieren, oder wenn ich Besorgungen u. Besuche zu machen habe so nehme ich ihn mit. Man kann schon die weitesten Wege mit ihm machen. Er ist magerer aber munterer u. ausgelassener als je, u. sein Sprechen setzt mich, obgleich ich es täglich höre, doch immer von Neuem in Verwunderung. Seine Neigung zu den Damen, aber, lieber Felix, ist noch immer dieselbe, heut hat sich die Hähnel zu Tisch bei uns melden lassen, da kann er die Zeit gar nicht erwarten, u. hat schon 20mal nach ihr gefragt. Eben war die Decker hier, bei der am Mittwoch Don Juan gesungen werden soll. Ich bedaure sehr, daß mir meine Partitur gestohlen ist, u. werde suchen, mir eine Andre zu verschaffen, dann lieber Felix, ich renommire da, u. setzte die Leute in Erstaunen indem ich die Zauberflöte aus der Partitur, u. das Opferfest vom Blatt spiele, das Letztere aber war eine unschuldige Renommege, es traf so mit meinem Cäcilienfest zusammen, daß ich nicht Zeit hatte, es durchzusehn. Im ganzen mache ich diesen Winter sehr viel Musik, u. bin ganz wohl damit zufrieden. Meine Sonntagmorgen erhalten sich ziemlich brillant, bis auf den letzten, der brillant klaterig war. Lebe wohl für heut.

50

Berlin, 25sten Januar 34

Ich hatte mir vorgenommen, Dir einmal zu Deinem Geburtstage recht ausführlich, lang u. weilig zu schreiben, und 4 Wochen vorher anzufangen, aber Gott weiß, wie es zugeht, wie mir die Tage jetzt fliegen, davon hast Du keinen Begriff, u. zu keiner vernünftigen Sache kann man kommen, so vielen Kühen hat man die Schwänze aufzubinden. Nebenbei ist es mir seit Deiner Abreise fast beständig so gegangen, daß ich meine Briefe an Dich, eine Stunde, ehe die Deinigen kamen, abgeschickt habe, u. das ist denn doch, mit Respekt zu sagen, absurd. Jetzt aber liegt einer vor mir, u. da muß ich Dir denn zuerst sagen, daß es mich sehr amüsirt, wie gewisse kleine Beziehungen, zufällige u. andre, sich immer zwischen uns wiederholen, u. auch in der Entfernung nicht ausbleiben. Als man mir Deinen Brief herüberschickte, worin Du von Deinen Proben des Don Juan schreibst, saß ich grade am Clavier, mit der Partitur des Don Juan vor mir, weil er den andern Abend bei der Decker gesungen werden sollte. Neulich, schreibst Du, Du habest auf die Cellos aus Fidelio phantasirt, u. da liegt auch richtig das Stück der Partitur aufgeschlagen vor mir, denn morgen habe ich lustige Sonntagsmusik, u. laß die Hauptstücke aus Fidelio singen.

Ich habe in dieser Zeit sehr viel einzustudiren u. zu musiciren gehabt, könnte ich nur einmal eine Sache mit so viel Proben einüben, als ich wollte, ich glaube wirklich, ich habe Talent dazu, u. auch es den Leuten deutlich zu machen aber die Dilettanten! Wäre ich Jean Paul, ich schallete hier ein Extrablatt über sie ein, an Stoff fehlt es mir nicht. Aber mit der Decker ist prächtig musiciren; das ist ein Talent! Sie war gestern hier, u. sagte gelegentlich, sie habe eine zärtliche Zuneigung für Dich, ich bat um Erlaubniß Dir das wörtlich zu Deinem Geburtstag schreiben zu dürfen. Du erhältst nachträglich zu Deinem Geburtstag von Deinen soeurs grises einen Ofenschirm, der sich wird sehn lassen. Du kannst Zick und Prege[r] einladen, danach zu studiren. Vorträglich aber bitten Hensel u. ich, den Violinspieler anzunehmen, der aus der Kiste herauskuckt. Ich hoffe Du hast ihn noch nicht, ich habe eine kleine Passion für das Blatt, u. es Vater zu Weihnachten geschenkt, nun wollten wir Dich auch gern daran Theil nehmen lassen. Hoffentlich schreibst Du uns vorher, wo Du ihn zubringen wirst, (nämlich Deinen Geburtstag) damit wir Dich da suchen. A propos, warum hast Du noch gar keinen Riß Deiner Stube geschickt? mit no. 1 Sopha 2 Flügel, etc. Ich bitte darum, nebst ähnlichem Portrait der Wirthstafel die Dich speist.

26sten. Eben ist mein Fidelio beendet, u. den Umständen nach, hat er sich sehr wohl befunden, u. das Publicum welches schon wieder so anfängt zu wachsen, wie damals, war entzückt. Die Decker hat wunderschön gesungen, u. alle Dilettanti leidlich. Wenn Du frägst, wer jetzt hier Tenor singt, so ist es H. v. Dachröden, der sich sehr viel Mühe giebt, u. eine hübsche Stimme hat, mit der er singt, u. ein hübsches Gesicht, mit dem er sitzt, nämlich im Attelier. Ferner ein Studentchen von 4 Zoll, Jörg, mit einer sehr hübschen Stimme, die wie eine Parodie von Mantius klingt, der singt Jaquino. Ferner Antonie Nölinchen, Busolt und Riese. Der arme schwerfällige Mann, der ein unglaublicher musikalischer Tölpel ist, hat es durch rührenden Fleiß dahin gebracht, nur die Hälfte der Fehler zu machen, die ich erwartete, Manches hat er sogar recht gut gesungen.—Kennst Du die Frau Wangen? Sie ist eine der schönsten Frauen in Berlin, wie Rose Behrend das schönste Mädchen, u. hatte heut ganz eigne Zöpfe, aus Gehorsam gegen ihren Mann, als aber die Musik aus war, nahmen Rebecka u. ich sie vor, u. meinten, das müßte noch etwas anders seyn, sie mußte sich hinsetzen, ich holte Kamm u. Staubmantel, u. sie wurde frisirt, da hättest Du Haar gesehn, das würde Dir gefallen haben. Wie ein Mantel, lang egal, u. vom schönsten Schwarz. Ich kann mich an der Frau nicht satt seyn.

28sten Gestern hat sich Möser einmal wieder zu Mozarts Geburtstag die Taschen gefüllt. (Du siehst wie musikalisch wir sind.) Der alte Fuchs befindet sich wohl dabei, u. das Publicum auch. Die Symphonie aus c dur ging ganz vortrefflich, u. erfrischte u. erfreute. Was ist das für ein prächtiges Stück, welche Lebendigkeit, u. Jugendlichkeit. Die Gesangstücke waren nicht alle günstig gewählt, u. Taubert spielte ein nicht sehr schönes Concert sehr unschön. Er spielt so sehr dilletantisch u. unfertig, u. kann keine Melodie schön vortragen. In der Thür stand H. Robert Müller, Dilettant aus Schottland.—Du willst ein Buch Sebastian u. ein Buch Walter? Das Buch Walter wird Dir Beckchen schreiben, es wird anfangen: der Zahn, der Zahn der ist heraus. Das Buch Sebastian könnte ich sehr lang machen, das Kerlchen ist allerliebst. Gestern hatte er bei Beckchen gegessen, u. kam wieder herunter, als wir noch bei Tisch waren, u. Ente u. Rüben aßen. Nach verschiedenen mißglückten Versuchen, noch einmal mitzuessen, fing er aufs Zärtlichste an zu schmeicheln, u. sagte: liebste Mutter, thu mir den einzigen Gefallen, gieb mir einen kleinen Knochen, wo *gar nichts* dran ist, dann will ich spielen, es wäre was dran. Und als er nun sah, daß wir uns des Lachens nicht enthalten konnten, fuhr er dreister fort: und dann gieb mir eine Rübe nach. Ist das nicht grade, wie ein Lorbeerblatt zu? Heut früh sagt er: ich habe Dich am allerliebsten, keinen Fremden hab ich so lieb wie Dich. Als Hensel aufwachte sagte er, die Augen wären ihm noch zugeklebt vor Schlaf, darauf fing der kleine Naseweis gleich an: im Basedow ist ein Jäger, der stellt ein Gefäß mit Leim hin, da kommen die Affen, u. kleben sich die Augen zu. Es ist gar zu niedlich, ihn etwas wieder erzählen zu hören, was er etwa einmal gelegentlich gehört hat, u. an der Art, wie ers wiedergiebt, zu erkennen, daß ers ganz richtig u. deutlich verstanden hat. Da ist er selbst.

[Fanny for Sebastian]

Gestern sagt er zum Vater: aber Vater, Du hast immer dieselben Farben, u. malst doch so verschiedene Bilder: Tante Beckchen, u. den Mohr u. die Juden, wie kann das wohl seyn? (Seine Redensart.) Neulich hatte er mir ein Glas Wasser in meine Pantoffeln geschüttelt, u. sagte nachher, als ich ihm die gehörige Moral darüber predigte, aber Mutter, Du hast mich doch lieb. Das war ja nur ungeschickt, das war nicht unartig.

Daß wir durchaus nicht hinter südlicheren Länden zurück sind, sondern blühende Krokus, grünblätterige Caprifolien, u. fingerlang aufgeschossene Hyacinthen, nebst der obligaten Ueberschwemmung im Garten haben, wirst Du wohl wissen. Mich persönlich ergötzt dieser Unwinter sehr, es ist mir noch nicht geschehn, mich mit einmaligem Heizen in meinem Zimmer behaglich zu fühlen. Dein Ofenschirm wird wohl diesmal als moutarde après diner erscheinen, u. Du wirst ihn Dir den Sommer über einpökeln müssen, indessen es komme ja mehr Winter, u. Du wirst ihn einstweilen als Herumsteherchen in der Stube auch nicht verschmähen. Hast Du schon von den neuen Eisenbahnprojekten in England gelesen, auf denen man (nämlich nicht auf den Projekten) in 4 Stunden nach Düsseldorf käme? O Hypercivilisation, wann wirst Du uns erreichen? Hensel hat Dir natürlich schreiben wollen, aber es natürlich bis heut verschoben, u. nun hat er natürlich eine Sitzung, also laß mich sein Schreiber seyn, u. Dir Alles sagen. Ich muß mich begnügen, u. nicht noch die andre Seite anzufangen, u. da Beckchen jetzt hier steht u. zu sieht, kann ich natürlich gar nicht weiter schreiben.

Adieu.

51

Berlin, 18ten Februar 34

Ich habe Dir vielen Dank zu sagen, lieber Felix, für Deine schöne Melusine, welche jetzt anfängt, es für mich zu seyn, nachdem sie mir allerdings eine sehr spröde Schöne gewesen. Deine Partituren sind überhaupt schwer, (ich triumphirte schon neulich, da ich die Zwischenacte zu Egmont sehr geläufig las) u. um diese an manchen Stellen sehr räthselhaft geschrieben, so daß ich mir den Genuß, wie billig durch einige Müh erkaufen muß. Indessen wie gesagt, ich fange an Licht zu sehn, u. sehr schönes Licht, wie ich es aber anfangen werde, das Stück Andere genießbar vorzutragen, weiß ich noch nicht. Moscheles' Redaction Eurer Zigeunervariationen wird Dich glaub ich, nicht erfreuen. Es ist nicht geschickt gemacht, gar Weniges drin, was ich Dir zuschreibe, u. die Zuthaten, z. B. die Introduction, sehr matt. Ich finde für die Herausgabe, hätt er den Character des Augenblicklichen ein wenig herausbringen sollen. Cependant! sage ich, u. Du sagst pah u. es ist abgemacht. Der Hofer gefällt mir sehr, u. muß sich an Art u. Stelle prächtig machen. Die beiden Lieder ohne Worte sind auch sehr hübsch, das Eine, was jungen Damen zu empfehlen ist, die, etc. werde ich wol ungespielt lassen. Junge, warum schreibst Du immer so rasend unbequem? Beethoven kommt Einem nach Dir ordentlich fingergerecht vor. A propos, als ich Deine Melusine zuerst in die Hände bekam, zog ich sogleich den Zettel heraus, der drin steckte, u. las wo dies Zeichen liegt, ist meine Lieblingsstelle. Noch wage ich nicht zu entscheiden, ists g dur? Mit Deinen Rebusen mußt Du uns doch alle zu Eseln, wir haben eben nur die Hälfte herausbekommen, u. von den beiden Letzten lagen wir in großen Streitigkeiten über die Lesarten: saufen ungeheuer, u. Bettler ging am Seegestade. Wir haben appellirt, u. ein halb Dutzend Wetten schweben. Aber diese Sympathie ist doch quite rührend daß wir drei Tage ehe Deine rebus ankamen, uns mit ähnlichen Malereien einen ganzen Abend vertrieben, u. beschlossen, Dir einen Bogen voll zu schicken. Jetzt wär es eine Retourkutsche. Du bist uns noch Rechenschaft schuldig über den Ball zu Deinem Geburtstag, Egmont, u. Dein 2tes Concert, von dem wir durch Kortüms wissen, daß es Statt gefunden. Sey weniger schweigsam. Schreibe überhaupt von Familien, die Du dort kennst, u. in denen Du Unglück anrichtest, schreibe mir einmal einen Privatbrief über les amours de Jacques in Düsseldorf, ich wills auch keinem Menschen wiedersagen, u.

wenn wir über die Herausgabe unsrer Briefe Contract abschließen, wollen wir verordnen, daß die Namen wegbleiben.

[S.]I.V.P.

[Hensel, Fanny for Sebastian]

Ich soll Dich erinnern an den Titel Deiner Symphonie für Schlesinger. Einer ähnlichen Theilnahme, wie Schleiermachers Tod erregt hat, weiß sich kein Mensch zu erinnern. Du wirst die Beschreibung seines Leichenbegängnisses in den Zeitungen gelesen haben, diesmal aber ist sie wirklich nicht übertrieben, es sollen 30-40000 Menschen auf den Beinen gewesen seyn, u. man hört kein ander Gespräch. An dem hast Du auch einen Freund verloren. Donnerstag giebt die Academie die h moll Messe. Fürchterlicheres wird man wahrscheinlich nie gehört haben. Der 2te Theil soll gar nicht studirt seyn. Versuche nun wohl zu leben, ich bin hungrig und muß frühstücken. Sage mal, wann kommst Du da dies Jahr nach Berlin? Du sprachst neulich was vom Mai, nimmst es lieber im Herbst Urlaub, u. kommst ordentlich zur Ausstellung u. bleibst lange? In jedem Fall hoffe ich doch, giebst Du unsrer guten Stadt den Vorzug, wenn Du reisest. Daß wir wegkommen dies Jahr, glaube ich schwerlich. Ich hoffe, daß Hensel fertig wird, indeß kann ich mir nicht verbergen, daß er hohes Spiel spielt. Die Sache ist schon auf Wochen gestellt, das geringste ernste Hinderniß giebt bösen Ausschlag. Gott gebe das Beste. Antworte darüber nicht. Uebrigens wird das Bild vortrefflich. Du glaubst nicht, wie alle übermalte Theile bedeutend hervortreten, ich glaube, es kann nicht verfehlen, wie alles Aechte, eine große Wirkung zu machen. Leb wohl.

52

Deine schöne Melusine habe ich nun ziemlich in der Gewalt, und große Freude dran. Das Stück plätschert ganz prächtig, u. Du hast den Wellen eine höchst anmuthige Mannigfaltigkeit gegeben. Uebrigens kenne ich das Mährchen gar nicht, was ist denn das für ein Seelöwe, der so bös in f moll angebrummt kommt, u. dann immer wieder durch das freundliche Wellenspiel beschwichtigt wird? Ich werde mir, wie Sir George eine schriftliche Instruction über die Ouvertüre ausbitten, oder doch eine Anweisung, *welches* Mährchen ich zu lesen habe? (Fatal, da nehme ich mir einen schönen Bogen, lasse mir eine neue Feder schneiden, u. will Dir einen recht sonntäglichen Brief schreiben, aber die Feder ist schlecht, und nimmt mir die ganze duftige Stimmung, Blüthenstaub, sagt Bärmann, mit. Täuschungen des Lebens!) Aber Du hast keinen Begriff, was für Sonne hinein scheint, eben mache ich das Fenster auf. Um auf Deinen Fisch zurückzukommen, so ist es doch ein ander Ding, wenn man zu Haus zusammen ist, Du mir einen ganz frischen Gedanken herüberbringst, u. mir nicht sagen willst, wozu er ist, den Tag drauf den zweiten, den dritten Tag Dich mit der Durchführung quälst, u. ich Dich tröste wenn Du meinst, Du könnest nun gar nichts mehr schreiben, u. am Ende das Werk dasteht, daß man meint, man habe Theil daran. Die hübschen Zeiten sind aber freilich längst vorüber. So erhalte ich nach Monaten ein Papier, worin mich freilich zuerst der Anblick Deiner Handschrift, und das Datum Deines Geburtstags erfreut, aber dann kommt das lange Fegefeuer des Sichdurcharbeitens durch eine fremde Partitur, ehe man zum Genuß gelangt, statt daß sonst die erste Bekanntschaft gleich durch reine Freude begleitet war. Diese habe ich aber jetzt auch bei der Melusine. Ich bin nun so weit, daß ich neue Entdeckungen in Kleinigkeiten mache die mich unendlich erfreuen. Einiges Wenige, was ich musikalisch vielleicht aussetzen möchte, verschiebe ich, denn ich fühle mich heut nicht zum Tadel aufgelegt.

28sten Februar. Einstweilen ist Dein letzter Brief, u. einer von Madame Moscheles angekommen, woraus wir die günstige Aufnahme Deiner Ouvertüre in London erfahren haben. Wann werde ich sie wohl zu hören bekommen? Ich habe ja, dumm genug, noch nicht einmal Deine Reformations[s]ymphonie gehört. Du hast doch gewiß die Idee, die Walpurgisnacht in Düsseldorf aufführen zu lassen, hast Du schon bestimmt, wann? Wenn Du einmal Gelegenheit hast, mir die Partitur auf ein Paar Wochen zu schicken, so würdest Du mich sehr erfreuen. Rückgelegenheit findet sich von hier immer durch den bekannten, gütrigen Portier. Löwe ist wieder hier, u. hat eine kleine Oper, mit Text v. Raupach gegeben, Devrient u. ich meinen, er würde hier Kapellmeister werden, es hat allen Anschein. Er hat eine Beharrlichkeit der Unart, die mich anfangs ärgert, jetzt aber belustigt. Ich weiß nämlich, daß er mich kennt, u. wir treffen zusammen, stehen neben einander, sprechen mit derselben Person, ohne daß er Miene machte, mich zu grüßen. Mit Marx hat er es noch besser gemacht. Ein Student erzählte ihm von seinem Verein bei der Universität, darauf frug er: Marx wer ist das? Marx giebt zwei Stücke fur Männergesang heraus, worin sehr schöne Sachen sind. Ich habe ihm, über das was mir falsch u. gefährlich schien, sehr offen meine Meinung gesagt, u. er hat fast Alles nach meinem Vorschlag abgeändert.

Eben wird mir gesagt, ich könne den Brief mit den Wachslichten abgehn lassen, wo er denn allerdings Gefahr laufen wird, mit angesteckt zu werden. Ich fürchte, das große Londoner Musikfest wird doch ziehn da überhaupt der Londoner Magnet für Dich keiner sonderlichen Verstärkung bedarf. Oder bist Du treu u. kommst her? Es wäre wol Noth, daß wir wieder einmal in Ruhe ein Paar Monate zusammen lebten. Devrient hat mir Deine Volkslieder gebracht, die mir ungemein gefallen, ganz besonders das 2te, u. im letzten die Vögel [u.] Abendwinde. Die Gedichte sind sehr reizend. Man sieht, was Heyne machen kann, wenn er einmal die Pointe aufgiebt. Was mir aber unbegreiflich ist, u. worüber ich Dich fragen muß, ist, warum Du Deine eignen, lieben Liederchen 4stimmig gesetzt hast, was mir weder zum Text, noch zu Deiner Auffassung davon zu passen scheint. Sprich, guter Ali. Noch einmal auf Deine Melusina zurückzukommen, so will ich Dir auch jetzt die Kleinigkeit sagen, die mir nicht dran gefällt, das ist also erstlich die erste Ausweichung nach der Dominante, ein Punkt, über den Du Dich selbst oft beklagt hast. Dagegen bist Du sehr schön wieder nach f dur gekommen. Der ganze Mittelsatz mit dem Gesange in as dur ist wunderschön. Dann kommt eine Stelle, die mir nicht gefällt, u. wo ich wetten möchte, daß Du Dich damit gequält hast. Es ist das Ende des Crescendo, welches zu dem forte führt.

etc. von da an schon, wo das Crescendo sich so wendet:

dann das folgende Forte, bis es wieder herunter u. nach g dur geht, wo es wieder wunderschön wird. Die benannte Stelle aber scheint mir eine Noth. In der darauf folgenden Durchführung, wo ich besonders die Stelle in c dur und g mit der Septime liebe, ist ein Takt, der mir nicht recht gefällt, es ist der in c dur vor dem schönen a dur, weil Du schon einmal länger in c dur warst. Ein großer Liebling ist die Clarinette mit der Verzierung, dann die beiden Bratschen unten, u. darauf das Thema wieder mit der schönen Flöte. Der ganze Schluß ist wunderschön. Und nun bin ich fertig. Du wirst finden, ich habe viel von Rellstab u. J. P. Schmidt profitirt. Es ist der Kuckuck, daß jede geschriebene Meinung über so etwas gleich so verdammt rezensentisch und hundemäßig klingt. Indem ichs jetzt wieder überlese, möchte ich den Brief lieber zerreißen, dann würdest Du aber nicht das Glück haben, außer den Wachslichten auch durch meine Weisheit erleuchtet zu werden, es sey also. Schreibe mir aber, daß ich ein Dummkopf bin, u. will die Hand küssen. Du schreibst über Deine Gesangsscene nur, daß eine obligate Violine für Beriot dabei sey, daraus schließen wir auf einen Sopran für die Malibran. Paßt der Schlüssel? Auf Deine Umarbeitung der Meeresstille bin ich neugierig. In der Regel sind die Zeitgenossen der ersten Auflage undankbar gegen die 2te, u. ich habe eine alte Liebe für das alte Stück mit seinen Fehlern. Gestern gaben die Ganze ein Concert, das wir aus musiksonntäglichen Rücksichten besuchten, u. das von lauter Modernismus zusammengesetzt war. Unter andern hackten die Herren Arnold u. Taubert ein neues Doppelconcert von Kalkbrenner ab, das nur in der Composition durch den Vortrag, u. im Vortrag durch die Composition übertroffen wurde. Leopold Ganz hatte eine Pastorale komponirt, die durch ein Glöckchen begläutet wurde. (Hier noch nie gehört!) Aber Moritz Ganz spielt prächtig, u. hatte wenigstens Themas aus Don Juan genommen. Außerdem die Ouvertüre aus Tauberts Zigeunern. Der hat so lange an Dir herumprobirt, u. Deine Themas mit dem Würfel durcheinander gerüttelt, bis er ein hübsches Motiv herausgebracht hat, das wie ein Irrlicht klingt, er hat es aber nicht vortheilhaft benutzt, u. für eine Opernouvertüre ist sie auch sehr lang. Lieber Felix, ich weiß gar nicht, wie wohl mir ist, schon 4 Wochen lang ruht der Zelter Goethesche Scandal, der 4te Theil ist noch nicht erschienen, u. so lange hat man Ruhe. Hoffentlich öffnet Dunkers großer Verlust bei dieser entreprise den Buchhändlern die Augen, u. wir bleiben vor ählichen[a] Gaben sicher, deren sich wieder manche vorbereiten. Unter andern, freue Dich! Bettina Arnims Correspondenz mit Goethe. Ich sehe Deine Gesichter von hier. Hegels Tagebuch, u. s. w. Adieu, leb wohl. Sebastian hat angespannt, sitzt auf dem Bock mit einem Posthorn um den Hals, u. fährt nach Düsseldorf. Er ißt jetzt allein, da wir erst nach 6 zu Tisch gehn. Eben kommt sein Diner. Leb wohl. Ich habe Dir nun zweimal nach einander geschrieben, u. heut einen schrecklich langen Brief, nun kannst Du auch einmal speciell antworten. Adieu.

---

[a]Fanny omitted "n."

53

Berlin, 12ten April 1834

Ich danke Dir, o Mond für Deine Sonnenstrahlen! sie sind zwar zeitig genug angekommen, um eine empfindliche Rache zu verhindern, die ich an Dir durch bedeutsames Sch[ ] zu nehmen gedachte. Jetzt nun habe ich meinen Kopf so voll für Dich, daß mich meine Ideen drücken, wie man es jüngst in französischen Blättern von Rossini sagte, weil er so lange nichts geschrieben hat. Also erstlich: heut geht mit Gelegenheit der Arconnatis, die wirklich dadurch ein Freundschaftsstück ausführen, der oft besagte Ofenschirm ab, in dessen Angelegenheiten ich Dich bitte, folgenden Theil meines Schreibens auszuschneiden u. wohl u. nett versiegelt, der Frau Bendemann hinzutragen, oder was gleich viel ist, selbst zu ihr zu gehn, u. ihr Nachstehendes vorzulesen. (Du kannst auch erst Vorstehendes nachlesen) Sehr werthe u. verehte Frau: werden wir (Rebecka u. ich) wol Verzeihung erwarten dürfen, wenn wir, ohne vorhergegangene Anfrage so frei sind, Sie mit einer weitläuftigen Besorgung zu belästigen? Da sie indessen meinen von Ihnen sehr verzogenen Bruder betrifft, u. die Zeit drängte, waren wir der Meinung daß (Paulinens Umstände erwogen) Sie die einzige Person in Düsseldorf wären, deren anerkannte u. längstgewürdigste Güte uns zu jener Anforderung ermuthigen könnte. Sie erhalten also unter Ihrer Addresse nächstens ein langes dünnes u. ein dickes Paket in Wachsleinewand, das eher wie alles Andere, als wie ein Ofenschirm aussieht, es aber dennoch ist. Ferner eine Arbeit, die wir äußerst sauber u. nett übergeben haben, u. die eben so ankommen möge, ferner ein Päckchen Schnur. Haben Sie nun die große Güte, Angesichts obiger Gegenstände einen Tapezier oder Tischler kommen, u. sie von ihm in gehöriger Weise zusammenfugen auch die Arbeit einschnüren zu lassen, u. dann das Ganze Felixen zu überschicken. Schließlich bitten wir, uns bald in den Stand zu setzen, wenigstens pecuniair unsre Schuld abzutragen, wenn wir auch für Ihre Güte zeitlebens Ihre Schuldenrinnen bleiben werden.

So sprich zierlich zu Madame Bendemann, u. dann warte der Dinge, die da kommen werden. Ich sage Dir noch nicht, welche Partie von mir, u. welche von Rebecka ist, Du magst erst errathen.

Deinen Brief erhielt ich heut früh, als ich mit Sebastian zusammen Kaffee trank, und so oft ich laut auflachte, frug er, was lachst Du? u. wann ich sagte, über den Brief, lachte er herzlich mit, u. sagte: wie sehr lustiger

Brief. Wilhelm reicht Dir von der Leiter herab die Hand. Er barbirt eben die Hohenpriester.

Hätte ich Dir gestern oder morgen geschrieben, so würde ich nicht verfehlt haben, bei Gelegenheit der heutigen Abreise Arconnatis, so zu schimpfen, wie wir es mit wirklich ganz Berlin seit 3 Wochen thun. Nie habe ich ein Publicum so einstimmig über eine Sache gefunden. Heut aber bin ich nicht schimpflich, sondern lustig, u. sage Dir daher blos, Du wirst Dich freuen, die Leute kennen zu lernen. D'epino ist ein herzensguter ehrlicher Kerl, sie eine feine, angenehme Frau. Sie waren überall und auch bei uns, viel u. gern gesehn, u. werden Dir von unserm Trio diesen Winter erzählen können. Die Art ihrer Abreise hat nun vollends Alles für sie in Bewegung gesetzt, u. sie nehmen die allgemeinste Theilnahme mit. Nun wollen wir uns noch ein wenig musikalisch unterhalten. Deine Gründe fürs 4stimmige will ich gelten lassen, besonders den Wohringischen. Würden wir hier alle 4 zusammen, u. hättens gesungen, so wäre es mir wahrscheinlich nicht eingefallen, etwas dagegen zu haben. Wer aber soll hier Tenor singen, wenn Du in Düsseldorf bist? Das verdammte Papier macht mich so philiströs, es wird einen gar nichts lebendig. Aber nun sage einmal, mein liebes Dummchen, kannst Du Dir wirklich einbilden, ego Deine Schwester wäre so ganz von Gott verlassen u. auf ihr Häuptlein gefallen, daß sie alles das von der Melusine nicht wüßte, was Du mir erzählst? Ich weiß Du kannst weitläuftige Erörterungen über alte Sachen nicht leiden, sonst würde ich Dir schreiben, wie viel ich davon weiß, u. längst gewußt habe, u. würde Dich über Dein Schelten schelten, dann würdest Du aber wieder über das Schelten des Scheltens schelten, u. so mit Grazie in infinitum. Stündest Du aber einmal hinter der Thür, und hörtest sie mich con amore e con espressione allein spielen, Du würdest mir ohne Weiteres glauben, daß ich sie für einen Fisch erkannt habe. Das Trio für F. P. schicke mir doch baldigst, das ist ja ein wahres Glück für mich. Habe ich Dir schon geschrieben, daß ich diesen Winter hier mit dem Trio v. Moscheles Glück gemacht hatte? Luise Dulcken läßt Dich sehr grüßen u. herzlich bitten, ihr das neue Rondo zu schicken, das Du gemacht hast. Sie spielt Dein Concert wirklich merkwürdig, ich hätte nicht gedacht, daß es außer Dir Jemand so wettern könnte. Natürlich spielst Du es unendlich phantastischer, besonders das Letztemal hier hast Du es ganz merkwürdig gespielt, u. mit ihrem Vortrag von Gesangstellen bin ich gar nicht einverstanden, aber es ist als wenn sie Feuer aus den Fingern schüttelte, u. ihre Kraft u. Rapidität ist wirklich bewundernswerth. Uebrigens ist sie abgesehn von ihrem Talent eine kluge gute liebenswürdige Frau, die sich ungemein wohl bei uns zu fühlen schien, u. mit der wir, Rebecka u. ich, in den wenigen Tagen wieder so intim[e] geworden sind, als wären wir, wer weiß wie lange, zusammen gewesen. Ein Jammer, daß sie diesen graulichen

Mann hat. Ich habe das tiefste Mitleiden mit ihr, u. leider die Ueberzeugung, daß es nie besser werden wird. Sebastian will schreiben:

[Fanny for Sebastian]

Wobei sich mein kleines Männchen wie ein junger Held benimmt. Du hast keine Idee, wie lieb u. brav das Kind ist. Er geht jetzt immer allein u. im Finstern zu Bett, hatte aber bis jetzt die Marotte, daß die Thür ein wenig aufstehn mußte. Seit kurzem hat er sich nun das auch abgewöhnt, u. brüstet sich mit seinem Heldenmuth. Gestern war er durch ein schmerzhaftes Augenwasser, daß ich ihm in sein armes schlimmes Augelchen drücken mußte, sehr weichmüthig gestimmt, zu Bette gegangen, u. sagte nach den vielen Küssen, die ich ihm immer beim Einschlafen geben muß (piangendo) Laß die Thür—(fièrement vivace) laß die Thür nicht auf, das kann ich gar nicht leiden. Das war wirklich komisch rührend. Uebrigens verspricht mir der Arzt (jetzt, da Bing langwierig krank ist, Dr. Stosch) daß es bald besser seyn, und gar nichts zu sagen haben soll. Felice, im Herbst mußt Du uns doch auf ein Paar Wochen besuchen, wenn Du auch weiter nicht reisest, womit ich sehr einverstanden bin, aber unsre Ausstellung mußt Du doch diesmal sehn. Bitte bitte!

Eben komme ich aus dem Garten zurück, wo der schönste hundekalte grüne Frühling blüht. Man kommt diesmal gar nicht zu dem angenehm erwartenden Frühlingsgefühl, wozu unsrerseits aber auch viel der Verkauf der wunderschönen Parkpartie des Gartens beitragen mag, in der wir nächste Woche das Vergnügen haben werden, Axt u. Säge aufräumen zu sehn. Was mich aber fast noch mehr als dies verdrießt, u. grämt, ist daß das Schuft von Gärtner ungestraft, aber nicht unbelebt den ganzen Rest des Gartens auf seine Art verstümmelt u. verdirbt, u. daß alle unsre Gegenvorstellungen auf unser Haupt zurückfallen, indem wir Alle nur eine Partei gegen den heiligen Bremer bilden. Dafür wollen wir uns aber nun wirklich ernstlich gegen ihn verbünden, u. sehn ob die vereinigten Kräfte 2/4 Kindern u. Schwiegerkindern nichts gegen die bekannte Betrügerei dieses Kerls vermögen werden, auf den ich wirklich keine geringe Malice habe. Wenn doch nur irgend ein Fremder unsrer Meinung würde! Wir wollen den General Braun in Vertrauen ziehn. Kann nicht vielleicht H. v. Wohringen etwas für uns? Du hast zwar seit Deiner Directorschaft sehr an Credit gewonnen, indem das traue ich Dir doch nicht zu, daß Du Bremer oder Carl aus dem Sattel heben könntest. Lieber Felix, glaube nicht, daß ich Taubert kopiren wolle, indem ich Dich kopire, u. den Brief erst beschreibe u. dann zulege. Ich finde aber die Methode sehr bequem, u. sage unverholen, daß ich sie nachmachen, u. noch allerhand erzählen will. Freu Dich doch nur nicht, auf den 4ten Theil Correspondenz, ich versichere Dich, er ist noch jämmerlicher als alle Andere, ich kann ihn vor Ekel u. Langeweile kaum zu Ende bringen. Von Marx liegt ein Exemplar seiner 6stimm. Männergesänge für Dich hier. Ich schicke es mit nächster prinzlichen Gelegenheit. Er ist jetzt sehr heiter u. muthig. Auch im Attelier geht Alles erwünscht u. frisch. Ein ungemein reizendes Bildchen von Burggraf (wozu Rose Behrend gesessen hat) u. eine runde Landschaft von Pohlke, die Du glaub ich schon gesehn hast, sind auf der Staffelei verkauft, Mehreres andre ist bestellt, u. an kleinem Portraitverdienst fehlt es den jungen Leuten nicht. Ein neuer Schüler ist vorige Woche eingerückt der eigen genug, Hübner heißt. Sie sind Alle voll Eifer, voll Liebe für Wilhelm, u. außerordentlich fleißig. Dir würde vieles gefallen, vor Allem aber glaub ich das liebliche Bildchen von Burggraf. Dabei fällt mir ein daß der mir neulich außerordentlich Erscheinung u. Behebung der Hähnel als Druidenpriesterin Norma gerühmt hat, Luise Dulcken fand aber diese Oper so gräulich, daß ich keine Courage dazu habe. Ich wollte Dir nur sagen daß ich die Hähnel lange nicht gesehn habe, eine Aufführung der Semele schleppt sich ihretwegen schon Monatenlang hin. Sie ist sehr beschäftigt u. muß jetzt auch in Potsdam singen, von wo göttlich emphatische Berichte in der Zeitung stehn. Wilhelm hat vortreffliche Zeichnungen von ihr u. der Dulcken gemacht. Ueber ihren Geburtstag wird Dir wohl Rebecka selbst schreiben. Weißt Du denn, daß ich in Briefwechsel mit Mary Alexander stehe, u. sie zärtlich liebe? Sie hat mich neulich um ein Stammbuchblatt gebeten, u. ich habe drei von den Liedern komponirt, die sie allerliebst aus dem Deutschen übersetzt hat, u. denen ich eine *Art* von Zusammenhang, so gut es gehn wollte, gegeben habe. Dazu hat W. eine kleine Arabeske gezeichnet, leider war der Raum auf dem von ihr geschickten Notenpapier sehr klein, aber ich denke es wird ihr Freude machen. Ihre deutschen Briefchen sind ja zum Küssen lieb. Dieser Tagen fangen wir eine Handarbeit für sie an. War das geplaudert? Sey aber nicht wieder so grausam, sondern schreibsam.

Deine F.

54

Sonntag, 27 April 34.
blaue Stube

Bülletin

Die Nacht war ganz ruhig u. gut, jetzt ist es Mittag, Mutter hat eben 2 Apfelsinen verzehrt, u. ist ganz munter, hat auch Erlaubniß, aufzustehn, wenn sie will. Das war ein Schreckschuß, lieber Felix, u. wer sie vorgestern Abend gesehn hat, hätte nicht an die Möglichkeit geglaubt, daß sie gestern wieder so erholt seyn würde. Gott sey Dank, daß es so vorübergegangen ist. Wir haben in dieser Woche rechten Wechsel erfahren. Unser letzter Brief war glaub ich, das Tollste, was Du noch in Düsseldorf erhalten hast, wir waren wirklich ganz exaltirt vor Lachen, Schreien u. Wundern, 2 Stunden drauf wurde Mutter krank. Die Agitation über Paul, worüber sie sich doch sehr freut, u. über Marianne, die sie im Grunde, wie auch Varnhagen, sehr lieb hat, mochten wol das ihrige dazu beigetragen haben. Uebrigens kann ich Dich versichern, daß sie, während die Krankheit am Aergsten war, jeden freien Augenblick dazu benutzt hat, von Marianne zu sprechen u. sich erzählen zu lassen, was der u. Jener darüber sagt. Paul nämlich ist ganz im Grund gebohrt, es spricht kein Mensch von ihm, nicht einmal wir. Mutter läßt Dir sagen, sie habe Nathan zum Rabbiner geschickt, um genau zu erfahren, wie alt die Braut ist: 49 Jahr, grade so alt, wie er.

Mutters Hauptübel besteht noch in heftigem Herzschlagen, wogegen sie Eis auf der Brust trägt, dies Mittel incommodirt sie gar nicht, u. thut ihr sehr wohl. Sie läßt Dir sagen, Deinen Arzt, wenn Du einen hast, darauf aufmerksam zu machen, daß Du auch die Disposition zu starkem Herzklopfen hast. Stosch sagt, man könne u. müsse früh dagegen etwas thun. Mit Stosch sind wir außerordentlich zufrieden, er ist sehr ernst, aufmerksam, examinirt bis ins kleinste Detail, u. hat obenein die unvergleichliche Eigenschaft, im Hause zu wohnen, so daß er vorgestern 5mal unten war, was man doch von keinem Andern, mit dem besten Willen, verlangen könnte.

Eben geht H. Bendemann weg, den Mutter einen Augenblick zu sehn verlangt hat. Er hat schon gestern Deine Sachen geschickt, für die wir bestens danken. Nein, mein Söhnchen, diesmal war ich nicht wieder solche Pute, den Zettel herauszuziehn, aber spielen könnte ich die Sonate noch nicht. Mutter hat sich Deine Zettel vorlesen lassen, u. dankt sehr für das

Album. Einen schönen Gräuel haben sie aus Hensels Zeichnung gemacht; da sie nichts daran getroffen haben, ist es mir fast lieb, daß sie den Namen auch nicht getroffen haben, er hat aber doch besonderes Pech mit Lithographie. Ueberhaupt enthält das g[em] nicht wenig Schund. Wenn gem von j[ämmer]lich käme, fände ich den Titel analoger. Deine beiden Stücke scheinen sehr hübsch zu seyn, ich habe sie nur bis jetzt gelesen. Aber Dein Frühlingslied ist etwa so wenig ähnlich wie Dein Bild. Denke Dir, daß ich unmoderne Personen von dem berühmten Hünten zuerst in diesem gem ein Hauptwerk, einen Walzer habe kennen lernen. Komponirt habe ich lange nichts. Ausgeschrieben! Was soll man machen? Soll man wie H. Hünten einen Walzer fürs gem schreiben? Hensels Bild rückt sehr vor, u. wird wunderschön. Ich hoffe, daß er, à moins d'accident, fertig wird. Tausend Grüße v. Marianne u. Varnhagen, sie gehn eben weg. Ueberhaupt haben Rebecka u. ich den ganzen Tag über Besuche zu empfangen, während wir abwechselnd drin bei Mutter sind. Lebe wohl, mein Herz, hoffentlich werden wir Dir morgen die besten Nachrichten zu geben haben.

Deine Fanny

Mutter grüßt noch tausendmal, u. läßt Dir befehlen, gesund zu bleiben. Dazu wird meine Erlaubniß ein Pferd zu halten, wol das ihrige beitragen. Adieu. Auch Vater läßt sehr grüßen.

55

Berlin 11ten Mai

Mutter geht es recht gut, lieber Felix, u. Abends vortrefflich: da sitzen wir Alle um den Theetisch, ganz wie gewöhnlich, u. Mutter ist munter, ganz wie gewöhnlich, morgens ist sie in der Regel etwas matt, u. war besonders gestern u. vorgestern, der druckender Gewitterluft wegen sehr abgespannt. Gestern Nachmittag hat es sich abgekühlt, u. heut ist sie auch viel muntrer. Diese Morgenmattigkeit ist eine Art von Nervenschwäche, die nach dem Blutverlust sehr erklärlich ist, u. die wir ja leidend in der Familie nur zu gut kennen, nur an Mutter bis jetzt nicht. Viel ist auch Hypochondrie dabei, sie ist des Krankseyns Gottlob nicht gewohnt, u. Du hast keinen Begriff, wie ängstlich sie ist, so daß auch jede Zerstreuung jeder Besuch ihre Stimmung günstig verändert. Am Nachmittag u. Abend, ich widerhole es, ist sie fast ganz wie sonst, munter u. theilnehmend, u. lachlustig u. spaßhaft, marschirt auch tapfer im Garten umher, u. macht, wie alle Welt, *noch immer,* Marianne u. Varnhagen zum Ziel ihrer Betrachtungen u. Späße. Deine Briefe freuen sie ungemein, schreibe nur recht fleißig, den Vorwurf Dir nicht treu berichtet zu haben, muß ich aber ablehnen. Wir haben Dir am dritten Tage der Krankheit geschrieben, eher konnten wir nicht, um Dich nicht unnütz zu beunruhigen, denn bis dahin schwebte die Sache, u. konnte sich von einer Stunde zur andern verändern. Sonnabend früh aber war die Gewißheit der Besserung eingetreten, u. von da an haben wir auch alle Tage fleißig u. treu geschrieben bis die Berichte nicht mehr so nöthig waren.

Deine musikalischen Berichte sind sehr erfreulich, mehr! Daß aber Euer Concert nicht voll war, verdrießt mich, Ihr habt es wahrscheinlich zu weit in die schöne Jahrszeit hinaus geschoben wo Eure Rheinischen Lebemenschen spaziren fahren u. Maitrank trinken. Das Trinken scheint bei Euch eine ungeheure Rolle zu spielen. Ist der junge Musikdirector aus Barmen nicht Rahlès? mir däucht der wohnt da. Die Sonate aus Fis gefällt mir sehr, u. ich spiele sie fleißig, denn sie ist à la Felix sehr schwer. Hab Dank dafür. Lieber Sohn an Gelegenheit würde es grade nicht fehlen, u. ich wollte Dir Deinen Idomeneo gern schicken, wenn er nur da wäre, aber der ist mit so manchen andern flötengegangen, ich suchte ihn diesen Winter, um die Decker die erste Arie draus, die ich ungeheuer liebe, singen zu lassen, fort war er. Ich bleibe dabei, wir müssen einen Hausdieb für Noten haben.—Schreibe doch ob der Ofenschirm wirklich gut angekommen ist, unabgestoßen, unbeschmutzt u. chiffonirt u. wie er Deiner Stube steht. Die ganze Zeit hatte ich Angst, er würde in der Zeit der ersten bösen Briefe angekommen seyn, u. Dir gar kein Vergnügen gemacht haben. Lebe wohl mein Schatz, ich will mit Mutter ein wenig in den Garten gehn. Gieb mir doch etwas auf zu komponiren aber nicht die Weltgeschichte, oder den dreißigjährigen Krieg, oder die Zeit der Päpste, oder die Insel Australien, sondern etwas wirklich Brauchbares, solid Existirendes. A propos, habe ich Dir denn jemal geschrieben, daß Elsholz uns eine Oper zu lesen gegeben hat, die er Dir schicken will? Der größte Scandal den ich je gelesen habe, ein Wettstreit der Abgeschmacktheit mit der Langweile, unglaublich. Es fällt mir eben ein, weil gestern eine neue Tragödie von ihm, König Harold, uns gelacht worden. Wir haben ihm auf die möglichst höfliche Art gesagt, daß Du eine Oper in *diesem genre* schwerlich komponiren würdest, denn N. B. er hat unsre Meinung über Deine Meinung verlangt, u. wenn Du sie bekommst, so ist es portofrei durch uns, nicht durch ihn, denn er soll nicht nur Elsholz sondern auch Geizhals seyn. Adies.

[Lea, Paul]

56

Berlin, 4 Juni 1834

Ich habe Dir eigentlich allerhand durcheinander zu schreiben, lustig, geschäftsmäßig, das Gegentheil, kurz viel. Wobei soll ich anfangen? Bei den Geschäften. An Henning habe ich geschrieben, aber noch keine Antwort. Schlesinger hat mir neulich einen Liebesbrief geschrieben, u. die Korrektur Deiner Symphonie eingelegt (4händige) die habe ich durchgesehn, aber eine solche Furcht vor Schelte, daß ich Dir lieber eine kleine Mühe als mir Gewissensbisse aufpacken will, u. ihm daher heut geantwortet habe, ich würde sie Dir erst schicken. Denn warum? Weil in dem Manuscr. Fehler sind, die ihres Gleichen suchen, u. so abgeschmackt sind, daß ich sie noch gar nicht fasse. Siehe Scherzo—Nun habe ich auch die Marxsche Partitur herausgesucht, u. will Dir einige Stellen bezeichnen, die mir sehr gefallen z. B. in No. 2 gefällt mir der Schluß des ersten Satzes, mit dem vielen e in seiner jetzigen Gestalt sehr gut, obgleich ich ihn zu lang finde. Den hättest Du aber hören sollen, wie er ihn mir im Manuscr. vorlegte, da gingen Bässe u. Tenore immer in einem fört zusammen mit dem e, so daß ich ihm sagte, es könne es kein Mensch singen vor Lachen. Das folgende Stück No. 2 finde ich auch gut, dagegen: wende dich Herr, gar nicht, u. das habe ich ihm auch gesagt, u. ihm überhaupt sehr viel gegen den 6stimm. Männergesang eingewandt. Es liege Alles viel zu nah an einander, als daß die Harmonieen Platz haben könnten, u. so wird es ein ewiges Gemurxe u. Geschnarre unfehlbar bleiben. Dieselbe Noth mit seinen Liedern. Es ist immer so viel gänzlich Unmusikalisches in seinen Sachen, es sind wol Gedanken, aber sie lassen sich nicht musikalisch gestalten, u. so bleibt es dem guten Willen, u. dem Zufall überlassen, ob man seine Absichten errathen kann u. will, denn dargestellt sind sie nicht. Suche ihm aber doch ein Wort über seinen Kirchengesang zu sagen, Du weißt wie empfindlich er ist, u. wie viel er auf Dich, u. allein auf Dich giebt.—Nun noch ein Wort auf dieser Seite, denn die andre wird ostensibel. Daß Du Vater in Baden besuchen willst, freut uns sehr, u. wir wollten Dich schon darum bitten. Mutter wird nämlich nicht mitreisen, wie sie Dir wol heut selbst schreibt. Stelle Dir aber deshalb ja keinen Rückschritt vor, im Gegentheil, es geht ihr sehr gut, aber Vater hatte ihr, unbegreiflicher Weise, diese Reise eingeredet, ohne Stosch zu fragen, u. der sagt nun, wie mir scheint, sehr vernünftig: da sie sich vor jeder Alternation u. Schreck besonders zu hüten hat, so ist eine Reise durchaus nicht anzurathen. Der Wagen kann umwerfen, sie kann an einem heißen Tage der Sonne mehr als nützlich ausgesetzt seyn, kurz tausend Kleinigkeiten, die sich zu Hause nicht vermeiden lassen, oder gänzlich wegfallen, u. die auf Reisen unberechnet sind. Nun darf aber Vater seiner Augen wegen nicht allein in Baden bleiben, er kann keine Bekanntschaft anknüpfen, nirgend hingehn, da ihn seine Kurzsichtigkeit scheu u. ängstlich macht. Zu jeder andern Zeit würden wir Hensels uns das größte Vergnügen daraus machen ihn zu begleiten, allein dies Jahr muß Hensel bleiben, u. ich bin ihm zu nöthig zu seiner Behaglichkeit u. Arbeitsstimmung, um ihn bei diesem wichtigen Werke verlassen zu können. Rebecka würde mit Walter reisen, wenn Du nicht könntest, aber da Du Dich schon halb dazu erbietest, so hoffe ich wird Dir der Vorschlag nicht unerwartet kommen, nach Baden zu gehen, wenn Vater hinkommt, u. die 4 Wochen mit ihm dazubleiben, die Reise kann er sehr gut mit Carl machen, nur dort braucht er jemand. Urlaub hast Du ja, u. arbeiten kannst Du in Baden. Du mußt aber so gut seyn, es ihm anbieten, denn wenn wir ihm den Vorschlag machen, so brummt er: Dich nicht stören, zufrieden lassen à la Majestät. Marianne Saaling ist eben hier angekommen, um Mittag zu seufzen, u. wir lösen uns mit Albertine ab, damit sie Mutter nicht den Kopf toll macht. Aehnlichen Skandal gab es nie. Halt abers Maul. Der gute Vater läßt sich da weich machen, das ärgert mich am Meisten. Ich bin verdrießlich, daß Mutter Dir die Infamie schreibt, die zuletzt in ihrem Brief steht, u. über die, wie über alle ganze schlechte Nachrede ich mich schon genug geärgert habe, ich will meine Hand ins Feuer legen, daß es blasse Verläumdung u. Unwahrheit ist, denn ich weiß es. Gestern war *nicht* der Stiftungstag des Atteliers, sondern gestern vor 8 T. Da war aber 10 Gr. Kälte, also wurde eine Festpartie nach Charlottenb. bis auf gestern verschoben, u. 1/2 11 frühstückte sämmtliches Attelier im Garten Brühe u. Sauerbraten u. etc. Dann gingen sie in die Sitzung der Academie wo Pohlke prämiert ward, u. 6 andre, worunter Kaselowsky u. Wagner, durch eine Kabale ausgeschieden, dann beging der alte Schadow die Lächerlichkeit, die zugleich eine Unwahrheit ist, zu sagen, die Ausstellung würde mager ausfallen, denn die besten Schüler wären nach Düsseldorf gegangen, dann gingen sie, u. wir fuhren nach Charlott. wo wir die Transfiguration, u. ein großes Bild v. Catel in der Kirche besahen, Rosa besuchte u. den Tag hier munter beschlossen. Zwei von den jungen Leuten waren noch obenein Geburtstagskinder. Na, leb wohl, dieser Bogen sollte einen Umschlag werden, u. ist über allem Plaudern selbst ein Brief geworden. Chopin möchte ich wol hören. Schreib doch was über Deinen Paulus, u. schick Deine Lieder. Ich habe von wegen Sympathie auch welche gemacht, aber leider nichts Größtes[,] nächste Woche wird bei uns Iphigenie gesungen, Bader Orest, ist das übel?

57

Ich muß, obwohl eine beschäftigte Festmutter, mich doch hinsetzen, u. einen Commentar zu dem Schreiben, was Dir Mutter wahrscheinlich in diesem Augenblick erzählt, damit Du nicht denkest, ich sey in Deiner Abwesenheit ganz dumm, oder eine Närrin geworden. Es ist übrigens eine sehr musikreiche Woche. Also: Mutter hat Dir doch gewiß vom Königstädten Orchester am Sonnabend erzählt, u. daß ich mit dem Stock wie ein Jupiter tonans da gestanden habe. Das ging aber folgendermaßen zu. Lecerf ließ seinen Scholoren spielen, u. zerklopfte sich die Finger dabei, da ging ich heraus, u. holte Dein weißes Stäbchen, u. gabs ihm in die Hand. Nachher ließ ich meine Ouvertüre spielen, u. stellte mich dabei ans Clavier, u. da flüsterte mir der Teufel in Lecerfs Gestalt zu, das Stöckchen in die Hand zu nehmen. Hätte ich mich nicht so entsetzlich geschämt, u. bei jedem Schlage genirt, so hätte ich ganz ordentlich damit dirigiren können. Es amüsirte mich sehr, das Stück nach 2 J. zum erstenmal zu hören, u. ziemlich Alles so zu finden, wie ich es mir gedacht hatte. Den Leuten schien es auch vielen Spaß zu machen, sie waren sehr freundlich, lobten mich, machten mir auch einige[r] Ausstellungen wegen unpraktikabel, u. kommen nächsten Sonnabend wieder. Da ist mir denn mit einem Mal eine ganz unerwartete Freude zu Theil geworden. Morgen läuft Iphigenie vom Stapel, die auch nicht übel besetzt ist.

Die Stimmgabel werde ich nächstens von Henning erhalten.

Wer ist der Spötter, der die schönen Verse gemacht hat?

Ich wollte ich könnte die Bachschen Motetten hören, giebst Du sie vollständig?

Auf Paulus bin ich nicht wenig begierig. Marx hat in Potsdam beim Schullehrermusikfest die erste seiner beiden Motetten aufgeführt, u. ist nicht wenig zufrieden mit Ausführung u. Aufnahme, die er dort gefunden.

Vale:—Heut ist Probe v. Iphigenie, es werden aber nicht viele dazu kommen.

13ten. Mein Briefchen ist vorgestern liegen geblieben, u. da kann ich Dir denn gleich Bericht abstatten über die Iphigenie, die sich sehr gut aufgeführt hat. Ich wollte Du wärst dabei gewesen, wie die drei Stimmen geklungen haben, u. wie die drei sich immer einander gesteigert haben, das hört man so leicht nicht wieder, es war wirklich wunderschön. Einen Strom von Klang, wie Bader u. Mantius in dem Duett hab ich nie gehört. Die Decker war auch vortrefflich bei Stimme, u. sang immer schöner bis zum Schluß, aber Bader war doch die Krone. Er hatte die Partie nie gesungen, u. kam gestern zur Probe ziemlich maussade, meinte auch, es läge ihm doch zu tief. Als er aber nur den ersten Akt gesungen hatte, war er schon ein ganz andrer Mensch, u. gestern hat er sich ein Mal übers andre bei mir bedankt, daß ich ihn zu der Partie veranlaßt hätte. Zu meiner großen Freude habe ich ihn mir auch so gewonnen, daß er sich ein für allemal angeboten hat bei mir zu singen, was ich wollte, wann ich wollte, Chor, Solo, etc. Und er soll singen, bei den Pforten der Hölle. Zunächst wahrscheinlich das Ave Maria, das im Kirchsprengel des Erzbischofs von Kölln erschienen, u. in Petersburg aufgeführt ist, und wovon ich noch jetzt eine lange Nase habe. Uebrigens waren 100 Personen gestern hier, die Eltern hatten Theil an der Fete genommen, u. mehrere Bekannte eingeladen, u. so kams, daß ich die Ehre hatte, den Oberbürgermeister, H. v. Bärensprung, die Familie Ölrichs aus Bremen, etc hier zu sehn. Unserseits waren mehrere Engländer hier, unter andern Lady Davy, die sehr viel von Dir zu erzählen wußte, u. eine liebenswürdige Frau ist. Sie sagte, sie hätte Cramer niemals mit solchem Entzücken von Jemand sprechen hören, als von Dir, er piquire sich sonst einiger Strenge.

Neben bei war mein Chor vortrefflich, 8 Soprane, 4 Alte mit der Thürrschmidt u. der Blano, im Tenor Bader u. Mantius, es war wunderschön, u. einige Sachen haben mich wirklich überrascht. Devrient, der den Thoas übernommen hatte, ließ wie gewöhnlich im letzten Augenblick ohne besonderen Grund, absagen, u. Busolt war so gefällig, für ihn zu singen.— Ueber Alles andre, war der Garten wunderschön, die Rosenhecke in voller Blüthe, u. das Lokal im Putz, sucht auch seines Gleichen.

Dazwischen sind nun alle Spuren von gestern weggeräumt, u. es bleibt nichts davon übrig, als einige verirrte Töne, die mir immer noch in den Ohren klingen. Addio, Mutter will auch noch schreiben, u. ich will Stimmen korrigiren, denn morgen rücken meine Königstädter wieder ein. Lebwohl, mein Söhnchen, laß bald von Dir hören. Hensel grüßt sehr, sein Bild avancirt mächtig, u. findet vielfache u. angenehme Anerkennung, daß der König Humboldt u. Bunsen hergeschickt hat, wird Dir Mutter geschrieben haben, es bleibt aber ganz uns, es ist uns nur geklatscht worden.

[Lea, Abraham]

58

Berlin, 18ten Juni 1834

Mein liebes Felixärmchen, wieder einmal will ich Dir erst Geschäftsbericht abstatten. Die Gabel erhältst Du mit nächster prinzlicher Post. Von Kalix konnte ich sie nicht contrasigniren lassen, weil der abwesend ist, u. ich nicht auf seine Rückkehr warten wollte. Der Instrumentenmacher Schulz der einstweilen bei mir stimmte, fand sie um eine Schwebung höher, als seine Gabel, u. so habe ich von Kubelius tastiren lassen, der sie mit zu Hause genommen, u. mit seiner Gabel verglichen hatte. Uebrigens sagt mir Schulz, daß Spontini immer noch in die Höhe triebe, so daß die jetzige heisige Stimmung ganz unvernünftig hoch ist, u. Henning sagt, man sey in Paris seit Kurzem um einen vollen halben Ton heruntergegangen. Es wäre doch interessant, wenn Du Dir zur Vergleichung eine Gabel aus Paris kommen ließest.—Die beiden Fugen aus e moll mußt Du unter Deinen Sachen in Düsseldorf haben, lieber Felix, ich schickte Dir damals Alles was Du irgend brauchen konntest, u. habe sie auch in den beiden zurückgebliebenen Mappen die nur ganz alte, oder unbeendete Sachen enthalten, nicht gefunden. Schreibst Du mir aber, daß sie entschieden nicht dort sind, so will ich noch einmal alles umkehren, u. sie aus der Erde zu stampfen suchen. Ferner erhältst Du mit dieser Sendung die Maryschen Lieder. Frägst Du mich um mein Urtheil, so sage ich: no. 1 gar nichts, no. 2 nichts, no. 3 wenig. Indeß hat no. 2 Marx außerordentlich gefallen, so daß er mir unbegreiflicher Weise fand, es sey eines meiner besten Lieder.

Sonntag sind meine Königstädter Herren wieder hier gewesen, es war ein Orchester wie eine Harlekinsjacke, an der Stelle der 2ten Flöte war ein Loch, sonst Trompeten, 4 Hörner, Pauken und alle Plunder. Die beiden Ganz thaten sehr wohl dazwischen. Einer der Herren hatte eine schaudervolle Ouvertüre mitgebracht, was mir aber ganz recht war, u. ich bat, wenn Einer von ihnen wieder einmal etwas zu probiren hätte, möchten sie es doch hier thun, wofür sie mir sehr dankbar waren, u. mir sämmtlich ihre Dienste abgeboten haben. Wenn es nun einmal wieder dazu kömmt, lasse ich Deine Melusine spielen. Meine Ouvertüre ging das letztemal sehr gut, u. schien ihnen Allen zu gefallen. Ueberhaupt habe ich die angenehme Erfahrung gemacht, daß mir die Leute freundlich u. gefällig sind, u. daß ich wohl ohne Furcht sie einmal in Anspruch nehmen kann. Vom Theater kann ich Noten haben, so viel, u. wann ich will.

Hensels Bild rückt ungeheuer vor, u. ich habe jetzt die Ueberzeugung, daß er, Unfälle abgerechnet, fertig wird. Der Pinsel fliegt ihm wirklich. Du wirst Dich über die wunderschönen, kraftvollen Gestalten freuen. Der Rahmen ist fertig, Du weißt, daß Uber nichts dafür nehmen will, sondern H. nur gebeten hat, ihn als Brustbild zu malen. Dies ist eine realle Anerkennung so wie Runges Lacklieferungen. Leider kann er das Bild nicht im Attelier in den Rahmen setzen, wird es also wahrscheinlich erst auf der Academie so sehn.

Stosch ist jetzt verreist, u. Mutter hat einstweilen Becker genommen, der ihr verordnet hat, früh aufzustehn, mit Vater der Brunnen trinkt, in den Garten zu gehn, u. ein Glas kaltes Wasser zu trinken, was ihr Alles sehr gut thut.

Lieber Felix, es ist 9 Uhr Morgens, Sebastian ist noch nicht gewaschen, meine Küche nicht bestellt, ich wollte blos den Brief anfangen, u. da ist mir die Feder weggelaufen. Vorgestern war Sebastians Geburtstag, der Junge war überglücklich. Von Rebecka hatte er ein lebendiges Lamm bekommen, das aber so wild ist, daß es alle Stricke zerreißt, u. sich gar nicht bändigen lassen will, ich glaube es ist ein verkleidetes Pferd. Als Kindergesellschaft hatte er sich, wie schon voriges Jahr, die Schüler eingeladen, unter denen Ratti sein entschiedenes Liebling ist. Gegen Abend spielten wir mit ihm Blindeküh, wobei er sich gar niedlich u. geschickt anstellte, sein Stimmchen veränderte so gut wie die Großen, u. es gar nicht aufhalten wollte vor Lachen u. Vergnügen.—Marianne u. Varnhagen sind jetzt declarirte Exbrautleute. Sie in Freienwalde, er sehr lustig, Beide benehmen sich, on ne peut pas plus mal. Die Geschichte ist so eklich, daß nicht einmal viel davon raisonnirt wird, [nun] denke?

Adieu Schatz.—Eben kommt Dein Brief. An Rosa werde ich noch heut schreiben, sie wohnt in Charlottenburg. Daß Dir der kleine Frank gefällt, freut mich sehr, Herrmann schildert seinen Character sehr liebenswürdig. Dieser ist uns aber diesmal unter uns gesagt, sehr abschmeckend u. schwerfällig vorgekommen, u. ich finde es auch natürlich, daß eine Lebensart wie die Seinige, bei vorrückenden Jahren dem der sie ausübt, alle Liebenswürdigkeit benehmen muß, dies zweck-u. thatenlose Umhertreiben kann Dir doch am Wenigsten gefallen.

Mache doch eine Ouvertüre zu Macbeth. Felix ich beschwöre Dich, schicke mir doch auf der Stelle eine Staffette mit dem Allegretto oder Mittelstückthema Deiner A dur Symphonie, ich quäle mich todt damit. Wahrscheinlich ists mir unterdessen schon längst eingefallen, aber never mind. Adieu. Wer hat denn Deine Scene gesungen? Malibran ist in Italien.

[Lea]

59

Berlin 1 Juli

[Lea]

Nur 2 Worte, denn ich [ ] heut den Vormittag verrechnet, verkramt, verwirthschaftet, ver . ver. ver. etc. Devrient kam vorgestern, mich zu bitten, in Euryanthe zu gehn, um die Großer zu hören, da habe ich mir dann auf eine originelle Weise ein Billet verschafft, die aber zu lang ist, sie zu erzählen: Sie hat den Umfang der zu Eglantine gehört, also v. ais unten bis h - c. oben. Eine sehr hübsche Höhe. Mittel-u. tiefe Töne erschienen mir schwächer. (Beckchen fand sie 2 T. früher ungeheuer stark.) Die Passagen machte sie so zur Noth, so daß man sieht, sie kann Geläufigkeit erlangen, aber ihr Vortrag ist noch gänzlich unausgebildet, ihr Spiel vollkommen roh, so daß sie wie Du denken kannst, eine schreckliche Eglantine war. Aussprechen that sie gar nicht, hübsch schien sie mir auch nicht, aber sie intonirt vollkommen rein, u. hatte, *wie ich höre*, die Partie in 8 T. gelernt u. sicher u. tadellos memorirt, was sehr viel ist. In Summa glaub ich, Du könntest wol eine Sängerin aus ihr machen. Indeß bitte ich zu bedenken, daß ich sie einmal, im großen Opernhause, als Eglan gehört habe, gewiß die unvortheilhafteste Art einer Anfängerin zu beurtheilen. Die Lenz gefällt mir ungleich besser. Indeß scheint die hier fest zu seyn, ich höre aber auch von der Großer, daß man sie hier zu engagiren denkt.—Devrient verlangte, daß ich Dir meine Meinung schreiben sollte, u. ich thats. Nun leb wohl.

Amalie zieht heut auch von mir, da sie ihr 4tes Kind erwartet.

60

Ich schreibe Dir wahrscheinlich vor unserm, wills Gott Wiedersehn zum letzten Mal, denn wenn die Feder merkt, daß Du bald kommst, so will sie gar nicht mehr rutschen. Ich hoffe, Du reist den 18ten ab, u. kommst direct hierher, denn auf der Eltern Reise baue nur gar keinen Plan, Du weißt erstlich, wie unschlüssig sie sind, wie wenig Lust Mutter jemals zum Reisen gehabt hat, u. nun die große Hitze dazu, die das Reisen wirklich sehr unbequem machen würde, ich halte es für viel wahrscheinlicher, daß Vater oder Beide Dich nachher zurückbegleiten, was auch für uns in sofern bei Weitem vorzuziehn wäre, als uns dadurch nichts von Deinem Urlaub entzogen würde, und Du die ganze Zeit hier zubringen könntest. Audi, et vidi, et inclina aurem tuam.

Bewundere meine Discretion, die mir nicht erlaubt hat, den an Fürst adressirten Paulus aus der Bande zu nehmen, um ihn erst zu lesen. Wie kommt Fürst unter die Propheten? Und habe Dank für das Stück Symphonie das mir große Freude macht, ich habe es eben erhalten, u. auch gleich 2mal mit Beckchen gespielt, mehr konnte sie nicht, denn sie befindet sich in der allergroteskesten Verzweiflung über die Hitze, die wirklich Alles übersteigt, was wir je gewohnt waren, zu ertragen. Mir geht es viel besser, ich zerschmelze nur ein Paar Stunden im Tage, u. halte mich größtentheils im Attelier, wo es leidlich ist. Am besten aber erträgt es Hensel, der den ganzen Tag, so lange er sehn kann, auf der Leiter arbeitet. Das Werk geht aber auch seiner Vollendung entgegen, u. Du wirst Dich dran freuen. Weichlich ist es eben nicht. Eben malt er dem Pilatus seine Candillen. Ich bin aber wieder abgekommen von Deinem Stück. Die Aenderung in der ersten Melodie gefällt mir nicht recht, warum hast Du sie gemacht? Um das viele a zu vermeiden? Die Melodie war aber natürlich u. schön. Die folgenden Veränderungen wollten mir auch nicht recht munden, indeß habe ich den weiteren Verlauf des Stücks doch nicht genau genug im Kopf, um eigentlich darüber urtheilen zu können. Im Ganzen glaub ich, gehst Du zu leicht daran, ein einmal gelungenes Stück später umzuarbeiten, blos weil Dir dies u. jenes dann besser gefällt. Es ist doch immer eine nüßliche Sache, u. wer sich einmal an eine Version gewöhnt hat, geht schwer daran, eine Abweichung zu dulden. Bring mir doch das Alte mit, wenn Du herkommst, dann können wir drüber disputiren.

Deine Vesper wurde neulich v. Marx im Studenten Concert gegeben, ging aber leider nicht gut, wie es denn sehr schwer seyn mag, einen so vollkommen volontairen Chor, der nicht, wie andre Academieen, durch die eifrigen Frauen zusammengehalten wird, zu einiger Einheit zu bringen. Was sich wunderschön machen muß ist das Solostück mit dem lamentirenden Baß, u. mächtig klang nach den vereinzelten Eintritten der 4stimmige

Auch der Schlußchoral muß, rein gesungen, wunderschön u. ruhig abschließen, aber sie detonirten sehr vor Hitze, u. da die Kirche leer war, so

schallte es noch obenein gewaltig, was der Deutlichkeit sehr Schaden that.
3ten Aug.

Vor allen Dingen melde ich, daß ich das Manuscript zurück erhalten, weil Herr Fürst verreist ist. Ich werde es nun bei mir behalten, bis ich erfahre, daß er wieder hier ist, wenn ich nicht andre Ordre von Dir erhalte.

Heut ist das Wetter sehr abgekühlt. Ein starker Sturm er- u. verjagt abwechselnd dicke Regenwolken, u. ich hoffe von des Königs Geburtstag mit dem Sonntag zusammen, daß sie sich den Spaß machen werden, den Leuten ihre Spazierkleiden unentgeltlich zu waschen.—Ich habe gestern einen bösen Tag mit angesehn, also gehabt. Hensel hat in 24 Stunden dreimal die entsetzlichsten Magenkrämpfe gehabt, so daß wir endlich gestern Abend in unsrer Verzweiflung zur Homöopathie unsre Zuflucht nahmen, welche Luise schon lange mit dem besten Erfolge braucht, u. welche denn auch diesmal, wol im Verein mit der Erschöpfung des Uebels, gute Wirkung that. Wahrscheinlich werden wir bei dieser Gelegenheit, aus Mangel an einem Arzt, zu dem wir eigentlich zutrauen hätten, an dem homöopathischen Stüler hangen bleiben. Stosch zieht weit weg, kommt nie von selbst, u. das ist für mich eine sehr unangenehme Eigenschaft.

Daß Steffens Rektor geworden, wird Dir Rebecka geschrieben haben, die Freude im Hause ist sehr groß.

Leb wohl.

61

4ten November 1834

So will ich Dir denn durchaus einmal wieder schreiben. Wie beschäftigt ich jetzt vor lauter Nichtsthun bin, das glaubst Du nicht, u. wie angelegen ich es mir besonders seyn lasse daß die Ausstellung nicht ohne kluge Leute ist. Dieser große Vehikel des angenehmen Müßiggangs fällt nun bald weg, u. dann wird sich wohl Alles wieder ins alte Geleise finden. Jetzt, so kurz vor Thorschluß, stehen noch große Kisten im Flur der Academie leere, wie ich nun erfahren habe, indessen kann doch nichts Erhebliches mehr fehlen, u. die Säle sind überreich besetzt. In neuster Zeit hat ein Bild eines Holländers, Maaß, das größte Aufsehn des Publicums, u. das Entzücken aller Kenner u. Künstler erregt. Es ist die lebensgroße, halbe Figur einer Italiänerin, im bekannten Bauerkostüm, welche, ihr schlafendes Kind in den Armen, vor einer Kapelle kniet, u. durch das doppelte Licht des Tages

u. der Altarlampe beleuchtet wird. Diese Beleuchtung nun, die Reflexe auf der Figur, das Zurücktreten des Hintergrundes, können die Maler nicht ausloben, während ich meine besondre Freude habe, an dem wunderschönen Köpfchen u. Aermchen des schlafenden Kindes, u. nur bedauern möchte, das Alles uebrige in die unförmlichen bunten Wickeln versteckt ist. Bendemanns Bild hängt auch seit einigen Tagen, gefällt mir aber auf der Ausstellung noch weniger, als in seinem Attelier, es sieht sehr grau u. nüchtern aus, u. die Inhaltlosigkeit fällt doppelt auf, da man Sohns, offenbar denselben Gegenstand behandelnde, mit der einen, wunderschönen Figur, daneben sieht. Auch den beiden Skizzen können wir es nicht abgewinnen, u. das thut mir leid, weil ich so gern mit Dir übereinstimme, aber besonders die Schäferscene mißfällt mir förmlich, u. den Andern hier im Hause geht es nicht besser. Im Allgemeinen glaub ich, kann man sagen, daß diesmal von den Düsseldorfer Bildern Stilkes am Besten gefällt. Köhlers, welches Du, wenn ich mich recht erinnere, nicht wohl leiden konntest, gefällt mir durch eine gewisse Heiterkeit u. Helligkeit, welche gegen die meist elegische Stimmung der dortigen Bilder vortheilhaft absteht, aber daß von altem Testament, u. der ägyptischen Retterin Mosis keine Spur darin ist, läßt sich wohl nicht läugnen.—Ich weiß nicht, ob man Dir geschrieben hat, daß Kaselowskys Bild sehr viel Beifall findet, u. gleich in der ersten Stunde nach seiner Ausstellung verkauft worden ist. Gestern haben Steffens u. der Landschaftmaler Dahl den Abend hier zugebracht, Hensel hat Dahl für sein Buch gezeichnet. Von den vielen hier anwesenden Düsseldorfer Malern hat keiner H. besucht. Sie scheinen darüber eine Verabredung zu treffen, da außer ihnen nicht leicht ein fremder Künstler unser Haus vorbeigeht. Stilke kann man darin nicht rechnen, da er ein alter Bekannter ist. Gruppe fährt fort, den kleinen Krieg gegen H. zu führen, er ist aber der Einzige, u. ich bin durchaus zufrieden mit der Aufnahme, die Meister u. Schüler diesmal finden. Mein Quartett habe ich fertig gemacht, u. dabei noch Deinen Rath was das Scherzo betraf, nach meinem besten Wissen benutzt. Ich werde es nun diese Woche probiren lassen. Wir haben durch die Zeitungen den Anfang Eurer Concerte, u. Theatervortstellungen erfahren, u. sind nun sehr begierig, von Dir das Nähere zu hören.

Gans ist zurück, sehr eingenommen von Italien, u. erzählt sehr lebendig u. hübsch von seinen Fährlichkeiten in der Schweiz, wo sie durch tollkühne Wanderungen auf zerstörten Straßen beinah ums Leben zukommen waren. Nun adieu, ich muß zur Veränderung auf die Ausstellung.

5ten. Heut Abend ist eine große Fête bei Paul, der die schönen, zu seinem Geburtstage ihm geschenkten Sachen einweihen will. Gestern sprachen wir seinen Lieutenant, der uns sagte, daß der Unteroffizier ihn für den besten im Exerciz nun erklärt habe. Uebrigens ist er noch immer äußerst unwirsch über seinen Dienst, u. es giebt häufige Streitigkeiten darüber. Gestern habe ich aus ziemlich zuverlässiger Quelle gehört, daß Dulcken schon wieder Bankerott gemacht hat. Er war vor kurzem hier, u. hat von einem hiesigen Tapisseriehändler, der sein Geschäftsfreund ist, eine Menge Sachen genommen, welche der ihm nun, wo möglich, noch in Hamburg abjagen will. Für die unglückliche Frau giebt es keine Hoffnung, wenn sie sich nicht von dem nichtswürdigen Menschen scheiden läßt, u. daran scheint sie gar nicht zu denken. Lafont, der süße, der uns so neue Nachrichten von Dir gebracht hat, kann noch zu keinem Concerte kommen, u. wird, fürchte ich, nicht viel ausrichten. Wenn man ihn sieht, kann man nicht umhin, sein Spiel veraltet zu erwarten, er ist so sehr ci devant jeune homme, hat so viel Aehnlichkeit von Neukomm, daß man bei seinem Anblick unwillkührlich daran denken muß, was seitdem die Kunst der Geige durch Paganini für einen Umschwung erlitten hat. Daß die Crelinger mit ihren Töchtern Gastrollen im Königst. Theater giebt, wirst Du aus Zeitungen wissen, daß man sich bei der ersten Vorstellung um Plätze geprügelt hat, ist eine Privatnachricht dazu. Pfui das schmeckt nach einem Zelterschen Briefe. Entsetzlich betrübt finde ich den Untergang des engl. Dampfboots. Solch ein unerhörter Fall erschüttert gar zu sehr das wohlgegründete Vertrauen. Brrr—Ich möchte jetzt nicht zur See gehn, das milde stürmische Wetter dauert fort. Fürchtet Klingemann nicht für seine Verdauung? Kein Wort von ihm in Deinem gestrigen Paulschen Briefe, woraus ich aber mit Freude sehe, daß ihr auch zu Templer u. Jüdin verstiegen habt. Das ist ja eine der schwersten Opern, u. wenn Euch die gelingt, könnt ihr wol Alles wagen. Daß Ritz einschlägt, freut mich herzlich, u. für ihn wird es ein unzuberechnender Vortheil seyn. Wie stehst Du nun mit ihm hinsichtlich der Direction? Dirigirst Du was u. wann Du willst à caprice, oder habt ihr auch das eingetheilt? Und was hast Du in Deinem ersten Concert gegeben? Adieu, lieber Felix, schreibe auch einmal wieder ordentlich. Deine F.

62

Berlin, 24sten Nov.

Habe Dank, o Clown, für Deinen lieben Geburtstagsbrief. Die Andere haben Dir seitdem geschrieben, also hast Du wohl von allen freundlichen Feierlichkeiten, Geschenk der jungen Leute, u. andern schönen Sachen, Thee im prächtig aufgeputzten Attelier, und vortrefflich aufgeführten Charaden, schon gehört. Ich glaube, wenn ich eine alte Frau seyn werde, werden mir noch solche Aufführungen Spaß machen. Gestern war der Geburtstag der Frau Steffens, den sie durch eine Gesellschaft in ihrer neuen, allerliebst eingerichteten Wohnung gefeiert haben. Man ist da immer in der besten Gesellschaft freundlichst aufgenommen, und ich wüßte mich keiner neuern Bekanntschaft zu entsinnen, über die ich mich immer so von Neuem gefreut hätte, als diese. Unter allen Entwürfen, die Du nennst und beabsichtigst, ist der des Trios nicht, das hast Du doch nicht aufgegeben? Bitte, mache es mir fertig, ich freue mich recht darauf.

Wilhelm hat mir eine Zeichnung zu meinem Geburtstage gemacht, die sehr schön wird. Mirjam, die Prophetin, die Pauk in ihrer Hand, die Weiber hinter ihr, Moses auf einem Berge, den Zug leitend, im Hintergrunde mit Beute Beladende, Theile des Heers, u. in dämmernder Ferne Pyramiden. Die Composition ist rund, u. sehr reich, schön und besonders. Ich hoffe, er wird es malen. Diese Zeichnung ist das erste Blatt, in einem schönen Buch, das wir uns zum Stammbuch eingerichtet haben.

27sten.

Du erhältst nun jetzt den 6ten Band v. Goethe Zelter, mit dem die Reihe geschlossen ist. Der Herausgeber hat sich die Mühe gegeben, hinten ein alphabetisches Verzeichniß anzuhängen in welchem Jeder, der das Abc weiß, ohne Mühe nachsehn kann, wo und wie oft er im ganzen Werk geschimpft oder gelobt worden, (Du—bists 58mal) was hier ziemlich gleich bedeutend ist. Figaro! würdest Du sagen, wenn Du hier wärst, ich kann Dir aber nicht helfen, es beleidigt mich von Anfang bis zum Schluß, daß in einem Lande ohne Preßfreiheit, wo also die zur Oeffentlichkeit bestimmten Personen sich der Oeffentlichkeit entziehn, harmlose Privatpersonen so plötzlich, wie von Räubern aus dem Busch angefallen, u. je nachdem den Herren die Dinte geflossen ist, besprochen und verlästert, auch mitunter ihnen die Ehre abgeschnitten wird. Von mir steht, ich spiele wie ein Mann, ich habe Gott oder Zelter zu danken, daß da nicht eine Unanständigkeit folgt, mit denen das Buch sonst wohl gesegnet ist. Vater wirst Du mehrere Mal hart getadelt finden, daß er Dich nicht nach Sicilien reisen lassen. In England würde ein solches Buch gar nicht gelesen, weil man der Persönlichkeiten gewohnt ist, u. es sonst kein Interesse hat, schön finde ich es aber unter keinen Umständen, u. immer u. ewig unzart, Privatleute zu veröffentlichen.

Streiten muß ich aber auch noch mit Dir. Nicht über die Bilder, denn das ist schriftlich zu weitläufig, u. wir sind mal zu sehr auseinander über den Punkt. Wir sprechen wol noch einmal darüber. Aber was schnaubst Du mich denn an, weil ich sage, Paganini habe das Geigenspiel verändert? Ist denn das nicht wahr? Spielt man denn heut, wie man auf der ersten Geige gespielt hat? Wer hat denn die Sache anders gemacht, als große Talente? Und wozu sind *Umschwünge in den Leuten*, wie Du sagst, wenn sie nicht auch außer sich etwas umschwingen? Mir scheint die franz. Zeitung ganz recht zu haben, wenn sie sich auch ungeschickt ausdrücken mag. Was willst Du denn anders, als weiterbringen, Dich u. die Kunst? Dazu bist Du doch wohl fleißig, u. nicht um so u. so viel Rießpapier zu beschreiben. Ich sagte u. rettete meine Seele, die aber doch wohl nicht in Gefahr bei Dir geschwebt hat, nicht wahr?

Gestern waren wir, o Wunder! im Theater, um die Töchter der Crelinger in Minna v. Barnhelm zu sehn. Ein Paar allerliebste Mädchen. Hübsche, natürliche Talente, u. so ausgebildet, daß man fast sagen möchte, es wäre für ihr Alter zu viel, wenn man nicht wieder hoffen müßte, daß ein so glückliches Naturell sich auch weiter hülft. Wir haben uns trotz der schlechtesten Plätze köstlich amüsirt.

Heut ist nun die letzte russische Majestät abgerutscht. Wie lumpenvagabundus sich Beide hier benommen haben, darüber ist nun ein Geschrei. Der Kaiser hat keine wohlthätige Anstalt beschenkt, die Kaiserin bis jetzt auch noch nicht, vielleicht kommt das noch. Da nahm sichs denn fast wie eine Satyre aus, daß der immens reiche, närrische Demidoff zur Feier ihrer Anwesenheit, den Armen 1000 rh schenkte. Von der Ausstellung, die ihretwegen 14 T. länger offen blieb, haben sie nicht für einen rh gekauft, u. die einzige grandiose Bestellung, die die Kaiserin gemacht hat, ist eine Kopie nach der Skizze v. Blancs Bilde. Ueberhaupt ist alles voll des Lobes ihrer Unfreundlichkeit, u. ihres kindischen u. würdelosen Betragens. Der Ausstellung haben sie entschieden an Schaden zugefügt, denn da sie den König nur Geld u. Zeit gebracht haben, hat weder er, noch der Kronprinz, noch sonst Jemand vom Hofe etwas gekauft, was eine unerhörte Sache ist. Nach Bildern von 20 Louis d'or hat die Kaiserin gefragt, u. sie waren ihr zu theuer.

Eben habe ich Deinen Brief an R. mit den Intendenzklagen gelesen, ich danke Gott, daß Du heraus bist. Lebe nun wohl, u.[a] will herüber, u. Vater vorlesen, aus Rankes Päpsten.

---

[a]Fanny may have meant "ich" instead of "u.," or else omitted "ich."

63

30sten Novbr.

Ich habe eben Deine Uebersetzung von Byrons Gedicht wieder gelesen, und finde es durchaus besser als Theremins. Bis auf den Schluß, der bei Th. unendlich schöner, ja ich möchte sagen, schöner als bei Byron selbst ist. Du mußt suchen, es noch zu ändern, u. mit, hell, aber ach! wie fern, zu schließen. Es klingt in dem Gedicht etwas Wunderbares, wie ich es fast nicht stärker ausgesprochen kenne. Es übt eine völlig magnetische Gewalt über mich aus, ich kann nicht wieder davon wegdenken.—Ich lerne ihn überhaupt jetzt kennen, zwar auf eine Weise die nicht die vortheilhafteste für einen Dichter ist, da ich seine Verse alle 8 Tage beim Lehrer lese, u. mehr oder weniger mühsam verstehe. Allein was durch alle diese Prosa durchdringt, das ist die Gewalt seines Rythmus, der wunderbare Klang seiner Verse in dieser widerstrebenden Sprache, das ist das tiefpoetische seines ganzen Wesens.

Mir ist dieser Tagen sein Leben in die Hände gefallen, das ich lese, u. das mich sehr interessirt. Es verdrießt mich immer, wenn wir, auch über Kleinigkeiten, nicht zusammen kommen können. Ich habe, seitdem Du andrer Meinung warst, versucht, mit Kritik an Loewes Komposition jenes Byroneschen Gedichts zu gehn, u. kann es nicht, weil es mich jedesmal wieder rührt, wenn ich nur dran denke. Ich finde es so ganz träumerisch schön, so, ich kann mich nicht andres ausdrücken, entfernt klingend, so in den Sinn der Worte eingehend, daß es mich mit fortreißt, sobald ich dran mäkeln will.

10ten. Ich hatte dies Blatt angefangen, mit dem Vorsatz, es gelegentlich, in guten Stunden, gar hinaus zu schreiben, u. so sey es denn. Heut den Tag über hatte ich mancherlei Verdrießlichkeiten, u. heut Nachmittag spielte ich 2 Trios durch, die ich mir, in Bezug, auf meine, Sonntag wieder anfangensollenden Musiken hatte geben lassen, von Reißiger u. Onslow. Ich wollte doch gar zu gern einmal etwas Neues bringen, u. das eine Onslowsche Thema hatte mir im Laden gefallen. Es war aber so mattes, lahmes, grundlangweiliges Zeug, daß ich im Durchspielen fast verschimmelte, u. nachher zur Erholung, die Litaney u. meine Lieblingsmotette: Gottes Zeit, spielte. Ah!! Dabei wird einem wieder wohl. Ich kenne keinen eindringlicheren Prediger als den alten Bach. Wenn er so in einer Arie die Kanzel besteigt, u. sein Thema nicht eher verläßt, bis er seine Gemeinde durch u. durch erschüttert oder erbaut u. überzeugt hat. Schöneres kenn ich fast nicht, als das Furchtbare es ist der alte Bund, wozu die Soprane so rührend einstimmen: ja komm Herr Jesu komm. Sebastian nicht Bach nimmt mir die Feder aus der Hand.

[Fanny for Sebastian]

23sten Dec. Da ich Dir nichts schicke, als mein Quartett, so wollte ich es doch nicht ohne Brief schicken, u. da ich vor Weihnachten nichts Vernünftiges schreiben kann, so lasse ich es bis nach Weihnachten liegen.

25sten. Dabei blieb es denn auch richtig vorgestern. Wir haben einen der lustigsten Weihnachten gehabt, u. nur bedauert, daß Du nicht dabei warst, bei meiner Kenntniß Deines Charakters glaube ich, Du hättest vor Lachen unter dem Tisch gelegen. Vorerst vielen Dank für Deine Sendung u. Dein liebes Bildchen, das uns Beiden die größte Freude gemacht hat. Meine Sendung kommt post festum.

[Fanny for Sebastian]

Relation. Rebecka und ich, wir hatten wieder zusammen aufgebaut, und zwar folgendermaßen: Von der Thür der grauen Stube an ging eine Allee abwechselnd von Weihnachtbäumen u. Tischen. Auf die Tische waren die Sachen, je nachdem sie zusammengehörten vertheilt, u. ihr Inhalt durch eine Tafel mit Rosinenschrift angegeben, so stand vor dem Tisch mit Kunstsachen: Chur, vor den Spielsachen: Gamet, u. s. w. Unser Kunsttisch war besonders brillant. Neue schöne Kupferstiche für die jungen Leute des Atteliers, eine allerliebste Zeichnung v. Hensel für Albertine: Paul als Soldat vorstellend, Walterchen v. Moser, als Geschenk von Rebekka für Mutter, eine schöne große Schweizerlandschaft von Lory von ihr für Dirichlet, viele Kupferwerke u. Bücher, dann war der Gypstisch sehr schön, auf dem Rebecka fürs Attelier eine kolossale antike Ariadnenbüste, mit dazu gehörigen Apollfüßen, u. einer Michel Angelo Hand aufgeputzt hatte. Es war eine Fülle von schönen Sachen aller Art, wie wir sie glaub ich noch nicht beisammen gehabt haben. Die beiden anwesenden Fremden, Lory u. Lafont, wurden beschenkt u. amüsirten sich vortrefflich. Nachdem Alles gehörig betrachtet war, (Mutter allerliebsten Aufbau hinter einen Schirm wird sie Dir wol beschrieben haben) wurde weggeräumt, et la chambre se constitua en théâtre, dessen Schauplatz die Tische war. Der Zettel besagt das Weitere. Das erste Bild, worin sie sämmtlich in Kostüm mit Nasen erschienen, wurde von dem einstimmigen Chor, Prinz Eugen begleitet, welches ich bei dieser Gelegenheit als dasjenige Lied kennen lernte, das in der Musik wahrscheinlich den tollsten Rythmus hat. Hast Du es je auf Noten gesehn?

Dann kam der Heirathsantrag, von Paul Albertine, u. Hübner als

Page dargestellt, das mußte ich aus kostümlichen Rücksichten versäumen, weil ich im Folgenden, der nach Hensels Zeichnung arrangirten Miriam zu thun hatte, u. die Pauke schlagen mußte. Beckchen mit der Harfe, u. Albertine mit Doppelflöten folgten mir, u. es soll sich sehr gut ausgenommen haben. Hierauf kam ein großer Effekt. Der Vorhang ging auf, ein einsamer großer Leierkasten stand da, von Pohlke in fabelhaft lumpigem Kostüm gedreht, der dazu den Dr. Eisenbart sang. Hinter dem Leierkasten aber saßen unsichtbar: Kaselowsky, Paul, Hübner, Löwenstein u. Wagner, u. ahmten mit ihren schönen Stimmen den Klang der Drehorgel so täuschend nach, daß anfangs gar nicht gelacht wurde, weil man es für einen wirklichen Leierkasten hielt. Nachher aber glaubten wir uns scheckig zu lachen. Ich empfehle Dir dieses Musikstück für Aufführungen in der Academie.

Den Bärentanz hat Dir Sebast. beschrieben, er war vortrefflich, u. das letzte machte Paul[s] Erfindung u. Geschmack alle Ehre. Die Pyramide bestand aus Schülern, Paul war der Gipfel. Jeder hatte ein Licht in einer, u. ein Geschenk in der andern Hand, u. einen Zettel aus dem Munde hängen, der den Empfänger bezeichnete. Sämmtliche Sachen kamen v. Paul, u. waren vortrefflich gewählt, u. sehr zweckmäßig u. hübsch.—Von den jungen Leuten habe ich sehr hübsche Zeichnungen nach ihren diesjährigen Bildern erhalten. Noch ganz zuletzt machten wir aus allerhand übrig gebliebenen Kleinigkeiten eine Lotterie fürs Attelier, die zu allgemeiner Belustigung diente. Am Erfreulichsten aber wird Dir, wie uns seyn, daß beide Eltern äußerst wohl u. vergnügt waren, Vater habe ich lange nicht so herzlich lachen sehn, auch meine alte Schwiegermutter war, so schwach sie auch jetzt ist, sehr munter u. froh, von den Kindern versteht sichs von selbst.

Auch wir hatten, insofern einen recht frohen Weihnachten, als sich die Angelegenheit mit dem Bilde kurz vorher so gut als entschieden hat. Sie ist nämlich dem Ministerium überwiesen, u. geht nun einen langsamen, aber wie Alle versichern, u. wir auch glauben, sichern Gang. Das ist mit ein Grund gewesen, warum ich Dir so lange nicht geschrieben habe. Hensel war krank vor Verdruß, u. [d]ann wieder verstimmt aus Krankheit, u. fest entschlossen, im Fall einer abschlägigen Antwort, ganz von hier wegzugehn. (Das aber, wie natürlich ganz unter uns.) Du kannst Dir denken, wie mich diese Aussicht, die eine halbe Nothwendigkeit war, so wie die ganze Unsicherheit unsrer Gegenwart gepeinigt u. verstimmt hatte. Ueber unsre jetzigen nächsten Plane ein andermal. Düsseldorf steht drin.—Nun noch in aller Eile, daß ich Deine beiden e moll Fugen nicht habe, ich glaube es Dir auch schon geschrieben zu haben, Du mußt sie unter Deinen Sachen finden. Ueber Deine Kirchenmusik Deine neuen Stücke die[a] noch nicht kenne u. vieles Andre, nächstes Jahr. Jetzt ist es 1/2 12, u. ich sitze in einer kalten Stube. Indessen da ich die Unmöglichkeit voraussehe, bei allen unsern morgenden Planen, ihn am Hochzeittage fertig zu machen, muß ich ihn heut gar hinaus schreiben. Fange nur beim 2ten Bogen zu lesen an. Seb. bittet, Du möchtest ihm doch auch einmal einen Brief schreiben. Leb wohl. Deine

F

[Hensel]

[a]Presumably Fanny omitted "ich."

64

Berlin, 27sten Dec. 1834

Ich schreibe, nicht blos als Federkiel, sondern als halbstündige Authorin.

Es waltet schon seit mehreren Wochen, und verschiedenen Hin- u. Herschreibungen ein so eigenthümliches Mißverständniß ob, mein lieber Felix, daß ich mich umgehend hinsetze, es endlich ins Klare zu bringen. Der Brief, den Dir Rebecka schrieb, auf den Brief den Du mir geschrieben hast, über den Brief den ich Dir geschrieben hatte, au sujet de Lafont, den ich damals noch gar nicht gehört—ist gar nicht aus R.s Kopf, wiewol aus ihrer Feder geflossen, sondern war der erste, den Vater dictirte. Wunderst Du Dich? Lies ihn noch einmal, u. die Schuppen werden Dir vom Auge fallen, u. Du wirst nicht begreifen, daß Du ihn nicht gleich so verstanden hast. Ich begreife es indeß sehr wohl, was man selbst weiß, denkt man gar zu leicht für jeden Andern auch begreiflich, u. so dachte Vater, Du müßtest auf der Stelle im Brief den Punkt erkennen, wo er angefangen zu diktiren. Ich fand es gleich nicht recht. Indeß ändert das eigentlich in der Sache nicht. Was *ich* Dir antwortete, war von mir, u. da wir einmal angefangen haben, uns in eine höchst würdige u. parlementarische Eröterung einzulassen, so wollen wir fortfahren. Je demande la parole, die Du mir von Düsseldorf aus gewiß nicht streitig machen wirst.

Daß die Zeiten sich ändern, und mit den Zeiten der Geschmack, und mit dem Geschmack der Zeiten auch wir, das läßt sich wol nicht ganz läugnen. Es giebt gewiß in der Kunst auch ein positiv Gutes, und ich hoffe, Du wirst mich niemals für so von Gott verlassen halten, daß ich das, was mir als Höchstes anerkannt haben, und immer anerkennen werden, der Mode unterworfen glauben sollte. Hannchen in den Jahreszeiten wird so wenig veralten, als Alceste, oder als der Evangelist Matthew. Nun aber giebt es doch im Guten eine unglaubliche Menge von Schattirungen, u. da sich die Kunst, oder das Schöne, oder der Geschmack nicht mit 2 mal 2, 4 demonstriren läßt, so wird es da einen Punkt geben (und der trifft glaub ich hauptsächlich die Execution) wo die Außenwelt, oder die Wandelbarkeit der Zeit, oder (schleiche Dich um das Wort herum wie Du willst) die *Mode* ihren Einfluß üben wird. Du erinnerst Du,[a] so gut wie ich, daß es eine Zeit gab, wo wir von Spohrs Musik unendlich entzückt waren. Jetzt sind wir es nicht mehr in dem Grade, nun ist aber doch seine Musik stehn geblieben, wir sind eben auch keine andre Menschen geworden, aber unser Verhältniß zu ihm hat sich geändert. Laß uns noch das einmal angeregte Beispiel von Violinspielern nehmen. Spohr hat gewiß in seinem Spiel unendlich viel positiv Gutes, was nicht vergehn wird, er hat aber auch daneben eine gewisse Süßlichkeit, u. diese Tendenz hat vielleicht in ihrer Zeit viel zu seinem Ruhm beigetragen. Nun kommt Paganini, u. spielt wild, phantastisch, stark, u. alle jungen Geiger bemühen sich es ihm nachzuthun, u. reißen die g Seite entsetzlich. Darauf höre ich Spohr nach einer Reihe von Jahren wieder, und unwillkührlich wird mir seine Süßigkeit mehr auffallen, als sonst, wenn sie sich auch an u. für sich nicht vermehrt hätte, weil ich die Ohren von einer entgegen gesetzten Richtung voll habe. Diesem Einfluß unterliegt natürlich zunächst das Publicum in Masse, die einzelnen Menschen mehr oder weniger, aber ganz frei glaube ich, kann sich Niemand davon sprechen. Es würde mir gar nicht schwer werden, noch Beispiele in Menge andrer Art anzuführen, wo uns Dinge oder Menschen, die uns vor einiger Zeit gefielen, jetzt fade u. langweilig, oder bizarr und unerträglich vorkommen. Solcher Wechsel trifft natürlich wie das Höchste und Beste seiner Art, aber daß auch das Gute, je nachdem es der Zeit gegenüber steht, mehr oder weniger gut erscheinen kann, scheint mir entschieden. Antworte hierauf, Clown! Soll ich diese ganze Korrespondenz in mein Streitbuch eintragen?

Lustig ist es übrigens, daß sich diese ganze Erörterung über ein dummes voreiliges Urtheil anspann, das ich über Lafonts Perücke fällte, denn weiter kannte ich damals noch nichts von ihm. Ich habe ihn seitdem im Concert gehört, wo mir sein klares, fleißendes, angenehmes Spiel ungemein gefallen hat, u. besonders sein reizender Vortrag melodiöser Stellen. Dann hat er einmal hier gespielt, wo ich ihm Variationen begleitete, u. dabei Gefahr lief, in mein erstes Urtheil über seine Perücke zurückzufallen, denn seine Compositionen, Variat. mit Herz und Kalkbrenner u. so w. sind doch wol von der Art, daß nicht einmal die äußerste Mode sie entschuldigen kann, u. es verdroß mich, daß die nette Geige nichts ordentliches spielt. Und nun habe ich geschwatzt u. geschwatzt, u. die Zeit versäumt in der ich mir Deine neuen Lieder einstudiren wollte, um sie morgen in pleno vorzutragen. Sie gefallen mir außerordentlich u. ohne *Aber*, ich halte sie mit für Deine Besten. Die Fugen sind vortrefflich, u. die kleine hat einen sehr schönen Fluß. An der großen gefällt mir der letzte Schluß nicht ganz, es wird da wieder dünne, nachdem es lange vollstimmig gewesen ist, u. auch in der Mitte ist eine Stelle, die mir wie ein Flick[en] scheint, es ist die nach dem p. cres. f., wenn der Baß das Thema in 8ven c dur bringt, u. dann nun von der Oberstimme imitirt wird, wie auch die Folgende Themastelle in f. Sonst ist sie prächtig, u. ich möchte sie schon erst von Dir spielen hören. Die kleine erinnert mich im Character an ein kleines Stück von Dir, welches mir eine Deiner liebsten Compositionen ist, u. trotz aller *Umschwünge*, oder Reforme oder Kirchenverbesserungen wahrscheinlich bleiben wird, ich müßte dann ein Türke werden, ein rechter Renegat. Ich meine, die kleine Quartettfuge, die mich sehr rührt, wenn ich nur an sie denke, u. an den, der sie schön spielte.

27sten Dec. Um nochmals auf besagten Umschwung zu kommen, will ich Dir einen Fall anführen, wo ich ganz Deiner Meinung bin. Ich war noch voriges Jahr sehr gegen die Homöopathie, u. besonders gegen das Selbstdispensiren der Aerzte; jetzt haben wir Stüler zum Arzt, er giebt mir u. uns Allen seine Pülverchen, ich bin damit zufrieden, u. Hensel besonders hat diese Behandlung gegen den Magenkrampf ganz vorzüglich gut gethan. Dessen ungeachtet aber kann ich es gar nicht leiden, wenn so manche homöopathische Neophiten sich anstellen, als wäre ihnen nun plötzlich das Himmelreich eröffnet, u. als wäre früher kein Mensch kurirt worden, ich bin gewiß frei von solcher Befangenheit, u. glaube es überhaupt so ziemlich zu seyn.

Heut habe ich meinen[b] Sonntagspublicum Deine neuen Sachen vorgespielt, Publicus war sehr entzückt. Das erste Lied, es dur, hast Du offenbar nur für das Clavier geschrieben, weil Du keine Worte dazu fandest, denn es ist ja ein wirkliches Lied u. sehr schön declamirt, Du hättest aber nur die Verfasser mehrerer von Dir komponirten Lieder, z. B. Egon Ebert, oder Voß drum angehn sollen, die hätten es Dir gewiß nach Deinem Sinn geschrieben. In dem 2ten Liede bitte ich um Erlaubniß eine Note zu ändern u. statt:

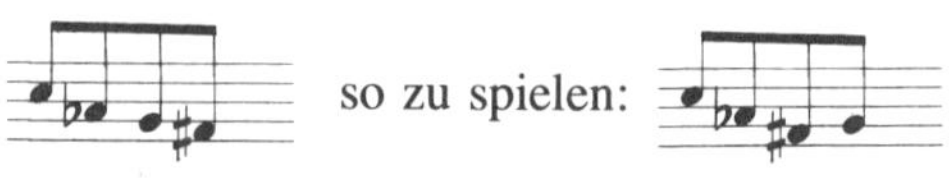

In diesem Liede ist eine Stelle, die mich jedesmal zwingt zu sagen: sehr hübsch! Es ist der Wiedereintritt ins Thema, der allerliebst ist.

Deine Nonnenstücke sollen sogleich abgeschrieben, u. Dir geschickt werden, wegen der Fugen habe ich Dir schon geantwortet, ich kann sie nicht finden, u. habe Dir auch damals, auf Dein ausdrückliches Verlangen, Alles geschickt was Du irgend glaubtest brauchen zu können. Nun aber höre ich auf, u. schreibe Dir nie wieder, bis Du mir einen ordentlichen Privatbrief geschrieben hast. Wetter, was denkst Du von mir? Du behandelst mich schlecht. Seit Du weg bist, hast Du ein einziges Mal an mich geschrieben, um mich zu meinem Geburtstag schlecht zu machen. Ist das recht? Nein Herr Ve——-tter. Hensel denkt Dir einen Privatbrief zu mit einer schönen Predigt über das Grün in Deinen Bildern. Nimm dies einstweilen als Verschreibung. Der schweizer Maler Lory, der jetzt hier ist, u. mehrere 100 Schweizer Prospecte in Wasserfarbe gemalt hat, würde Dich interessiren. Ich bekomme auch ein Bild von ihm, wofür ihn Hensel zeichnet.

---

[a]Fanny mistakenly wrote "Du" instead of "Dich."
[b]Fanny mistakenly wrote "meinen" instead of "meinem."

65

Berlin, 16ten Januar 1834[a]

Das war einmal ein ordentlicher Brief, u. Du sollst bedankt seyn. Nun habe ich Dir wieder viel zu antworten, u. viel zu sagen, u. da Dir die Tagebuchart des vorigen Briefes behagte, so will ich auf alle Fälle wieder anfangen, wenn auch der Brief dann eine Weile wieder liegen bleibt, was ich nicht verhindern werde, denn die Tage fliegen jetzt. H. v. Sybel sagte uns gestern in den Jahreszeiten, Du habest wieder Verdruß gehabt, wir sind recht gespannt auf Briefe von Dir, hoffentlich ist es nicht so arg, aber doch immer unangenehm genug, Du hast schon viel Verdruß zu bestehen gehabt, u. was das Schlimmste ist, ich fürchte, es ist immer nicht der Mühe werth, u. was mir gewiß scheint, ist, daß Du nicht über Deinen Contrakt in Düsseldorf bleiben wirst. Leipzig würde mich der Nähe wegen sehr freuen, u. ich hoffe immer noch, es kommt zu Stande. Nun will ich Dir, ganz unter uns, unsre nächsten Plane sagen. Du weißt aber welch ein Rad zwischen

Berlin u. Düsseldorf geht, u. kannst Dir denken, daß uns dran gelegen ist, es auch dort nicht vor der Zeit bekannt werden zu lassen, ich bitte Dich also sehr, gieb, wie Du zu sagen pflegst, der Welt das erste Beispiel. Wir werden Dich nächstens besuchen. Ist Dir das angenehm? Wir haben nämlich nach Paris geschrieben, um uns zu erkundigen, ob dies Jahr dort Ausstellung ist. Wenn es ist, u. die Unterhandlungen hier nicht gar zu langsam gehn, u. der König es erlaube (Du siehst noch viele wenns) so gehn wir mit dem Bilde nach Paris, u. kommen denn über Düsseldorf u. besuchen Dich auf 8 Tage, worauf ich mich freue wie ein Kaninchen. Findet die Combination mit dem Bilde nicht statt, so gehn wir wahrscheinlich doch nach Paris, nur etwas später, ungefähr im April, u. halten uns einige Tage in Weimar, Frankfurt u. Düsseldorf auf. Kannst, u. willst Du uns dann nach Ffurt entgegen kommen, so haben wir etwas mehr Zeit mit einander zuzubringen, u. reisen zusammen zurück. Wird das nicht lustig? An unsre Pariser Reise denken wir dann die in ein Seebad zu knüpfen, u. so werden wir im Ganzen etwa 4 Monate abwesend seyn. Du frägst nach dem Stande der Bildangelegenheit, u. da will ich Dir sagen, daß das Ministerium ein Gutachten von der Academie gefordert, u. der alte Schadow zu H. gesagt hat: er würde zufrieden seyn. Sie haben zugleich das Bild taxiren müssen, u. wenn sie dabe[i] nur irgend honnett verfahren, so ist es H. sehr angenehm, dem Fordern auszuweichen.

2[0]sten: Welchen furor Deine Lieder hier machen, das kann ich Dir gar nicht beschreiben, ich spiele sie überall, u. regelmäßig fallen ein Paar Damen dabei in Ohnmacht. Unter andern in unserm Künstlerkränzchen, wo sie Alle sehr unverständige fanatici parla[ ] sind, u. Walzer u. Seb. Bach lieben, haben sie mir aufgetragen, Dir schriftlich die Hände zu küssen. Für die eine Stelle in der Fuge will ich Deinem Wunsch gemäß eine Aenderung vorschlagen.

22sten. Als ich neulich anfangen wollte zu schreiben, kam Marx u. blieb sosehr lange, als er fort war, schrieb ich obige 3 Zeilen, da kam ein andrer Besuch, u. dann wars zu spät. Also: könntest Du nicht nach dieser Stelle

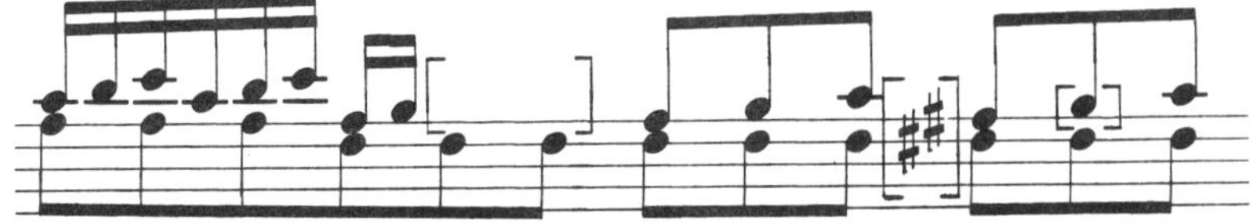

mit Uebergehung einer ganzen Zeile gleich ins unisono kommen? Es müßten denn einige Noten geändert werden. Der Schluß dachte ich ließe sich auch leise etwas voller machen.

Seitdem ist Dein letzter Brief von Vater angekommen, da ich fast nicht zweifle, daß Du Leipzig wählen wirst, so freue ich mich unendlich auf Deine Nähe. Da kann man denn ein Paarmal des Jahres zum Concert herüberreisen, u. überhaupt einmal irgend einem whim nachgebend, sich heut Abend entschließen u. morgen Abend bei Dir seyn. Und wie ehrwürdig wirst Du, (Schülerin des Plato) Dich an das alten Seb. Bachs Stall u. Stuhl ausnehmen. Ach hättest Du je solche Musik gemacht, wie ich heut! Laß mich die kaum geheilte Wunde nicht wieder aufreißen, Blankensee hat mit mir gespielt. O weh, das soll ein Gesicht seyn, das die Junge [raus]blökt, es ist aber nicht zu erkennen.

[Fanny for Sebastian]

Dies ist seine eigenhändige Unterschrift, Du wirst mit einiger Mühe einige Druckbuchstaben herausfinden, die fing er neulich Abends einmal plötzlich u. ohne alle Unterweisung an zu schreiben, u. zwar viel deutlicher u. besser als hier oben. Das Kind hat wirklich ausgezeichnete Fähigkeiten, u. es ist ein doppeltes Glück, für ihn, daß er nicht Eltern hat, die ein Wunderkind aus ihm machen wollen, denn das bin ich überzeugt, würde man mit der leichtesten Mühe können.

Nun rückt Dein Geburtstag heran. Wenn Du künftig in Leipzig bist, so können wir uns Dir einmal sammt u. sonders bescheren, was einen hübschen Tischvoll ausmachen würde. Für diesmal bekommst Du v. Rebecka u. mir ein englisches Stahlstichwerk, Ansichten v. Granada. Diese Stahlstiche Drucke u. Bände der Engländer sind eine kindische Liebhaberei von mir, obwohl sie mir Hensel beständig als Virtuosenwerk vorwirft, er hat doch selbst auch Freude daran.—Wir haben erfahren, daß das Gutachten der Academie ganz außerordentlich ausgefallen, u. von Allen einstimmig genehmigt worden ist, wir wollen suchen uns eine Abschrift davon zu verschaffen.

Hast Du erfahren, daß neulich in einer Gesellschaft bei Rebecka eine Versöhnung mit Droysen stattgefunden hat? Zu meiner großen Freude, denn theils habe ich ihn persönlich sehr gern, und theils kann ich überhaupt Auseinanderkommen mit alten Freunden nicht leiden. Er wird uns nächstens wieder besuchen.

---

[a]She mistakenly wrote "1834" instead of "1835."

66

Mit Lafont habe ich in der letzten Zeit ziemlich viel Musik gemacht. Er spielt wunderhübsch das muß wahr seyn, in einer eleganten, nobeln, einfachen, älteren aber nicht veralteten Weise. Aber seine Prätentionen auf Singen sind unbegreiflich lächerlich, u. das ganze Männchen ist u. bleibt eine ridicüle höchst veraltete Erscheinung. Er hat gestern mit der Decker hier Musik gemacht, sie sang seine große Bravourarie prächtig vom Blatt, aber dann setzte er sich hin, u. schrieb ihr einige Romancen auf, u. sang mit ihr, hoch u. tief, mit Läuferchen u. Trillerchen das man sich kaum des Lachens enthalten konnte, u. daß mir hundertmal die schöne Geschichte v. Pückler, von dem Triller der engl. Dame einfiel.

Lebe wohl, ich bin ganz dumm geworden, [u. kann] gar keinen ordentlichen Brief mehr [schreib]en. Auch bin ich jetzt Lector geworden, [u. le]se drei verschiedenen Leuten drei verschiedene Autoren des Tags vor. Morgens Vater die Zeitung, Nachmittags Hensel den Shakespeare, u. Abends Sebastian den Löhr. Jetzt will ich die eine Lektorenpflicht erfüllen.

27sten Da wir heut Antwort aus Paris erhalten haben, so kann ich Dir noch in diesem Brief nähere Nachricht über unsern Reiseplan geben. Alles vorausgesetzt, daß der König uns Reisegeld giebt, denn sonst bleiben wir zu Haus, u. wischen uns das Maul, es ist aber kaum zu begreifen.

Mit der Ausstellung in Paris ist es für dies Jahr nichts. Die Bilder müssen bis zum 18ten Febr. spätestens da seyn, u. dies ist wenn selbst hier Alles in ordnung wäre, ein Ding der Unmöglichkeit. Die Ausstellung dauert bis zum ersten Juni; unser Plan ist nun, gegen den 1sten Mai von hier abzureisen, um gemächlich, mit gehörigem Aufenthalt reisen zu können, u. noch das Ende der Ausstellung zu sehn. Dann gleich ins Seebad zu gehn, wahrscheinlich nach Dieppe, u. wieder nach Paris zurückzukommen, da sie wie Du wissen [mag]st, dort den herzbrechenden Unsinns [ ] die neuen Bilder vor den alten [ ] aufzustellen, welches während dieser [ ] Zeit unsichtbar bleibt. Wir müssen also zurück um das Museum zu sehn, u. denken dann noch irgend eine hübsche Rückreise zu machen, wie wissen wir selbst noch nicht. Ich hoffe nun, daß Du nicht verhindert seyn wirst, uns Anfangs Mai in Düsseldorf zu erwarten, oder uns bis Ffurt entgegen zu kommen.

[Rebecka]

67

Berlin 17ten Februar 1835

Ich habe Dir für 2 Briefe zu danken, und will einmal erst ordentlich beantworten, was zu beantworten ist. (Verzeih, ich sehe eben, ich habe den Brief verkehrt angefangen, will ihn aber dennoch weiter schreiben.) Die beiden Stücke, die Du verlangt hast, sind in Begriff abzugehn, das Eine hab ich nur noch nicht vom Notenschreiber zurück. Was nun das Herausgeben betrifft, so wollte ich Dich fragen, ob Du auch nicht vergessen hast: wer nur den lieben Gott läßt walten, es gefällt mir sehr, u. wenn ich unter den 2 genannten zu wählen hätte, so wäre es Christe du Lamm Gottes. Von "ach Gott vom" gefällt mir ganz besonders das erste Stück, u. vorzüglich vom unisono an, wo es sehr ernsthaft u. schön bis nach a dur hinein geht. Die Arie ist wunderlich und schön wie die Worte. Aber das Letzte Stück möchte ich Dir stark anfechten. Du mußt nur nicht glauben, daß ich Dir eine retour Kutsche schicke, das ists gewiß und wahrhaftig nicht. Aber das fängt in fis. moll an, u. schließt in a moll oder vielmehr in c dur, durch wenige Modulationen hindurch, u. doch glaube ich hätten die Worte da die allergrößte Standhaftigkeit u. ein Beharren im Choral erfordert. Wären wir beisammen so würden wir uns leicht darüber verständigen, so bitte ich Dich aber, antworte mir darauf, u. sage mir in wiefern Du vielleicht seit den Paar Jahren, die über die Composition vergangen sind, andrer Meinung geworden bist.

Die Arie aus: wer nur den lieben Gott, bringt mich darauf, Dir zu sagen, daß ich in mehreren Solosachen Deiner kleinen geistlichen Musiken eine Art von Gewohnheit finde, die ich nicht gern Manier nennen möchte, u. nicht recht zu benennen weiß, nämlich etwas übereinfaches, welches mir Dir nicht ganz natürlich zu seyn scheint, eine Art von kurzen Rythmen z. B. die etwas kindliches aber auch etwas kindisches haben, u. mir der ganzen Gattung sowohl, als auch Deiner ernsten Art die Chöre zu behandeln, nicht ganz angemessen scheint. Ich habe hier vorzüglich die Arie aus der Weihnachtsmusik im Sinn, wo ich mir wohl denken kann, wie Du dazu gekommen bist, aber auch in mehreren andern scheint mir das Prinzip das Nämliche zu seyn. Wenn es Zeit hätte, bis wir uns sehn, so wäre es wohl hübsch, wenn wir die Auswahl zusammen machen könnten, denn ich habe nicht alle die Musiken, die ich nicht besitze, genug im Kopf, um Dir meinen weisen Rath zu ertheilen.

Habe Dank für die ordentliche Kritik meines Quartetts. Wirst Du es einmal spielen lassen? Weißt Du, daß ich finde, wir schreiben uns jetzt sehr ordentliche Briefe; vielleicht nicht ganz so lustig, als da ich mit Beckchen zusammensaß, u. eine der andern immer zu tollerm Zeuge die Feder aus der Hand nahm, aber vernünftig u. über ordentliche Gegenstände. Mir ist es ganz recht, wenn es dabei bleibt. Die ganze vorige Woche konnte ich Dir nicht schreiben, weil ich sehr fleißig Dein Rondo brillant einstudirt habe. Dies ist nun gestern, Sonntag Vormittag mit doppelter Quartett u. Contrabaßbegleitung, vom Stapel gelaufen, unter allgemeinem Beifall, u. ich war toll genug, es, obgleich sehr unwohl hustend, u. matt wie eine Fliege, zweimal zu spielen, solche Lust hatte ich daran. Ich habe eine Arie für den Sopran gemacht, die würde Dir in Bezug auf Form u. Modulation besser als mein Quartett gefallen, sie hält sich ziemlich streng, u. zwar hatte ich sie fertig, ehe Du mir darüber schriebst. Ich habe nachgedacht, wie ich, eigentlich gar nicht excentrische oder hypersentimentale Person zu der weichlichen Schreibart komme? Ich glaube es kommt daher, daß wir grade mit Beethovens letzter Zeit jung waren, u. dessen Art u. Weise wir billig, sehr in uns aufgenommen haben. Sie ist doch gar zu rührend u. eindringlich. Du hast Dich durchgelebt u. durchgeschrieben, u. ich bin drin stecken geblieben, aber ohne die Kraft durch die die Weichheit allein bestehn kann u. soll. Daher glaub ich auch, hast Du nicht den rechten Punkt über mich getroffen oder ausgesprochen. Es ist nicht sowohl die Schreibart an der es fehlt, als ein gewisses Lebensprinzip, u. diesem Mangel zufolge sterben meine längern Sachen in ihrer Jugend an Altersschwäche, es fehlt mir die Kraft, die Gedanken gehörig festzuhalten, ihnen die nöthige Consistenz zu geben. Daher gelingen mir am besten Lieder, wozu nur allenfalls ein hübscher Einfall ohne viele Kraft der Durchführung gehört.

ich will mir alle al- le Mü- he ge- ben

Kennst Du Eugene Aram? Ich habe es noch nicht ganz aus, u. werde Dir im nächsten Brief meine Meinung darüber schreiben. Thue Du desgleichen, dann wollen wir sehn, wie unsre Urtheile zusammen stimmen.— Höre mal, wenn Du aber dieses Frühjahr nicht in Düsseldorf wärest, das würde uns einen garstigen Strich durch unsre Rechnung machen, denn daß Du des stärksten mit dem Reiseplan stehst, cela va sans dire. Wenn Du nach England mußt, so kann ich freilich dagegen nicht viel einwenden (es würde auch nicht viel helfen) aber Leipzig dachte ich könntest Du im Juni so gut besuchen, als im Mai, u. wir müssen, wenn wir überhaupt noch reisen, doch zur bestimmten Zeit in Paris seyn. Nicht reisen würden wir übrigens nur im Fall nicht vorherzusehender Hindernisse. Das einzige vorherzusehnde wäre die übermäßige Verzögerung unsrer Angelegenheit, u. die ist allerdings möglich, bis jetzt sind schon drei Gutachten wegen der Art der Ausstellung gefordert u. gegeben, da sie nun Alle gut und achtend ausgefallen; so ließe sich daraus freilich auf eine baldige Erledigung der Sache schließen, aber unerforschlich sind die Wege des Kabinetts.

Sey aber in Düsseldorf!

Freitag sind wir auf fete bei Heydemanns, mit denen wir uns ebenfalls wie mit Droysen, ausgesöhnt haben. Was sagst Du zu Louis Heirath von der die Welt spricht? Du hast sie doch gewiß gewußt, noch ehe sie sich gekannt haben. Ich finde sie sehr out of the way, u. gar nicht in Louis Weise dem ich ein sehr unschuldiges, liebliches 16jähr. Mädchen, so à la Marie Mendheim, zugetraut u. gegönnt hätte. Ich möchte der Liebe rathen, sich bei Dr. Jüngken in die Cour zu geben, aber ich fürchte, sie hat den schwarzen Staar, u. es wird in diesem Leben ihr nicht mehr zu helfen. Louis gefällt mir eigentlich außerordentlich. Er hat ein so ungemein feines, durchgebildetes Wesen, so vernünftig ohne kalt, stolz ohne beleidigend, im Gegentheil mild u. wohlthätig dabei. Nur etwas in seiner durchaus honneßten Seele habe ich nie begreifen können. Das Protegiren von Verhältnissen, die nicht protégeable sind, z. B. Paul, wo durchaus keine Veranlassung war, zu verheimlichen, u. die Verheimlichung zu unterstützen, u. wo er doch eine förmliche Intrigue einfach den Umständen angemessen, aber doch immer eine Intrigue geführt hat. Und nun hat er sich selbst in ein Verhältniß hinein protegirt, das ich am wenigstens begreife.

Daß Dich Granada amüsirt, freut mich. Ich denke es in Düsseldorf bei Dir ordentlich zu sehn, hier hatten wir nicht Zeit dazu, u. Hensel hat es nicht einmal durchgeblättert. Dein Geburtstag muß ja sehr nett gewesen seyn. Euer Concert ist gut, u. daß Du wirklich mit Ritz zufrieden bist, freut mich ungemein. Er kam mir immer etwas hochfarend vor, u. ich fürchtete, er möchte Dir Verdruß machen. Nächsten Sonntag lasse ich Gottes Zeit, u. wenn ichs zusammen bringen kann, Dein ave Maria singen. Solls Herr Riechers oder H. Stümer haben? Denk doch, wenn ich Deinen Paulus nicht auf der Reise zu hören bekäme! Pray, laß mir doch die beiden größern Capricen, die Du hier spieltest, abschreiben, ich spiele diesen Winter immer Deine Sachen, u. sie machen so schrecklich viel Glück. Adieu, mein Herz, der Brief ist wieder plauderhaft u. lang geworden. F

Hensel u. Luise grüßen sehr, übrigens Alle. Beckchen hat Stunde bei Pohlke, und wird dieser Tage schreiben. Sie macht sehr nette Fortschritte im Zeichnen, u. ist im Englischen unser Polstern. Die Heber weiß zu meinem Trost nicht mehr, als ich.

68

Berlin, 8ten März 1835.

Ich will Dir ohne Aufschub Deine Hauptfrage beantworten, lieber Felix. Vater wird höchst wahrscheinlich in diesem Jahr noch nicht operirt werden können, obgleich das Uebel seit einigen Monaten bedeutende Fortschritte gemacht hat. Jüngken war vor ein Paar Tagen bei ihm, und äußerte sich sehr unbestimmt darüber, was er doch nicht thun würde, wenn er die nahe Befreiung wahrscheinlich fände, auch liegt es am Tage, und muß jedem Lamm einleuchten, daß Vater von dem Punkt, der eine Operation zuläßt, noch weit entfernt ist. Das Licht thut ihm noch weh, so daß er es nicht ertragen kann, auch kann er sich in den Stuben noch vollkommen zurechtfinden, ja sogar, wiewol mit Mühe, einige Worte lesen. Es ist übrigens unbeschreiblich, mit welcher Geduld u. Liebenswürdigkeit u. Milde er dieses Leiden erträgt, u. wie überhaupt mit jedem Jahr seine vortrefflichen Eigenschaften mehr hervortreten, u. sein Character sanfter u. gütiger wird. Wir thun natürlich alles Mögliche, ihm die Zeit zu verkürzen, u. Eine von uns bleibt immer Abends zu Hause, wobei uns die Männer treulich Beistand leisten.

Wenn ich es doch nur einzurichten wüßte, zum Musikfest in Cölln zu seyn, diese Frage geht mir beständig im Kopf herum, u. ich weiß sie doch gar nicht zu beantworten, indessen denk ich, kommt Zeit, kommt Rath, auf jeden Fall freue ich mich ganz kindisch auf diese Reise. Ich weiß nicht, ob ich Dir neulich geschrieben habe, wo Hensels Bild hinkommt, will aber mit Gans sagen, es ist besser Du erfährst es zweimal, als gar nicht, in die Garnison Kirche, der deshalb ein Paar Fenster zugemauert werden, grade über dem Sängerchor. Man wird es von unten aus der Ferne, u. von oben nahebei sehn können, u. Hensel ist in jeder Beziehung sehr mit dem Platz zufrieden. Ich freue mich besonders, daß nun doch endlich eins seiner Werke dem Publicum ohne Weiteres zugänglich seyn wird, was bis jetzt noch mit Keinem der Fall gewesen ist.—Ich billige es außerordentlich, daß Du ein Gesetz veranlassen willst, daß auf Musikfesten nichts mehr vom Dirigenten gegeben werden soll. Wenn das nicht förmlich ausgesprochen wird, so ist es allerdings unhöflich, ihn nicht dazu aufzufordern, u. nicht alle Dictoren sind so bescheiden als mein Bruder, den mir die Bescheidenheit zu nennen verbietet. Vater hat so von Weitem die Idee, vielleicht nach Ffurt zu Deinem Paulus zu kommen, schreibe ihm aber noch nicht, daß ich es Dir geklatscht habe. Ich hoffe immer, Du kommst mir einmal näher damit denn unmöglich kann ich, wenn wir eben nach Hause gekommen sind, schon wieder so weit reisen, wenn es Leipzig wäre, ging es eher. Kommst Du einmal wieder her, so mußt Du, die Bilde zu Ehren, in der Garnisonkirche schöne Musik machen. Diese Ostern höre ich, soll die Passion dort gegeben werden. Es ist schade, daß Du ihnen nicht alle große Bachsche Musiken so schön vorgeschnitten u. mit Sauce bereitet hast, denn was die Tölpel selbst versucht haben, ist doch spurlos wieder untergegangen.

Gestern wurde bei der Decker der Don Juan gesungen, den ich begleitete. Der Musikdirector Grell u. der Organist Schneider standen zu meinen Seiten, u. paßten mir auf den Dienst, ich habe Grell aber nicht den Gefall than[a], einen Fehler zu machen. Gerechter Gott wie sieht der Mensch aus! u. was für ein Rüpel ist er! Als die Arie der Elvire kam, öffnete er zuerst seinen weisen Mund, u. sagte zu seinem Nachbar: die Arie hat ein sehr schönes Orschester.[b]

Heydemanns, wie die Welt sagt Braut, ist die Frau von Siebold, die Wittwe des berühnten man midwife, eine hübsche, sehr kokette, u. nicht ganz unzweideutig berufene Frau. relata refero. So viel ist gewiß, daß er alle Tage bei ihr, u. sie sehr viel bei H.s ist, u. daß sie sich alle Mühe geben soll, ihn an sich zu ziehn, haben wir aus guter Hand. Meine Wahl wäre sie eben nicht, indeß daran wird ihm blutwenig gelegen seyn. Wir haben sie einen Abend da gesehn, u. da machte nicht er, sondern Albert u. Minna ihr die Cour, das ist schon sehr verdächtig. Da hast Du was Geklatschtes.—Lieber Felix, ich hänge mich um, ich schieße mich auf, ich bringe mich todt. Deine Nonnenstücke, die ich noch vor 4 Wochen für Dich abschreiben lassen, sind fort, wie weggeblasen. Sollte ich sie Dir aus Versehn mit den Abschriften geschickt haben, so bitte, lasse sie mit erster Gelegenheit von dieser Spatzierfahrt zurückkommen, ich besitze jetzt den nettesten Chor von 10 Sopranen, 2 Alten, 1 Tenor, und 5 Bässen die sollen, relaxa facinora, singen.

Eben lese ich in der Spen. Zeitung die Inhalte von Halevys Jüdin. Lieber Felix, das ist ja wieder ein außerordentlicher Fortschritt der künstlerischen Freiheit, da werden die Leute auf dem Theater in siedendem Oehl gebraten. Solche neue, sublime Idee hat Shakespeare nie gehabt. Wo wirst Du einen vernünftigen Text herbekommen! Schaff Dir nu[n] um Gotteswillen einen. Leider hat Cherubini auch von Scribes Verrücktheit zu leiden gehabt, namentlich ist der Schluß unbegreiflich schlecht. (Ich rede v. Ali Baba) Es ist doch kurios, was die Oper für einen Gang seit 50 Jahren genommen hat, u. wie sie jetzt, nach meinem Gefühl wenigstens, an einem Uebermaße dessen leidet, was ihr damals gänzlich fehlte. In Ali Baba erdrücken sich die ensemblestücken einander u. mit den dicksten ensemblestücken ist es schon nicht mehr gethan, sie müssen alle noch mit

Chor gefüttert, seine liebenswürdigste Eigenschaft, die rasende Lebhaftigkeit, wird am Ende ungenießbar, weil sie durch gar keine Ruhe getragen u. unterbrochen wird. Das war mir wenigstens der Eindruck des ersten Hörens, sobald es wieder gegeben wird, werde ich wieder hingehn, um die viele, wunderschöne Musik wo möglich besser zu fassen. Es schien mir sehr sorgsam u. gut einstudirt, u. namentlich das Orchester vortrefflich zu seyn.

Lebe wohl, mon ami, es ist so schönes Wetter, daß ich noch einen Augenblick ausgehn will.

---

[a]Fanny omitted the "ge" prefix.
[b]Actual spelling, presumably in imitation of Grell's speech.

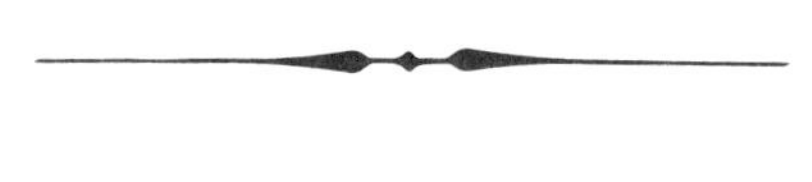

69

Berlin, 19ten März 1835.

Ich will Dir nur in der Kürze heut meine Freude auszudrücken suchen, lieber Felix, daß wir höchst wahrscheinlich zum Musikfest kommen werden. Wir haben nämlich im Widerspruch mit unsern Pariser Nachrichten hier von wohlunterrichteten Personen erfahren, daß der Salon schon am 1sten Mai schließt, was mir auch bei alljähriger Ausstellung sehr glaublich ist. In dem Fall würden wir nicht gut ohne große Uebereilung die Ausstellung noch erreichen können, sondern im Gegentheil, zu meiner großen Freude, unsre Abreise ein wenig verzögern, u. mit Dir in Cölln zusammentreffen. Ich habe vor einigen Tagen an Leo geschrieben, u. sobald ich durch seine Antwort Gewißheit erhalte, werde ich Dir officiell die Ehre übertragen für uns Wohnung in Cölln zu bestellen, u. mich unter die Altistimmen[a] zu enroliren. Wie schade daß wir nicht zusammen werden wohnen können, um Dich werden sich doch gewiß, die um den Honeur sieben Städte, wenigstens 7 Häuser, zanken, u. wir möchten in keinem Fall einquartirt werden. Ich werde Dich dann bitten, mir so früh als möglich zu melden, wann Du nach Cölln gehst, u. die Proben beginnst, ich möchte deren gern so viel als möglich mitmachen. Auch frage ich an, ob es wol möglich ist, daß Du den Tag nach dem Feste mit uns nach Düsseldorf zurück gehst, u. dort einige Tage ruhig mit uns lebst, denn von irgend einer Art von Mittheilung wird in Cölln keine Rede seyn können, u. man möchte doch auch ein Wort mit einander sprechen, u. ich muß doch auch den Paulus hören. Ich freue mich so kindisch auf diese ganze Reise, daß ich es gar nicht beschreiben kann. Dieser Anfang mit u. dem Cöllner Fest, dann nach Paris u. zuletzt ins Seebad—an Plane liegt es gewiß nicht, wenn die Reise nicht gelingt. Nun Gott gebe seinen Segen dazu. Eben kommt die Idee auf, die Rückreise mit dem neuen Dampfboot von Havre nach Hamburg zu machen, wozu ich der Schnelligkeit wegen sehr geneigt bin, denn wenn man sich so lange in der Welt umhergetreten hat, pflegt man sich nach Hause zu sehnen. Indeß läßt sich über die Rückreise nichts bestimmen, so lange man noch nicht aus dem Hause ist.

Deine Ouvertüren sind angekommen, u. ich werde sie jetzt gleich durchspielen. Verzeihe diesen ganz dummen Brief, aber ich habe jetzt wörtlich nichts als die Reise im Kopf, u. wollte Dir diese Nachricht, von der ich glaube, daß sie Dir auch Vergnügen machen wird, doch gern gleich mittheilen.

Alles ist wohl u. grüßt.

Deine Fanny

Glaube nur nicht, daß ich das kronprinzliche Exemplar verzögere, das ist beim Buchbinder, aber Breitkopf hat den Eltern eine geschickt.

---

[a]Fanny misspelled the word.

70

Berlin, 8ten April 35

Es sey bei den Pforten der Hölle, laß mich in den Alt eintragen. Wir werden einige Tage vor dem Musikfest eintreffen, um noch die letzten Proben mitzumachen, ich werde es aber kennen, denn wie das in der Ordnung ist, saß ich gestern am Clavier u. spielte die ersten Noten des ersten Chors von Salomon, als Dein Brief ankam, worin Du Dich freust, ich freue mich auch, das kannst Du glauben. Bestelle uns also Quartier, aber mit der schönen Idee des Zusammen Einquartirens wird es nichts werden. Wir kommen nicht allein sondern mit Sebastian u. Minna, aber ohne Dienstboten, u. es ist doch ein Ding der Unmöglichkeit, zu wildfremden Leuten, die nicht Wirthsleute sind, 4 Mann hoch einzutreten, u. zu sagen: lieber Mann, da sind wir. Dazu gehört wenigstens oheimische Unbefangenheit, die wir lieder nicht haben. Ob Ihr mich mit Eurem flüssigen Kräuterkissen, das Ihr mit dem poetischen Namen Maitrank beehrt, u. das doch nur die schlechteste Copie von Bischof ist, versöhnen werdet, das ist mir sehr zweifelhaft. Indessen will ich, sobald es mir schmeckt, gern gestehn, daß ich mich geirrt habe. Eins will ich Dir aber sagen, wenn Du einen ungehörigen Lärm von mir machst, u. die Leute gar auf mein Spiel gespannt werden, so komm ich gar nicht. Ich habe ohnedies eine so unvernünftige Furcht vor Dir, (und außerdem vor keinem Menschen weiter, außer ein bischen vor Vater) daß ich ja eigentlich nie in Deiner Gegenwart ordentlich spiele, u. z. B. accompagniren, was ich wirklich gut machen kann, das weiß ich selber würde ich nie versuchen, wenn Du da bist. Ich sehe schon jetzt, wie Du mich in Düsseldorf quälst, u. wie ich mich ängstige, und wie ich pudle und pfusche u. mich ärgere. Da nun vollends, wo sie gewöhnt sind, Alles was ich irgend spielen könnte, von Dir zu hören. Und nun wollen wir noch einmal einen andern Gegenstand reiflich überlegen. Vater hat neulich wieder gegen Jemand geäußert, er wünsche zum Oktober zu Deinem Oratorium nach Frankfurt zu kommen. Ist es nun schon gewiß daß diese Aufführung statt findet, u. bleibst Du die letzten Monate vorher, Aug. u. Sept. in Düsseldorf, so solltest Du die Eltern einladen, Dich dort zu besuchen, u. diese Monate etwa abwechselnd in Düsseldorf u. Horchheim zuzubringen. Ich habe verschiedene Gründe, dies sehr zu wünschen. Erstlich glaube ich die Eltern werden sehr viel Vergnügen mit aller Gemächlichkeit haben können. Zweitens aber will ich Dir im Vertrauen sagen, daß Beckchen böse auf uns ist, weil wir des Musikfestes wegen unsre Reise etwas verschoben haben. Sie glaubt, oder giebt ihrer üblen Laune wegen vor zu glauben, daß sie in ihren Reiseplanen dadurch gestört werde. Da wir aber Beide von Anfang an den Plan hatten, ein Seebad zu gebrauchen, u. man das nur in einer ganz beschränkten Jahreszeit kann, so waren wir immer übereingekommen, 4 Wochen ungefähr zusammen wegzubleiben. Daß nun aus diesen 4 Wochen vielleicht 6 werden, ist doch nicht von solcher Wichtigkeit, daß sie ihre Reise deshalb aufzugeben nöthig hätte, um so mehr, als unsre Abwesenheit in den Sommer fällt, wo die Tage lang sind, das Wetter gut, Vater viel im Freien seyn, u. also das Vorlesen weit weniger vermissen wird, als im Winter? So ungerecht ich also ihre Beschwerde auch finde, so unangenehm ist es mir doch, daß sie meinetwegen brummt, u. Du kannst glauben, daß es mir die Freude an der Reise recht dämpft. Wenn aber jener Plan zu Stande käme, der würde Alles ins Gleiche bringen. Sobald ich St[üler] sehe, spreche ich Mutters wegen mit ihm, ich bezweifle nicht, daß er sie wird reisen lassen. Bei Vater bedarf es kaum einer Frage, da es die Aerzte voriges Jahr sogar wünschten, sein Fuß geheilt ist, u. sich mit seinen Augen wenig verändert hat. Ueberlege u. schreibe mir, aber bald. Daß Du meines zweiten Beweggrundes nicht ermähnst, versteht sich von selbst. Wir haben unsre Reise insofern abgeändert, als wir von Cölln aus erst in ein Seebad und dann nach Paris zu reisen gedenken. Hast Du also Zeit u. Lust uns zu begleiten, so schmeiß Dich ein wenig mit ins Meer.

Wagner u. Pohkle reisen morgen nach Paris zur Ausstellung, und werden uns dort erwarten und zum Winter zurückkommen. Die beiden jungen Leuten haben sich auf ehrenvolle Weise die Mittel zu dieser Reise erworben. Ueberhaupt steht es im Attelier sehr gut, es ist *Alles* von der letzten Ausstellung verkauft. Leb wohl, mein bester Felix, wie freue ich mich.

71

Berlin, den 8ten Oktober 1835.

Ich muß Dir ein Paar Zeilen schreiben, um mich wegen der Geschichte mit Baron Speck zu rechtfertigen, lieber Felix, sonst schimpfst Du auf mich wie nichts Guts, u. hältst mich für die ärgste Klatsche. Du weißt aber am Besten aus eigner Erfahrung, wie oft gewisse Dinge eine Wirkung thun, die man sich eben gar nicht denkt. In den ersten fünf Minuten unsres Hierseyns, wo man, wie Du das kennst, noch Alles anfängt, zu reden, u. noch ehe man halb fertig ist, Alles andre, mußte ich natürlich von Dir gleich Rechenschaft geben, ich freute mich des Guten, das ich berichten konnte, Vater frug, ob Du angenehmen Umgang hättest, ich bejähte, er frug weiter ob Du etwa beim Baron Speck gewesen wärest, u. da fuhr mir Dein Absagebillett über die Zunge. Nachher that es mir leid, u. ich bat richtig Mutter, die Sache auf sich beruhen zu lassen, u. Deine Erziehung zu vernachlässigen, bei Vater versäumte ichs, als ich aber, 8 T. drauf, den Brief an Dich für ihn schrieb, u. merkte, wo er hinaus wollte, [erhob] ich Einspruch, konnte aber, als ehrlicher Secretair nicht umhin, zu schreiben, was mir diktirt ward. Er behauptete, Du würdest es nicht merken. Pardon! und erzähle mir deshalb nie in meinem Leben eine Geschichte weniger, ich will mich aber künftig besser in Acht nehmen.

Wir haben heut meine Schwiegermutter begraben. Zum ersten Mal in meinem Leben habe ich Sterben, u. alle die darauf folgenden Prozeduren so in der Nähe gesehn, es ist etwas wunderbar feierliches darin, ein Leben ausgehn zu sehn, u. in dem Augenblick den Faden für das Weitere zu verlieren, es war aber in diesem Falle durchaus nichts Widriges oder Schreckliches darin, sie starb bei vollem Bewußtseyn, sehr ruhig, u. mit dem Wunsch der Erlösung. Wie froh bin ich daß wir noch zur rechten Zeit gekommen sind.

Eben ist ein Brief v. Rebecka gekommen, die um 2 Tage später bei Dir eintrifft. Wenn sie wüßte, daß sie Moscheles concert dadurch versäumt, würde sie es nicht thun. Sie hat wieder einen Treffer, daß sie grade zu Deinem kommt, u. mir thut es sehr leid, die Händelschen Partituren u. Chopin um einen Tag versäumt zu haben. Vielleicht wären wir leichter über ihn einig geworden, wenn wir ihn zusammen gehört hätten. Ich kann nicht läugnen, daß ich finde, es fehlt ihm zu sehr eine ganze, wichtige Seite, nämlich die Kraft, um für einen vollendeten Künstler gelten zu können. Sein Spiel ist nicht grau in grau, sondern rosenroth in rosenroth gefärbt, wenn er nur je ein bischen bisse! Aber er ist ein allerliebster Mensch, u. wenn Du [glaubst], daß seine Idyllen mir kein Vergnügen gemacht haben, so irrst Du Dich entweder, oder ich habe mich falsch ausgedrückt.

Devrient läßt sagen, er nehme seinen Auftrag wegen der Leipziger dramatischen Autoren (nebbig!) zurück, bitte aber um Deine Unterschrift. Die andern sind einstweilen eingelaufen. Grüße Moscheles, u. sage ihm, wie leid es uns thut, ihn nicht zu sehn. Hat denn Chopin wirklich Sinn für Händelsche oder Paulische Partituren? Hä, hä, glaubs nicht.

Liebe Rebecka, Du wirst unendlich interessant seyn, ich bin noch grade fertig mit meinen Reisegeschichten, u. nun kommst Du mit einem frischen Vorrath, das trifft prächtig. Vergiß nur nicht, daß u. warum Du mich kohlschwarz triffst, u. erschrick nicht darüber. Wenn Du die schöne Mlle. Pensa siehst, so grüß sie mir viel tausendmal. Ich konnte mich neulich durchaus nicht auf ihren Namen besinnen, weil ich immer H. Mecum im Kopf hatte. Bringst Du meine Bonner Wäsche mit? Bring mir auch die Partitur mit, die ich bei Hauser ließ, u. grüße die lieben Leute bestens.

Adieu Ihr dummes Volk, macht daß ihr wiederkommt.

72

Berlin, 29sten Oktbr. 35

Mein liebes Felixelchen, seit Deiner Abreise ist Tag um Tag vergangen, u. ich habe mich nicht stimmen können, Dir zu schreiben. Das liebe Leipzig giebt einem durch angenehme Nähe so die Empfindung, als könntest Du etwa einmal zur Thüre herum treten, u. da kommen täglich Leute, die Dich gesehn, von Dir gehört, etc. es ist gar hübsch. Wäre nur eine Eisenbahn dahin, dann wäre es gar ein Spaß.—Dein Hauser ist ein lieber Mensch, u. wird bei uns schrecklich verhätschelt. Du weißt, das können wir, wenn wir Einen mögen. Morgen tritt er als Diable auf, u. hat so höllische Moren, daß wir Alle mit ihm bange sind. Ach es war nicht seine Wahl, ist uns aber lieb für ihn, denn es wird eine Knallvorstellung. Eichberger tritt mit ihm auf, u. die großen Elslers, König, sonstiger Hof u. unsre lieben Freunde, die russischen Offiziere werden drin seyn, u. so Gott will, wird es ihm gelingen. Wäre nur das Theater ein Zimmer, u. die große Oper ein deutsches Lied, das kann man nicht besser singen als er, so wie seine Stimme wunderschön zum Clavier klingt. Ich habe mich ganz in ein Lied v. Hauptmann verliebt: komm heraus, tritt aus dem Haus. Wie Du mich aber, seit Du Hauser kennst, hast behäbig nennen können, weiß ich nicht. Er hat ja alle Behäbigkeit der Welt in sich geschluckt, so daß für einen andern ehrlichen Menschen gar nichts übrig geblieben ist.

Neulich haben bei uns Dienstagskränzchen begonnen, welche fortan zwischen uns 3 Geschwistern abwechseln werden. Der Anfang war sehr lustig, Du hast keine Idee, was sie für tolles Zeug gemacht haben. Es soll die Einrichtung stattfinden daß um 9 Uhr mit dem Thee zugleich Stichwörter u. der ganze Plunder gegessen wird. Dies wurde schrecklich bespöttelt u. bekrittelt, keiner wollte schon Appetit haben, u. es endete damit, daß Alle Alles u. noch Einiges aßen. Hauser lachte wie ein Kobold über alle Possen die vorgetragen wurden, u. dann machten wir noch bis Mitternacht Musik, tanzten, etc. Es war übrigens Niemand da, als Eltern u. Geschwister, Hauser, einige Schüler u. Franz Woringen, der anfängt ein wenig aufzuthauen u. lustig zu werden.

Deine Noten sind längst beim Schreiber, lieber Felix, ich hatte sie Koch gegeben, der voriges Jahr immer für mich schrieb, da kommt heut ein Andrer, Kowalsky, u. sagt, Koch habe eine Anstellung bekommen, könne nicht weiter schreiben, er habe früher für Dich gearbeitet u. ich solle ihm die Arbeit lassen. Das habe ich einstweilen gethan, u. ihn so sehr gedrängt als möglich. Sobald ich sie erhalten kann, schicke ich sie hin.

30sten Heut ist Pauls Geburtstag, und wir sind Abends bei Albertinen, wo wir Kindermusik machen werden. Wir schenken ihm einen avant avant la lettre, d. h. Probedruck von der schönen Tiriana auf unserm Museum von Kaspar hübsch gestochen. Hauser denkt nach dem Theater zu kommen. Solchen Katzenjammer wie der arme Kerl hat, habe ich nie gesehn. Grüße Madame Hauser bestens, Sebastian grüßt Moritz u. Joseph, u. läßt sie bitten, bald herzukommen. Den Moritz als Chorknaben möchte ich sehn, er muß allerliebst aussehn.

Adieu, mein Junge, ich muß ausgehn u. es ist schlecht Wetter. Du bist auch jetzt schreibfaul, Hauser schmachtet nach einem Brief von Dir, so sehr es ihm seine Behäbigkeit erlaubt.

Deine F.

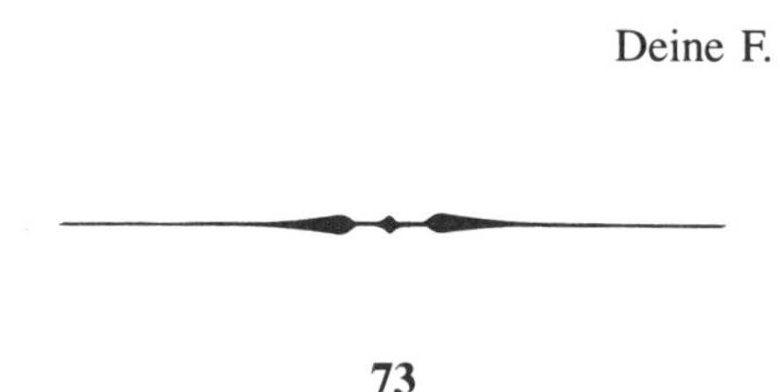

73

Berlin, 7ten Novemb.

Es freut mich, Dir sagen zu können, daß mir Hauser sehr gefallen hat, lieber Felix. Wir waren Alle zusammen im Figaro. Er war nicht nur weit über meine Erwartung, was nichts Positives ist, sondern weitaus besser, als wir ihn zuletzt in Leipzig gesehn hatten. Seine Stimme füllt das Opernhaus sehr gut, u. klingt sehr voll u. schön, besonders gegen die Tiefe, wogegen ihm die Höhe von es an, unsicher ist. Uebrigens hört man durchweg den musikalisch gebildeten Sänger, besonders beim Accompagniren, was er vortrefflich versteht, u. wozu auch seine Stimme sich sehr schön eignet. Uebrigens können sie ihn meines Erachtens, hier gar nicht missen, sie müßten denn überhaupt Lust haben, ohne Oper fertig zu werden, wozu sie freilich Miene machen, denn sie können jetzt effektiv Don Juan nicht besetzen, sie haben keine Donna Anna. Er war gestern zum Grafen bestellt, es ist aber nichts ausgemacht. Als er mir die Unterredung erzählte, mußte ich laut lachen, denn sie klang so natürlich wie alle Deine Geschichten von ihm, daß eins wie das Exempel; und das andre wie die Probe heraus kam. Wäre er [ ][a] aus allen diesen Geschichten, es paßt so [ ] doch erst [ ]. Adieu, me[ ] Lebwohl. Dr. Reiter bringt Dir Deiner Sachen. D[a][ ] [g]roßen Bibliothek werden wir wohl bis zum [ ] verschieben müssen, [ ] klimatischen Ursachen. Geordnet ist Alles.

---

[a]Multiple blotches in the manuscript.

74

Berlin, 9ten Novemb. 1835

Es thut mir leid, daß ich nicht gleich alle Deine Aufträge ausführen kann, lieber Felix. Die Ouvertüre zur Medea habe ich trotz alles Schickens u. Treibens noch nicht erhalten können, sobald ich sie habe, geht sie ab.

Die Partitur v. Haydn, u. ein Stück aus Medea bringt Dir der Dr. Reiter mit diesem Brief. Und hier die Stelle aus der as dur Sonate.

Eben wird mir die Ouvertüre zu Medea bestimmt auf heut versprochen, sollte nun Dr. Reiter schon fort seyn, so schicke ich sie mit Post nach, da ich nicht weiß, ob ich auf Herrn Limburger damit warten darf. Habt Ihr viel Solche in Eurem comité?—Steffens waren gestern Abend hier. Was mir das Spaß macht, wenn so alle Tage Leute kommen, die Dich den Tag vorher gesehn haben, das ist gar zu angenehm. Hauser sang gestern Abend wunderschön, ich habe wirklich nie eine weichere, ich möchte sagen rührendere Baßstimme gehört, die Tenore haben das wol eher, daß es Einem wunderlich ums Herz wird beim Klang ihrer Stimme. Hast Du einmal die Arie v. Mozart: mentre ti lascio o figlia, von ihm gehört? Diese, nebst dem Liede v. Hauptmann u. dem aus dem Wasserträger, bilden das Haupt- u. Lieblingsrepertoir. Heut hat sich die Hähnel zu Tisch anmelden lassen, Hauser ißt auch bei uns, wenn es erst Eisenbahn zu Dir giebt, lade ich Dich früh ein, u. Du kommst zu Mittag, u. ißt ein Lieblingsgericht. Hauser ist ein eben solcher Lecker, wie Du, über Confitüren kann er komplett in Enthusiasmus gerathen. Woringens schreiben von einem Düsseldorfer Gerücht, daß Immermann nach Leipzig als Director käme. Ich hoffe, es ist nicht wahr, es würde Dir doch gewiß sehr unangenehm seyn. Ich kann mir übrigens denken, daß die Malice Antheil an einem solchen Entschluß seinerseits hätte. Adieu, lieber Felix, Reiter kommt um 11, die Sachen für Dich abzuholen, u. ich muß mich noch anziehn, u. herausgehen. [Addio.] Diese Woche bekomme ich wol einen Brief von Dir.

75

Berlin, 18ten Nov. 1835

Dank für Deinen Brief, lieber Clown, ich setze mich eigends für ihn bestens zu beantworten, sitze auf Deinem Clavierstühl, den ich vor meinen Schreibtisch gestellt habe, u. denke behaglich Deiner. Hauser sitzt auf dem Sopha, u. hat Kopfschmerzen u. spricht schon seit gestern Nachmittag kein Wort. Sage es aber seiner Frau nicht, denn es hat keineswegs etwas zu sagen, er ist nebenbei der erste Hypochonder Deutschland, was er zusammenschleppen läßt von Mitteln Senf und Meerrettig u. eine Prise, und Eihaube auf seine schlimme Nase, u. das gelbe für seinen schlimmen Hals, u. Aepfelwasser in Eimer [ ] Leinsamenthee u. Hafergrütze, u. Fußbäder u. den Teufel u. seine Großmutter. Neulich war er eines Abends hier weg mit 3 Flaschen u. Töpfe bepackt, ich warnte ihn, Niemanden drüben so in die Hände zu fallen, sonst wäre er d[ ] Neckereien 8 Tage nicht los geworden. Das beherzigte er, u. ließ uns erst vorausgehn, zu sehn ob das Feld rein wäre. Abends schläft er um 8 Uhr ein, u. dann wird er entweder gekniffen oder zu Bett geschickt. Wenn er sich aber aus seiner Faulheit u. Hypochondrie aufrafft u. bei Stimme ist, singt er wirklich wunderschön. Ich habe Sonntag meine Musik wieder angefangen u. Liebster Gott, wann werd ich sterben, u. Herr, gehe nicht ins Gericht singen lassen, das Rezit. aus dieser Cantate: Wohl aber dem, sang Hauser wunderschön u. mit allgemeinem Beifall. Es war überhaupt sehr gut besetzt, u. ich habe Freude dran. Das nächste Mal denke ich mich zu erfrechen, Dein Concert zu spielen, ich will einmal sehn, ob es beißt. Gewiß bin ich der Meinung daß der es dur Rondo zehnmal besser ist, als das aus la, Du hast über den Verfasser kein Urtheil. Und hier komme ich mit einem Sprunge auf Dein Verzeichniß. Seine Schönheit muß Dich so geblendet haben, daß Du gänzlich folgenden Artikel übersehn hast, der mit allen Buchstaben drin steht: *8 Pack Briefe*. Ich will ihn aber bei dieser Gelegenheit dahin berichtigen, daß es 7 Pack Briefe sind, u. das 8te laut Aufschrift: Brieftaschen u. Kleinigkeiten enthält, die wir nicht untersuchen wollten. Ich habe sie Alle in einen Schrank geschlossen, von wo sie das Tageslicht nicht wieder erblicken werden, bis Du sie einmal abforderst. Nimm aber bei dieser Veranlassung zugleich das Geständniß, daß als mir beim Auspacken der Kiste das erste dieser Pakete in die Hände fiel, ich es unbesonnen erbrach, ohne nach der Aufschrift zu sehn. Ich gebe Dir aber mein Ehrenwort, daß ich keinen einzigen Brief auch nur von außen besehn, sondern das Paket, als ob es brennte, bei Seite geschoben habe. (Hauser schläft) Noch muß ich bemerken daß von den zahlreichen Stimmen, die wir verzeichnet haben, fast keine Partie vollständig ist. Ueberdies ist das Verzeichniß, daß gar keine Ansprüche auf Schönheit macht, durch seine raisonnirende Treue bemerkenswerth, u. der Graf mag seine Diener loben. Nun höre ich in welcher traurigen Alternation ich mich befinde. Als Dein Limburger Baumeister oder Baumeister Limburger hier war, u. ich ihm vorspielen sollte, brachte ich unter andern die etudes v. Cramer mit hinüber, u. spielte Einige, die mißfielen, aber Vater sehr. Ich versicherte ihm indeß, er müsse sie Alle hören, sonst machtest Du mich Weihnachten todt, u. er mache mich vor Weihnachten todt, wenn ich sie Alle spielte, sagte er. Welchen Todes soll ich nun sterben? Sebastian sagte neulich zu der, Dir wol noch von Alters her bekannten Freistädtl: nun wollen wir ein Concert machen. Was wollen wir vornehmen, Beethoven oder Onkel Felix?

Das arme Kerlchen hat schon sehr lange den Husten, u. er u. wir schlafen keine Nacht ungestört. Uebrigens ist fast kein Mensch gesund, das ganz ungewöhnliche Wetter mag wol mit Schuld seyn.

Wenn Pixis in Leipzig ist, so ist Mme. Camille Pleyel hier, ich bin neugierig auf sie als schöne Frau u. gute Clavierspielerin. Gute Sitten braucht man ja nicht von ihr zu lernen. Zu Deiner Melusine möchte ich schon nach Leipzig kommen, wenn nur, wenn, wenn alle wenns nicht wären. Schick mir doch die Partitur von Deiner Walpurgis, die Stimmen hab ich hier, ich möchte einmal was draus singen lassen. Du schickst mir auch nicht die Stücke die ich mir aussuchen durfte, u. Du mir abschreiben lassen wolltest, jetzt stecken sie längst wieder in der rothen Mappe, Du weißt sie nicht mehr, u. ich muß erst wieder nach Leipzig kommen, u. sie noch einmal aussuchen. O Clown, u. nicht ein Wort schreibst Du, ob Du die Ouvertüre zur Medea bekommen habest, die eine Stunde nach Abreise des Dr. Reiter eintraf, u. ihm einen Tag drauf in Deine Arme nacheilte. Grüße doch den Dr. Reiter, er ist ein netter Mensch, u. sieht Stengler so ähnlich daß ich Gefahr laufe, beide in meinem Gedächtniß zusammen zu rühren, u. beim Wiedersehn Einen für den Andern zu halten. Hier wird fortwährend Hauser für Hensel gehalten, eben hat das Stück wieder gespielt. Er schläft aber nun nicht mehr, denn es kam ein Besuch u. störte ihn, sonst stünde ich Dir dafür.

Lebe wohl, mein Herz. Hensel grüßt. Er hat mir zu meinem Geburtstag die Farbenskizze der Mirjam geschenkt, die mir außerordentlich gefällt. Ich bin überhaupt sehr schön beschenkt worden. Unter andern mit einem And. v. Beethoven aus f dur, das ich gar nicht kannte, aber wunderschön finde. Du sollst es in Düsseld. gespielt haben.

76

Berlin, 11ten Dec.

Du läßt gar nichts von Dir hören, lieber Felix! Wie geht es Dir, was machst Du? Wir hoffen auch auf Nachricht durch Hauser, der Dir die Neuesten von uns gebracht hat, u. erfahren nichts.

Der heutige Tag wird Dir schwer seyn, wie uns. Er ist aus einem heitern Freudentag zu einem ernsten memento mori geworden. Allein das Glück haben wir gehabt, u. nichts kann uns die Erinnerung daran rauben. Haltet mein Andenken in Ehren. Das thun wir, u. wollen versuchen es so zu thun, daß wir unser Leben lang sein Beispiel vor Augen haben, das heißt in seinem Sinne handeln.

Rebecka schläft heut zum erstenmal vorn, u. ist sehr mit ihrem Umzug beschäftigt. Mutter will Dir selbst einige Zeilen schreiben. Wie ist Davids erstes Auftreten abgelaufen?

Leb wohl, liebster Bruder, u. schreibe bald. Mittwoch reist Paul zu Dir, wenn die Kälte so anhält, werdet ihr leiden.

[Lea]

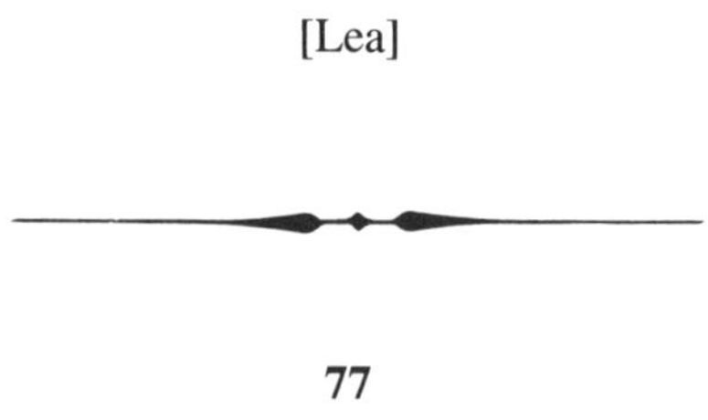

77

Berlin, 5 Januar

Mutter hat mich gestern nicht mitgenommen, da muß ich denn allein nachlaufen, u. sehn, ob ich die Post einholen kann.

Wir haben das neue Jahr schlecht genug angefangen, mit doppeltem Köchinnenwechsel (wärest oder hättest Du eine Frau, so würdest Du wissen, was das heißt, in drei Tagen drei Köchinnen zu haben) einem kranken Mann, Hensel lag den 2ten zu Bett, u. solchem Hauskreuz. Gott gebe uns ein wenig Ruhe jetzt, wir könnens brauchen.

In dem Te Deums habe ich fleißig gespielt, u. tiefsinnige Betrachtungen angestellt, welche durch die darüber gestellten Jahreszahlen sehr erleichtert wurden, wie die früheren weit perückenhafter u. formbelasteter, die späteren besonders das Dettinger frei u. Händelsch eigenthümlicher erscheinen. Sehr liebe ich das: to thee all angels cry aloud. Indessen kenne ich sie noch nicht Alle, u. werde Dir weiter darüber schreiben.

9ten Wenn ein Brief von mir 2 Tage liegen bleibt, kommt er mir so abscheulich dumm vor, daß ich ihn in den meisten Fällen gar nicht abschicke. Indessen wenn ich mich bedenke und fasse, sehe ich wohl, daß ich schwerlich am 9ten einen bessern Brief schreiben werde, als am 5ten, u. wenn denn jener wieder bis zum 11ten liegen bleiben müßte, finge es abermals einen neuen an, u. so fort.

Uebermorgen wollen wir eine Paulussitzung halten, mit Devrients u. Woringen. Hauser ist in Hypochondrie u. Schmutz begraben, u. ich glaube jetzt nicht, daß sein Aufenthalt hier irgend eine Annehmlichkeit für uns haben wird, er ist zu wunderlich. Heut vor 8 Wochen ergötzte sich Vater sehr an seinem Gesange. Geht es Dir auch so? Mich überfällt so oft die Erinnerung an ihn, wie an einen Entfernten, so daß ich denke: ich hab ihn ja so lange nicht gesehn, u. dann kommt erst die Wahrheit nach.

Wärst Du doch hier, es ist mir gar zu wehmüthig daß wir nun so auf unbestimmte Zeit aus einander sind. Ich möchte Dich so gern in Leipzig besuchen, fürchte aber, es wird diesen Winter nicht gehn. So, nun breche ich wieder ab, u. ärgre mich morgen von Neuem.

12ten Heut will ich nun diesen Wisch blindlings abschicken, ohne ihn wieder zu lesen, ich bringe jetzt keinen ordentlichen Brief zu Stande, obgleich Beckchen findet, es sähe bei mir aus, wie bei einer ästhetischen Dame. Meine Wohnstube ist wunderhübsch, mit den schönen Kupferstichen, Noten, Instrument u. Schreibtisch, es ist mir aber doch nicht ganz heimlich darin, weil Du es nicht kennst, und es gehört gar zu notwendig zu meinem Leben, daß Du Alles darin kennst u. gutheißest. Darum ist es mir auch so leid, wirklich nicht aus Eitelkeit, daß ich Dir schon so lange nichts Musikalisches recht habe zu Dank machen können. Habe ich es denn früher wirklich besser gemacht, oder warst Du nur leichter zu befriedigen?

Unser Paulus ist wieder auf morgen verlegt. Von den drei dazu nöthigen Personen können heut vier nicht. Seit ich es vom Notenschreiber zurück habe, spiele ich es mit Freude und Erbauung. Vater ist mir immer so sehr gegenwärtig, dabei, als wenn ich es ihm vorspielen könnte. Addio. Leb wohl, grüß David, laß bald von Dir hören.

78

Berlin, 26sten Januar 36

Mein lieber Felix, ich hoffe Du wirst nicht böse seyn, wenn ich Dein Gebot umgehend zu schicken um *einen* Tag übertrete, da Du es doch noch zur rechten Zeit, ja einen Tag früher bekommst. Mittwoch, morgen gebe ich es auf die Post, und Freitag ist es dort, Sonnabend brauchst Du es, wie Du schreibst. Du kennst die Liebenswürdigkeit der hiesigen Arbeiter, seit 14 Tagen ist der Auszug beim Notenschreiber, u. auf mehrfaches Erinnern antwortet er immer, er sey bald fertig, als ich nun gestern die Noten fordern lasse, findet sichs, daß er erst eben angefangen hat. Er wird nun, auf mein entsetzliches Schelten u. Brummen, die Nacht durch schreiben, u. morgen früh fertig seyn. Aber fertig oder nicht, schicke ich den Auszug auf mein Wort morgen ab. Besten Dank für die Melusina, wir wollen uns oft dran erfreuen. Dein Winterbildchen ist sehr schön, Du machst jetzt große Fortschritte, mache mir doch auch einmal wieder eins. Rebecka amüsirt sich prächtig mit dem Blumenmalen, u. hat für die kurze Zeit wirklich schon sehr viel gelernt. Ich lese fleißig englisch, schreibe Wörter auf, u. lerne sie auswendig, bemühe mich auch, meinem sehr verfallnen musikalischen Gedächtniß zu Hülfe zu kommen, u. lerne ordentlich Musik auswendig. Deinen Geburtstag wollen wir durch unsern Paulus feiern, u. vielleicht non nobis da zu nehmen.

Sebastian, der den ganzen Winter in der Stube zubringen müssen,[a] ist erst zweimal ausgefahren, heut aber ist das Wetter so schön u. freundlich, daß ich ihn zum erstenmal ein wenig zu Fuß aus führen will, er hat sich Gott sey Dank, wieder sehr erholt. Da aber die Sonne nicht wartet, addio, nächstens mehr.

Nun habe ich Mutter und Sebastian spatziren geführt. Sey doch so gut, da es doch wahrscheinlich noch lange dauert, bis Dein Auszug gedruckt wird, was Du davon fertig hast, dort abschreiben zu lassen, u. mir herzuschicken. Mutter will das an uns wenden,[b] damit wir eher die Freude haben, es zu hören. Und nun leb wohl.

[Rebecka]

---

[a]Fanny erroneously wrote "müssen" instead of "muß."

[b]Fanny wrote "wenden," but this does not fit grammatically and logically; "senden" fits here, so perhaps she made a mistake. The latter is assumed for the translation.

79

3 Febr.

Lieber Felix, Gott erhalte uns Dich, u. was wir sonst noch Gutes haben, u. schenke Dir seinen besten [Se]gen. Was ich Dir jetzt am Meisten wünsche, weißt Du, es möge Dir gelingen, wie so Vieles in Deinem Leben, Vater hat es immer lebhaft gewünscht.

Den Schiller, den Du im Berliner Paket findest, einen als ein Andenken von [un]s, diese einbändigen Editionen sind [g]ut auf Reisen mitzunehmen. Du wirst [z]war nicht: Freude schöner Götterfunken daraus komponiren, ich wüßte auch für jetzt noch nicht, was sonst, aber so wenig [ ] mir hätte träumen lassen, daß sich aus den Druiden so herrliche Musik [ ]achen ließe, wie Du gethan, so wenig kann ich wissen, was in einem jeden Gedichtband schlummert.

Kennst Du eine Cantate v. Bach aus e dur, die Hauser hat: wohl dem, [der] sich auf seinen Gott recht kindlich kann verlassen. Es ist der alte Choral des blinden Leiermanns von der neuen Promenade. Kennst Dus nicht, so lasse ich den ersten Chor abschreiben u. schenke ihn Dir noch nachträglich zum Geburtstag. Ich finde ihn wunderschön, er ist so einer von den St[ ] im Lande.

Hensel läßt sehr grüßen u. glückw[ünschen,] Seb. ebenfalls. Er ist jetzt Gott sey Dank ganz gesund, wie wir Alle. So viel h[aben] wir lange nicht sagen können.

Leb wohl, u. schreibe mir auch einm[al.] Hensel hat eine Zeichnung von mir gemacht, für Mad. Kiéné, die darum gebeten, über die wieder große Parteienkämpfe im Hause waren. Dirichlet hat sie nicht erkannt u. Paul ist mit Wuth dagegen, alle andre Leute dagegen finden sie sehr schön u. ähnlich. Adieu zum zweitenmal.

Denke an Deine

Fanny

80

Berlin, 4ten Februar 1836

Ich will Deiner Aufforderung nachkommen, u. Dir einmal einen rechten Kantorbrief schreiben, voller Quinten u. Faxen, aber nein. Wir haben gestern die anwesenden Nummern des Paulus gesungen, zum zweitenmal, u. bitten nun recht dringend um mehr, nämlich den Anfang, es geht schon sehr gut. Im ganzen wüßte ich gar nichts auszusetzen, es folgt Alles schön u. natürlich auf einander u. steht in gutem Verhältniß. Meine Tadel sollen nur Einzelnheiten betreffen, u. damit Du zugleich siehst, daß ich mein Urtheil als mein subjektives, u. nicht à la Rezensent als *unsres* hinstellen will, erzähle ich Dir gleich als ehrlicher Mann, wie erbaulich es ist, daß bei einer Stelle die ich nicht leiden kann, Devrient jedesmal mit stiller Inbrunst zu sich selbst sagt: wunderschön. Nun rathe, was das für eine ist. Ja einigen Rezitativ. (in denen mir übrigens, beiläufig gesagt, die Hauptkraft des Werks zu liegen scheint) sind müßige oder zu moderne Stellen. Am ersten, mit dem darauf folgenden Chor, Choral, u. 2ten Rezit. wüßte ich gar nichts auszusetzen. Das Alles ist grandios u. schön. Wunderschön der ganze erste Theil der Arie in b moll, bis zu den Worten: Herr thue meine Lippen auf bis zum tempo 1mo. Diese Stelle scheint mir matt, namentl. die Wiederholung der Worte. Der Schluß ist wieder sehr schön. Das folgende Rezit. fängt sehr schön an, so ruhig u. heiter u. gelassen. Es ist eine meiner Lieblingsstellen, bis nach den Worten: denn siehe, er betet. Die folgenden Worte bis zum tempo scheinen mir zu unbedeutend u. modern. Ist Allo con moto nicht eine zu schnelle Bezeichnung für diese Stelle? Im folgenden Stück kommt die Stelle über die ich mit Devrient verschiedner Meinung bin. Es ist der Eintritt der Alte mit den Worten,: denn der Herr hat es gesagt, wonach 2 Takte später die Soprane eben so kommen. Das scheint mir, mit der Begleitung zusammen, nicht recht ernsthaft. Ich glaube, Du hast das Thema erst als Kontrathema zum ersten erfunden, u. mit dem zusammen klingt es auch nachher sehr schön, auch sogar allein, wenn die andern Stimmen dazu kommen, nur dieser doppelte Eintritt auf denselben Noten will mir nicht gefallen.

Und nun zu guter Letzt will ich mich noch gegen eine Stelle des letzten Sopranrezit. erklären, u. zwar gegen die Worte: und ging hin u. ließ sich taufen, welche mir nicht ihrer Wichtigkeit gemäß behandelt scheinen.

Und nun bin ich fertig.

Hauser u. Paul haben auch viel geschuhuht, u. wollten den Schluß der letzten Fuge mit dem hohen a u. dem Quartsextenaccord zu modern finden. Ich erklärte ihnen aber sehr bestimmt, er würde nicht geändert, denn er wäre wesentlich Felixsch. Ueberdieß ist das Singevolk höchst erbaut, u. die Chöre singen sich sehr leicht, und wir haben Alle große Freude dran, u. eine Beruhigung, daß Vater doch noch etwas davon in Düsseldorf gehört hat. Daß ich daran nicht Theil genommen, wird mir ewig leid seyn.

5ten Feb. Gestern waren wir zum erstenmal im Concert u. zwar im Israel in Egypten, u. da habe ich wieder Grimm u. Aerger geschluckt. Wie dieser Lump das schöne Talent, die Singacademie herunter gebracht hat. Kein einziger Stimmeneintritt in der ganzen Musik ging gut, u. wer sie nicht vorher kannte, war nicht im Stande auch nur eine Ahnung davon zu bekommen. Beständig mußte ich an die Orgel u. die Cöllner Chöre denken. Und nun die eine Rungenhagensche Posaune, die er obligat zu Allem setzt. Den Gesang der Mirjam ließ er mit 2 Hörnern u. einer Pauke begleiten. Nebenbei ist es auch nicht wenig schade, daß die Lenz, diese allerliebste Sängerin, ihre Stimme so ganz verloren hat. Du erinnerst Dich doch wie sie die Königinn der Nacht sang, jetzt bringt sie mühsam fis, u. g fast gar nicht heraus. Ich wollte erst kaum glauben, daß sie es wäre.

Dabei fällt mir ein: glaubst Du denn, daß Händel selbst die Orgel zu seinen Sachen gespielt hat? Denn da die geschriebenen Orgelstimmen nicht da sind, so müßte der Organist, wenn er es nicht selbst gewesen ist, doch wohl nur die Ziffern begleitet haben.

Dein Mozartsches Concert möchte ich wol gehört haben. Seit 7 Jahren, also eigentlich grade von der Zeit Deiner vollen Ausbildung an, sind wir nun nicht mehr zusammen, u. ich habe Dich fast gar nicht öffentlich spielen hören, u. wären wir nicht diesen Sommer nach Cölln gekommen, hätte ich gar keine Anschauung von Deinem öffentlichen Treiben. Und hier sitzt unterdessen ein Affe, u. verdirbt alle Jahr 6 Concerte mit den besten Mitteln, u. so viel Proben, als er dazu braucht. Pfui!

Nun will ich schließlich noch einmal auf mich zurück kommen, so unangenehm es auch ist, Advokat in seiner eignen Sache zu seyn, wir sind ja gewohnt, rund heraus mit einander zu reden. Du hast in Leipzig gesagt, ich möchte lieber keine geistliche Musik mehr machen, weil mein Talent dazu nicht neigte. Nun habe ich seit meiner Rückkunft, oder vielmehr seit 8 T. mehrere meiner frühern Sachen der Art durchgespielt, u. muß vorausschicken, daß ich der Meinung bin, es gäbe keinen strengeren Beurtheiler, als ein ehrlicher Mensch über seine eignen frühern Sachen ist. Vieles, ja das Meiste hat mich so ennüyirt, daß ich mit Mühe die Geduld aufbringen konnte, es durchzuspielen, Manches aber, z. B. die Arie: o daß ich tausend Zungen hätte, u. einige Chöre u. Rezit. aus der sogenannten

Choleramusik, hat mir so gut gefallen, daß ich mich, so närrisch das klingen mag, recht daran erfreut habe, weil ich da[ ] für eine Probe halte, wenn Einem die eignen Sachen nach längerer Zeit, u. nachdem man sie ganz in Vergessenheit gerathen lassen, wieder gefallen. Indessen was Du sagst fällt ein bei mir auf einen steinigen Boden, u. ich bin mißtrauisch geworden, wiewol ich im Allgemeinen glaube, es jetzt besser machen zu können, als damals, u. mich schon dran gemacht hätte, Einiges umzuarbeiten, wenn nicht Dein Interdict mich störte.

Hensel hat mir vorgestern an Deinem Geburtstage eine hübsche Ueberraschung gemacht, indem er in den Hintergrund seines Bildes die Figur eines Knaben gemalt, die lustig Horn bläst, u. mit langen braunen Haaren Dir ähnlich sieht. Ich glaube das Bild wird sehr schön. Vaters Bemerkungen hat er Alle noch benutzt.

Adieu, das war mal ein ganz handwerkmäßiger Brief. Schreibe mir bald wieder. Kommst Du nicht nach beendeten Concerten her?

81

Berlin 20 Februar 1836

Ich ziehe es vor, Dir die Noten gleich zu schicken, lieber Felix, da Du mir versprichst, sie bald zurück zu senden. 14 Tage sind fast zu wenig, für Stimmen ausschreiben, Leute zusammenkommen, etc. Aber halte auch Wort. Und bitte auch um das Rondo aus e dur. Ist das im Pariser Album schon gedruckt? Rebecka u. ich tragen die Ouvertüre zur Melusina mit vielem Ausdruck schön vor, es wäre schon der Mühe werth, daß Du nach Berlin kämest, um das zu hören. Ueber Davids Engagement freue ich mich herzlich, seinet- u. Deinetwegen, ich glaube es wird ein Grund mehr für Dich seyn, die Stelle fortzubehalten. Grüße ihn herzlich von mir u. sage ihm, er sey immer noch der alte Favorit, ich habe vor einigen Tagen auf dem Museum mit Rührung das Bild wieder gesehn, nach dem wir ihm vor vielen Jahren den Namen Haustürke gaben. Aelte Zeiten!

Wirst Du denn nach Düsseldorf gehn? Wenn ich doch hinkönnte! Deine polnische Judengeschichte ist sehr gut. Der Kerl ist wirklich ein Phänomen, er macht hier furore. Wenn ich nur begreifen könnte, wie Holz auf Holz Ton geben kann. Lebe aber wohl.

[Lea]

82

Berlin den 1sten Juny

[Rebecka]

Hier sind wir, lieber Felix! So geschwind zurückgereist, daß sie hier geglaubt haben, wir wären unser Geist, Montag 1/2 9 Abends waren wir hier u. haben 2 Nächte geschlafen. Beckchen hab ich, Gottlob, quite charming gefunden, sie wird nicht müde, erzählen zu hören. Wie schön war es in Düsseldorf u. wie höre ich noch immer Paulus vor Ohren. Sobald Reb. wohl genug ist, daran Theil nehmen zu können, laß ich singen, zu meinem Vergnügen u. deren im Hause. Dieser Brief trifft wohl mit Dir zugleich in Ffurt ein, grüße alle lieben Bekannte, u. laß bald von Dir hören. Auch was Du noch am Paulus thust, möchte ich wohl wissen.

83

Berlin, 28sten Juni 1836

Ich bin so lange nicht dazu gekommen, Dir zu schreiben, lieber Felix, daß ich mich heut, Dienstag den 25sten Juni Nachmittags um 5 eigen dazu in den Garten hinsetze u. somit loslege; eigentlich habe ich Dir nichts zu schreiben, denn bei uns geht es still u. häuslich zu, u. wird es nächstens noch viel mehr, denn heut über 8 T. rutscht Beckchen ab, Dein Frankf. Brief war sehr hübsch u. ergötzlich, Rossini der die h moll Messe anhört ist für mich ein unvergeßlich komisches Bild. Was Du über Eckermann schreibst, habe ich fast wirklich einige Tage früher an Klingemann geschrieben. Das Buch hält sich interessant bis zum Ende, nur daß ich finde, daß Eckerm. eigene, mehr [ ] simple Bemerkungen immer posserlicher werden je öfter sie sich wiederholen. Es ist unbegreiflich, wie jemand, der Verstand genug hatte, Goethe so nachzuschreiben, nicht genug hat, die Armuth dieser raisonnements einzusehn. Ist Dir nicht aufgefallen, wie manches drin ist, was Vater eben so gesagt hat? Bei jeder Zeile mußte ich dran denken, was er darüber gesagt, u. wie er sich manches Zusammentreffens gefreut haben würde.

Ich habe neulich den ersten Theil des Paulus singen lassen, u. werde in diesen Tagen den 2ten vornehmen. Schreibe doch wie es mit der Herausgabe steht, u. wann er erscheint. Ferner bitte ich, Dich um Angabe des Tempos von o siehe, wir preisen selig, u. des Anfangs der Arie des Paulus: Herr sey mir gnädig, mit dem Mälzlschen Metronom, ich war in Streit mit Paul darüber. Es thut mir sehr leid, daß ich nicht vor Düsseldorf den ganzen Paulus kannte, es hat zwar auch seinen eignen Reiz, die Sachen so fertig kennen zu lernen, aber man hat doch mehr Genuß, wenn man schon voraus jede Note weiß, die da kommt. Ich wollte aber, Du hörtest einmal die Sopranarien von der Decker, sie sang sie prächtig.

Sebastian hat zu seinem Geburtstag einen Vogel u. eine Armbrust bekommen, u. hat gleich so gut ins Schießen gefunden, daß er den ersten Tag gleich den ganzen Vogel herunter [ ], so hat er gestern zum ersten Mal boccia gespielt mit den Großen, u. es ganz vortrefflich ging. Er hat viel Geschick u. Grazie zu körperlichen Uebungen, so ist es allerliebst, ihn sein Gärtchen selbst begießen, hacken u. bearbeiten zu sehn. Der kleine gute Dicke hilft ihm treuherzig dabei, der Junge hat ein allerliebstes Gemüthchen, u. wenn er Sebastian lieber Freund, oder lieber Bruder nennt, so hört sich das gar niedlich an. Heut ist herrliches Wetter, u. einer der schönsten Tage, die wir noch hatten, wir haben lange von den eigensinnigsten Wind- u. Wetterlaunen zu leiden gehabt. Klingemann, der Verräther hat noch nicht geschrieben, weißt Du was von ihm? Es stehn Dir ganz besondre Berliner Freuden bevor, ich muß Dich nur darauf vorbereiten, damit Dir die Ueberraschung nicht schade, in Frankfurt wirst Du Herrn Rex! u. in Scheveningen H. v. Varnhagen sehn.

Grüße Tante Schlegel, Veits, Hiller, u. Andre, dessen gutes Gesicht ich wol einmal wieder sehn möchte. Daß Du ihm ähnlich gefunden wirst, ist um so sonderbarer, als Du eigentlich von Vater keine Aehnlichkeit hast, sondern entschieden in Mutters Familie siehst. Sebastian hat von ihm den Schädelbau, worüber ich mich jeden Tag freue. Möchte ihm [ ] was dr[ ] ist ähnlich werden, was ich dazu thun kann, will ich mir Mühe geben, nicht zu versäumen. Ueberhaupt fällt mir oft ans Herz, welche schwere Verantwortung man doch übernimmt, indem man ein Kind auferzieht. Ich kann dabei nichts thun, als das Beispiel der Eltern möglichst nachzuahmen suchen, es ist nur, so etwas ahmt sich nicht nach, u. die Fälle sind ja auch verschieden. Gott möge uns helfen, u. er wird es, nach Vaters Wahlspruch, wenn wir uns helfen.

Lebe wohl, bester Felix, schreibe mir bald einmal. Was wirst Du nach der Redaction des Paulus arbeiten? Nimmst Du nicht einmal die früheren Symphonieen wieder vor?

Heut Abend ist bei Rebecka eine große Fete [?].

84

Berlin, 30sten Juli 1836.

Es fällt mir nicht ein, böse zu seyn, oder eigene Briefe für mich allein zu verlangen, liebster Felix, auch hätte ich Dir gewiß auf Deinen vorigen Brief schon geschrieben, allein es geschah mir, daß ich mich hinsetzte, Papier u. Feder nahm, u. als ich mich nun besann, was ich Dir schreiben sollte, nichts wußte, es ging mir, wie nach Humboldt den Affen, die deshalb nur nicht reden, weil sie nichts zu sagen haben. In Deinem letzten Brief aber ist so manches mir Erfreuliche, daß ich, obgleich sich seitdem nichts Erzählbares zugetragen hat, recht gut weiß, was Dir zu schreiben. Es hat mich darin unter Andern eines jener kleinen Zusammentreffen erfreut, die sich in unserm Leben öfters wiederholen, u. die ich nicht gern Zufall nennen möchte, daß Du zum ersten seit Deiner Kindheit Goethes Leben wieder liest, u. daß mich seit mehreren Wochen eben dieselbe Lektüre beschäftigt; das kömmt nun wol bei uns beiden durch Eckermann, allein manche Tausend Menschen mögen das Buch lesen, u. doch nicht danach Goethes Leben. Ich dachte mir auch, wenn ich einmal wieder nach Frankfurt komme, muß ich die Stadt in Bezug auf sein Leben kennen lernen. Ich lese jetzt den 4ten Band Hensel vor, wie ich es auch eben mit dem Eckermann gemacht.

Ferner beschäftigt mich Dein Frankfurter schönes Mädchen nicht wenig, Du glaubst nicht, was ich für Verlangen nach Deiner Braut habe, ich fühle so sehr, daß Dir das wohlthun wird. Ich könnte Dir wenn ich Sancho wäre, eine ganze Menge Sprichwörter anführen, um Deinen guten Entschluß zu beschleunigen: Frisch gewagt, ist halb gewonnen, wer das Glück hat, führt die Braut heim, wenn sie Dir schenken die Kuh, so laut mit dem Stricke zu, wer den Teufel verschlucken will, muß ihn nicht lange ansehn, u. noch manches Andre, was nicht hierher paßt. Ich habe mir nun fest in den Kopf gesetzt, Du machst diesmal Ernst, u. wenn Du Dich nun im Haag in Doris Zelter verliebst, u. es wird wieder nichts draus, so werde ich höchst disappointed seyn. Dabei fällt mir ein, daß ich Dich so recht eigentlich verliebt noch gar nicht gesehn habe, alle Deine großen Amourschaften (siehe Rosalie Mendelssohns ungedruckte Werke) waren auswärts, u. ich bin doch gar zu neugierig wie Dir das steht. Das Alles sind nun schlechte Späße, aber im bittersten Ernst möchte ich gar zu sehr, daß Du Dich verheirathest.

Zwei sehr hübsche angenehme Proben des Paulus habe ich gehalten, so lange die Decker hier war, nun aber stiebt Alles dermaßen auseinander, daß ich wol glaube, ich werde die ganze Sache bis auf den Herbst verschieben müssen. Daß Du Dich so mit dem Clavierauszug gequält hast, thut mir sehr leid, hättest Du mir nur einen Theil der Arbeit abgegeben, ich hätte es schon fleißig u. gut machen wollen. Uebrigens wird mir der Paulus bei näherer Bekanntschaft immer lieber, u. der schwachen Sachen, oder die mir wenigstens so vorkommen, sind sehr wenige, von denen wir gesprochen haben. Ich bin nun sehr neugierig, wie Du noch wirst geändert haben, hast Du wirklich noch den ersten Chor weggelassen? nur nicht, der du die Menschen, die Arie ist mir sehr ans Herz gewachsen.

Mit der Musik ists hier klateriger als je. Wozu sie den Hauser engagirt haben, möchte ich schon wissen, er tritt nie auf. Ich habe, da es Hensel wünschte, wieder Sonntags zu spielen angefangen, aber Ganzens sind nicht hier, u. mich von Alevin mit Vergnügen begleiten zu lassen, dazu bin ich wirklich zu verwöhnt. Ich habe, wie der gestrenge Herr befohlen, fortgefahren, Clavierstücke zu machen, u. es ist mir zum ersten Mal gelungen, etwas zu Stande zu bringen, das brillant klingt. Ich weiß zwar nicht genau, was Goethe mit dem dämonischen Einfluß meint, von dem er zuletzt so viel spricht, doch soviel ist klar, daß wenn dergleichen existirt, Du es in Bezug auf mich ausübst. Ich glaube, wenn Du mir im Ernst vorschlügst, ein guter Mathematiker zu werden, so würde ich keine besondre Schwierigkeit dabei finden, eben so wie ich morgen keine Musik mehr würde machen können, wenn Du meintest, ich könne keine machen. Nimm Dich daher mit mir in Acht.

So wie es ein junges Deutschland giebt, [so giebt] es auch ein langweiliges, das Beckchen in [Eiger] u. ein odiöses, das Du in Scheveningen findest. Mad. Robert u. H. v. Varnhagen können Einem schon die Palmen u. die Austern verhaßt machen. Verliere aber diesen Brief nicht am Meere, sonst findet ihn Einer von denen u. liebt mich dafür.

Adieu, Hensel grüßt bestens. Heut reist Dirichlet, u. dann wird Mutter unser Tischgast seyn. Sie hört auch gewöhnlich zu, wenn ich Hensel vorlese, was mir viel Freude macht. An das Vorlesen knüpfen sich für mich die schönsten Erinnerungen.

Lebe wohl u. bleibe mir gut.

Deine Fanny

85

Berlin, 19ten Oktober 1836

Ich habe Dir für ein allerliebstes Lied zu danken, lieber Felix u. thue es von ganzem Herzen, Du hast mich sehr damit erfreut. Dann aber will ich mir aufs Maul schlagen, u. stilleschweigen, bis Du allen Leuten in der Welt u. zuletzt auch einmal mir wirst geschrieben haben. Man sagt gewöhnlich, wie es in den Wald hinein schallt, so schallt es auch wieder heraus, das ist aber bei uns nicht der Fall, ich habe diesen ganzen Sommer unaufhörlich geschallt, ohne auch nur ein einziges Echo zu hören. Nun nehme ich Dir das wahrhaftig nicht im Mindesten übel, ich weiß wie es bei Dir zugeht, indessen da doch das Schreiben anstatt des Gesprächs dasteht, so hat es auch die Aehnlichkeit von demselben, das wenn Einer immer allein spricht er am Ende sich u. den Hörer ermüdet.

Daß Du mir keinen vollständigen Auszug des Paulus hast schicken können, thut mir sehr leid, ich hätte es so gern diesen Herbst noch im Gartensaal singen lassen u. daran wird nun nicht mehr zu denken seyn, wenn der gedruckte kommt, passen die Stimmen nicht, die ich habe, u. müssen erst neue geschrieben werden. Hast Du etwas Näheres über die Aufführung in Liverpool gehört? War Klingemann dort? Sollte er darüber schreiben, so schicke uns doch seinen Brief.

Von Cecilen habe ich einen Brief erhalten, zum Küssen. Wäre ich so uneigennützig wie Mutter, so schickte ich ihn Dir, aber ich hüte mich wohl, Du giebst ihn doch nicht wieder. Sie schreibt mir auf meine Bitte die ganze Geschichte Eurer Bekanntschaft u. Verlobung, mit einer liebenswürdigen Naivetät u. Einfachheit, daß man sie wirklich von Herzen liebgewinnen muß. Von allen Seiten überschüttet man uns dermaßen mit ihrem Lobe, daß michs nach grade anfängt herzlich zu langweilen, daß ich sie nicht kenne, vorzüglich, da mir Paul wieder in Erinnerung gebracht hat, daß wir einen Brief von Emmeline an Souchays hatten. Wir Schafköpfe, hätten wir den nun nicht selbst abgeben können!

Von der Ausstellung soll ich Dir schreiben, das wird mir aber etwas schwer, da ich mir zwar wohl, Du aber schwerlich, Unparteilichkeit genug zutraust, die Sache wie ein andrer Zuschauer zu betrachten. Von den französ. Land- u. Seeschaften wirst Du wol zur Genüge gehört haben. Wenn man so etwas nicht kennt, hört man sehr leicht schon zuviel davon. Soviel kann ich Dir sagen, daß sie vortrefflich sind, dagegen die historischen Bilder die sie uns geschickt haben, nichts weniger, daß ich aber eine Franzosenmanie hier deutlich anmarschire, u. sich auf den Platz der Düsseldorfer setzen sehn. Die Berliner haben bei aller Ihrer unleidlichen Kälte eine Art von Schwefelholzfeuer, das einen Augenblick brennt, u. eine Stunde danach stinkt, sie thun immer zu wenig oder zu viel. Von Hensels Bild mag ich Dir nichts sagen, es hat zuviel vom Eigenlob, wenn man die Seinigen lobt, u. so am Ende glaubt mir Niemand, Du auch nicht, daß ich das Bild auch wunderschön finden würde, wenn es nicht von meinem Mann wäre. Sonntag kommt es zur Ausstellung, nebst einer Skizze und Studienkopf zu einem sterbenden Moses, u. einigen Rähmen[a] mit Zeichnungen, deren er in der letzten Zeit wieder vortreffliche gemacht hat. Daß Moser den Beerschen Preis gewonnen wird Dir Mutter geschrieben haben. Hensel läßt Dir herzlichst grüßen, u. läßt Dir sagen, es wäre sehr unrecht, daß Du nicht auf ein Paar Tage uns u. die Ausstellung besuchst. Könntest Dus, wäres sehr schön. Wir sehn Dich sonst gar nicht als Bräutigam. Auch Cecile sähe ich gar gern als Braut, u. mit ihrer Mutter und Schwester. Sie wird nachher gewiß nicht weniger liebenswürdig, aber sie wird doch anders seyn, kennte sie gern auf alle Weise.

Lebe wohl, grüße Sie herzlich, u. sage ihr, wenn die gehörige Anständszeit vorüber wäre, würde ich ihr antworten. Wenn ich meinem Hange nachlebte, so würde ich mich in demselben Augenblick hinsetzen, wo ich einen Brief von ihr erhalte um ihn sogleich zu beantworten, aber das schickt sich nicht, u. ich bin wohlerzogen.

Deine Fanny

---

[a]Fanny does use the umlaut.

86

Berlin, 28sten Oktr. 1836.

Habe Dank, bester Felix, für Deinen lieben Brief. Aber entschuldigen auf drei Seiten hättest Du Dich nicht sollen, so war es nicht gemeint, u. zwischen uns soll u. wird es ja wohl nicht zu Mißverständnissen kommen. Und da Du so ein ehrlicher Mann bist, u. Briefe wiedergiebst, so sollst Du auch die beiden lieben von Cecile haben. Herr Schunk bringt sie Dir mit, u. Du kannst sie mir durch Paul wiederschicken. Den kannst Du zum Israel erwarten; Alexanders kommen Sonntag, u. dann wird er sich aufmachen, sobald er Alles übergeben hat. Der Israel wird prachtvoll werden, Orgel u. Kirche zusammen hat man seit Menschengedenken nicht zu Händel gehört. Wollt ich könnt es hören. Noch etwas gutes Herbstwetter könnten wir auch brauchen. Seit Hensels Bild auf der Ausstellung ist, war keine Stunde Sonnenschein, u. den könnte es doch brauchen, denn da sie 12 neue Säle gebaut haben, so fehlt es natürlich an Platz, ein Bild gehörig zu hängen, da die besten Plätze an den Fenstern durch breite Thüren eingenommen sind, drei Viertel des Raumes ganz unbrauchbar, u. das letzte Viertel mäßig dunkel ist. Ueber diese Geschichte von dem Neubau, den der alte Schadow ganz im Stillen mit dem Architekten der prinzlichen Ställe verübt hat, darf ich gar nicht reden, sonst fange ich jedesmal an zu wüthen, u. Du sagst: eine wüthende Gere. Es ist aber das Aergste, was wir hier in langer Zeit vollbracht haben, u. das will was sagen. Uebrigens können wir mit der Aufnahme die das Bild findet, nicht anders als zufrieden seyn.

Du frägst, was ich komponirt habe, u. ich antworte, Deiner Aufgabe gemäß, ein halb Dutzend Clavierstücke. Ich werde sie Dir durch Paul schicken, hast Du Zeit so spiele sie einmal durch, oder laß sie durch einen Deiner Schüler spielen, u. laß mir was drüber sagen. Ich habe so viel von der Natur Deines Schülers, daß es mir immer am Besten gelingt, wenn Du mir sagst: mache doch das oder das. Ich bin in der letzten Zeit wieder viel angegangen worden, etwas heraus zu geben, soll ichs thun?

Nächste Woche müssen wir eine förmliche musikalische Sauerei[a] geben, wovor mir schon heut (verzeih) mies ist. Es ist uns nämlich eine italiän. Sängerin empfohlen, die an Schönheit u. Stimme ein wahres Meerwunder seyn soll, dazu will ich dann Deckers bitten, u. Curschmann u. Röschen, die jetzt überall herum singen, u. dann mögen sie trillern. Dazwischen spiele ich ein zartes Lied, wo möglich so zart wie Curschmann, oder soll ich die 33 Variat. von Beethoven spielen? Bei Deckers fangen auch die Opern wieder an.

Ich muß doch noch einmal auf die Ausstellung zurückkommen. Ich habe noch keine gesehn, bei der das Interesse so gespalten, so wenig ein allgemeines gewesen wäre. Das alleinige Düsseldorfer Regiment hat aufgehört, sie haben mit Recht ihr Publicum, u. werden es behalten, u. Hildebrandt ist diesmal ihr vorzüglichster Vertreter. Dann haben die Franzosen den größten Beifall, von hier sind auch einige bedeutende Sachen da, herrliche Landschaften von Rom, Mehreres von Deutschen, die in Paris studiren, eine herrliche Landschaft von [Konckonck], die ich Dir wol zu sehn wünschte, ein Wald im Winter, Roberts Erndte, u. ein prächtiges Bild seines Bruders, so daß von allen Seiten her Schönes u. Interessantes in Menge vorhanden [sind], u. man durchaus nicht sagen kann, die Ausstellung habe einen Mittelpunkt, das macht sie aber vielleicht nur noch interessanter. Lebe wohl o Felix u. habe weniger zu thun. Komponirst Du denn jetzt etwas? u. was? Werden denn Deine Symphonieen nie vor Tageslicht kommen? Wann wird sichs entscheiden, ob Du in Leipzig bleibst, oder nicht? Grüße Cecile, jetzt werde ich ihr in diesen Tagen schreiben.

Deine F.

---

[a]A combination of "Soiree" and "sauer."

87

Berlin, 16ten Novbr. 1836

Lieber Felix, sey schönstens bedankt für Deinen lieben Brief, der mich sehr erfreut hat. Ich finde nun zwar eigentlich, zwischen 16 u. 61 Jahren müßte man keinen Geburtstag haben (obgleich ich jeden Geburtstag der Andern sehr gern habe u. feiere) aber für mich habe ich den eigentlichen Apparat von Kuchen u. Zubehör längst abgeschafft. Aber ein Brief, ein freundliches Gesicht (jenes soll dieses ersetzen), eine liebe Zeichnung von Sebastian, wer sich darüber nicht freuen wollte, der müßte wol noch älter als alt seyn.—Was mir sehr leid thut, ist daß Du gar nicht aus dem gehetzten Leben herauskommen kannst, denn ich weiß u. sehe an Hensel, dem es auch oft so geht, wie sehr das aufreibt u. die Nerven angreift. Auch dafür hoffe ich von Deiner Verheirathung sehr viel. Die viel Zeit wirst Du nicht schon durch das Zuhauseessen ersparen, u. wie angenehm wird das Tischchen seyn. Du wirst überhaupt so gern zu Hause seyn, daß Du Mittel finden wirst, es zu können, u. das wird Dir sehr wohl thun.—Daß Ihr übrigens den Israel nicht wiederholt, finde ich sehr schade, es wäre der doppelte Genuß für dieselbe Mühe, u. wie es den Directoren für das Frühjahr schaden soll, begreife ich nicht, ich dächte im Gegentheil.

Von der Art u. Weise habe ich nun wohl durch den Salomon eine Idee, indeß mag es mit einer tüchtigen Kirchenorgel doch noch anders klingen. Frank sagte mir, sein Bruder habe die ganze Orgelstimme geschrieben, ist das wahr, oder hat der kleine Frank geflunkert? Wie ich hier ganz u. gar aus jeder Musik herauskomme, die ich mir nicht selbst vormache, davon hast Du wirklich keinen Begriff. Ich höre im eigentlichsten Sinne des Worts keinen Ton, u. was sollte ich auch hören? Wie Möser Jahr aus Jahr nie dieselben Symphonieen in derselben Reihenfolge herunterkratzen läßt, oder wie Ries ziemlich sauber aber sehr langweilig ein Quartett nach dem andern spielt? Da bin ich sogar abonnirt, gehe aber niemals hin. Oper haben wir nicht, von Academieconcerten werde ich wol Joseph in Egypten v. Händel hören, weil ich das nicht kenne, u. daher weniger fühlen werde, wie sie es verderben. Ueber diesen gänzlichen Mangel an Anstoß von außen verfalle ich nun selbst auch in eine solche musikalische Apathie, daß ich wirklich in Jahr u. Tag keine eigentliche Musik gemacht habe. Indeß habe ich beschlossen, mich herauszureißen, u. Ende des Monats mit Deinem Psalm u. den drei Nonnenstücken wieder anzufangen, die ich sehr hübsch besetzen kann. Die Decker ist nach wie vor äußerst gefällig u. liebenswürdig gegen mich, auch haben wir vorige Woche bei ihr eine sehr wohlgelungene Aufführung v. Marschners Templer gehabt.—Daher kannst Du denken, wie erfreulich es mir ist, daß Du mit meinen Clavierstücken zufrieden bist, woraus ich doch sehn kann, daß ich noch nicht ganz mit der Musik zerfallen bin. Schicke sie mir nur wieder, ich werde sie an Dir abschreiben lassen, dafür laß Du mir das aus c moll à la Thalberg, zukommen. Die Ausstellung wird Sonntag geschlossen weshalb wir den heutigen schönen, trüben Tag benutzen wollen, noch einmal hinzugehn, auf klares Wetter können wir doch nicht mehr warten. Wir haben allerdings Ursach, mit dem Erfolg ganz gut zufrieden zu seyn, lieber Felix, was uns aber viel mehr als das, hier hält, weißt Du ja, u. kannst es Dir denken. Indessen müssen wir daran denken u. thun es auch alles Ernstes, in einigen Jahren einmal ein Jahr in Italien zuzubringen. Für Hensel ist es ein Bedürfniß, u. mein Wunsch stimmt natürlich mit ein. Was nun das jetzige Schulenwesen betrifft, darüber habe ich meine eigene Gedanken, die sich bei dieser Ausstellung sehr bestätigt haben. Um eine eigentliche Schule zu bilden, dazu gehört, daß wie im Mittelalter durchgängig, u. heut zu Tage nur allein in München, eine gemeinsame große Aufgabe Lehrer u. Schüler lange Zeit hindurch beschäftige. Wie ist es aber möglich, daß 3. oder 400 junge Maler, jeder jedes Jahr ein Bild malen können? Die ohnehin schon schwachen Kräfte zersplitten sich, die Gegenstände wiederholen sich ins Unendliche, u. es ist natürlich, daß endlich wie in Düsseldorf, ein Leithammel voran springt, u. 100 andre den Sprung nachzuthun versuchen. Mit Hensel ist es wieder etwas anders. Er betreibt die Sache ohne alle Koketterie, u. nur im Interesse seiner jungen Leute. Daher entbläßt er sie, sobald sie irgend auf eignen Füßen stehen können, u. hat es immer wieder mit neuen zu thun, die ihm weder künstlerisch noch persönlich, so viel Interesse einflößen können. Doch hat er diesmal die Freude, die 2 einzigen Preise, die im ganzen Staat für dies Fach vergeben werden, in sein Attelier gekommen zu sehn, Kaselowsky ist schon fort, Moser wird im Lauf des Winters gehn, dann ist die ganze erste Generation, mit der wir uns sehr eingelebt hatten, zerstoben, u. daß er nicht Lust hat, das in infinitum so fort zu treiben, kannst Du Dir wol denken.

Ich habe immer so einen Gedanken im Hinterh[aupt], sollte denn der gar nicht ausführbar seyn, daß wir uns einmal Alle aufmachten, u. einen Sommer in schöner Gegend, am Rhein, oder in Baden, oder in Dresden, still mit einander zubrächten. Was meinst Du dazu? Sollte das nicht möglich u. sehr hübsch seyn? Oder am Genfer See. Du hast uns auch noch gar nicht die froh[e] Versicherung gegeben, uns Cäcilien zu bringen sobald sie Dein ist, wir hoffen zwar Alle sich[er] darauf, möchten es doch aber auch gar zu gern hören. Und wie gern sähen wir sie erst noch als Mädchen. An meinem Geburtstage war Marianne mit ihren Kindern hier, u. denen haben wir wieder recht viel von [ ] gesprochen. Alle Menschen kennen sie j[ ] nur wir nicht, das ist doch recht grausam. Grüße sie tausendmal, u. sage ihr, sie so[lle] uns einstweilen gut seyn. Ihre Briefe sind gar zu lieb. Was beschreibt sie denn von der Verlobung falsch? Widerlege sie. Neulich hat sie wieder ein allerliebstes Briefchen an Mutter geschrieben. Mutter, Beckchen u. Hensel, Alles grüßt Dich bestens. Es ist Alles wohl, bis auf den Schnupfen der die [Runden] gemacht hat, und jetzt an mir hält, Hensel hat viel am Zahnweh gelitten, sich einen ausreißen lassen, u. laborirt trotz aller Kaps[el]gallen, fortwährend am Magen.

Sein voriges großes Bild wird in sehr großem Dimension, sehr gut lithographirt der Stein ist heut noch auf die Ausstellung gekommen, wir hoffen Dir zu Weihnachten einen Abdruck zu [schicken]. Ich bitte Dich aber sehr, dies Alles streng unter uns zu lassen. [ ] zu können. Leb wohl u. bleib mir gut.

Deine F.

88

[Lea]

Berlin, 22 Novbr.
am Tage der heil. Cäcilia.

Wozu Dir Glück gewünscht sey.
Eigentlich wollt ich Dir gleich nach Empfang eines Briefs aus Leipzig v. Paul u. Albertine schreiben, die so gar viel Erfreuliches gemeldet haben, wie viel Fortschritte Dein Orchester gemacht, wie munter u. glücklich zu seyst,[a] Paul schreibt, noch viel vollkommner geworden, wie angenehm Deine dortige Situation, u. was uns natürlich sehr erfreulich, daß alle Aussicht auf Verlängerung Deines dortigen Aufenthalts sey, denn das Bewußtseyn, sich in 18 Stunden sehn zu *können*, [is]t doch gar beruhigend u. erfreulich. Daß Du Cäcilien ein Stammbuch machst, u. Lieder von mir drin haben willst, ist sehr hübsch, auch Hensel ist wie natürlich sehr gern bereit, [ ] u. einer Vignettenbeisteuer. Sage nur bald, was u. wie Dus willst, kurz vor Weihnachten [hä]ufen sich immer die Arbeiten etwas, [ka]nn ich Papier nehmen, wie ich will, oder soll ich ins Buch schreiben?

Was mein Herausgeben betrifft, so stehe ich dabei, wie der Esel zwischen zwei Heubündeln. Ich selbst bin ziemlich neutral dabei, es ist mir aufrichtig gestanden, einerlei, Hensel wünscht es, Du bist dagegen. In jeder Andern Sache, würde ich natürlich dem Wunsch meines Mannes unbedingt Folge leisten, allein hierbei ist es mir doch zu wichtig, Deine Beistimmung zu haben, ohne dieselbe möchte ich nichts der Art unternehmen.

Gestern habe ich hier einen italiänischen Improvisator gehört, Bindocci, von dem die, welche ihn das erstemal schon besucht hatten, ganz entzückt waren. Sey es aber, daß ich nicht genug italiänisch verstehe, oder daß mir die ganze Art u. Weise zu fremd ist, seine *gesungen* vorgetragenen Gedichte machten mir den Eindruck des Lächerlichen u. unleidlich Ermüdenden. Viel besser gefielen mir seine gesprochenen Improvisationen, u. sein eigentliches Talent scheint mir das rasche Ausfüllen gegebener Reime, namentlich zu komischen Thematen. Ueberdies scheint mir die ganze Sache leichter als sie aussieht, die gegebenen Themata, besonders solche die etwas ferner liegen, läßt er sehr aus dem Spiel, u. ergeht sich mehr in Allgemeinheiten, die er längst in der Gewalt haben muß, eine große Reimleichtigkeit u. Geistesgegenwart gehört wol vor allem dazu.

Heut essen Mutter, Dirichlets, Julie Schunk u. Marianne Saaling hier.

Mit Julien gehe ich vorher auf die Ausstellung. Ich glaube das arme Kind ennüyirt sich hier ziemlich, die Beneke ist immer kränklich u. geht fast gar nicht aus, u. bei ihnen im Hause ist es auch sehr still.

Leb wohl, mein lieber Felix, grüße in Leipzig u. Frankfurt u. bleibe mir gut.

Deine Fanny

---

[a]Fanny mistakenly wrote "zu seyst" instead of "Du seyst."

89

Ich wollte Dir noch einmal recht ausführlich über den Paulus schreiben, u. Dir danken lieber Felix, da ich nun aber höre, daß diese Zeilen Dich *frühestens* in der Abreise begriffen, antreffen, will ich Dir nur glückliche Reise wünschen, u. ein Mehreres nach Frankfurt richten, wo Dir, so Gott will, die Freude nicht fehlen wird.

Ich meinerseits freue mich nicht wenig darauf, den Paulus, so gut es meine Kräfte gestatten, singen zu lassen, schon weniger auf Weihnachten, noch weiß ich nicht recht, ob wir ihn lustig zubringen werden. Die Bilderchen zu den Liedern für Cäcilie hat Hensel angefangen, u. wir werden sie Dir nach Ffurt. schicken. Möge sie damit zufrieden seyn.

Wenn Ihr uns nun aber nicht von Frankfurt aus zum Weihnachtsgeschenk eine bestimmte Zusage schickt, *wann* Ihr herkommt, so werden wir böse. Bei uns müßt Ihr wohnen, die blaue u. die gelbe Stube stehn zum Sommer für Euch bereit. Kannst Du Jeanrenaud's bereden, noch vor der Hochzeit nach Leipzig zu kommen, so kommen wir auch hin, eigentlich möchte ich sie doch gar zu gern noch als Mädchen sehn.

Döhler habe ich mit großem Vergnügen mehrere Male gehört, besonders im Zimmer. Man hat hier so selten Gelegenheit etwas zu lernen, daß ich mich immer doppelt freue, wenn es einmal geschehn kann. Er hat bescheidner Weise im Hotel de Russie Concert gegeben, das aber ganz voll war, hoffentlich spielt er noch öfter.

Und nun, addio, viel Glück u. Freude in Frankfurt, u. viel Grüße an Cäcilie, ihre Mutter u. Schwester, Veits u. die Schlegel. Denk unser, wenn Du froh bist.

Deine Fanny

Ein sehr böses Subjekt,—Herr von Schramm, der Violine zu spielen vorgiebt, reist nach Leipzig, u. will Dir durchaus empfohlen seyn, was mir Deine Abreise glückliche Gelegenheit giebt, abzulehnen. Indessen habe ich versprechen müssen, Dir seine Ankunft anzuzeigen, u. mich mit meinem Gewissen abzufinden, habe ich das hiermit gethan.

Heut ist der 11te December.

[Lea]

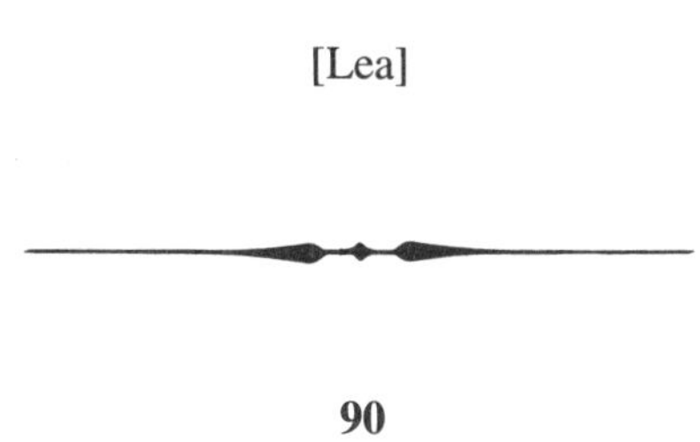

90

Berlin, 19ten Dec. 1836

Hier ist also unsre Beisteuer zum Album, lieber Felix. Die eine, sehr schön ausgeführte Zeichnung möge der andern, die nur im Umriß erscheint, zur Entschuldigung dienen, ich habe darauf bestanden, daß sie so ergehn sollte, sonst hätte sie gar nicht kommen können. Zum dritten Bogen hat Luise die Verzierung übernommen, u. mit der ihr, in solchen Dingen eigenen Grazie ausgeführt. Mögt Ihr zufrieden seyn. Nun wünsche ich nur, daß Du nicht etwa auch des Westes feuchte Schwingen für Cecile erwählt habest, sonst plumpe ich mörderlich. Erkläre auch Cecilen, warum sie ein gedrucktes Lied bekommt, sonst denkt sie, ich habe kein andres gemacht. Für Dich, lieber Felix, baue beikommende Hefte Stahlstiche auf, welche anzügliche Punkte enthalten. Und Gott schenke Euch, u. uns Allen eine frohe Weihnachtszeit, u. gebe, daß wir sie nächstes Jahr zusammen zubringen.

Gestern habe ich eine sehr schöne Probe des ersten Theils von Paulus gehalten. Bader war da, u. sang Einiges wunderschön, u. war selbst sehr ergriffen von der Musik. Ein junger Bassist vom Theater, Böttcher, der eine wundervolle Stimme hat, wird den Paulus singen, ich hoffe gut. Mein Chor jubelte, ich kann Dir nicht sagen, was ich für Freude gehabt habe. Berger, den ich neulich in Döhlers Concert traf u. mit dem ich Freundschaft erneuerte, war hier, u. saß neben mir beim Spielen, es war wie immer, als müßte er sagen stehn Sie auf Faniska, ich wills Ihnen vorspielen. Er hatte eine außerordentliche Freude über die Musik, u. ich kann Dir nicht sagen, wie sein Anblick mich rührt, er sieht so sehr übel aus, u. ist so still geworden.

Mit Deinen meisten Aenderungen bin ich sehr einverstanden, aber nicht mit Allen. Unter andern hätte ich eine Ohrfeige eben so gern genommen, als daß Du die Stelle geändert hast: welcher gemacht hat Himmel u. Erde u. das Meer, die war eine meiner Lieblingsstellen. Ferner, warum Du, die von mir sehr geliebte Sopranarie ausgeschlossen, begreife ich nicht, ich hätte viel lieber die kleine aus f dur, oder die Altarie gemißt.

Dagegen freue ich mich, daß Du in der Stelle der Erscheinung die Zwischenreden[a] an Baß u. Tenor vertheilt hast, u. bedanke mich noch besonders für die Aenderung: denn der Herr hat es gesagt. Warum hast Du nicht noch, wie es Deine Absicht war, gegen das Ende einen lebhaften Chor eingelegt?

Heut reist Madame Schunk mit Julien wieder zurück. Sie glauben bestimmt, daß Madame Jeanrenaud mit Cecilen u. Julien nach Leipzig kommt, betreibe Du die Sache, dann sehn wir uns auch, sonst wol schwerlich in diesem Winter.

Ich habe Mutter zugeredet, auch noch ein Blatt für Cecile zu schreiben, worüber sie sich zwar freuen wird. Rebecka wird leider nicht fertig, u. ärgert sich sehr darüber.

Wie unser Weihnachten werden wird, wissen wir noch gar nicht, nicht einmal bei wem, ob hier oder drüben, das soll heut ausgemacht werden. Wir rücken immer mit einer solchen Armee an, diesmal allein 12 Schüler, daß wir wirklich Niemanden zumuthen können, uns aufzunehmen.

Leb wohl, mein Schatz. Grüß herzlich Deine Cecile, u. ihre Angehörigen, u. freue Dich Deines Lebens. Hensel grüßt herzlich.

Deine Fanny

---

[a]Kuzhals-Reuter, *Oratorien,* 110, incorrectly transcribes this word as ''Geschichtenrede'' in her quotation of this passage.

91

Berlin, 20sten Jan. 1837

Vor allen Dingen gratulire ich, daß Cecile nach Leipzig kommt, und wie ihre Mutter schreibt, doch wenigstens 3 Wochen bleibt, Du wirst also während der übrigen Zeit Deines Bräutigamstandes wenig mehr allein seyn. Den 23sten.

Bewundere mich, wie viel ich in diesen 3 Tagen geschrieben habe, theils war ich nur unwohl, u. theils ist gestern der Paulus vom Stapel gelaufen, wovon ich Freitag Abend Probe hatte, Sonnabend mußte die Wohnung ziemlich umgedreht werden, u. da konnte ich denn nicht wieder dazu kommen. Ich überlasse es übrigens Mutter Dir davon zu erzählen, die eine außerordentliche Freude daran gehabt hat. Was mich besonders erfreut hat, war daß Berger sich bei dieser Gelegenheit einmal wieder zuthulich u. freundlich gezeigt, u. mit großem Interesse allen Proben beigewohnt hat. Alle Singenden, u. vor Allen Bader haben auch ihre große Freude daran gehabt, der hat ganz herrlich gesungen. Aber auch Stümer mit seiner wenigen übrigen Stimme sehr schön, die Decker vortrefflich, u. Bötticher hat sich alle Mühe gegeben. Er hat eine wundervolle dicke Stimme, ist ungemein musikalisch, aber sein Gesang ist noch etwas plump u. steif, u. nichts wird ihm so schwer als ein piano. Der müßte sich recht auf dem Theater aussingen können, aber sie halten ihn hier, geben ihm jährlich mehr, damit er bleibe, u. beschäftigen ihn nie. Man glaubt wirklich den Unsinn nicht.

Ich habe insofern einen ziemlich unangenehmen Winter, als Hensel fast beständig unwohl ist, u. keine Nacht schläft. Sobald es Frühjahr wird, treibe ich ihn aus. Ob ich mitgehn werde ist noch die Frage. Von der Grippe übrigens sind wir ziemlich verschont geblieben, die sonst hier wie toll umgegangen ist.

Grüße Cecilen, ich schreibe ihr nächstens. H. v. Liphart hat die Arie wieder mitgenommen, u. hoffentlich richtig abgeliefert. Daß meine Tempi richtig waren, habe ich gesehn, der erste Theil hat gerade 10 Minuten kurzer gedauert, als in Düsseldorf, was nach Abrechnung 2er Arien, die hier ausfielen, grade auskömmt. Die Sopranarie nämlich habe ich doch nicht eingelegt, mir aber abgeschrieben für ein andermal, u. die Altarie wegen kränklichen [Aus]bleibens der Thürrschmidt weg [lassen] müssen. Die Decker ist in andern Umständen u. piept, hat aber doch in den Hauptchören tüchtig mitgesungen.

Lebe wohl.

[Lea]

92

Berlin, 27sten Janr. 1837

Ich glaube, ich habe Dir vorigen Montag einen ziemlich dummen und confusen Brief geschrieben, Hensel war die Nacht nicht wohl gewesen, und ich hatte nicht ausgeschlafen auf den Paulus, und war sehr müde, nun habe ich aber Mittwoch Deinen lieben Brief bekommen, und danke Dir dafür. Wie froh bin ich, daß Du keine weitere Sorge hast, als wann Jeanrenauds kommen, wir seufzen jetzt einmal wieder nach Eisenbahn, dann wäre es doch keine Frage, daß Ihr uns besuchtet, u. so ist es leider auch keine Frage. Eigentlich ist es doch abscheulich, nur eine starke Tagereise auseinander zu seyn, und sich nicht zu sehn. Mutter beabsichtigt, zum Paulus nach Leipzig zu kommen, und auch Tante Levy, ich denke sie werden zusammen fahren, meine Reise ist unwahrscheinlich geworden, lieber Felix, in dieser Zwischenzeit, und ich setze Hensel zu, allein zu fahren. Ob der nun aber nicht doch grünere Jahreszeit abwarten wird, das ist die Frage. Das bitte ich Dich aber inständigst, halte uns nur diesen Sommer nicht zu kurz, gönne uns ein ordentlich Stückchen Zeit, damit man sich nicht blos guten Tag, und adieu sagt! Pauls kommen Ende Aprils, und werden, denke ich, ohne Unterbrechung hier bleiben, u. dann können wir Alle zusammen ein hübsch Leben führen. Paul ist unendlich glücklich über Dein Glück, u. was mir sehr gefällt, gewißermassen stolz über Deine Liebe, als wenn er die Liebe erfunden hätte, das finde ich aber sehr hübsch. Wie freut mich, was Du von Davids schreibst. Das ist wirklich auch eine von den Geschichten, die man nur nach dem Erfolg beurtheilen kann, geht es gut, haben die Leute Recht gehabt.—Meine Autorschaft, bestehend in einem Liede, hat mir gar keinen Spaß gemacht, lieber Felix, im Gegentheil, war mir das Geschrei und Posaunen, das Schlesingers von diesem, eigentlich doch ganz erbärmlichen Dinge von Album gemacht haben, sehr zuwider. Namentlich konnten sie sich gar nicht zufrieden geben, über die wundervolle Ausstattung, nun braucht man nur das schlechteste französische oder englische Ding der Art zu sehn, um zu begreifen, daß das hiesige sehr jammervoll ist. Uebrigens ist mir mit dem Leipz. Album etwas Komisches begegnet. Ich hatte erst für Cecile das Byronsche Lied komponiren wollen: there be none of et., u. ließ es liegen, als mir Rebecka sagte, sie wisse kein englisch. Als ich danach las, Du habest für das Leipz. Album etwas gegeben, ging ich in einen Musikladen, um zu sehn, was? Unterwegs fiel mir mein englisches Lied wieder ein, u. ich machte es in Gedanken gar fertig, u. trete in den Laden, fordre das Album,

u. schlage auf: there be none. Ich will es mir nächstens geben lassen, und abschreiben, es war aber sehr komisch. Diesen Winter ist außer dem Mühlspiel, wovon Du wol schon gehört hast, auch der Punsch bei uns Mode, den Minna so vortrefflich zu bereiten versteht, daß Mutter sogar (Du kannst sie damit necken) sich hin u. wieder zu einem halben Glas verleiten läßt. Vorgestern Abend waren Devrients hier, mit denen wir nach langer Zeit einmal wieder, einen recht angenehmen Abend hatten. Die armen Leute kommen nur gar nicht aus dem Hauskreuz heraus, beständig Krankheiten u. Noth. (Verzeih den Klex, ich sah ihn erst jetzt beim Umwenden, u. habe nicht Lust, deshalb einen andern Brief zu schreiben.) Ries hat zum 4ten in einem Concert Deine Melusine angekündigt, das wird einmal wieder eine schöne Execution werden.

Grüße Hiller wieder von mir. Bei [d]em habe ich mich recht muthwillig um den Ruf [ ] gebracht, der Musikdirector der Sphärenmusik zu seyn, so dumm uncoquett will ich aber auch nie wieder seyn. Wie geht Schelble? Setzt Hiller immer noch den Cäcilienverein fort? Und werden sie ihn nicht verbeißen? Darf man gegen Jeanrenauds äußern, daß man sich über die Flucht der Frankfurter Studenten freut? oder sind sie aristokratisch? Die Strasb. Jury hat hier im Hause große Streitigkeiten u. Dirichlet gegen Alle zuwege gebracht. Was sagst Du davon? Leb wohl, Alles grüßt Dich.

Deine Fanny

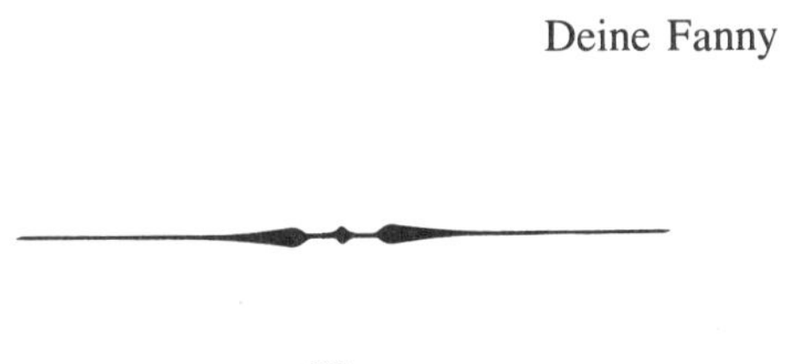

93

Berlin, 13ten April 1837.

Damit Ihr seht, liebe Kinder, daß ich noch vorhanden bin, u. was noch mehr ist, mich wohl befinde, will ich Euch ein Lebenszeichen geben. Der abermalige Unfall hat mich ganz ohne meine Schuld betroffen, u. ich befand mich bis zum letzten Augenblick so wohl, daß ich die besten Hoffnungen hegte. Auch bin ich sehr leicht davon gekommen, u. jetzt nach noch nicht 14 Tagen fast als wäre nichts geschehn. Wenigstens ist mein Kopf durchaus frei u. leicht, wenn auch die Beine noch nicht recht mitkönnen. Aussehn thu ich sehr miserabel, indeß wird sich auch wohl das geben mit der bessern Jahreszeit, *wenn* wir Eine bekommen. Wir waren recht neugierig zu erfahren, wo Ihr die große Schneekatastrophe überstanden hättet, u. sind nun durch Euren heutigen Brief aus Strasburg darüber belehrt. Daß Ihr unter Euren Planen oder Nichtplanen unser auch nicht mit einem Worte gedenkt, thut uns wohl leid, u. ich habe schon ganz die Hoffnung aufgegeben, Cecile in diesem Jahr zu sehn. Ich werde Berlin nicht verlassen. Sobald alles grün ist, treibe ich Hensel aus, nach Dresden, von wo aus er nach der sächsischen Schweiz zu Fuß gehn, u. da malen wird. Wäret Ihr in Leipzig, so reiste ich mit, u. käme unterdessen zu Euch, so aber bleibe ich in min Hus. Bei den andern versteht es sich von selbst. Wie freue ich mich Eures Glücks, u. wie goutiren wir, Hensel u. ich, Euer planloses Umherschweifen, das ich sehr angenehm für eine junge Ehe finde. Ich freue mich auch auf Deine Flitterwochenpräludien, von allen Wochen in die man kommen kann, sind die Flitterwochen unstreitig die angenehmsten. Mein zu guter Mann hat mich so gepflegt, daß ich ihm nach all dem Krankenstubenst[ ] doppelt einen Athemzug in frischer Luft gönne. Nun aber lebt wohl, ich habe Euch weiter nichts zu sagen, daß wir Euch lieb haben, das wißt Ihr, dabei bleibts, es kommt nichts dazu, u. nichts davon. Wilhelm u. meine Schwägerinnen grüßen bestens.

Eure Fanny

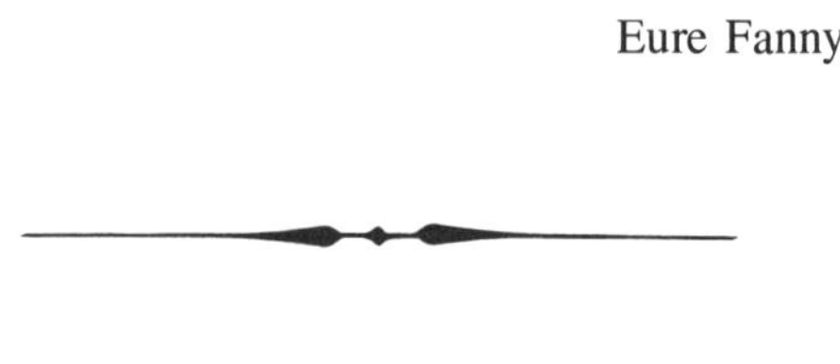

94

Berlin, 2ten Juni 1837
Regen Sturm u.
Kälte.

Dein gestriger Brief, lieber Felix, hat mir die Zunge gelöst, die mir etwas eingefroren war, wie kanns bei dem Wetter anders seyn, und ich werde nun wie ein Mühlrad klappern, daß Du mich am Ende wieder aufhören heißt. Zuerst muß ich Dir sogleich sagen, daß Alexander und Mad. Schunk, und wer Dir sonst gesagt haben mag, daß wir oder ich Dir die englische Reise übel nehme, sich gänzlich geirrt hat. So etwas ist mir auch im Traume nicht eingefallen, ich sehe die Wichtigkeit und Annehmlichkeit dieser Reise viel zu gut ein, wünsche viel zu sehr sie selbst einmal mit meinem Mann zu machen, als daß ich sie irgend Jemand der sie verdient, mißgönnen sollte am wenigstens Dir. Auch sind wir weit entfernt, die Prätention zu machen, daß Du, um uns zu besuchen, irgend etwas aufgeben solltest, daß

Dir nützlich oder erfreulich seyn kann. Weil aber doch die Sache einmal zur Sprache gekommen ist, so will ich Dir aufrichtig sagen was daran ist. Daß Ihr nicht von Leipzig hergekommen seyd, was Ihr so gut ohne irgend ein Opfer gekonnt hättet, wäret Ihr dem Plane gefolgt, den ich Euch gleich anfangs angab, u. der doch nachher zur Aufführung kam, das habe ich zwar nicht übel genommen, denn das ist der rechte Ausdruck nicht, aber sehr schmerzlich empfunden, und wohl hier u. da ausgesprochen. Mad. Jeanrenauds Gründe für ihre schnelle Rückreise haben mir niemals einleuchten wollen, und der Erfolg hat auch gezeigt, daß ich nicht so unrecht hatte, denn die Hochzeit ist recht gut von Statten gegangen, ohne daß sie drei Wochen vorher da gewesen wäre, und Mad. Souchay ist auch nicht so unversöhnlich gewesen. Wenn Deine Beschäftigungen Dich abgehalten haben, länger als ein Paar Tage hier zu bleiben, so hätten diese hingereicht, Cecile herzubringen, u. auf länger, als ein Paar Tage war ja auch der ganze Besuch nicht versprochen. Indessen das sind lauter "hätte u. wäre" mit denen nichts zurückzurufen ist. Schade ist es nur, daß der Verlust für uns unersetzlich ist, denn Cecile als Mädchen zu sehn, ist nun in diesem Leben nicht mehr möglich. Hätten wir reisen können, so wären wir natürlich nach Leipzig gekommen, obgleich Du auch das im Anfang nicht zu wünschen schienest, so aber war das unmöglich, u. ich danke Gott, daß ich mich nicht von meinem Wohlbefinden habe verleiten lassen, es doch zu wagen, weil ich mir sonst wegen meines Unfalls die größten Vorwürfe gemacht haben würde. Ich denke also lieber Bruder, Du wirst es mir nicht verdenken, vielmehr ein Zeichen meiner Liebe darin sehn, daß ich mich durch dies Mißlingen in eine unbehagliche Stimmung versetzt fühlte. Wenn Du an die Zeit zurück denkst, wo wir beständig zusammen waren, wo ich jeden Gedanken sogleich erfuhr, der Dir durch den Kopf ging, u. Deine neuen Sachen auswendig wußte, ehe Du sie einmal aufgeschrieben, wenn Du Dich erinnerst, daß unser Verhältniß, schon durch die gemeinsame musikalische Beschäftigung ein gewiß auch unter Geschwistern seltenes war, so wirst Du mir zugeben, daß es grade für mich eine seltsame Entbehrung ist, Dich Jahr und Tag auf eine Weise beglückt zu wissen, wie ich sie immer so lebhaft für Dich gewünscht habe, und Deine Geliebte, Deine Frau gar nicht einmal zu kennen. Alle Beschreibungen helfen nichts, sie machen nur irre. Dazu kommt noch, daß ich auch für die Zukunft wenig Aussicht habe, denn eine Reise im Winter hierher—wie leicht, ja wie wahrscheinlich wird die auf eine oder die andre Weise unausführbar werden, u. so können noch von jetzt an gerechnet, Jahr und Tag drüber hingehn, ehe wir uns sehn. Drei Jahre sind es bereits, seit wir uns nur auf Tage u. in der Hetze begegnet sind. Zum Unglück hat mein Mann eben so wenig in Leipzig zu thun, als Du in Berlin, u. so wird der Wunsch, einmal wieder einige Zeit mit Dir zusammen zu seyn, wol unter diejenige gehören, nach deren Erfülling zu streben man sich versagen muß; man lernt Manches mit der Zeit. Um nun mit einem Mal Alles zu sagen, so kam es mir so vor, als habe diese Entfernung, die an mir gewiß immer spurlos vorübergehn wird, Dich nicht ganz unverändert gelassen, wenn auch nicht was mich, doch was die Meinigen betrifft. Ich weiß mich der Zeit nicht zu erinnern, daß Du nach Hensels Arbeiten, nach Sebastians Fortschritten gefragt, da habe ich mir denn auch nach u. nach abgewöhnt, von ihnen zu reden, denn dergleichen Mittheilungen wollen angeregt seyn u. Wichtigeres habe ich doch nicht zu berichten. Sage mir daß ich mich irre, u. ich will es sehr gern glauben.

Das sind so ungefähr die Gründe, lieber Felix, weshalb ich in der letzten Zeit das Maul gehalten habe. Du siehst, es ist alles Andre eher, als der Schatten einer Mißbilligung Deiner englischen Reise. Ich wußte Dir wirklich nichts zu sagen, was mir der Mühe werth geschienen hätte, und wenn Dich nun dieser erste Brief, den ich Dir wieder schreibe, herzlich ennüyirt, so verzeih mirs, ich käme so gern wieder in den alten, dummen Ton, der Dich so oft lachen machte, wenn ich nur könnte. Vor Allem zeige nur Cecile diesen Brief nicht, sie bekommt sonst, wie man hier sagt: einen Graul vor der brummigen Schwägerin, Du nanntest mich aber von jeher Grimmhild, u. mußt mir schon erlauben, so viel von meinem Grimm beizubehalten, als ich mit aller Mühe, die ich mir gebe, nicht abzulegen vermag. Und nun basta.

Der musikal. spleen, über den Du Dich mokirst, kam ganz natürlich daher, daß ich den Winter wenig Musik gemacht u. gehört habe u. dann drei Virtuosen nacheinander kamen, Döhler, die Wieck, u. Henselt. Du weißt, ich lasse mich überhaupt sehr leicht niederschlagen, hatte damals angegriffene Nerven, u. kam mir unbeschreiblich veraltet vor. Seitdem aber habe ich mich wieder erholt, u. mir Chopins Etüden angeschafft, von denen ich einige fleißig übe. Henselt hat in seinem Concerte ein Paar Etüden von Chopin, u. ein Paar sehr hübsche von sich, überaus delicat u. rapid gespielt, das war aber auch das Beste. Das an sich etwas langweilige Trio v. Hummel hat er so vorgetragen, wie wir es in früher, guter Zeit aus Spaß thaten, u. Schmöckerio so nannten. Ich glaube, diese Vortragsart wird überhaupt wieder Mode werden, denn da diese ganze Virtuosität ein Modenartikel ist wie Porzellan Kleider u. Lithographieen, so muß sie auch Schritt mit diesen halten, u. den Schnörkelstyl wieder hervorsuchen, wie in der Kunst jetzt Ludwig XIV Perrücken Mode sind, wenigstens bei Engländern u. Franzosen.

Die Variation. eigener Composit. die Henselt am Schluß spielte fand ich bei aller Schwierigkeit so wenig brillant, u. so häßlich, daß sie mich sehr degoutirten, wie überhaupt dies ganze Concertwesen. Von diesen drei Clavierspielern hat keiner ein ordentliches concert, keiner mit Begleitung gespielt, sondern Etüden, Variat. u. s. w. Nächstens werden sie vor dem Publicum eine Stunde geben.—Wenn ich es zusammenbringen kann, so werde ich diesen Sommer wieder Musik machen, ich glaube aber kaum, da meine Freunde, die Ganze in Baden sind u. ich gar zu wenig Musiker kenne. In der Oper war ich ein Paarmal, u. habe Armide, trotz der theilweise sehr mangelhaften Aufführung, mit unbeschreiblichem Vergnügen gehört. Die Faßmann, deren Mittel allerdings für diese Rolle nicht hinreichend sind, singt sie aber doch mit einer solchen Aufopferung aller Kräfte die sie hat, mit einer solchen Hingebung an die Sache, daß sie Manches ihr fehlende dadurch ersetzt, u. man ihr schon gern manches nachsieht, weil sie doch gute Musik singt, u. wie es den Anschein hat, mit Respekt singt. Auch Spontinis Direction hat mich amüsirt, obgleich ich manches gern anders gehabt hätte, sie war aber doch lebendig, u. das Orchester klang. Ueberdies waren 8 oder 10 Vorstellungen der Armide krankevoll, u. die Nachtwandlerin, worin ich die Löwe sah, nicht. Nun sage man noch, daß ein Publicum nicht gern gute Sachen hört, wenn man sie ihm nur g[ebe], das hiesige hat nur die Energie nicht, das Gute zu fordern.

Auf Deine Fugen freue ich mich sehr. Die Lieder habe ich mir nur auf eine Stunde zum Ansehn kommen lassen, weil ich wußte daß wir sie bekommen, ich werde Dir darüber schreiben, wenn ich sie besser kenne. Unter den Aelteren gefällt mir das Sonntagslied, u. auf Flügeln des Gesanges, unter den Neuen das Reiselied von Heine am Besten. Den Anfang davon finde ich wunderhübsch, die Stelle aber wo die 16tel aufhören gefällt mir nicht ganz. Uebrigens ist es mir immer sehr eigen, Sachen von Dir zuerst gedruckt zu sehn. Ich habe gleich ein Urtheil drüber wie über Compositionen von Mendelssohn, es ist mir dann gar nicht als wären sie von Felix. Gestern habe ich "farewell" von Byron componirt, u. ehe Dein Brief kam, hatte ich die Idee, es Dir anstatt eines Briefes zu schicken, denn es gefällt mir.—Was ist das für ein Psalm, den Du komponirt hast? u. ist er deutsch oder lateinisch? Schreibe mir doch, was Du für die nächste Zeit für Arbeitsplane hast. Wirst Du nicht bald die komische Oper schreiben, auf die ich schon so lange warte? Ich möchte so gern einmal ein Liederspiel schreiben, hätte ich nur einen Text dazu.

Heut ist ein Wetter, daß man keinen Hund heraus jagen möchte, der Regen strömt den ganzen Tag, Kälte, Sturm. Ich habe die Ueberzeugung, daß wir diesmal keinen Sommer bekommen. Der ganze Garten steht in unbeschreiblicher Herrlichkeit, u. kaum drei Tage haben wir gehabt es zu genießen.—Mutter, über deren letzten Brief Du Dich so sehr gefreut hast, ist Gottlob zum Bewundern frisch heiter u. gesund. Gott erhalte sie so. Lebe wohl. Tausend Grüßen an Cecilen.

Ich bitte Dich sehr, Mad. Jeanrenaud bestens für Ihren so gütrigen freundlichen Brief zu danken, den ich gewiß nächstens beantworten werde.

Woringens, nach denen Du frägst, sind wohl, wir haben kürzlich Briefe v. ihnen gehabt. Daß Ferdinand Rath in Liegnitz geworden, wirst Du wol wissen. Eben so daß Louis Heyd. ein brillantes Examen gemacht, u. nun seine Frau heirathen wird.

95

Hier schicke ich Dir besagten Hammel, an dem ich keinen rothen, oder sonstigen Strich gemacht. Dabei fällt mir ein, daß vorgestern in der Spenerschen Zeitung in einem Bericht über die Thierschau in Stargardt gestanden hat: der Herr Regierungsrath, Graf v. Itzenplitz gewann, wie stets, den für den besten Schafbock ausgesetzten Preis. Dabei fällt mir ein, daß Dorn gestern erzählt hat, im Park zu Mannheim folgenden Anschlag gelesen zu haben: wer diese Anlagen beschädigt, riskirt nach den Gesetzen des Landes behandelt zu werden.

Gestern habe ich eine brillante Probe des Paulus gehalten. Im Gartensaal, mit einem Chor von 40 Personen, der nächsten Sonntag bis auf circa 50 anwachsen wird, das kommt Dir nun sehr lächerlich vor, wir aber haben große Freude daran. Denke also liebe Cecile, nächsten Sonntag zwischen 11 u. 2 an uns. Danach brauche ich nicht zu berichten, daß Alles wohl ist. Leider wird die Decker diesmal nur einen Theil der Solis singen, sie ist ihrer Entbindung nahe, und sehr leidend.

Adieu, liebste Kinder, ich muß ausgehn. Laßt bald von Euch hören. Cecile ist doch hoffentlich wohl? ich schließe es daraus, daß Felix nicht das Gegentheil geschrieben hat.

Eure Fanny.

96

Ich nehme also meine neuliche Kondolenz und Mitjammer zurück, liebe Cecile, finde Dich gar nicht zu beklagen, pauvre homme der Du mit allen möglichen Comforts zu Bingen am Rhein wohnst. Voriges Jahr war ich mit Paul u. Albertine auch einen Tag dort, u. es ist meiner Treu wunderschön. Bewohnt ihr ein Gasthaus zu welchem man durch einen kleinen Garten gelangt, mit 2 Belvederes an beiden Ecken? den Namen habe ich vergessen, aber da waren wir damals. Uns vergeht hier der Sommer bei großer Einförmigkeit der Lebensweise äußerst schnell. Woringens werden nun wol einigen Wechsel hineinbringen. Vorige Woche waren wir 2 Tage auf dem Lande, 4 Meilen von hier, um Sebastian abzuholen, der schon einige Tage früher mit Luisen hingefahren war. Es war eigentlich das erstemal, daß ich hier in der Gegend wo im Lande war. Wären nur alle Wege hier, so wie sie von der Chaussee abführen, nicht so trostlos. Die Aufenthalt dort fanden wir sehr angenehm. Die Leute sehr freundlich, gastfrei, u. das Besuchen u. Durcheinanderreisen bei den benachbarten Gutsbesitzern fast so stark, wie in glücklicheren Ländern.

Einstweilen haben wir hier überall das durch M. J. Herz verbreitete Gerücht von Felixens Abreise nach England weiter gebracht. Lieber Felix, daß Du unter die Musiker die einen schlechten Lebenswandel führen, auch Meyerbeer rechnest, der seine Frau verläßt, das habe ich nur mit Naserümpfen lesen können, da Du selbst in Begriff stehst, Deine Frau so böslich zu verlassen. An ihrer Stelle würde ich diese Veranlassung ergreifen, mich von Dir scheiden zu lassen, sie klagt ja ohnehin in allen Briefen, daß sie es nicht bei Dir aushalten kann. Sehr wenig habe ich gegen das Präludium u. die Fuge einzuwenden, die Du in London spielen willst, warum dieses nicht?

Weißt Du denn, daß jetzt die Gluckschen Opern hier wieder gegeben werden? Wenn auch Eichberger als Admet ein wahres Schlächter, u. Blume als Hercules der Ochs dazu ist, so kann ich doch nicht läugnen, daß ich sie mit wahrer Freude wiedergehört habe. Die Faßmann, deren Mittel eigentlich bei Weitem nicht ausreichend sind, singt u. spielt mit solcher Aufopferung aller Kräfte, die ihr irgend zu Gebot stehn, daß sie die Partien nicht allein durchführt, sondern wirklich schön durchführt. Man muß nun freilich nicht an die Milder denken, deren Organ allein, fast ohne daß sie damit gesungen hätte, an vielen Stellen so wunderbar wirkte, aber man freut sich doch, die Töne einmal wieder zu hören, u. nach 10 u. 20 Jahren dasselbe Publicum wieder zu sehn, welches damals keine Glucksche Oper ungehört ließ. Der erste Rang ist leer, wie früher, alles Andre durchaus voll, u. namentlich die jüngere Generation, die die Milder nicht recht mehr gehört hat, höchst entzückt. Von dieser erzählt man, sie sey gefragt worden, ob sie Alceste von der Faßmann gehört hätte, u. darauf geantwortet haben: nein, ich habe die Rolle einmal von der Milder gehört, u. will sie nun nie wieder hören. In Aeußern erinnert die Faßmann, wie Hensel sehr richtig abbrachte, an die Flaxmanschen Gestalten.

Lieber Felix, mache mir einmal einen Begriff, von Deinem Psalm, wie der Hirsch schreit. Schreit er 4stimmig oder 8, a capella, oder mit Begleitung? Und von Deinem Concert möchte ich auch etwas wissen. Daß Du wieder ein Oratorium machen willst, freut mich. Man kann doch nun einmal keine komische Oper aus der Bibel machen, die möchte ich freilich am liebsten jetzt von Dir hören.

Meine Musiken müssen sich jetzt ohne die Decker behelfen, gegen die der Gansdarmenmann nur eine Strippe ist. Ich behaupte immer, sie bekommt kein Kind, sondern ein Haus. Daß Woringens sie nicht mobiler treffen, thut mir leid. Lebt übrigens wohl. Es ist Mittag, u. ich bin noch im Schlafrock, u. eben klingelt es, o weh! Geht das anderswo auch so, daß wenn man sich grade einmal verspätet hat, alle Leute kommen, u. wenn man gut angezogen ist, kein Mensch? Ich bitte wohl zu leben, und mich Madame Jeanrenaud bestens zu empfehlen.

Eure Fanny

[Rebecka]

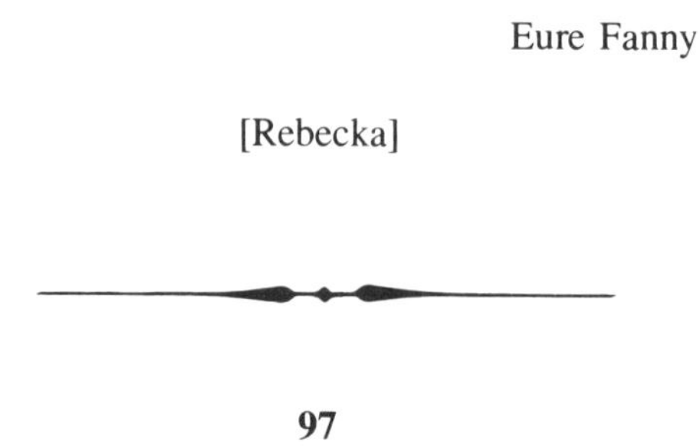

97

31 Juli 1837

Ich will heut nur anfragen, ob ich die beiden Kanonen richtig gelöst habe.

und no. 2

mit dem bin ich nicht sehr sicher. Der letzte Takt klingt so nichtswürdig, wie ich es einem so wohltönenden (beinah hätt ich geschrieben wohlriechenden) Meister wie Du bist, nicht gern zutrauen möchte. Fällt mir einstweilen eine richtigere Lösung ein, so lasse ich sie Dich durch den Telegraphen nach Coblenz wissen. So wichtig wie manches, was damit gemeldet wird, ist es auch. Heut habe ich mich über die Badische Kammer gefreut, die einstimmig ein Gesuch um Protest gegen das Regierungspatent erlassen hat. Dies wird übrigens hier in sofern weniger besprochen, als man meinen sollte, da sich Niemand findet, diesen ungeschickten Tölpel zu vertheidigen, der so grob in sein neues Königthum hineingelumpt ist. Die besten Legitimisten wagen es nicht recht, u. wo man einer Meinung ist, hat das Gespräch bald ein Ende. Von Woringens wissen wir leider noch immer nichts, wenn ihnen nur nichts dazwischen gekommen ist, das wäre gar zu schade. Einstweilen reist hier Alles ab, was noch bis jetzt übrig geblieben war, u. sie behalten nur unsre Liebenswürdigkeit, um sie zu unterhalten.

Weiß denn kein Mensch was von Klingemann? Von Euch bekommt man auch darüber keine Antwort. Der Unart hat verschiedene Briefe verschiedener Mitglieder dieses Hauses sehr unbeantwortet gelassen. Ompteda ist in Hannover angekommen, die Kanzlei wird aufgelöst, was wird denn aus ihm?

Adieu, lebt wohl, freut Euch des Lebens, weil noch das Lämpchen glüht, u. denkt meiner in Nebenstunden.

Empfiehl mich Deiner Mutter liebe Cecile.

98

Berlin, 29sten August 1837.

Wir beeilen uns, Dir die gewünschten Nachrichten zu geben, lieber Felix, die Gott sey Dank, sehr befriedigend über uns Alle lauten. Bis jetzt wußten wir nicht recht, wann u. wohin wir Dir nach England adressiren sollten. Die Cholera ist, wie Du aus den Zeitungen sehn wirst, ziemlich stark hier, aber wir leben vorsichtig, ohne Angst, u. was das Beste ist, ungemein vergnügt mit unsern lieben Gästen. Daß diese lieben Leute meiner Ueberzeugung nach grade weil die Cholera hier ist, länger bleiben, als sie anfangs wollten, verdient auch bemerkt zu werden, ich glaube, das macht ihnen so leicht kein Fremder nach. Nun sind sie in der 4ten Woche hier, u. es scheint ihnen hier sehr gut zu gefallen. Da Rebecka ziemlich unbeweglich ist, u. Mutter in der Hitze nicht ausgeht, so sind mir größtentheils die honneurs von Berlin anheim gefallen, die ich denn auch mit meinem lieben Mann zusammen, mit möglichster coquettrie gemacht habe. Abends haben wir Musik, oder dumm Zeug gemacht, u. in diesen Paar Wochen mehr gelacht, als vorher in einigen Jahren. Franz hat das von seinen Schwestern immer gepriesene komische Talent nach 4jährigem Schweigen auf eine Weise herausgekehrt, die alle unsre Erwartungen weit übertraf, u. ich versichere Dich, er ist ein ganz bedeutender komischer Schauspieler. Sie geben uns improvisirte Vorstellungen im rheinischen Dialekt, in denen er eine stehende Figur dat Hännesche, vorstellt, ich versichere Dich, Du würdest unter den Tisch fallen, wenn Du das einmal sähest. Der alte Mann ist unverändert liebenswürdig u. frisch, es ist wirklich eine wahre Erquickung, mit diesen vortrefflichen Menschen zu leben.

Gestern, zugleich mit Deinem u. Ceciles Brief kam einer von Ferdinand Woringen an seinen Vater, der viel von Euch schreibt. Wir freuen uns sehr, mündlich noch mehr von ihm zu hören.—Die arme Decker hat vor einigen Tagen nach vielen Leiden ein todtes Kind geboren, zum Glück ist sie selbst wohl. Sie sah wirklich in der letzten Zeit zum Erschrecken aus.

Sage Klingemann, ich ließe ihn recht herzlich, nicht grüßen, keiner im Hause läßt ihn grüßen, denn er ist ein Verräther. Es liegen auch einige englische Lieder für ihn u. seine kleine Miss da, die soll er nächstens nicht haben. Wir wissen u. A. noch immer nicht, in welcher Eigenschaft er in England bleibt.

Adieu, lebwohl. Ich überlasse Mutter die Feder. Ich habe das

Schreiben verlernt. Hast Du Deine schöne Paulinische Partitur mit nach England genommen?

[Rebecka, Lea]

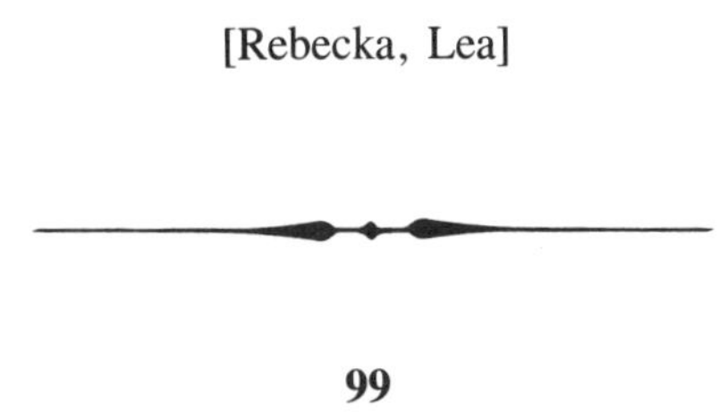

99

Berlin, den 12 Dezbr. 1837

[Luise Hensel, with signatures of Sebastian,
Margarethe Mendelssohn, Marie Mendelssohn]

Nicht später als gleich setze ich mich hin, u. schicke Dir anbei das von ehrenwerthen Männern unterschriebenen Zeugniß meiner Unschuld und der singacademischen Verläumdung. Ich höre von Dir, wie Du in Leipzig gesagt hast: Fanny muß sich doch aber auch immer in meine Angelegenheiten mischen, oder: wer hat denn Fanny geheißen, da in meinem Namen Antwort ertheilen? oder irgend eine andre Süßigkeit, kurz ich wette Du schimpftest, aber nein!

Auf Clara Novello freue ich mich sehr, wir wollen alles Mögliche thun, ihr den Aufenthalt angenehm u. nützlich zu machen. Vieuxtemps habe ich gehört, er spielt vortrefflich. Er spielte Sonntag vor 8 T. hier Variationen v. Bériot, dann mit mir u. Ganz das d dur Trio v. Beethoven, dann kam Davide penitente woraus die Decker die Sopranpartie famos sang, die Arie zwar aus b dur, aber unglaublich brillant, u. ich hatte ihr eine lange Cadenz gemacht, womit sie furore machte. Es waren 120-30 personen hier, u. es war fast unser brillantester Musikmorgen. Der ganze kleine Vieuxtemps gefällt mir recht gut, er hat etwas recht Anspruchloses, Gefälliges, das man jedem hoch anrechnen kann, der seit seinem 7ten Jahre als Wunderkind durch die Welt geschleppt wird. Sie machen ihm hier unerhörte Schwierigkeiten u. Kabalen, d. h. Möser u. Consorten. Leider steht hier immer Alles blank gegen einen Fremden, der Concert geben will, sage das aber der Novello nicht.—Ich gratulire übrigens zur neuen Wohnung, wünsche sie mit Gesundheit zu verzehren, u. freue mich auf das Zusammenkommen im Frühjahr. Dann werdet Ihr unsre Gäste. Liebe Cecile, alle Leute verlieben sich hier in Deine Zeichnung, mehr noch, als ins Bild für welches ich aber immer eine große Liebe behalte.

Eure Zusammenkünfte bei Hofrath Keil müssen recht interessant seyn, ich weiß aber auch warum Felix sie nicht versäumen will, oder ist diese Neckerei nicht mehr an der Tagesordnung? Lebt wohl. Ich wünsche Cecilen die besten Nachrichten aus Frankfort.

Eure Fanny

100

Berlin, 15ten Januar 1838.

Du hast einen so schönen lustigen Brief geschrieben, lieber Felix, trotz Ohrenpein u. Frost, daß ich nicht umhin kann, sogleich zu antworten. Ach, wenn man nur wüßte, wie es jetzt die Briefe bei Euch treffen, ob sie nicht in ein freudevolles Ach u. Wehgeschrei hinein fallen. Nun Gott mache es kurz u. gut. Wenn irgendwo, so ist das kurz in diesem Fall gut. Das Zeugniß, welches ich Dir kürzlich überschickt, u. auf welches Du heut antwortest, gelte Dir ein für allemal dafür, daß ich mich nicht unberufen in Deine Sachen mische. Wenn Dir z. B. Ad. Mt. Schlesinger schreibt, ich habe erlaubt, daß er Dein facsimile herausgiebt, so halte dafür, daß er lügt. Oder wenn Dir der Archiver Werner (Mann einer schlechten Schauspielerin) einen Text schickt, mit dem Bemerken, ich habe ihn in Deinem Namen angenommen, und ihm 1000 rh von Dir davon versprochen, so sey überzeugt, daß ich ihm höflich zu verstehn gegeben habe, ich glaube nicht, daß Dir ein Text von ihm sehr schmecken würde, Du wärest höchst sonderbar, u. oft kritisch u. gefährlich, indeß könne man nicht wissen, Du wohntest in Leipzig, u. ein Brief an Dich, frankirt auf die Post gegeben, träfe Dich stets den 2ten Tag in erwünschten Wohlseyn. So rede ich, u. so höre mich in meiner Weisheit reden, wenn sie Dir auch das Gegentheil schreiben, gewöhnlich setze ich noch hinzu, auf Antwort von Dir sey schwer zu rechnen, Du wärst ein vielbeschäftigter Mann, der Ortographie nicht sehr sicher, u. Dein Secretair sey krank. Was nun übrigens die Geschichte mit dem Paulus betrifft, so ist sie höchst sonderbar. Meine Rolle als Souffleur hat aber wenigstens das bewirkt, daß ich viel Unheil von dem edlen Apostel habe abwenden können. Mutter scheint Dir geschrieben zu haben, daß Rungenhagen mich schriftlich gebeten hat, den Proben beizuwohnen, u. ihn durch meine Meinung zu erquicken. Darauf ging ich vorigen Dienstag hin, u. entsetzte mich ganz so, wie Du es beschrieben, u. empfand all das Fingerjucken, u. all die Qualen die Du kennst, wie ich die Neelerei, u.

Grell sein Sauigeln auf dem Clavier hörte, u. mir dachte: wenn Du nun da oben säßest, ginge das Ding doch gleich. Lichtenstein setzte sich zu mir, u. hörte mein Seufzen. Mache dich auf, fingen sie richtig die Hälfte zu langsam an, u. da rief ich ganz unwillkührlich aus: Gott sieh uns bei, das muß ja noch einmal so schnell seyn! Lichtst. bat mich, ich möchte ihnen ein Licht aufstecken, u. sagte mir, der Musikdirector Schneider hätte sie versichert, man könne sich nach dem Metronom nicht richten. Da versicherte ich sie, sie könnten sich auf mein Wort danach richten, u. sie möchten es nur in Gottesnamen thun. Darauf ging ich Freitag wieder, in den kleinen Academiesaal, wo ich seit Zelters Tode nicht gewesen war, u. wo mir alle möglichen Geister Lebender u. Verstorbener entgegen traten. Da kam nun Rungenh. nach jedem Chor zu mir heran, u. frug mich, ob es so recht gewesen wäre, u. da sagte ich ganz offen, ja oder nein, wie es mir geschienen hatte. Im Ganzen aber fand ich eine solche Veränderung zum Guten, daß ich ganz freudig überrascht war, u. anfing Hoffnung zu fassen. Sonnabend war R. über eine Stunde bei mir, u. ließ sich Alle Soli vor mir vorspielen. Freitag sprach ich auch noch Ries, der mich um vieles fragte, u. unter andern, wie mir die Tuba gefallen hätte, die sie in der Kirche an all den Stellen zugesetzt hatten, wo die Orgel steht. Nun ist besagte Tuba ein Monstrum, welche alle Stellen, zu denen sie gebraucht wird, zu besoffnen Bierbrauern macht. Ich fiel also auf die Knien, u. bat sie ihrer selbst zu schonen, u. die Tuba zu Hause zu lassen. Rungenh. hob mich auf u. gewährte mir meine Bitte. Gestern war nun die erste große Probe, die weit über meine Erwartung ausfiel. Ich kann Dir zu meiner Freude sagen, daß ich über vieles ganz entzückt war, die Chöre die nun im richtigen Tempo genommen wurden (einige etwas zu schnell) sangen mit einem Feuer u. einer Kraft, u. auch nuancirt, wie man es nur verlangen kann. Das gute alte Merinohaupt hat sich wirklich die redlichste Mühe gegeben, u. Alles war erstaunt über seine Lebhaftigkeit. Viele haben gemerkt, aus welcher Ecke der Wind bläst. Ich habe mich aber sehr ruhig verhalten, mich nicht zum Don Quixote des Paulus gemacht, u. mir hoffentlich keine Feinde gemacht, es sey denn der Tubaist. Heut war Ries noch einmal bei mir, ich habe allen guten Rath in diesen Tagen ausgegeben, den ich nur in der Speisekammer hatte, nun bin ich ganz dumm. Ich muß erst einmal wieder mit zusammenkommen, u. was lernen. Schade ist es doch, daß Du diese Aufführung nicht dirigirst, sie wäre famos geworden, u. Du hättest sehr wenig Mühe davon gehabt. Morgen ist nun die Generalprobe, auf die ich sehr neugierig bin.—Auf die Novello freue ich mich sehr. Ich habe für Sonntag den Titus angesetzt, mit Dein Vorbehalt, daß sie, wenn sie aufgelegt ist, von più di fiori singen soll. Die Decker singt Vitellia, die Faßmann, die mich ganz ohne mein Zuthun aufgesucht, u. sich zu allem erboten hat, Sextus, ich denke, es soll hübsch werden. Wir haben Mutter einen

Floh ins Ohr gesetzt, daß sie der Novello eine Fete geben soll. Dirichlets u. wir haben beide kein Geld (ich bin erschrecklich klamm diesen Winter) sonst thäten wirs.

Heut früh fand ich Mutter an ihrem Schreibtisch sitzend, aufs Ernsthafteste beschäftigt, in ihr gewisses Buch, 10-12 neue lächerliche Anzeigen einzukleben. Das ist doch hübsch, im 61sten Jahr noch solche Lust am Spaß zu haben.

16sten. Sage mir doch, wie weit Du mit Planché bist, das interessirt mich natürlich sehr. Ueberhaupt, was werden wir im Frühling zu plaudern haben, u. wie freue ich mich darauf. Von den Cantaten von Bach, deren Du erwähnst, bitte ich Dich mir einige nach eigner Wahl abschreiben zu lassen, u. baldigst herzuschicken. Ich bin diesen Winter sehr in den Mozart hineingerathen, als Gegengewicht könnte einiger neue Bach nicht schaden. Eben schickt die Singacademie 6 Billette mit der Einladung, sie zum Paulus zu beehren. Sie werden gar genteel.

Adieu, mein Schatz. Empfiehl mich Mad. Schunk u. Mad. Jeanrenaud, u. grüße eine gewisse Cecile von mir. Wenn Du den Brief in der Nachtlampe findest, wirst Du denken, dieselbe käme von mir, aber nein, aber empfehlen kann ich sie sehr ich habe eine solche, Cecile wird sich in Wochen an dem netten Schein an der Decke ergötzen.

Lebt wohl besten Leute, der Meinige grüßt.

101

Berlin, 19ten Janr. 1838

Ich will Dir einen summarischen Bericht über den Paulus abstatten, lieber Felix, denn da ich im Ganzen zufrieden war, wirst Du nicht von mir verlangen, daß ich ins Einzelne gehe, u. Dir die Fehler aufzähle. Es war bei Weitem die beste Aufführung, die seit Zelters Tode hier statt gefunden, man hat sich redliche Mühe gegeben, u. gethan was man konnte, mehr ist am Ende von keinem Menschen zu verlangen. Wärst Du hier gewesen, es wäre eine welthistorische Aufführung geworden. Das Publicum war entzückt, u. da stelle ich mich am Ende noch zufriedener, als ich wirklich war, denn einen guten Eindruck der Art muß man nicht durch Tadel schwächen, wenn er gleich gerecht wäre. Die Sopranpartie habe ich übrigens noch nicht so schön gehört, als diesmal von der Faßmann. Das ist eine wahre Sängerin für solche Musik, einfach, nobel, klar im Vortrag, mit schöner, heller Stimme. Ich glaube sie müßte Dir gefallen. Clara Novello war mit Mutter drin, (wir waren alle zerstreut,) u. hat sich sehr amüsirt. Sonntag wird sie hier die zwei Arien der Vitellia singen, die Decker die übrige Vitellia u. Parto dazu, die Faßmann den übrigen Sextus.

Das im Concert liegende Paket habe ich gestern abgeschickt, da es mir vorgestern in meiner Weisheit gar nicht einfiel, nachzusehn, ob noch etwas drin wäre. Den H. Dr. Meysenburg kenne ich nicht, habe sogar seinen illustren Namen nie vorher gehört, u. werde ihn auch nicht weiter sagen.

Aber alle Leipziger, die ich in diesen Tagen gesprochen, klagen Dich an, bester Felix, daß Du Dich zu sehr anstrengst, zu viel probirst, etc, und ich habe es ja auch gesehn, wie Du ganz u. gar keine Ruhe hast. Cecile! ich rufe Dich an, wende all Deinen Einfluß auf, u. vor allen Dingen, gebt uns, oder laßt uns geben Tag um Tag Bericht, wie es mit Felixens Ohren geht. Es sind ja bei Euch so viele, die einmal ein Wort schreiben können.

Durch Ries' Tod ist nun der Cäcilienverein wieder vacant. Wenn Du nur nicht hingehst, das wäre mir gar nicht lieb.

Was sagst Du zu der Londoner Börse? Das Feuer frißt viel in diesem Winter.

Sage mir, womit Du jetzt eben beschäftigt bist. Kommen die Nonnenstücke der neue Psalm nicht bald heraus? Es ist recht, daß Du den Seb. Bach auf die Rheinischen Musikfeste bringen willst, ich finde immer: Du Hirte Israel, sehr geeignet dazu. Heitreres hat er wol schwerlich gemacht. Oder soll es etwas Ungedrucktes seyn? Vergiß nicht, mir ein Paar von den Cantaten zu schicken.

Adieu. Schreibt bald, wie sich Felixens Ohren befinden. Ueberhaupt Details. Wie ihr lebt. Ich höre ja leider, daß trotz aller meiner, u. Clarus Weisheit, die Wohnung feucht ist. Ist es das Schlafzimmer auch? Wo eßt Ihr? Wo wohnt Mad. Jeanrenaud? Adieu.

Eure Fanny.

Mann u. Schwägerinnen grüßen bestens.

Hast Du die Lieder v. Mad. Mathieux zu Gesicht bekommen? Es sind ein Paar sehr hübsche darunter.

102

Berlin, 2ten Febr. 38

Viel Glück zum morgenden Tage, lieber Felix. Das größte Geschenk was einem Menschen gegeben werden kann, ist doch ein andrer Mensch, der ihm gehört, das möge Dir Deine liebe Frau bringen, u. wohlgewaschen, gebadet u. eingewickelt möge es Dir aufgeputzt werden. Nebenbei freue ich mich Dir melden zu können, daß die blaue Grütze, die Du für die Novello so sehr gefürchtet hast, ihr gar nicht so übel bekommt, u. daß die niedliche kleine Person hier eben so sehr gefällt, als es ihr gefällt. Daß sie bei ganz gefülltem Opernhaus gesungen, weißt Du schon, nun hat sie aber gestern ihr Concert im großen Saal gegeben, u. ihn ganz u. gar mit dem elegantesten Publicum angefüllt gehabt, der ganze Hof, Alles comme il faut, u. der schönste Beifall. Im Opernhause war ihre Haltung etwas ängstlich, da sie, ein wenig kahl angezogen, ohne irgend etwas in den Händen zu halten, in unbeweglicher Ruhe da stand. Da dies allgemein auffiel, hatten wir es ihr gesagt, u. sie zum gestrigen Concert aufs Beste herausgeputzt. Sie hielt einen Fächer v. Rebecka, u. einen Blumenstrauß v. Paul in der Hand, trug einen Kranz, den ich ihr geschenkt, u. alle unsern Schmuck, u. sah allerliebst aus. Ich bin neugierig, sie nun zu sprechen, ich bin gewiß, sie wird außerordentlich zufrieden seyn, seit der Sonntag u. Paganini ist solch ein Concert nicht gemacht worden. Sage mir doch, ob ihre Art Händel zu singen, z. B. das rasche Tempo, das ich sehr goutire, in England allgemein ist. So lieblich u. fein sie als Concertsängerin ist, glaube ich doch, daß ihr Plan, in Italien auf die Bühne zu gehn, gewagt ist, zum Dramatischen scheint es ihr an Beweglichkeit u. Feuer zu fehlen. Was sagst Du? Meinst Du nicht auch? Neulich waren wir mit ihr in einer sehr brillanten Gesellschaft zusammen, wo alle Juden u. alle Schauspieler waren, u. wo unter A. das Finale aus Don Juan wirklich wunderschön gesungen wurde. Das sogen. Maskenterzett v. der Faßmann, der Novello u. Mantius, so schön, wie ich es noch nie gehört. Bader, der krank gewesen war, hörte sie den Abend zum erstenmal, u. war ganz entzückt. Uebrigens scheint sie den Leipz. jungen Herren, nicht übel den Kopf verdreht zu haben, Euer Vetter Schunk, u. der Dr. Weber, die ihr nachgereist sind, stehn rechts u. links neben ihr, wo sie ist, u. sperren Maul u. Nase auf. Montag ist nun ein großer Kuhschwanz bei Paul, nur Pamina bleibt davon, wir können diesen Winter keine Feten geben, wir sind sehr klamm.

Morgen feiert Hensel seine silberne Hochzeit mit dem Feldzug v. 1813. Man wird alt, ehe man sichs versieht, ist das bischen Leben vorbei.

Adieu, diese mörderische Bemerkung paßt schlecht an das Ende eines Geburtstagsbriefs, ich will also lieber singen: freut Euch des Lebens. Grüße mir tausendmal die liebe Cecile. Habe einen vergnügten Tag, aber einen stillen, denn Cecile liege im Bette, u. das Kleine bringe Dir ein Ständchen. Adieu, ihr lieben Leutchen.

Fanny

Hensel grüßt u. beglückwünscht bestens.

[Sebastian]

103

Berlin, 14ten Fbr. 1838

Obgleich ich Dir eigentlich nichts zu schreiben habe, als noch einmal viel Glück, so will ich doch an meinem Theil bestens danken, für die vielen, pünktlichen, vortrefflichen Bülletins. Seit denen über den Schlaf u. die heitre Laune des Erzherzogs v. Oestreich in Venedig, habe ich keine gelesen, die mich so interessirt hätten. Cecile scheint ihr Weibermetier außerordentlich vortrefflich zu verstehen, Gott erhalte sie dabei. Ueber die große Jungenhecke (der Senior nimmt eben hier in der Stube mit einem andern Jungen eine Schreib- u. Rechnenstunde) haben wir viel Spaß. Möchte doch Paul ein Mädchen dazu anschaffen! Er wird zur Taufe kommen mit Albertinen, u. freut sich sehr darauf. Ist schon bestimmt, wie der Junge heißen soll? Cecile wird gewiß wieder wunderschön werden, an Gestalt u. Farbe und Allem, wenn sie erst aufersteht. Morgen, wenn es nach hieseigen Regeln geht, verläßt sie das Bett. Uebrigens scheint man auch dort die armen Frauen schmählichem Hunger preiszugeben, wenn anders Cecile nicht ein großes Fresserchen ist. Ihre Klagen rühren mich sehr, da ich weiß wie mir immer die Wassersuppen vorgekommen sind.

Ries sprach Paul 2 Stunden nach seiner Ankunft, hier ist er aber noch nicht gewesen. Jetzt wird es jährig daß Ihr uns so abscheulich in April schicktet, hoffentlich macht Ihr es nun bald wieder gut. Schicke mir Deinen Psalm aber voraus, daß ich was zu singen habe, für meine Sonntage. Das wußt ich nicht, daß Du noch mehr Stücke dazu gemacht hattest. Ach das Dilettantenconcert! Hätte ich nur Humor, ich erzählte Dir Geschichten davon. Sie lachen mich hier im Hause schrecklich aus, weil ich Curschmann immer die Stange gehalten habe, wie Beckchen behauptet, um doch von *einem* hiesigen Musiker gut zu reden, u. wie ich behaupte, weil er der einzige hier v. Metier ist, der Lebensart hat, u. nicht mit den Fingern Suppe ißt—was hilft mir aber alle seine Lebensart, wenn er die erste Gelegenheit, als Dirigent aufzutreten, benutzt, um ein so niederträchtiges, schauderhaftes Concert zu arrangiren, wie die Welt noch nicht gesehn. Als Ob Du ein Diner so arrangiren wolltest: Suppe: Zuckerwasser. Beefsteak: ein Bonbon; Gemüse: ein Baiser. Fisch (komm ich dazwischen, mit einem ordentlichen Stück, weil ich ihm durchaus seinen Willen nicht habe thun wollen, u. auch ein Stück von ein Dutzend Takten spielen.) Braten: ein Stück Zucker, Dessert: Alles Obige, daß Dich die—!

Uebrigens habe ich bis jetzt keine Angst, wenns nur nicht noch kommt. Der Erfolg der Novello erhält sich, sie macht completten furore, u. man kann jetzt vor der Hand sagen, wo sie singt, ist es voll. Neulich, in Ganzens Concert hat sie sich, auf meinen Rath, einige Lieder selbst begleitet, (wir waren schon fort, weil wir ganz hinten im Vorzimmer stehn mußten) u. soll damit den Berliner ganz besonders entzückt haben. Wir sehn sie jetzt sehr selten, denn sie wird zerrissen, wie Du das hier kennst. Nun lebe wohl. Hensel grüßt allerbestens u. Cecile ganz besonders. Er hat eine sehr schöne Zeichnung v. Mariannens drei Töchtern gestern abgeliefert, die zu unsrer großen Freude den einstimmigsten Beifall erhalten hat. Jetzt überarbeitet er die aus dem Danke für den König von Sachsen noch einmal. Lebt wohl, Ihr Besten. Empfiehl mich Mme. Jeanrenaud, lieber Felix, u. grüße Mme. Schunk u. Julie aufs Herzlichste.

Deine Fanny

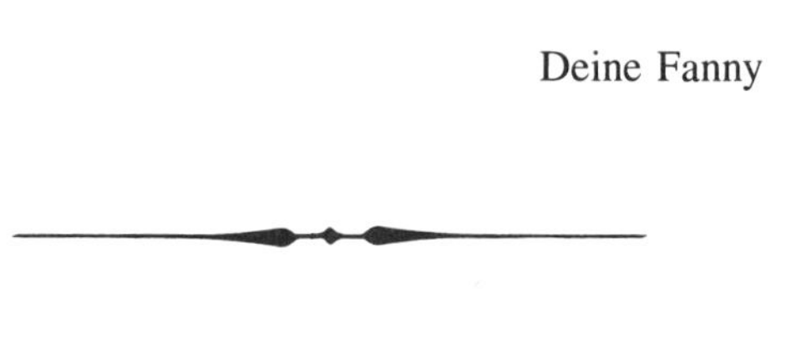

104

Berlin, 21sten Feb. 1838

In der Hoffnung, daß Deine gute Gesundheit Dir erlauben wird, jetzt selbst einen Brief zu lesen, u. in der guten Absicht, Dir eine gesunde Langeweile zu bereiten, adressire ich an Dich liebe Cecile, u. will Dir einmal selbst sagen, wie wir uns freuen über Dein musterhaftes Wochenbett u. alle Deine weiblichen Tugenden. Gewiß macht es Dir unendliche Freude, Dein Kindchen an der Brust zu haben, und selbst zu nähren, und wie freue ich mich darauf, Dich so zu sehn! Deine vortreffliche Ruhe ist auch eine der zum Nähren so unentbehrlichen Eigenschaften. Wie gut, daß Felix kein Kind zu nähren hat. Ueberhaupt hat die Natur wol gewußt, was sie that, als sie uns das Departement des Kinderbekommens, mit Allem was dazu gehört, überließ; einen Mann möchte ich einmal sich dabei anstellen sehn! Doch ich will das Läuten lassen, denn wer weiß, am Ende leidet Deine Mutter noch nicht, daß Du einen Brief liesest, u. liest ihn Dir vor, und dann schäme ich mich vor ihr. Ueberhaupt habe ich schreckliche Furcht vor Deiner Mutter—

Unser vielbesprochenes Dilettantenconcert ist denn vorgestern mit glänzendem Erfolg vom Stapel gelaufen, 2300 rh war die Einnahme, die Kosten fast null. Welche Masse von kleinen Eitelkeiten, großen Prätensionen, bedeutender Unliebenswürdigkeit aber dabei zum Vorschein gekommen ist, glaubt man kaum. Toller wie die Kunstreiter sind solche Dilettanten, wenn sie sich einmal ihrer Bestialität überlassen. Mutter wird Euch geschrieben haben, wie komisch auch die kleine süßstimmige Novello sich herausgelassen, u. mit Händen, Füßen, u. Lunge sich als Prima donna dargestellt hat. Es war übrigens eine poetische Freiheit, sie unter die Dilettanten zu rechnen. Heut giebt sie ihr letztes Concert. Von mir wollte ich Euch noch erzählen, daß ich mich, mir selbst unbegreiflicher Weise fast gar nicht geängstigt habe, u. ziemlich unbefangen gespielt. Es ist mir lieb, doch einmal auch diese Erfahrung gemacht zu haben. Schade, daß das Arrangement des ganzen Concerts so spottschlecht war, es hätte doch für dasselbe Geld so wunderschön seyn können. Wenn die Novello mir zu Gefallen noch einen Tag zugiebt, sie will eigentlich Sonnabend reisen, so denke ich Sonntag endlich einmal den schon dreimal angesetzten Don Juan zu geben, worüber ich Euch dann weiter berichte. Ries hat mir viel Erfreuliches von Euch erzählt, namentlich auch von Felixens neuem Psalm, der, nachdem, was er mir davon sagt, eine ganz neue Gestalt bekommen haben muß. Wie freue ich mich darauf. Auch von dem neuen Quartett hat er mir erzählt. Eigentlich ist es ganz überflüßig, daß ich Euch schreibe, Mutter schreibt so oft u. so hübsch, daß ich doch nur als 5tes Rad am Wagen komme, u. Euch nie etwas Neues zu erzählen habe, ich thue es aber zu meinem eignen Vergnügen. Wenn Ihr hier seyd, wollen wir aber ein lustiges Leben führen, u. ich glaube, was die Stadt betrifft, so wird selbst Felix in seiner Berserkerwuth gegen uns arme Berliner, nicht läugnen können, daß die sich fortwährend verschönerte Schade übrigens, daß ihr, für Dich, in keiner günstigen Jahreszeit kommt, etwas früher wäre die Stadt, was Vergnügungen betrifft, u. etwas später unser Haus, des Gartens wegen, angenehmer gewesen. So werdet Ihr allein mit unsrer liebenswürdig[en] Gesellschaft vorlieb nehmen müssen. Indessen, wir wollen uns vertragen, mein großer Zank mit Felix vom letzten Mal brennt mir noch auf der Seele.

Lieber Felix, ich habe gestern ein Briefchen von der guten Mme. Kiené bekommen, die noch nach der alten Weise lebt, Dich u. uns Alle aufs Zärtlichste liebt, u. Dich herzlich grüßt. Wenn Du einmal Zeit hast, so schreibe doch der lieben alten Frau ein Wort, sie wird es dankbar anerkennen. Ich werde ihr auch baldigst antworten. Lebt wohl, ich muß Sebastian eine Stunde geben. Dem geht es, Gott sey Dank, diesen Winter, wie dem Fisch im Wasser. Wie wird denn Euer künftiger großer, kleiner Mann heißen? Haben große Debatten darüber statt gefunden? Lebt wohl Ihr Lieben!

Eure Fanny

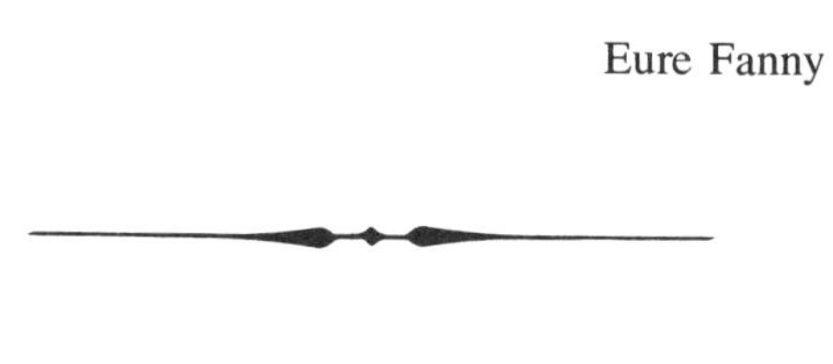

105

Berlin 7ten September 1838

Du lieber Engel, Du süßes Lamm, daß Du die Masern hast, u. Dein liebes klares Gesicht voller Flecke, das ist ja ganz abscheulich. Solchen Sonntagskindern, wie Du bist, sollte nie etwas fehlen. Hätte ich nicht mein Kind zu pflegen, u. meinen Mann zu erwarten, kurz hielten mich nicht die nächsten Pflichten, ich wäre auf der Stelle hingekommen, Dich zu hätscheln, u. Dir, wenn Felix ausgehn muß, nach Kräften die Zeit zu vertreiben, es war meine erste Bewegung, der ich aber nicht folgen konnte. Wenn ich nach uns Allen schließen soll, so ist übrigens in diesen Augenblick die eigentliche Krankheit vorbei, u. morgen lasse ich Dich aufstehn, u. Brühsuppe essen. Wir erwarten nun mit einer Art von Humor, wer von dieser 2ten Masernauflage weiter wird angesteckt werden, Mutter, Mad. Dirichlet, Minna u. ich, u. sämmtliche Leute sind noch übrig. Mir für mein Theil wäre es nur höchst fatal, etwa krank zu seyn, wenn mein Mann kommt, den ich nächste Woche erwarte, zu einer andern Zeit wäre es mir viel gleichgültiger. Wenn Carlchen seine Oehrchen steif hielte, so wärs ein Wunder, ich kann Dich übrigens versichern, liebste Cecile, daß es mit den Kindern ein Spaß ist. Zwei Tage hatte Sebastian Fieber, u. er fiebert u. phantasirt eben so leicht, wie Felix, dann war er gleich wieder munter, hatte Appetit u. die beste Laune. Uebrigens hat er im Fieber die possierlichsten Einfälle, daß man nicht lassen kann, drüber zu lachen, u. jetzt geht er in einem langen Schlafrock in der Stube spatzieren, zum todtlachen. Es fehlt ihm nichts als die Pfeife im Munde, zum volligen Philister.

Rebecka haben einige Austern, die ich ihr verehrt, vortrefflich geschmeckt, sie ist vorgestern zuerst aufgestanden, hatte gestern einen Anfall von heftiger Migraine, die aber bald vorüber ging, u. wird übermorgen herunter zu Walter gehn, der auch morgen aufsteht. So sehn wir doch nun Licht, das war aber wirklich fatale Zeit, nach der schönen dieses Sommers. Wenn das schöne Wetter nur noch eine Weile fortdauert, um Euch Maserkranken auch zu Gute zu kommen, für meines Mannes Ueberfahrt wünsche ich es auch nicht wenig. Vorige Woche, grade in den Tagen, wo Sebastian krank wurde, sausten die unheimlichsten Stürme, ach Cecile, da war mir schrecklich zu Muth wenn ich an die Ueberfahrt dachte, u. dann wieder an das fieberkranke Kind. Bunsen hat, wie mir Hensel schreibt, eine tolle Reise über Meer gehabt, einige 50 St. v. Rotterdam nach London, und davon 10 in Lebensgefahr auf einer Klippe festgesessen, u. Alle seekrank.

In unserm Garten ist eine so günstige Veränderung vorgenommen worden, daß ich mich recht ärgere, sie nicht schon bei Eurem Hierseyn vorgeschlagen zu haben. Es ist mir aber nicht früher eingefallen, wer kann dafür? Von dem dickem Fliedergebüsch, das die ganze Länge unsrer Wohnung entlanglief, ist aber die Hälfte weggehauen, so daß der kleine Taxus kaum unserm Balcon gegenüber, nun allein steht, u. wir eine freie Aussicht auf den Grasplatz haben. Auch von dem andern Fliedergebüsch ist ein großer Theil weggenommen, das schafft uns Luft u. Licht im Hause, u. sieht viel hübscher aus.

Lieber Felix, wenn Singliedern die Worte weggenommen werden, um sie als Concertstück zu brauchen, so ist das ein richtiges Gegenstück zu dem Experiment, Deinen Spielliedern Worte unterzulegen, die andre Hälfte von der verkehrten Welt. Ich bin schon lange alt genug, um Manches was in der jetzigen Zeit geschieht recht abgeschmackt zu finden, das mag denn dazu gehören. Soll man nun aber nicht eine ungeheure Meinung von sich bekommen (nein, man soll nicht) wenn man sieht, daß die Späße, womit wir uns als halbe Kinder die Zeit vertrieben haben, jetzt von den großen Talenten nacherfunden, u. als Futter fürs Publicum gebraucht werden? Das Publicum ist aber mitunter unbeschreiblich genügsam, u. dann einandermal überaus strenge. Kurz, das Publicum das ist ein Mann. Mutter habe ich, seit Ihr fort seyd, schon 2mal mit ins Theater geschleppt, wir haben Correggio, u. Hamlet von Löwe gesehn. Beim Correggio standen wir aber immer doch, als es Gold regnete, bei einer 2ten Vorstellung war Gern krank, u.—Seydelmann ersetzte seine Stelle, u. spielte den Wirth. Mutter wollte erst nicht gehn, amüsirte sich aber nachher sehr gut.

Nun lebt wohl, beste Kinder, es ist Nachmittag, ich muß Sebastian, der heut ziemlich lange auf war, zu Bett bringen. Mutter, Dirichlets, Minna grüßen herzlich, u. wünschen beste gute Besserung.

106

Berlin, 14ten Decbr. 1838

Lieber Felix, die Schulz war gestern u. heut hier, um über die Sache mit mir zu sprechen, sie wünscht sehr, daß ihre Tochter sich mit Euch einige, was sie mir aber gesagt, was in dem Briefe der Direction gestanden, war ganz anders, als was Du geschrieben hast, sie meinte nämlich, es wäre die Rede, ihre Tochter schon dies Jahr für eine halbe saison zu engagiren, u. Du schriebst nur von einem Concert. Was sie Dir geantwortet, weiß ich ebenfalls nicht, mich aber hat sie gebeten, Dir zu sagen, daß sie für diesen Versuch kein Honorar, wol aber freie Reise u. Aufenthalt für sich, ihre Tochter, u. ein Mädchen wünschte. Ich bestelle, was mir aufgetragen. Ich glaube übrigens, wenn Ihr Euch einigt, daß Ihr an der Hedwig Schulz eine gute Acquisition machen werdet. Sie hat gestern den Gabriel in der Schöpfung wirklich recht sehr gut gesungen, die Stimme ist schön u. klangvoll u. sie hat schon recht viel gelernt. Vieles fehlt Ihr freilich noch, u. A. macht sie einen Triller, für den sie am Ende riskiren würde, die Treppe herunter geworfen zu werden, wie Frl. Schlegel, dafür aber glaube ich, riskirst Du nicht, daß sie den Triller macht, wenn Du es ihr verbieten, denn sie ist ein sehr artiges, gelehriges Mädchen. Ferner beim Aushalten des Tons nimmt sie zu plötzlich ab u. zu sie hat das noch nicht recht in der Gewalt, aber sie ist noch im Lernen begriffen, sie wird nicht schlechter, sondern besser werden, u. wenn Du Dich ihrer annimmst, was Du ja mit Mancher gethan, die es nicht so verdient, u. sie ein wenig zustutzest, glaube ich, wird sie den Ansprüche erfüllen, die die Leipziger an eine bei ihnen engagirte Sängerin zu machen gewöhnt sind. Ich bemühe mich übrigens gegen mein Interesse, diesen Bund zu schließen, denn in Ermanglung der Decker, auf die nach Neujahr nicht mehr zu rechnen ist, würde sie mir, wenn ich wieder anfange Musik zu machen, von großem Nutzen gewesen seyn. H. v. Dachröden sagte mir gestern, daß er auch schon auf sie reflektirt hätte. Ich glaube nicht, daß man so leicht irgendwo zwei Dilettantinnen finden wird, die die Sopranpartieen in der Schöpfung singen, wie gestern die Schulz u. die Curschmann.

Hier geht, Gott sey Dank, alles gut. Rebecka war heut aus, u. es geht ihr seit jener Zahnkatastrophe ganz gut, Gott gebe, daß es dabei bleibe. Wenn wir doch einmal wieder Weihnachten zusammen seyn könnten, leider hat das Fest die üble Gewohnheit, im Winter zu seyn, wo alles Kinderreisen äußerst beschwerlich ist. Diesmal werden wir keine allzubrillant Stimmung aufzubauen haben, und die thut doch immer das Beste dazu. Die armen Woringens, die werden ein trauriges Fest haben. Ich bin recht gespannt, was sie für die Zukunft beschließen werden.

Neulich waren wir mit Sebastian u. Walter zum erstenmal im Theater, das war dann sehr lustig anzusehn, es war die Zauberflöte. Während des ganzen ersten Akts saßen sie mit offnen Mäulern u. einem grimmigen Ernst da, nachher erst faßten sie Muth, sich zu amüsiren u. zu lachen.

Adieu, lieber Leute, Cecilchen, Du könntest mir auch einmal wieder schreiben, küß Carlchen, u. erzähl ihm von der lächerlichen Tante. Ach! wie hübsch war das, wenn die beiden lieben Kinder so zusammen in den Garten getragen wurden.

Lebt wohl.

Eure Fanny

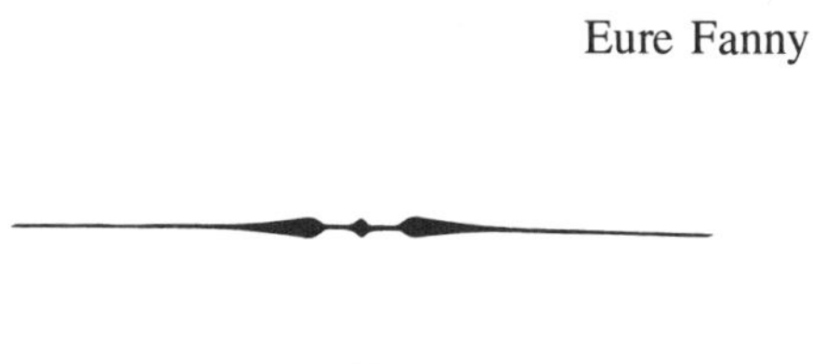

107

Berlin, 6ten Janr. 1839

Lieber Felix, ich bin ein sehr schlechter Minister des Auswärtigen gewesen, u. fürchte, Eure Kammer wird mir den Abschied geben, wie auch die Adresse auf diesem Brief, ausfallen möge, die Schulz tritt nächste Woche als Gräfin im Figaro auf. Für die hiesige Bühne wird sie von geringem Nutzen seyn, denn ich halte ihre Stimme noch nicht für geeignet, das Opernhaus zu füllen, für Euren Saal wäre sie sehr gut gewesen, u. so geschieht wieder, was so oft, sie stellt sich nicht auf den Platz den sie ausfüllen könnte. Es thut mir leid, um Euretwegen, um ihretwegen u. um meinetwegen, daß ich Euch nicht habe dienen können. Euer groß Thier, Thalberg, ist auch nun hier, er war bei Mutter, die hat ihn aber für sich behalten, morgen werden wir mit ihm bei Alexander essen, ich höre aber leider, daß er nicht in Gesellschaft spielt, u. von den Paar Concerten, wird man nur wenig lernen können. Diese Hexenmeister muß man eigentlich spielen sehn, ich werde, um so viel Nutzen als möglich davon zu haben, mir die Sachen die er spielt, vorher geben lassen, um sie zu kennen. Die Herren machen sichs wirklich unerhört leicht mit ihren Schwierigkeiten nicht einmal eine Probe brauchen sie, weil sie Alles ohne Begleitung spielen, u. so ist Alles aufs meiste Geld in der kürzesten Zeit berechnet. Ich weiß wol, Du bist jetzt der mildeste der Milden, u. ich bin überzeugt, daß Thalberg wunderschön spielt, aber dies Wesen kann ich doch nicht loben, dafür bin ich das Charivari. Ein großes Vergnügen haben wir vorgestern Abend gehabt, wo uns Seydelmann wieder einmal vorlas. Er hatte den Antonio im Tasso gewählt, weil er die Rolle nächstens spielt, u. wie er sagte, nicht genug bei Stimme sey, um ein ganzes Stück zu lesen, da hatten wir Andere denn, mit ruhmwürdiger Aufopferung uns bereit finden lassen, die übrigen Rollen abzuhaspeln, u. lasen auch meist nur die Scenen, in denen Antonio erscheint. Mit welcher Feinheit, Liebenswürdigkeit, Ironie u. Würde er diese Rolle nimmt, das kann man sich kaum vorstellen, selbst wenn man ihn kennt, es ist ein Meisterstück. Nachher las er noch auf Begehren die Kraniche des Ibycus, u. dann auf eignen Antrieb, den Kampf mit dem Drachen. Er war so erfreut über unser Entzücken, daß er sich erboten hat, zu lesen, was u. wann wir wollten, u. wir werden gewiß nicht zögern, Gebrauch davon zu machen. Es waren 17 Personen hier, grade so viel, als unser Wohnzimmer bequem faßt, u. der Abend war überaus angenehm. Nun aber Frank! Wir hatten schon munkeln hören daß, nachdem sich ganz Europa ihm *ergeben* hatte, er sich am Ende Leipzig ergeben würde, und es ist mir für Dich überaus erfreulich. Wenn die Frauen für einander passen, wird es eine unschatzbare Vermehrung Eures kleinen Kreises seyn. Grüß ihn mir recht herzlich, ich möchte diesen alten Freund wol einmal wieder sehn. Schlage ihm doch von meinetwegen vor, wenn er Meubles hier kaufen will, das in Person zu thun, ich will mit ihm herum laufen, u. ihn erst in die schlechtesten Magazine führen, damit er nun so länger hier bleibt, u. ihn am Ende doch zufrieden stellen. Grade als er mir in diesen Tagen durch Deine Briefe wieder recht nahe gerückt war, fiel mir seine famose Etüde in die Hande, mit der Unterschrift: sanft u. etwas abgeschmackt, aber nicht zu langsam. Wenn er sie bei sich verlegen will, so werde ich sie ihm schicken, er könne ja da er den Autor gut kennt, den Rest des Dutzends bei ihm bestellen, u. statt Portraits, die Charakteristik vordrucken lassen, die ein andrer, eben so berühmter Autor, ich, von ihm gemacht hat. Beabsichtigt er noch, sein erstes Kind von einer Löwin säugen zu lassen, u. ist seine Frau mit der Wahl dieser Amme einverstanden?

Daß Du Deinen es dur Psalm herausgiebst, ist mir sehr lieb, ich liebe Vieles drin ganz außerordentlich, namentlich Anfang u. Schluß. Wo stehn die Recensionen von Goethe aus den Jahren 72 u. 73? Hast Du die Briefe an die Gräfin Stolberg aus der Urania 39 gelesen? Das ist kurioses Zeug.

Im Ganzen finde ich bestätigt Goethes Nachlaß wieder recht die allgemeine Regel von den Nachlässen. Was ein kluger Mann dem Publicum entzieht, daran verliert das Publicum auch nicht viel, denn der kluge Mann hat seine Gründe. Indeß kann man sich gar manchmal über seine Herausgeber, u. seine Korespondenten, u. seine Erben, u. ihn selbst ärgern, u. braucht dann nur wieder eine Scene aus dem Tasso, u. einen Gesang aus Herrmann u. Dorothea zu lesen, um ihm mit Herz u. Seele u. jeder bessern Empfindung deren man fähig ist, anzugehören. Wohl uns, daß wir ihn gehabt haben. Ich glaube, er würde zufrieden gewesen seyn, wenn er Seydelmann den Antonio hätte lesen hören.—Seitdem haben wir bei Mutter gegessen, u. uns einmal wieder über Alles herumgezankt. Ich denke, ich höre Dich lachen, wenn wir so ernsthaft übers Kaisers Bart streiten. Aber Cecile, meine Cecile, Du hast mir seit Ihr weg seid, ein einziges kleines kleines Briefchen geschrieben, ist das wol halb recht? Es haben Dich zwar alle Leute lieb, die Dich kennen, aber so lieb wie ich haben Dich doch nicht viel Leute.

7te

Gestern Abend trank das große Thier bei Mutter Thee, Du weißt es ist niemals so langweilig bei uns, als wenn ein großer Mann da ist, diese Erfahrung bestätigte sich auch gestern. Unter den Aehnlichkeiten die er zu haben beschuldigt wurde, nenne ich Dir nur Lord Wellington, die schöne Vittoria, u. Lida Bendemann. Suche Dir einen davon aus. Ich habe à peine seine Bekanntschaft gemacht. Vorher hatte ich mir vorgenommen, ihn zu bitten, mir Gelegenheit zu geben ihn im Zimmer zu hören, aber dann fand ich ihn so virtuosich, so vernehm u. mit sich selbst zufrieden, daß ichs lieber unterließ, u. wie immer in solchen Fällen, meine Fischberedsamkeit laut werden ließ. In Rußland wird er Paul treffen, der uns gestern eröffnet, daß er in 8 Tagen nach dieser Bärenhöhle reisen müsse. Er läßt Albertine hier, was ich auch in Rücksicht auf die Jahreszeit sehr vernünftig finde, u. wird daher hoffentlich bald wiederkommen.

Woringens sind in hohem Grade angegriffen, u. das Leben in ihrem Hause scheint ihnen ganz unerträglich zu werden. Ferdinand ist, wie Du wissen wirst, noch dort, Franz beabsichtigt die Mädchen Ostern herzuholen, u. Rebecka hat gestern den sehr vernünftigen Vorschlag gemacht, daß sie mit ihr nach dem Seebade reisen sollten, eine Cour, die Elisen längst verordnet worden. Wenn dieser Plan zur Ausführung kommt, so wird er für beide Theile sehr heilsam seyn. Ferdinand wird in etwa 8 T. hier durchkommen, u. von ihm werden wir wol Manches Nähere hören. Ich hoffe, sie bleiben für die Zukunft hier.

Ich muß Dich doch noch für Deinen Lichtschirm u. Dein Bildchen für Rebecka loben, die beide allerliebst gerathen sind. Mache doch einmal einen runden Lichtschirm, auf die Lampe zu setzen, die sehn so hübsch aus. Mir könntest Du auch einmal wieder ein Bildchen malen, u. bei Cecile habe ich auch noch ein Pimpernüßchen zu Gute. Heut glaube ich, soll das Bildchen für Mutter kommen. Adieu, lieben Leutchen. Felix eine ungerechtere Beschuldigung ist nie vor ein Tribunal gebracht worden, als die, daß ich Dir kurze Episteln für lange schriebe, 3 lange u. eine kurze für eine, à la bonne heure. Thalberg hat etwas von dem Dreyschock erzählt, das ist wirklich fabelhaft, daß er die [18]te Etüde v. Chopin im Baß mit Oktaven spielt. Th. sagt: wenn der Mann Geschmack hätte, spielte er uns Alle todt, u. dabei sieht er aus wie Honig mit Zucker gekocht, u. ein klein Tröpfchen Rum. Die Prunellenfrau hat hier das Gerücht verbreitet Carlchen hätte 3 Zähnchen, wenn das wahr ist, wie kannst Du Rabenmutter denn nichts davon schreiben? Nun lebt aber im Ernst wohl. Ich bin heut sehr schreibselig, wie ihr sehr. Weißt Du, daß Henselt in Rußland zu 3 Ducaten Stunden giebt?

Adieu, mein Mann grüßt Euch bestens. Wenn Du einmal eine Landschaft auf [der] Ausstellung gäbest, würde das Pub[licum] gewiß Deine Frau nicht auspischen, aus doppelten Gründen.

Eure Fanny

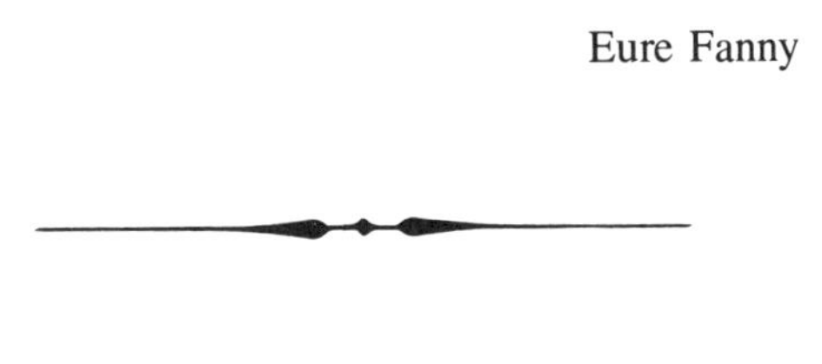

108

Viel Glück zum dritten Februar, lieber Felix und liebe Cecile! Mögt Ihr festhalten, was Ihr habt, besser kommt es doch nicht, und Gott sey Dank, daß wir uns Alle dasselbe wünschen und sagen können. Leider hab ich wenig Aussicht, Euch in diesem Jahr zu sehn, wohl aber denk ich, kommt Rebecka bald, so bald es milde wird, und der gönne ich auch vor Allem eine Erholung und Zerstreuung. Wie lange haben wir nun schon keinen unsrer Geburtstage zusammen verlebt. Welch ein dummer Druckfehler in unsrer Geschichte, daß wir nicht in einer Stadt leben. Nur wenigstens so oft als möglich laßt uns zusammenkommen, das Leben ist kurz!

Von Paul laufen täglich schneeige Berichte ein, von Tilsit ab ist er zu Schlitten gefahren. Albertine ißt in der Familie herum, alle Tage wo anders.

Gestern Abend haben wir ein gruseliges Vergnügen gehabt, Seydelmann las uns Richard III vor, jedesmal wenn man ihn gehört, meint man, so habe er noch nie gelesen. Wie eine Tigerkatze war er, wenn er so im Lesen warm wird u. anfängt zu agiren, das ist wirklich prächtig.

Mit dem Musikmachen habe ich diesen Winter besonders Pech. Noch hat es mir nicht gelingen wollen, anzufangen, u. wenn es nun nicht bald geht, so wird es ganz u. gar zu spät; u. ich gebe es auf.

Kommt denn die Shaw nicht her? Schick sie doch! Die Garcia las ich heut ist für die Season in London zu den philharmonischen Concerten engagirt. Es würde mich recht freuen, sie dort zu sehn. Thalberg giebt morgen sein 4tes Concert, außer einem für die Armen, im Opernhause, worin er gespielt hat. Sein drittes war schon als Abschiedsconcert angekündigt, dies hier als letztes. Ob er ein Allerletztes wird folgen lassen, weiß ich nicht, aber so viel ist gewiß, daß er kein Virtuosenkünstchen verschmäht.

In diesem Kistchen lieber Felix, findest Du ein Alabasterbüstchen Shakespeares, womit ich Dich bitte, Deine Stube zu schmüken. Mein Mann vereinigt sich mit mir zu allen guten und besten Wünschen. Sebastian will Dir in seinem Besenstyl noch selbst gratuliren. Lebe wohl, liebster Bruder, Gott schenke Dir lange und frohe Tage. Jemehr Virtuosen ich kennen lerne, jemehr danke ich Gott mit pharisäischem Hochmuth, daß Du nicht geworden bist, wie diese, so leer u. so eitel.

Rebecka behauptete neulich, Mutter packe immer meuchlings für Dich ein, da wir gewöhnlich erst nach Abgang der Pakete erfahren, daß, u. was sie geschickt hat. Lebt wohl, liebste Kinder, denkt unser, wenn Ihr froh seyd.

Eure Fanny

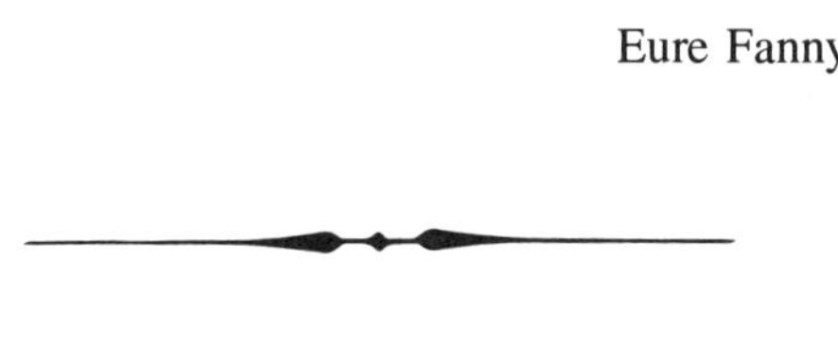

109

Erstens noch einmal alles Glück und alles Gute, liebster Felix, von neuerm Datum als das im Schächtelchen befindliche. Zweitens gleich zur Sache. Ich kann Dir nicht läugnen, daß mich die Nachricht von Deiner Reise nach England, zu einer so nahen u. doch Andern Zeit als die unsre, uns Beide sehr bewegt hat. Läßt es sich denn mit Deinen Planen u. Interessen nicht vereinigen, die Reise von Düsseld. aus, nach dem Musikfest zu machen? Wenn ich fragen darf, weshalb gehst Du nach England? Deiner Oper wegen? Opfern mußt Du freilich nichts deshalb, denn alle menschliche Dinge sind unsicher, u. wenn Du etwas opfertest, um uns da zu treffen, u. wir könnten nachher etwa doch nicht kommen, so würde mich das sehr betrüben. Wenn es aber seyn könnte! so könnten wir auch wol allerseits manche Freude, u. was in England auch nicht zu verachten ist, manchen Vortheil davon ziehn, z. B. zusammen wohnen if it will suit you, etc. Bitte, schreibe mir darüber, u. bald. Du kannst denken, es würde meine gruselige Furcht vor L. sehr überwinden helfen, wenn ich wüßte, Dich da zu treffen. Hensels Bilder sind in diesem Augenblick in british institution . . . bewegt, wie es äußerliche Dinge nur können, begreifst Du wohl.

Die Shaw ist nun da, eine recht nette lebhafte Person, ich war gestern gleich mit ihr in Läden, daß wir für sie thun werden, was möglich, geht ohne sagen, leider kann ich diesen Sonntag noch nicht Musik haben, was ihr vielleicht vortheilhaft wäre, sondern erst nächsten.

Lebt wohl Ihr Lieben.

Eure Fanny

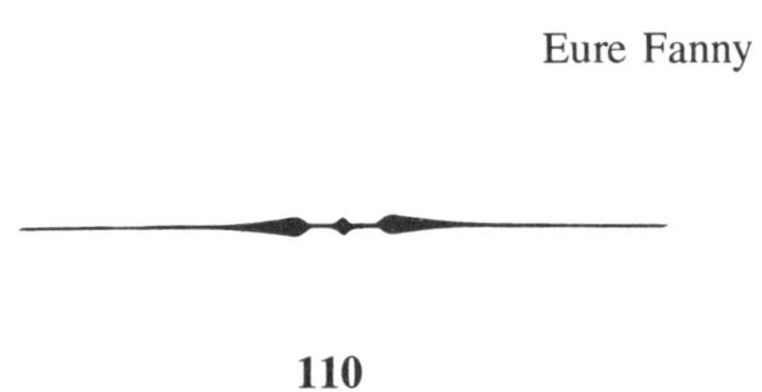

110

Berlin, 26sten Febr. 1839

Lieber Felix! Du hast mich, als Du mir das letzte Mal schriebst, so derb mit ganz Berlin ausgezankt, daß ich mich bis jetzt noch nicht von meinem Schreck habe erholen können, ich muß es aber doch einmal wieder wagen, wieder vor Deinem Angesicht zu erscheinen, sey es auch nur, um Dir Bericht abzustatten, daß ich Deinen Auftrag, wegen der Doberaner Harmoniemusik sogleich pünktlich ausgerichtet. Zwar nicht auf so vornehmem Wege, als Du dachtest, der Kammerherr u. Theaterintendant, H. v. Dachröden, lebt in Strelitz, u. seine Seele weiß nichts von Schwerin, aber der H. Hofmusikus P. Lappe in Schwerin ist gebeten u. angewiesen worden, Dir die Noten direct nach Leipzig zu schicken. Hast Du sie erhalten, bitte so melde mirs, hast Du sie in weniger Zeit noch nicht, bitte ein Dito, dann als dann soll uns der Lappe nicht durch die Lappen gehn.

Rebecka denke ich, wird zu Euch kommen, indeß muß dazu vollkommnes Wohlseyn u. schönes Wetter sich vereinigen, u. das hat bis jetzt noch nicht geschehn wollen. Ich rede nur gelinde zu, denn man übernimmt eine Verantwortung zu so etwas zu treiben, u. so viel Lust sie auch zu dieser Reise hat, so ist sie doch noch sehr low spirited.—Gestern war Mme. Shaws Concert im Theater, wo Parkett u. erste Ranglogen voll waren, das Uebrige nicht. So recht will es hier leider nicht mit ihr gelingen, wie sie es doch so sehr verdient, u. wie es der Novello gelang. Dabei findet sie ganz ungetheilten Beifall, u. enthusiastische Verehrer, aber sie traf es nicht gut, u. man muß ihr zur Ehre nachsagen, daß sie das Concertgebermetier noch nicht so recht versteht. Da traf sie mit Ole Bull zusammen, der besser mit den Taschen der Leute bescheid weiß, mit der Familie Lewy, die unmündig ist, u. daher interessirt, u. sie, mit ihrem nobeln einfachen Gesange, u. ihrem natürlichen Wesen, kann gegen solche Künste nicht streiten. Dabei ist sie aber immer zufrieden, u. das ist das Beste. Sie gefällt mir ungemein wohl, u. allen Leuten hier. Bei uns hier hat sie zweimal Sonntags gesungen, u. Alles entzückt, besonders durch die Arie aus dem Paulus.—Dabei fällt mir Paul ein, der sehr hübsche amüsante Briefe aus Petersburg schreibt, u. uns ein recht anschauliches Bild von dem Leben dort giebt, das ich keineswegs reizend finde. Albertine bildet sich ein, er käme bald wieder, ich glaube aber, es wird noch ziemlich lange dauern. Heut war die Faßmann bei mir, die nun verreist, u. nach Woringens Aufforderung nach Düss. zu gehn denkt, sie sagt mir aber, sie wisse noch gar nichts Näheres. Weißt Du nicht, wie es steht, u. ob man auch auf sie rechnet? Sie ist öfter bei der Shaw gewesen, um sich von der den Messias mit engl. pikanten Sauce einstudiren zu lassen, mehr Bescheidenheit kann man doch von einer Sängerin nicht verlangen.

Geht denn Cecile diesmal mit zum Musikfest? Ich denke doch. Deinen Psalm möchte ich schon von dem Chor hören, das wird sich prächtig machen. Kommt Dein neuer Psalm nicht bald? Ich möchte ihn gern noch singen lassen.

Wen in aller Welt hat denn der Liphart geheirathet? Das ist eine närrische Familie mit Heirathen, plötzlich sitzt er da im Concert u. hat eine Frau. Wie geht es Franks? Gefällt es ihnen in Leipzig? Hast sie[a] die Welt noch mit keinem Fränkchen vermehrt?

Grüße Carl, den Läufer, den Schwätzer, u. Cecile, die ich nun einmal nicht leiden kann, u. ich fürchte, in diesem Leben lern ichs nicht mehr indeß, da sie nun doch einmal meine Schwägerin ist, muß ich mich mit ihr vertragen, was hilft das Alles? Adieu, ihr lieben Leute, Alles grüßt.

Eure Fanny

Von Kling. u. Fanny Horsley hatte ich vorige Woche Briefe. Der v. Kling. war der erste längere u. muntrere seit langer Zeit. In dem, was Du mir über meine Unruhe über die englische Reise schreibst, hast Du gewiß Recht, das fühle ich selbst, was ist aber da zu thun? ich glaube gar nicht, daß ich meinem Mann eine Wohlthat erweise, wenn ich mitreise, ich glaube, ich werde ihn mehr hindern als fördern, u. das beunruhigt mich nur mehr. Uebrigens schreiben mir meine bekannten u. unbekannten Correspondenten so freundlich u. zutraulich, daß mich das billig über die Furcht erheben sollte. Sobald wir Näheres bestimmt haben, sollt Ihrs wissen, bis jetzt mag ich noch gar nicht von der Reise reden. In diesen Tagen geht die Mathieux bei Dir durch. Sie will nach Bonn, um sich von ihrem Mann scheiden zu lassen, u. der närrische Mann will nicht. Ist Dir so etwas schon vorgekommen? Laß den Brief nicht in den Papierkorb fallen, damit sie ihn nicht findet u. liest. So diese ganze 4te Seite ist ein postscript. Weiblicher Pferdefuß.

---

[a]Fanny mistakenly wrote "Hast sie" instead of "Hat sie."

111

Berlin, 4ten März 1839

Lieber Felix! Eine Stunde nach Sicht war ich bei la Fass, und will Dir meine ganze Weisheit auskramen. La Fass verlangt es nicht besser, als die Alceste zu spielen, an einem Hercules, der zugleich der Oberpriester tragiren könnte, wird es auch nicht fehlen, denn Bötticher ist ja engagirt, wenn Ihr nun noch einen Berliner Tenor braucht, so nehmt doch Eichberger, der spielt den Admet, und kann immer reisen, wenn die Faßmann reist, weil er nur mit der zusammen spielt. Was nun die Bedingungen betrifft, da frug ich, u. sie wußte nicht, u. meinte, u. dachte, u. da sagte ich wieder, was sie denn in andern Mittelstädten für eine Rolle bekäme, u. da kam denn heraus, 25-30 fr d'or, für eine große Rolle. Ich glaube wenn Ihr Dialog in die Alceste einlegt, kriegt Ihrs billiger, ich glaube auch, sie läßt mit sich handeln, wenns Euch zu viel ist.

Was nun die übrigen Forderungen betrifft, so will sie keine Summe, sondern die Reisekosten, sie kommt von ihrer jetzigen Reise erst noch zurück, u. so läßt sich ihr so ziemlich nachrechnen. Als ich schüchtern frug: wie werden Sie reisen u. zur Antwort erhielt: mit Extrapost, gab ich mir im Interesse des Düsseld. Musikvereins alle Mühe, ihr mit Beredsamkeit die Schönheit der Natur am Rhein zu schildern, u. versicherte sie, wenn sie mit Schnellpost bis Mainz, u. von da Dampfbootaliter hinab glitte, würde ihre Seele sich ergötzen an der smaragdenen Fluth, u. was mir die Begeisterung noch mehr Poetisches einflößte. Darauf erwiderte sie, da Bötticher auch hinreiste, könnten sie ihn mitnehmen u. drei Personen extra reisten nicht theuerer als 3 mit der Schnellpost. Das ist rather wahr, u. da ich wohl fühlte, daß meine Befugnisse hier at an end wären, schloß ich mit einem refrain zum Lobe des Rheins, u. ging zum Haus Bericht zu erstatten. Hier bin ich nun erst durch ein großes Paket mit unzähligen graziösen Geschenkchen u. Briefen von Luise[n] aufgehalten, u. nun weißt Du Alles, aber noch nicht, daß etwaige Mittheilungen die Faßmann bis Ostern in Bremen, später in Hannover (mit Respect zu sagen), treffen, u. daß sie in etwa 5 Wochen wieder hier ist. Sie ist übrigens so niedlich, u. ihre langen blonden Locken sind so schön, daß sie gewiß in Düsseld. sehr gefallen wird.

Beckchen hat Dich an mich gewiesen, um Dir zu erzählen, daß unter Allem, was die Shaw schön singt, ein Paar Arien aus dem Orpheus doch oben an stehn, das ist wirklich first rate music. Morgen essen sie noch bei uns nachdem sie heut Abend ihr letztes Concert gegeben haben wird. Wenn es nur voller wird. Ich fürchte fast nein, so etwas liegt immer in der Luft, u. ich habe nicht viel munkeln gehört. Morgen bitte ich Miss Forrester dazu, eine sehr nette Engländerin, bei der wir Unterricht nehmen.—Ueber den gekikksten (oder schreibst Du gekixten?) Ton in der Symphonie habe ich nicht 3 Takte, sondern drei Stunden gelacht, weil ich das von hier höre. Bei so etwas lachen alle Leute nur der Sänger nicht, der läßt das Lachen wol bleiben. Liebe Nessel, Du bekommst nächstens einen aparten Brief von mir, da wollen wir uns weiter zanken. Ueber die Mathieux stimme ich sehr mit Dir überein, u. daß das Fräulein Frank Carlchens Windeln zerreißt, dazu brauchte sie keine halbe Prinzeß zu seyn.

Felix, ich bin so melancholisch wie ein Brummkater, aber der Sekt ist nicht Schuld daran. Wie viel plagt man sich im Leben für nichts. Lebt wohl, ich muß nur anfangen zu schließen, denn wenn ich erst die Thür in die Hand nehme, dauert es wenigstens noch eine Seite. Ich höre, Benikes reisen nach Leipzig, wenn ihr sie seht, macht doch ein Compliment von mir, u. fragt, was wir ihnen denn eigentlich gethan haben? Ich möchte es wahrhaftig gern wissen. Neulich auf einer Sauree bei Mariannen, haben wir uns des Nichtgrüßens befleißigt. Dafür grüßt mir aber Miss Schunk, ich meine Julie u. ihre Mutter, die ist eigentlich das beste Frauenzimmer aus der Familie. Aber die Welt ist dumm, die Welt ist schlecht, wird täglich abgeschmackter.

H. Lappe werde ich nächstens was am Zunge flicken, der Lump antwortet auch nicht einmal. Nun wird es Ernst, adieu, lebt wohl. Denkt meiner wenn ihr Suppe eßt, wie ich eben thun will.

Eure Fanny

112

Berlin, 28sten April 39

Lieber Felix, ich bin Dir noch den Dank schuldig für das liebe Briefchen, das mir Drouet gebracht. Mutter, die beste u. fleißigste Berichterstatterin, der ich mehr traue, als Rellstab, (das der Horcherin) wird Dir geschrieben haben, in wiefern ich ihm zu dienen gesucht, ich habe nämlich, was ich noch nie gethan, seinetwegen an den Grafen Redern geschrieben, für den er keinen Brief hatte, und zwar mit gutem Erfolg, denn er hat drei Tage darauf im Opernhause mit vielem Beifall gespielt. Auf eine Morgenmusik mit Publicum bei uns ging ich wol aus, er aber nicht recht [ein], u. in seinem Interesse hielt ich es für das Beste, daß er im Theater spielte, u. kein eignes Concert gäbe, wozu mir Zeit u. Umstände nicht günstig schienen. Nun muß ich Dir aber eine Klatscherei schreiben, u. mich im Voraus deshalb entschuldigen, Du weißt freilich wohl, daß es meine Art in der Regel nicht ist, aber never mind, ich entschuldige mich doch zu klatschen, weil ich mich schäme. Die Frau v. Faßmann war heut früh bei mir, um mir zu erzählen, die Novello sey zu ihrer Tochter gekommen, u. habe ihr erzählt: *sie* sey zum Musikfest in Düsseldorf engagirt wolle aber die Arien aus dem Messias mit der Faßmann theilen; auch zur Rolle der Alceste sey sie aufgefordert, wisse aber noch nicht, ob sie sie annehmen solle, da sie noch nicht auf der Bühne gewesen, auch nicht fest genug im Deutschen sey. Auf die Aufforderung der Frau v. Faß. ihr die Briefe des comité zu zeigen, wußte sie natürlich nichts-vonzubringen, u. die kam nun zu mir, um sich zu erkundigen, ob ich etwas von diesem seynsollenden Engagement der Novello wüßte? C'est du pack, pflegt einer der ersten Componisten unsrer Zeit zu sagen. Da nun aber die Faßmann wie Du willst, eine protégée, oder eine Protectrice von mir ist, so habe ich nicht unterlassen wollen, Dir Obiges zu klatschen, um Dich an fett zu setzen, was Dir bei Deiner Magerkeit in keiner Hinsicht schaden kann.

Erzähle mir doch einmal, thu es aber wirklich, wann Deine drei Quartette erscheinen? Ein wahres Meisterstück von eleganter Ausgabe ist Deine Sonate mit Cello. Sind das Spiel- oder Singlieder, die jetzt erscheinen? Mit Deinen Liedern ohne Worte hast Du wieder gutes Unheil angestiftet. Sie kommen mir dabei vor, wie der Wirth, der alle Weine aus einem Faß zapft, Alles komponiren sie, Lieder, Etüden, *Refrain mir Chor*, Notturnos, Capricen, Duette, Liebeslieder, alles aber aus dem selben alten Clavierfaß gezapft. Henselt hat die Kunst erfunden, die Instrumentalmusik unanständig zu machen, er könnte ein Patent drauf nehmen, dem Uebel-stand zu bloßen Etüden keine schlüpfrigen Texte wählen zu können, hat er glücklich durch die Ueberschriften abgeholfen. Lißzt hat die Kunst erfunden, die musikalische Ortographie, welche mir doch dazu vorhanden zu seyn scheint, um die Musik damit *lesen* zu können, so glücklich zu verwirren u. zu entstellen, daß es ihm gelungen ist, seine ohnehin schon sinn- u. zusammenhanglosen Compositionen mit Hülfe der Schreibart noch sinn- u. zusammenhangloser zu machen. Wäre das Chaos nicht schon vor Erschaffung der Welt durch den lieben Gott erfunden worden, so könnte Lißzt ihm die Erfindung streitig machen. Nun will ich aber aufhören, die Uebrigen zu rezensiren, sonst sagt Cecile wieder, ich habe ein Zörnchen. Gegen sie aber habe ich keines, sondern ein Liebchen, oder vielmehr eine dicke, große Liebe, welche ich Dir hiermit auftrage, ihr zu Füßen, um den Hals oder auf den Mund zu legen, mich Mad. Jeanrenaud u. Mad. Souchay in aufsteigender Linie der Verehrung zu empfehlen, Tante Schlegel, der ich nächstens schreiben werde, herzlichst Du grüßen, Dich eben so von meinem Mann grüßen zu lassen, u. zu bleiben mein treuer Bruder

Felix Mendelssohn Bartholdy

[Rebecka, Lea]

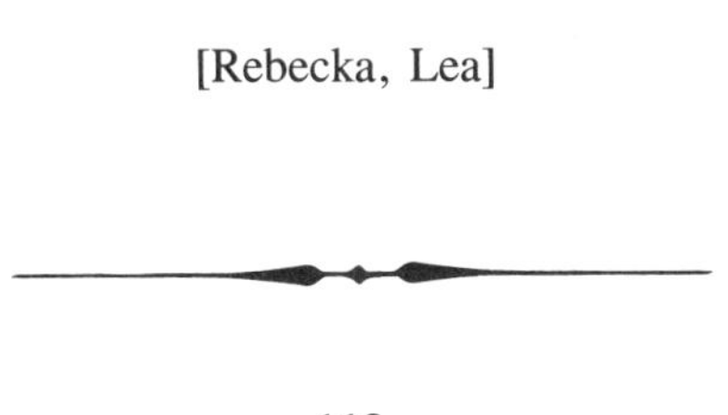

113

Berlin, 8ten Mai 39.

Ich will Dich nicht länger ohne Nachricht lassen, lieber Felix. Es ist Gottlob, Alles wohl, Rebecka hat sich brav gehalten, u. diese überaus traurigen 8 Tage haben wenigstens ihrer Gesundheit nicht geschadet. So eben kommen wir von Gans Beerdigung zurück. Studenten trugen ihn den langen Weg, eine unabsehbare Menschenmenge, die ganze Universität, u. Alles was ihm kannte, folgte zu Fuß. Er liegt auf dem Oranienburger Kirchhof nah bei Hegel u. Fichte. Seit Schleiermachers Tode habe ich solche Sensation nicht gesehn. Es ist nicht zu sagen, wie viel jeder seiner Freunde verliert, wie überaus wichtig er grade hier war, mit seiner seltenen Freimüthigkeit, mit seinem unermüdlichen Eifer, der überall durchzugreife[n][a] wußte, wo es recht war u. Noth that. Er war aber auch ein sehr glücklicher Mensch, wie wir in diesen Tagen vielfach besprachen. Er hat fast nie ein Unglück, oder nur eine ernste Widerwärtigkeit erfahren. Alles,

Annerkennung so wie Opposition war für ihn ein Gegenstand der Freude, u. er hat sein Leben so recht nach allen Seiten hin genossen. Unstreitig fingen seine Kräfte an, zurückzugehn, u. so kann man ihn wol selig preisen, daß er dahingegangen, bevor diese Abnahme ihn selbst bemerklich u. schmerzlich ward. Wenn man das Leben nicht nach Tagen u. Jahren mißt, sondern nach dem, was seinen Werth ausmacht, so hat er ein langes Leben geführt.

Lebe wohl bester Felix, mögen diese bewegten Tagen Dich u. Cecile nicht allzusehr angreifen. Ich denke immer noch daran, wie Du vor drei Jahren nach 8 Tagen noch nicht ausgeschlafen hattest. Hoffentlich hören wir bald von Euch. Aus Frankfurt haben wir einen Brief erhalten. Lebt wohl, grüßt Woringens.

Eure Fanny

[Rebecka]

---

[a]Fanny omitted the "n" at the end of this verb.

114

München, 23sten September 39

Ich muß Dir vor unsrer auf morgen festgesetzten Abreise noch danken für Dein schönes Rezept zur italiänischen Reise, bester Felix. Ich werde ihm bestens nachzuleben suchen. Was die Portraitgallerie in Florenz betrifft, so habe ich Deine Bemerkungen darüber nur einmal gelesen, weil ich beabsichtige, meinerseits auch dergleichen anzustellen, u. sie dann zu vergleichen, nur Einiges, was sich seiner Wahrheit wegen zu tief eingeprägt hat, werde ich wol abschreiben, denn daß Rafael herrlich, u. Carlo Dolce ein Narr ist, wer möchte das bezweifeln? Was ich Dir ferner erzählen will, ist, daß ich Delphine Handleys Bekanntschaft gemacht habe, u. mit sehr großem Vergnügen. Sie ist eine allerliebste Person, u. ein vortreffliches Talent. Dein erstes Concert habe ich, außer von Dir, noch nicht so spielen gehört. Wir gingen zu ihr, u. fanden sie so überaus freundlich, wie ichs Dir gar nicht sagen kann, wir machten gleich etwas Musik, u. sie luden uns auf den andern Abend zum Thee ein, wo sie uns eben jenes Concert ganz glorios vorspielte. In welchem Andenken Du im Hause stehst; das ist ganz unbeschreiblich. Sie wissen jedes Wort, das Du gesprochen, jede Bewegung, die Du gemacht hast. Was mir an ihrem Spiel noch besonders gefallen hat, das ist ihr geistreiches Präludiren, das findet man so selten bei Frauenzimmern. Ich sage Dir, sie hat mir tausendmal besser gefallen, als der keuchende Dreyschock. Mein Mann hat sie gezeichnet, worüber sie ganz entzückt war.

Deine Lieblinge auf der Pinakothek habe ich wol behalten, u. mir aufgesucht. In ihrer jetzigen Gestalt aber kennst Du sie noch nicht. Etwas Prachtvolleres, als die beiden Rubenssäle, die 95 Bilder von ihm enthalten, wird es wol nicht leicht irgendwo geben. Man muß erstaunen, über diesen gewaltigen Geist. Erinnerst Du Dich denn des Portraits der Frau v. Vandyk, mit ihrem Kinde? Die Frau sieht so vornehm aus, u. fein, u. ein bischen traurig, u. ein klein bischen langweilig. Und seines Portraits eines Antwerper Organisten? Das ist ein ganz ähnliches Bild aller Tenoristen, man meint, er müsse gleich singen: dies Bildniß ist bezaubernd schön, u. sich selbst damit meinen. Und der junge, blonde Vandyk selbst ist auch nicht so übel. München ist eine interessante Stadt. Wir sind nun 14 Tage hier, u. haben eigentlich nur nothdürftig alles gesehn, wir könnten sehr gut das doppelte hier brauchen. Denn was für neuere Kunst, u. Kunstgewerbe hier geschieht, ist im hohen Grade wichtig u. bedeutend, die Glasmalereien, die Fresko- u. Wachsgemälde, die Gebäude, die gehauene u. gegossene Skulptur, die Porzellanfabrik, alles ist in seiner Art neu u. wichtig. Du kannst Dir denken, wie es meinen Mann interessirt hat, so Vieles Neue in seinem Fach zu sehn, u. die Künstler wiederzusehn, die er meist von Rom aus kannte. Ich kannte keine Seele hier, u. habe also meinem Kopf nicht wenig voll von neuen Sachen und Menschen, es ist aber immer angenehm, einmal wieder zu erproben, daß man in der Fremde gern gesehn, u. freundlich aufgenommen wird. Die Glyptothek haben wir nur ein einziges Mal, u. obenein flüchtig gesehn. Aber der Herbst treibt uns über die Berge, u. wir haben die höchste Bergfahrt vor, die man, mit Extrapost, in der ganzen Welt machen kann, wir wollen über das Stilfser Joch. Du weißt, welche Passion ich von meiner Jugend an hatte, einmal solche Straße zu sehn, u. jetzt soll es mir zu Theil werden, u. mein Mann einen ihm noch ganz neuen Theil v. Italien kennen lernen. Hoffentlich sind wir nun in 4-5 Tagen aus der sehr empfindlichen Münchner Herbstluft heraus, u. im Frühling drin. Wir gehn über die Seen nach Mailand, u. wenn wir schönes Wetter bekommen, so wird es eine einzig herrliche Reise werden. Wenn Du oder Cecile in diesen Tagen nach Berlin schreibt, so bitte ich Euch, Ihnen zu bestellen, daß sie sich nicht ängstigen sollen, wenn sie etwas lange nichts von hören.[a] Es wird vielleicht 8 Tage dauern, ehe wir schreiben können, u. da wir uns zugleich in starken Tagereisen entfernen, so braucht der Brief um so längere Zeit. Es ist doch ein eigne[b] Gefühl, so über die Alpen aus dem Vaterland zu gehn. Ich denke es mir ähnlich, als wann man über die See geht. Dagegen ist eine flache, willkürliche Grenze nichts. Wenn Du Frank siehst, lieber Felix, danke ihm für seinen Brief. Lascia passare haben wir uns leider, vor der Hand nicht verschaffen können, u. werden also zunächst der östreich. Douane verfallen. Ein gutes Geduldsübungsmittel. Liebe Cecile, Hebaba, u. Tata[r], u. [Orja] grüßen u. küßen das süße Carlchen. Halt Du Dich wol, mein liebes Herz, u. laß uns zu rechter Zeit Gutes hören. Bis circa 20sten Oktbr. schreibt uns poste restante nach Venedig. Adieu geliebten Geschwister!

Eure Fanny

---

[a]The word "uns" omitted by mistake.
[b]The "s" ending is omitted.

115

Rom, den 1sten Januar 1840

Mein erstes Geschäft im neuen Jahr soll seyn, Euch, Ihr lieben Geschwister einmal wieder zu schreiben, denn ich habe so lange nichts von Euch gehört, daß ichs nicht recht mehr aushalten kann. Von Cecilen habe ich noch gar keinen Brief seit ihren Wochen gehabt, u. von Felix seit Venedig nicht. Nun schenke Euch Gott frohe Zeit, und erhalte Euch Euer Glück in diesem Jahr, wie in allen kommenden, und lasse uns Alle, bald und froh wieder zusammen treffen. Schreibe mir doch, lieber Felix, ob wir Hoffnung haben, Euch bei unsrer Rückkehr in Berlin zu treffen oder ob wir Euch in Leipzig, oder Frankfurt, oder irgend wo anders suchen müssen, denn sehn *müssen* wir uns in diesem Jahr, ich muß das süße Carlchen sehn, u. mein erstes Nichtchen kennen lernen.—Hier leben wir recht sehr angenehm, wir haben eine behagliche, sonnige Wohnung, bis jetzt fast beständig das schönste Wetter, u. sehn, da wir keine Eil haben, die Schönheiten Roms mit aller Muße, nach und nach. Nur von Musik habe ich, seit ich in Italien bin, noch nichts Erbauliches gehört. Die päpstlichen Sänger habe ich 3mal gehört, einmal in der sixtinischen Kapelle am ersten Adventssonntag, einmal ebendaselbst am Weihnachtsheiligabend, und

Weihnachten in der Peterskirche. Eigentlich, muß ich Dir sagen, bin ich erstaunt gewesen, die Ausführung nicht vollkommener zu finden. Sie scheinen grade jetzt keine besondern Stimmen zu haben, u. singen durchaus nicht rein. Ich hatte bis jetzt immer nicht Gelegenheit gehabt, mich vorher zu unterrichten (was ich zu Ostern gewiß nicht versäumen werde) was, u. von wem gesungen würde, da habe ich denn nur auf den Klang gehört, u. der hat mich eben nicht recht befriedigt. Man kann sich nicht so geschwind von seinen gewohnten Vorstellungen losmachen. Eine Kirchenmusik in Deutschland, mit einem Chor von ein Paar hundert Sängern, u. verhältnißmäßigen Orchester, fällt nicht nur das Ohr, sondern auch noch die Erinnerung so an, daß mir die Paar Sänger, namentlich in den weiten Räumen der Peterskirche, sehr dünn vorkamen. In den Musiken sind mir einige Stellen als schön aufgefallen. Namentlich am Weihnachtsvorabend eine, wo, nachdem sich die Stimmen lange einzeln hingeschleppt hatten, ein lebhafter, 4stimmiger, fugirter Satz in a moll eintrat, der sehr wohl that. Ich hörte nachher, es sey der Moment gewesen, in dem der Papst in die Kapelle trat, denn von den Ceremonien sehn die Frauenzimmer leider gar nichts, da sie hinter einem Gitter, weit ab sitzen, u. die Luft überdies von Kerzen u. Weihrauchdampf verfinstert wird. Die Functionen in der Peterskirche am Weihnachtstage konnte ich dagegen, wenigstens theilweise, sehr gut sehn, und fand sie sehr prächtig und unterhaltend. Einen Weihnachtsbaum hatten wir natürlich, Sebastians wegen aufgebaut, von Cypressen, Myrthen u. Orangezweigen. Die Zweige waren wol schön, aber es fehlte doch am Besten, u. ich hatte den Tag mit Sebastian um die Wette Heimweh. Mein Mann, liebe Cecile, hat mir ein sehr schönes Schränkchen mit Elfenbein eingelegt, geschenkt, u. ich ihm eine Skizze von Paul Veronese, die ihm sehr gefiel, u. die er selbst ein wenig zu restouriren denkt, denn das hat sie nöthig. Man sieht hier gar zu schöne Dinge, besonders Alterthumskram, aber auch die Marmorarbeiten u. geschnittenen Muscheln reizen mich sehr, wenn nur nicht alles so erschrecklich theuer wäre. Rom soll in dieser Hinsicht sehr verloren haben, besonders seit vorigem Jahr, wo Alles überfüllt war, u. die Römer die tollsten Preise gefordert u. erhalten haben. Dies Jahr soll es eben so in Neapel seyn. Mit Schadows sind wir viel zusammen. Er sieht sehr krank aus, erholt sich aber doch hier, u. klagt weniger, als im Anfang. Es freut mich, Dir sagen zu können, daß sie freundlich gegen uns waren, u. Du kannst wol glauben, daß wir es von Herzen gern erwidert haben. Schadow freut sich, wenn ich ihm vorspiele, u. findet, daß es ihn einigermaßen an Dich erinnert, er ist Dein sehr warmer Freund. Der alte Santini läßt Dich sehr grüßen, u. bitten, Du möchtest ihm ein Stückchen Manuscript schicken. Der gute alte Mann besucht uns öfters, u. erzählt von seinem Steckenpferd, seiner Bibliothek. Alle mögliche Damen haben mit Entzücken von Dir gesprochen, u. mir mit Stolz erzählt, Du hättest sie besucht, u. ihnen vorgespielt, Du kennst sie aber gewiß nicht mehr dem Namen nach, u. ich will auch Cecile nicht kränken, u. von Luise Nitschmann sprechen. Aber Deinen Rath muß ich jetzt haben. Da Du nicht nach Wien gegangen bist, mir also kein Instrument hast aussuchen können, sage mir, wie ichs anfangen soll, um eins zu bekommen? Ich habe bei Landsberg eins gespielt, von "Felix Groß" in Wien, das mir, besonders das erstenmal, sehr gefallen hat, es hat einen vollen schönen Ton, u. eine gute Spielart, obgleich, wie alle Wiener, nicht sehr präcis. Nun hatte ich aber in Monaten, nichts gehört u. gespielt, als die erbärmlichsten Klapperkasten, so daß ich nicht zu entscheiden wage, wie viel dieser Umstand zu meiner Zufriedenheit mag beigetragen haben. Kennst Du Instrumente v. Groß? u. räthst Du mir dazu? Und weißt Du Jemand in Wien, dem Du für die Auswahl vertrauen könntest? Ich muß Dir gestehn, daß mir Schunks Instrument, welches, wenn ich mich recht besinne, Hauser ausgesucht, gar nicht gefallen hat. Was sagst Du dazu? Bitte, antworte mir einmal ordentlich, geschäftsmäßig auf alle diese Punkte, denn ohne Deinen Rath mag ich doch nicht beschließen. Verzeih, daß ich Dir zu Deinen vielen Geschäften u. Störungen noch einige aufpacke. Solltest Du nicht Zeit haben, so bitte, trage Cecilen auf, was sie mir darüber schreiben soll, mit deren Zeit habe ich schon weniger Mitleid, u. sie hätte mir wol schon einmal schreiben können. Aber bitte, thu es bald, ich möchte doch gern, wo möglich, ein Instrument finden, wenn wir nach Berlin kommen, u. über dem Hin- u. herschreiben u. Schicken vergehn reichlich die noch übrigen Monate unsrer Reise. Kannst Du mir solche Instructionen geben, daß ich von hier direct nach Wien schreiben kann, so will ich Dir gern die Mühe eines Briefes dorthin ersparen.— Findest Du auch, wie ich, Rom von jeder, auch der kleinsten Höhe, so wunderschön? Ganz entzückt war ich von der Aussicht beim Thurm der Cecilia Metella, u. finde überhaupt diese ganze Gegend überaus schön u. anziehend. Wir waren beim herrlichsten Wetter dort, wie auch neulich in der villa Mills, wo wir Alles blühend fanden; Millionen Rosen u. andre Blumen, dazwischen die herrlichen immergrünen Bäume, u. nach allen Seiten eine bezaubernde Aussicht. Das Clima genieße ich mit wahrer Wonne, ich kann Dir nicht sagen, wie wohl ich befinde; auch Sebastian bekommt es sehr gut, u. er sieht besser aus, als je. Wir sind außerordentlich mit ihm zufrieden, das Kind ist wirklich so liebenswürdig, wie man in seinem Alter nur seyn kann. Ich glaube, einen solchen Winter, wenn man ihn einmal gekostet hat, wird man ewig regrettiren, ich möchte wahrhaftig keine Italiänerin seyn, u. überhaupt nichts anders, als eine Deutsche, wenn wir aber unser liebes Vaterland ein wenig nach dem Süden rücken könnten, das wäre doch gar nicht so übel. Mutter schreibt mir gestern, sie hätten in Berlin am 19ten 12 Gr. Kälte gehabt, u. wir leben hier noch immer ohne Mäntel u. fast ohne Feuer. Das ist denn doch ein materieller Lebensgenuß, der mit zu den größten gehört. Und diese Vegetation das ganze Jahr hindurch! Jeden Tag sehe ichs, u. jeden Tag überrascht u. erfreut es mich von Neuem.

Lebe wohl, lieber Felix, küsse Cecile u. Deine Kinderchen von mir. Was arbeitest Du jetzt? Laß es mich erfahren. Mein Mann und Sebastian grüßen bestens.

Deine Fanny

116

Rom, 4ten März, 1840

Lieber, lieber pater, peccavi! aber es ist durchaus nicht meine Schuld, denn während ich Dich über Berlin schelten ließ, lag, oimé! hier auf der Post sechs, sage sechs Wochen lang, der schönste Brief eingepöckelt! Bis zu seiner Krankheit ging mein Mann oft hin, obgleich wir schon lange keine poste restante Briefe mehr erwarteten, sondern Euch Allen Valentini aufgegeben hatten, aber schon damals müssen sie ihn ihm vorenthalten, die asinacci! wie in Venedig, wo ich Ceciles Entbindung auch 8 Tage später erfuhr, als nöthig. Neulich nun, schicken wir einen Brief nach der Post, Kaselowsky brachte ihn hin, u. wir baten ihn, beiläufig einmal nachzufragen, u. zurück kommt der wunderschönste Brief, den ich sechsmal hinter einander gelesen, u. mich sechshundertmal dabei todtgelacht habe, Du siehst aber ich lebe noch. Du begehst wahrlich einen Raub an meiner Gesundheit, wenn Du mir nicht öfter schreibst, denn Du glaubst gar nicht, wie gesund es mir ist, mich krank zu lachen. Deine vortrefflichen Fragen und Rathschläge will ich der Reihe nach beantworten. Was ich in Rom treibe? Mich herum die ersten 2 Monate. Wir haben einen ordentlichen giro gemacht, u. sind noch lange nicht fertig. Den 3ten Monat meinen Mann gepflegt, u. nicht weiter gekommen als Monte Pincio, wo ich oft mit Thränen spazieren ging, weil ich spazieren gehn *sollte* u. mich doch so ängstigte und grämte. Dann kam Carneval, u. da mein Mann eben wieder anfing etwas vertragen zu können, so haben wir ihn mit vielem Plaisir mitgemacht, u. ich habe mich amüsirt, wie ichs nie gedacht hätte. Gestern Abend haben wir moccoli gehabt, u. nun ists aus, u. wir werden wieder anfangen uns ein wenig herumzutreiben, denn leider geht die köstliche Zeit auf die Neige, u. es muß noch viel, gar viel geschehn bis Ostern. Wohnen thun wir in der via del Tritone, die in piazza Barbarini ausläuft. Wenn wir um 2 Ecken gehn, sind wir auf der passeggiata auf monte Pincio, und die Nähe dieses sonnigen Spaziergangs mit erträglicher Aussicht war uns schon oft, besonders während Wilhelms Genesungszeit, sehr angenehm. Broccoli als Salat habe ich noch immer nicht gegessen, obgleich Du es mir schon zweimal zur Pflicht gemacht, verzeih diese Nachlässigkeit, ich habe ihn aber eben auf morgen bestellt. Gott, die Madame Tizian, im Palast Sciarra, liebe ich ja schon erschrecklich seit Florenz, wo sie in den Uffizien, leider nicht in der Tribüne, unter dem Namen Flora, mit einem weißen Hemde u. einer Handvoll Blumen hängt, u. eben so viel von einer Göttin als von einem Racker hat. Ferner ist sie zu schauen im Palast Barbarini, mit einer Haarperücke à la Bellin, einem vollgesprengelten Kleide, (Mein Mann sagt, das hat er mit seinem Blut gemalt) u. einer dicken, herabhängenden Kette, (mein Mann sagt: daran liegt Tizian) u. gar keinem abgewelkten Gesicht, aber böse sieht die schöne Kröte aus, und hat ihm gewiß das Leben sauer und süß gemacht. Woher sollte ich armes Thier wol alle Kardinäle kennen? Ich bin ja kurzsichtig u. komme gar nicht in die sixtinische Kapelle hinein, u. auch in der Peterskirche dem Heiligthum der Kappen u. Schweife, gar nicht nah. Ich sehe die Herren nur, wenn ihre Schweife ihnen aufgewickelt werden, u. dann sehn sie nichts weniger als schön aus. A[m] vi. Von päbstlichen Quinten habe ich schon Weihnachten eine deutliche Anschauung bekommen, das ist ja immer der refrain.

Wenn das nicht Quintissime sind, dann weiß ichs nicht. Sonstige Kirchenmusik habe ich nur erst einmal in St. Maria Maggiore gehört, wo die vera cella angedudelt wurde, ich habe aber genug. Die Nonnen auf trinità wollte ich aus Schwesterliebe gern hören, man kommt aber jetzt schwer hinein, u. ich werde mich einmal hinter meine fromme Cousine stecken müssen.— Vorgestern fand hier ein Fest welches, was das Local betrifft, wol einzig in seiner Art war, eigentlich ein Ball auf dem Kapitol, zum Besten der Cholerawaisen. Man fuhr hinauf durch das Forum, welches mit unzähligen Fackeln erleuchtet war, in deren Schein die alten Säulengeister ganz eigen schauerlich und phantastisch dastanden. Der Kapitolplatz selbst mit dem Marc Aurel u. den Dioskuren sah auch prachtvoll aus in dem Fackellicht. Leider regnete es in Strömen, bei mondhellem Abend müßte der Anblick noch unendlich prächtiger gewesen seyn. Ueberhaupt war der Karneval gar nicht vom Wetter begünstigt, die ersten Tage hatten wir bitterböse Tramontane, u. zuletzt Regenwetter. Selbst der Moccoliabend mußte mit Regenschirmen begangen werden, hat mich aber dennoch unendlich amüsirt. Das Wesen ist so toll, daß es wieder poetisch wird, die zahllosen beweglichen Lichter, das tolle lustige Geschrei, die so vielfach beleuchteten Maskenkleidungen, die beständigen Angriffe die man abzuwehren suchen muß, die Bemühungen, die ausgelöschten Lichter, wieder anzustecken. Alles das verwirrt Einen so, daß man zuletzt nicht mehr weiß wo Einem der Kopf steht. Eine ganz besondre Virtuosität haben die Italiäner im Aussprechen des "senza moccolo", welches von allen Seiten ertönt, sobald sich Jemand ohne Licht, oder mit ausgelöschtem Licht sehn läßt, Spott, Verwunderung, Mitleid, tiefstes Bedauern, Frage, Triumph, Alles legen sie hinein, und es ist zum Todtlachen, wenn man so von allen Seiten angebrüllt wird. Dagegen ist das: sia ammazzato, welches Goethe gehört hat, nicht mehr Mode.

Hillers Entschluß, in Leipzig fleißig zu seyn, macht ihm alle Ehre. Grüß ihn recht sehr von mir, u. sage ihm wie leid es uns war, ihn nicht in Mailand zu treffen. Wir haben überhaupt auf dieser Reise Pech mit Menschen gehabt. Eine ganze Saison in Rom zu seyn, und nicht eine einzige Person von großer Auszeichnung zu treffen, ist doch wirklich schade. Voriges Jahr war Liszt vier Monate hier, wie gern hätte ich den ungarischen Magneten gehört! Hast Du je etwas Lächerlicheres gehört als diese Säbelumgürtungsgeschichte? Lablache hätte sich auch wol können von mir in Italien hören lassen, ich fürchte sehr, er, oder ich werden Alle, ehe ich ihn kennen gelernt habe. Halt! was für ein Psalm von Dir ist denn jetzt aufgeführt? Kommt, laßt uns anbeten, oder, als Israel aus Egypten zog? Nimm Dich nur in Acht, daß der europäische Congreß nicht meint, Du habest Ibrahim im Sinn gehabt, als der aus Egypten zog, um die Schlacht bei Nisib zu schlagen. Antworte mir aber ernstlich darauf, u. auch auf das Piano, ob ich eins von Felix Groß Bürger in Wien, nehmen soll? Von Graff möchte ich keins, sie sind zu leicht, u. ich habe eben an einer Mme. Hensel hier ein warnendes Beispiel gesehn, wie man sich verwöhnen kann. Die Frau hat drei Monat lang einen alten leichten, ausgespielten Klapperkasten gehabt, u. nun ein andres, gewöhnliches Wiener Instrument bekommen, ich habe sie gestern gehört, u. ich versichere Dich, sie kann gar nicht drauf fort, sollte sie gar in einiger Zeit nach Leipzig kommen, so würdest Du sehn, daß sie nicht mehr spielen kann: aller Anfang *ist schwer*. Ach und componiren! Ich habe es erst eben nach Berlin geklagt, daß mir gar nichts mehr einfällt, nichts Gutes u. nichts Schlechtes. Dio mio! Abraham wird alt! Nun gehe ich aus Deiner Stube hinaus, u. zu Cecilen. Guten Tag, lieber Schatz! Wenn ich noch Platz hätte, würde ich Dich schelten, daß Du so viel pumpst, schreiben sollst Du, öfter, oft, daß mir Deine Briefe lieb u. erfreulich und interessant sind, kannst Du schon glauben. Die schönsten Kindergeschichten von Carlchen, z. B. muß ich über Berlin erfahren. Tante Hund hat mich sehr ergötzt. Ich gratulire zum Pianino. Wenn ich Dich einmal wieder besuche, wollen wir stille Musik zusammen machen. Das ist doch noch ein schönes Geschenk! Ich bin hier aber auch sehr hübsch beschenkt worden. Von Elsasser habe ich eine sehr schöne Oelskizze u. eine prächtige Federzeichnung bekommen, Catel malt mir auch etwas. Außerdem haben wir uns selbst mit mehreren Sachen beschenkt, an denen Ihr auch wol Vergnügen haben werdet, wenn Ihr sie einmal seht. Hoffentlich aber finden wir Euch in Berlin, u. Gott gebe, daß wir Alle da gesund zusammentreffen mögen, am Vergnügen soll es dann nicht fehlen. Mit diesem frommen Wunsch will ich schließen, und Dich bitten, uns allen Schunks zu empfehlen, auch sonstigen Leipziger Freunden. Und bitte, bitte! schreibt bald wieder, Ihr glaubt gar nicht, was es uns für Vergnügen macht. Mein Mann und Männchen grüßen bestens. Eure Fanny.

Kaselowsky bittet, ihn Dir lieber Felix angelegentlichst zu empfehlen.

117

Rom, 10ten Mai 1840.

Liebster Felix, ich danke Dir für Deinen lieben lustigen Brief vom 7ten April, es war mir um so lieber, durch Dich Deine Reise nach Berlin erfahren zu haben, als der Brief aus Berlin, der mir Deine wirklich erfolgte, glückliche Ankunft anzeigte, unbegreiflicher Weise fast 3 Wochen unterwegs geblieben ist, so daß ich schon anfing, mich zu ängstigen. Ihr seyd grade im rechten Augenblick nach Berlin gekommen (für uns freilich nicht) denn nach Woringens Abreise, u. bei Beckchens Zuständchen, fürchteten wir, es möchte ein wenig zu still im Hause werden, bis wir, als neue Leute, neues Leben, u. neue Geschichten mitbringen könnten. Wenn ich nur absähe, wenn wir uns sehn können, u. wo! Ich habe mein Auge auf Frankfurt geworfen, das wir jedenfalls passiren werden, u. das Ihr doch auch wahrscheinlich nicht liegen lassen werdet. Lieber wäre es mir freilich, wir träfen uns in Leipzig, Euch da zu Hause, u. unsre Reiseschlange bisse sich in den Schwanz, u. Ihr gäbt uns wieder ein Paar Tage Quartier. Es verlangt mich herzlich, Euch zu sehn, u. mit Dir unsre Reise durchzusprechen. Ich kann Dir gar nicht ausdrücken, wie glücklich wir uns hier fühlen, wie unbeschreiblich es mir gefällt. Wir haben unsere Aufenthalt hier noch bis Ende des Monats verlängert, u. ich sehe mit Gram die Zeit unter den Fingern verrinnen, wir konnten uns wirklich nicht trennen, u. auch jetzt thut mir das Herz weh, wenn ich an die Abreise denke. Zum Glück steht uns noch Neapel bevor, worauf ich mich denn freilich auch nicht wenig freue. Wir denken nur ganz kurze Zeit in der Stadt selbst zu bleiben, u. die Excursionen von Castellamare aus zu machen, wie man uns mehrfach gerathen. Vielleicht läßt sich dabei auch Zeit zu einigen Seebädern erübrigen. Wir haben hier einige Wochenlang ein Wetter gehabt, daß es eine Wonne war, sich in der Luft zu befinden, u. sie einzuschlucken, während dieser Zeit haben wir fleißige Spazierfahrten in der Campagne gemacht, die ich nicht mehr lieben könnte, wenn ich ein Maler wäre, u. neulich auch einen köstlichen Tag in Tivoli zugebracht. Das Albanergebirg steht uns noch bevor. Das habe ich nun den ganzen Winter in seiner unendlichen Lieblichkeit da liegen sehn, oft Umwege gemacht u. Höhen erstiegen, um es nur zu sehn, wenn ich es ein Paar Tage nicht vor Augen gehabt hatte, u. empfinde doch gar keine Ungeduld, hinzukommen. Ueberhaupt bin ich nun lange genug in Rom, um das eigentliche Reisefieber ganz los zu seyn, ich sage schon mit Zelter, ich bin zu jung, um Alles zu sehn, u. wenn man auf den Punkt gekommen ist, dann fängt der Genuß erst an. Ich werde gewiß Manches nicht gesehn haben, wenn wir abreisen, aber die Lieblingspünkte immer wieder, u. Genuß u. Freude habe ich hier gehabt, in Fülle. Heut über 3 Wochen sind wir in Neapel, so Gott will, da wird es uns wol auch nicht mißfallen.

Die Lisztsche Zeit in Leipzig hätte ich wol erleben mögen. Hier höre ich erstaunlich viel von ihm reden, er war voriges Jahr 4 Monate hier, mit Ingres u. den musikal. Pensionairen befreundet, wie wir, u. da erzählen sie mir denn immer von ihm. Es thut mir sehr leid, ihn nicht getroffen zu haben, denn er muß hier besonders menschlich gewesen seyn, u. hat keine Concerte gegeben, sondern bei sich gespielt, u. bei Ingres, was soviel man wollte. Er hat 2 seiner Arrangements Beethovenschen Symphonieen an Ingres zugeeignet, u. ihm dieser Tage geschickt. Wenn ein toller Regen, der seit vorgestern Nacht fast ununterbrochen strömt, so gut seyn will, nachzulassen, so gehn wir heut Abend hin, u. ich sehe mir das tolle Zeug an. Hier sind sie entzückt von der Art, wie er die Symphonieen v. B. spielt, Du scheinst es weniger zu seyn. Ich bin neugierig, Dich erzählen zu hören, wie das eigentlich ist. Das Concert von Bach hätte ich hören mögen von Euch dreien. Denke Dir, daß ich es diese Woche auch spielen werde, mit einer Dänin u. einer Italiänerin, Beide recht gute Clavierspielerinnen, es wird aber doch einiger Unterschied stattfinden. Ich sage Dir, die Franzosen bewundern jetzt nichts, als *Bacque*, es ist zu komisch. Das Concert aus d moll habe ich wenigstens schon ein Dutzendmal spielen müssen, u. sie möchten sich immer auf die Köpfe stellen vor Entzücken. Auch für Dich sind sie ein vortreffliches Publicum, u. das muß man ihnen nachsagen, zuhören thun sie gut u. angenehm, u. behalten nach 1maligem Hören, wie man es nur verlangen kann. Der alte Santini quält mir die Seele aus, so oft er mich sieht, Du sollst ihm Musik schicken, ich werde ihm etwas hier lassen müssen, was ich von Dir mitgebracht habe, ich sehe er läßt mich sonst nicht fort. Er ist aber ein gut alt Männeken, bei Weitem der Leidlichste unter den Langweiligen hier. Denn das ist die Schattenseite von Rom, die vielen, unausstehlich ennüyanten Leute, besonders unter den Offiziellen, u. namentlich wieder unter den offiziellen Deutschen. Gott! was für Leute! doch still, ich habe meinem Mann versprochen, brieflich über Niemanden zu raisonniren, mündlich aber lasse ich mir das Maul nicht stopfen, u. da Beckchen hier fehlt, muß ich Charivari und Figaro in einer Person seyn. Doch bin ich hier in besonders rosenfarber Laune, u. lasse Manche u. Manches gelten, was zu Hause schwerlich Gnade fände. Ich glaube, die Luft flößt mir etwas von ihrer unendlichen Milde ein.—

11ten Der Regen ließ gestern richtig nach, wir waren auf der Academie, u. ich habe die Lißzt-Beethoven-Ingreschen Symphonieen gesehn. Sehr gut ist, daß er in der Vorrede sagt, er wolle dadurch beitragen sie zu popularisiren, wenn das der musikal. Popülus oder Pöbel jemals spielt, so laß mich hängen! Bei allem dem Apparat zweifle ich keinen Augenblick, daß Du sie zehnmal schöner spielst. Ich gratulire zum glücklichen Gelingen von Hillers Oratorium. Wenn Du Dir einmal mit mir so viel Mühe giebst, so mache ich auch eins. Daß ich den Buchdruckerjubel nicht irgendwo in Deutschland erlebt, thut mir wirklich leid. Wenn eins, so ist das ein schönes Fest, u. das Drucke auf offner Straße entzückt mich. Ich möchte mal sehn, wie die Mönche hier so ein Fest begingen, gewiß mit einem Requiem. Hast Du hier eine große Messe bei den Armeniern gehört? Das ist die schauderhafteste Katzenmusik, die meine Ohren je gehört, u. Miau! war auch das einzige Wort, das deutlich zu verstehn war. Dabei haben die Leute so schöne ernsthafte Köpfe, u. der Bischof ist ein so ehrwürdiger Greis, daß man nicht weiß, ob man sich wundern, oder die Leute bedauern soll, die ihren Gott auf eine so menschenfresserische Weise angrunzen. Dagegen singen die Griecher sehr gut. 3stimmige Männerchöre, ordentlich komponirte Musik, rein, stark u. sicher vorgetragen, weit fester, als die päpstlichen Sänger, die das Miserere beidemal in h moll anfingen, u. einmal in g, einmal in f moll schloßen. Darüber müssen wir auch noch viel sprechen. Wenn Spontini nicht schon Vorschläge zur Verbesserung der

Kirchenmusik gethan hätte, so würde ich mich mir Sr. Heiligkeit in Rapport setzen, denn eine Verbesserung thut wahrlich Noth, u. da Magnus, der Ketzer, einen Kardinal malt, so kann man gar nicht wissen. Ich höre, Otto Nicolai hatte [die] Absicht, Director der päpstlichen Kapelle zu werden, Katholik u. Priester, was man dazu seyn muß, das war er Alles willig auch zu werden, das war ihm alles Wurscht. Da der Plan aber mißglückt ist, hat er sich der Oper in die Arme geworfen, u. ist jetzt in Turin. Wenn Hiller im Juni nach dem Comersee zurückgeht, so ist es sehr möglich, daß wir ihn im Juli dort sehn, wir waren nur einen Tag am Comersee, noch dazu bei Regenwetter, u. es ist so himmlisch schön da, daß wir wohl, wenn es sich machen läßt, von Mailand aus noch Como sehn möchten, wo wir nicht waren. Es ist übrigens unmöglich, bei *einer* Reise nach Italien Alles zu sehn, wenn man auch noch so viel Zickzack fährt, Parma u. Perugia, was mein Mann Beides noch nicht kennt, werden wir wol diesmal auch aufgeben müssen. Es ist zu fatiguant, mitten im Sommer durch ganz Italien zu reisen, 6 Tage allein von Rom nach Florenz, u. wir werden deshalb, wenn Sebastian u. ich es nur irgend ertragen können, von Neapel nach Livorno dämpfen.—Liebes Cecilchen, habe Dank für Deine lieben Zeilen aus Berlin. Sie schreiben mir so viel Böses von Dir, u. Du sollst so häßlich jetzt aussehn, daß ich ordentlich ungeduldig bin, Dich zu sehn, um mich zu überzeugen, ob das Alles wahr ist. Auch Deine Kinder kann kein Mensch im Hause leiden, das muß Dir nun besonders unangenehm gewesen seyn. Das Talent zum Singen hat Carlchen in meiner Abwesenheit ausgebildet, der Junge muß jetzt zum Fressen seyn. Auf die Bekanntschaft meines ersten Nichtchens bin ich sehr gespannt. Was es nun heuer für Kinder in Berlin geben wird? Kein Brief ist gekommen, der mich nicht von neuen Hoffnungen unterrichtet hätte, nächstes Jahr wird Alles kribbeln u. wibbeln. Lebt nun wohl, geliebten Leutchen! Hoffentlich fällt kein Schnee, bevor wir uns gesehn. Nach dieser Reise ist es mir noch mehr Bedürfniß als sonst. Mein Mann grüßt herzlich. Er ist fleißig beim Studienmalen, u. bringt einige sehr schöne Köpfe mit. Wir sind jetzt Gottlob Alle gesund, u. seitdem erfreue ich mich eben gar so sehr meines Lebens. Du weißt, lieber Felix, was für ein Luftfisch ich bin, u. kann Dir denken, mit welcher Wonne ich diese Himmelsluft athme. Nach einigen Regentagen hat es sich heut wieder aufgeklärt, u. wir können nun wieder dem herrlichsten Wetter entgegen sehn. Es ist jetzt für uns eine solche Zeit, in der man jede Minute lebendig fühlt, in der jede Stunde einen Pulsschlag hat, den man versteht. So ist es mir auch, wenn wir mit Euch, Lieben zusammen sind. Möge es bald wieder geschehn!

Eure Fanny.

118

Berlin, 28sten September 1840

Lieber Felix! dieser Brief soll Dich empfangen wenn Du aus England zurückkommst, u. damit Du Dich nicht übereilst, ihn zu lesen, will ich Dir gleich jetzt sagen, daß gar nichts drin stehn soll, nur etwas Geplauder. Ich will Dir einen guten Rath geben, wie Du mir mehrere nach Rom. Wenn Du wieder nach Italien reisen willst, suche Dir ein Werk darüber zu verschaffen, das ich jetzt eben mit großem Interesse gelesen habe, u. das mir besser gefällt, als Alles, was ich je über diesen vielbeschriebenen Gegenstand gelesen, es wird aber etwas schwer halten, es Dir zu verschaffen, denn es ist meines Wissens noch rarer, als die Nibelungen von Decker, die nur in 106 Exemplaren, u. die Ausgaben englischer Großen, die nur in 3. oder 4 existiren, es giebt nämlich nur ein einziges Exemplar davon, im Manuscript, u. wir sind in dieser Beziehung nicht besser dran, als vor der Erfindung der Buckdruckerkunst. (eine zeitgemäße Bemerkung.) Es sind mit einem Wort, die Briefe eines reisenden Musikanten, der nebenbei mein ältester Bruder ist. Ich kann Dir gar nicht ausdrücken, wie mich die Briefe interessirt haben, jetzt, wo mir Alles so frisch vor der Seele steht, was Dich vor zehn Jahren bewegte. Wer übrigens dran zweifeln möchte, daß zehn Jahre eine lange Zeit sind, der braucht nur Briefe zu lesen, die so alt sind. Es ist schrecklich! Wie wenig von allen darin genannten Menschen u. Verhältnissen übrig ist. Alles gestorben, verdorben, auseinander. Man muß Gott danken, wenn nur das zusammen Gehörige auch wirklich zusammen bleibt, u. sich nicht von einander trennt, es scheide denn der Todt. Und darauf habe ich denn, wenn ich mich recht besinne, eigentlich kommen wollen, u. Dir einmal wieder sagen, wie ich mich Deines Lebens u. Webens freue, u. wie gut es mir gefällt, daß wir zufällig Geschwister geworden. Mein Gott, ich möchte ja gern stolz seyn auf meinen Bruder wenn ich nur vor lauter Behaglichkeit u. Freude dazu kommen könnte. Ich meine, innerlich, denn, daß ich gegen Fremde stolz darauf bin, versteht sich von selbst. Es ist wirklich ein arger Fehler in unserm Leben, daß wir nun schon zehn Jahre, u. wahrscheinlich auch unser übrige Lebenszeit nicht zusammen zubringen, sonder höchstens alljährlich ein Paar Tage, wie gestohlen, in Eil u. Hast, da es uns doch Allen nicht schaden könnte, wenn wir zusammen wären. Das ist noch das Leidlichste an Berlin, daß es wenigstens nur eine Tagereise von Leipzig ist, Dresden gefiele mir aus dem Grunde noch weit besser, weil es viel näher ist, wenn ich mir nun täglich u. stündlich Rom zurückrufe, u. mir denke, wie herrlich wir da gelebt, u. wie gern ich einmal auf längere Zeit zurück möchte, so muß ich gleich dabei denken, wie ich Euch dann gar nicht mehr sehn würde. Und so ist in der Welt nicht alles Wünschenswerthe zu vereinigen. Aber das muß ich Dir im Vertrauen sagen, da ich Dir gern Alles sage, wie wir uns Beide noch gar nicht wieder in Berlin finden kommen. Rom hat Dir ja denselben Eindruck gemacht, wie uns, denn[a] einer Ruhe u. Bewegtheit zugleich, die Ruhe war uns auch sehr auffallend u. erquicklich, u. nun kann ich Dir gar nicht sagen, wie uns das scharfe Berliner Wesen, die harte, trockne Kritik über Alles, empfindlich gewesen ist, u. noch ist! Wenn es mir nur wenigstens dazu dient, mein Theil daran, dessen ich mir wol bewußt bin, loszuwerden, wie ich den besten Willen dazu habe. Das ist ein böser Thema! Wie freut es mich, daß wir in so vielen Dingen übereinstimmen, was Italien betrifft. Namentlich ist der Eindruck von Rom ganz derselbe gewesen, auch im Verhältniß zu Neapel, obgleich ich finde, daß Du dem doch im Ganzem ein wenig Unrecht thust, denn die Schönheit ist doch gar zu göttlich da! Auch über Florenz u. namentlich die Gallerie, u. Rafaels Portrait sprichst Du ganz meine Gedanken aus, nur besser, als ich sie hatte. Aber über zwei Bilder in der Tribüne sind wir verschiedener Meinung. Das weibliche Portrait v. Rafael Fornerina genannt, hat Dir nicht gefallen, Du findest etwas Ordinaires darin, u. v. der Venus v. Tizian sagst Du, es würde Dir fromm vor Schönheit dabei. Das ging mir nun grade umgekehrt, die Venus von Tizian ist mir etwas zu toll, u. das Portrait von Rafael finde ich so über alle Maaßen schön, daß ich mich nie dran habe satt sehn können. Wilhelm sagt, er sey wieder andrer Meinung, u. ihm gefielen sie Beyde über alle Maaßen. Der Mann hat am Ende recht.

Wenn man so alte Zeit in Briefen wieder erlebt, u. da sieht, wie manche Befürchtung, wie manche Sorge man gehabt, die Einem die schönsten, theuersten Stunden verbittert, u. wie dann das Befürchtete ausgeblieben, dagegen so manches geschehn, worauf man gar nicht gerüstet war, wenn man dann weiter denkt, wie das immer so fort geht, wie ich jetzt die 5 Tage in Leipzig gar nicht genießen können, weil mich die Sorge um Deine Reise nach England fast verzehrt, wie nun diese Reise jetzt zum größten Theil schon so glücklich zurück gelegt ist, u. Dir statt Unheil, Freude u. Vortheil gebracht hat, wenn man überzeugt ist, daß *das leben* heißt, so sollte man wirklich nach einigem Leichtsinn trachten, um das was man eben hat, fröhlicher zu genießen u. um die Zukunft unbesorgt zu seyn, die eben deshalb fast immer anders kömmt, als man sie erwartet, weil man sie nicht ergründen kann und soll. Aber das ist auch Gabe, wie Alles andre, wer sie hat, soll sie nicht ausbilden, denn sonst wird er wie Backhausens, die eben hier sind, in 14 Tagen nach Mexico abreisen, u. davon sprechen, wie wir von einer Fahrt nach Charlottenburg, Potsdam kommt uns schon ernsthafter vor. Die wilden Kinder wollen sie an langen Stricken angebunden herum laufen lassen, damit sie nicht über Bord fallen, und zu alle dem lachen sie, es ist wirklich glücklich, das Leben so leicht nehmen zu können.

Ferner muß ich Dir sagen, wie es mich amüsirt hat, daß wir Alle, um die Zeit Deiner Abreise von hier, Jeanpaulisirten, u. wie Du Dir nach u. nach in Rom einen ganz eigenthümlichen, Felixschen Styl herausgeschrieben hast, ich glaube fest, dieser Brief schmeckt wieder ein bischen nach der alten Zeit, da ich mich so mit Lust wieder hinein gelesen habe. Was kann uns Menschen glücklicheres begegnen, als wenn wir uns der Unsrigen freuen u. rühmen dürfen, u. was bin ich darin glücklich, ich mag nun meines Mannes, oder meiner Eltern u. Geschwister im weiten Sinne, denken. Cecile gehört auch nicht wenig dazu, lieber Felix, u. so oft ich sie einmal wieder gesehn habe, kann ich Gott nicht genug danken, für die Güte, die er Dir bewiesen, indem er Dich unter allen Frauen, die es giebt, die hat finden lassen, die am Meisten für Dich paßt, u. Dich am Glücklichsten machen kann. Und eben so dürfen wir mit Vertrauen weiter hinaussehn, Dein Carlchen ist ein lieber Engel, u. unsre Jungen hier sind auch gar gute, prächtige Kinder. Ich wollte, Du sähest sie jetzt zusammen, es ist wirklich eine Freude, sie könnten nicht mehr an einander hängen, wenn sie Brüder wären, sie sind unzertrennlich, u. haben sich noch nicht ein einziges Mal gezankt. Nächste Woche kommen sie zusammen in die Schule, freilich nicht in eine Classe, aber sie freuen sich doch sehr drauf. Wenn man sie so Arm in Arm in den Garten gehn sieht, ist es wirklich eine Freude.

Jetzt habe ich mir Dein Trio vorgenommen, u. übe es, es ist aber sehr schwer. Wenn ich einmal wieder anfange, Musik zu machen, soll es das Erste seyn. Es ist mir aber noch gar nicht danach zu Muth. Ich bin sehr verwöhnt worden, auf der Reise, durch ein überdankbares Publicum beständig zum Spielen getrieben u. aufgefordert zu werden, bald um Dieses, bald um Jenes gebeten, u. immer in Athem erhalten, das läßt man sich gar zu gern gefallen, es ist aber unrecht von mir, ich muß das nicht nöthig haben, u. will auch durchaus suchen, drüber weg zu kommen. Es ist aber doch ärgerlich, daß Niemand hier ist, mit dem man so recht Musik machen kann, vielleicht wenn Woringens kommen.

Nun kann ich doch aber unmöglich einen Brief abschicken, in dem gar nichts steht, also will ich Dir wenigstens sagen, daß Albertine in die Stadt gezogen ist, u. sich sehr wohl befindet, Beckchen wartet. Die Buchdrucker haben hier eine klaterige, nachträgliche Feier gehabt, u. eine sehr hübsche Ausstellung, in der u. A. eine Gutenbergsche Bibel zu sehn ist, unsre Kunstausstellung giebt viel zu reden, nämlich leider sehr wenig, u. werde ich den Bericht darüber in meinem nächsten Stück nachliefern. Ich versichere Dich, wenn man aus verschiedenen Gründen Antheil an der Kunst nimmt u. nehmen muß, u. etwas mehr Spleen als Freude am Leben hätte, könnte man sich nach solcher Kunstausstellung todtschießen. So viel Unwahres, Nachgeäfftes, Breitgetretenes, u. so wenig Erfreuliches, habe ich leider noch nie hier beisammen gesehn. Das liegt an Vielem, hauptsächlich aber daran, daß sie in Deutschland Alles todthetzen, u. daß jede Stadt von drei Einwohnern jetzt wenigstens eine Ausstellung von vier Bildern haben will.—Mit solchem Rabengeschrei will ich aber nicht schließen, sondern mit der Bitte an Cecile, uns einige Details über Deinen Birminghamer Aufenthalt zu geben, da Du selbst wol gleich wieder von Geschäften überhäuft seyn wirst. Lebt wohl Ihr liebsten [Leute], lieber Felix, finde diesen langen Brief, worin gar nichts steht, nicht gar zu dumm, ich mußte einmal wieder mit Dir plaudern, u. Dir mein schwarzes Herz zeigen. Sind die beiden Julien wieder eingerückt? Wie geht es Ceciles Schwester u. Mutter. Mein Mann grüßt herzlichst u. ich bin Eure

Fanny

Ich muß Dir noch in Eile erzählen, wer gestern Sebastians Partner im Bocciaspiel war, u. eine Partie gegen ihn verlor, kein andrer als Bökh; ist das nicht sehr komisch? Dirichlet ist auch jetzt ein wüthender Bocciaspieler, u. fordert alle Menschen dazu auf.

---

[a]Fanny wrote "denn" instead of "den."

119

Berlin, 9ten Decbr. 1840

Lieber Felix, ich will Dir sogleich Bericht erstatten, wie ich Deine ochsige Commission ausgeführt. Erstlich sah ich im Adressbuch nach Rungenhagens Sprechstunde (Heinrich Beer hat auch eine) u. da ich fand 7. 8. Morgens u. 4 Uhr Nachmittags, so mußte ich versuchen, ob er wohl auch zu einer andern Stunde sprechen könne, denn von 7. 8 ist meine Schlafstunde, u. 4 meine Freßstunde, ich ging also getrost nach dem Caffee diesen Morgen hin, geschmückt mit allen Reizen, die die Jahreszeit bietet, als: item: eine rothe Nase, mit item einem Eiszapfen dran, etc, u. warf mein Anliegen auf den Herrn Rungelhägelchen, u. der erhörete mich, u. war sehr graziös, u. meinte, er u. Alles was er besaße, wäre zu Deinen u. meinen Diensten. Gerathe jetzt aber nicht in Wuth, weil Du glaubst, ich dächte, diese Partituren gehörten ihm, ich weiß recht gut, es war nur eine Redensart von mir; sie gehören Zelter auch nicht, sondern der Academie. Da ich nun in der Nebenstube Schülerinnen quietschen hörte, sagte ich, (ich besitze nämlich Lebensart) ich wolle ihm das Verzeichniß der Sachen zuschicken u. wolle ihn nicht ferner stören, er aber: ich lasse Dich nicht, schreibe nur hier die Titel auf, u. darauf schmiß ich ihn aus Höflichkeit heraus zu seinen Schülerinnen, nachdem er mir Papier u. Feder angewiesen hatte. Eine Feder aber sage ich Dir, die war so grob! daß Zelter in seinen gröbsten Stunden höflich dagegen war, dur konnte man allenfalls damit schreiben, aber moll gar nicht, u. dann lag ein blauer Lappen auf dem Tisch, damit wischte ich sie ab, sie war früher noch niemals abgewischt worden, auch glaube ich, seitdem sie der Gans ausgerissen worden, noch nicht geschärft. Kurz mit der Feder schrieb ich Alles auf, Breneus ist da, und ein Flutenconcert wahrscheinlich auch, u. hoffentlich wirst Du Alles zur bestimmten Zeit bekommen können, das ich indessen nicht gewiß versprechen kann, da ich nicht der Notenschreiber bin, u. wenn ich er wäre, würde es *viel* länger dauern. Als ich wegging, sah ich auf dem Clavier stehn Lieder ohne Worte, dem Frl. v. Woringen zugeeignet, "sehet, welch eine Liebe."—Als ich den Name Nitschmann in Deinem Briefe las, freute ich mich schon, denn ich dachte, Du wolltest dem armen L___chen wirklich was zu verdienen geben, ich stehe noch immer in Relation mit ihr, u. werde sie wahrhaftig nächstens wieder Noten schmieren lassen, denn sie ist eben so scheuslich,[a] aber eben so elend, wie jemals, und Suppenmarken und eine wollene Jacke wont do.

Paul schreibt Dir wie ich höre, noch, daß er heut plötzlich nach Hamburg reisen muß, das ist eine recht verdrießliche Geschichte, seit wir zurück sind, waren wir doch noch nicht ein einziges Mal Alle zusammen. Wann werden wir einmal wirklich Alle zusammen seyn, das heißt auch mit Euch? Ich mag wohl sagen, ich sehne mich danach, Dich einmal anders, als blos so lange zu sehn, um guten Tag u. adieu zu sagen, u. seit drei Jahren sind wir nicht anders zusammen gewesen. Aperçus willst Du? Erblickungen? Blicke? Die Jagd mit Siegfrieds Tode giebt ein prachtvolles 2tes Final, der dritte Akt muß mit Chriemhild u. ihren Frauen anfangen, wie sie aus ihrer Thür tritt, u. den todten Siegfried da findet, daraus kannst Du eine Polonaise mit Chor machen. Sollte Sir übrigens für den Erfolg der Oper bange seyn, so würde ich als captatio benev. von einem Doppelchor von Hunnen und Nibelungen, "sie sollen ihn nicht haben," nach der Melodie von "ei du lieber Augustin", singen lassen, so:

sie
sollen
ihn
nicht
haben

Ist das nicht wunderschön daß die hannov. Censur das Lied verbietet, u. der Kronprinz es komponirt? Adieu! Sonnabend habe ich Dir geschrieben, warum hast Du denn Montag noch nicht den Brief gehabt? Leb wohl, grüß Cecile u. den Engel v. Carlchen. Mein Mann grüßt bestens. Deine Fanny

---

[a]Fanny mistakenly wrote "s" instead of "ß."

120

Daß Rungenhagen ein dicker Esel ist, u. ein gehörnter dazu nicht im Stande, 3 Namen in seinem dummen Kopf zu behalten, bezeuge ich hierdurch mit meiner Namensunterschrift. Der Rest dessen was Du verlangt hast, u. was nicht in der Bibliothek der Academie seyn soll, will ich noch heut drin suchen. Ich bin gestern in eine schwer zu beschreibende Berserkerwuth gegen ihn gerathen. Dein Psalm ist göttlich! das Breiteste was Du gemacht. Lebwohl! Der lieber Gott duldet allerhand Gethier in seiner Langmuth, darunter sind die Beherrscher der Singacademie einige der Nutzlosesten. Die Post wartet nicht. Adieu.

121

Berlin, 13ten Januar 1841

Lieber Felix! ich hätte Dir gar zu gern nicht eher wieder geschrieben, als bis ich Dir den Rest der von Dir bestellten Sachen hätte zuschicken können, 3 Partituren hast Du doch durch den Prof. Puchte richtig erhalten? Allein es wird mir zu lange u. mein Gewissen treibt mich, mich wenigstens bei Dir zu entschuldigen. Nimm es mir ja nicht übel! ich habe es diesmal falsch u. dumm angefangen, u. entziehe mir Deine Aufträge nicht, ich will sie gewiß ein andermal mehr zu Deiner Zufriedenheit auszuführen suchen. Wenn Du nur durch diese fatale Verzögerung nicht in Verlegenheit geräthst, dann wäre ich untröstlich. Bitte, schreibe mir ein Wort, sage mir, ob Du auch nicht böse bist, u. ob ich Dir einzeln schicken soll, was ich habe, bis jetzt das Violinconcert. Mein Instrument habe ich nun seit 14 Tagen, u. es hat Sonntag Vormittag sein Probestück vor versammelten Publicus mit allgemeinem Beifall abgelegt. Ich habe nun freilich dies u. das daran auszusetzen. Die mittleren Octaven:

sind merklich schwächer als das Uebrige, namentlich als der sehr schön u. vollklingende Baß, u. dann hat es den Fehler, an dem, an den Dein erstes englisches auch litt, man hört bei p spielen etwas neben dem Ton, das sehr unangenehm klingt. Trotz dessen muß ich sagen, es ist ein gutes Instrument, besser als die hiesigen, die mir nun ein für allemal nicht gefallen, besser als die Graffschen, Pauls z. B. klingt unglaublich klapperig u. schlecht nach so kurzem Gebrauch, nicht so gut als die *besten* Streicherschen, aber bei Weitem besser als das, was er für Schunk geschickt hatte, u. was blieb mir anders übrig, da wir nicht 1000 rh für ein englisches ausgeben können? Das Deckersche ist pracht[voll], dagegen kommt Einem freilich alles Andre gerin[g] vor, sie ist sehr glücklich darüber.—Ich wollte, ich könnte Euch jetzt einmal in unsre Wohnung führen, es ist gar zu hübsch jetzt bei uns. Die ganze blaue Stube mit mitgebrachten, alt u. neuen Bildern ausgeschmückt, u. außerdem in jedem Winkel angenehme Reiseerinnerungen. Jeder freut sich darüber, wer zu uns in die Stube tritt.—

14ten Januar. Gestern Abend kam Dein vortrefflicher Brief mit Sendung. Du Rachsuchtiger Mensch! der nie vergessen kann, daß ich einmal vergessen habe! Deine vortrefflichen Rathschläge, was Tempi u. Vortrag betrifft, werde ich gewiß nicht verloren gehn lassen, u. versuchen, es nächsten Sonntag heraus zu bringen. Habe schönsten Dank dafür. Daraus sehe ich denn auch, daß die Andere Euch schon von unserer Zimmeraufputzerei geschrieben haben, u. daß ich einmal wieder wiedergekäuet habe. Die Sonate v. Beeth. werde ich ohne Frage mit Eckert spielen. Habe Dank für die Cadenz, sie ist sehr interessant. Du willst mir also nicht erlauben, sie als Beilage zu meiner musikal. Zeitung zu gebrauchen? Sebastian hat v. Henry Schlesinger zu Weihnachten die Musikschule v. Moscheles u. Fetis bekommen (Beckchen behauptet, was wir ordentliches hätten, käme von Henry) u. da habe ich mit Vergnügen einen alten Bekannten expreß für die Methode komponirt, gefunden. Ich schicke nun also mit nächster Fahrposten, was ich habe. Das Flötensolo von Fritzen habe ich immer noch nicht auftreiben können, ich werde damit von Pontius zu Pilatus geschickt. Indessen hoffe ich bald dazu zu gelangen.

Lebe also wohl, grüß Cecile, der Gott eine glückliche Stunde schenke, u. küß die englischen Bälzer, deren Concert ich lieber hören möchte, als manches Andre.

Addio.

Wenn Ihr diesen Winter Deine Symphonie Cantate nicht mehr braucht, kannst Du mir nicht durch Fahrpost oder Gelegenheit die Partitur u. circa 20 St. schicken? Ich will auch Grell um die Tempi fragen.

122

Berlin, 29sten Januar 1841

Lieber Felix! nachdem ich Dir die Nachricht gegeben, daß Rebecka sich wieder einen Zahn hat ausziehn lassen, u. nun sich wohl befindet, Gott gebe auf lange! denn es war gestern einmal wieder ein schrecklicher Tag! will ich Dir von Eckerts Oratorium berichten, das mich doch sehr überrascht hat, ich finde es für das Alter namentlich, ein sehr schönes Werk. Um zuerst auf le moral, wie der Franzose sehr französich sagt, zu kommen, so war der Saal etwa halb voll, u. er wird knapp auf seine Kosten gekommen seyn, war indeß, als wir ihn nach der Aufführung sprachen, sehr vergnügt. Die Chöre gingen vortrefflich, höchst brillant u. lebendig, das Orchester, so so lala, von den Solosängern war Mantius u. Böttcher sehr gut, alles

Andre schlecht, u. leider die Hauptpartie höchst kläglich, so wie denn bekanntlich jetzt alle unsre Sängerinnen tragisch, komisch, brillant u. solide, durch die einzige Faßmann repräsentirt werden, der arme Eckert war auf die Hofkunz angewiesen, u. die that was sie kann, sie kann aber leider blutwenig. Seine Schule verläugnet Eckert eben mich,[a] es hat uns sehr amüsirt, wie er Dein Dirigiren, man kann eben nicht sagen, kopirt, aber sehr gut angenommen hat, er hat es äußerst hübsch gemacht, sah nett dabei aus, u. war voller Leben, was ich ihm früher am Wenigsten zugetraut hätte. Du mußt ihm etwas göttlichen Odem in die Nase geblasen haben. Was nun die Musik selbst betrifft, da begegnet man Dir auf jedem Schritt und Tritt, das finde ich aber ganz recht, da es selten zur förmlichen Nachahmung wird, u. da es doch auch an originellen Zügen, u. sehr guter, tüchtiger Arbeit nicht fehlt, das meiste Fehlerhafte drin scheint mir jugendlich, u. ich glaube gewiß, er ist auf dem besten Wege, Dank sey es Dir, den er denn auch wahrlich anbetet. Ich glaube, er wäre zur Stunde schon ein recht tüchtiger Dirigent.

Sonntag hab ich, wie Du bereits von Mutter wissen wirst, Deinen Psalm singen lassen, der nach 2 Proben überraschend gut ging. Es war ein, für die blaue Stube, imposanter Chor von 25 Personen versammelt, u. er ist grade jetzt sehr gut komponirt, so daß es wirklich mächtig klang. Wir nahmen ihn zu Anfang, u. mußten ihn am Schluß wiederholen. Wie freue ich mich darauf, Deinen Lobgesang einzustudiren! Bekomme ich ihn bald? Glaube mir, daß es mir höchst empfindlich ist, Deinen Auftrag wegen der Musik so schlecht ausgeführt zu haben. Was ich nun noch erhalte, werde ich zurück behalten, da Du es doch vor der Hand nicht mehr brauchen kannst, u. bitte nur: straf mich nicht in Deinem Zorn, sondern glaube, daß ich durch Schaden klug geworden bin, u. ein andermal meine Sache besser machen werde.

Der Luise Nitschmann habe ich, hoffend, daß Ceciles Eifersucht nicht bei Nennung ihres Namens von neuem erwachen wird, in Deinem Namen für einen rh. Holzmarken gegeben, u. werde, wenn Du nichts dagegen hast, in einiger Zeit dasselbe thun. Von uns bekommt sie Suppenmarken u. Arbeit u. so kann sie wenigstens existiren. Wenn es uns gelänge, aus diesem elenden Gerippe wieder eine menschliche Gestalt herzustellen, so könnten wir wirklich sagen, wir hätten ein gutes Werk gethan. Leb wohl lieber Felix, beste Grüße an Cecile, u. die Kinderchen.

Eure forever Fanny

---

[a]Fanny may have meant "nicht" instead of "mich," as the latter does not make sense here; "nicht" is assumed for the translation.

123

Berlin, 2ten März 1841.

Es ist wol in den Jahrbüchern unsrer Correspondenz noch nicht da gewesen, daß ich erst in der dritten Woche auf einen Deiner Briefe geantwortet hätte, lieber Felix, aber bei uns stand Alles auf dem Kopf, oder war vielmehr, wie Humboldt sagt, horizontal. Als Dein Brief ankam, lagen wir Beide, mein Mann u. ich, krank zu Bette, ich habe mich rasch wieder herausgemacht, mein Mann aber war recht übel dran. Dann kam die Reihe an Beckchen, und an meinen armen Bax, der zehn Tage mit offnen Frostwunden an beiden Füßen dagelegen, u. erst seit vorgestern wieder einigermaßen auf den Beinen ist. Er hat sich diesen Grad des Uebels meist durch seinen Fleiß zugezogen, da er schon die letzten 14 Tage nur mit Mühe nach der Schule hinkte, u. dennoch nicht zu bewegen war, auch nur einen Tag zu fehlen, er hat nun 8 *Primus*stellen eingebüßt, u. wenn Du Dich noch aus Deiner Schulzeit erinnerst, was das für einen Jungen heißen will, so wirst Du Dich nicht wundern, daß es bittre Thränen kostete, als wir ihn endlich zwangen, zu Haus zu bleiben. Der Winter ist aber auch endlos hart u. böse, ich versichere Dich, die Schneemassen, die wir nun schon seit vier Monaten ununterbrochen im Garten liegen sehn, ermüden meine Seele, [?] noch mehr als meine Augen. Noch jede Nacht gefrorne Fenster, am Tage ein bischen nothdürftiges Thauwetter in der Sonne, doch ihr werdet wol die nämliche Klage zu führen haben, u. aus Euern Fenstern mag es diesen Winter auch wüst genug ausgesehn haben. Uebermorgen findet wieder ein sogenanntes Dilettantenconcert statt, ziemlich als moutarde après diner, da doch hoffentlich die größte Noth für diesmal vorüber ist. Ich werde Dein Trio spielen, eigentlich hätte ich sollen für den Concertsaal die Serenade wählen, aber die liegt mir gar nicht fingerrecht, u. ich habe sie noch nicht können spielen lernen, während das Trio, das vielleicht nicht weniger schwer ist, mir bequem liegt, u. da ich das öffentliche Spielen doch gar nicht gewohnt bin, so muß ich dazu etwas wählen, das mich nicht beunruhigt. Diese Sorge wird übermorgen beseitigt seyn, dann kommt eine große Andre. Ich weiß nicht, ob eins der Geschwister Dir schon geschrieben hat, daß wir zu Mutters Geburtstag eine fête monstre beabsichtigen, wozu wir drei Familien uns vereinigen wollen. Nun ist bekanntlich nichts schwerer, als dergleichen zu allseitiger Zufriedenheit zu arrangiren, wo Viele mitzureden haben, u. unter uns gesagt, ich fürchte, wir fallen uns noch in die Haare, vor dem 16ten März.

Wie ist es aber mit Euch? kommt Ihr? wann kommt Ihr? Die Gartenwohnung über uns, die Paul für den Sommer gemiethet hat, steht zu Euerm Empfang bereit, sobald Ihr Euch meldet.—Wenn Du bedauerst, unsre Sonntagsmusiken nicht zu hören, so bedaure ich wol mit etwas mehr Recht, Eure Concerten nicht zu hören, Deinen Lobgesang hätte ich gar zu gern einmal mit Orchester gehört. Wenn Du übrigens herkommst, soll Dir die beste Sonntagsmusik vorgeritten werden, zu der ich fähig bin, obgleich ich schon heut sehe, wie ich mich ängstige, u. gar nichts anzufangen weiß, u. Dich zu allem um Rath frage, obgleich ich mich recht gut zu behelfen weiß, wenn ich allein bin. Weißt Du denn gar nichts Neues für meine Sonntage? Nächstens will ich einmal die Lieder von Spohr mit Clarinette zum Vorschein bringen, denn mein Orchester, dessen Hauptgeiger Alevin zu werden droht, hat sich um den jungen Herrn Gareis, des alten Herrn Gareis ältesten Sohn u. Clarinettisten, vermehrt. Wäre nur ein ordentlicher Geigerdilettant da! Mit Deinen Rechnungen hat es ja Zeit, bis Du herkommst.

Und nunmehr lebe wohl! Carl liefert die schönsten Kindergeschichten, die es nur giebt, daß er den Prediger zur Ruhe verwiesen, vergess ich ihm nie. Grüß Cecile, wie freue ich mich, wieder einige Zeit mit ihr zuzubringen, denn wir Alle nehmen mit Gewißheit an, daß Ihr Alle herkommt u. dann wollen wir ein vergnügtes Leben haben. Lebt Alle wohl!

Eure Fanny

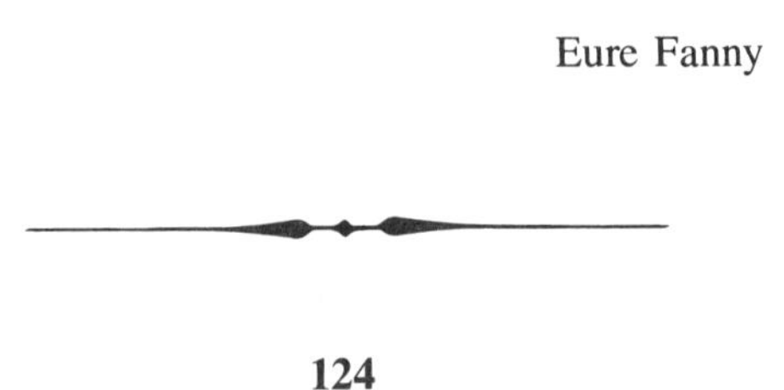

124

Berlin, 13ten Juli 1841

Wenn man zu danken, und zu gratuliren hat, so muß man Feder, Dinte u. Papier, diese Eselsbrücken der Abwesenheit, zu Hülfe nehmen, da man noch immer das Volk ist, das im Dunkeln wandelt, u. nicht weiß, wann es Dich, großes Licht, zu sehn bekommen wird. Ich dachte, nun wäre es mit dem Schreiben für einige Zeit vorbei, aber nein.—Ich gratulire also, Herr Musikd'me, daß Du jetzt die höchste menschliche Würde nächst dem Hofrath u. Papst erreicht hast, Kapellmeister ist ein hübscher Titel, insofern er wenigstens anzeigt, was für eine Art von Mensch man ist, während ein Dr. eben so gut ein Zahnbrecher, oder Accoucheur, Gott sey bei uns! seyn kann.—Was nun den Dank betrifft so sage ich ihn Dir erst recht herzlich für Dein bittersüßes Reiselied, wovon Du mir hier schon eine u. die andre Wendung vorgespielt hattest. Mit den Liedern von der Lang nun ist es wieder einmal komisch gegangen. Mehrere Tage vorher hatte mir Trautwein ein Pack neuer Sachen geschickt, u. just den Tag ehe Paul zurück kommt, spiele ich es durch, finde, nach vielen Neuigkeiten, bei denen ich nicht über die ersten zehn Takte fortkommen kann, die Lieder der Lang, die mir so gut gefallen, daß ich sie spiele u. wieder spiele, u. mich nicht davon trennen kann, u. sie endlich bei Seite lege, um sie zu behalten, den ganzen Tag habe ich, besonders das eine Altlied, gesungen u. allen Leuten davon erzählt, da kommt Paul den andern Morgen, u. bringt sie mir von Dir. Es war mir ordentlich angenehm, daß mich das Schicksal diesmal davor bewahrt hatte, ein Papagei zu seyn, wenn ich Dein Urtheil über etwas kenne, bin ich immer ungewiß, ob ich nur nachfinde, oder wirklich auch finde. Die Sachen sind so recht musikalisch in tiefster Seele, die Modulationen oft so sinnreich u. eigen, daß ich große Freude daran habe. Wenn ich sie in München kennen gelernt hätte, würde ich ihr gewiß schreiben, um ihr das auszusprechen.—Hier haben wir jetzt die Pasta, die um dabei anzufangen, eine sehr liebenswürdige, freundliche, einfache, wirklich angenehme Frau ist. Auf der Bühne habe ich Norma, u. einige Scenen aus Othello u. Semiramis von ihr gesehn. Norma war, schon als ganze Vorstellung, bei Weitem das Bedeutendste. Ich kann Dir nicht sagen, wie freudvoll u. leidvoll mir dabei zu Muthe war. Ihre Meisterschaft ist ganz außerordentlich, die Nüancen in der Stimme, namentlich ein gewaltiges Crescendo, ihre Art Rezitativ vorzutragen, deren Du Dich ja gewiß erinnerst, einzig, die nobelsten u. geschmackvollsten Verzierungen, (die aus Othello, welche Du damals aus Paris schriebst, habe ich wohl behalten u. unverändert wiedererkannt,) nun aber haben die Mängel der Intonation, die sie immer soll gehabt haben, dermaßen zugenommen, daß sie, namentlich in den tiefern Tönen fast fortwährend zwischen einem 8tel u. einem 4tel Ton zu tief singt, was das für eine Qual ist, das kann man nicht aussprechen. Es ist so arg, daß man zuweilen ganz in Verwirrung geräth u. nicht mehr weiß, was man hört. Nun muß man sich also fortwährend über dies Leiden hinwegarbeiten, um zur Bewunderung ihrer Größe zu gelangen, daß dabei kein eigentlicher Genuß stattfinden kann, denkst Du Dir wol, u. doch hatte sie in der Norma Momente, die ich nie vergessen werde. Ihre hohen Töne sind übrigens viel reiner, u. je länger sie singt, je mehr klärt sich ihre Stimme. Daher sind auch (daher paßt hier gar nicht, setze ein anderes Wort dafür) ihre größten Enthusiasten die nicht-Musikalischen, z. B. mein Mann, der förmlich böse wird, wenn mich ihr unrecht Singen stört.—Beckchen hat gestern wieder sehr wohl u. vergnügt aus Heringsdorf geschrieben, auch der Mama gefällt es sehr dort.

Gestern früh habe ich Woringens auf die Post begleitet, die auf einige Monate nach Liegnitz reisen, jeden Tag fast fällt etwas von unserm Kreise ab, u. wir haben diesen Sommer nicht die mindeste Reiselust, Italien hält noch vor, u. wird es bei mir wol noch lange.

Ich höre von einem neuen Psalm von Dir, der wunderschön seyn soll, u. von ernsthaften Variationen, auf die bin ich denn sehr neugierig.—Adieu, lieber Felix, lebe wohl, grüße Cecile u. die süße kleine Heerde, auf Wiedersehn!

Deine Fanny

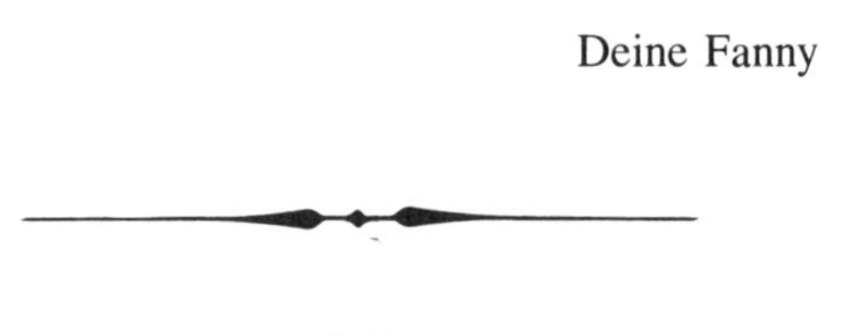

125

Berlin, 5ten Decbr. 1842

Ich habe recht lange versäumt, Dir, lieber Felix, für Deinen lieben Geburtstagsbrief, und die sehr willkommne Lodoiska zu danken, u. kann eigentlich nichts zu meiner Entschuldigung anführen, als die verschiedenen Zweckämpfe, die seit einigen Wochen von Jedem im Hause gegen die Husten, Hals- u. Zahnschmerzen, Nasenbluten, u. was weiß ich, was sonst noch für Ungethüme von Gegnern geführt worden sind, u. woran mein Theil mich unfähig macht, einen Brief wie Du es nennst, zu schleudern, so daß ich ganz zufrieden bin, wenn die Feder nur stille ihren Weg schleicht. Doch hat mich das Nasenbluten diesmal lange nicht so heruntergebracht, wie voriges Jahr, eine tüchtige Erkältung hilft jetzt nach. Dazu haben wir seit gestern einen ganz englischen Nebel, der zugleich die Luft verfinstert, u. in Tropfen niederfällt, die wahre lange Nacht, die jetzt den kürzesten Tagen noch auf die Beine hilft. À propos von englisch, was sagst Du zu der Weltgeschichte, die dort wieder gemacht wird? China u. Kabul mit derselben Post, das ist fast unverschämt. Ihre Verhältnisse sind so kolossal, daß Einem Alles andre dagegen wirklich wie Schulbegebenheiten vorkommt, ich finde, wenn man eben an die englische Weltstellung (verzeih das Wort, ich weiß nicht gleich ein unbedeutenderes, was dasselbe sagt) gedacht hat, muß man darauf erst an das heutige Mittagessen denken, wenn man irgend etwas anders der Mühe werth halten soll, zu geschehen. Ich muß mir nur immer vorstellen, wie bodenlos der Kaiser des Reiches der Mitte, u. seine ste[illegible]pröckige Armee sich muß gegrault u. gewundert haben, als die barbarischen Krebse ihnen so auf den Pelz rückten; es mag wol schwer seyn, das Wort auszusprechen, das eine vieltausendjährige Consequenz umbringt. Der englische Gesandte, der Dich jedesmal, wenn er mich sieht, aufs härtlichste grüßen läßt, nahm die Glückwünsche, die ich ihm neulich deshalb abstattete, Alle für sich, da man ein Regiment nach ihm benannt. Das schien ihm für den Augenblick doch noch wichtiger, als Kabel[a] u. Tischin-Kiang-Fu.—Die Austin ist hier, u. wird den Winter über bleiben. Ich wünsche recht, daß es ihr hier gefallen möge, ich habe sie sehr gern. Sie ist doch ein Blaustrumpf im besten Sinn.—Du hast die Oper von Lachner gehört, schreibe mir doch, wie sie Dir gefallen hat, u. auch, was Du von Rienzi gehört hast, Lachners Oper scheint ja nicht recht durchgreifen zu können. Der Clavierauszug v. Halevy seiner mißfällt mir sehr. Recht gemeine Motive mit großer Prätension u. unendlicher Länge ausgelegt. Meyerbeer ist auch wieder hier. Warum wird denn sein Prophet niemals une vérité? Na, u. Fanny Elsler habe ich auch gesehn, u. kann von den großen Fortschritten nicht viel finden. Habe aber, NB. keinen Nationaltanz gesehn, sondern ein Characterballet, Blaubart, in dem ich ihr eigentliches Spiel sehr manierrt u. unschön (ihren Anzug ganz abscheulich) aber ihre Tänze sehr leicht, anmüthig u. sicher, ganz nach ihrer frühern Art, gefunden habe. Man sieht, sie ist eine größere Virtuosin, als die andern, aber in demselben Prinzip. Es ist auch wirklich unwahrscheinlich, daß eine Tänzerin zwischen 30. u. 40 noch so große Fortschritte sollte gemacht haben.—Da wir einmal bei modernen Productionen sind, so empfehle ich Dir, liebe Cecile, Thomas Thyrnau, wohlverstanden, Dir, nicht Felix, denn für Männer, ist das keine Kost, mußt Du aber einmal wegen eines Schnupfens, oder sonst aus einem Grunde, drei Tage zu Hause bleiben, so laß es Dir holen, u. ich glaube, Du wirst Dich dabei amüsiren. So haben wir Weiber hier wenigstens Alle gethan.—Daß es mit der Aufstellung des Bachschen Denkmals bis zu seinem u. Frühlingsanfang bleibt, ist mir ganz recht, hoffentlich kann ich dann dabei seyn, u. zugleich Deine Symphonie u. irgend etwas anders Gutes erwischen. Du willst den Leipzigern noch diesen guten Geruch neben vielen andern hinterlassen, u. ich gönne es Dir u. ihnen, obgleich sie jetzt wieder nicht wenig krähen, daß Du nun den Winter über noch dort bleibst. Grüße sie von mir, insofern sie Schunk, Schleinitz, David, etc. heißen, u. insofern sie Deine Kinder sind, küsse sie, das wird Dir wol kein Opfer seyn. Ich lasse Carl u. Marie sagen, ich hätte ein niedliches Kanarienvogel das sitzt im Fenster unter den Blumen, u. die beiden ausgestopften Vögel daneben, u. wenn sie wieder kommen, sollen sie auch eine neue Eisenbahn haben. Die Meinigen grüßen bestens, u. wenn ich im Nebel nicht mehr sehn kann, meinen Namen zu unterschreiben, so wirst Du mich wol ohnehin kennen.

---

[a]Fanny incorrectly spelled it ''Kabel'' this time.

126

Berlin, 17ten Januar 1842.[a]

Herzlichen Dank, mein bester Felix, für Deinen lieben Brief, und Deine freundliche Einladung, die wir mit allem Dank annehmen. Zuerst aber die Frage, Du hast doch gleich die Partituren erhalten? Ich habe sie angesichts Deines Briefs einpacken lassen. Was nun unser Zusammenkommen betrifft, so dürfen wir Dich wol kaum noch in diesem Monat erwarten, da Du gar nichts davon schreibst—wir stellen uns mit unserm Besuch ganz zu Deiner Disposition, Sebastian hat bis jetzt seine Bedingungen gehalten, so daß ich ihn sogar mit gutem Gewissen mitnehmen kann, auf seine Ferien können wir nicht warten, denn sie kommen erst kurz vor Ostern wieder, Hensel wird also, wenn es so weit ist, auf einige Tage Urlaub für ihn bei seinem Director nachsuchen, was nun ihn selbst betrifft, so soll ich Dich fragen, ob Du ihm wol zu Deinem Bilde sitzen könntest u. möchtest, dann wird er mit tausend Freuden mitkommen, aber ohne bestimmte Arbeit, das liegt außerhalb der Gränzen meiner Macht. Schreibe uns also, wann Du uns haben willst, wann Cecile uns brauchen kann, u. wenn dann nicht besondre Hindernisse eintreten, so kommen wir, zu Zweien oder Dreien. Meines Mannes Fuß ist zwar immer noch nicht ganz gut, aber er geht damit aus, u. in Kurzem, hoffe ich, soll es damit besser gehn.

Wir leben wie Ihr, still, Woche um Woche bei Dirichlets, u. uns des Abends. Wenn wir so über den Hof gehn, an der Treppe vorbei, die wir so viele Jahre täglich auf u. abgestiegen sind, das ist immer ein bittrer Moment, u. wenn die immer hellen Saalfenster dunkel da stehn. Wir haben gute Zeit gehabt, u. eine frohe Jugend, wie Wenige, u. es vergeht keine Stunde, in der ich nicht dankbar gerührt daran zurück dächte.

Uebrigens ist Berlin in diesem Winter unbeschreiblich graulich. Einbrüche sind ganz alltäglich, u. man erzählt sich die gräulichsten Details dabei, u. A. hat sich H. v. Webern Nachts mit 2 Spitzbuben in seinem Zimmer herumgebalgt. Dabei ist unser Haus jetzt so sehr einsam, u. namentlich das Gartenhaus nur allein von uns bewohnt, daß wir uns mehr als gewöhnlich einschließen, u. ich doch zuweilen das Gruseln nicht lassen kann, namentlich wenn es stürmt, u. Alles klirrt u. klappert u. rasselt, als wollte es Einem über den Kopf zusammen fallen.

Was Du mir von dem dänischen Componisten schreibst, ist ja sehr interessant, der wird sich gefreut haben über Deinen Brief. Es thäte Noth, daß wir einmal wieder ein großes Talent bekämen, es ist gar zu wenig

Nachwuchs da. Auf Deine Umarbeitung der Walpurgisnacht bin ich auch sehr neugierig. Du weißt, wie schwer ich aus Gewohnheit dieser Art herauskomme, ich will mir aber alle Mühe geben. Wenn Du mir nur mein schönes Alt-Solo hast stehn lassen, womit ich, als junge Frau, als alte Frau, so viel Glück gemacht habe, die Erinnerungen an solche Triumphe verwischen sich nicht.—Ich wußte gar nicht, daß Du so viel Sachen von mir hättest, um 2 Bände zu füllen, ich werde Dir gewiß, da Du es wünschest, wieder Material liefern, ich weiß ja ungefähr, was Dir gefällt.—Liebe Cecile, ich höre zu meiner großen Freude, daß es Deiner Julie so viel besser mit ihrer Gesundheit geht. Grüße sie mir recht herzlich, und sage ihr, daß ich sie *sehr* lieb habe. Sollte ich sie nicht bald sehn, so schreibe ich ihr, ich denke aber das Erstere. An Deine liebe Mutter habe ich in diesen Tagen geschrieben. Küsse mir die geliebten Kinder, Carl soll mir schreiben, was ich ihm u. Mariechen mitbringen soll, für Paul wird sichs finden. Adieu, Ihr Liebsten, lebt wohl, und behaltet uns lieb.

Eure Fanny

---

[a]Fanny mistakenly wrote 1842 for 1843.

127

Berlin, 2ten März 1843.

Wir sind glücklich angekommen, gut gefahren, gut genährt, Dank sey es Cecile, die uns unglaublich verproviantirt hat, zu unsrer Schande aber muß ich gestehn, wir haben fast Alles aufgegessen, wobei besonders Sebastian Wunder geleistet hat. Der Brief, lieber Felix, war den Abend vorher um 11 abgegeben worden. Es ist uns sehr wohl, ein Paar Tage in Eurer lieben Nähe gewesen zu seyn, schon die süßen Kinder so viel zu sehn, ist die größte Freude, die man genießen kann, u. ich denke an Jedes von ihnen mit ganz besondrer Zärtlichkeit. Habt Dank für Eure Gastfreundschaft, wie für Alles Gute, das Ihr uns erweist, u. besonders dafür, daß Ihr eben da seyd, das ist sehr schön von Euch.—Rebecka sitzt tief im Kramen u. Räumen, u. grüßt für heut herzlich. Sebastian, lieber Carl, hat gestern große Angst gehabt, wieder in die Schule zu gehn, das Leben bei Dir hat ihm gar zu gut gefallen. Alles grüßt sehr herzlich, u. ich thue desgleichen, da dieser Zettel nur eine telegraphische Depesche ist. Lebt wohl, liebe Cecile, schone Dich recht!

Eure Fanny

Felix, schreibe Memoiren!

128

Berlin, 28sten März 1843.

Ihr laßt so ganz u. gar nichts von Euch hören, daß ich einmal wieder anklopfen muß. Eigentlich warten wir jetzt schon täglich auf Nachrichten von Cecile, u. wahrscheinlich verschiebst Du auch aus dem Grunde das Schreiben von Tage zu Tage. Wenn es noch lange dauert, kommst Du doch am Ende mit dem Palmsonntag in Verlegenheit. Hier ist Alles beim Alten.

Seydelmann ist todt, wie Du wirst erfahren haben, u. somit denn das Theater für mich vor der Hand aus, ich werde so leicht nicht wieder Lust dazu bekommen, es sey denn, um den Berliozschen Erfolg mit anzusehn, von dem ich gewiß weiß, daß man nichts vorher wissen kann. In der Hauptmannschen musikal. Zeitung stand ein sehr hübscher Aufsatz über ihn, zu musikalisch für einen Philosophen, u. zu philosophisch für einen Musiker, von wem mag er seyn? Da wir nun einmal bei musikalischem Kapitel sind, will ich sogleich mich eines Auftrags entledigen, den ich, wiewol ungern, übernommen habe. Musikdirector Lecerf geht weg von hier, vor der Hand nach Dresden, u. wünschte zu wissen, ob Du wol meinst, daß jetzt in Leipzig etwas für ihn zu thun sey? Ich bin vielleicht selbst die unglückliche u. unschuldige Ursache davon, indem ich ihn auf den Tod des Musikdirector Polenz aufmerksam gemacht habe. Das war, in dem Augenblick namentlich, ein frappant trauriger Fall, unmittelbar nach dem so sehr schön eingerichteten Jubiläumsconcert; das muß man den Leipzigern lassen, daß sie das verstehn. Dein Bachsches Denkmal bleibt nun noch verhüllt, wie lange? Die beiden Büsten, für deren Besorgung ich bestens danke, stehn auf meinen beiden großen Notenschränken, u. sehn sehr gravitätisch aus. Mir gefällt besonders sehr die von Bach, bei Händel macht sich die Perücke ein bischen gar zu breit.—Hier war in diesen Tagen ein schönes Werk ausgestellt, eine Reiterstatue Friedrichs d. Großen von dem Amazonen Kiß, die für Breslau in Erz gegossen wird. Besonders den Kopf fand ich ganz außerordentlich schön, geistreich, u. edler, als ich es bei Friedrichs Häßlichkeit für möglich gehalten hätte. Er hat ihn jung, als Sieger über Schlesien, dargestellt.—Unser Frühjahr ist, wie wir es schon seit 3 Jahren haben, ostwindig, trocken u. kalt-sonnig, mir das antipatischste Wetter von der Welt, auch hat Alles Husten u. Schupfen, hier im Hause, wie in der ganzen Stadt. Liebe Cecile, nächsten Mittwoch soll Margarethens Hochzeit seyn, wenn es noch vor allen Krankheiten dazu kommt, Clärchen hat das Scharlachtfieber, weshalb wir uns auch gar nicht sehn, u. noch mehrere aus der Oppenheimschen Familie sind krank. Ißt Mariechen noch so gern "hunte hute Nute"? Schönsten Dank für die vortreffliche Chocolade, die Albertine uns von Dir gebracht hat. Grüß mir die lieben Kinder, wenn ich wieder nach L. komme, muß mir Carl von seiner Reise erzählen, das war zu schön den Morgen! Adieu, liebste Cecile, mache Deine Sache so gut, wie immer, u. behalte mich lieb. Adieu liebster Felix, u. prächtigste Kinder. Mein Mann u. Sebastian husten u. grüßen.

Fanny

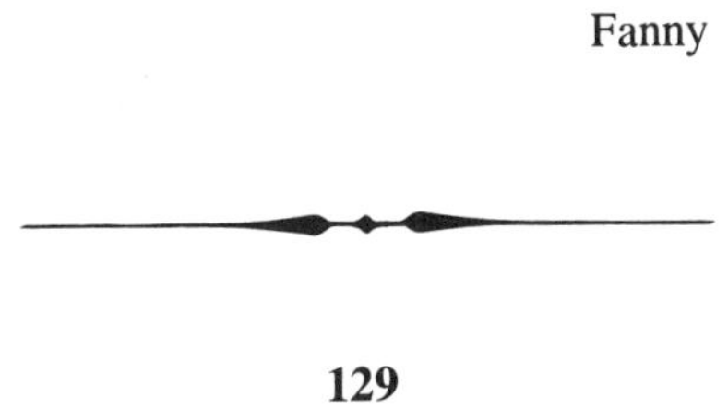

129

Berlin, 17ten April 1843.

Das war eine große Täuschung! Ich wußte nicht, wie ich Deinen Brief geschwind genug aufreißen, u. auseinander halten sollte, um zu sehn, ob ich einen Neffen, oder eine Nichte mehr zu lieben hätte, u. finde eine Partitur! Cecile, Du Zauderer! wird Dir nicht selbst die Zeit lang? Du armer Kerl, mußt dann die schönste Zeit des Jahrs im Zimmer zubringen! Die Partitur, lieber Felix, erfolgt hierbei, soll der Chor bei der Einweihung gesungen werden?

Vorige Woche waren wir sehr allein, beide Männer abwesend, Dirichlet ist es noch, Hensel ist am Sonnabend zurückgekommen, von einer sehr angenehmen kleinen Reise nach Braunschweig, wo er sehr gern gesehn, u. folglich sehr gern ist. Schreibe mir doch einmal den Namen Deines seltsamen Braunschweiger Freundes, lieber Felix, ich möchte wissen, ob er ihm nicht vorgekommen ist? Er läßt sich sehr empfehlen, u. Cecile bitten, sie möchte doch einige Rücksicht auf ihn nehmen, damit er vor seiner englischen Reise noch Gevatter seyn könne. Dirichlet schreibt, daß Jacobys Zustand sehr bedenklich ist, leider wird er wohl nicht lange mehr leben, u. Dirichlet wendet doppelte Aufmerksamkeit auf jedes Wort, das dieser bedeutende Mann ihm sagt. Er hat auch eine Vorlesung v. Walesrode gehört, den andern Jacoby kennengelernt, u. wird mit Schön bekannt gemacht werden. Wenn wir noch die liebe Leipziger lesen dürften, würden wir diese Reise nach Königsberg gewiß interpretirt sehn.

Durch Zufall war grade auch Bökh in der vorigen Woche abwesend, so daß wir eine ganz herrenlose Schaar waren. Jetzt sind Woringens bei uns, noch auf einige Tage, ehe sie uns ganz verlassen, sie hatten kein Bett u. keinen Stuhl mehr bei sich. Ihr Umzug ist für uns ein so großer geselliger Verlust, wie wir nur je einen erlitten haben.—Jetzt müßtet Ihr hier seyn, Kinderchen, der Garten ist schon wunderschön, ein wehmüthiger Anblick für uns, die Pfirsich u. Mandeln stehn in voller Blüthe, die Sträucher sind ganz grün, Alles andre schickt an zum Schönwerden, u. das ist eben für mich das Allerschönste.

Lebt wohl, Ihr liebsten Leute, laßt uns [b]ald Gutes hören, u. küßt die geliebten Kinder. Beny ist jetzt hier, mit dem spreche ich, so oft ich ihn sehe, von Carlchen, den er auch etwas lieb hat.

Eure Fanny

130

Berlin, 2ten Mai 1843.

Lieber Felix! Diese Zeilen erhältst Du durch Herrn Gounod, unsern römischen, u. Hausers Wiener Freund. Es thut mir sehr leid, daß er in diesem Augenblick nach Leipzig geht, wo er Dir vielleicht sehr in die Queer kommen, u. Cecile gar nicht sehn wird, da er aber nun unmittelbar nach Paris zurückkehrt, u. Dich doch gar zu gern vorher sehn wollte, so ließ es sich nicht anders machen. Sey ihm so freundlich, als es unter den grade obwaltenden Umständen möglich seyn wird, er hat gute Zeit mit uns verlebt, u. ist ein talentvoller Mensch. Habe noch nachträglich Dank für die Einladung zur Bachfeier, die ich gewiß gern mitgemacht hätte, da ich aber kürzlich dort war, u. in diesem Frühjahr wieder hinzukommen denke, fürchtete ich, Ihr würdet denken, ich sey besorgt, daß der Weg nicht ohne kluge Leute bleibe. Die schade,[a] daß Du selbst das Fest nicht recht hast genießen können, die erste Nachricht davon, u. von Deiner Grippe erhielten wir durch Pauline, die jetzt hier ist.

[Rebecka]

Die letzten 4 Wochen hier waren so voller Ankommen u. Abreisen, wie es mir nicht leicht vorgekommen ist. Woringens werden wir so bald nicht verschmerzen lernen, die fehlen uns gar zu sehr! Kaselowsky haben wir ganz geheilt entlassen, dem ist es auch nicht wenig schwer geworden, sich von uns zu trennen. Es freut mich wahrhaft, daß der erste Gebrauch, der von des seligen Vaters Stiftung gemacht worden ist, so gute Früchte getragen hat, es ist ein gutes Omen für die Nachfolgenden. Dann ist Hensel abgereist u. wiedergekommen, Dirichlet abgereist u. wiedergekommen, Marie u. Margarethe mit ihren Männern nach Italien, Hauser u. Gounod etc. sind vorübergezogen, jetzt wird nun wol Ruhe kommen.

Lieber Felix, nun muß ich Dich noch mit einer Bitte belästigen. Der Leipziger Käferlieferant hat wirklich eine bedeutende Sendung an Sebastian adressirt, von der wir die Hauptsachen für den kleinen Mann behalten haben, den Rest, so wie das Geld nimmt Gounod mit zurück. Willst Du wol so gütig seyn, ihm Beides gegen Quittung zu schicken?—Ist es denn wahr, liebe Cecile, daß Du die schönste Rococo Porzellanuhr vom König v. Sachsen bekommen hast? So wurde uns erzählt. Ach Leute, man hört gar nichts von Euch, Ihr schreibt so wenig, daß es ein Jammer ist. Es heißt auch, Du kämest in diesem Monat her, was dürfen wir hoffen? Können wir uns darüber freuen!—Seit einer Stunde sitze ich wie ein Narr, u. revidire die Käferrechnung für Sebastian, u. schreibe die berlinischen Namen ab. Ganz will es mir aber auch nicht stimmen, er bekömmt einen Käfer mehr, u. einige gl. weniger zurück, als es nach der Addition mit den hierbleibenden seyn sollte. Der alte Mann wird sich wol geirrt haben. Er kann aber zufrieden seyn, wir haben ihm die Hälfte seines Krams abgenommen. Dohrn der hier ist, hat übrigens einige Hauptstücke mit unverhohlener Bewunderung betrachtet, auch Sebastian mit aufs zoologische Museum genommen, u. ihm Käfer gezeigt, die 200 rh. kosten. Wenn H. Frank nur nicht einmal solche herschickt! Ich lasse ihn bitten, (das wird wol Gristel oder Fette freundlich bestellen) vor der Hand nichts herzuschicken, wenn wir einmal nach Leipzig kommen, wollen wir ihn aufsuchen. Leb wohl, lieber, bester Felix! Meine Herzens Cecile, an die ich tausendmal des Tages denke, ob sie jetzt wol ach u. weh schreien muß? Grüß u. küsse mir die geliebten Kinder.

Deine F.

3ten [Rebecka]

Nun Gott sey Dank, und tausend u. noch einmal tausend Segen u. Glück Euch geliebten Geschwister! Wie freue ich mich, daß die arme Cecile endlich ihre Last los ist, u. ihre Sache wieder so meisterhaft gemacht hat. Sie mußt aber auch für uns Alle arbeiten.—Diesen Brief sollte Dir Gounod heut überbringen, da er aber gestern krank geworden ist, u. wol noch einige Tage wird hier bleiben müssen, nehme ich ihn (große Verwirrung zwischen dem Brief u. Gounod) wieder aus dem Couvert, u. lasse ihn alleine laufen. Kommt *er* (nun wieder der Andre) in ein Paar Tagen nach, so bringt er die hierin angekündigten Käfer u. das Geld, u. den Empfehlungsbrief läßt Du wohl als solchen gelten. Lebt wohl, lasse ja alle Tage Nachricht kommen, was haben denn die Kinder zu dem neuen Geschwisterchen gesagt? Carl hat doch gewiß sehr schöne Bemerkungen gemacht. Nun, Gottes bester Segen bleibe mit Euch. Eure F

Tausend Grüße u. Glückwünsche von meinem Mann u. Minna.

---

[a]Should be "Schade."

131

Berlin, 14ten Mai 1843.

Diesmal kommt also nun der wirkliche Gounod, beladen mit Käfern, Geld dafür, u. brennender Begierde, Dich kennen zu lernen. Ich hoffe, er wird auch Cecile einen Augenblick sehn können. Schreiben will ich weiter nicht, da wir uns ja hoffentlich in ein Paar Tagen sehn, wenn Du noch, wie Du es verheißen, den 20sten herkommst. Dein Violinspieler hat sich noch nicht gemeldet. Seit der Eisenbahn brauchen die Leute immer ein Paar Wochen, von Leipzig hierher zu kommen, da sie sich in allen kleinen Nestern aufhalten u. Concerte geben. Habt Ihr denn auch so abscheuliches Wetter, wie wir, kalte Sonne, schneidender Ostwind, u. gräulicher Staub. Heut findet ein Dilettantenconcert Statt (ich habe keine Schuld u. keinen Theil daran) worin die schöne Pomowitz das Melodram aus Antigone declamirt. Adies, ich werde unterbrochen.

Deine F

132

Berlin, 4ten Juni 44.

Lieber Felix, ich muß Dich abermals mit meiner infamen Pote[a] (königl. Worte) belästigen, um Dir Nachrichten von Beckchen zu geben, die Dich erfreuen werden. Ich habe nämlich zu meiner großen Ueberraschung einen glückseligen Brief aus Palermo erhalten, nachdem sie zuletzt aus Neapel zweifelhaft über die Reise geschrieben hatte. Die Ueberfahrt geschah bei dem schönsten Wetter, u. sie schreibt ganz entzückt. Ich bin so froh, daß sie die Freude hat, Sicilien zu sehn, schon giebt es keinen bessern Beweis für ihr Wohlbefinden, als die rasche Ausführung dieses Plans. Da ich vermuthe, daß Ihr Euch jetzt schriftlich nicht werdet zu finden wissen, wollte ich Dir diese Nachricht nicht vorenthalten.—Was erlebst Du wieder für interessante Zeit in old England! Heut erfahren wir O'Connels Verurtheilung. Kein Roman ist so spannend wie diese ernste Wirklichkeit. Wie beide Theile ihr Spiel zu Ende bringen werden, das ahnde ich nicht. Wenn O'Connel die Caution leistet, so unterschreibt er sein Todesurtheil. Klingemann soll mir eine Privatcorrespondenz darüber schreiben, ich möchte gern wissen, was *er* u. *man* denkt.

Hier beschäftigen uns andre politische Fragen. Die Vase für Devrient—die Feier für Thorwaldsen. Wenn Du Ersterer die Ehre erweisen willst, ihr Deinen Namen beizufügen, so gieb bald Nachricht, denn der Porzellenmaler steht mit eingetrunktem Pinsel, u. wartet nur auf Dich. Letzere, die Thorwaldsenfeier hat sich dadurch vor andern Demonstrationen der Art ausgezeichnet, daß noch viel mehr Böcke dabei geschossen worden, als gewöhnlich. Untern andern ist *aus Versehn* der König u. der ganze Hof nicht eingeladen worden, ferner haben sie noch ein Paar Kleinigkeiten vergessen, Beuth u. Humboldt. Wie groß die Bestürzung war, als die Feier so unhöflich ablief, kannst Du Dir denken. Kopisch hatte eine Kantate gedichtet, die auf so hohem Kothurne umherging, daß es fast ein paar Stelzen waren. Was Taubert dazu für Musik gemacht hat, das hörst Du von drüben. Die Introduction war der Trauermarsch aus Antigone, er hatte ihm zwar ein kurzes Mäntelchen u. ein dünnes Mäskchen angethan, aber der alte Junge war doch gleich zu kennen. Um sich die Arbeit zu erleichtern, nahm er auch fast durch das ganze Stück nur Männerchöre, die mit halben Versen gegen einander Ball spielten, obgleich die Frauen da saßen, aber wenn er gleich mit gemischten schon angefangen hätte, wäre doch die Portraitähnlichkeit nicht so heraus zu bringen gewesen. Dann kam ein Uebergang aus der Trauer in die Freude des ewigen Ruhmes, das feierte er mit Festklängen, tut, tut, tut, tut, 4 Accorde aus dem Sommernachtstraum, Posaunen, Frauenstimmen, das ganze machte sich wirklich sehr hübsch u. brillant. Es ist ein kurioses Talent, das der Taubert hat, so gutklingend anständige, gutgearbeitete Musik zu machen, u. dabei gänzlich mit fremden Kälbern zu pflügen, wenn mir das widerfährt, so schieb ichs auf die Bluthsverwandschaft. Aber er hat wirklich kein Recht dazu—Donner.

Aber ich habe Dir ja nur 2 Zeilen schreiben wollen—verzeih. Den lieben Kinderchen geht es ja Gott sey Dank besser, wie mir die liebe Cecile schreibt. Albertine u. ihrem Pflänzchen geht es ebenfalls vortrefflich. Lebewohl, Alles grüßt. Laß bald von Dir hören.

Fanny

---

[a]Fanny wrote "Pote" instead of "Pfote."

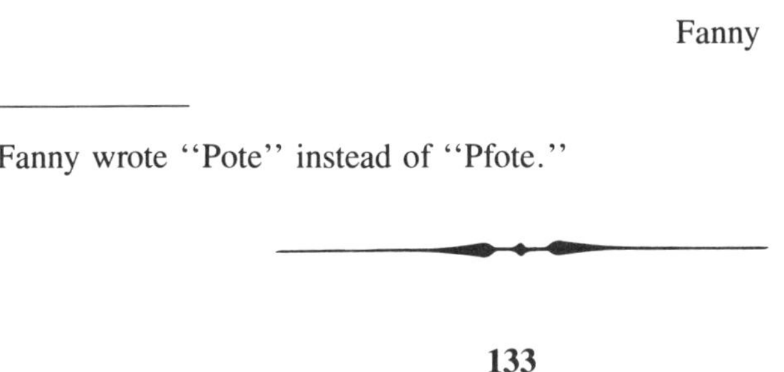

133

Berlin, 30sten Juli 1844

Lieber Felix, ich muß Deinen melankolischen Sodener Brief, worin Du mit viel Anschaulichkeit Dein Verhältniß zu Eichbäumen u. ihren Bewohnern schön aus einander setzest, nur gleich beantworten, u. mir wahrscheinlich Rüffel zuziehn, die ich aber gewiß nicht verdiene. Das Stück, das Du wegen Deines verwundeten Knies zu meiner Hochzeit (schon über halb silbern) nicht fertig gemacht hast, habe ich auch nachher nie erhalten, kann es Dir daher auch nicht schicken. Hier sehe ich ein Lächeln u. ein Ave Maria um Deine Lippen schweben, dafür habe ich aber jetzt eine Zeichnung aufzuweisen, die Jahrelang verschwunden, in einem vielsagenden römischen Patent wieder zu Tage kam, kurz ich habe das Stück nicht, u. habe es nie gehabt, u. Du mußt es schon auswendig neu machen, es wird doch alles anders. Dein Sodener Leben muß aber eine schöne Idylle seyn, wenn ich Dich so sehe, will es mir scheinen, als kennte ich Dich noch nicht ganz, denn wenn Du Zeit hast, habe ich Dich noch nie gesehn, Du wirst darauf antworten, Du mich noch nie, wenn ich keine habe, eigentlich möchte ich einmal eine Reise mit Dir nach einer *Gegend* machen, u. Dich kennen lernen, wie Du die Tage im Grase liegst, u. nichts zu thun hast, habe aber keine Furcht, ich hänge mich doch nicht an, so kennst Du mich schon. Nebenbei müßt Ihr dort ganz ander Wetter haben, als wir arme Hunde, das im Grase liegen wollten wir ohnehin schon bleiben lassen, wenn wir nur wenigstens auf einer Bank unterm Baum sitzen könnten, aber davon ist in diesem Sommer hier keine Rede. Alle Sorten schlecht Wetter wechseln miteinander ab, nur kein gutes. Seit 2 1/2 Monaten haben wir nicht einen ganz schönen Tag gehabt. Von Rebecka habe ich gestern einen Brief aus Sorrent mit dem Deinigen zusammen erhalten, so gut macht es die Post nicht oft. Sie leben wie die Götter in Frankreich, u. haben sich die Antwort nach Zürich bestellt, wollen aber erst Ende Septembers wieder einrücken. Ich hoffe, daß sie wenigstens halb so verliebt in ihre Wohnung seyn wird, als ich es bin, ich bringe meine meiste Lebenszeit da zu, u. richte ein, u. richte wieder aus, bis ich Alles so wunderschön finde, daß gar nichts drüber geht, zanke mich einen Tag mit dem Wirth, u. den andern mit der Wirthin, die Beide nicht wollen, daß ich die Fenster aufmachen soll, weil die Mahagonythüren von der Sonne leiden, ich will aber nicht, daß die Menschen von Mangel an Luft leiden sollen, u. thue es doch. Wahrhaftig, ich finde mich dies Jahr sehr philosophisch u. fast alt, da ich ruhig hier bleibe, Alles reisen sehe u. höre, u. kaum ein lebhaftes Verlangen danach habe, eigentlich hab ichs aber doch, u. vertröste mich schon mit der heimlichen Hoffnung auf übers Jahr, wo ich denke, daß wir mit unserm *erwachsenen* Sohn ein bischen aufkratzen wollen, in seinen Ferien. Er wird Dir aus seiner Residenz Interbock schreiben, wohin er gestern auf 3 Tage mit Matusch gegangen ist, auf die Weise folge ich Deinem Befehl, seinen Brief nicht zu lesen. Unter allen schönen Dingen, die Du schreibst, steht aber nicht ein Wort von Wiederkommen, wäre ich nicht hier in Berlin, ich würde es Dir gar nicht übel nehmen, daß Dir so mies davor ist, aber ich freue mich doch nicht wenig auf Euch u. die gar zu lieben Kinder, die doch mancherlei Interessantes hier versäumen, mehr als ihre Eltern, junge Ziegen, junge Hühner, junge Störche. A propos—Andersen läßt Dich u. besonders Cecile zärtlich grüßen. Daß Du ihn hast Märchen erzählen hören, weiß ich, denn ich erinnere mich, daß Carl drüber geweint hat, (der Junge hatte Recht) hast Du ihn aber jemals diese kinderlichen Geschichten mit unglaublich naivem Vortrag vor lauter alten Leuten verbringen hören, wie ich gestern Abend? Das ist über alle Naturgeschichte, u. muß selbst gehört werden, wenn man es glauben soll. Ich versichere Dich, ich war in Begriff, wieder an den Klapperstorch zu glauben, u. Pappe zu fordern, so kindlich kam ich mir vor.—Von Klingemann hat Paul einen prächtigen Brief bekommen, der viel gute Nachrichten über Dich in London erhält. Wie gern möchte ich den prächtigen Menschen einmal wiedersehn! Nun verspricht er wieder zum Oktober, u. wird auch dann nicht kommen. Du schreibst, Du komponirst viel, aber nicht was, denn bei einem Heft bestellter Orgelsachen wirst Du es wohl, wenn Du einmal fleißig bist, nicht bewenden lassen. Ich meine, da Du so viel Zeit in Soden hast, (das sollst Du nicht umsonst gesagt haben), schreibst Du mir einmal wieder einen so prächtigen lustigen Brief, u. sagst mir mehr davon, u. so will ich Dir denn auch erzählen, daß ich nach meiner Art fleißig bin, u. einen kleinen Roman in Liedern komponire, den mein Mann während des Brunnentrinkens für mich gemacht hat, für Dich ist oder wäre das auf einen Zahn, Du schreibst in 3/4 St. so viel Noten, wie ich in 3/4 Jahren, aber ich gebe mir sehr viel Mühe darum, es soll wieder so ein Heftchen mit Vignetten werden.

Nun Dir meinen Dank, liebe Cecile, für Deine lieben Zeilen, worin Du mir sagst, daß es Dir besser geht, etwas Lieberes kannst Du mir gar nicht sagen. Ich meine, die Milchkur wirst Du hier vielleicht mit unsern Ziegen fortsetzen können, wir haben eine vollständige Trinkanstalt diesen Sommer hier im Garten, die 3 milchenden Ziegen versorgen mehrere Personen, u. die Brunnenpromenade ist auch trotz a[ ] schlechten Wetters sehr lebhaft. Vielleicht wird die frische Milch auch für Felixchen recht zuträglich seyn. Grüß Deine liebe Mutter, ich schreibe ihr heut noch nicht, danke ihr sehr für ihren freundlichen Brief, den ich nächstens beantworten werde. Daß wir Benekes aus London hier, aber leider nur im Fluge gesehn haben, wirst Du wissen. Doch ist es immer angenehm, Personen von denen man so viel gehört, wenigstens von Anges[icht] zu kennen, wenn es auch viel mehr nicht geworden.

Mein Mann grüßt bestens, es geht ihm wohl, doch niemals wohler, als so lange er Brunnen trinkt, was in diesem Herbst noch einmal geschehn soll. Marianne ist mit Marieen nach Ostende gereist, die Charlottenburger grüßen bestens.

Eure Fanny

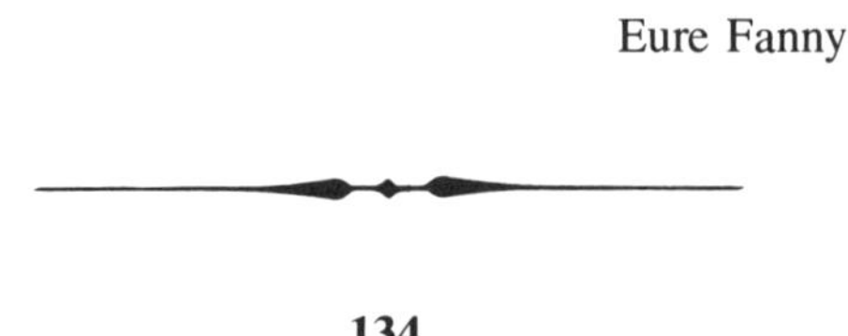

134

Berlin, 21 Decbr. 1844

Gott sey Dank, lieber Felix, daß es bei Euch soviel besser geht, u. möge es dabei bleiben, u. täglich besser werden. Ich weiß nicht, ob Cecile es mag, daß man ihr ähnliche Fälle erzählt, aber ich kann nicht umhin ihr zu sagen, daß Bertha Friedheim ein sehr niedliches Kind von jetzt 5 Jahren hat, das ganz dieselben Krankheiten, Masern, Keuchhusten, u. in Folge davon dieselben Unterleibsleiden hatte, u. sich gänzlich wieder erholt hat. Ich habe Dir für 2 liebe Briefe zu danken, denn als ich den Meinigen neulich kaum abgeschickt hatte, kam Dein erster. Deine Orgelstücke habe ich zum Abschreiben gegeben, denn obgleich Dir[a] vollkommen traue selbst was das Stück zu meiner Hochzeit betrifft, so möchte ich doch das Heftchen gern mitnehmen, u. kann es Dir deshalb nicht in Natura schicken. Halt mir die übrigen bereit, ich hole sie mit im Sommer von Dir ab. Ach Gott! Das sind alles Plane,[b] u. wenn wir nicht gewußt hätten, daß der Mensch denkt u. Gott lenkt, so hätten wir es doch in diesem Herbst lernen müssen. Wissen wir doch noch nicht einmal gewiß, ob wir reisen, wir haben seit 14 T. kein Wort von Florenz gehört, u. wer weiß, was der nächste Brief bringen mag. Das Wetter ist jetzt prächtig, u. wenn wir so davon begünstigt würden, so wäre die ganze Sache wirklich nicht so gefährlich. Ich bin jetzt ungeduldig fortgekommen, um mit eignen Augen zu sehn, u. dann könnt Ihr Euch auch auf vollständige u. ehrliche Berichte verlassen. Aber ganz ruhig bin ich, lieber Felix, u. weder furioso ma non tanto noch agitato ma con ich weiß nicht mehr was, u. dazu mag wol ein tüchtiger Anfall von Nasenbluten beigetragen haben, den ich bald nach Deiner Abreise bekam. Ich habe wahrhaftig noch nicht Zeit gehabt, mich recht con amore über Dein Nicht-Hierseyn zu grämen, die Paar ersten Tage nach Deinem Fortgehn war ich so abgespannt von allen Ereignissen der letzten Zeit, daß ich nur so vegetirte, u. dann kam Alles andre wieder, was Einem den Kopf brummen macht. Bei Alle dem macht mir, u. uns Allen Dein Bild die größte Freude. Ich würde mich sehr betrübt haben, daß es nach Rußland sollte, wenn ich nicht von Anfang an so eine gewisse innere Beruhigung gehabt hätte, es würde wol nicht fortgehn. Auch hatte sich Paul schon erklärt, es nicht weglassen zu wollen, als Du noch hier warst wollte aber nicht, daß wir es Dir sagen sollten, ich weiß nicht, warum. Hensel macht es mit Noth u. Sorge in einzelnen Momenten fertig, denn die Besuche, um es zu sehn, so wie das Elsassersche, nehmen kein Ende u. heut hat er endlich seine Thür schließen müssen, (nur für Humboldt nicht, der im höchsten Grade zufrieden damit war) weil er es doch zu Weihnachten an Paul abliefern will. Ja ja, mein Felix, wann, wie, wo werden wir uns wiedersehn? Ich wollte, es stellte mir Einer einen gültigen Wechsel darüber aus, den der liebe Gott zur rechten Zeit honorirte!

Bin ich denn in Stimmung Dir zu erzählen, u. Du anzuhören, daß ich gestern zum erstenmal das Opernhaus u. die Lind als Norma genossen habe? Leider wird sie wol keine andre Rolle singen, solange ich hier bin. Ihre Stimme ist von der haarscharfen Reinheit, die an u. für sich so erquicklich wirkt, dabei außerordentlich u. vorzüglich schön in den höhern Tönen bis b, ihre Fertigkeit ist nicht grade hervorragend, aber ganz ausreichend um jede große Rolle damit zu singen, Triller sehr gut, Vortrag u.

Ausdruck, soviel man in dieser weicherlichen Musik beurtheilen kann, sehr stark u. schön, wie auch das Spiel. Von der Kraft ihrer Stimme kann ich nichts viel sagen, da wir einen elenden Platz hatten, wo wie ich vermuthen muß, die Hälfte des Klanges verloren ging. Was nun aber das Innre des Theaters betrifft, da bin ich mit Mephistopheles des trocknen Tones satt, muß wieder recht den Berliner spielen. Alles Gold, Roth, Silber, Weiß, Sammt, Gyps, Gas,[c] Stuck, Putz, Pracht aller Art ist nicht im Stande, die Tapezier u. Buchbinder Seele zu überkleistern, die im Grunde aller Verhältnisse u. Formen lebt. Hiltls Geist schwebt über jeder Loge! Sonderbar genug, das frühere Theater, das so recht in der Blüthe des Zopfes erbaut war, hatte die einfachsten, schönsten, edelsten Formen, die ich je an irgend einem Theater der Welt gesehn habe, u. dies, aus unsrer eklektischweisen Bauzeit, die alle Style von Ptalemäus bis Semper liebt, wählt sich die schönste Perücke, um hinunter zu kriechen.

Mögt Ihr ein vergnügtes Fest haben, u. keins Eurer Kinder Euch Sorge machen. Wir werden heilig Abend bei Paul zubringen. Welche Beruhigung für die liebe Cecile, in dieser traurigen Zeit ihre Mutter in der Nähe gehabt zu haben. Grüße die gute Madame Jeanrenaud doch recht herzlich von mir, u. empfiehl mich der Frau Souchay. Hensel grüßt Alles aufs Beste. Sebastian hat ein sehr gutes Schulzeugniß bekommen, u. ist auch von seinem Director, den wir auf Anlaß der Reise gesprochen haben, persönlich sehr gelobt worden. Der arme liebe Carl muß soviel studiren schon! Liebe Cecile, ich habe unter Beckchens Kinderwäsche ein Hemdchen von ihm gefunden, das ich Dir mit irgend einer Gelegenheit zuschicken werde.— Lebt wohl Ihr Lieben, Liebsten! Möge uns der Himmel froh u. glücklich wieder zusammentreffen lassen.

Deine Fanny

Das allerliebste Reiseausgabebuch, was Du mir vor drei Jahren schenktest, schließt seine Vignetten mit Florenz, wobei steht, ist fortzusetzen. Ist das nicht sentimental? Ich werde es jetzt in Gebrauch nehmen.

---

[a]Fanny omitted "ich."
[b]Fanny omitted the umlaut; see note "a" to letter 24.
[c]It is possible she meant to write "Glas."

135

Florenz den 4ten März 1845

Mein lieber Bruder und Musicus! Wir haben uns leider so viel Krankheits- u. Gottlob soviel Gesundheitsbriefe zu schreiben gehabt, daß es wol auch einmal wieder Zeit wäre, ans Handwerk zu denken. Gott! weiß ich denn, ob Du Deine 7te Transcription aus Robert le diable fertig hast? Oder welche Oper von Verdi (Donizetti ist bei uns in Italien veraltet) Deinen Genius jetzt am Meisten beschäftigt? Oder ob Du diesen Winter in Deinen Concerten mehr die Fantasie aus Lucia, oder den Walzer über den Choral aus den Hugenotten, dieser genialsten Erfindung Meyerbeers gespielt hast? Bin ich über das Alles aufgeklärt, namentlich auch darüber, ob Du vielleicht auch gelegentlich ein neues Trio schreibst, ich erlaube Dir, die Themas der Berliner Academie dazu zu benutzen, wenn Du es nicht vorziehn solltest, Dich einmal selbst in der Erfindung zu versuchen, so will ich Dir von meinen eignen Fortschritten in der Musik zu Erbauung u. Nacheifer erzählen. Ich bin noch gar nicht in der Oper gewesen, was man dabei lernt, das glaubst Du nicht! Ich habe die Absicht, die Kunst, die sich viel zu sehr von der Natur entfernt hat, wieder auf den ursprünglichen Weg zurück zu führen, u. studire deshalb mit großem Eifer die Aeußerungen der jüngsten Nichte meiner Laune. Es ist dabei ein gewisses Murxen vorherrschend, ein mezzoforte welches sehr interessante Effekte bei der Uebertragung ins Orchester verspricht. Wenn Berlioz die 50 Flügel placirt haben wird, die ihm nöthig scheinen, würde ich ihm rathen, an jeden eine Amme mit einem Wochenkinde zu setzen, die alle ein paar Stunden vorher gehungert haben müßten, ich bin überzeugt, das Publicum, namentlich die Mütter der Kinder, würden sehr gerührt seyn. Was nun vollends meine Ausbildung im Technischen betrifft, so ist die ganz ungeheuer, ich habe mir in dem hiesigen milden Himmelsstrich den rechten Zeigefinger erfroren, grade da, wo er aufgesetzt wird, u. sage nun jedesmal autsch! wenn ich ihn brauche, u. auch das kann ich Dir als einen ganz neuen, u. sehr brauchbaren Effekt empfehlen.

Dabei fällt mir aber ein, daß ich Dir eigentlich etwas zu schreiben habe, u. zwar Folgendes: Hast Du Dich am 6ten März ganz Taufe gefühlt, so fange am 12ten wieder von vorne an, u. fühle noch einmal. Auf den Tag ist sie nun nämlich—so Gott es will—unwiderruflich bestimmt, u. meine Abreise nach Rom auf den 15ten. Nach allem Vorstehenden hielte ich es fast für überflüssig, Dir noch besonders zu versichern, daß Mutter

u. Kind sich des Wohlsten befinden, wenn ich nicht wüßte, daß Du die exacte Wissenschaft liebst, also, Beide sind in vortrefflichstem Wohlseyn, u. resp. Humor, u. erholen, u. bleichen sich zusehends, in dem die Eine ihre Röthe, die andre ihre Bräune mehr u. mehr verliert, Beiden schmeckt Essen u. Trinken, beide nehmen zu, u. ich bin mit Beiden höchst zufrieden. Hoffentlich wird Dein nächster Brief auch schon etwas Zuversichtliches klingen, Dein ersten, der vorgestern ankam, sah man noch die Besorgniß zwischen den Zeilen an. Liebe Cecile, Deine Schilderung von dem kleinen Frank in einem wollnen Rock hat uns sehr zu lachen gemacht, denn ungefähr so war unser armes Bambino die erste Nacht beschaffen, es war in eine wollne Jacke von Dirichlet ohne sonderliche Anmuth gekleidet, ein Aermel über den Kopf gezogen, der dann lang herunter schleppte, aber schon den Vormittag konnte ich es, halbwege anständig gewickelt, zu Beckchen bringen, u. jetzt, da wir grade unsere kleine provisorische Aussteuer beendet haben, kommt auch die Kiste von Berlin, u. die sieben magern Jahre sind vorüber. Was Ihr lieben Geschwister mir nun in der nächsten Zeit von Nachrichten zugedacht habt, das laßt nur über Florenz u. Beckchen gehn, die natürlich wissen wird, wie lange uns die Briefe in Rom treffen. Dort will ich noch Ostern mitnehmen, alles meiner musikalischen Erziehung wegen, die ich diesmal durchaus poussiren muß, sehr viel trägt auch dazu die geistreich anregende Conversation eines Franzosen bei, der mit uns in einem Hause wohnt, von Profession Sprachlehrer, von Passion lutherischer Propagandist, u. dabei ein sehr lahmes musikal. Steckenpferd reitet. So oft er mich auf dem Corridor hört, singt er

u. wenn er bei uns Thee trinkt, frägt er, ob ich Don Juan liebe? Worauf ich denn erwidre, mein lieber Monsieur, das frägt man nicht. Nun laß Dich aber im Ernst bitten, mir einen schönen musikalischen Brief zu schreiben, u. mich wissen zu lassen wovon die Rede ist, wie Jacoby sagt, damit ich nicht gar zu strohdumm werde, was Einem leicht geschehn kann, wenn man das Glück hat, ein halb Jahr in Italien bleiben zu können, wie ich jetzt. Lebe nun wohl, bleibe gesund mit Deiner lieben Hälfte u. Deinen 4 Vierteln, empfiehl mich der lieben Madame Jeanrenaud, die ich mich sehr freue, wiederzusehn, u. bleibe mir gut.

[Rebecka]

136

Rom, den 3ten April 1845

Lieber Felix, unsre Korespondenz soll also, damit das Rad recht rund bleibe, über Florenz hin u. zurück gehn, so lange wir hier sind, was aber nicht gar lange dauern wird. Du hast wol bereits durch Beckchen u. Paul erfahren, wie übel es uns im Anfang hier gegangen ist, um so mehr Freude ist es mir, Euch jetzt nur gute Nachrichten geben zu können, Hensel ist in voller Genesung, noch etwas schwach, aber gesund, u. jede Vorsicht wird angewendet, daß es beim Guten bleibe, u. wir keine Rück- u. Unfälle weiter zu beklagen haben mögen. Auch Sebastian u. ich nehmen uns sehr in Acht, obgleich ich für meine Person nie einen übeln Einfluß vom Klima verspürt habe, sondern mich wo möglich hier noch mehr wie der pont neuf befinde, als zu Hause. (unbeschrieen, schreibt Beckchen hier drüber, wenn ich es nicht selbst thue.) Und so kann ich denn auf ein sehr angenehmes Thema übergehn, nämlich Deine Vorschläge zum Familiencongreß, die wir gern annehmen. Früh werdet Ihr doch wahrscheinlich nach dem furchtbar harten u. späten Winter nicht aufs Land ziehn, wenn wir also unserm u. Beckchens allerersten Plan treu bleiben, u. Mitte Juni von Florenz abreisen (früher möchten wir nicht gern) so können wir in der ersten Hälfte des Juli in Soden seyn, u. das ist wol für Euch u. Paul die rechte Zeit. Da Ihr für den Sommer dort etablirt seyd, so schadet es auch nicht, wenn Einer von uns ein wenig auf den Andern bei Dir wartet, da man doch schwerlich von Florenz u. Berlin grade auf den Tag zusammentreffen kann. Rückt dann die Zeit näher, so wird sich davon reden lassen, ob Ihr Gebrüder Euch nicht ein bischen weiter vorschiebt, u. uns etwa bis Freyburg entgegen kommt, wo wir doch bei Woringens jedenfalls Station machen werden. In Soden denke ich dann, soll Hensel Brunnen trinken, giebt es Marienbader in Frankfurt? Doch gewiß. Und noch eins, kann man wol in Soden ein Zimmer haben, worin Malen möglich ist? Cecile, Du weißt ja, nicht zu niedrige Fenster, u. etwas Wand dahinter. Wollt Ihr in unserm Interesse einmal bei schönem Wetter eine Spazierfahrt nach Soden machen, u. sehn ob es eine Wohnung mit so einem Möbel giebt, so will ich dafür versprechen, daß wir so lange bleiben wollen, bis Ihr uns die Thür von Soden weist. Und nun gebe Gott aller Schwäche Stärkung u. aller Gesundheit Bestand, so können wir, nach vielen Stürmen, einer frohen, ruhigen Zeit entgegen sehn. Sehr schön war es, lieber Felix, wie 2 Tage nach Abgang meines Briefs mit den musikalischen Fragen, Deine Antwort darauf kam.

Besonders freue ich mich auf das Trio, wenn ich es nur noch werde spielen können, Du kannst Dir gar nicht denken, wie ich mich zurückgegangen fühle, u. wie schwach meine Hände geworden sind, hätte ich nicht seit undenklicher Zeit so sehr wenig Musik, u. so sehr viel andre Sachen im Kopf gehabt, würde ich mich ernstlich darüber grämen. Daß Du eine Oper suchst, ist mir sehr lieb, denn es steht geschrieben, suchtet so werdet ihr finden, u. Du wirst schon finden. Was nun die Beantwortung Deiner Fragen betrifft, so will ich Dir zuerst erzählen, daß der Ritter Landsberg, von dem Du nichts wissen willst, u. der ein großer Lumpus ist, einen Erardschen Flügel an einen Russen auf *einen* Monat für 35 Scudi vermiethet hat, u. daß Du in unsern Augen Unrecht hast, Mme. Sabatier zu sehr zu hassen, wir haben sie ganz angenehm, u. sehr freundlich u. gefällig gefunden. Deinen Intimus, den Marchese Martellini haben wir freilich in Florenz nicht gesehn, wohin er noch nicht zurückgekehrt war, wol aber auf der Durchreise in München, u. wol in Florenz seine Frau u. Töchter, die sich bei mir durch einen höchst gebildeten musikal. Geschmack sehr insinuirt haben, als ich nämlich zuerst da einen Besuch machte, ging ich an einem Zimmer vorbei, worin das h moll Quartett v. Mendelssohn gut gespielt wurde, u. sie kennen Alles von diesem genialen Compositeur, u. lieben ihn, u. haben ihn sich von Kopf zu Fuß beschreiben lassen, u. waren so außer sich über die Zwischenacte vom Sommernachtstraum, die ich da zum erstenmal seit Berlin gespielt habe, daß ich, wie gesagt, ein sehr günstiges Urtheil über diese Familie bekommen habe. Eckert ist nicht mehr in Rom, wol aber Fränkchen, den ich gestern gesehn, u. der sich wirklich aus einer Schwarzwurzel zu einem häßlichen, aber ganz anständigen Jüngling herausgemuffelt hat. Der Director der päpstlichen Kapelle ist nobody (Abbate Garombo), der älteste von den Bassen taktirt, weiter gehören ja keine Kenntnisse dazu, meinen sie. Ich hoffe es zu erleben, daß die päpstliche Musik eines schönen Morgens Alle wird, da sie sich gegen die Reform mit den Knabenstimmen, wie gegen jede andre in der Welt sperren, u. die alten nach u. nach so alt werden, daß nächstens Alles aufhört. Den Palmsonntag in Rom habe ich in der Diligence auf der Landstraße gefeiert, u. daher kein Urtheil darüber mir erlauben wollen. Broccoli all' insalata essen wir täglich, lieber Felix, auf Deine Gesundheit, gestern schickte mir Charlotte Thygeson welchen aus ihrer Villa, u. unser vortrefflicher Francesco, der Koch, Kellner, Hausmädchen, kurz Mädchen für Alles ist, u. dessen Toilette in abgeschnittenen Schlafröcken besteht, die irgend eine alte Engländerin hier vergessen hat, u. dessen Küche nichts anders als italiänisch spricht, bereitet sie schön zu. Kennst Du riso di Germania? Das ist eine Sorte grober Graupe, die wir zur Abwechselung probiren wollen, denn sonst kennt der Italiäner nur riso di Pasta, u. pasta di riso. Lebwohl, für heut, ich will Beckchen nicht gar zu sehr beeinträchtigen. Grüße Cecile u. die lieben Kindern. Hoffentlich habt Ihr jetzt endlich gut Wetter, wenn auch nicht so schönes, wie wir, u. das Felixchen verliert die letzten Reste seiner bösen Krankheit. Gott erhalte ihm u. Euch Alle.

Eure Fanny

H. Schmitz ist sehr freundlich u. gefällig, u. hat mir bei meiner Abreise die größten Dienste geleistet. Danke doch H. Bernus, wenn Du ihn siehst, für die Empfehlung.

Lieber Felix, eben schreibt mir Beckchen, daß sie Dir einen Br. von mir geschickt hat. Du wirst finden, daß ich Deine theure Schwester bin, was Postgeld betrifft, verzeih!

[Sebastian, Rebecka]

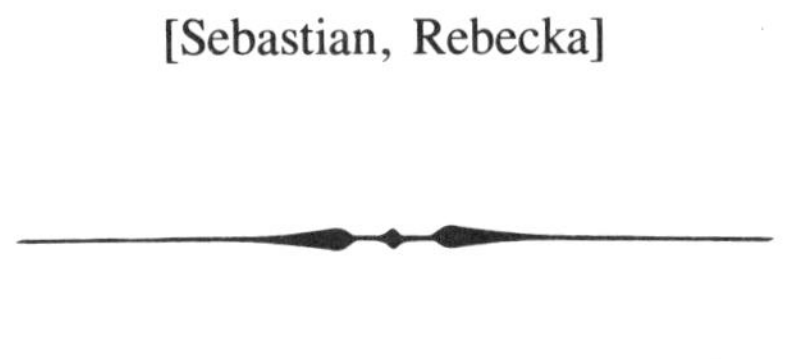

137

Berlin, den 4ten August 1845.

Lieber Felix, vorgestern sind wir denn also, unserm Plan gemäß, mit dem 2ten Zuge glücklich hier angekommen, nachdem es noch den Morgen, recht schief hätte gehn können. Die Postchaise, in die Rebecka des Regens wegen gestiegen war, warf eine Viertelstunde vor Halle, also recht eigentlich vor Thorschluß, um, indem das Rad abflog, wie bei Cronthal, Rebecka selbst hat eine starke Beule an der Stirn, u. eine kleine Contusion an der Hand davon getragen, die Andere alle, auch Walter der vom Bock herabfiel, waren ganz unverletzt. Ich schreibe Dir diesen kleinen Unfall hauptsächlich deshalb, daß Johann recht auf die Räder Achtung giebt. Sie ist übrigens sehr wohl, u. heut herumgestiegen, Einkäufe machen, auch mit ihrer Wohnung sehr zufrieden. So weit wären wir also, u. nun bleibt das Einpassen in das Hauskleid des Lebens noch übrig. Zwei Abende lang war der Garten prächtig erleuchtet, uns zu Ehren, und diese Feierlichkeit "vom schönsten Wetter begünstigt". Pauls sind beide sehr wohl, u. wohnen noch im Hause, für Dich wird bei Beckchen eingerichtet. Das ist so ziemlich das Einzige, was zu melden wäre. Eben bekomme ich die erste spenersche in die Hand, u. die ist so voll Hersky u. Ronge, Lichtfreunde u. Jesuiten, Juden, Protestanten u. Neukatholiken, daß mir ganz nach Religiönskrieg zu Muth wird, ich rieche lauter Pech u. Schwefel. In Italien duselt man so fort zwischen Kunst u. Lebensgenuß, daß man sich wirklich hart gewöhnt, wieder von so unbequemen Dingen viel zu hören, es ist eine Verwöhnung, wie mit der italiänischen Musik, die Einem auch die Ohren so verweichlicht, wenn man sie viel hört, daß jede gesunde Modulation wie eine Anmaßung klingt. Nun solltest Du meinen, das Wiedersehn mit Heinrich sollte mich über jede sonstige Lebensentbehrung fort gehoben haben, aber nein pflegten wir sonst zu sagen.

Lebe wohl, wenn in Deutschland der 30jährige Krieg anbricht, so gehe ich wieder nach Italien. Cecile glückliche Reise mit Deiner lieben Schaar. Liebe Madame Jeanrenaud, behalten Sie uns in freundlichem Andenken.

Fanny.

138

Berlin, den 20sten Septbr. 1845

Lieber Felix! Wozu sind die dummen Streiche in der Welt, wenn sie nicht begangen werden sollen? Ich habe einen recht herzlich dummen gemacht, indem ich das Arrangement mit dem Flügel, was Du mir anbotest, abgelehnt habe, u. bin jetzt in Begriff, ihn durch einen zweiten, vielleicht eben so dummen, wieder gut zu machen. Böse Beispiele verderben gute Sitten, ach nein, das paßt eigentlich gar nicht hierher, Wohlhaben verwöhnt die Menschen, das ist wieder kein Sprichwort, ich armer rat de campagne war so zufrieden mit meinem ländlichen Wiener, bis der stolze rat de ville mich einmal zu seinem Gastmahl einlud, u. dahin ist der Geschmack an der Hausmannskost, mit einem Wort, ich bin so vollkommen disgustirt, daß ich gar nicht mehr spielen mag, u. brauche, wenn ich überhaupt die ganze Musikmachen nicht jetzt an den Nagel hängen soll, einen vollen, schweren, etwas bärbeißigen Flügel. Ist ein solcher vorhanden? Hast du Dich schon danach umgethan? Dann muß ich ihn haben, u. wenn am Ende des Jahrs das Deficit zu groß ist, verkaufe ich meine Perlen, mein Schwanenhals kann ohne sie bestehn.

Sehr haben wir uns gefreut, aus Ceciles Brief an Rebecka zu sehn, daß sie so wohl u. munter ist, u. daß es ihr in der neuen Wohnung gefällt. Unser Hausverkauf schwankt noch immer, ich wollte, es wäre erst entschieden, wir sind natürlich am Meisten dabei persönlich interessirt, da wir große Prätensionen von Wohnung, Atelier u. Garten haben, u. gar nicht wissen, wie sich das Alles vereinigen lassen. Ich neige noch immer für einen Hausbau.

Am Tage Deiner Abreise erhielten wir die Nachricht von dem Tode unsers lieben Elsassers, u. des Architekten Hallmann, mit dem wir ebenfalls sehr befreundet waren, u. ihn in der letzten Zeit in Rom fast täglich gesehn hatten. Heut bekomme ich Nachricht aus Liegnitz, von wo wir erfahren hatten, daß Rosa u. Elise Beide am Nervenfieber krank lägen, Beide schreiben ein Paar Zeilen mit Bleistift aus dem Bette, u. liegen seit 6. u. 7 Wochen, die größte Gefahr ist zwar vorüber, doch soll besonders Elise sehr schwach seyn. Und so hat es wieder mancherlei Gram u. Sorge gegeben!

Lebt wohl, Gott erhalte Euch, u. lasse der lieben Cecile die nächste Zeit leicht werden.

Vorgestern ist die Antigone im neuen Palais vom Stapel gelaufen. Hensel hatte ein Billet geschickt bekommen, u. ist drüben gewesen, es soll recht gut gegangen seyn. Viele herzliche Grüße an Mad. Jeanrenaud, Frl. Jung u. die Kinder nicht zu vergessen.

Fanny.

Lasse mich also bitte, bald etwas von einem Flügel hören.

139

Berlin den 2ten Februar 1846.

Was hier am 2ten Februar abgeht, wird ein 3ten in Leipzig seyn, u. gratuliren, u. das soll es auch, u. zwar recht herzlich, Du machst jetzt ein ehrwürdiges Familienhaupt aus, wenn alle Deine fünf beim Geburtstag erscheinen. Gott erhalte sie Dir zu. Alle Dein anderes Glück, amen.—Hier geht es überall gut, Paul wird übermorgen seine erste Ausfahrt halten, u. alle Kinder sind wohl, Florentinchen hat nach den Masern ein ganz anderes Gesicht bekommen.

Diese Woche wissen wir uns vor Kunstgenüssen nicht zu fassen. Heut Leonard mit Deinem Concert, morgen Feldlager mit der Lind, wozu uns das Schicksal zwei Billette zugeworfen, (eine würdige Feier Deines Geburtstags,) Ende der Woche im Theater. Armen Concert mit der Lind,

Mittwoch der Sommernachtstraum, wo fange ich an? wo höre ich auf? Ihr habt ja auch die Lind wieder in Leipzig gehabt, hat sie was gethan dort? Ich habe sie nicht wieder gesehn, man trifft sie schwer, u. da ich nicht sehr andringender Natur bin, so weiß ich nicht, wie wir recht zusammenkommen sollen. Mit meinem Flügel bin ich fortwährend sehr zufrieden, er macht mir große Freude, u. gefällt allen Leuten, die ihn hören. Es ist erstaunlich, was er brillant klingt, neulich spielte ich auf einem kleinen Pleyelschen Flügel, u. es war mir gar nicht möglich, etwas wie Ton daraus zu ziehn, während ich auf meinem das schönste ff. mit meinen lahmen Armen zu Stande bringe.

Diesen Brief will ich aber nicht abgehn lassen, ohne mit einem Vorschlag herauszurücken, den wir Beide schon lange auf der Zunge haben. Ich kann Dir nicht läugnen, es ist uns Beiden nicht angenehm, daß das einzige Bild von Hensel, welches bei Dir hängt, ein altes u. auf keine Weise geeignetes ist, ihn, um mich neu auszudrücken, würdig bei Dir zu vertreten, besonders seitdem Du Cecile u. Carl von Magnus hast malen lassen. Das sieht mir nicht verwandschaftlich u. nicht freundschaftlich genug aus. Hensel macht Dir also folgenden Vorschlag, den ich hiermit unterstütze; Du mögest ihm Rebeckas Bild zurückgeben, u. erlauben daß er statt dessen eine Wiederholung des Deinigen für Cecile mache, welches ja Dir selbst, und allen Verwandten hier, namentlich Paul, so wohl gefallen. Ihr thut gewiß keinen schlechten Tausch, u. uns erweist Ihr eine Gefälligkeit, also dächte ich, wäre der Vorschlag annehmbar. Bitte, antworte uns hierauf.

Liebe Cecile, ich schicke morgen eine Schachtel mit kleinen Sächelchen für die Kinder ab, die Schuh für mein liebes Felixchen habe ich aber nicht können fertig machen lassen, weil ich sein Maaß nicht habe. Bitte, laß sie erst machen, ehe die andere die kleinen Arbeiten bekommen damit das liebe Kind nicht leer ausgeht. Es ist alles meine eigne Fabrik. Nun lebt wohl, Ihr Lieben, Alle den vergnügtesten Tag morgen, u. dann lauter folgende danach. Hensel grüßt u. gratulirt bestens. Eure Fanny

[Sebastian]

140

Jenny Lind geht nach Leipzig, u. wünscht einen Empfehlungsbrief an Dich, in der Hoffnung, daß sie mir vielleicht auch einen giebt, wenn ich einmal zu Dir reise, will ich ihr ihre Bitte nicht abschlagen. Wie lebt Ihr? wir Alle krank, kränklich, unwohl. Hensel ist schon seit fast 4 Wochen recht leidend, u. gar nicht auf dem Strumpf, ich war es 14 Tage lang, Mama Dirichlet u. Beckchens jüngste Kinder haben die Grippe, gestern ist Sebastian eingesegnet worden, das sind die Zeitereignisse. Zu den Begebenheiten aber, die sich nicht ereignet haben, gehört die Athalia, die Du mir durch Taubert nicht geschickt hast, bitte thu es doch, morgen über 14 T. möchte ich wieder Musik haben. Wie schön ist es jetzt schon, wie früh, die Mandeln haben abgeblüht, Pfirsich u. Aprikosen sind dabei, in einigen Tagen blühen die andern Obstbäume, hat man denn in der Königstraße eine Ahndung davon? Ich habe Cecile vor einiger Zeit ein gewisses Mannel geschickt, wofür mich die Kinder, fürchte ich, gar nicht lieben werden, sie hat es ihnen doch hoffentlich nicht gesagt? Ich erfahre heut aus der Zeitung, daß Du einen Sängerverein in Cölln dirigiren wirst, u. ihnen auch ein neues Stück versprochen hast. Du hattest wol noch nicht genug zu thun? Wirst Du denn Dein neues Oratorium in England aufführen? Laß doch irgend etwas von Deinem vielbewegten Planen in unser stagnirendes Leben hören. A propos, willst Du wol so gut seyn mir das Lied abschreiben zu lassen u. mit der Athalia zu schicken.

Solltest Du einmal dran denken, wenn Du Dr. Härtel siehst, so danke ihm doch für seine freundlichen Zeilen, u. die Uebersendung der Seiten. Es hat gehulfen, u. ich bin in Begriff, Berlin das erste Beispiel zu geben, daß man ohne Calixe leben kann. Mit dem alten habe ich mich überworfen, u. den jungen mag ich nicht, es ist aber noch Jemand hier, der mit weniger Prätension eine Seite aufziehn u. sie auch stimmen kann.

Lebet wohl geliebte Bäume, u. schüttelt einmal Eure Aeste, daß mans hier hört. Was macht meine Freundin Marie? Denkt sie noch an Caffee u. Kuchen? Jetzt haben Cléments wieder eine Kuh, das würde ihr

Vergnügen machen. Warum habe ich nichts von den Kindern hier! ich bin gar zuviel allein u. dann fange ich Grillen.

Lebtwohl!

Eure Fanny.

141

Liebe Cecile, Deinen Brief erhielt ich neulich, eben als ich einige Zeilen an Felix durch die Lind-Post abgeschickt hatte. Schönen Dank. Von Devrients habe ich auch directe Nachricht gehabt. Kommt denn Felix nicht noch auf ein Paar T. her, ehe er ins Weite geht, u. macht er das Oratorium für England. Die Reihe von Musikfesten am Rhein muß ganz hübsch werden, wäre ich nicht dies Jahr eine so arme Kirchenmaus, ich ginge gern hin. Grüße an alle liebe Kinder. Bleibst Du denn ganz sitzen, während *er* schwärmt? Lebwohl!

Lieber Felix

Ich habe versprochen, beifolgenden Brief zu bevor- etc. worten, u. thue es hiermit. Ich glaube die Friedheim hat mit deshalb einen Leipziger Flügel gewählt, um das Vergnügen zu haben, Dir einen Brief zu schreiben. Bitte, gieb Walter die Stimmen zur Athalia mit, bitte vergiß es nicht. Er wird seine Würde als Reisender fühlen, u. sie nicht in Cöthen liegen lassen, ich freue mich so sehr darauf, sie singen zu lassen, ich finde sie sehr plaisirlich. Aber Peri— impossibile. Ich kann diesem Schumann keinen Geschmack abgewinnen. Cecile, reiche mir die Hand. Lebt wohl, heut ist Geburtstag, worüber Walter das Nähere specifiziren wird. Wenn er nur nicht zu blöde ist.

Adieu! F.

142

Lieber Felix, diese schöne schwarze Taube kann ich nun doch unmöglich wegfliegen lassen, ohne ihr ein Blättchen in den Schnabel zu stecken. Ein grünes, ungeschriebenes hätte es diesmal werden können, wie Du die Korespondenz eigentlich verlangest, hätte ich Dir nicht Einiges zu sagen. Erstens bin ich entzückt von der Wahl Deines Textes für den Cölner Musikverein, das ist einmal wieder so ein glücklicher Griff, wie Du ihn zu thun verstehst, u. worin eigentlich die ganze Arbeit schon enthalten ist. Ich wollte wol, ich könnte diese schöne Reihe von Musikfesten mitmachen. Zweitens herzlichen Dank für das von mir sehr geliebte Lied, lasse ich es hier singen, so muß ich den Titel ändern, sonst machen sich die Leute lustig über die Tafel, an der nichts zu essen ist. Drittens we[ ]e[a] ich, Du hast mir ja viel zu wenig Stimmen zur Athalja geschickt, ich bitte Dich, gieb Paul noch einmal doppelte mit, was denkst Du von meinem Chor? Und dabei grade will Keiner zurückbleiben, darauf freuen sie sich Alle und ich am Meisten. Also bitte, vergesst es alle Beide nicht, ich lasse Marie bitten, daran zu erinnern.

Und somit lebt Alle wohl, u. seyd herzlich gegrüßt, wie Ihr geliebt seyd.

Fanny.

---

[a]It looks like "wenne," but this is not a word. Perhaps Fanny meant to write "wähne," or perhaps "wenne" or "weene" is an earlier spelling of "wähen."

143

Berlin, 22sten Juni 1846.

Mein lieber Felix, sey einmal recht barmherzig u. recht liebenswürdig, u. nachdem Du Europa u. die angränzenden Länder erfreut, erfreue u. erquicke auch einmal wieder die Deinigen. Komm entweder auf ein Paar

Tage incognito her, u. erzähle, erzähle, erzähle den ganzen lieben langen Tag, oder wenn das nicht seyn kann, schenke uns wenigstens eine Stunde, u. schreibe einen langen, ausführlichen Brief. Ich lasse diesmal all Dein Beschäftigtseyn nicht gelten, u. mache auch einmal einen Anspruch an Deine Zeit, ich denke ich thue es nicht zu oft, bilde Dir ein, es säße irgend ein Schlemil eine Stunde länger bei Dir, dann würdest Du ihn auch nicht zur Thür heraus werfen, kurz laß uns etwas mitgenie[ßen] von dem vielen Prächtigen, das Du erlebt hast, in Cölln muß es gar zu schön gewesen seyn, u. gieb mir einen Begriff, wie 2000 Männerstimmen klingen, von 10 weiß ich es wohl. So was muß ich doch auch einmal hören. Und was war denn in Lüttich los? Denn daß Du nicht hast dirigiren wollen, weil die Musik zu schlecht ging, glaube ich doch schwerlich, angedenkens der Zweybrücker Sängerin, der Du den Taktstock vor die Nase gehalten, Du hast wol vorher beichten sollen, oder dergl.? Kurz laß hören, ich sterbe vor Neugier vielerlei zu wissen. Das ist nun Alles im großen Styl der Existenz, unsre kleine Taschenausgabe lebt aber diesen Sommer auch sehr vergnüglich u. angenehm, ich mache sehr viel Musik u. habe Spaß daran, was wie ich glaubte, für dies Leben schon vorbei wäre, u. freue mich überhaupt meines Lebens mit rechtem Bewußtseyn. Ich weiß nicht, ob es nach recht schwerer, böser Zeit ein verdoppeltes Bedürfniß des Athmens ist, aber ich habe seit meiner Jugend den Tag nicht so genossen, wie diesen Sommer, wo uns denn überhaupt Gott sey Dank heitre, ungestörte Zeit verliehen ist. Ich wollte, ich könnte dasselbe von Rebecka sagen, aber ihre trübselige Laune scheint sich leider so festgesetzt zu haben, daß ich gar kein Ende davon absehn kann. Ich denke manchmal es sey unrecht von mir, mich dagegen gewissermaßen abgestumpft zu haben, u. mich jetzt meines eignen Glücks zu freuen, wie ich es wahrlich lange nicht gekonnt, aber mein Mann hat doch den ersten Anspruch auf mich, u. wenn ich dem das Leben verbittre, dadurch daß ich mich mit um alle Freudigkeit bringen lasse, so ist das am Ende doch auch nicht wohlgethan. Sie wohnt jetzt mit Mama u. den kleinen Kindern hier bei uns oben, wo Ihr zuletzt wart, die Kinder sind so prächtig u. liebenswürdig, daß sie wahrlich schon allein hinreichen müßten, sie heiter, froh u. dankbar zu erhalten. Ich versichere Dich, lieber Felix, das so täglich u. stündlich zu sehn, es ist recht böses Leiden, u. ich danke Gott doppelt, daß ich im Stande bin, jetzt gegen zu halten, u. ein wenig Lust u. Freude im Hause zu verbreiten, im Winter vermochte ich es nicht, da ging ich fast mit zu Grunde in dieser bodenlosen Uebellaunigkeit.—Pauls wohnen im Thiergarten, u. da sehn wir uns leider nicht oft, sie sitzen in ihrem Garten, wir in unserm, Jeder hat Besuch, nur Sonntags kommen wir in der Regel zusammen, die Kinder sind auch dort ganz allerliebst, die kleine Nachwelt macht uns gar zu viel Vergnügen. Ueber seine 4 Wände hinaussehn muß man freilich nicht, dann giebt es zuviel Unerquickliches, hast Du u. A. schon gehört, daß sie hier das Reisestipendium für die jungen Künstler eingezogen u. [?] die Tasche gesenkt haben? Ueberall erweitert man die Mittel u. erleichtert die Wege für Kunstbildung, u. hier ist es, als ob sie nicht eigentlich darauf bedacht wären, die einheimischen Künstler mit Füßen zu treten. Ich bin begierig auf das neue Statut der Academie, das wird auch ein lieb Kind seyn! lebwohl, das Thema kommt am Schluß wieder, das ist zwar auch schon eine alte Jacke, aber wenn auch, erzähle oder schreibe.

Und grüße Cecile u. die Kinder, wie Alles Euch herzlich grüßt.

Deine Fanny.

144

Berlin, 9ten Juli 1846.

Mein lieber Felice, habe Dank für Deinen Brief mit den schönsten Nachrichten, worunter Du die vom Milchreiß freilich oben angestellt hast. Ich hätte immer noch mehr Nachrichten vertragen können, denn wenn Du Dir einbildest, Cecile habe viel geschrieben, so sitzest Du, wie man hier sagt, auf einem dicken Irrthum. Cecile ist zu behäbig, um Details zu schreiben. Doch weiß ich es dankbar anzuerkennen, daß ich der Schlemil war, dem Du eine halbe Stunde geschenkt hast. Warum auch nicht? Soll ich mir nicht einbilden, Dir eben soviel werth zu seyn, als Spohr? Ein so bescheidener Lump werde ich doch nicht seyn. Eigentlich wäre das ein Contract den wir mit einander abschließen könnten, daß Du nach jedem Musikfest, jedem großen Ereigniß einen langen Brief schriebest, damit man doch auch etwas davon hätte. Kommen wir nach langen[a] Zeit einmal zusammen, dann geht doch von den Einzelheiten zu viel verloren, u. wie Gans sagte, so etwas hört man viel lieber zweimal, als gar nicht. Nun geht wieder ein ganzes Oratorium von Dir in die Welt, u. ich kenne keine Note davon. Wann wird das mal an uns kommen? Eigentlich sollte ich Dir jetzt gar nicht zumuthen, diesen Quark zu lesen, beschäftigt wie Du bist, wenn ich Dir nicht hätte schreiben müssen, um Dir etwas mitzutheilen. Da ich aber von Anfang an weiß, daß es Dir nicht recht ist, so werde ich mich etwas ungeschickt dazu anstellen, denn lache mich aus, oder nicht, ich habe zu 40 Jahren eine Furcht vor meinen Brüdern, wie ich sie zu 14 meinem Vater gehabt habe, oder vielmehr Furcht ist nicht das rechte Wort, sondern der Wunsch, Euch u. Allen die ich liebe, es in meinem ganzen Leben recht zu machen, u. wenn ich nun vorher weiß, daß es nicht der Fall seyn wird, so fühle ich mich rather unbehaglich dabei. Mit einem Wort, ich fange an herauszugeben, ich habe Herrn Bocks treuer Liebesbewerbung um meine Lieder, u. seinen vortheilhaften Bedingungen endlich ein geneigtes Ohr geliehen, u. wenn ich mich aus freier Bewegung dazu entschlossen habe, u. Niemanden von den Meinigen verklagen kann, wenn mir Verdruß daraus entsteht, (Freunde u. Bekannte haben mir allerdings lange zugeredet) so kann ich mich anderseits mit dem Bewußtseyn trösten, die Art von musikal. Ruf, die mir zu solchen Anerbietungen verholfen haben mag, auf keinerlei Weise gesucht oder herbeigeführt zu haben. Schande hoffe ich Euch nicht damit zu machen, da ich keine femme libre, u. leider gar kein *junges* Deutschland bin, Verdruß wirst *Du* hoffentlich auch auf keine Weise dabei haben, da ich, um Dir jeden etwa unangenehmen Moment zu ersparen, wie Du siehst, durchaus selbständig verfahren bin, u. so hoffe ich, wirst Du es mir nicht übel nehmen. Gelingt es, d. h. daß die Sachen gefallen, u. ich mehr Anerbietungen bekomme, so weiß ich, daß es mir eine große Anregung seyn wird, deren ich immer bedarf, um etwas hervorzubringen, im andern Falle, bin ich so weit, wie ich immer gewesen bin, werde mich nicht grämen, u. wenn ich dann weniger oder nichts mehr arbeite, so ist ja dann auch nichts dabei verloren. "Das ist der wahre Grund von unserm Zweck u. [Heil]".

Ist es wol möglich einmal den Derwischchor von Leipzig geliehen zu bekommen, oder geht das nicht? Für jetzt brauche ich ihn auf keinen Fall, denn nächsten Sonntag habe ich die letzte Musik für diesen Sommer. Meinen Hauptbassisten Behr bekommt Ihr ja nach Leipzig. Ich glaube, er wird ein sehr guter komischer Sänger werden, nur muß er sich ein bischen vor allzuvielen Narrenspossen hüten. Anlage zur Komik hat er gewiß. Was sagst Du zu diesem göttlichsten Sommer? Ihr thut mir so leid, daß Ihr ihn in der Königsstraße verbringen müßt, ich genieße den Garten so, wie noch nie, u. liebe ihn zärtlicher, als je, vielleicht eine Ahndung, daß wir ihn bald verlieren, es spuken wieder allerlei Verkaufs u. gräuliche Niederreißungs u. Straßendurchbrechungsplane, aber Pourtollès wäre ein rechter Narr, wenn er es nicht kaufte.

Lebt wohl, Ihr lieben Leute, grüße mir die beste Cecile, u. alle fünf Kinder, Hensel grüßt ebenfalls.

Deine Fanny.

Noch eins wollte ich Dich bitten, wenn H. v. Keudell, den Du ja kennst, sich in diesen nächsten 14 T. bei Dir meldet, u. Dir vielleicht noch etwas die Queere bei Deiner Arbeit kommt, nimm ihn doch freundlich auf, er ist jetzt sehr viel in unserm Hause, u. ein guter musikal. Kumpen, mit dem feinsten Gefühl für Musik, und einem Gedächtniß, wie ich es außerdem nur bei Dir kenne. Die wie 150 No. Schubert, 130 No. Beethoven, einige 60 No. Mendelssohn, u. solche Kleinigkeiten mehr weiß er auswendig u. spielt sehr gut.

Die Obige.

---

[a]Fanny wrote "langen" instead of "langer."

145

Mein lieber Felix, da kommen die Trauben u. Feigen wieder, u. da sie, wie ich sehe, so gar vortreffliche Advocaten sind, u. da Du so sehr müstig bist, so will ich Deinen Brief beantworten, gähnt auch. Wenn ich auch kein anders Vergnügen von der Herausgebe meiner Lieder hätte, als diesen Deinen Brief, so würde es mir schon nicht leid thun, denn er ist sehr liebenswürdig, u. hat mich auf drei Tage lustig gemacht, wäre ich es nicht ohnehin. Warum ich meine Lieder nicht an Dich adressirt habe? Zum Theil weiß ichs, zum Theil nicht, ich wollte Cecile als Vermittlerin in Anspruch nehmen, weil ich doch so eine Sorte von bösem Gewissen Dir gegenüber hatte, denn allerdings, wenn ich bedenke, daß ich vor 10 Jahren fand, es wäre zu spät, u. jetzt, es wäre grade die äußerste Zeit, so ist das rather lächerlich, so wie ich mich auch lange bei dem Gedanken empört habe, auf meine alten Tage mit op. 1 anzufangen. Da Du nun aber so überaus liebenswürdig dabei bist, will ich Dir auch bekennen, wie entsetzlich mausig ich mich gemacht habe, u. daß nächstens 6 4stimm. Lieder kommen, von denen Du kaum eins kennst. Ich hätte sie Dir gern erst mitgetheilt, aber Du kamst doch nicht, u. schriftlich geht das nicht. Meine Freitagssänger haben sie gern gesungen, u. unterstützt von dem guten Rath, der mir hier zu Gebote steht, habe ich mir Mühe gegeben, es so gut zu machen, als ich kann. Ich werde so frei seyn, dem Dr. Mendelssohn ein Exemplar zu schicken.

Aber nun, noch einmal schönen Dank u. schönen Dank! Was hast Du mir für Freude gemacht, durch den Beethoven, u. wie kommt mir der zu Recht, da ich nächsten Sonntag etwas Musik machen will, u. eine Stunde, ehe Dein Brief kam, Taubert fragte, ob er mir gar nichts Neues empfehlen könne, u. ob er denn nichts von den Ruinen von Athen wüßte? Nun kann ich die Sachen grade noch ausschreiben u. probiren lassen. Ich habe mich gestern den ganzen Vormittag dran erfreut. Wie liebenswürdig, u. wie ganz menschlich ist er in dieser Musik, nur bei dem Derwischchor kehrt er den alten Brummbär gar zu prächtig heraus. Das einzige, was mir an Deinem Brief gar nicht gefallen hat, ist die Unbestimmtheit Deiner Herreise, u. daß ich von Deinem neuen Oratorium dessen *Namen* ich jetzt freilich erfahren habe, (ich habe auch Gegenstände zum Necken) auch weiter noch nichts weiß, während doch das ganze Birminghamer Publicum, von denen vielleicht Wenige so viel Freude daran haben werden, als ich, klug ist, u. Chor u. Orchester sogar sehr klug. And a tremendous affair it is, sagte der Bericht der Morning chronicle, die mir mein Freund, Lord Oxenpantoffel sogleich zuschickte, von einer der encoreten Nummern. Kurz, ich bin sehr ungeduldig. Muß denn das so lange dauern, bis Alles gedruckt ist? Das kann wirklich lange dauern, u. darüber wird man nicht nur alt u. grau, sondern noch älter u. noch grauer. Komme Du bald! Es ist lange her, daß wir uns nicht sahen, u. es sieht, Gottlob, jetzt recht heiter u. gut bei uns aus. Beckchen wohnt noch hier, wird aber in nächster Woche hinüber ziehn. Hensel u. sie brauchen eine Art von Traubencur im Garten. Seb. ist mit sehr guter Censur nach Prima versetzt, und lernt jetzt in den Ferien fleißig bei Biermann aquarelliren. Frank wird vorläufig hier wohnen, u. zwar auf dem Leipziger Platz, was uns sehr angenehm ist, u. unsre Wintergeselligkeit nur aufs Erfreulichste beleben kann. Alles grüßt Euch Alle aufs Herzlichste, Mama läßt Dir sagen, wie gerührt sie von Deinem guten Andenken ist. Beckchen läßt fragen, ob Behr die Pferde von Walter für Carl abgegeben? Wie gehts denn meinem Freunde Behr dort? Entzückt er Leipziger, oder wenig? Mit einer Traubenschachtel, die vorgestern fix u. fertig gepackt dastand, hat sich die tragische Begebenheit ereignet, daß sie dann nicht abgehn konnte, die heutigen sind etwas verregnet, u. Du wirst finden, daß sie die Mittagshöhe ihrer Vortrefflichkeit leider überschritten haben. Wespen, Spatzen, u. lange Trockenheit haben an der Blüte ihrer Schönheit genagt. Schicke indeß die Schachtel doch wieder zurück, vielleicht finden wir noch einmal etwas Eurer Würdiges. Lebt wohl, lebt wohl, Ihr lieben Leutchen. Das man sich jetzt in 7 Stunden erreichen kann, ist allerdings sehr schön, wenn nur nicht doch 7 Monate u. mehr drüber hingingen, ohne daß man sich sieht, wie Figure zeigt.

F.

Hensel grüßt tausendmal.

146

Mein lieber Felix, hier mit dieser Schachtel kommt ein Brief, wie Du ihn gern hast, ein grünes Blatt, oder eine blaue Traube. Weiter sollst Du Corespondenz[meider] denn auch nichts zu lesen haben. Ich aber liebe sehr die Briefe schwarz auf weiß, u. wünschte wol, Du theiltest uns die letzten Capitel Deiner Biographie mit, u. auch den nächstzuerlebenden Band, wann Du zu kommen denkst, wann etwas aufzuführen, nur ungefähr, u. Cecile kommt doch wol einmal wieder mit? Ja? Was sagst Du zu diesem unerschöpflich wunderbaren Jahr? Wir genießen u. genießen, u. können uns nicht satt Luft schnappen, es thut mir nur leid, daß die liebe Cecile nichts davon gehabt hat, der Garten war zu schön, u. nie haben wir auch solche Traubenlust gehabt, die Spaliere brachen unter der Last. Cecile soll so gut seyn, mir die Schachtel wieder zu schicken, dann kommt sie nächste Woche gefüllt wieder. Adieu, mein liebster Bruder, ich freue mich nicht wenig drauf, Dich bald wieder zu sehn, es ist lange her, seit wir nicht zusammen waren. Beckchen wohnt noch hier, u. ist wohl.

Eigendorff kommt, lebt wohl!

Deine F.

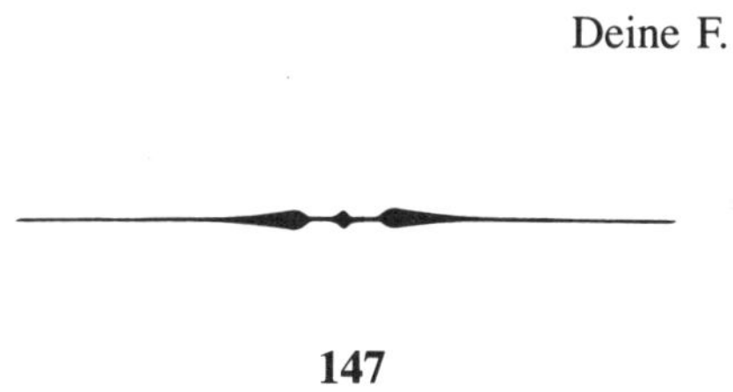

147

26sten Oktbr. 46.

Ich muß Dir heut einen Zettel schreiben, der kein Blatt u. keine Traube ist, u. zwar in andrer Leute Angelegenheiten. Vor ein Paar Tagen war Mad. Hildebrandt, die Tochter v. Bernhard Romberg bei mir, um zu fragen, wenn u. wo sie Dich in der Welt antreffen könnte, u. ob Du sie wol freundlich aufnehmen würdest, wenn sie mit ihrem Sohn zu Dir käme, Dein Urtheil über musikal. Talent zu erbitten, das Letztere glaubte ich ihr versprechen zu können, ich muß in solchen Fallen immer daran denken, wie Vater mit Dir zu Cherubini reiste, über das Erstere versprach ich mich zu erkundigen, vielleicht erfahre ichs bei der Gelegenheit auch. Die Frau wohnt jetzt in Hamburg, u. will mit ihrem Sohn nach Leipzig oder Berlin reisen, lieber hierher, wenn sie Dich hier zu treffen weiß. Einstweilen höre ich nun, daß sichs mit Deinem Herkommen wieder ganz ins Ungewisse verschleppt, u. betrübe mich darüber. Ja, wenn nur das Leben nicht auf diese Weise sachte zu Ende ginge, ein Jahr nach dem andern, ohne daß man etwas von einander hat. Es sind nun schon beinah wieder 9 Monat, daß wir uns nicht gesehn. Es ist traurig!

Ich danke Dir sehr für Comala. Peri, Ossian, lauter Nachkommenschaft von der Walpurgisnacht. Sowie Du es aber möglich gemacht hast, aus dieser kurzen, einfachen Ballade das allerinteressanteste Werk zu machen, (das letzten Sonntag wieder mit Enthusiasmus hier gesungen worden, mein kleiner Chor weiß es auswendig, u. fiel vollstimmig ein, als ein neuer Solosänger in der Probe fehlte) so kochen die Andere breite Bettelsuppen, u. werden, wie ich sehr fürchte, von der Langenweile zu Grabe getragen. Verzeih, wenn ich voreilig urtheile, ich habe das Gadesche Stück erst einmal gespielt, u. unter dem Einfluß des Mißtrauens gegen den Ossianschen Text, der mir denn doch gar zu einförmig erscheint, nur der Geisterchor bringt etwas anders in die ewige Klage. Zum Sonntag kann ich nichts mehr daraus singen lassen, u. dann ist für diese Season das letzte Concert, aber zum Frühjahr werde ich es dann ganz singen lassen, mich überhaupt mit Wuth in die Opposition, d. h. die moderne deutsche Musik werfen, wenn sie Einem auch nicht immer schmecken will, man muß darin mit gutem Beispiel hier vorangehn, wo sie so unglaublich faul vornehm gegen alles Neue sind, ich sage Dir, wenn irgend ein hier Angestellter u. Bezahlter sich so viel Mühe um die Sache gäbe, wie ich u. noch ein Paar Dilettanten, es würde manches anders herauskommen. Gades Symphonie habe ich bei Taubert durchgesetzt, u. sie ist in der ersten Soiree recht gut gespielt worden, u. hat mir wieder unglaubliches Vergnügen gemacht, besonders das Andante, das in seiner süßen, liebenswürdigen Einfachheit meine wahre Liebe ist.—Was thust Du denn jetzt? Womit bist Du beschäftigt?

Hensel muß noch immer das Haus hüten, seine Wunde ist noch nicht zu. In derselben Zeit hatte sich Mama Dirichlet den Fuß vertreten, u. mußte einige Tage liegen, vorgestern haben die beiden Lahmen ein rührendes Wiedersehn gefeiert. Es ist doch schade, daß Du die Ausstellung gar nicht siehst, sie ist recht interessant, u. daß kein einziges Bild ganz ausschließlich die Aufmerksamkeit in Anspruch nimmt, halte ich für keinen Nachtheil, die Berliner sind gar zu unausstehlich wenn sie verliebt sind, diesmal vertheilt sich Liebe u. Haß, u. dabei kann man bestehn. An Stoff zum Streiten fehlt es zwar nicht, aber es kommt doch nicht zu Mord u. Todtschlag.

Beckchen wirst Du recht vortheilhaft verändert finden, wenn Du nicht zu lange ausbleibst, u. der Winter sie nicht unterdess wieder angreift. Wenn ich an die elende, traurige Zeit denke, die wir voriges Jahr mit ihr durchzumachen hatten, kann ich Gott nicht genug danken, daß es sich so über jede Erwartung gebessert hat. Leb wohl, mein lieber, lieber Felix: das ist das Einzige, was mich zuweilen traurig macht, daß wir so fern von einander leben, u. sowenig von Dir hören. Grüß Cecile u. die lieben Kinder, hier grüßt Alles. Ist Mad. Jeanrenaud noch dort?

F.

148

Mein lieber Felix, hier erhältst Du durch Deine Frankfurter Freunde einen Theil der Dinge, die Du gewünscht hast, Alles habe ich leider nicht auftreiben können. Nämlich zuerst Deine Geographie habe ich nicht gefunden, glaube auch, daß Du vor einigen Jahren Alles der Art, was noch hier vorhanden war, mitgenommen hast. Zweitens, nun schäme ich mich aber, u. werde 8 Tage lang in Domino u. Marke umher gehn, habe ich die Gartenzeitung nicht finden können, u. wie es sogar bequem ist, Alles auf andre Leute zu schieben, so muß zehn Jahre lang die Schuld von allem Unfindbaren Albertine tragen, die, als wir zuletzt in Italien waren, hier gewohnt, u. mir Alles ausgeräumt hat, bis auf meinen Schreibtisch. Ich finde sie aber, u. schick sie Dir, sobald sich der erste Zipfel davon sehn läßt. Dagegen erhältst Du die Briefe vom lieben sel. Vater, u. was sich in den bei Rebecka u. mir befindlichen Briefen v. Klingemann Poetisches zerstreut fand, so wie meine neuen Pimpernüßchen. Ich hätte gern gesehn, die beiden Hefte wären zusammen gekommen, oder vielmehr gar nicht getheilt worden, will aber nun doch nicht verzögern, Dir die erste Hälfte zu schicken, es hilft ja nichts, vielleicht hast Du sie schon wieder eher gesehn als ich. Du armer Felix, das fehlt Dir auch noch, daß Du einem Berliner einem[a] Empfehlungsbrief an mich geben mußt, ich habe das inliegende Würstchen richtig erhalten, u. es gleich auf den andern Tag zum Trio eingeladen. Es soll diesen Winter immer an dem dritten Sonntag, der uns zufällt, gefeirt[b] werden, wenn Violinen da sind, ich bin zu allen Humoren aufgelegt, u. will lustig leben. Vorgestern waren die Bernus' bei uns in kleiner Gesellschaft, u. gestern waren sie bei Paul in kleiner Gesellschaft, u. die beiden kleinen Gesellschaften waren ganz dieselben, was Paul, der vorgestern verreist, u. also nicht bei uns war, gestern zu seinem großen, u. sehr komischen Schrecken erfuhr, es hat aber gar nichts geschadet.

Hensels Fuß ist immer noch nicht besser, es zieht sich nun schon in der 5ten Woche hin, heut aber macht es ernstliche Anstalt zum Heilen. Beckchen ist Gott sey Dank, recht wohl diesen Winter, speriamo daß es so fort geht, dann kann das Leben recht angenehm werden. Unser kleiner täglicher Kreis hat sich jetzt sehr hübsch abgerundet, u. Frank ist eine außerordentliche Verbesserung, man kann wirklich nicht angenehmer im näheren Umgang seyn, als er es ist.

Nun lebt wohl, Ihr lieben Leute. Ich seufze, ich seufze, daß Euer Kommen nun wieder in nebelhafte Ferne gerückt ist, Gott bessers. Grüß Cecile u. alle liebe Kinder. Ich habe lange nichts Ausführliches von ihnen gehört, u. möchte das besonders gern vom Felix u. der Lili. Lebt wohl, der arme Johann thut mir recht leid, u. ihr auch dabei.

Eure Fanny.

---

[a]Fanny wrote "einem" instead of "einen."
[b]She omitted the third "e" in "gefeiert."

149

Berlin, den 2ten Januar 1847.

Ich muß nur einmal mein Tagewerk mit dem grünen Blatt anfangen, sonst gelingt es mir wieder nicht, Euch zu schreiben, Ihr lieben Geschwister. Zuerst habe Euern besten Dank für die wohlschmekende Sendung, u. die guten Nachrichten. Liebe Cecile, was ich diesmal für Freude von Felixens Aufenthalt gehabt habe, das kann ich Dir gar nicht sagen, es war nicht so unruhig um ihn her, als gewöhnlich, er blieb den ganzen Morgen zu Hause, hat mir Elias vorgespielt, u. erzählt, es waren prächtigen 8 Tage. Er hat zwar bei uns gefroren, aber sein gutes Gewissen, daß er mir so große Freude gemacht hat, muß ihn noch hinterher warm halten. Der Winter ist bös, u. wir haben in unserm dünnen Sommerpalästchen viel zu leiden, dafür war es auch den größten Theil des Jahrs desto schöner. Weihnachtsabend war Alles bei uns, u. wir hatten einen sehr schönen Aufbau, der große Orangebaum war Weihnachtsbaum, (diese Mittheilung ist eigentlich für Marie) in den Zweigen durch ausgehöhlte Citronen erleuchtet, um den Kübel ein Kranz von Lichtern, die Erde mit Moos, u. dieses mit bunten Zuckerplätzchen bedeckt, die Thüren mit Taxusbogen bekleidet, u. Alles voll Blumen, Lichtern, vielen Gypssachen, die wir verschenkt haben, u. die sich zum Ausputz sehr hübsch eignen. Nachher spielten wir sämmtliche 3 Kindersymphonieen, welche am Sylvesterabend "unter Mitwirkung des berühmten Virtuosen, H. Ernst" wiederholt wurden. Ich weiß nicht, ob Du Dich erinnerst, Felix, zu einer derselben ein agnolo gesetzt zu haben, welches Paul auf einem kleinen weißen Pudel mit vielem Beifall schön verträgt.

Das wäre nun Alles recht gut, wenn nur die Heidelberger Geschichte erst entschieden wäre, die liegt uns aber Allen recht in den Gliedern. Wenn es an einer Verschlepperei hier scheiterte, das wäre doch ganz abscheulich, denn im Grunde wünschen doch Alle, u. er nicht am letzten, daß er bleibe. Seine Freunde haben Alle ihre Schuldigkeit gethan, dagegen ist nichts zu sagen. Bis auf diese böse Ueberraschung am Schluß war das Jahr im Allgemeinen sehr gut, ich wünsche mir in mancher Beziehung mehr solche. Am Reichsten war es freilich für Paul, 2 Kinder in einem Jahr, das will was sagen. Albertine ist auch diesmal etwas angegriffen, u. erholt sich langsamer, doch ist sie wohl.

Nun lebt wohl, Ihr lieben Leute, habt ein gutes Jahr, mit all Euern Kindern, u. mögen wir viel zusammen kommen, das wünsche ich mehr, als ich es hoffe.

Hensel grüßt bestens u. wünscht ebenfalls viel Glück zum neuen Jahr.

Eure Fanny

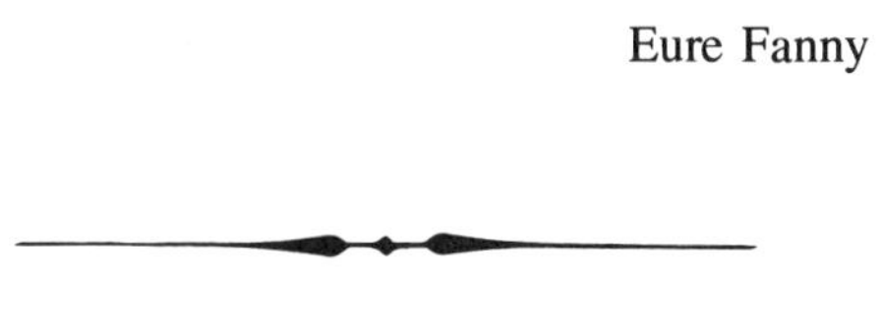

150

Berlin, den 1sten Februar

An dem Tage, an dem alle Völker sich durch Deputationen dem Throne Ew. musikalischen Majestät nahen, wage auch ich, Dir schönstens zu gratuliren, Herr Bruder, u. Dir ferner so viel Glück zu wünschen, als Du, Gott sey Dank! hast, u. verdienst u. vertragen kannst. Eigentlich müßte man Reihe herum Deiner Frau, u. allen Deinen Kindern zu Deinem Geburtstag Glück wünschen, u. dann käme es nur alle 7 Jahre an Dich, ich fürchte nur, Felixchen u. Lili ist fast eben so wenig mit einem Briefe gedient, als Dir, u. zur Strafe dafür sollst Du ihn eben lesen, u. Chocolade u.

Kuchenkrümel darauf fallen lassen, u. ihn auf den Tisch werfen, zu allen Ständchen u. Blumen, u. Damenarbeiten, u. dem Gedicht v. Herrn v. Webern, u. einem Band sonstiger Gedichte, u. allen Besuchen, u. allen Beweisen der Freude, die alle Leute von sich geben, daß Du vor so u. so viel 30 Jahren in Hamburg angefangen. Damit ist uns freilich Allen gedient, u. sehr. Ich schicke Dir leider nichts, als meine 4stimmigen Lieder, u. bitte Dich, spiele sie der lieben Cecile, die immer ein gütiges Publicum für mich ist, vor, ein andres Exemplar folgt dieser Tage durch Eigendorfsche Gelegenheit für Mme. Frege. Es hängt sehr angenehme Zeit an diesen Liedern, u. darum sind sie mir lieber, als andre meiner Pimpernüßchen.

Dieser Tage habe ich einen Brief aus Wien erhalten, der wesentlich nichts enthielt, als die Anfrage ob "auf Flügeln des Gesanges" von mir wäre, u. ich möchte überhaupt ein Verzeichniß von den Sachen von mir schicken, die verkappt in der Welt umherlaufen, es scheint, sie sind selber nicht pfiffig genug, die Spreu von Weizen zu sondern. Darauf muß ich nun meinen ganzen Witz zusammen nehmen, denn blos zu antworten: ach, meine Herren, leider nein! das fände ich rather platt, u. so dumm werde ich auch nicht seyn, ihnen meine Paar Sächelchen mit Fingern zu zeigen, ich hab es halt so besser, aber unverschämt will ich auch nicht seyn, kurz, ich muß beinah eben so im Dunkel lassen, als der Magistrat unsre Straßen, seit er die Erleuchtung übernommen. Sonntag taufen wir nun bei Albertine, wenn nur ihr Bruder keinen Queerstrich macht, der ist leider im letzten Stadium seiner Krankheit. Das Kind ist ganz allerliebst u. sieht Käthchen sehr ähnlich, da es nun auch dieselbe Amma hat, so wird die Aehnlichkeit wol noch wachsen. Ach, wenn ich Eure Kinder doch einmal wiedersehn könnte, das ist nun Alles wieder ein Jahr lang in die Höhe geschossen. Ich glaube, liebe Cecile, ich war neulich ein so undankbarer Lump, daß ich dem lieben Mariechen gar nicht für ihre niedliche Arbeit gedankt habe, bitte thue es für mich, u. sage ihr, sie hätte mir viel Freude damit gemacht. Und Dir lieber Felix, habe ich noch zu danken für Dein Trio u. Dein Liederheft, Beides schon vielfach gebraucht, u. für die Zeitung mit dem Beethovenschen Brief, der sehr interessant ist, dergl. sollten Härtels öfter publiciren. Der Lind ihre Angelegenheiten in London haben sich ja häßlich verwickelt, es sieht mir bald so aus, als würde sie gar nicht hingehn können. Wer wird dann die Partie in der neuen Oper von Dir singen, von denen die Zeitungen uns erzählen? Wie weit ist der Elias? Natürlich bekommen wir ihn diesen Winter hier nicht, u. dann wird er im Sommer überall gegeben, u. wir haben wieder das Nachsehn. Wofür stehn wir denn an der Spitze der Civilisation?

Mit Dirichlet ist leider noch alles auf dem alten Fleck. Er hört weder von Heidelberg noch von hier etwas, u. fängt an, sehr verdrießlich zu werden. Ich fürchte nur, es ist dem Minister hier ganz recht, wenn er geht, denn sonst hätte er, nach den Schritten, die die Facultät gethan hat, u. da er den Willen des Königs in demselben Sinne weiß, sich längst rühren müssen. Daß sie ihm die Schleife angehängt haben, wirst Du wol wissen.

Sonst leben wir ganz vergnügt, jeder nach seiner Weise fleißig, u. sehen dabei viel Leute. Sebastian, denke Dir, liebe Cecile, ist ein vollständiger Jüngling, u. beliebter Tänzer, weshalb er aber, natürlich nicht das Geringste von seinen Studien versäumen darf, heut ist er auf einem Ball bei der alten Mad. Magnus, o Felix, wir werden alt, da haben wir auch in früheren Jahrhunderten getanzt. Lieb ist es mir, daß er auch nicht einen Spur von Narrheit oder Ziererei zeigt, er hat andre Fehler, aber im Ganzen sind wir doch recht mit ihm zufrieden. Hensel hat sein großes Bild unter Farbe, u. arbeitet an verschiedenen Sachen gleichzeitig, er läßt tausendmal herzlich grüßen, u. Glück wünschen, wie auch Seb., dessen Rückkehr von der Schule ich nicht erwarten kann, um dieses grüne Blatt, welches ein blauer Brief ist, zur Eisenbahn zu schicken. Ich danke Dir auch noch, daß Du vor Weihnacht 8 Tage hier gefroren hast, es war sehr hübsch, u. im Grunde friere ich doch schon 17 Jahre hier, die Sommermonate ausgenommen, u. befinde mich ganz wohl dabei.

Lebt Alle wohl, u. laßt etwas von Euch hören.

Eure F

Appendix A: List of the Letters

No.	Green Books No.	Date	Destination	Page No.
1	I 2	28 October [1821]	[Leipzig]	1
2	I 5	[29 October 1821]	[Leipzig]	3
3	I 6	3 November 1821	[Weimar]	4
4	I 7	Berlin, 6 November 1821	[Weimar]	7
5	I 7c	[8 April 1825]	[Paris]	8
6	I 9	Monday, 11 April [1825]	[Paris]	9
7	I 8	25 April 1825	[Paris]	12
8	I 12	29 April [1825]	[Paris]	15
9	I 14b	Berlin, 16 February [1827]	[Stettin]	18
10	I 16	[after 16 February 1827]	[Stettin]	20
11	I 32	[PM 25 October (1828)]	Brandenburg	21
12	I 39	Berlin, 18 April 1829	London	23
13	I 41	Berlin, 24 April 1829	[London]	28
14	I 43	1 May 1829	[London]	32
15	I 66	[c. 6 May 1829]	[London]	35
16	I 47	7 May 1829	[London]	37

17	I 50	20 May 1829	[London]	39
18	I 51	Berlin, 27 May 1829	London	42
19	I 56	3 June 1829	London	43
20	I 55	4 June [1829]	[London]	47
21	I 58	Thursday, 11 [June 1829]	[London]	51
22	I 64	Berlin, 29 June 1829	[London]	57
23	I 65	1 July 1829	London	59
24	I 69	[PM 8 July (1829)]	London	61
25	I 70	[PM 8 July (1829)]	London	66
26	I 73	13 July [1829]	London	68
27	I 79	15 August 1829	[London]	73
28	I 82	Berlin, 21 August 1829	London	76
29	I 84	[31 August (1829)]	London	79
30	I 90	Leipziger Strasse No. 3 21 September [1829]	London	83
31	I 95	Berlin, 28 September 1829	London	86
32	I 98	[3 October 1829]	London	90
33	I 100	Berlin, 8 October [1829]	London	92
34	I 97	[PM 3 November (1829)]	London	94
35	I 59	[c. early November 1829]	[London]	96
36	II 16	Tuesday, 18 May 1830	[Weimar]	96
37	II 19	[22 May (1830)]	[Weimar]	99
38	II 23	30 May 1830	[Munich?]	101
39	II 45	[PM 29 June (1830)]	Munich	102
40	II 52	Berlin, 5 July [1830]	Munich	103
41	II 54b	[c. 9 July 1830]	[Munich]	105
42	II 63	[c. end of July 1830]	[Salzburg?]	106
43	II 87	Berlin, 22 April 1833	London	108
44	II 90	[c. 8 May 1833]	London	109
45	II 93	Thursday, 16 May [1833]	Düsseldorf	110
46	II 128	Berlin, 22 October 1833	[Düsseldorf]	111
47	II 133	Berlin, 2 November 1833	Düsseldorf	114
48	II 150, 149	Berlin, [23 November 1833]	[Düsseldorf]	116

49	II 158	Berlin, 1 December 1833	[Düsseldorf]	118
50	III 15	Berlin, 25 January 1834	[Düsseldorf]	120
51	III 47	Berlin, 18 February 1834	Düsseldorf	124
52	III 78	[c. 27 February 1834]	[Düsseldorf]	127
53	III 96	Berlin, 12 April 1834	[Düsseldorf]	132
54	III 118	Sunday, 27 April 1834	Düsseldorf	137
55	III 140	Berlin, 11 May [1834]	[Düsseldorf]	139
56	III 165	Berlin, 4 June 1834	[Düsseldorf]	141
57	III 170, 171	[11 June 1834]	[Düsseldorf]	144
58	III 181, 333	Berlin, 18 June 1834	[Düsseldorf]	147
59	III 194	Berlin, 1 July [1834]	[Düsseldorf]	150
60	III 237	[c. 1 August 1834]	[Düsseldorf]	151
61	III 304, 305	4 November 1834	Düsseldorf	153
62	III 320	Berlin, 24 November [1834]	[Düsseldorf]	156
63	III 309, 338	30 November [1834]	[Düsseldorf]	160
64	III 341, IV 221	Berlin, 27 December 1834	Düsseldorf	164
65	IV 6, 106	Berlin, 16 January [1835]	[Düsseldorf]	168
66	IV 219, 220	[PM 29 January (1835)]	[Düsseldorf]	171
67	IV 13, 218b	Berlin, 17 February 1835	[Düsseldorf]	173
68	IV 21	Berlin, 8 March 1835	[Düsseldorf]	177
69	IV 24	Berlin, 19 March 1835	Düsseldorf	180
70	IV 27	Berlin, 8 April 1835	Düsseldorf	182
71	IV 120	Berlin, 8 October 1835	Leipzig	184
72	IV 134	Berlin, 29 October 1835	Leipzig	186
73	IV 142	Berlin, 7 November [1835]	Leipzig	188
74	IV 146	Berlin, 9 November 1835	Leipzig	189
75	IV 155	Berlin, 18 November 1835	[Leipzig]	190
76	IV 181	Berlin, 11 December [1835]	Leipzig	193
77	V 7	Berlin, 5 January [1836]	Leipzig	194
78	V 10	Berlin, 26 January 1836	[Leipzig]	196
79	V 16	3 February [1836]	[Leipzig]	197

80	V 21	Berlin, 4 February 1836	Leipzig	199
81	V 31	20 February 1836	Leipzig	203
82	V 95	Berlin, 1 June [1836]	[Frankfurt]	204
83	V 103	Berlin, 28 June 1836	Frankfurt	205
84	V 112	Berlin, 30 July 1836	[Scheveningen?]	207
85	V 129	Berlin, 19 October 1836	Leipzig	210
86	V 132	Berlin, 28 October 1836	Leipzig	214
87	V 135	Berlin, 16 November 1836	[Leipzig]	216
88	V 139	Berlin, 22 November [1836]	Leipzig	221
89	V 146	11 December [1836]	[Leipzig]	223
90	V 149	Berlin, 19 December [1836]	Frankfurt	225
91	VI 5	Berlin, 20 January 1837	Leipzig	227
92	VI 9	Berlin, 27 January 1837	[Leipzig]	229
93	VI 32	Berlin, 13 April 1837	[Freiburg]	231
94	VI 43	Berlin, 2 June 1837	[Frankfurt]	233
95	VI 47	[PM 19 June (1837)]	Frankfurt	238
96	VI 56	[after c. 10 July 1837]	Frankfurt	239
97	VI 60	31 July 1837	[?]	242
98	VI 63	Berlin, 29 August 1837	London	244
99	VI 151	Berlin, 12 December 1837	[Leipzig]	245
100	VII 17	Berlin, 15 January 1838	Leipzig	247
101	VII 20	Berlin, 19 January 1838	[Leipzig]	251
102	VII 39	Berlin, 2 February 1838	[Leipzig]	254
103	VII 36	Berlin, 14 February 1838	Leipzig	256
104	VII 66	Berlin, 21 February 1838	Leipzig	258
105	VIII 48	Berlin, 7 September 1838	Leipzig	260
106	VIII 118	Berlin, 14 December 1838	Leipzig	262
107	IX 12, 11	Berlin, 6 January 1839	Leipzig	264
108	X 238	[c. 3 February 1839]	[Leipzig]	268
109	X 259	[c. 4 February 1839]	[Leipzig]	270
110	IX 70	Berlin, 26 February 1839	[Leipzig]	271

111	IX 80	Berlin, 4 March 1839	[Leipzig]	274
112	IX 142a	Berlin, 28 April 1839	[Frankfurt?]	276
113	IX 152	Berlin, 8 May 1839	Düsseldorf	278
114	X 65	Munich, 23 September 1839	[Leipzig]	279
115	XI 1	Rome, 1 January 1840	Leipzig	281
116	XI 77	Rome, 4 March 1840	Leipzig	285
117	XI 143	Rome, 10 May 1840	Leipzig	289
118	XII 89	Berlin, 28 September 1840	Leipzig	294
119	XII 161	Berlin, 9 December 1840	Leipzig	298
120	XII 215	[after 9 December 1840]	[Leipzig]	301
121	XIII 16	Berlin, 13 January 1841	Leipzig	302
122	XIII 41	Berlin, 29 January 1841	Leipzig	304
123	XIII 99	Berlin, 2 March 1841	[Leipzig]	306
124	XVI 10	Berlin, 13 July 1841	[Leipzig]	308
125	XVI 147	Berlin, 5 December 1842	[Leipzig]	310
126	XVII 29	Berlin, 17 January [1843]	Leipzig	313
127	XVII 37	Berlin, 2 March 1843	Leipzig	315
128	XVII 163	Berlin, 28 March 1843	Leipzig	316
129	XVII 206	Berlin, 17 April 1843	[Leipzig]	318
130	XVII 234	Berlin, 2 May 1843	[Leipzig]	319
131	XVII 255	Berlin, 14 May 1843	[Leipzig]	323
132	XIX 284	Berlin, 4 June 1844	[London]	324
133	XX 42	Berlin, 30 July 1844	[Soden]	326
134	XX 217	Berlin, 21 December 1844	[Frankfurt?]	329
135	XXI 92	Florence, 4 March 1845	Frankfurt	332
136	XXI 129	Rome, 3 April 1845	Frankfurt	334
137	XXII 44	Berlin, 4 August 1845	Frankfurt	337
138	XXII 111	Berlin, 20 September 1845	Leipzig	339
139	XXIII 76, 77	Berlin, 2 February 1846	Leipzig	341
140	XXIII 233	[before 11 April 1846]	[Leipzig]	343
141	XXIII 233	[11 April 1846]	[Leipzig]	344

Appendix B: Biographical Timeline for Fanny and Felix

1805

14 November: Fanny is born in Hamburg.

1809

3 February: Felix is born in Hamburg.

1811

Family moves from Hamburg to Berlin.

1816

All 4 children are baptized as Christians; Fanny and Felix receive piano instruction from Marie Bigot in Paris.

1818

28 October: Felix's first public piano performance.

1819

Felix and Fanny probably begin their study of theory and composition with Zelter; 11 December: earliest extant pieces by Fanny and Felix respectively—a lied by each in honor of their father's birthday.

1820

1 October: Fanny and Felix enroll at the Singakademie.

1821

Fanny meets Wilhelm Hensel at a Berlin art exhibition; November: Felix visits Goethe in Weimar.

1822

Family adds the surname Bartholdy; July-October: family travels to Switzerland and visits Goethe in Weimar on the return trip.

1823

Spring: Felix's confirmation takes place; August: Felix, Abraham, and Paul journey to Silesia; the Mendelssohns' musicales begin around this time.

1824

Summer: Felix, Abraham, and Rebecka visit Doberan.

1825

22 March-25 May: Felix visits Paris with Abraham and sees Goethe in Weimar on the return trip; Spring or Summer: family moves into the estate at Leipziger Strasse 3.

1826

Summer: Felix composes the Overture to *A Midsummer Night's Dream;* Fanny travels to Doberan.

1827

February: Felix makes a brief journey to Stettin for the premiere of the Overture; 29 April: Felix's opera, *Die Hochzeit des Camacho*, is produced and given only one performance; May: Felix matriculates at the University of Berlin; August-October: Felix takes a tour of the Harz Mountains; three of Fanny's lieder are published under Felix's authorship in his Opus 8.

1828

October: Felix makes a brief journey to Brandenburg.

1829

January: Fanny becomes engaged to W. Hensel; 11 March: revival of the *St. Matthew* Passion at the Singakademie takes place under Felix's leadership; 10 April: Felix departs for England, accompanied by Abraham and Rebecka as far as Hamburg; 21 April: Felix arrives in England; late July-9 September: Felix visits Scotland with Klingemann; 17 September: Felix sustains a knee injury, delaying his trip home; 3 October: Fanny marries W. Hensel; 7 December: Felix returns to Berlin; 25-26 December: celebration of parents' silver anniversary.

1830

13 May: Felix begins his lengthy *Bildungsreise*; 20 May: Felix visits Goethe in Weimar; 6 June: Felix arrives in Munich; three of Fanny's lieder are published under Felix's authorship in his Op. 9; 16 June: Fanny gives birth to her son, Sebastian; 13 August: Felix arrives in Vienna; 9 October: Felix begins his lengthy Italian visit.

1831

Fanny assumes an ever-increasing role in the organization and leadership of the Sunday musicales; August: Felix visits Switzerland; September-October: Felix visits Munich; November: Felix travels to Düsseldorf, via Stuttgart, Heidelberg, and Frankfurt; December: Felix arrives in Paris for an extended stay.

1832

23 April: Felix arrives in London; July: Felix returns to Berlin; End of the year: Felix becomes a candidate for the leadership of the Singakadmie, to succeed Zelter.

1833

22 January: Rungenhagen is selected over Felix to direct the Singakademie; 26-28 May: Felix conducts the Lower Rhenish Music Festival in Düsseldorf, and Abraham attends; 5 June-4 August: Felix and Abraham visit London; 1 October: Felix assumes the position of Music Director in Düsseldorf.

1834

March: Felix begins work on the music of *St. Paul;* 18-20 May: Felix attends the Lower Rhenish Music Festival in Aachen; Spring: Felix is made a member of the Berlin Academy of Fine Arts; September: Felix visits the family in Berlin; 23 October: Felix returns to Düsseldorf.

1835

Early months: Felix negotiates with Leipzig for a position; 7-9 June: Felix conducts the Lower Rhenish Music Festival in Cologne, which Fanny, Rebecka, and their parents attend; End of June: Felix returns to Berlin with his parents; Summer: the Hensels journey to Paris to attend an art exhibition, then vacation in Boulogne on the return trip; 27 September: the Hensels arrive in Berlin; 4 October: Felix conducts his first concert as musical leader of the Leipzig Gewandhaus; 14 October: Felix and Moscheles accompany Rebecka back to Berlin for a two-day visit; 19 November: Abraham dies.

1836

March: Felix is awarded the doctorate by the University of Leipzig; 22 May: Felix conducts the premiere of *St. Paul* at the Lower Rhenish Music Festival in Düsseldorf, which Fanny and the family attend; Early Summer: Felix substitutes for Schelble as leader of the Frankfurt Caecilienverein; Felix meets Cecile Jeanrenaud; August: Felix vacations in Scheveningen with Schadow senior and junior; 9 September: Felix becomes engaged to Cecile; 2 October: Felix resumes his duties in Leipzig; Christmas: Felix spends the holiday with the Jeanrenauds in Frankfurt.

1837

January: a composition by Fanny, *Die Schiffende,* is the first published under her own name; 16 March: Felix conducts *St. Paul* in a Leipzig church; 28 March: Felix marries Cecile in Frankfurt; Late Spring and Summer: Felix and Cecile take a honeymoon tour in Germany, Switzerland, and France; 27 August-end of September: Felix visits England and conducts *St. Paul*; 1 October: Felix resumes his concerts in Leipzig.

1838

7 February: Felix's first child, Carl, is born; 27 February: Fanny performs in public for the first time, playing Felix's first Piano Concerto at a charity concert; February-March: Felix introduces "historical concerts" in Leipzig; 3-6 June: Felix conducts the Lower Rhenish Music Festival in Cologne; Summer: Felix visits the family in Berlin, and Cecile meets them for the first time; Early September: Felix returns to Leipzig, and contracts the measles upon his return.

1839

19-21 May: Felix conducts the Lower Rhenish Music Festival in Düsseldorf; Late May-early August: Felix travels to Frankfurt, to Horchheim, to Frankfurt; Summer: Fanny vacations with Rebecka in Heringsdorf; 21 August: Felix returns to Leipzig; End of August: Fanny spends a week with Felix on her way to Italy; 6-8 September: Felix conducts a music festival in Brunswick; End of September: Fanny crosses the Alps and enters Italy for the first time; 2 October: Felix's second child, Marie, is born; October: Fanny visits Milan and Venice; Mid November: Fanny visits Florence: End of November: Fanny arrives in Rome for an extended stay.

1840

April: Felix writes a letter to the Saxon ministry urging the establishment of a Leipzig music academy; May-June: Felix and his family live in Berlin; 2 June: Fanny leaves Rome; 24-25 June: Felix conducts the commemoration concert for the European invention of printing; 8-10 July: Felix conducts a music festival at Schwerin, which includes *St. Paul*; c. 15 July: Felix visits the family in Berlin for three days on his return trip; 3 September: Fanny visits Felix in Leipzig on her return from Italy; 11 September: Fanny arrives home in Berlin; 18-c. 30 September: Felix visits England; 11 December: the new Prussian King (Friedrich Wilhelm IV) offers Felix the position of director of a Berlin music academy to be established, and lengthy negotiations commence.

1841

18 January: Felix's third child, Paul, is born; 4 April: Felix conducts his concluding concert in Leipzig, and is appointed Kapellmeister to the King of

Saxony; End of May: Felix assumes his duties in Berlin; Summer: Felix is given the title of Kapellmeister to the King of Prussia; July: Felix spends a few weeks in Leipzig; Autumn: Felix divides his time between his duties in Berlin and Leipzig; Christmas: Felix spends the holiday in Berlin.

1842

3 March: Felix returns to Leipzig for a performance of his *Scotch* Symphony; Spring: Felix lives in Berlin; 15-17 May: Felix conducts the Lower Rhenish Music Festival in Düsseldorf; June-early July: Felix visits England; Mid July: Felix visits Cecile's family in Frankfurt; August: Felix vacations in Switzerland with Paul and their wives; 2 October: Felix conducts the opening Gewandhaus concert; 9 October: Felix returns to Berlin; 22 November: the Prussian Domchor is set up under Felix, and he is granted the title of General Music Director by the King of Prussia, thereby forced to give up his title of Saxon Kapellmeister; December: Felix returns to Leipzig and sets plans in motion for the establishment of a Leipzig music conservatory; 12 December: Lea dies.

1843

c. 20 February-c. 1 March: Fanny visits Felix in Leipzig; 9 March: Felix conducts a concert commemorating the centennial anniversary of the Gewandhaus concerts; 3 April: the Leipzig Music Conservatory is opened; 23 April: Felix conducts the concerts accompanying the unveiling of the Bach Monument in Leipzig; 1 May: Felix's fourth child, Felix, is born; August: Felix conducts music in Berlin celebrating the thousand-year anniversary of the Reich; September-November: Felix travels frequently between Berlin and Leipzig to fulfill his obligations in both cities; 25 November: Felix moves into the front house at Leipziger Strasse 3 with his family; 30 November: Felix conducts the first of the Berlin subscription concerts, with Taubert.

1844

End of April-early May: Felix has serious disagreements with the Berlin authorities, and moves his family to Frankfurt; 10 May-10 July: Felix visits London to conduct the Philharmonic and other concerts; Summer: Felix vacations in Soden with his family; 31 July-1 August: Felix conducts at the Zweibrücken Festival; 30 September: Felix arrives in Berlin to resume his duties, and lives with the Hensels; 30 November: Felix leaves Berlin; early December: Felix spends time with his family in Frankfurt, and his son Felix is very ill; c. end of December: Felix declines an invitation to conduct a festival in New York in 1845.

1845

2 January: Fanny leaves Berlin for a trip to Italy to assist the ailing Rebecka; 19 January: Fanny arrives in Florence; Mid March: Fanny travels to Rome to

meet up with Hensel, whom she discovers has been ill; 20 May: Fanny returns to Florence; 15 June: Fanny leaves Florence with Rebecka and her new baby, Flora; Summer: Felix, Fanny, and the family vacation together in Soden and then the Rhine area; 2 August: Fanny arrives in Berlin; Early September: Felix moves back to Leipzig; 19 September: Felix's fifth child, Lili, is born; 5 October: Felix resumes the conductorship of the Gewandhaus concerts; November: Felix travels to Berlin for performances of his works; 3 December: Felix returns to Leipzig.

1846

Early months: Felix is working steadily on *Elijah*; 31 May-2 June: Felix conducts the Lower Rhenish Music Festival in Aachen; Mid June: Felix conducts a series of concerts in various Rhenish cities; 26 June: Felix returns to Leipzig; Summer: Fanny receives offers to have her music published; c. 17 August: Felix arrives in London; 26 August: Felix conducts the premiere of *Elijah* in Birmingham; 6 September: Felix begins his journey back to Leipzig; late 1846: Fanny's Opp. 1 and 2 are issued; Christmas: Felix spends the holiday with the Hensels in Berlin.

1847

Early January: Felix is back in Leipzig; 12 April-9 May: Felix visits England; 13 May: Fanny composes the lied *Bergeslust,* to be her last composition (Illustration 13); 14 May: Fanny suffers a stroke and dies; c. 15 May: Felix, in Frankfurt, learns of Fanny's death; Summer: Felix vacations with family members in Switzerland; 17 September: Felix arrives in Leipzig; October: Felix's health worsens; 9 October: Felix undergoes an attack, possibly a stroke; 28 October: Felix has a second attack; 3 November: Felix undergoes a fatal stroke; 4 November: Felix dies.

Glossary and Index of Names

References can pertain to works. Italicized numbers indicate notes, non-italicized denote textual references, or a combination of textual and note references.

ALEXANDER family: family that Felix befriended during his 1829 visit to England; includes Sir Alexander, and the daughters Margaret (1791-1861), Anna-Joanna (1793-1859), and Mary. 42, 397.

ALEXANDER, Mary (1806-1867): Fanny corresponded with her and composed a few of her English texts. 136-*37*, 147, 462, 470.

[ ], AMALIE: presumably a servant of Fanny. 150, 472.

ANDERS, [Mlle.]: a Berlin friend of Felix and Fanny in the late 1820s, who possibly had some romantic feelings for Felix. 95, 433.

ANDERSEN, Hans Christian (1805-1875): Danish poet, novelist, and author of fairy tales. 327, 595.

ANDRÉ, Johann Anton (1775-1842): Frankfurt composer and music publisher. 206-*07*, 512.

ARCONNATI, D'Epino: exiled from Italy for political reasons; lived in Belgium, but made frequent trips to Berlin and the Rhine area; friend of Fanny. 132-33, *136*, 459-60.

ARNIM, Bettina von, née Brentano (1785-1859): writer, and leading member of Berlin's *litterati*. 130, 458.

ARNIM, Countess: possibly the wife of Adolf Heinrich, Count von Arnim-Boyssenburg (1803-1868). 89, 429.

ARNOLD, Carl (b. 1794): pianist, and composer of piano music, lieder, and opera. 130, 458.

ATTWOOD, Thomas (1765-1838): English composer and organist. *101*.

AUBER, Daniel-François-Esprit (1782-1871): French opera composer. 60-*61*, *206*, 409.

AUSTIN, Sarah, née Taylor: member of the Taylor family that Felix befriended at Coed Dû in England in 1829. 311, 585.

BACH, August Wilhelm (1796-after 1860): important figure in Berlin church music; organist, Professor at the Academy of the Arts; composer. 42-*43*, 398.

BACH, Johann Sebastian (1685-1750): composer and organist; held position at Leipzig from 1722-1750. xxii, *xliii*, 13, 25, *27*, 35, 39, *41*, 44-45, 47, 89, 100, *101*, *124*-125, 145-*46*, 161, *164*-65, 169-70, 176-78, *180*, *186*, 191-*92*, 198, 205, *207*, 240-*41*, 249-*50*, 253, 291, 299-*300*, 302-*03*, 311-12, 317, 319, *334*, 378, 385, 393, 396, 400, 428, 436, 455, 468, 479, 483, 486-87, 491, 493, 502, 507, 511, 533, 540-41, 569-70, 576, 578, 585, 588, 590, 630, 633.

BACKHAUSEN family: friends of the Hensels c. 1840. 296, 573.

BADER, Carl Adam (1789-1870): tenor at the Berlin court opera after 1820; honorary member of the Singakademie. xxvi, 26, 30, 143, 145, 225, 227, 254, 387, 389, 467, 468-69, 523, 525, 542.

BÄRENSPRUNG, Friedrich Wilhelm Leopold von (1779-1841): mayor of Berlin; father of famous dermatologist, Friedrich Wilhelm (1822-1864). 145, 469.

BÄRMANN, Heinrich Joseph (1784-1847): Munich clarinettist; Felix composed two pieces for clarinet and bassethorn (Opp. 113, 114) for Heinrich and his son Karl. 127, *131*, 456.

BÄRMANN, Karl (1811-1885): clarinettist; son of Heinrich Joseph. 127, *131*, 456.

BAGGE, Baron: a Parisian friend of the Mendelssohns; could be the son of the Parisian Baron Bagge (d. 1791) described in the *ADB*. 10-*11*, 376.

BARTHOLDY, Jacob Salomon (1779-1825): brother of Lea MB; converted to Christianity in 1805 and adopted the name Bartholdy; Prussian diplomat in Rome from 1815, where he championed the visual arts. 67, *288*.

BAUR, Albert (1803-1866): friend of the Mendelssohns; corresponded with Felix in the 1840s. 44-45, 399-400.

BENECKE, Henriette, née Souchay (1807-1893): Cecile's aunt, wife of F. W. 275, 557.

BENECKE, Paul Victor Mendelssohn (d. 1944): grandson of Felix; possessor of the Green Books; Senior Fellow at Magdalen College, Oxford. xlvi.

BENNETT, William Sterndale (1816-1875): English composer; good friend of Felix. *243*.

BERGER, Ludwig (1777-1839): Berlin composer, pianist, and piano pedagogue; taught Fanny, Felix, Taubert, and Henselt. xxii, 2, *126*, 225-27, 369, 523, 525.

BÉRIOT, Charles-Auguste de (1802-1870): Belgian violinist and composer; husband of soprano Maria Malibran; founder of the Franco-Belgian school of violin playing. 130-*31*, 246, 458, 537.

BERLIOZ, Hector (1803-1869): French composer, conductor, and critic; met Felix in Rome in 1831; toured Berlin during the 1842-1843 season. 316, 332, 588, 599.

BERNUS DU FAY, Franz (1808-1884): Frankfurt senator; acquaintance of Felix. 336, 360, 603, 617.

[ ], BERTHA: a servant for the Hensels c. 1830. 102, 437.

BEUTH, Peter Christian Wilhelm (1781-1853): Prussian official. 324, 593.

BIERMANN, Eduard (1803-1892): Berlin landscape painter. 355, 614.

BIGOT, Marie, née Kiené (1786-1820): pianist; taught Fanny and Felix during their 1816 trip to Paris. xxii, 9, 376, 629.

BINDOCCI, [ ]: Italian improvisor. 222, 521.

BING, [Frau]: a friend of the Mendelssohns. 7, 374.

BLANC, Louis Ammy (1810–1885): genre and portrait painter; lived in Düsseldorf after 1833; student of Julius Hübner. 157, 478.

BLANKENSEE, Georg Friedrich, Count von (1792-1867): poet, violinist, and composer; close friend of W. Hensel; Berlin patron of the arts. 170, 487.

BLANO, [Mlle.]: sang alto in Fanny's chorus in the mid 1830s. 145, 469.

BLUME, Heinrich (1788-1856): Berlin opera singer and actor; gained fame as Don Giovanni, and sang Heinrich VI in Spontini's *Agnes*. 60, 240, 409, 533.

BOCK, Gustav (1813-1863): co-founder of Berlin music-publishing firm of Bote & Bock (1838), which published Fanny's Opp. 1-3, 6, 7, and a *Pastorella* in an anthology (1848). 349, *352*, 612.

BÖCKH, Philipp August (1785-1867): researcher of antiquity; lived on ground floor of Leipziger Strasse 3 from 1840-1846; advised Felix on the *Antigone* music. 297, 318, 575, 590.

BÖTTICHER, Louis (1813-1867): bass, formerly hornist; specialized in opera and oratorio. xxvi, 225, 227-*28*, 274, 304, 523, 525, 556-57, 579.

BOGUSLAWSKY, Wilhelm von (1803-1874): Prussian jurist and amateur composer. 40, 396.

BONAPARTE, Napoleon I (1769-1821): general and emperor of France. 3, *255*, 371.

BOUCHER, Alexandre (1770-1861): French violinist; toured Germany and other countries after 1820; last public concert in 1829. 1-4, 9, *11*, 369-70, 376.

BRAHAM, John (1774-1856): English opera singer and composer. *65*.

BRAUN, Johann Karl Ludwig (1771-1835): military general; lived at Leipziger Strasse 3 at least in late October 1833. 112, 135, 445, 461.

BREMER, Friedrich Franz Dietrich, Count (1759-1836): Hanoverian diplomat. 135-*36*, 461.

BRÜHL, Carl Friedrich, Count von (1772-1837): Intendant of the Berlin royal theater from 1815-1830; after 1821 an honorary member of Zelter's Liedertafel. *6*.

BRUNSWICK, Wilhelm, Duke of (1806-1884): reigned from 1830, when his brother, Karl II, was forced from office through an uprising. *366*.

BÜSCHLEG, [Frl.]: an acquaintance of Fanny c. 1829. 43, 399.

BULL, Ole (1810-1880): Norwegian violinist and composer; toured extensively beginning in 1836. 272, 555.

BULWER-LYTTON, Edward George (1803-1873): English novelist. 175-*76*, 490.

BUNSEN, Christian Josias, Baron von (1791-1860): diplomat; part of Prussian embassy in Rome from 1824, where he hosted W. Hensel, and Felix in 1830; ambassador to London in 1842; supportive of the plans in 1840 to establish a large musical institute in Berlin. 146, 261, 469, 547.

BURGGRAF, Karl (b. 1803): Berlin genre and portrait painter; student of W. Hensel. 135, 462.

BURIDAN, Jean (d. c. 1358): French philosopher. 222-*23*, 521.

BUSOLT, J. E.: bass at the Berlin royal opera between 1822 and 1831. 121, 145, 451, 469.

BUTE, Mine: presumably an aunt, or great-aunt, of Fanny and Felix, who lived in London. 44, *47*, 400.

BUXTON, Edward: member of the English music-publishing firm of Ewer & Co. *345*.

BYRON, George Gordon, Lord (1788-1824): English poet admired by Fanny and Felix, who both set a few of his poems in English. 160, *163-64*, 229, *231*, 236, 526, 531.

CALIXE; see Kalix.

CARADORI-ALLAN, Maria, née de Munck (1800-1865): soprano; best known as a concert and oratorio singer; performed often in England. *150*.

[ ], CARL: possibly a servant of the Mendelssohns. 22-*23*, 86, 142, 385, 427, 467.

CASPAR, Fanny, née Levin: presumably wife of Johann Ludwig Caspar. 2-*3*, 370.

CASPAR, Johann Ludwig (1796-1864): physician and writer; wrote libretti for four youthful stage works by Felix. 2-4, 6, 15, 370-73, 379.

CATEL, Franz (1778-1856): painter; spent several years in Rome. 143, 288, 467, 568.

CERVANTES, Miguel de (1547-1616): Spanish writer. *11*, 208-*10*, 249, 513, 539.

CHERUBINI, Luigi (1760-1842): influential composer, theorist, and pedagogue working principally in Paris; 1822 director of the Conservatoire; 1825 passed favorable judgment on the sixteen-year-old Felix. *xl*, 179-*80*, 187-*90*, 192, 310, *312*, *334*, 358, 493-94, 499, 501, 503, 584, 615.

CHINA; Tischin-Kiang-Fu, Emperor of: of Manchu dynasty. 311, 585.

CHOPIN, Frederic (1810-1849): Polish pianist and composer; met Felix in May 1834. xxvi, 143-*44*, 184-*86*, *231*, 235, 267, 498, 530, 552.

CHORLEY, Henry F. (1808-1872): English writer, and close friend of Felix. xxiv.

CIMAROSA, Domenico (1749-1801): Italian opera composer. 33-*34*, 391.

CLARUS, Johann Christian August (1774-1854): Leipzig physician and official. 253, 541.

CLAUREN, H. (1771-1854): Romantic writer; alias for Karl Heun. *23*, 384.

CLÉMENTS family: family of the Hensels' gardener; lived in the basement of the main house at Leipziger Strasse 3 from c. 1838 to 1848. 344, 607.

CORNEILLE, Pierre (1606-1684): French dramatic poet, especially of classical tragedy. 3, 371.

CORNELIUS, Peter (1783-1867): Painter, active in Munich. 280-*81*, 561.

COTTA, [Frl.]: a friend of the Mendelssohns in the late 1820s. 40, 396.

CRAMER, Johann Baptist (1771-1858): pianist, composer, and music publisher; settled in England c. 1791; entered music publishing in 1805. 17, *95*, *101*, 145, 191, 380, 469, 503.

CRELINGER, Auguste, widowed Stich, née During (1795-1865): Berlin actress between 1812 and 1862; mother of Bertha Crelinger and Clara Stich. 155, 157, 476, 478.

CRELINGER, Bertha (1818-1876): Berlin actress. 155, 157, 476, 478.

CURSCHMANN, [Mme.]; see Behrend.

CZERNY, Carl (1791-1857): Austrian composer, pianist, pedagogue, and writer on music. 197

DACHRÖDEN, [Herr] von: tenor in Fanny's opera performances; presumably also the theater Intendant who resides in Strelitz. 121, 263, 271, *273*, 452, 548, 554.

DAHL, Carl (b. c. 1813): landscape painter; a member of the Düsseldorf school. 154, 475.

DAVID, Ferdinand (1810-1873): violinist, composer, and music editor; close friend of Felix; 1826-1829 in Berlin Königstadt orchestra; 1829-1835 in quartet of Baron von Liphart in Dorpat; from 1836 concertmaster of the Leipzig Gewandhaus orchestra; from 1843 head of the violin department at the Leipzig Conservatory. xxvi, 20-21, 25, 29, 79-80, *82*, 194-95, 203-*04*, 229-*30*, 312, 383-84, 386, 388, 421-22, 504-05, 510, 526, 585.

DAVY, Jane, Lady, née Kerr (1780-1855): wife of Sir Humphrey Davy; a leading social figure in Rome and London. 145, 469.

DECKER, Pauline, née Schätzel (1811-1882): Berlin opera and oratorio singer; studied with Heinrich Stümer; debuted as Agathe in *Der Freischütz*; retired from opera in 1832 upon her marriage to Rudolf Decker. xxvi, 25-26, 112, 115-17, 119, 121, 140, 145, 171, 178, *202-03*, 206, 208, 215, 217, 227-28, 239, 241, 244-46, 251, 253, 263, 302, 386, 444, 447-48, 450-51, 465, 468, 488, 493, 512, 514, 517, 519, 525, 531, 536-37, 541, 548, 578.

DECKER, Rudolf Ludwig (1804-1877): publisher; husband of Pauline Schätzel. 87, 215, 294, *303*, 427, 517, 572.

DEETZ, [Herr]: a messenger for the Mendelssohns in 1829. 42, 397.

DELMAR, Baron: possibly the former Berlin banker Ferdinand Moritz Levy, who became Baron Delmar in 1810, had extensive French business connections, and was living in Paris in at least 1815. 69, 415.

DELOI, Emilie, née Riedel: an acquaintance of Fanny; in Paris in mid 1820s. 9, 376.

DEMIDOV, Anatoli Nikolaevich (1812-1870): Russian traveler and patron of art. 157, 478.

DEVRIENT, Eduard (1801-1877): singer, actor, stage director, theater manager, and author; active in Berlin, Dresden, and Karlsruhe; close friend of the Mendelssohns in the late 1820s; in 1829-1830 lived at Leipziger Strasse 3. 25-*27*, 29, 42-45, *47*, 63, 97, 112, 114-15, *120*, 128, *132*, 145, 150, 185, 194, 199, 230, 324-*25*, 344, 386-87, 389, 398, 400, 411, 435, 444, 446-47, 456-57, 469, 472, 498, 505, 508, 527, 593, 608.

DEVRIENT, Therese, née Schlesinger (1803-1882): singer; married Eduard in 1824; a good friend of Fanny, whom she had met at the Singakademie. 20, 63, 97, *99*, 194, 230, *325*, 344, 383, 411, 435, 505, 527, 608.

DIRICHLET, Felix (1837-1838): second child of Rebecka. *273*.

DIRICHLET, Flora (1845-1912): third and youngest surviving child of Rebecka. 332-*34*, 341-*42*, 599-600, 605, 634.

DIRICHLET, [Mme.] (b. c. 1768): Rebecka's mother-in-law. 260, 309-*10*, 343, 347, 355, 359, 546, 583, 607, 610, 614, 616.

DIRICHLET, Peter Gustav Lejeune (1805-1859): mathematician; husband of Rebecka Mendelssohn Bartholdy. 111, 161, 177, *185-86*, *190*, 198, 209, 222, 230, 249, 261, 297, 313, 318, 320, *328*, 333, 362, 365, 444, 480, 492, 507, 514, 521, 527, 540, 548, 575, 586, 589, 591, 600, 619-20.

DIRICHLET, Rebecka, née Mendelssohn (1811-1858): younger sister of Fanny; talented in music (soprano), and especially good at languages, notably Greek and English. xxviii, xxxv, *xliii*, liv, 1, 3, 7, 10-*11*, 15-17, 19-22, *27*-28, 30-*31*, 35, 38-42, 45, 47-51, 53-54, 58-61, 63-64, 69-71, 74-76, *78*-81, 83, *85*, 87-89, 91-97, 99-102, 104-107, 109-111, *113*-14, 116, *120*, 122-23, *126*, 132-34, 136, 138-*39*, 142-*43*, 148, 150-52, 158-*59*, 161-64, *167-68*, 170, 172, 174, 176-*77*, 183-87, *193*-97, *201*, 203-06, 209, *212-13*, *216*, 218, 226, 229, *232*, *236-37*, 244, 249, 254, 256, 260, 263, 266, 268-69, 271, *273*, 275, 277-79, 289, 291, 296-97, 303-04, 306-07, 309, 313, 315, 318, 320-21, *323*-26, *328*, 331, 333-38, 342, 345, 347, *352*, 355, 357, 359-60, 369, 371, 374, 376, 379, 382-84, 388, 390, 393, 395-98, 400-02, 404-05, 408-11, 413, 416, 418-24, 427, 429-44, 446, 448, 452-53, 459-60, 464,

EBERS, Sophie: possibly a daughter or sister of Moritz Ebers (1802-1837), banker and porcelain manufacturer. 112, 444.

EBERT, Karl Egon (1801-1882): Bohemian poet; editions of his poetry first issued in 1824. 167, 484.

ECKERMANN, Johann Peter (1792-1854): writer; close associate of Goethe; compiler of *Gespräche mit Goethe . . . 1823-32* (1837). *120*, 205, *207*-08, *210*, 511, 513.

ECKERT, Carl (1820-1879): violinist, pianist, and conductor; toured extensively. 303-05, 336, 579-80, 602.

EHRHARDT, [Herr]: presumably a family acquaintance. 106-07, 441.

EICHBERGER, Joseph: tenor at Berlin royal opera between 1834 and 1842; later a voice teacher in Königsberg. 186, 240, 274, 499, 533, 556.

EIGENDORFF, [Herr]: an acquaintance or a messenger who made frequent trips between Berlin and Leipzig in 1846 and 1847, often carrying Fanny's letters to Felix. 357, 363, 615, 620.

EINBRODT, [Herr]: friend of Fanny and Felix in the late 1820s; also in London in 1829. 20, 58, 86, 383, 408, 426-27.

ELSASSER, Friedrich August (1810-1845): painter; lived in Rome from 1832; friend of the Hensels and Dirichlets. 288, 330, 339, 568, 597, 605.

ELSHOLZ, Franz von (1791-1872): writer, playwright, and librettist. 140-*41*, *224*, 465.

ELSLER, Fanny (1810-1884): celebrated ballet dancer; 1843 received a Doctorate in Dancing Arts at Oxford. 311, 585.

ENGLAND; Edward, Prince of Wales (1841-1910): eldest son of Victoria; reigned as King Edward VII from 1901. *319*.

ENGLAND; Victoria, Queen of (1819-190l); reigned 1837 to 1901; expressed admiration to Felix for *Italien,* Fanny's lied published in his Op. 8 collection. *224*, 266, 551.

ERNST, Heinrich Wilhelm (1814-1865): Berlin violinist and composer. 362, 619.

FASCH, Carl Friedrich (1736-1800): Berlin composer, conductor, and harpsichordist. *14*, 94-*95*, 433.

FASSMANN, Auguste von (b. 1817): opera singer; debuted in Berlin in 1836; specialized in German classical opera, especially Gluck; also sang oratorio, including *St. Paul.* xxvi, 235, 240-*42*, 249, 251, *253*-54, 272, 274-78, 304, 531, 533-34, 539-40, 542, 555-58, 580.

FREISTÄDTL, [ ], née von Alters; presumably a Berlin friend of Fanny and Felix. 191, 503.

FRIEDHEIM, Bertha: possibly a friend of Fanny. 329, 345, 596, 608.

FUCHS, Aloys (1799-1853): Austrian musicologist and critic. 122, 452.

FÜRST, Julius (1805-1873): Orientalist; studied Semitic languages; worked on text for Felix's oratorio, *St. Paul.* 151-*53*, 473-74.

FÜRSTER, Ernst: a friend of Fanny and Felix in the early 1820s. 3, 371.

GADE, Niels (1817-1890): Danish composer; a good friend of Felix, and his successor at the Leipzig Gewandhaus. 314, *316*, 358-59, 586, 616.

GANS, Eduard (1798-1839): Professor of law in Berlin; student of Hegel; teacher of Felix at the University of Berlin. 21, 69, 79-80, 93-94, 106, 110, 114, *141*, 154, 178, 278, 349, 384, 416, 421-22, 432-33, 440, 443, 446, 475, 492, 559, 611.

GANZ, Leopold (1810-1869): violinist; concertmaster in the Berlin royal orchestra in 1836; with his brother Moritz, a frequent participant in Fanny's musicales. 130, *132*, 147, 209, 235, 257, 458, 470, 514, 531, 544.

GANZ, Moritz (1806-1868): cellist; concertmaster in the Berlin royal orchestra in 1836. 130, 147, 209, 235, 246, 257, 458, 470, 514, 531, 537, 544.

GARCIA, Pauline Viardot; see Viardot-Garcia.

GAREIS, Albert (1811-1860): Berlin clarinettist; son of Gottlieb Gareis; engaged at the royal chapel in 1834. 307, 582.

GAREIS, Gottlieb (d. 1859): Berlin violist. 307, 582.

GAROMBO, Abbate: director of the Papal Chapel when Fanny visited Rome in 1845. 336-*37*, 602.

GERN, Albert Leopold (1789-1869): Berlin actor. 261, 547.

GIRSCHNER, Christian Friedrich Johann (1797-1860): composer and music theorist; studied under Zelter; composed operas, sacred music, lieder, and instrumental music. 97, 109, 435, 442.

GLUCK, Christoph Willibald (1714-1778): composer of opera, whose works embodied many aspects of reform and were highly influential on contemporaries and later composers. 12, *14*, 22, 63, *65*, 109-*10*, 112, 143-44, 165, 235, *238*, 240-*41*, 274-75, 277, 309, 377, 384, 411, 443, 445, 467-68, 483, 533-34, 557-58, 583.

GOETHE, Johann Wolfgang von (1749-1832): writer, scientist, statesman; the Mendelssohns were great devotees of the man and his works; Fanny

folk-type instrument used in Poland and Russia, with which he toured Western Europe beginning in 1834. *204*.

GUTENBERG, Johann (c. 1397-1468): inventor of printing with movable type in Europe. 291, *293*, 297-*98*, 570, 574.

HÄHNEL, Amalie (1807-1849): mezzosoprano opera singer; engaged in Vienna in 1829, Berlin (Königstadt) in 1831, and Berlin royal opera in 1841. 110, 119, 135-36, 189, 443, 450, 462, 501.

HÄRTEL, Dr. Hermann (1803-1875): co-owner of Breitkopf & Härtel publishing firm; a director on the board governing the Gewandhaus concerts. 344, 607.

HALÉVY, Jacques-François Fromental (1799-1862): French opera composer, pedagogue, and music writer; from 1827 taught at Paris Conservatoire; *La Juive* his greatest success. 179-*80*, 311-*12*, 493, 585.

HALLMANN, Anton (1812-1845): architect and painter. 339, 605.

HANDEL, George Friedrich (1685-1759): Baroque composer of German extraction who gained fame in England; greatest successes in opera and oratorio. xxii, 12-*13*, 15, *18*, 22, 33, 63, *66*, 110-14, *116, 119*, 136, *181*-82, 184-*86*, 194-*95*, 200, 214-*15*, 217, *219, 250, 253*-54, 272-*73*, 276, 317, 377, 379, 384, 392, 412, 443-46, 462, 495, 498, 504-05, 509, 516-519, 542, 555, 558, 588.

HANDLEY, Delphine Hill, née Schauroth (1813-1887): pianist; Felix met her in Munich in 1830, was captivated by her personally and pianistically, and dedicated his g-minor Piano Concerto to her. 107, 279-*81*, 560-61.

HANOVER; Georg, Crown Prince of (1819-1878). 299, *301*, 577.

HANSMANN, Otto Friedrich Gustav (1769-1836): Berlin choral conductor. *180*.

HARTKNOCH, Karl Eduard (1796-1834): composer and pianist; grandson of Johann Friedrich Hartknoch (1740-1789), who had founded a music-publishing firm; pupil of Hummel. 5, 373.

HASSE, Johann Adolph (1699-1783): prolific composer of mostly vocal music, including several Requiems. 13-*14*, 378.

HAUPTMANN, Moritz (1792-1868): composer, theorist, and pedagogue; 1843 on the faculty of the Leipzig Conservatory; became editor of the *AMZ* in 1843. 187, 189-*90*, 316, 499, 501, 588.

HAUSER, Franz (1794-1870): Bohemian baritone, voice teacher, and collector of Bach manuscripts; sang in many opera houses, including Leipzig (1832-1835) and Berlin (1835-1836); in 1837 retired from the stage and

HELLWIG, Carl Friedrich Ludwig (1773-1838): Berlin royal music director and court cathedral organist; composer. 39, 396.

HENNING, Carl Wilhelm (1784-1867): violinist, conductor, and composer; music director at the Königstadt theater from 1824 to 1826; taught Felix violin, and a member of their musical circle. 141, *143*, 145, 147, 466, 468, 470.

HENNING, [Mme.]: wife of Carl Wilhelm Henning. 35, 393.

HENSEL, Louise Johanne, née Trost (1764-1835): mother of Wilhelm Hensel; poet. 162, 184-*86*, 481, 497.

HENSEL, Luise (1798-1876): poet; sister of Wilhelm Hensel; lived at Leipziger Strasse 3 from 1833 to 1836. 108-*09*, 113, 115, 118, 152, 176, 225-*26*, 232, 240-*41*, 245, 253, 275, 442, 445, 447, 449, 474, 491, 523, 528, 533, 537, 541, 557.

HENSEL, Sebastian (1830-1898): Fanny's only child; later director of the Hotel Kaiserhof in Berlin, and author of a family chronicle. *xxvii*, xxxv, xlvii, l, 103-08, 110-112, 114-16, 119, 122-23, 125, *127*, 130, 133-34, 148, 161-63, 170, 172, 182, *185*, 187, 191, 197-98, 206, 217, 234, 240, 245, 255-*57*, 259-61, 263, *267*, 269, *281*-82, 284, 288, 292, 296-97, 303, 312-15, 317, 320-*21*, 327-*28*, 330, 334, 337-*38*, 342-43, 355, 365, 439-48, 450, 452-53, 455, 458-59, 461, 471, 480-82, 487-88, 495, 500, 503, 506-07, 512, 518, 530, 533, 537, 543, 546-49, 553, 563-65, 568, 571, 574-75, 579, 585-87, 589, 519, 595, 598, 601, 603, 606-07, 614, 621, 630.

HENSEL, Wilhelm (1794-1861): painter, draftsman, poet; husband of Fanny from 1829; Berlin Professor of Art, and Court Painter. xxv-xxvii, xxxiii, *xli*, 33-35, 37-38, 40-42, 44, 46, 48-63, 66-69, 72, 74-79, 81-87, 89-96, 99-101, 103-08, 110-11, 113-*18*, 121-23, 125-*27*, 133, 135-*39*, 142-*44*, 146, 148-*49*, 151-52, 154, 156, *158*, 161-63, 166-67, 169-72, 175-*79*, *181*, *185*-86, 192-94, 198, 201-*03*, 208-09, 211-*15*, 217-*18*, 222-23, 226-27, 229, 232-34, 241, *243*-44, 249, 253, 255, 257, 260-61, 267, 269-70, 272-73, 277, 280-82, 284-86, 288, 291-93, 295-97, 300, 306, 309, 312-14, 317-18, 321, 327-28, 330-*31*, 334-35, *337*-43, 347, 351-*52*, 355, 359-60, 362, 365, 391-92, 394-99, 401-07, 409-11, 413-14, 416, 418-27, 429-37, 439-46, 448, 451-53, 455, 460, 462, 464, 467, 469-70, 473-75, 477, 480-82, 484-85, 487-88, 492, 503-04, 507, 510, 513-14, 516-22, 524-26, 528-29, 534, 536, 540-42, 544, 546-47, 552-555, 559, 561, 563, 565-66, 568, 570-71, 573-75, 577, 581, 583, 585-86, 589, 591-92, 596-98, 601, 603-07, 610, 612, 614, 616, 618-19, 621, 629-31, 634.

HILLER, Ferdinand (1811-1885): conductor, composer, pedagogue, pianist; very close friend of Felix, who recommended him for study with Hummel (1825-1827); also aligned with Berlioz, Chopin, and Liszt; replaced Felix as conductor of Leipzig Gewandhaus concerts in 1843 and 1844; wrote a book of memoirs on Mendelssohn (1874). 206, 230-*31*, 287, *289*, 291-93, 512, 527, 567, 569-71.

HILTL, [ ]: Prussian court decorator. 330, 598.

HOFFMANN, Johann (1805-after 1860): tenor at the Berlin royal opera; debuted in 1829 as Max in *Der Freischütz* and left in 1835. 112, 444.

HOFKUNZ, Aurora: soprano at the Berlin royal opera; active at the Singakademie from 1838 to 1846; left the stage in 1846 upon her marriage. 304, 580.

HOFMEISTER, Friedrich (1782-1864): Leipzig music publisher and bibliographer. *101*.

HOGARTH, George (1783-1870): English music critic; on London *Morning Chronicle* from 1831 to 1845, then on London *Daily News* from 1846 to 1866. 80, 422.

HOLTEI, Carl (1798-1880): poet and playwright. 249-*50*.

HORN, Wilhelm: presumably a friend of Felix and Fanny in the late 1820s and early 1830s. 55, 69, *71*, 100, 406, 415, 436.

HÜBNER, [ ]: pupil of W. Hensel. 135-*36*, 462.

HÜBNER, Julius (1806-1882): painter of historical subjects and portraits in the Düsseldorf school; studied with W. Schadow; married Eduard Bendemann's sister, Pauline. 80, *136*, 162, 423, 481.

HÜBNER, Pauline, née Bendemann (1809-1895): married Julius Hübner in 1829. 30-*31*, 80, 115, 132, 319, *321*, 389, 423, 447, 459, 591.

HÜNTEN, Franz (1793-1878): composer and piano pedagogue; almost all his pieces are piano arrangements or pieces based on contemporary operas, and were intended for amateurs; he did not perform in public. 138, *231*, 464.

HUMBOLDT, Alexander von (1769-1859): geographer, geologist, and naturalist; close friend of the Mendelssohns; Fanny attended his lectures in 1825; set up an observatory for magnetism at Leipziger Strasse 3. 146, 207, 306, 324, 330, 469, 513, 581, 593, 597.

HUMMEL, Johann Nepomuk (1778-1837): Austrian pianist, composer, pedagogue, and conductor; became Kapellmeister in Weimar in 1819; toured extensively and was one of the most important pianists; Felix took some lessons from him in Weimar in 1821 while visiting Goethe. xliii, 4-7, *11*-12, 235, *238*, 371-74, 378, 530.

IMMERMANN, Karl (1796-1840): writer for the stage; from 1832 to 1837 played a great role in shaping German theater history in his position as theater director in Düsseldorf; Felix worked with him there between 1833 and 1835 as opera Intendant but resigned out of dissatisfaction and frustration. 112, 114, *120*, *159*, 189-*90*, 444, 446, 501.

INGRES, Jean Auguste Dominique (1780-1867): French painter; from 1834 head of French Academy in Rome; Fanny met him during her trips to Italy in 1840 and 1845. 290-91, *293*, 569-70.

ITZENPLITZ, Count von: Stargard bureaucrat in mid 1830s. 238, 532.

JACOBY, Gustav (1804-1851): mathematician in Königsberg from 1826 to 1843; made frequent visits to the Hensels in late 1843; in 1844 he helped out Dirichlet financially in Italy. 318-*19*, 334, 590, 600.

JACOBY, Dr. Johann (1805-1877): brother of Gustav; lived in Königsberg; physician, political writer, and Prussian delegate. 318-*19*, 590.

JACQUES, Clara: presumably a neighbor or friend of the Mendelssohns. 117, *318*, 448.

JEANRENAUD, Cecile; see Mendelssohn Bartholdy.

JEANRENAUD, Elisabeth, née Souchay (1796-1871): Cecile's mother. 212, *222*-24, 314, 516, 522, 587.

JEANRENAUD, Julie; see Schunck.

JOACHIM, Joseph (1831-1907): Austro-Hungarian violinist, composer, conductor, and teacher; went to Leipzig in the spring of 1843, and Felix advised him on his general and compositional education. 323, 592.

[ ], JÖRG: a young student of W. Hensel who sang in Fanny's musicales. 121, 451.

JÜNGKEN, Johann Christian (1793-1875): famous Berlin oculist, who treated Abraham Mendelssohn Bartholdy in the early 1830s. 175, 177, 491-92.

JUNG, [Frl.] S.: governess to Felix's children. 341, 605.

KALIX, [ ]: trusted musical acquaintance in Berlin. *143*, 147, 344, 470, 607.

KALKBRENNER, Friedrich (1785-1849): pianist, pedagogue, composer; studied at the Paris Conservatoire; 1825 to 1835 at the height of his performing career. 12, 130, *132*, 166, 377-78, 458, 483.

KASELOWSKY, August (1810-1892): painter; a student of W. Hensel; lived in Italy from 1840 to 1850. 143, 154, 162, 218, 285, 288, 320, 467, 475, 481, 519, 565, 568, 591.

KASPAR, [ ]: Berlin printer. 187, 500.

KAULBACH, Wilhelm von (1805-1874): painter of portraits and historical subjects. 280-*81*, 561.

KEFERSTEIN, [Herr]: acquaintance of Felix in London in 1829, possibly a musician. *47*.

KEIL, Johann Georg (1781-1857): Doctor of Law; member of the board of directors of the Gewandhaus concerts from 1831; a founder of the Leipzig Conservatory. 246-*47*, 537.

KEUDELL, Robert von (1824-1903): a close musical friend of Fanny in the later years of her life. 351, *353*, 612.

KIENÉ, [Mme.]: mother of Marie Bigot; lived in Paris. 9, *11, 196*, 198, 259, 376, 507, 546.

KIND, [Dr.]: presumably the physician in London treating Felix's knee injury in 1829. 89, 429.

KISS, August (1802-1865): sculptor; student of Rauch; between 1835 and 1838 he worked on his main piece, *Amazon on Horseback Fighting with a Tiger.* 317, 589.

KLEIST, Heinrich von (1777-1811): dramatic poet. 100-*01*, 437.

KLINGEMANN, Karl (1798-1862): official at the Hanoverian legation in Berlin, and from mid 1827 in London; Felix's closest lifelong friend; also friends with Fanny; wrote poetry and libretti, and wanted to author texts for Felix's oratorios. *11*, 13, 15, 17, *28*, 34, *47*, 53, 55, 64, 70-*71*, 80-*82*, *85*-87, 89, 91, 94-95, 99, *101*, 106, 109, *132, 137, 139, 149,* 155, *201-02*, 206-*07*, 211, 243-45, *259*, 272-*73*, *301*, 324, 327, *352*, 360-*61*, 378-79, 381, 392, 405-06, 412, 416, 422, 427-29, 431, 433-34, 436, 440, 442, 476, 512, 515, 535-36, 555, 593, 595, 617, 630.

KLOPSTOCK, Friedrich Gottlieb (1724-1803): poet and dramatist; his poems had wide-ranging influence; his *Odes* (1747-1780) set by many composers. 33, 392.

KOCH, [ ]: Berlin music copyist; perhaps Friedrich Koch, who signed a letter to Felix on behalf of the Berlin Singakademie. 187, 499.

KÖHLER, Andreas (1811-1840): painter. 154, 475.

KÖSTLIN, Reinhold (d. 1856): Swabian poet; husband of Josephine Lang. *310*.

KOHLREIF, [ ]: presumably an amateur musician in the circle of Fanny and Felix in the late 1820s. 20, 383.

KONCKONCK, [ ]: presumably a German landscape painter. 215, 517.

LECERF, Julius Amadeus (1789-1868): public voice teacher and music director at several Berlin private schools between 1829 and 1843; composer of opera, sacred vocal music, lieder, and instrumental music. 144, 316-*17*, 468, 588.

LE FORT, Auguste von; see Medem.

LENZ, Bertha; soprano at Berlin royal opera from 1832 to 1838. 150, 200, 472, 509.

LEO, [Auguste]: Parisian banker, but originally from Hamburg. 180, 494.

LÉONARD, Hubert (1819-1890): Belgian violinist, composer, and teacher; between 1845 and 1848 concertized extensively throughout Europe, especially Germany. 341, 605.

LESSING, Gotthold Ephraim (1729-1781): philosopher, dramatist, and critic; good friend of Moses Mendelssohn. 157, *159*, 477.

LEVY, Moritz: possibly a friend of Abraham Mendelssohn, or a relative on Lea's side; perhaps a banker. 86, 427.

LEVY, Sarah, née Itzig (1761-1854): Lea's aunt; a lively salon personality, with considerable musical training. *xlii*, 229, 526.

LEWENHAGEN, [Herr]: a friend of the Mendelssohns in the late 1820s. 40, 396.

LEWY, Eduard (1796-1846): hornist; made many tours after 1836 with his three children: Karl (hornist and pianist), Richard (hornist), and Melanie (harpist). 272, 555.

LICHTENSTEIN, Karl August (1767-1845): German composer, theater manager, poet, conductor, and singer; settled in Berlin in 1823 and appointed to the opera in 1825; composed 17 operas; wrote 4 libretti, including *Die Hochzeit des Camacho* for Felix in 1825. 248, 539.

LIMBURGER, Jacob Bernhard (1770-1847): architect and merchant; longstanding treasurer of the Gewandhaus concerts, and after 1799 a member of its board of directors. 189, 191, *193*, 501, 503.

LIND, Jenny (1820-1887): soprano; formal debut in 1838; visited Berlin in 1844, 1845, and 1846; sang under Felix at a Gewandhaus concert in December 1845; London debut in May 1847. 330-*31*, 341-44, 365-*66,* 597, 605-08, 620.

LINDENAU, Leopold (1806-1859): Hamburg violinist. 10, 376.

LINDNER, [ ]: Berlin actress c. 1830. 100, 437.

LIPHART, Carl von: patron of the arts; supported a private string quartet; father of Sophie David (1807-1893). 228, 272, 525, 555.

LIPINSKI, Gustav Carl (1790-1861): Polish violinist; rival of Paganini; concertmaster in Dresden. 2, 4-*6*, 370-71, 373.

MAGNUS, [Mme.]: presumably the mother of Eduard *et. al. 90*, 365, 621.

MAGNUS, Martin: presumably a relative of Eduard, Gustav, and Fanny; a friend of Fanny and Felix in the late 1820s. 60, *90*, 409.

MALIBRAN, Maria, née Garcia (1808-1836): Spanish mezzosoprano; elder sister of Pauline Viardot; studied voice with her father; debuted in opera in 1814; married de Bériot in March 1836, and died in September. 45, *47*, 130, *150*, 400, 458, 471.

MALON, [Mlle.]: presumably an acquaintance of the family in the late 1820s. 81, 423.

MANTIUS, Eduard (1806-1874): tenor; at Berlin royal opera from 1831 to 1857; also an oratorio singer. 105, 112, 121, 145, 254, 304, 444, 452, 468-69, 542, 579.

MARSCHNER, Heinrich (1795-1861): composer of German opera between Weber and Wagner; conductor at the Hanover opera from 1830. *101*, 155, 217, *219*, 476, 519.

MARTELLINI, Marchese: Florentine nobleman well acquainted with Felix. 335-*37*, 602.

MARX, Adolph Bernhard (1795-1866): music critic, theorist, and composer; editor of the *BAMZ* from 1824 to 1830; close friend of Felix until the mid 1830s; Professor of Music at the University of Berlin in 1830; most of his compositions vocal; presented original ideas on thematic-formal analysis of music. xxvi, 12, 29, *31*, 33, 35, 43, 48-49, 53, 70-*71*, 80, *82*, 97, 103-07, 128, *131*, 135, *136*, 141-47, *149*, 152, 169, *203*, 377, 388-89, 391-93, 398, 401-02, 405, 416, 422, 435, 438-41, 456, 462, 466, 468, 470, 473, 486.

MATTHIEUX, Johanna Kinkel, née Mockel (1810-1858): composer of lieder; friend of Bettina von Arnim as well as Rebecka. 253, 273-*76*, 541, 556-57.

MATUSCH, L.: educator; lived at Leipziger Strasse 3 from 1844 to 1845 when tutor to Sebastian. 327, 595.

MECUM, [Herr]: presumably an acquaintance of the Mendelssohns in the mid 1830s. 185, 498.

MEDEM, Auguste: a close friend of Fanny, Felix, Klingemann, and their circle in the 1820s; married Le Fort. 53, *56*, 70, *105*, 405, 416.

MEDEM family: family friendly with the Mendelssohns in the late 1820s, which included their daughters Auguste, Jette, and Constanze. 53-54, *56*, 405.

78, 481-82, 487-88, 492, 495-97, 499, 504-05, 507, 509-12, 574, 591, 611, 615, 617, 630-31.

MENDELSSOHN BARTHOLDY, Albertine, née Heine (1814-1879): married Paul MB in 1835; friend of the Mendelssohns in the late 1820s. 74-*75*, *139*, 143, 161-62, *176*, 187, *219*-21, 229, 239, 256, 266, 268, 272, 297, 317, 325, 338, 347-48, 360, 362-63, 418, 467, 480-81, 500, 521, 526, 533, 543, 551-52, 555, 574, 589, 594, 603, 610, 617, 619-20.

MENDELSSOHN BARTHOLDY, Albrecht (d. 1936): son of Carl MB, Felix's eldest child; married his first cousin, Dora Wach, in 1905; possessor of the Green Books. xlv, xlvi.

MENDELSSOHN BARTHOLDY, Carl (1838-1897): first child of Felix; became Professor of History in Heidelberg and Freiburg. xlvi, 256-60, 263, 267, 272, 275, 281-82, 284, 288-*89*, 292, 296, 300, 307, 309, 312, 314-15, 317, 319, 321, 325, 327, 330-31, 334, 336, 338, 341-43, 345, 348, 351, 355, 359, 361-63, 365, 543-44, 546, 549, 552, 555, 557, 562, 565, 568, 571, 574, 577, 582-83, 585, 587, 589-92, 594-95, 598, 603-08, 611-12, 614, 617-19, 620, 631.

MENDELSSOHN BARTHOLDY, Cecile, née Jeanrenaud (1817-1853): Felix's wife; descended from a Frankfurt family with patrician French lineage on her maternal side (Souchay). xxxviii, xlvi, 208-*09*, 211-*16*, 218-*19*, 221, 223-34, 236, 239-*41*, 243-44, 246, 249, 251, 254-63, 266-68, 272-*73*, 277, 279-81, 283-85, 288-*89*, 292, 296-*98*, 300, 303, 307, 309, 311, 313-21, 323-25, 327-31, 333-36, 338-39, 341-45, 348-49, 351-53, *356*-57, 359, 361, 363, 365, 513, 515-16, 520-33, 535-37, 540-47, 549, 551-52, 555, 559-65, 568, 571, 574-75, 577, 579, 582, 584-96, 598, 600-01, 603-08, 611-13, 615, 617, 618-21, 631-33.

MENDELSSOHN BARTHOLDY, Ernst (1846-1909): eldest surviving child of Paul and Albertine MB. 362-63, 365-*66*, 619-20.

MENDELSSOHN BARTHOLDY, Felix (1843-1851): fourth child of Felix and Cecile. *317*, 321, 325, 327-28, 330-*31*, 334, 336, 338, 341-43, 345, 348, 351, 359, 361-63, 365, 592, 594-96, 598, 600, 603-08, 611-12, 617-20, 633.

MENDELSSOHN BARTHOLDY, Katherine (b. 1846): daughter of Paul and Albertine MB; died in childhood. 362, 365-*66*, 619-20.

MENDELSSOHN BARTHOLDY, Lea, née Salomon (1778-1842): mother of Fanny and Felix; highly educated, with knowledge of many languages and a deep appreciation of the music of J. S. Bach. xxi, xli-xlii, xlv, 1, 4, 6-7, 13, 15, 17, 19, *23*, 27, 29, 33, 38, 40-42, 48, *50*, 58, 60, 62-64, 66-67, 69-70, 76, 81-*82*, *85*, 87-89, 92-93, 101-04, *108*-12, 114, 116, *120*, 137-46, 148-51, 161-62, 181-84, 187, 194, 197-*98*,

MEYERBEER, Giacomo (1791-1864): opera composer; composed French and German operas; from 1842 to 1849 general musical director at the Berlin royal opera, succeeding Spontini. 12, 186, *188, 206-07, 238*, 240, 311-*12*, 332, 341-*42*, *366*, 378, 499, 533, 585, 599, 605.

MEYSENBURG, Emil von: Doctor of Law. 251, *253*, 541.

MICHELANGELO (1475-1564): Italian Renaissance painter, sculptor, and poet. 161, 480.

MILAN, [Mlle.]: singer. 9, 376.

MILDER-HAUPTMANN, Anna (1785-1838): singer and actress; operatic debut in 1803 in Vienna; sang many times in Berlin opera; participated in first performance of revived *St. Matthew* Passion (March 1829). 15, 25-*28*, 42-44, 48, 240, *242*, 379, 386-87, 398, 400-01, 533-34.

MILTIZ, Carl Borromäus von: writer and librettist; occasional contributor to the *AMZ*. 55-*56*, *120*, 406.

MÖSER, Karl (1774-1851): Berlin composer, violinist, and conductor; Kapellmeister at Berlin royal opera; 1813 began string quartet evenings that later became symphony concerts; presented Berlin premiere of Beethoven's Symphony No. 9. xxvi, 15, *17*, 122, 200, *202*, 217, 246, 379, 452, 509, 518, 537.

MOLIÈRE, Jean Baptiste Poquelin (1622-1673): French playwright of satiric comedies that mocked the foibles of society. 3, 371.

MOORE, Thomas (1779-1852): Irish poet. *95*.

MOSCHELES, Charlotte, née Embden (1805-1889): wife of Ignaz Moscheles; compiled his memoirs after his death. *38*, 128, 456.

MOSCHELES, Iganz (1794-1870): German pianist, composer, and conductor; lived in London from 1821 to 1846; from 1846 head of the piano department at the Leipzig Conservatory; close friend of Felix. xxiv, 12, 34, 45, 70, *73*, 115, 124, *126*, 134, *136, 149*, 184-*86*, 303, 378, 392, 400, 417, 447, 454, 460, 498, 579.

MOSER, Julius (1805-1879): painter; became student of W. Hensel in 1831; lived in Rome from 1840 to 1847. 161, 212, 218, 480, 516, 519.

MOSEVIUS, Johann Theodor (1788-1858): conductor; first active in Königsberg, then after 1816 in Breslau; furthered chamber music, and also founded musical teaching institutions; performed many of Felix's works; championed Bach. 27, 29, 387-88.

MOZART, Franz Xaver Wolfgang (1791-1844): composer and pianist; youngest surviving son of Wolfang A. Mozart; Berlin included on his first extensive tour between 1819 and 1821; composed both vocal and instrumental music. 1, *3*, 369.

O'CONNELL, Daniel (1775-1847): Irish political leader; an important force representing Irish interests in Parliament; helped to end Sir Robert Peel's Conservative government in 1835; imprisoned in late 1843 for political agitation, but the charge dropped, and he was released in 1844. 324, 593.

OEHLENSCHLAGER, Adam Gottlob (1779-1850): Danish poet and playwright. 261-*62*, 547.

ÖLRICHS family: presumably friends of the Mendelssohns, from Bremen. 145, 469.

OETZEL, August: friend of Fanny in the late 1820s. 30, 389.

OETZEL, Luise: friend of Fanny in the late 1820s. 30, 389.

OMPTEDA, Ludwig Karl Georg (1767-1854): Hanoverian diplomat; ambassador in Berlin until 1823; held cabinet position in Hanover until 1831; then associated with Hanoverian legation in London until the death of William IV (June 1837), King of Hanover and England. 243, 535.

ONSLOW, Georges (1784-1853): French composer of English descent; composed operas and miscellaneous instrumental music. 9, *11*, 160, *164*, 375, 479.

OPPENHEIM family: related to the Mendelssohns; Lea MB had an uncle Mendel Oppenheim; Margarethe Mendelssohn married Otto Georg Oppenheim in 1843; his brothers Marco and Alexander were in Berlin in the winter of 1843-1844; much later, Paul MB, Felix's child, married Else Oppenheim, and then Enole Oppenheim; when Abraham MB lived in Paris, he worked for the banking firm of Fould, Oppenheim, & Co., probably related to his wife's family. 317-*18*, 320-*21*, 589.

OSSIAN: legendary Gaelic poet; the tales are told by the old, blind bard, Ossian; they were popularized by the inauthentic eighteenth-century "translations" of James MacPherson, and quickly criticized by Samuel Johnson as forgeries. 358-*59*, 616.

PAGANINI, Nicolò (1782-1840): virtuoso violinist; touted as the first in the string of legendary nineteenth-century virtuoso performers; toured Germany 1829 to 1831, enjoying great success in Berlin in the spring of 1829, with eleven performances; met Goethe in Weimar, and Spohr in Kassel; received a mixed response in Paris in 1831; his international career ended three years later. xxvi, xxxvi, 29-*31*, 33-37, *144*, 155, 157-*59*, 165, 254, 389, 391-93, 476-77, 483, 542.

PASTA, Giuditta (1797-1865): great dramatic soprano in the 1820s; premiered the role of Desdemona in Rossini's *Otello* in Paris (1821), as well as many Bellini roles written especially for her. xxvi, 309-*10*, 583.

PAUL, Jean; see Richter.

PENSA, Auguste Elisabeth (1804-1885): daughter of Maria Catharina Pensa, née Belli (1767-1857), and a merchant. 185, 498.

PETERS, Ulrike (d. 1832): close friend of Fanny in the 1820s. 21, *23*, 29, *31*, 100, 384, 389, 436.

PISTOR, Betty (b. 1808): daughter of the Berlin government minister, Carl Pistor (1778-1847); close friend of Felix and Fanny in the 1820s; married Adolph Rudorff in 1832. *51*, 69, *82*, 87, 416, 427.

PIXIS, Johann Peter (1788-1874): pianist and composer; studied music in Vienna; most of his pieces are virtuosic piano compositions; contributed one variation to the collaborative *Hexameron* (with Liszt, Thalberg, Herz, Czerny, and Chopin). *14*, 192-*93*, 503.

PLANCHÉ, James Robinson (1798-1880): English dramatist; wrote libretti, including *Oberon* for Weber; worked on a libretto for Felix in 1838, but abandoned the project. 249-*50*, 540.

PLATO (c. 427-347 B.C.): Greek philosopher. 170, 487.

PLEYEL, Camille Marie (1811-1875): French pianist, teacher, and composer; dedicatee of many piano works; from 1848 to 1872 taught piano at the Brussels Conservatory. 192-*93*, 503.

POGWISCH, Ulrike von (1804-1875): sister of Goethe's daughter-in-law, Ottilie. 97, *99*, 435.

POHLENZ, Christian August (1790-1843): predecessor of Felix as conductor of the Gewandhaus concerts (1827-1835); organist at the Thomaskirche and leader of the Leipzig Singakademie. 316, 588.

POHLKE, Carl Wilhelm (b. 1810): Berlin painter; a student of W. Hensel. 135, 143, 162, 176, 183, 462, 467, 481, 491, 497.

POMOWITZ, [Frau]: Berlin amateur actress. 323, 592.

POURTALÈS, Friedrich, Count von (1779-1861): Berlin minister of protocol; lived at Leipziger Strasse 3 from 1843 to 1850. 351, 612.

PRAUN, Sigismond Otto von (1811-1830): violinist; attempted to emulate Paganini; toured Berlin in 1829. 30, 389.

PREGER, [ ]: presumably an associate of Felix in Düsseldorf. 121, 451.

PRUNELLE, [Frau]: acquaintance of Felix and Cecile in Leipzig and of the Hensels in Berlin. 267, 552.

PRUSSIA; Albrecht, Prince of (1809-1872). 84, 425.

PRUSSIA; Augusta, Princess of, née of Saxe-Weimar (1811-1890): married Prince Wilhelm of Prussia in 1829. *45*.

PRUSSIA; Friedrich II, King of (1712-1786): dubbed "the great;" reigned 1740 to 1786; patron of the arts, flutist, composer, and librettist; his compositions written before the Seven Years War (1756-1763). 299-*300*, 303-*05*, 317, 576, 579, 588-89.

PRUSSIA; Friedrich Wilhelm III, King of (1770-1840): reigned 1797 to 1840. *6*, 26, 44, 62, 84, 146, 152, 158, 169, 172, 186, *243*, 387, 399, 410, 425, 469, 474, 478, 486, 488, 499.

PRUSSIA; Friedrich Wilhelm IV, King of (1795-1861): reigned 1840 to 1861; a patron of music, who hired Felix as Kapellmeister and urged him to organize and direct a new Berlin musical academy. xxxviii, 5, 158, 181, 324, 365, 373, 478, 495, 593, 621, 632-33.

PRUSSIA; Wilhelm, Prince of (1797-1888): married Princess Augusta of Saxe-Weimar in 1829; became Prussian King in 1861, and first Kaiser of Germany in 1871. *45*.

PTOLEMY (2nd century A.D.): Greco-Egyptian mathematician, astronomer, and geographer. 330, 598.

PUCHTE, [Professor]: presumably a professor in Berlin or Leipzig c. 1840. 302, 578.

PÜCKLER-MUSKAU, Hermann, Prince von (1785-1871): writer of travel literature; close friend of the Varnhagens; he and his wife divorced in 1826, although they continued to live together. 171, 488.

RAHLÈS, Ferdinand (1812-1878): musician in Solingen c. 1834. 140-*41*, 465.

RAMLER, Karl Wilhelm (1725-1798): poet, translator, and theater director; compiler of anthologies by contemporary poets. *116*.

RANKE, Leopold von (1795-1886): historian; began giving lectures in 1825 at the University of Berlin. 158-*59*, 478.

RAPHAEL (1483-1520): Italian Renaissance painter, working mainly in Rome. 117, 143-*44*, 279, 295, 448, 560, 573.

RATTI, Eduard (b. 1816): painter of historical and genre themes; pupil of W. Hensel in the 1830s. 148, 471.

RAUCH, Christian Daniel (1777-1857): sculptor; friend of W. Hensel; prominent member of the Berlin Academy of the Arts. 48, 401.

RAUPACH, Ernst (1784-1852): librettist and playwright; settled in Berlin in 1824; translated choruses for Felix's *Athalia*. *61*, 128, *131*, 456.

REBENSTEIN, [Lebrecht Gottlieb], Count von (1788-1832): actor and singer. 100, 437.

REDEN, Elise: daughter of F. L. W. Reden; musical amateur. 32-33, 391.

REDEN, Franz Ludwig Wilhelm, Baron von (1754-1831): Hanoverian ambassador to Berlin; lived at Leipziger Strasse 3 between 1825 and 1831, as the embassy was situated there. 31-32, 390-91.

REDERN, Friedrich Wilhelm, Count von (1802-1883): composer; Brühl's successor as Intendant at Berlin royal theater, 1832 to 1842; then Intendant of court music in Berlin. 30, 188, 276, 389, 500, 558.

REICHA, Anton (1770-1836): Czech composer; active as a teacher and theorist in Paris. *11*.

REICHARDT, Johann Friedrich (1752-1814): German composer and writer on music. *120*, 299-*300*, 576.

REISSIGER, Carl Gottlieb (1798-1859): Saxon composer and Kapellmeister; succeeded Weber in 1826 as music director at Dresden opera; later court Kapellmeister. 13, 160, *164*, 378, 479.

REITER, [Dr.]: friend of the Mendelssohns. 188-89, 192-*93*, 500-01, 503.

RELLSTAB, Ludwig (1799-1860): writer on music, and author of novels; music critic at the *Berliner allgemeine musikalische Zeitung*, at the *Vossische Zeitung* (= *Berlinische Zeitung*), and later at *Iris*. xxvi, 33, 43, 60-*61*, 100, 129, 276, 392, 399, 409, 436, 457, 558.

REMY, August (1800-1872): painter; became Professor at the Berlin Academy of the Arts. 30, 389.

REUSS, [Karl August von] (1793-1874): forest warden. *270*.

REY, Louis-Charles-Joseph (1738-1811): cellist and composer; wrote chamber music, operas, and vocal music. 115-*16*, 447.

RICHTER, Johann Paul Friedrich, pseud. Jean Paul (1763-1825): novelist; his writings extremely popular with Fanny and Felix in their youth. 121, 296, 451, 574.

RIDDERSTOLPE, [Mme.]: member of the Hensels' social circle in their early married life. 93, 432.

RIECHERS, [Herr]: singer who participated in Fanny's musicales. 176, 491.

RIEMER, Friedrich Wilhelm (1774-1845): friend of Goethe, and editor of many Goethe writings, including the *Goethe-Zelter Correspondence*. *120, 156*.

RIES, Ferdinand (1784-1838): pianist and composer; pupil and companion of Beethoven; active in England 1814 to 1824, then returned to native Germany; involved with Lower Rhenish Music Festivals. 251, *253*, 541.

RIES, Pieter Hubert (1802-1886): Berlin violinist and composer; younger brother of Ferdinand Ries; settled in Berlin in 1824 as part of newly-formed Königstadt theater orchestra; member of court orchestra in 1825. 217, *219*, 230, 248-*50*, 256-*57*, 259, 519, 527, 539, 543, 545.

RIESE, [Herr]: amateur Berlin singer. 121, 452.

RIETZ, Eduard (1802-1832): violinist, conductor, and singer; after a nerve injury in his left hand he performed less often; founded and then directed the mostly amateur Philharmonic society (1826); close friend of Felix and the Mendelssohns; died of tuberculosis. xxvi, 2-4, 9-10, 13-15, 17, 21, 25-*27*, 29, 37-*38*, 40, 42-44, *47*, 49, 79-*81*, 87, 93-*94*, *124*, *314*, 370-71, 375-76, 378-81, 386-88, 394, 396, 398, 400, 402, 421-22, 427, 432.

RIETZ, Julius (1812-1877): cellist, conductor, and composer; brother of E. Rietz; successor to Mendelssohn in Düsseldorf in 1835; Kapellmeister at theater in Leipzig (1847-1854), and successor to Gade as Gewandhaus Kapellmeister in 1848; taught composition at Leipzig Conservatory; edited Felix's collected works between 1874 and 1877. xxvi, 10-11, 35, 93, 155, 176, 376-77, 393, 432, 476, 491.

ROBERT, Friederike, née Braun (1795-1832): poet; wife of writer Ludwig Robert; close friend of Fanny and Felix, both of whom set her poems. 6, 10, 21, 40, 209-*10*, 373, 376, 384, 396, 514.

ROBERT, Ludwig (1778-1832): writer; brother of Rahel Varnhagen; lived in Berlin from 1803 and belonged to his sister's circle; married Friederike in 1822; close with the Mendelssohns. 21, 215, 384, 517.

ROBERT, [Victor] (1813-1888): painter in Berlin exhibition of 1836; presumably related to Ludwig Robert. 215, 517.

RODE, Pierre (1774-1830): French violinist and composer; Professor of Violin at the Paris Conservatoire; settled in Berlin in 1814, but returned to Paris c. 1817. 9, 12-*14*, 17, 375, 377-78, 380.

RÖDER, [Herr] von: musical amateur in Berlin in the late 1820s. 33, 391.

RÖSEL, Samuel (1768-1843): painter; friend of W. Hensel. 2, 8, 20, 93, 370, 375, 383, 432.

RÖSTELL, [ ]: Berlin friend of Fanny and Felix. 100, 103, 436, 439.

ROMBERG, Bernhard Heinrich (1767-1841): cellist and composer; lived in Berlin for several periods, including 1816 to 1819; lived in Hamburg after 1820. 358, 615.

RONGE, Johannes (1813-1887): chief founder of the German/Christian Catholic denomination, for which he was excommunicated. 338, 603.

ROSEN, Friedrich (1805-1837): Orientalist; in circle of Felix's Berlin friends from 1824; resided in London from 1828; his younger sister Sophie later married Karl Klingemann. 27, 34, 88, 94-95, 109, 114, 387, 392, 428, 433, 442, 446.

ROSSINI, Gioacchino (1792-1868): Italian opera composer. 12, *14*, 132, 205-*07*, *267*, 309-*10*, 378, 459, 511, 583.

ROTHSCHILD, Amschel Mayer (1773-1855): head of the Frankfurt Rothschild bank. 109-*10*, 443.

ROUSSEAU, Jean Jacques (1712-1778): Swiss-French philosopher, author, political theorist, and composer. 53, 404.

RUBENS, Peter Paul (1577-1640): Flemish painter. 280, 561.

RUNGE, Philipp Otto (1777-1810): Romantic painter. 148, 471.

RUNGENHAGEN, Karl Friedrich (1778-1851): Berlin conductor, composer, and music director; successor to Zelter as director of the Singakademie from 1833, having competed successfully against Felix for the position; viewed as a musical conservative. xxvi, xliii, 39, 94, 109-*10*, 200, 248, 298, *300*-01, *325*, 396, 433, 443, 509, 538-39, 575-77, 630.

RUSSIA; Aleksandra Fedorovna, Czarin of (1781-1860): the former Princess Charlotte of Prussia, daughter of King Friedrich Wilhelm III; married in 1817, effecting a close relationship between Prussia and the court in St. Petersburg. 43, *45*, 157-*59*, 399, 478.

RUSSIA; Nicholas I, Czar of (1796-1855): reigned 1825 to 1855. *61*, 157, *159*, 478.

SAALING, Marianne (1786-1868): noted Berlin beauty; close friend of the Mendelssohns; moved to Berlin in the 1820s and lived with her sister Julie and her husband, Karl Heyse; maligned for her later, although short-lived, engagement to Varnhagen. *3*, 21, 137, 138-*39*, 141, 143, 148-*49*, 222, 384, 463-65, 467, 471, 521.

SABATIER, [Mme.], née Benezaet (b. 1822): singer, pianist, and composer of songs and operettas; member of the Hensels' circle during their stay in Rome in 1845; married Sabatier in 1839; sang frequently in salons and concerts, but refused to sing in opera. 335, *337*, 602.

SANDON, Lord: English acquaintance of Felix during his stay in London in 1829. 44, *47*, 400.

SANTINI, Fortunato (1778-1862): Italian music patron; possessor of an impressive music library; Felix visited him in Rome in 1830. 283, 291, 563, 570.

SAXE-WEIMAR: Augusta, Princess of; see Prussia.

SAXONY; Friedrich August II, King of (1797-1854): reigned 1836 to 1854. 257, *310*, 320, 591, 632-33.

SCHADOW, Friedrich Wilhelm von (1788-1862): painter and writer; founder of the Düsseldorf school of painting (1826); brother-in-law of Eduard Bendemann; Felix studied drawing with him in Düsseldorf (c. 1833 to 1835), lived at his house for a while, and was a close friend. 143, 283, 467, 563.

SCHADOW, Johann Gottfried von (1764-1850): sculptor and draftsman; leading representative of North German classicism; in 1815 became the director of the Academy of the Arts in Berlin; father of Friedrich Wilhelm Schadow and Lida Bendemann. 169, 214, 486, 517.

SCHÄTZEL, Pauline; see Decker.

SCHAUHEIL, [ ]: trombonist, presumably in Düsseldorf. *126*.

SCHAUM, [ ]: German writer who translated English into German. 112, 444.

SCHAUROTH, Delphine; see Handley.

SCHECHNER, Nanette (1806-1860): opera singer; performed throughout Germany and Austria; first sang in Berlin in 1827. 55, 63, *65*, 406, 411.

SCHELBLE, Johann Nepomuk (1789-1837): founder and director of the Frankfurt Caecilienverein; a good friend of Felix. 230-*31*, 527, 631.

SCHILLER, Friedrich von (1759-1805): dramatist, poet, and historian. *3*, 198, 265, *267*, *345*, 507, 550.

SCHIRMER, Johann Wilhelm (1807-1863): painter; Felix's painting teacher while he lived in Düsseldorf. *117*

SCHLEGEL, Dorothea von, née Mendelssohn (1765-1839): eldest sibling of Abraham MB; separated from her first husband, Simon Veit, in 1799, and lived with Friedrich Schlegel, whom she married in 1804; from 1830 lived in Frankfurt; only member of the Mendelssohn family to attend Felix's wedding, on 28 March 1837. 206, 224, 277, 512, 522, 559.

SCHLEGEL, [Frl.]: singer, presumably an amateur. 262, 548.

SCHLEGEL, Friedrich von (1772-1829): philosopher, critic, and writer; a leading figure in German Romanticism; second husband of Dorothea Mendelssohn. 22-*23*, *85*, *210*, 384.

SCHLEIERMACHER, Friedrich (1768-1834): Protestant theologian; friend of F. Schlegel; moved to Berlin in 1810 and became Professor at the University; also translated Plato. 125, *127*, 278, 455, 559.

SCHLEINITZ, Heinrich Conrad (1802-1881): lawyer and notary; from 1834 on board of directors of the Leipzig Gewandhaus; a founder of the Leipzig Conservatory; also appeared as a tenor. *204*, 312, 585.

SCHLESINGER, Adolph Martin (1769-1838): Berlin music publisher; opened a music store in 1810 and began the publishing business in 1811. xxiii, xli, 18, 100-*01*, 125, *127*, 141, *216*, *223*, *226*, 229, *230-31*, 247, 382, 436, 455, 466, 526, 538.

SCHLESINGER, Henry: friend of Sebastian; presumably a member of the music-publishing Schlesinger family. *19*-20, 303, 383, 579.

SCHMIDT, Johann Philipp Samuel (1779-1853): influential music critic at Berlin's *Spenersche Zeitung* from 1815 to 1845; author of miscellaneous musical essays in *Caecilia* and the *AMZ*. *116*, 129, 217, *219*, 457, 519.

SCHMITZ, Philipp Moritz (1765-1849): diplomat; in 1828 effected the first Zollverein in Germany; lived in Munich. 336, 603.

SCHNEIDER, Georg Abraham (1770-1839): hornist, oboist, composer, Berlin Kapellmeister, pedagogue; became music director of the royal theater in 1820 and Kapellmeister in 1825; taught at the Prussian Academy of the Arts; a prolific composer. 178, 248, 493, 539.

SCHÖN, Theodor von (1773-1856): leader in Königsberg of the united provinces of West Prussia-Danzig and East Prussia-Königsberg between c. 1824 and 1842; accomplished many social reforms, including the building of highways. 280-*81*, 318, 561, 590.

SCHORNSTEIN, J. E. Hermann (c. 1811-1882): music director in Elberfeld. *141*.

SCHRAMM, [Herr] von: violinist. 224, 523.

SCHRÖDER-DEVRIENT, Wilhelmine (1804-1860): operatic soprano. *150*.

SCHRÖDTER, [Herr]: acquaintance of Felix in Düsseldorf. 118, 449.

SCHUBERT, Franz (1797-1828): Austrian composer famous for lieder; Felix presented the public premiere of his C-major Symphony in Leipzig. 351, *353*, 613.

SCHUBRING, Julius (1806-1889): pastor in Dessau; helped fashion libretto for *St. Paul;* first became acquainted with the Mendelssohns in the spring of 1825. 12, 45, *186*, *242*, 378, 400.

SCHULZ, Hedwig (1815-1845): Berlin opera singer between 1839 and 1842; taught by her mother, Josephine, and by H. Stümer; entered Singakademie in 1836 and was a featured vocalist. 262-64, *267*, 548-49.

SCHULZ, [Herr]: instrument maker in Berlin. 147, 470.

SCHULZ, Josephine (1790-after 1860): mother of Hedwig Schulz; singer at royal court opera between 1810 and 1830. 30, 262-*63*, 389, 548.

SCHUMANN, Clara; see Wieck.

SCHUMANN, Robert (1810-1856): composer, music critic, and pianist; close friend of Felix, whom he met in 1835; championed his music through his writings in the *NZM*. xxiii, *47*, 345, 358-*59*, 608, 616.

SCHUNCK, Julia Louisa, née Bauer (1789-1862): mother of Julie and Cornelie; related to Cecile MB. 226, 233, 249, 257, 275, 524, 528, 540, 544, 557.

SCHUNCK, Julie, née Jeanrenaud (1816-1875): sister of Cecile MB; married Julius Schunck in 1839. 212, *222*-24, 226-*27*, 229-30, 257, 297-*98*, 516, 521-22, 524, 526-27, 544, 575.

SCHUNCK, Julie (1819-1899): cousin of Cecile MB; married Kissel. 226-*27*, 275, 297, 557, 575.

SCHUNCK, Martin (c. 1788-1872): cousin of Cecile MB. 254, 542.

SCHUNCK, Philipp Daniel: father-in-law of Julie Jeanrenaud Schunck. 283-*84*, 564.

SCHWANTHALER, Ludwig von (1802-1848): south German classical sculptor. 280-*81*, 561.

SCHWARZ, [Herr]: Berlin merchant. 47, 401.

SCOTLAND; Mary, Queen of [= Mary Stuart] (1542-1587): Elizabeth I had her executed because she was a Roman Catholic and a potential threat to Elizabeth's throne. *103*.

SCOTT, Sir Walter (1771-1832): Scottish novelist and poet; met Felix in 1829. *155*.

SCRIBE, Eugène (1791-1861): French dramatist; one of the most significant librettists, writing for Meyerbeer, Auber, and Halévy, among others. *6*, 179, *366*, 493.

SEIDLER, Caroline, née Wranitzki (1790-after 1860): singer at the Berlin royal opera; sang guest roles in 1816 and engaged between 1817 and 1836. 5, 373.

SEMPER, Gottfried (1803-1879): famous neo-classical architect. 330, 598.

SEYDELMANN, Karl (1793-1843): actor; from 1838 at the royal theater in Berlin. 261-*62*, 264-65, *267*, 268-*69*, 316, 547, 550-52, 588.

SHAKESPEARE, William (1564-1616): famous English dramatist; Fanny and Felix nurtured on him. 3, *55*, 61, *65*, 69, *102*, 148-*49*, 172, 179, *203*, 261, 268-69, *366*, 371, 410, 415, 471, 488, 493, 547, 552-53.

SHAW, Mary, née Postans (1814-1876): English contralto; debuted in London in 1834; introduced to Leipzig by Felix in 1838; also sang later in

STENGLER, [Herr]: described as resembling Dr. Reiter. 192, 503.

STETZER, Mine: friend of Fanny. 87, 427.

STICH, Clara (1820-after 1860): actress and singer; daughter of Auguste Crelinger, stepsister of Bertha Crelinger; debuted on Berlin stage in 1834; member of the Singakademie. 155, 157, 476, 478.

STILKE, Hermann (1803-1860): Düsseldorf painter. 154-*55*, 475.

STOLBERG, Louise Auguste Henriette, Countess of (1799-1875): poet; acquainted with the famous literary figures, including Goethe, Schiller, and Heine. 265, 551.

STOSCH, [Dr.]: physician to the Mendelssohns in the mid 1830s. 134, 138, 142, 148, 152, 461, 463, 466, 471, 474.

STOSCH, [Frau] von: amateur Berlin musician; perhaps related to Dr. Stosch. 33, 391.

STÜLER, [ ]: Berlin physician practicing homeopathy. 152, 166, 183, 474, 484, 496.

STÜMER, Johann Daniel Heinrich (1789-1857): Berlin tenor in opera and oratorio, and composer; from 1811 to 1830 engaged at the royal opera; among his voice students were Pauline Decker and Hedwig Schulz; sang the role of the Evangelist in Felix's revival of the *St. Matthew* Passion in March 1829. 25-26, 176, 227, 387, 491, 525.

SYBEL, Heinrich von (1817-1895): Prussian historian and politician; member of the Committee for the Lower Rhenish Music Festival. 168, 485.

SYDOW, [Frl.]: Berlin friend of Felix in the late 1820s who was very fond of his music; perhaps related to Emil von Sydow (1812-1873), a Prussian colonel, military geographer, and cartographer, who lived in Berlin. 95, 433.

TALLEYRAND, Charles Maurice de (1754-1838): French statesman; represented Louis XVIII at the Congress of Vienna; paradigm of a witty, cynical diplomat. *263*.

TAUBERT, Carl Gottfried Wilhelm (1811-1891): composer, conductor, pianist, and pedagogue; 1831 assistant conductor of the Berlin court orchestra; 1840s involved with royal opera under Felix and Meyerbeer, and music director between 1845 and 1848; taught at the Academy of the Arts after 1865. xxvi, 112-*13*, 122, *124*, 130, *132*, 135, 324-25, 343, 355, 359, 444, 452, 458, 461, 593, 607, 613, 616, 633.

TAYLOR family: of Coed Dû, England; John Taylor and his wife, his son John, and his daughters Honora, Anne, and Susan; Felix spent several happy days with the family in September 1829. *101*.

VEIT, Moritz (1808-1864): Berlin writer, book dealer, politician. *163*, 206, 224, 512, 522.

VEIT, Philipp (1793-1877): painter; Fanny's cousin; younger son of Dorothea Mendelssohn and her first husband, Simon Veit. 206-*07*, 224, 512, 522.

VERDI, Giuseppe (1813-1901): Italian opera composer. 332, 599.

VERKENIUS, Ernst Heinrich Wilhelm (1776-1841): member of the Cologne Committee for the Lower Rhenish Music Festival. *310*.

VERONESE, Paolo (1528-1588): Italian Renaissance painter of the Venetian school. 283, 563.

VIEUXTEMPS, Henri (1820-1881): violinist and composer; studied with Bériot; 1833 taken on a tour through Germany. xxvi, 246-*47*, 537.

VIO, [Mlle.]: opera singer at the Berlin Königstadt theater c. 1829. 44, 400.

VONHALLE, [Herr]: an employer of Paul MB c. 1829. 69, 415.

VOSS, Johann Heinrich (1751-1826): poet; works set frequently by both Fanny and Felix. 167, 484.

WACH, Dora: daughter of Lili MB; granddaughter of Felix and Cecile; married cousin Albrecht MB in 1905; possessor of the Green Books. xlvi.

WACH, Lili; see Mendelssohn Bartholdy.

WAGNER, Franz (1810-at least 1864): painter; pupil of W. Hensel. 143, 162, *164*, 183, 467, 481, 497.

WAGNER, Richard (1813-1883): opera composer; became acquainted with Felix in 1835. 311-*12*, 585.

WALESRODE, Ludwig (1810-1889): journalist; had pseudonym of Emil Wagner; friendly with Johann Jacoby; did political writing in the 1840s. 318, 590.

WANGEN, Blandine: Berlin acquaintance of Fanny. 115, 122, 447, 452.

WARSCHAUER, Robert (1816-1884): husband of Marie Mendelssohn; cousin of Fanny and Felix. 320-*21*, 591.

WEBER, [Dr.] Carl Friedrich (fl. 1827-1859): presumably an acquaintance of Felix in Leipzig. 254, 542.

WEBER, Carl Maria von (1786-1826): opera composer and conductor; *Der Freischütz* highly successful and influential. 2, 5, *14*, 18-*19*, 30-*31*, 100, 112, 150, 382, 389, 436, 444, 472.

WEBER, [Herr] von: a neighbor in Berlin. 313, 586.

WORINGEN, Rosa von: daughter of Otto; good friend of Fanny from c. 1834; dedicatee of Felix's *Lieder ohne Worte,* Op. 38. 236, 240-41, 243-*45*, 297, 309, 318, 320, 335, 339, *341*, 532-36, 574, 584, 590-91, 601.

WÜRST, Richard (1824-after 1860): Berlin composer; studied composition with Felix in Leipzig from 1843 to 1847; designated royal music director in Berlin in 1856. 360-*61*, 617.

ZELTER, Carl Friedrich (1758-1832): Berlin composer, conductor, and teacher; director of the Singakademie from 1800 to 1832; promotor of J. S. Bach; close friend of Goethe; taught both Felix and Fanny theory and composition; his lieder style very influential. xxii, xxxvi, 1, *3*-7, 13-*14*, 17, 21, 25-26, 38-39, 43, 48, 53-54, 63, *65-66*, *82*, 94, 107, 118-*20*, 130, 133, 135-*36*, 155-58, 251, 290, 298, *300*, 369, 371-72, 374, 378, 381, 384-87, 395-96, 398, 402, 404-05, 412, 433, 441, 449-50, 458, 460-62, 476-77, 539-40, 569, 576, 629, 631.

ZELTER, Doris (1792-1852): daughter of Carl Friedrich Zelter; friend of Fanny; accompanied her father and Felix to Weimar in 1821. 4, 6-*8*, 208, 371, 373-74, 513.

ZICK, [ ]: presumably an associate of Felix in Düsseldorf. 121, 451.

Index of Fanny Hensel's Compositions

I. Published Works

In Felix's Zwölf Gesänge, Op. 8 (pub. 1827) xxiii, *19, 216,* 630.
No. 2: *Heimweh* (c. 1824) *19.*
No. 3: *Italien* (1825) *19.*
No. 12: *Suleika und Hatem* (1825) *19*-20, *146, 222-23, 226.*
In Felix's Zwölf Lieder, Op. 9 (pub. 1830) xxiii, 100-*01, 216,* 436, 630.
No. 7: *Sehnsucht* (before 1830) *101.*
No. 10: *Verlust* (before 1830) *101, 146.*
No. 12: *Die Nonne* (1822) *101, 146.*
Die Schiffende (pub. 1837; n. d.) xxiii, xli, *216, 222-23,* 225-*26,* 229-*31, 356,* 523, 526, 631.
Schloss Liebeneck (pub. 1839; n. d.) *356.*
Sechs Lieder, Op. 1 (pub. 1846) xxiii, xxxviii, xlii, 353, *356,* 613, 634.
No. 3: *Warum sind denn die Rosen so blass* (1837) 354, *356.*
Vier Lieder für das Pianoforte, Op. 2 (pub. 1846) xxiii, 360-*61,* 617, 634.
No. 1: Andante in G (1836) 217, *219-20,* 519.
Gartenlieder: Sechs Gesänge für SATB, Op. 3 (pub. 1846) xxiii, *346,* 353, *356,* 363, *366,* 620.
Six Mélodies pour le Piano, Op. 4 (pub. c. 1847) xxiii.

Six Mélodies pour le Piano, Op. 5 (pub. c. 1847) xxiii.
Vier Lieder für das Pianoforte, Op. 6 (pub. c. 1847) xxiii.
Sechs Lieder, Op. 7 (pub. c. 1847) xxiii.
Vier Lieder für das Pianoforte, Op. 8 (pub. 1850) xxiii.
Sechs Lieder, Op. 9 (pub. 1850) xxiii.
No. 4: *Die frühen Gräber* (c. 1828) *34*.
No. 5: *Der Maiabend* (1830) 98.
Fünf Lieder, Op. 10 (pub. 1850) xxiii.
No. 5: *Bergeslust* (1847) *xliii*, 364, 634.
Trio, Op. 11 (pub. 1850; 1846) xxiii, 360, 617.

II. Unpublished Works

Lied for Father's Birthday (1819) xxii, 629.
Erster Verlust (c. 1821) *7-8*.
Piano Sonata in F (c. 1821) xxv, 3-4, 371.
Die Spinnerin (1823) 10-*11*, 377.
Piano Sonata in c (1824) 8, 375.
Die frühen Gräber (double bass, 2 cellos, viola; 1829) 33-*34*, 392.
Lieder von Fanny für Felix, 1829 xxv, 46, 48-*51*, 77-*78*, 100-*01*, *196*, 401-02, 420, 436.
No. 1: *Stören möcht ich* 49, *51*, 403.
No. 2: *Grüner Frühling* 50-*51*, 403.
No. 3: Grave 64, *66*, *71*, 413.
No. 5: *Hochland* 50-*51*, *71*, 403.
No. 6: *Wiedersehn* 47, 50-*51*, 401, 403.
Nachtreigen (double chorus; 1829) 57-*58*, 77-*78*, 407, 420.
Präludium in F for Organ (1829) 88, 91-*92*, 428, 430.
Festspiel (1829) *85*.
Präludium in G for Organ (c. 1829-33) 91-*92*, 430.
Overture in C for Orchestra (early 1830s) 144, *146*-47, *149*, 468, 470.
Lobgesang (c. 1831) 201-*02*, 509.
Cholera Music (1831) 201-*03*, 510.
Zum Fest der heiligen Cäcilia (1833) 116, *118*, 448.
Once O'er My Dark and Troubled Life (1834) 136-*37*, 147, *149*, *196*, 462, 470.
I Wander Through the Wood and Weep (1834) 136-*37*, 147, *149*, 462, 470.
What Means the Lonely Tear (1834) 136-*37*, 147, *149*, *196*, 470.

Index of Felix Mendelssohn's Compositions

I. Published Works with Opus Numbers

II. Other Works